THE QUEENSBAY SMALL TOWN ROMANCES

DINNER FOR TWO
ROUGH HARBOR
THE IVY HOUSE
CHASING A CHANCE

DREA STEIN

Dear Reader,

Thanks for checking out my new series. Happy reading...and for a free bonus, please check out my website at http://dreastein.com/

Cheers,

Drea

Dinner for Two - Darby & Sean's Story

Book 1 - The Queensbay Series

Drea Stein

Chapter 1

Darby Reese looked at the box on the counter, a feeling of disbelief washing over her. This could not be happening, not on her first day in charge. She had planned everything successfully down to the last detail, and now it was all going to go fall apart because of one old man.

True, this wasn't the first time Felix had made a mistake with a food order. But seriously, what was she going to do with a mix of shitake and oyster mushrooms when what she really needed was a simple box of white button caps? She'd lose money the first day if she made that kind of substitution.

She sighed and tucked a loose strand of reddish-brown hair more firmly behind her ear as she put the box of exotic mushrooms off to the side. The deli had been doing business with Felix for over thirty years, and Felix hadn't been young back then, which meant that now he was way past his sell-by date.

Still, she knew her dad always waved off Felix's mistakes, not wanting to make a fuss or hurt his friend's feelings. Some things were more important than business, her dad always said, which could explain why The Dory, her family's deli, hadn't changed in more than thirty years either. Darby had tried to coax her father into making changes, suggesting he update the menu, perhaps add a fresh coat of paint to the seating area, even going so far as to offer to take on the project herself. But he had always waved her off, telling her that she shouldn't worry about things like that. Focus on school, on getting a job.

And look where that had gotten her. She had played by all the rules, all right, and it had gotten her exactly where her dad wanted her to be. Unfortunately, it also made her miserable. *Deep breath*, she told herself. Today was the start of a new beginning and she wasn't going to second guess herself out of it.

Going through the rest of the food delivery, she checked off the items against her printed list. She could have done it all in her head, but this was no time to be winging it. Her parents had left for their three-week trip to Italy yesterday afternoon and now, finally, fully, she was in charge—and she planned on running a tight ship.

She hummed as she put the rest of the ingredients away. The sun was barely up, but she was happy to be here, to be surrounded by the comforting feel of the kitchen she had known all her life. Every pot and pan was familiar, every bowl in its place. Her dad, if not interested in the artistic aspects of cuisine, at least kept a tidy kitchen.

He'd hemmed and hawed about her taking time off from her "real job" to help out at The Dory while he was away. Since this was exactly the opportunity she'd been waiting for, to have the place all to herself, she'd come up with a story to explain it: she was leaving one position and starting another much more lucrative one, but she had a whole month off, and there was nothing more she wanted to do than to spend it in Queensbay.

She sighed. At least the last part was true. She hoped her parents would forgive her a few white lies if all worked out. After all, wasn't that what parents were supposed to do? Even if you knew you were going to disappoint the hell out of them?

Luckily, her dad had never searched the Internet to check out her story. The law firm of Werther and Associates simply didn't exist, and there was no job waiting for her because she hadn't ever applied for a new one after quitting her old one. But all that wouldn't matter if these few weeks went as planned.

"You have *got* to be kidding me." The voice was authoritative and, truth be told, downright accusatory.

She looked up as a man stormed into The Dory's kitchen.

"Excuse me?" she said, blinking, not quite sure what anyone else was doing here at this ungodly hour of the morning. She glanced over his shoulder, saw that the back door was still swinging shut, and deduced that she must not have locked up after Felix had left.

"How could you keep fish out like that? Are you insane? And is that raw chicken? And ..." The man was tall, topping out at just over six feet with short, mussed, blondish hair, dark eyes, and impressively large biceps, which were not in any way disguised by the fitted black t-shirt he wore. She let her eyes do a quick assessment of the rest of his body and yes, she was pretty sure that his muscles continued in a nice long, lean line underneath the shirt as well.

She managed to draw her eyes back up, wiping her hands on the simple black apron she wore, wondering just what in the bloody hell someone with the kind of body that was seldom seen outside the pages of a magazine was doing in her kitchen first thing in the morning.

"There they are." Apparently recovered from the sight of fish and raw chicken, both of which had been on their way to the large, industrial refrigerator, the man focused on the box of mushrooms. "There are my babies," he practically cooed, as he picked up the box of fungi and cradled them in his arms. "How dare you take these?" He turned fully to look at her.

She was overwhelmed by him. Oh, god. Yes, there was no mistaking it. There he was. In the flesh. Sean Callahan, with his caramel-colored eyes and a deadly look on his face. What in the name of kitchen gods was he doing here? She had to fight to keep her heart from beating a rapid fire tattoo against her chest. She hadn't seen him in months, and yet still she could feel her stomach heave and her palms start to sweat just by being in his presence.

"Take them?" She finally found her voice. She felt like a tornado had just swept through the room, to say nothing of how her body was feeling, like she had just stuck her hand in an electrical outlet. He hadn't changed at all and, she was embarrassed to admit, he still had that effect on her, even after what had happened.

"My chanterelles, my criminis? You ordered the button tops."

She took a step back. His tone was definitely accusatory, and she drew herself up. This was her kitchen, after all, and if there was one immutable law of the kitchen, it was the authority of the head chef. No matter what other chef might appear.

"Yes I did and I need them." She hoped her voice didn't betray any of the emotions that were currently flaming through her body. She had thought that she was over—so over—any feelings Sean Callahan could ignite in her. "And until you can produce button mushrooms, you can just put those down." She used her best voice, the one that successfully cowed opposing attorneys.

"Ha, I threw them out. No one in their right mind would use them," he said, with a flick of his hand, so easily consigning the poor, innocent mushrooms to the rubbish bin.

He had taken a step closer to her, and she fought the desire to back down. Something danced in his eyes, and she wondered if he recognized her. Determined to show that she was still in charge, she felt a lick of anger spit through her. This was the Sean Callahan she knew, the temper she expected. "You threw my ingredients out?"

It was she who took a step closer to him this time, noticing his fine, dark eyebrows and the way his nose would have been classically straight and handsome, if it hadn't so obviously been broken.

One of those eyebrows rose up a fraction, and a hint of a smile ghosted across his full, heavy lips. "Listen, sugar, you can put the knife down. I didn't mean all that about the mushrooms. They're just some fungi, right?" His voice had definitely changed from accusatory to conciliatory.

She glanced down. She did indeed have a knife—a small one—in her hand. She let it drop on the countertop. Sean Callahan, with his doe-like eyes, devilish grin, and quick temper, had strong opinions about most things— that she knew all too well, but she didn't think he was going to hurt her.

"They might just be ordinary fungi to you, but I did need them for today's soup," she told him, searching his face for some sort of sign of recognition. But she saw none of that, only that saucy, cocky grin. She wondered if it could be possible, if really, he had no idea who she was. The thought should have calmed her racing heart, but it didn't, and instead she felt the warm prick of heat racing up her neck and onto her face.

"Ahh, yes, and I need these for my stir fry," he said. Without really thinking about it, the two of them had inched closer.

"Felix has been a bit off lately," she said, her mind racing, her mouth and brain not quite connecting but feeling that she needed to offer an explanation—any kind of one.

"Felix?" Callahan echoed, his eyes narrowing. His attention never left her, and she again saw the light dancing in them.

"From Gourmet Deliveries," she explained. "I assume we share the same food delivery service. Felix must have mixed up the mushroom order." Half of her brain was working quite rationally, in the precise, ordered way that had made her a successful lawyer. The other half was noting that her body had not recovered from the instantaneous reaction it seemed to have any time Sean Callahan was around.

"Ah, yes, that must be it." He hadn't blinked, and she found herself almost mesmerized, stupefied by him, until she had to drop her own eyes to break the connection.

"We haven't met, have we?" Sean asked, his voice thick with the question, smooth and dripping with charm.

She reared up, not sure whether to be offended that she had made no lasting impression on him, or to do a happy dance that he did not remember their last disaster of a meeting.

"I feel like perhaps we met somewhere? The South Beach Food Festival? No? Then at the party that the Food Network gave?"

She froze. He had moved closer to her, so that their hands, both of them leaning against the large butcher block counter, were close together. He shifted his weight, and in a move so smooth, his head was almost touching hers. He lifted his hand and oh-so-casually brushed the top of hers, sending an electric thrill straight through her—and sending her stomach into backflips worthy of an Olympic gymnast.

"None of those places?" He raised one eyebrow.

She felt her pulse thud into overdrive.

"Well, perhaps I can cook you dinner sometime? I'm kind of a chef, you know. Maybe you've seen me on TV?" He leaned in and was practically whispering in her ear. His warm breath stirred her hair, and she felt her legs almost give way.

Suddenly she sniffed. "Oh no," she cried, springing into action. She brushed past him, barely managing to push him out of the way. Faint, gray smoke streamed from her oven, and the unmistakable smell of burning baked goods filled the air.

Grabbing a kitchen towel, she yanked the oven door open, and a snake of smoke wrapped around her. She pulled the tray out and dumped in on the counter so hard that all the cookies, browned as they were, did a little dance in the air before settling back down.

"I forgot to set the timer," she said to herself, before she remembered that she wasn't alone.

He was still there, arms crossed as he looked at her with one eyebrow quirked up and a self-satisfied smirk on his face. He was obviously waiting for the answer to his question, and she was almost certain he thought it would be a yes.

Had she just been about to fall for one of the oldest lines in the book? From a smug, arrogant jerk of a man who had no idea who she was? What, did he think that just because he was Sean Callahan, that anyone he batted those big brown eyes at would just drop their panties for him? Well, at least the impending disaster of burning cookies had brought her to her senses.

"I know exactly who you are," she said, through gritted teeth, "and unless you can bring back my mushrooms, you can get the hell out of my kitchen."

"Look, sugar, I'm very, very sorry about your cookies. But perhaps we can get together for coffee, maybe compare recipes some time." His voice still had that gravelly quality, the one that sent little whispers of anticipation up and down her back. Okay, so he was a really attractive arrogant ass.

Steeling herself, telling herself to be strong, she said, "Get out. I open in thirty minutes for breakfast. So get out. And don't call me sugar."

She turned on her heel. The cookies were an experiment, and not essential to today's menu. But in another forty minutes, the morning rush would be here for coffee and egg sandwiches and, hopefully, for her light-as-air scones, which she had made and had managed not to burn. She didn't have time to argue over the comparative values of mushroom types.

There was the sound of something suspiciously like laughter, and then she heard the back kitchen door open and bang shut.

She glanced over at the place where she had been unpacking the delivery. Sean Callahan was gone, without even an iota of recognition on his part. And sure enough, the mushrooms were gone as well. Groaning, she realized that would just be one other thing she would have to handle today. Welcome to life in a restaurant.

Chapter 2

The appearance of Sean Callahan in her kitchen that morning had unnerved her, but it had also inspired Darby. After all, here was a man who had once cooked for the President. Simple button mushrooms were no longer good enough for her, nor was plain beef soup. Her father had said that she was free to come up with her own daily specials, as long as they were, in his words, "not too fancy, and didn't cost an arm and a leg."

Taking that as all the license she needed, she had pulled out one of her favorite recipes, one for wild rice and chicken soup, with a touch of cream and baby Portobello mushrooms. If she were going to make a splash with The Dory while she was in charge, she might as well start off right.

As she worked, her mind wandered. Sean Callahan. What was he doing here in Queensbay? Up until recently, he'd been a hotshot New York City chef, running one of the hottest kitchens in town and starring on his own cooking segment on one of those late night shows. He'd taken the food world by storm in just a few years, rising from virtual obscurity to managing some of the finest restaurants in town, cooking for celebrities to becoming kind of one himself. Well, you had to be a foodie, really, to know who he was, but among a certain segment of the food-loving public, Sean Callahan had been the man. It didn't hurt that he was just plain yummy to look at.

Of course, among the people who worked in the industry, he had a developed a reputation for having a bit of a temper. But since the end result was usually too good to pass up—great food, great press, and celebrity diners—everyone had turned a bit of a blind eye and his star had seemed to be rising.

And then all of a sudden, he'd just dropped from view. Like a day-old dinner special. She'd figured he'd have landed somewhere, but it was certainly odd for the former chef du jour to wind up in Queensbay of all places. Sure, the village was a nice place to visit, especially if you liked boating, but he'd come here to cook, not sail; otherwise, why would he be so concerned about his mushrooms?

She took a deep breath, trying not to remember the way he had looked—confident, arrogant even—in the tight black t-shirt that had showed off those well-muscled biceps. While not quite bulging, they certainly showed a dedication to some sort of regular exercise routine—or just excellent genes, she mused as she chopped some fresh tarragon. It just wasn't fair that a face and body like that could belong to someone with such a terrible personality. Or maybe that was exactly fair, she thought.

He hadn't recognized her, of course. She couldn't decide if that was a good thing or more salt rubbed in the wounds of her humiliation. Obviously, her last encounter with him had made much more of an impression on her than on him. But then again, he'd been Sean Callahan then, at the apex of his career, and she was just Darby Reese, another nameless culinary student. No reason she should have made a lasting impression on him the way he had on her.

But today, he'd walked into her kitchen and, unless her radar was totally off, she was fairly sure that Sean Callahan had been putting the moves on her. His eyes had held hers so intently, that it had made her heart hammer in her chest. Ugh, she had to be a total glutton for punishment if she was even thinking of going there. And besides, Sean Callahan was a known player. Why, it seemed like every other day there had been a story linking him with another actress or model.

So there was no reason why his caramel eyes should have lit up in recognition at seeing her, no reason why his pulse should have matched her racing one. Girls like Darby, good girls, who followed the rules and played it safe, didn't make pulses quicken and hearts flutter. She'd been told that more than once by her last boyfriend. Nope, Sean had just been making the moves because he probably tried it on just about every girl he could.

She sighed. Of course he put the moves on everyone. He was Sean Callahan, the infamous Chef Sexy and for all he knew, she was just some girl working in the kitchen of the village's favorite greasy spoon. He was probably looking for just another notch on his ladle.

"I got the heavy cream and those mushrooms you needed," Caitlyn Montgomery said, breezing in through the back door of The Dory's kitchen with a cloth shopping bag slung over her shoulder and her phone in one hand. She was apparently trying to text, her thumb moving furiously over the screen, and talk to Darby at the same time. Predictably, she did not succeed. "Hell's bells!" she yelled as she hit her hip bone on the pointy edge of a stainless steel prep counter.

"Caitlyn," Darby said, gritting her teeth. Her friend's exclamation had been loud enough that several customers were staring back into the kitchen with interest. It was also enough to pull her out of her obsessive Sean Callahan thoughts.

"Fine, fine," Caitlyn huffed, and there was a clatter of plastic and keys as she threw her stuff down on the prep area.

"Not here," Darby hissed, trying not to get raw onion on Caitlyn's expensive phone in its even more expensive Italian leather case.

Rolling her eyes, Caitlyn took her keys, purse, and phone back to the counter that Darby had designated just for that purpose.

Satisfied that at least someone was listening to her today, Darby turned her attention back to the pile of onions.

"Okay, so you needed cream, mushrooms, this long stem wild pilaf rice …" Caitlyn clacked back over to the prep area in her elegant sandals and started to pull items out of the grocery bag.

"You're a lifesaver. Thanks for picking that stuff up. I know you're on your way to work."

Caitlyn Montgomery, with hair so dark it was almost black, and cool, gray eyes, stood there in her summer-weight business suit with her arms crossed and an interested expression on her face. She was a year or so older than Darby and almost like a big sister to her. They'd grown up in Queensbay together, until Caitlyn had left for college and later London. She'd only recently returned to the States, and she and Darby had reconnected as if no time had passed.

"What's that?" Caitlyn said, as a phone vibrated. "Oh, it's yours." She picked up the phone from the shelf where Darby had placed it, glanced at the screen, and said, "Uh oh, it's your dad."

"What is he saying?" Darby asked. She spared a glance for Kelly, the longtime employee who was working the front. It was past the morning rush, and most of the customers were ordering muffins and scones with their coffee, instead of egg sandwiches.

"Don't forget to rest the freezer on Tuesday, the invoice from Felix needs to be paid, you're low on chicken broth—you know, all the exciting stuff."

"Nothing about the view, the food?" Darby said.

She had gotten one message from her mom, soon after her parents had landed in Milan. Her mother had immediately sought out chocolate hazelnut gelato and texted Darby a picture. But the trip, after all, had been her mother's idea: a three-week-long tour of Italy, including a stay in an authentic Tuscan palazzo. It was the trip of a lifetime, a promise her father had made to her mother years ago but had never made good on.

Truth was, Reg Reese would much rather have been keeping watch over Queensbay Harbor and sneaking out early for an afternoon of fishing and beer than sipping Chianti under the Tuscan moon. But Aggie, Darby's mother, had finally found a "great deal" and had Reg reluctantly packing his bags.

"Nope. Just instructions. I did get one from him, too, asking how you were doing," Caitlyn said, finding one of the thick, plain white mugs and pouring herself a cup of coffee from the carafe Darby had set aside.

"And what did you say?" Darby said, trying to keep her voice neutral.

"The truth."

Chapter 3

The knife slipped, and Darby almost cut her knuckle off as she searched Caitlyn's face. "How could you—"

"Got you," Caitlyn said with a laugh, her gray eyes dancing with mischief, "and watch it with that knife. I thought that was the first thing they taught you in those fancy cooking classes, how to handle the sharp, pointy things."

"You'd better watch it," Darby said, as her heart rate returned to normal, and she continued to add to the pile of onions in front of her. "I can debone a whole fish in thirty seconds."

"Oh, I'm scared," Caitlyn said, her black eyebrows rising up above the rim of the white coffee cup.

"Well, what did you tell him?" Darby asked, when she could no longer stand the suspense. She had thought her dad was above spying on her, but at least he had gone to someone friendly to her point of view.

Caitlyn shrugged. "That you're doing fine. It's only the first day, after all. I mean, how bad could things go on the first day, right?" Caitlyn's eyes were no longer dancing and instead she shot a long, considering look at Darby.

There was a pause, the only sounds the jingle of the bell above the door and Kelly's voice as she called out goodbye to a customer.

"What is it?" Darby had long ago learned to read into Caitlyn's silences.

"Are you sure about this, chucking your career? You spent three years in law school, two in practice."

"It was three years in practice. And I hated every minute of it," Darby almost exploded, since she could remember every moment of the soul-sucking time.

"But you seemed to be doing well at it," Caitlyn said.

Darby sighed, tried to keep her temper in check. No one had said this plan would be easy, which was why she had stopped sharing it. But it seemed as if today, the world was aligned against her. First *uber* chef Sean Callahan had burst into her kitchen accusing her of theft and now Caitlyn, one of her oldest friends, was questioning her meticulously drawn up plans. "And I thought you were on my side."

Caitlyn held up her hands. "I am, of course. You know I'm always on your side."

Darby sighed, into another one of Caitlyn's silences. "Well, what is it now?"

"It's just your dad's so proud of you. I mean seriously, every time he gets a chance to slip it in, he does ... 'My daughter, the lawyer.' Ugh. It would be obnoxious if it wasn't so cute," Caitlyn said, then took a sip of her coffee.

Guilt rose in Darby. Unlike Caitlyn, she had a close, loving family that was invested in her every success. This was part of the whole problem, why something so simple just wasn't. She threw down the knife and scrubbed a hand over her face. "It's just ... it's that I can't do it anymore. Sitting in an office, behind a desk all day, looking over papers. It's killing me. I want to cook, and I know it was never something he wanted for me, but it's what I want. I know how proud he is, but I can't spend all my life living out someone else's plan. You, of all people, should understand that."

Caitlyn searched her face, and then gave a single nod of her head. "You're right; I do understand that."

"So you'll keep it under wraps for a while longer?" Darby asked desperately. Queensbay wasn't exactly a small town, but it operated like one. Nothing really stayed secret for long.

Neither of her parents knew that she had ditched her job for an intensive course at the New York Culinary Academy last fall. After that, she'd done an internship in the kitchen of an upscale French-inspired restaurant on the Upper East Side where she had been yelled at, had food thrown at her, and generally been belittled, all in the name of haute cuisine. It had all been in the name of preparing her for her next big step.

She had always loved to cook, but this was a whole new experience. The temper, the passion, the excitement—they were like nothing she had experienced in law school, where everything was dry and dull, reduced to simple black and white. She had absolutely loved it and knew she couldn't go back to her old life.

Cooking was all about the nuances and flavors. She had worked in restaurants all through high school, college, and law school to make her spending money. But it was only in the last year—as the realization that a life working at a big law firm lay ahead of her—that she knew with a fierce certainty she had to get out. She even had a plan. After all, her dad wasn't getting any younger but The Dory wasn't going anywhere.

"Look, I tried to tell my dad what I wanted to do. I even made him an offer to buy him out. He just laughed at me. Said that I was meant for 'better things'."

Darby shook her head. She had hoped that offering money would show her father how serious she was, how she wanted to be part of the family business, take it over from him, even buy it outright if that's what it took.

Caitlyn was rooting around for a chocolate chip cookie, prying off the lid of the airtight plastic container Darby had placed them in. She'd had to bake a new batch after Sean Callahan had ruined the first.

Caitlyn took a bite of her cookie, eyes closed as she savored the way the chocolate mixed with the sugar, butter, and flour to create the perfect melt-in-your-mouth flavor.

Darby knew this because the cookies were her specialty—a giant confection of chocolate and sugar and fat that no one could resist.

"Man," Caitlyn said, "I swear these are the best yet. What could he possibly mean by 'better things' when you can make these?"

Darby smiled. She knew at the end of the day she could count on Caitlyn, even if her plan was sneaky, underhanded, and on the crazy side.

"Your dad is going to flip when he comes home and finds that you've changed the entire menu around on him," Caitlyn said.

"Look, if he doesn't see things my way, then he can always change it back."

"And what will you do?" Caitlyn stopped chewing and looked at her.

"There are other storefronts in town."

"With commercial kitchens, a half block from the marina?" Caitlyn pointed out.

"Well, no, and I would hate to go into competition with my dad, but I'm prepared to play dirty." Darby looked at her friend. "I quit my job, I gave up the lease on my apartment. I dumped my boyfriend because he thought I didn't have the guts for it. I've saved every penny for years to make this happen, even when I didn't know what I was saving it for. Come hell or high water …"

"Fine," Caitlyn shrugged, not letting Darby finish. "I get it. You're playing for keeps. Just remember, you have just about three weeks for your grand plan. Plus, I'll make you a bet."

"What kind of bet?" Darby asked. Caitlyn had always loved to gamble. With her, everything had always been a competition. The stakes could have been anything, from a dollar to the promise of tracking down a cute guy's number, to a crazy dare like jumping into Queensbay Harbor in the middle of winter.

"I bet that if you can increase The Dory's revenue by, say, fifty percent, in the three weeks he's gone, then maybe, just maybe, your dad won't go ballistic when he finds out you quit your promising career to keep the populace of Queensbay in baked goods."

"Okay?" Darby couldn't exactly see how this was a bet. "So if I win, I get to work at The Dory and preserve family harmony and you get to eat cookies for the rest of your life?"

"Correct," Caitlyn said, smiling.

"Well, what do you get if I lose?"

"Your secret cookie recipe," Caitlyn said.

Darby's eyes widened. "It's a secret for a reason."

"Well, then, don't lose," Caitlyn said, as she grabbed her stuff and started to sashay her way out of the kitchen.

"Actually, I don't see how you can lose—either way, you get cookies," Darby called after her.

"Exactly!" Caitlyn said. Just before she went through the door, she called out, "Your dad wanted me to remind you to go to the Chamber of Commerce meeting today. It's at the Village Hall."

The door slammed, and Darby swore. She had forgotten she'd promised to go to the Chamber meeting. Just another thing that would keep her out of the kitchen. She glanced up at the clock and realized she had only another hour before the lunch crowd started to come in. She'd better get moving if that soup was going to be ready.

Chapter 4

He looked at his assembled collection of basil, garlic, pine nuts, and olive oil. Pesto. He'd been trying to teach one of the line cooks the right way to make pesto, but somehow he found himself staring at the dark green of the basil and thinking about eyes.

Not just any pair of eyes, but the ones belonging to the woman who'd been in the kitchen at The Dory, the little deli where someone had suggested he might find his mushrooms. He'd barely noticed it on his first walk through town, but when he'd approached, he'd been struck by its good location. Not too far off the water, in a sturdy brick and wood building, just as quaint as all the others in this typically quaint town.

The inside space was a decent size, with a serving counter and some tables, but the place could have used a paint job, inside and out. He'd gone through the back—force of habit when he entered a kitchen—and been pleasantly surprised to see that, if not modern, at least it had been clean.

The woman standing there had been plainly taken aback to see him, her mouth drawn into a startled O that had quickly turned to annoyance. Her eyes had flashed, and he had immediately thought of the green of fiddlehead ferns. Or the green of dried sage. Not brilliantly green, but a dusky, earthy green. They had stared at him quite hotly, rightly annoyed at his intrusion.

He'd been so disconcerted by the eyes, by the way she had looked, that he had forgotten to use any of his charm. "Roguishly charming" was what his kindergarten teacher had called him, and the description had been apt, since all his life he'd relied on that charm to keep him out of trouble. But there had been something about her that had rendered him speechless or, worse yet, incapable of polite speech. So he had done whatever he did when he felt like he needed to get a handle on the situation—gone on the offensive.

Okay, so maybe, when it had just been about the mushrooms, he'd been rude. But then he had seen her eyes, and what? He'd needed—no, he had been overwhelmed by the sense that he knew this woman, that he had to get to know her. So, what had he done?

15

He shredded the basil efficiently, still thinking. He'd tried to find out where he knew her from. But she had just stood there, silent, eyes boring into him, until he had tried one of the oldest lines in the book. Real smooth move. No wonder her eyes had hardened with anger and those cute, little lips had grown tight and thin. He didn't think she was a woman that responded well to pick-up lines. There had been something distinctly elegant about her long, lean body and fine-boned features. Classy types like her usually didn't want to give him the time of day.

"Excuse me, Chef?" The voice was hesitant, and Sean turned to see one of his line cooks standing there. "Was this what you were looking for, the broth?"

He looked. "I said beef, not chicken." The line cook's hand shook, and Sean sighed, resisting the urge to yell. After a rocky start at the restaurant, he'd done his best to be nicer because - hell, he *wanted* to be a nicer, better person. He didn't want to be that guy, the one the whole world already thought they knew.

And this was his chance. His shot at redemption, his chance to get back into the big leagues. He couldn't mess this up. He'd made a promise to himself that he would do whatever it took to get it all back.

"I don't think we have any more," Kevin, the line cook, managed to say.

Sean suppressed his second sigh. The entire kitchen staff of the Osprey Arms had been a pretty sorry lot. Well, he supposed *sorry* was too harsh a word. They were rather average, and that's just what this restaurant was, too. Or had been. He'd been here almost three months and was whipping them into shape, but there was still a lot of work to do.

The restaurant had an amazing location, nestled right on the edge of Queensbay Harbor, and was the first dining establishment anyone who tied up at the busy marina saw. But until recently, its specialties were baskets of fried shrimp and frozen cod. That was, until Chase Sanders, a local businessman, had bought the whole complex, a hotel and restaurant combo. Sean had met Chase a few years ago, and he had been the first person Chase called when the deal on the Osprey Arms closed. Chase had offered him the chance to be a full partner in developing an upscale steak and seafood place. At first, Sean hadn't been interested, not wanting to leave the rush of the big city for a small town in Connecticut that no one had ever heard of.

But Chase was a patient guy. After Sean had found himself out of a job and out of favor, Chase had called again. Being a stand-up guy, Chase hadn't changed the deal. A full partnership and the authority to design a new menu and run the restaurant the way Sean wanted. All of a sudden, what had seemed like a step down a few months earlier now appeared to be the perfect way to make the climb back to the top. Eventually, even his publicist had come around, and so far Sean had been here a few months, working hard to make the restaurant into something unique—a high end, yet friendly placed that served impeccably prepared gourmet food.

But in order to do that, he needed to raise everybody's standards, and it started with the staff. That was one of the first lessons Big Mac had taught him back in the kitchen of that simple rib joint in Indiana. It all came down to how well your team worked ... well, as a team. You couldn't serve over a hundred dinners a night flying solo, whether it was filet mignon or chicken and biscuits. And if it took some shouting to make it happen, well then so be it.

"Well, then, add it to the list," Sean said, pleased that his voice was calm. He almost went back to his chopping, but he turned. "Hey, kid, you from around here?"

Kevin turned and nodded, plainly too scared to speak.

"You know that deli up on Main?"

"The Dory," Kevin nodded, and Sean could see him relax a fraction. "Good sandwiches," the cook added and then shuffled his feet as if aware that offering an opinion on food was a dangerous thing to do.

"Who owns it?"

"The Reeses. Owned it for years, I think, even when my grandmother was alive."

"Reese," Sean said. "Thanks," he added over his shoulder. Well, that girl hadn't been more than twenty-seven or twenty-eight, so probably not the Reese who had owned it for years. She looked like she was in charge, though—Sean could always tell—so maybe she was a family member.

There had been something in the way she looked at him. Or maybe it had been how she looked: short khaki shorts, plain white sneakers, a simple gray V-neck t-shirt, an apron around her waist. Her hair, that red-gold color, had been pulled back in a ponytail, but some of it had escaped, waving about her face. She had a nice, trim figure, the kind that begged you to touch and feel. She had even smelled good, like vanilla and flour.

But the way she had looked at him, hand clenched around the handle of the knife. Like she had known exactly who he was, what kind of person he was—and hadn't liked what she was seeing.

He'd gotten used to that. The recognition. He knew, truly, that he wasn't famous. But even a few appearances on late night TV, plus that flattering profile by the reporter who wanted a good table at his last restaurant had been enough to get him "recognized." And at first, it had been nice, the recognition. He had taken full advantage of it. He was a kid from a small town in the Midwest. The fame had been what he had always imagined it would be like, from the guys who were asking for a table at your restaurant, to the girls who wanted to get close to you. The money hadn't been so bad either, but that had seemed beside the point when he'd been everyone's darling. So what if he ran a tough kitchen. It wasn't easy staying on top.

Then there had been a few of those not-so-flattering stories. About his late nights and how the food he cooked seemed to look better than it tasted. And there had been the rumors of his temper. Greatly exaggerated for the most part. Okay, so maybe that was the one part they had gotten right. And his fall had been just as swift as his rise. All of a sudden, people had looked at him with, what—a certain kind of wariness, like they expected him to start yelling and throwing things.

He'd seen the whisper of fear that ran through the staff at the Osprey when Chase introduced him. One of the waitresses had even quit on the spot, saying she wouldn't work for a thug. Sean knew that he had a lot of work to do to repair his reputation. So far, things were coming along okay. His staff was starting to treat him like a normal person, and he found that he liked the pace here in Queensbay. He was calmer and that meant that he yelled less. He was able to focus more on the food, and that made him happier than he'd been in a long time. And since he was a partner, it turned out the money wasn't so bad either.

His last dinner was served by nine, ten at the latest. He'd been going to bed at a reasonable hour, had even started to get up and go for a run along the beach in the mornings. He'd even been working on some new recipes and hoped to pull them together in a cookbook. The restaurant was starting to get a reputation for serving locally sourced, seasonal food. All things considered, life was going much better than he had hoped. So it made no sense that some girl who looked good in an apron should be occupying so much of his thoughts.

"What are those?" Sean sniffed, as one of the waitresses walked by carrying a pink-and-white-striped cardboard box. The aroma had caused a stir in the restaurant as most of the staff gravitated toward her.

"Cookies. From The Dory. Darby's back in town while her parents are on vacation. She's baking them for the store."

Kevin was the first to scoop one up. "These are amazing. Remember when she used to make them for the football games?" There was a general murmur of agreement.

The Dory. Darby Reese. That meant she must be the daughter of the owners. Now that he knew a name, Sean tried to search his memory, to see if he could remember her. No, there was nothing. "Let me try."

The staff cleared a path for him.

He looked in the box, saw it was piled high with chocolate chip cookies the size of his palm, studded with big, dark chips of chocolate. They were a perfect golden brown. He selected one and felt every eye on him as he took a bite. The chocolate and dough melted in his mouth. "Wow," he said, surprised. "These are really good."

The waitress flashed him a relieved smile. "Darby knows how to bake 'em."

"And she's easy on the eyes," said another waiter, a college kid with shaggy hair.

There was a nervous ripple of laughter as Sean let a hint of a smile cross his face before he shut it down. "That's enough. Back to work." Somehow the thought of that pimply kid commenting on Darby's good looks unsettled him.

The staff scattered, and Sean worked with them, helping them with their techniques, identifying skills they needed to work on.

After an hour or so of talks and making notes, he stepped outside for a breath of fresh air. There was a view of the water, even here, from the back door of the kitchen. Queensbay Harbor was a huge indent on the coastline of Connecticut, ringed by beaches and hills, with the village at the very apex of it and houses fanning up and out on either side. The harbor, even on a weekday, was busy with the hum of motorboats and the snap of crisp white sails.

There was the faint tang of salt and something else—seaweed, he guessed, because until he'd come to Queensbay, he'd never been this close to saltwater. The town was cute, hugging the Connecticut shoreline and was filled with houses and stores that had been built over two hundred years ago and, except for new paint, looked like they hadn't been touched. Everything had a look of prosperous self-assurance about it, as if Queensbay and the people in it were sure of their place in the world. All in all it had a simple and quiet feel and was just what the doctor, or rather his publicist, had ordered.

Get out of the city, keep a low profile. Be successful, keep his nose clean and then, just maybe, he'd get another shot at the big leagues again. So far things were going according to plan. His publicist planned to have him back in the city by September, but now, standing here looking at the broad expanse of the harbor, at the dark green hills that ringed it and the sapphire-blue sky, overhead, he wasn't so sure that he wouldn't miss the place just a bit.

He was about to go inside, thinking it was time to give the staff a lesson on mushrooms, when his phone beeped. It was an alarm. Chase had asked him to go to the Chamber of Commerce meeting, something about getting more established as a businessman in town. Sean had seen right through that. There was no way Chase wanted to sit through a meeting on a glorious summer afternoon, so he was pawning the obligation off.

He sighed. Another freakin' meeting. He'd much rather be in the kitchen.

Chapter 5

Darby was running late, mostly because she wanted to change out of her work clothes, but she couldn't help taking a moment to enjoy the sunshine as she walked the few blocks that separated The Dory from Village Hall. She waved at people she knew—friends of the family, men and women she'd known all of her life. She caught sight of a pair of cute earrings in the window of The Garden Cottage and made a mental note to pop back in later to try them on.

It felt nice, right, to be here, even if it was under false pretenses. For just a moment, she let the sun warm her cheeks and took in the sight of the harbor spread out before her. She had missed the water, she admitted to herself. Four years of college, three years of law school, and three more working—and every day, she had missed being able to see the water. It would be perfect to be able to wake up to this every morning. Surely, her dad would be able to understand her need to come home, if nothing else.

Queensbay had always been a summer town, a haven for boaters. They docked at the marina or anchored in the harbor, creating flotillas of party boats. Other sightseers came by train or car to grab a room at the Osprey Arms and spend a day or two poking around the antique stores and knickknack shops, exclaim over the neat, well-kept houses behind white picket fences, hear a live band play along the waterfront, and have dinner while watching the sun set over the harbor. Though small, Queensbay always felt just busy enough, never too small or too big.

And it didn't end with summer. Fall was soccer and apple picking time, time for pumpkin carving and leaf pile jumping. Almost as much as the summertime, she loved that season, when you could build a crackling fire indoors, when it was time to lay on the soup and casseroles, to hunker down and pull out the sweaters and cozy up. Queensbay was her home and everything that meant. Some part of her had known that she would always wind up here, no matter how many times her dad had told her to go off and spread her wings.

The town, too, was growing. It was no longer quite as sleepy as she remembered from childhood. The relocation of a few big companies and the expansion of the local hospital meant that more people were discovering the charming little village on the water. It was now home to folks year round, both young families with kids and to double-income, no kid, executive couples.

Her dad complained about them, saying they were too fancy, with gourmet tastes. All of a sudden, pastrami on rye with a side of slaw wasn't okay anymore. These customers wanted fresh chicken with pesto mayonnaise on a crusty roll, topped off with a cappuccino and biscotti.

She shook her head as she walked, noting all around her the signs that Queensbay was changing. There was a new designer boutique on the corner and a fancy ice cream shop that served a cone as big as a dinner platter. She'd suggested to her dad that maybe it was time to update things a bit; fix The Dory up, add in a few new menu items. But he'd only sniffed and muttered, saying if his sandwiches weren't good enough for them, then they could shove off. Since The Dory was the only deli in town and apparently had the profits to prove it, she knew her dad didn't have much motivation to keep up with the times. Still, she hoped to show him that a little change could go a long way.

Village Hall appeared before her, an impressive brick building that anchored the downtown portion of the village. Well over a hundred years old, the building was a familiar local landmark. All charm, however, ended at the front door. Inside, it was like any government building, with beige walls and gray carpet.

She took the wide steps up to the entrance, pushed through the double-height door and onto the first floor. She had to climb the stairs up to the second-floor conference room where the Chamber of Commerce meeting was to be held. The room was only half-filled, and she breathed a sigh of relief that she wasn't late. Apparently, a Chamber meeting in the middle of a summer afternoon wasn't on the top of anyone's priority list.

"Well, well, Darby, you're looking quite well." Mayor Peyton came over and gave her both a kiss on the cheek and a handshake. He was about the same age as her father but with an impressive set of jowls that was a testament to his politician's "man about town" status. Mayor Zander Peyton was the type of man who never cooked at home when he could eat out, who never drank alone when he could buy a round, and who never turned down a cup of coffee even if it meant hearing the gripes of the populace of Queensbay. He'd been the mayor for a record four terms and counting, and when not running the business of the village, he was a high school science teacher.

"Thank you, Mr. Mayor. It's nice to be back in town," she said, genuinely glad to see him. He had been her science teacher too, and until he pointed out the comparisons between cooking and chemistry, she'd dreaded the class. Since then, she had appreciated the technical aspects of cooking as much as the artistic side.

"Glad you could make it to our meeting today. It's always nice to have some fresh, young voices around the table," he said, giving her shoulder a final, friendly squeeze.

Alone now, she surveyed the scene. The conference room had a gray-beige rug, a fake wood table, and serviceable chairs. The room was starting to fill up with the members of the council: all the men and women who owned businesses in the village proper and in the outlying commercial areas. More than a few nodded and waved to her.

Joan Altieri, the owner of The Garden Cottage, came over to her, sliding into the chair one over from her, her hair bleached and styled in a pixie cut for the summer. "How are you holding up with your parents out of town?"

Darby's mom and Joan had been friends for years, and she was sure that her mom had asked Joan to check up on her.

"Just fine," Darby answered. "Made it through the breakfast rush without a hitch."

She nodded, trying to sound like she was in control. Lunch had been easy, too—slow, almost, compared to the crush she was used to from her jobs at restaurants in the city. And maybe, if she were honest with herself, a bit slower than the way she remembered lunch at The Dory had been. It might be time to look over the books at The Dory, to see if things were really as sunny as her father kept saying they were.

"I keep telling Reg you missed your calling going into law," Joan said.

Darby froze. "What do you mean?"

Joan squeezed her hand. "I hear you've been making your cookies again. I tell you, the whole town just waits until you get a chance to stop by and bake us up a batch. Seems like you could make yourself quite a fortune if you just concentrated on making those cookies."

Darby managed a nod, hoping that the panic didn't show. As a lawyer, she'd grown pretty good at keeping a poker face, but it was harder to do that around people she had known all her life. She certainly wasn't ready to let anyone besides Caitlyn know that she had quit her job and was planning to convince her dad to let her join him in the family business.

"Who knows? Maybe your dad will bring us back some new recipes. All of a sudden, I feel like Queensbay is becoming so cosmopolitan," Joan said. "Why, my sales are up twenty percent this season alone—and not just because I raised my prices, mind you. Used to be we had more browsers than tourists, but now I feel like we've got our own little bit of fancy. I mean, you've heard what they've been doing to the Osprey Arms?"

Darby looked at Joan, whose eyes flickered behind her half-moon glasses. "What are they going to do?" she asked, her mind still thinking about what Joan had said.

"You haven't heard then? Chase Sanders bought the Osprey Arms and got himself a partner to run the restaurant. They want to turn it into a real steak and seafood place. No more baskets of fried shrimp." Joan said it with a bit of a sigh, like she was going to miss the old menu.

Darby could almost agree. The Osprey Arms, like The Dory, was an institution, with a menu that never changed. People didn't go there for the food, really; they went because there were white tablecloths and heavy duty silverware and a bar where they could order real drinks, all while looking out over the water. She had celebrated her high school graduation at the Osprey Arms, where she had had a stuffed flounder filet and her father had ordered the shrimp scampi with a side of pasta.

"And it's some chef … oh dear, I can't remember his name, but my Ben tells me that he's a hit with all the cool kids, or whatever you say." Joan shook her head and continued. "I never heard of him or whatever show he's on, but he's quite something to look at. All dark eyes and blonde hair and boyish charm." Joan nodded authoritatively.

Darby felt her heart sink as she realized she'd just discovered why Sean Callahan was in her town. Apparently, just about everyone could fall for that easy charm. But she could personally attest to what it felt like to be on the receiving end of one of his tirades. Her dismay turned to anger. *The bastard didn't even remember me,* she seethed on the inside.

That just made the fact that she'd felt a pull of attraction toward Sean Callahan all the more irritating. She knew he had a temper and a reputation as a bad boy. And there was no way, she, Darby Reese, budding business owner, was going to fall for the likes of Sean Callahan. Just because a guy had cute dimples and great upper body strength, didn't make him eligible bachelor material. She'd learned that lesson the hard way. She was so over bad boys.

After all, when a guy had showed up on a late night talk show with his own segment, titled "Date Night Delight," where he taught whatever pretty young thing of the moment how to cook something, you knew that he had to be trouble. The subtext wasn't all that subtle, since that was how Sean had gotten his Chef Sexy nickname. If she just remembered that and focused on her own agenda, then she should be able to steer clear of Sean Callahan. No need for him to ever figure out where they'd met before.

"Order, order." Mayor Peyton had taken his seat at the head of the table and banged his small gavel. The room hushed quickly as people rushed to fill the seats.

She only half-listened, trying to ignore her annoyance at knowing Sean Callahan had invaded her town by trying to remember where she had seen a recipe for an avocado salad. It might be something that she wanted to try out on the menu this week, if only she could dig it up.

A murmur ran through the room, and she looked up to see him standing in the doorway, politely pushing his way into the room. Once again, Sean Callahan looked as if he'd walked out of an ad for a men's clothing magazine rather than the kitchen. He still wore his black t-shirt, paired with dark jeans. She was suddenly very aware that his arms and the rest of his body were as well-muscled as his shoulders. His blondish hair was windblown, more disheveled than it had been that morning, and he wore a lip-curling grin on his face as he maneuvered around the legs of chairs and eased himself into the cramped space between her and Joan Altieri.

His dark eyes raked over her, and a shiver ran through her. It took her only a moment to recognize it for what it was and only a second longer to tamp it down and tell herself that it was just an obvious reaction to a man who had all the parts nicely arranged. There was no way she could ever be attracted to Sean Callahan, not after their history—even as forgettable as it was to him. Still, she was happy she had managed to run home and change out of her work clothes into something more benefitting a hopeful small business owner.

Mayor Peyton, in the middle of something about a noise ordinance, nodded politely at the newcomer but kept on with his droning. She felt the familiar heat on her skin as Sean Callahan's arm brushed against hers. She moved it quickly, but not before she knew that the red splotches of embarrassment were shooting up her arms, across her neck, and probably onto her cheeks. It was a problem with having the coloring of a redhead. Most of the time, she was able to minimize it, but her body's internal temperature was spiking at her nearness to him.

She felt his eyes on her, and she dared to turn her head quickly. He had the audacity to wear a smile—a comfortable, I-am-in-command type of smile. He gave her a quick nod and a grin as if the tirade in her kitchen—her kitchen!—had never happened.

She tried for a frosty glare, but that only seemed to amuse him, as if he enjoyed the challenge. He looked at her for an instant, and when she didn't return his smile, he gave her a wink and settled himself more fully so that his elbow brushed hers. She retracted her arm as if she'd been scalded, but that only made his smile grow even wider.

She forced herself to look at the worn, scratched, fake wood surface of the table, trying to get her breathing to return to normal. So what if she was sitting next to Sean Callahan? So what if he had been on national TV teaching America how to properly cook a *coq au vin*, chatting with the pretty blonde actresses and flirting away? He was an ass. They'd met just two times, and at both of them, she had been subjected to his bruising flak and he still had no clue who she was—probably hadn't even bothered to find out her name.

Willfully, she focused again on what Mayor Peyton was saying, hoping that the minute details of village life would be an effective distraction from the way her body was reacting to the nearness of Sean. She sighed. It was no good. Her whole body was buzzing just from being close to him. Not knowing what else to do, she started to go over the articles of the Universal Commerce Code in head, a truly boring piece of law that required almost total concentration on her part.

Chapter 6

The meeting had taken almost two hours. Well, one hundred and thirteen minutes, to be precise. And when a minute meant the difference between limp pasta and the perfect al dente bite, he knew that these were one hundred and thirteen he would never get back.

Sean had been daydreaming. Well, not daydreaming so much as lost in his thoughts. He'd been trying to work through why his latest recipe wasn't working in an effort to distract himself from the palpable antagonism he felt rolling off of Darby Reese and directed toward him.

He had studied her when he thought she wasn't looking, noticing the way her hands were small and delicate, yet with long fingers. Her nose was straight with just a slight turn at the end, and when her nostrils flared as his arm brushed against hers, he was hit with a jolt of attraction so sharp, he wondered just what it would be like to get her really angry.

One scowl was what she had given him, and he found himself not caring about the difference between a porterhouse and sirloin but instead thinking only about what it would be like to kiss those lips. He'd struck out big time with her before, but surely she'd be willing to give him a second chance? After all, they'd just met; he couldn't have done anything wrong yet. Or could he have?

Somehow, between his not paying attention and being hyper aware of her next to him, the meeting concluded, and it was time to go. Like a shot, Darby was out of her seat and headed toward the door before he had a chance to react.

Sean got up in a panic and then tried to look cool. He knew where to find her. Still, he knew he needed to apologize. Sure, he'd said he was sorry this morning, but he needed to give her a real apology. No woman could resist that, right?

Pushing through the crowd of people, with an easy smile on his face, he ignored the looks of people who he knew wanted to talk to him. He was supposed to stop, say a few words. Chase had told him to be friendly, but now he was on a mission.

He moved quickly. "Wait!" he called. She was down the stairs now, onto the tiled floor of the lobby. He picked up the pace, thought wildly for a second about using the wood-carved banister for a faster lift, but instead took the wide, shallow steps two at a time.

He caught up with her on the walkway in front of the village hall. His arm reached out to catch her.

She spun around, her hair blowing about her face, her eyes narrowed slits. "Don't touch me," she snapped.

He took a step back, held up his hands. He'd just wanted to talk to her. What kind of crazy lady act was this? "Darby, right?" He put on his best, biggest smile, the one his publicist had told him to use when he was on TV and nervous as hell.

Her hands were on her hips. She wore some sort of pale pink halter top and a skirt that was striped like penny candy. Long, tan legs traveled down to a pair of strappy sandals. For a moment, he had a brief, hot vision of what they might look like wrapped around him, but then he willed it away.

There was a decidedly annoyed look on her face as she stood, waiting for him. He'd been right. Her eyes weren't a bright green, but a dusky shade like dried sage. And her hair wasn't brown, as there was too much red in it. Like chestnuts. He had to shake his head to stop the culinary comparisons. Thinking in food was both a benefit and a curse in his line of work.

"I'm Sean Callahan." He stuck out his hand.

She looked at it, shrugged and said. "We met already, remember?"

He did his best to keep smiling, but her hostility was wearing him down. "Yeah, about that."

"I assume your mushrooms worked out for you?" Her tone was frostily polite as she turned and began to walk.

Surprised, he had to move quickly to keep up with her. "You know, I have plenty more," he said, "if you need some. I didn't mean to send you back to the store." Friendly. If you were friendly, then someone else was supposed to be friendly back, right? Apparently, this one wasn't going to give him an inch.

She looked at him, and he noticed that she had a small smattering of freckles across the bridge of her nose and cheeks. "I managed to improvise." Her tone was clipped, and it didn't take a genius to deduce that she was pissed at him.

He ran a hand through his hair. Usually he didn't have to work this hard to get a girl to like him. Women seemed to find him charming, at least at first. Until they got pissed off when he decided it was time to move on. Unfortunately, Darby seemed to have moved straight on to the pissed stage, without even giving him a chance. Okay, so he'd not been on his best behavior that morning, at least until he'd gotten a good look at her.

He turned on his high-wattage smile, the one that always worked, and tried his best bad-boy-turned-sorry look. "Sorry, sugar, it was a bit of a crazy morning. I hadn't had my coffee yet. You know how that goes, right?"

He waited. There was nothing, not a nod or the slowing of her step, so he had to lengthen his stride to keep up with her. He fell in beside her, enjoying the way her long, strong arms moved in time with her pace. This was no little mouse of a woman. He had the distinct vision of a lioness loping along the plains, as matched her determined pace.

"So," he said, but Darby didn't stop, "you're the owner of The Dory?"

"My father is. He's on vacation. I'm running it for the rest of the summer." She kept her answers short, staccato bursts of information.

"Do you work with your dad a lot?" He tried again.

"No," she answered. They passed the fish market, a half-open building, and the gray-haired woman behind the counter yelled out a hello to her. Darby lifted a hand in greeting but didn't slow down.

"So, are you between jobs then? I mean, I feel like maybe I've seen you before."

"You ask a lot of questions," she said and shot him a look that he was sure was meant to intimidate. Instead he just became more determined.

"Sorry, I didn't mean to be nosy, but it just seems ... I don't know ... that you're familiar. Sugar, you're so sweet; I'm sure we've met before."

Darby gave him a withering look. "Does that line really work with girls?"

He took a deep breath and decided to start over. He would find out where they had met before; he just needed to finesse her a bit. "So, you're not a chef, but your cookies taste like they were baked by a professional. Made me wonder where you were trained."

He was hoping the compliment would disarm some of the hostility, but instead it only seemed to enrage her.

"Are telling me you have no idea who I am?" Darby stopped in the middle of the sidewalk, her arms folded, glaring at him. He thought that anger made her look even more desirable, the way her cheeks flushed and her eyes danced.

"Should I?" He kept his voice light, while his mind raced. Okay, so he was right. They had met before. But where? Seriously, looking at her, the long legs, tan, shaped arms, the angry eyes and blowing hair, he wasn't sure he, or anyone, for that matter, could have forgotten meeting her.

Had he already tried to ask her out and been shot down? Or worse yet, maybe she had tried to hit on him and he had—what would he have been thinking?—turned her down? There had been a lot of late nights in his past, and he couldn't be sure he could remember every single one of them in perfect detail.

He looked at her, taking in the red-gold hair, the splay of freckles across her cheeks, the sage-green eyes with the slight catlike twist to them and the pert nose that turned up just a bit at the end.

"No idea?"

Baffled, he shook his head and held up his hands in defeat.

With a huff, she turned on her heel and started away from him.

"Hey there," he reached out and grabbed her arm lightly, but she shook it off.

"Get your hands off of me," she hissed, barely turning around.

"Nope," he said, and moved so that he was in front of her, blocking her way. "You're not going to get away with that."

"Get away with what?" Her voice rose.

"Teasing me like that," he said, keeping his voice light. Two could play this little game. He was aware that they were in the middle of the sidewalk and that a few people, like the young girl who worked in the used bookstore, had stopped whatever they were doing and were watching them.

"Teasing you?" Her voice dipped down to a snarl.

If he'd been a smart man, he later thought, he would have backed down then and there, but curiosity and desire—desire to know more about her, to see what other reactions he could provoke from her—kept him marching forward.

"You have some nerve," Darby said.

"Some nerve to what? You won't tell me what you're talking about." Now he was the one who was pissed, and he knew his tone showed it.

"Nice to know I'm so forgettable," Darby said, her arms folded over her chest, her stance protective.

"Forgettable." He took a step, closing the space between the two of them. He could smell her. Cinnamon and sugar, like the baker she was. "There is nothing forgettable about you."

"Apparently, that's where you're mistaken."

"So you admit it, we have met before." He moved closer, mesmerized by those eyes. The fire had quieted in them, replaced by a hint of ice, but as he moved closer, they opened in alarm.

His hand touched her arm, and it was like an electric shock through them both, he could tell. She nearly took a step back, but recovered and stood her ground. Her lips were cherry red, drawn back in a slight O of surprise.

"Please, enlighten me. Put me out of my misery because ... ," he dropped his head down, close to her ear so that he was sure no one else could hear them, "I can't stop thinking about you." As he said it, he realized that, while it sounded like just another cheap pickup line, it wasn't—at least to him. She had been in his thoughts all day.

"We have met. About a year ago." Her voice was breathy, and he moved even closer into her, meeting no resistance. Her pulse fluttered at the base of her neck, and he desperately wanted to know what it would be like to touch his lips against it, to have his hands in her mass of red-gold waves, to feel her lips warm and soft beneath his.

"A year ago." One part of his mind raced to remember twelve months ago. As it was, he was having trouble remembering ninety seconds ago. The other part of his brain couldn't think but for her.

"The Culinary Academy, New York."

Something was coming back to him, and he maneuvered even closer to her. She didn't rear back this time, and he could smell her breath, sweet like peppermint and oranges, as it fanned around him.

"You were a guest instructor. The class was making a classic steakhouse dinner."

"Rib eye, onion rings, and creamed spinach." His heart lurched as memories started to come back. So far, she hadn't moved away

31

from him, and he was so close that they were almost touching. But he knew where this ship was going, heading straight for the rocks, not a lighthouse in sight.

"Exactly. Apparently, my spinach wasn't up to snuff, which you made abundantly clear, in front of everyone."

"That was you. Under the chef's hat." It all came flooding back to him. He'd been under a lot of stress then and had taken it out on the students. In particular, her. He'd made an example of her. Her creamed spinach had not been bad; it had been awful. Too salty, as if it had been cooked in a bath of seawater. And what was even worse is that he was sure he'd been flirting with her just before that. No wonder she was mad at him.

"But how could that be? I've tasted your food." He was genuinely puzzled. There was no way that this Darby, the one who made cookies so exquisite they were chocolate heaven, could be the same chef as that Darby who had ruined spinach. "What happened?"

"Does it matter? The fact is you were an ass then and, judging by your behavior this morning, you're still an ass, so you can just get out of my way." She took a step back, their whispery, electric connection broken. Her eyes were like ice now, hard and angry, and she pushed around him, walking past him.

All around him, there were people enjoying the fine weather, eating ice cream cones, window shopping, but he ignored them all as they surged around him, watching the retreating figure of Darby Reese, feeling anger and shame at the person he had been.

Chapter 7

"So, you actually met him?" Caitlyn was looking at her as Darby banged into the kitchen of The Dory.

"Who?"

"Sean Callahan. The new chef who's working with Chase? You're muttering his name, plus a few other interesting words. I take it you met him? Word on the street is that he's more delish than a hot fudge sundae."

Darby thought about the broad shoulders, the disheveled blonde hair, and the caramel-colored eyes. And the grin, the one he kept flashing that displayed deceptively boyish dimples.

"Yes," she answered because there was no use denying it. She felt something buzzing through her—anger, resentment … god, even that tight little curl of attraction again. She needed to do something with her hands. She grabbed an apron, then found the flour and a bowl and banged them down on the counter.

"I knew it," Caitlyn said, clasping her hands together. "There's something about his hands."

"His hands?" Darby spoke loudly over the water rushing from the faucet as she washed her own hands in the large stainless steel sink.

"Don't you ever watch those chefs on TV? They all have the most amazing hands. Strong, long boned. You know, the kind of hands—"

Darby cut her off. "Don't even go there. He's a jerk."

"How do you know? What did he do?" Caitlyn had reared up, and Darby felt a wave of relief flow through her. She could always count on Caitlyn to have her back. She shrugged, busying herself getting her ingredients together.

"Oh no you don't." Caitlyn wagged a finger at her. "I know you. You aren't saying something. I can tell."

Darby rolled her eyes but then figured she might as well tell. Caitlyn could be relentless. "I met him once before."

"You met him, and you never told me?"

Darby shook her head. "Let's just say it wasn't my finest moment."

Caitlyn jumped down from the counter she was sitting on. "Oh, do tell," she said, her eyes alight with interest.

"Don't you have a job?" Darby decided to make some bread. It was a soothing process, and that was exactly what she needed.

"It's time for my late afternoon break and I need another cookie and an iced coffee."

"We're closed," Darby pointed out.

"So? Kelly let me in, said I just had to wait for you to get back. And now you're avoiding the topic at hand. Just how do you know Chef Sexy?"

Darby sighed. "It was at one of my cooking classes. I was still working as a lawyer, you know, but taking classes on the side, testing the waters. And Sean Callahan was one of our guest instructors—you know, this hot new chef there to give us encouragement about our future."

"Hot chef," Caitlyn said, laughing, "You made a funny."

"Do you want to hear the story or not?" Darby asked, not in the mood for Caitlyn's jokes.

Caitlyn waved a hand. "Oh please, keep going."

"We were supposed to make a traditional steakhouse meal. Rib eye, onion rings, creamed spinach."

"I'm getting hungry just thinking about it." Caitlyn closed her eyes.

"Well, don't," Darby told her.

"What happened?" Caitlyn's eyes flew open.

"I don't know." Darby shook her head. She actually had an idea, but it was hard to prove. "My creamed spinach tasted like it had been dipped in seawater and left out in the sun to bake off."

"Ugh," Caitlyn held up her hands. "Not so hungry anymore."

"And, of course, somehow the heat on my cooktop was turned up too high, and my steak was a rubbery gray lump. And I won't even tell you what happened to the onion rings."

"So, you had a bad meal. Happens to all of us." Caitlyn tried to sound encouraging.

Darby shook her head. "But I was top of my class, and I make amazing creamed spinach."

"True. So then what happened?"

"Sean Callahan did. And, well, let's just say I learned exactly why he had a reputation for being not such a nice guy."

Darby had to suppress a shudder at the memory. She had been yelled at before. Try being a first year associate at a law firm. One of the partners there had been both a screamer and a book thrower. Luckily, her aim had been terrible. Still, she hadn't really cared about her job there. But cooking … she had poured everything she had into that meal, hoping that a big name chef like Sean Callahan would love it and validate her dream of wanting to quit being a lawyer and run a restaurant, even a small deli in a small town.

"So what happened? I mean, to your spinach?"

Darby shrugged. "I can't be sure, but you remember Will, the guy I almost got engaged to? I think perhaps he was jealous. You see, Sean came around tasting our work in progress and was actually really nice. Will saw and, well, he was the most jealous guy I've ever met. I think he might have sabotaged me."

She knew she couldn't prove it, and she and Will were old history, but being told that she should rethink her career choice by Sean Callahan had smarted. More than smarted. She had almost been reduced to tears, but had fought it off, vowing to work harder and even smarter. And watch her back. It wasn't the last time another chef had tried to ruin her food. Chefs were a passionate lot.

"Why do you think that?" Caitlyn asked.

"Because Will stepped forward with the most perfect spinach anyone had ever tasted."

Caitlyn narrowed her eyes. "And let me guess, it tasted just like yours?"

"Just about," Darby nodded.

"So you think he stole your creamed spinach and passed it off as his own?"

"I could never prove it, but yeah, I think. Too much salt is a rookie mistake."

"And you're no rookie," Caitlyn agreed. There was a pause, and Darby focused on the flour she was working into dough.

"So, what happened with Sean today? What did he do? Remind you of your mistake?" Caitlyn asked, her gray eyes wide with sympathy.

"Worse. He apparently remembered nothing about me or the incident. It was like it never happened," Darby said and looked up from where she was kneading her dough. "Well," she amended, "he did try every cheesy pickup line in the book on me, so I guess I made some sort of impression on him."

"What an ass," Caitlyn said, dismissing Sean.

Darby shook her head. "I think Sean Callahan probably yells at a hundred people every day. Several times a day. You should have seen what he said to the pastry students about their *apple tartine*. Now that was something fearsome to behold." Darby tried to make her voice light, make it sound like she was over the whole ordeal.

But it still hurts, she thought. She had wanted to impress Sean Callahan that day, to prove to herself and the world that quitting her nice, steady, secure job to open a restaurant wasn't such a crazy idea. And he had shaken her faith in herself—or rather, Darby thought, she had let him shake her own faith.

"Well, how are you going to show him?" Caitlyn asked.

"Show him what?" Darby stopped mixing her dough and looked at her friend.

"That you're an amazing cook."

"Umm, why would I do that?"

"You need to cook for him again." Caitlyn said it matter-of-factly, as if it were an everyday occurrence to make a meal for a celebrity chef.

Darby made a scoffing sound. "And how do you propose I do something like that?" She gestured with her knife to her cutting board. "Send him over dinner on a cart? Should I dress like a sexy French maid too?"

Caitlyn shrugged one shoulder. "I'm more of a big picture thinker, so I'll leave the details to you. Can I have my cookie, now that I've listened to all your problems? Please, being a good friend makes me hungry."

Darby laughed. Caitlyn had cheered her up, and maybe, just maybe, she was on to a way that Darby could restore her pride.

Chapter 8

Sean nursed his morning coffee. He'd stayed up late, going over menus and working on some recipes for the cookbook he was developing, and he was enjoying easing into the day. He was sitting at the empty barroom of the Osprey Arms waiting for the prep meeting, which was supposed to start in ten minutes.

His phone buzzed, and he reached for it, reading the text before pushing it away. His publicist was working overtime on his big "comeback," but seriously, a job hosting a cooking show in Japan? He texted back one word: *No* and received a predictable response: *But you're a huge hit there.*

He didn't even bother to answer, just took another sip of his coffee and stared pensively out over the water. He'd thought after being asked to leave, well, fired really from the restaurant in New York that everything would blow over with enough time. But he was finding that perhaps it wasn't the case. He'd sort of accepted the fact that he might not be able to live it down or get back to where he had been—which, strangely, didn't bother him as much as it might have a few months ago.

Things were going well here, the Osprey Arms' new menu proving to be a success. People were all of a sudden showing up by land and sea to check it out. Sure, they might not be celebrities or models as they were in the city, but the customers here were more appreciative and even more genuine. And then there had been that review. Sure, it was just in the region's local paper, but what had it said was: "Sean Callahan's food finally lives up to all of its hype." Coming to Queensbay meant that he was able to focus on what he loved doing—cooking.

A waitress walked by, and an enticing aroma wafted up in the air.

"What's that?" He held up a hand to stop her. She froze, like a deer caught in the headlights.

"What's what? This?" She held up a brown paper bag. "I'm sorry. I was going to just finish it up and get started on my shift." The waitress was babbling, clearly afraid he was going to yell.

"Let me see," Sean said. He knew the waitress was worried she'd done something wrong, but he didn't care. Whatever was in that bag smelled too delicious to let her pass by without finding out what was in there.

An egg sandwich appeared, and he took it from her. He put it on the bar, spread out on its white paper wrapping.

"Homemade bun. Thick-cut bacon. Fresh eggs. Chives. Goat cheese," he said, cataloging the ingredients.

He looked at the waitress.

"You can have it," she said, and he could hear the quiver in her voice.

He didn't need to be invited twice. He picked it up, took a bite. The bread was delicious, fresh and tasty, the bacon thick and juicy, and the egg was fried crisp. The goat cheese gave the right amount of saltiness to the whole thing.

"Where did you get this?"

"The Dory," the girl managed to stammer. She was the one who had brought the cookies in yesterday. Apparently, she was a big fan of the place.

"Here." Sean reached into his pocket and pulled out a couple of bills. "Go get yourself another—and some for the rest of the crew. On me."

The girl hesitated for only an instant before she grabbed the money and was gone.

Sean took another bite of the sandwich. It was just an egg sandwich, but everything was perfection. He knew he'd been right about Darby the first time. Whatever else she was, which was certainly mad as hell at him, she was still an excellent cook. He'd had one of The Dory's egg sandwiches a couple of weeks ago, when her dad had been cooking. It had been fine, adequate even, but this ... this was, he thought as he took another bite, amazing.

One of the things that had attracted him about the opportunity with Chase and the Osprey was the fact that there wasn't a lot of competition in Queensbay for really good food. However, if Darby Reese kept cooking like this, then he might be in for a run for his money.

He'd been thinking about her every moment since she had told him to leave her alone. Now that she had reminded him about it, the incident played over and over in his head.

He remembered her now. How he had been intrigued by her those eyes and the quiet, intent concentration she put into everything she was doing. She was different than a lot of the other students. A bit older, more put together, and focused.

He'd been asked to be a guest instructor at the Culinary Academy to a group of hopeful chefs. These days, it seemed like everyone dreamed of becoming a chef, running a fancy restaurant, getting a job on TV. None of them really considered all the hard work, the intensity of working in an overheated environment trying to serve a hundred dinners at once. No one had wanted to hear his story about the years spent at a no name rib and fried chicken joint in a small town. Or how it was important to know and respect your ingredients, to know your basic techniques. Everyone just wanted to be famous.

The head instructor had told him to be real so that the kids would get a taste of what it would be like in a busy kitchen: all heat and passion and little tolerance for mistakes. He had gone hard on the soup round and felt like an ass. Then he'd been more helpful with the spinach, checking in on the students, tasting as they went, hoping to find someone's he could say something nice about. And he had with Darby's, or so he had thought. It had been good, delicious even ... and, well, she'd been easy on the eyes. He even remembered that now. So he had planned on picking hers to show that he could be a good guy as well.

And then when she had brought it up to him, it had been, what—ruined? Like drinking saltwater, he remembered. The instinct to criticize was almost habitual, but perhaps he had gone too far out of surprise. Darby had withstood his abuse reasonably well, he recalled now, her face immovable under her chef's hat.

And then he had moved on to the steak and onions and then to the dessert. Had he even noticed that she had disappeared? Anyway, the top student had been Will Green, who had done everything well, including the creamed spinach that now, as he swallowed another bite of Darby's truly wonderful egg sandwich, reminded him of someone else's.

"Son of a bitch," he said, everything falling into place.

Chapter 9

"You need how many sandwiches?" Darby looked at Chloe like she had three heads.

"Twelve," Chloe repeated firmly.

"It's a bit late and I have to switch over to the lunch menu," Darby said, trying to talk her out of it. The goat cheese breakfast sandwich had been a special and had just about sold out, pleasing Darby since she had adjusted the price upwards to give her a better profit margin and hadn't gotten one complaint about it.

Her first few days at The Dory were going well. She had managed to spruce up the dining area a bit with some potted flowers and a good cleaning, but there was still more that could be done.

Chloe shifted from one foot to the other. She was a local girl, a few years younger than Darby. "Please, Darby, please? I'll buy you a beer at Quentin's."

"Are you even old enough to drink?" Darby asked, checking the water level in the coffee maker.

"I'm going to be a senior at UConn," Chloe answered, with a huff in her voice.

"That doesn't answer my question," Darby said sternly.

"Look, Sean Callahan really liked them. I showed up for work, and he took mine and told me to get another one and sandwiches for the whole crew."

Darby almost let the water overflow the coffee pot she was refilling. "Sean Callahan wants them?"

"Yes. Please don't make me say you ran out." The look on Chloe's heavily freckled face was scrunched up in pure terror.

Darby let herself have a smile. "Okay, done—but you have to promise to run back to the Osprey with them. I don't want them to get cold."

"Thank you, thank you, thank you!" Chloe was practically on her knees in gratitude. "The beer is on me."

"You can save the beer. Don't worry; I'll find some other way you can pay me back."

Darby went back to the grill herself. So, Sean Callahan had a craving for her breakfast special. She was getting the chance to cook for him and she hadn't even needed to don any kind of costume.

Chapter 10

"Can we talk?" Sean came up to her as she was locking The Dory's door. It was almost five, and The Dory usually stopped serving lunch around two. Darby knew her dad did it so he could head down to the docks, take his boat out, and get a little fishing in before the sun set.

Still, a quick look through the books and her observations led her to believe that they were missing out on a lot of revenue by closing early. There were plenty of people who needed a mid-afternoon pick-me-up, like a cookie and iced coffee. She had stayed open later and already pulled up profits for the day. It was something else she meant to point out to her dad when he came back.

"Why?" she said, straightening up. Her back ached, and her feet were sore. Though she was used to putting in longer days than this, there was something about being on her feet all day that was a lot more demanding than sitting behind a desk.

"I think I owe you an apology," Sean said, running his fingers through his hair, making the blonde tips stand on end.

He needs a haircut, she thought, fighting back the strong desire to rearrange it for him. He wasn't some cute little boy that needed to be taken care of. He was cruel; she had to remember that, despite the completely different signals her body was sending her brain.

She dropped the key in her bag and started to move up the street. She knew that she needed to stay away from him, try to circumvent the little jolts of attraction that started to shoot off whenever he was around.

"What for? Yelling at me when I served bad food? Or not remembering me after the fact?"

He took her arm again, this time gently spinning her around. "Both," he said, his voice contrite, his eyes the color of dark ginger beer.

Bewitched by those eyes, she managed to nod and then, without another word, turned on her heel and headed up High Street. Sean fell into step beside her.

"You're still here," she said.

"You never said 'apology accepted'," he pointed out.

"What are we? Four years old?" She swallowed. She hadn't said anything because she didn't trust herself. She worried that her voice might quiver. For months, she had dwelled on the incident, wondering if she could have done something different. More than anything, she was mad at herself for being too trusting, for not really understanding the stakes of the game. What had she thought? That Sean Callahan would be so entranced by her food that he would immediately offer her a job, her dreams thereby achieved in one easy step. But nope, it never worked that way.

"Fine, apology accepted," she said, praying that he would leave her alone—and knowing she would be sorely disappointed if he did.

It had been another perfect day in Queensbay, with a blue sky and strong breeze, but now there was a different feel to the air. A bank of gray clouds was building out to the east, and the breeze had quickened. Still, over the town, sun reigned.

She sniffed.

"What are you doing?" Sean asked.

She hazarded a glance up and explained, "The air. It's changed. Rain's coming."

"Still looks sunny to me." Sean pointed toward the blue sky out to the west.

"Look out to the east, out over the water, toward the ocean. Looks like a squall is coming through."

"Guess I'll have to trust you on that," Sean said, his voice light.

She stared into those liquid brown eyes and tried to control the reaction in her body, the way her stomach did a flip flop before sending out a call for the rest of her to do a happy dance. Seriously, she knew that Sean Callahan was not a good person. Why, then, did she feel that familiar tightening, the clutch of desire just south of her churning stomach?

Something almost like a giggle escaped from her. She told herself not to be so nervous. She had nothing to worry about. Sean Callahan had sought her out. If she had been one of her clients and this had been a negotiation or some sort of a deal, she would have told her client to act cool, collected, let Sean do all the talking, see what he wanted. See where this was going to go.

"Nice little town," Sean said, in the tone of voice that meant he was trying desperately to find something to say that wouldn't get him in trouble.

"It is," she answered in the same tone.

He gave a little laugh.

"What's so funny?"

"Are you a typical New Englander, only saying one word when two will do? I mean, I've heard of people like you, but I didn't think they actually existed."

He flashed a smile at her, and she caught a glimpse of his dimples. Her breath almost caught again, and she shook her head.

"I talk. It's just ... I have a lot on my mind."

"Really?" He looked over at her speculatively and waited a moment, before he said, "You can't leave a guy hanging like that, you know. You can't say you have a lot on your mind and just let it go. It's the kind of statement that's begging for a followup."

"It's just stuff. You know, did I remember to order enough eggs for the morning rush? Do I need to get a new coffee supplier? Those types of things. It's nothing."

He shrugged. "Sounds like the stuff I worry about all the time. Perils of running a restaurant."

They stopped, and Sean looked expectantly at her.

"This is my place." She opened an ornately scrolled iron gate that sat in front of a small lawn bisected by a gravel and stone path. The house it led to was a tidy little Queen Anne Victorian, painted a dark cream, its trim in a contrasting shade of white. It was one of many homes that lined the streets of the village as it worked its way back from the water. The lots closer to downtown were a little smaller, and the house was diminutive, rather than expansive, but as she had inherited it from her grandmother a few years back, she had no reason to complain.

In the first few years that she had owned it, she had rented it out, but last month, when the last lease had been up, she'd decided not to rent it, telling her parents she needed a place to escape from the city on the weekends.

"It's cute," Sean said, leaning back to take it in.

Like many Victorians, the house had more height than width, with a fanciful little square tower on one side, which was accessed through a panel in the ceiling in Darby's bedroom.

"Thanks," she said, pushing the off-kilter gate that led to a flagstone walkway. She'd spent most of her free time this summer painting, pruning, planting, and cleaning the place up. It was finally starting to look the way it had when her grandmother had been in her prime. Sean was still following her, and she didn't know how to say anything to shake him. Worse yet, she wasn't sure she wanted to.

She led the way up the path, noticing that the pots of begonias needed more water. He followed her up onto the porch. She didn't know what she was supposed to do, whether to ask him in or not. He had apologized; she had accepted. Business completed. Still, he showed no sign of going anywhere, and finally her good manners won over.

"We could go inside, but it's probably cooler out here." She motioned to the wicker couch on the porch. She had given it a new life with a coat of crisp white paint, and Caitlyn, who was surprisingly skilled with a sewing machine, had whipped up some striped cushions for her.

Sean sank onto the couch. "You can see the water," he said appreciatively, craning his neck to catch a view of it.

"Barely. Can I get you a drink?" Darby offered, more because she wanted one, and Sean didn't seem in any hurry to leave.

"I don't want to put you out," he said, but his tone was hopeful.

"You're the one who followed me home," she pointed out. "Anyway, coffee's always on ice here," she said, trying not to sound elated at the prospect of spending more time with him.

"Iced coffee it is." Sean nodded and gave her another one of his smiles that would have had her blushing if she hadn't turned and hurried through the screen door.

She went into the kitchen, telling herself to cool it. He had come to her, so again there was no reason to be nervous. He had apologized, right? Did that mean they were starting over? Did she want to start over? They were grownups, right, and there was no use denying that she found him attractive. And he felt the same way, she assumed, judging by his remarks the other day.

She sighed, reminding herself that Sean was used to hanging out with celebrities and models. Bright, attractive, well-put together: she might use all those words to describe herself, but she'd never once been asked to model. Was he trying for another notch on his ladle?

Just go with it, she told herself. She wasn't a lawyer anymore; she didn't need to analyze everything from every angle. She was allowed to simply enjoy being in the presence of a really cute guy, right? After all, it was about time her hormones kicked in and showed there was still some life left in them. And just because she acknowledged finding him attractive, didn't mean she had to act on it. Or did it?

She put that thought out of her head as she grabbed the jug of coffee she brewed every morning and put in the fridge to cool during the day. She threw it onto a tray, along with some tall glasses, a bowl of ice, and a small pitcher of cream.

She poked her head into the small powder room that had been squeezed under the stairs. She looked … well, as good as one could look after a day spent in a hot kitchen. She pulled her hair back, trying to smooth down the wisps that were curling even more because of the humidity of the approaching storm.

Lipstick, she really should wear lipstick, but to run upstairs and find some would only keep him waiting, and he probably had to be back at work.

So she took her tray, and her smile, and headed out onto the porch.

"You were right." Sean nodded at the sky. The storm had rolled in fast, the pewter-gray clouds tumbling in on a strong wind that was tossing the trees so that the leaves showed their silvery underbellies. In the distance, Queensbay Harbor was flecked with whitecaps, the water a seething, metallic thing, almost as if it were some sort of beast coiling to strike.

She nodded. She was seldom wrong about the weather, especially when it was happening on her harbor. She busied herself pouring coffee. "That's living on the water for you."

"I wouldn't know," Sean said.

"No?" she asked, curious despite herself.

"I'm from Indianapolis, well, not even. A small town about a hundred miles away."

"I'm guessing there's no water there?"

"No, not really, at least nothing like this." He gestured toward the harbor.

She looked out at it. She loved the water, always had. "No, it's definitely a force of nature to behold."

Sean seemed to take up most of the couch, but there was nowhere else to sit, unless she decided to lean back against the railing, which probably wasn't a good idea with the way the wind was whipping around. A small branch, leaves still attached, flew by.

Trying not to get too close to him, she sat on the edge of the couch and watched as he poured himself some coffee.

"Hmm," he said, after he had added some cream. "You must grind those beans yourself."

"Every morning," she admitted, taking a sip of her own coffee. The temperature had dropped, which was a welcome change from the earlier heat. Rain wouldn't be too far behind. Probably lightning and thunder would come as well. "But you didn't come here to talk about my coffee, did you?"

Sean looked her over, and she had to fight back a nervous reaction to check her hair, check her lips, anything to make sure that he wasn't staring at her for the wrong reason. His eyes, the color of a dark ginger beer, danced with effervescence. *God, could he be any hotter?* she thought and then put the thought away, deeply away.

"Not about the coffee, though I might have to ask you for the name of your supplier."

"We'll see," she said. The truth was, she had her own personal beans delivered monthly from a small company in Portland. And there were some things that were meant to be kept under wraps.

"You were sabotaged," he said, finally.

"What?" She looked at him.

"That's what happened, right? Someone poured salt in the spinach before you gave it to me? I tasted it before. It was incredible, and then when I tasted it in front of the class ..." He trailed off.

"It tasted like seawater. I know. It's my grandmother's recipe. Trust me, it never tasted like that."

"So somebody dumped salt in it." He sounded triumphant, pleased with himself at having figured it out.

She shrugged, shifting a little on the couch. "Actually, I think someone took mine, gave me his, and poured salt into it. I can't prove it, but what I made didn't taste like that."

"You should have said something," Sean said, running his hands through his hair in frustration. She wondered why he was bothered by this now.

"Like you would have believed me? It would have sounded like an excuse. Look, I'm a lawyer. Trust me, I have heard just about all of them. And none of them ever sound like anything but an excuse. You were upset and rightly so—the dish that you tasted was a disaster. But don't worry, it was only spinach. I've suffered much worse from clients and partners. You went easy on me."

As she said it, she realized it was true. It had only been spinach and she had moved on and forward—and become better because of his criticism. Still, she thought, she wasn't about to thank him for it, not when he looked so cute being apologetic.

"Then why did you leave the class? I looked for you, afterwards to talk to you, but ..."

She laughed, amused at his discomfort. "Not because of you. Well, at least, not just because of you. I had a work emergency. I wasn't quite ready to quit my day job back then, so I had to go back to the office. I was just taking the class for fun, really."

Sean looked at her, one eyebrow slightly raised. "It was a professional level class. People don't take it just for fun."

"What can I say? My idea of fun is a little different than everyone else's."

"Who did it? Who do you think poured the salt in it?" Sean asked.

"Does it matter?" She didn't really want to discuss this.

"I think I have an idea," Sean said, his voice dropping to a throaty whisper that had a delightful shiver running down her back, one that had nothing to do with the sudden drop in temperature.

"Those are good things to have, usually," she managed to respond, her stomach clenching at the hope that perhaps his voice might suddenly whisper something naughty in her ear.

"It was Will Green, wasn't it? Do you know I hired him? Because of that class." Sean shifted uncomfortably, and anger flashed across his face.

"I know. Probably. The guy was a jealous bastard with a temper. And he was a sneak."

"You seem to know him well."

She hesitated, and then decided it was better if it were out in the open. "We dated. Actually we more than dated. So I saw firsthand how determined he could be to get his own way."

"Did he hurt you?" All of sudden, Sean's voice was loud again, his eyes hard and unreadable.

"No." She shook her head. "He was a controlling manipulative bastard, and he had a way of making me doubt myself. Needless to say, he shook my faith in the intentions of the other sex. We hadn't really started to date then, but I think he was jealous that you were giving me some attention. So he got back at me."

"Why would he try to get back at you?" Sean asked.

"I told you he was a sneak. I think he was more jealous of my cooking skills than of me with other men. He kept stealing all my family recipes and passing them off as his own. It just took me a while to figure it out."

"So, did it get serious between the two of you?" Sean said, his voice cool.

She sat back. She really didn't like to remember her time with Will. He hadn't hurt her, at least not physically. But he'd done a good job of luring her in. Maybe, just for a bit, she had thought he was the one. But then her good senses had kicked in and she'd seen all the things he did in an attempt to try to prove he was in control. Little things, to undercut her and undermine her confidence. At first had been things like showing up late, leaving her waiting at places, then it had been the verbal put downs, and finally the last straw—stealing her family recipes. It galled her that she had stood for it, even holding out hopes that maybe they'd get engaged. But she had figured out, finally, just how manipulative he was, and then she had walked away fast enough.

"Sort of. But I ended it. Well, at least according to me. I am sure if you ask him, he'd tell a completely different story."

Sean gave a bitter laugh. "We're not exactly on speaking terms either. I did hire him, but then I had to fire him. It got a little ugly."

"Ugly?"

Sean looked down into his coffee. "It might have gotten a little physical."

She tried to quash the feeling of triumph. "Is it wrong to say I hope you won?"

Sean sighed. "Maybe the battle, but not the war. Turns out nobody likes a boss who punches people. Let's just say it wasn't my finest hour."

"Why did you fire him?" She knew she should stop talking about it, but she couldn't resist satisfying her own curiosity.

"I fired him because he was giving away the kitchen's secrets to one of our competitors. Before I knew it, we were yelling, and then … I don't know." Sean stood up, his large hands clenched at his sides.

She thought for a moment. "Let me guess … he pretty much goaded you into throwing the first punch, then cried foul and got you in trouble?"

He shot her a look. "How did you know?"

"Like I said, I dated him. That was totally his style."

Sean laughed bitterly. "Funny thing is, I hadn't thrown a punch in years. I mean, when I was a kid, that was the only way I knew how to settle things. I know I have a temper, and I know I yell at people, but like I said, I haven't used my fists in years. I thought I had that part of me under control. But he pushed every button I had."

She shook her head. "It's a pretty foolproof scam, you know—trick someone into getting so mad that it looks like they're the ones that started it. Works on schoolyard bullies and bosses."

Sean gave a bitter laugh. "Before I knew it, I was the one who was fired and Will had my job. He even threatened to sue me."

She felt for him, remembering the way Will had manipulated her. "I'm sorry. Is that why you left the city? One moment you were all the rage, and then, well, you just sort of disappeared."

She regretted the words as soon as they were out of her mouth. She hadn't meant to get so personal with him, but then again she almost never talked about Will.

Sean didn't seem to mind, he just nodded and said, "One of the reasons, I guess. I worked for a group of investors at this big restaurant. They liked me when I was on TV and hanging with the city's celebrities, but not so much when they had to hire a lawyer to defend me against that lowlife. So they asked me to leave. When I didn't want to, they fired me and advised me to keep a low profile and get the hell out of Dodge. Or in this case, Gotham."

She looked at Sean and saw that he was truly upset. "It doesn't sound fair."

Sean shook his head and he sank back down onto the couch. "Truth is, I did punch a guy—warranted or not—and they were right. I was wound up tight, ready to blow. So here's to lessons learned— and using them to become a better person."

"And watching our backs." She realized she had settled in on the couch closer to him, no longer guarding her space. Their glasses clinked, and their eyes locked. She could feel the cool wind whipping around them, and realized, out of the corner of her eye, that the storm had come in and borne down on them with a vengeance, yet all she could do was stare at Sean's face, taking in the way his eyes bore into hers.

Their heads were almost touching, and one of his hands reached out and tugged at a strand of her hair that had blown loose. His finger traced down the skin of her cheek lightly, and she shivered, turning in to his touch. Her mind was racing as, almost unbidden, they moved even closer to each other. She knew she shouldn't be doing this, but she risked looking into his eyes and was lost. The question was there, in his intense gaze, and she knew she was matching the heat in them with her own.

Seamlessly, words unnecessary, they moved toward each other, their lips touching. At first, his kiss was tentative, but she responded to it, leaned into it, and he took her lead, his mouth hot and hungry on hers, his arms pulling her up and closer to him. She heard his glass being set down and felt hers being lifted from her hand, and then his arms were around her, pulling her close.

He pushed back once, searched her face, and then covered her mouth with his. A moan escaped her as she felt her body tense in response to his kisses. Electricity snaked through them, matching the ozone in the air.

He leaned over her, so her back was on the couch, and she could feel the delicious weight of his body over hers, feel the strength in his arms. She loved the way his lips were brushing down her neck, her chin, down to her chest, flirting with the curve of her breasts underneath her top.

She didn't know how long they would have stayed like that, or what would have happened next. And then it came, just as she had predicted, a boom of thunder so deafening that they sprang apart.

"Oh," she said, as a spear of lightning cracked over the harbor.

"I'm sorry." Sean sat up, backing away from her, the expression on his face wary, unreadable.

She was very aware that her heart was racing and that her hair clip had come undone and that her eyes were open wide in shock.

"I didn't mean to," he stammered.

She sat up, too, but he rose and took a step back, nearly tipping over a small side table.

"Look," Sean cleared his throat and his voice was steady, "thanks for the coffee. I guess I better head back now. Dinner rush and all that."

She nodded. The temperature had dropped, and she wrapped her arms around her, hugging herself close, all of a sudden cold in just a t-shirt, or maybe it was from the waves of coldness rolling off of Sean.

He was backing away, turning to face the top of the steps. "Thanks again for the coffee."

And with that, he practically ran down the steps, down the flagstones and out the gate. It swung shut behind him, the low squeal of the hinges muted by another roll of thunder that caused her to flinch. A slash of lighting forked across the roiling black sky over the harbor.

Sean all but jogged down the sidewalk, and he disappeared around the corner just as the first of the big, fat raindrops splattered down.

Had she just been jilted by Sean Callahan? *Ugh*, she thought, banging her head against the column. It was for the best, she thought. Sure, they had shared a moment, but this was still Sean Callahan standing in front of her. He was a guy known for his Get Laid dinners, wild nights, bad temper and now for firing people by punching them out. Really, truly, she needed to stay away, especially if the torrent of emotions she was experiencing was any indication. She needed to concentrate, focus, while she was here. She had a bad habit of getting too wrapped up, forgetting herself. But not this time. Now, with her plan, there could be no distractions. *Men,* she thought. Chefs were even worse. Maybe all he wanted from her were her beans.

Chapter 11

Sean didn't really stop to think until he was back in the kitchen of the Osprey Arms. He yelled at the line chef and felt marginally better, and then remembered he wasn't supposed to yell at all. But after his afternoon with Darby, he felt like he had to take his stupidity out on somebody. And then, of course, he realized he had no one to blame but himself.

With a sigh, he set down his knife, straightened up and called the guy over.

"Sorry about that, buddy. I don't think I was clear. I want you to prepare the vegetables this way."

He went over the technique, slowly, patiently, and this time Kevin got it. Sean clapped him on the back.

Feeling better, Sean took off his cap and went out the back door into the small alley. The rain storm had been short but violent. What had Darby called it? A squall. In and out. He'd gotten a thorough soaking by the time he'd reached the restaurant, which had done nothing to cool down the heat running thorough him. He felt like a randy teenager who had just gotten in his first grope under the bleachers. Not even if he threw himself in the waters of Queensbay Harbor would it be enough to cool him down.

What had come over him? There was just something about her, the way she had looked at him, had listened to him.

"God, what was I thinking?" he muttered. He'd gone to see Darby to apologize. To do the right thing. To make amends for being a jerk. And then what had he done? He'd kissed her—god, he had practically jumped her on the creaky wicker couch on her porch in front of the whole village. He had wanted to kiss her, kiss her so hard she would call out his name and beg him for more. There was something about the way those dusky green eyes looked at him, inviting him to confess, making him feel forgiven.

She was a good girl. Not in a prim way, not at all, judging by the way she had responded to him. Still, he just knew that Darby Reese was a good girl. The type of girl who ran her dad's restaurant for him while he was on vacation. The type of girl who everybody liked, who baked cookies to help out the team, who probably kept her books sorted in alphabetical order.

He ran a hand through his hair. She was a good girl, which was exactly the reason he needed to stay away from her. She deserved better. Yes, he was trying to be a better person, but he wasn't there. Truth was, when he had punched Will Green, all he had thought was that the guy had deserved it, that it had felt good. Very good to feel his hands connect with another person's face. Just like old times. In fact, if some of the busboys hadn't pulled him off, he wasn't sure he'd have been able to stop.

Before that moment, he had thought he'd put his past behind him, that he'd never become the kind of man he'd been shaping up to be. And then one little worm of a guy had pushed his buttons, and he'd gone right back to being the type of hothead who couldn't be trusted.

But with Darby it was all of a sudden important to him that she thought more of him. The knowledge surprised him. He walked to the railing of the dock. A mother duck and her ducklings were swimming around. He knew they often came here, looking for handouts. Sean pulled the lettuce he had set aside from the pocket of his chef's uniform and tossed it into the water. There was a flurry of interest, some quacks, and soon momma and babies were happily feasting.

He smiled at the scene, and then his thoughts turned to her again. He'd gone to explain himself, and suddenly he'd been thinking along entirely different lines. Like how her freckles were like flakes of cinnamon dusted across her pale skin. How the sun, before it had been subsumed by the clouds, had gilded her hair red, and how all he had wanted to do was twine his hands through it.

And her lips. She had licked them and then bitten them as she had listened to him, with an intensity that told him she was taking it all in, and it had driven him crazy. He hadn't been able to stop himself—and well, she hadn't exactly told him no, had she? No, she had damn near given him a gold-stamped invitation.

He scrubbed his hands through his hair. He didn't know why he cared what she thought. She had accepted his apology. In fact, she was only here for a little while, and perhaps with any luck, so was he. He hadn't come here to get involved with a woman. He'd come here to do a job. An important one. Getting involved with someone like Darby Reese wasn't on his agenda. Couldn't be on his agenda. He had his own redemption to work on. He couldn't bring anyone else along for the ride. Except there was something about her, something that had made him want to ask if they could start over.

Someone called his name from the inside. Swearing to himself, he put his hat back on and went into the heat of the kitchen.

Chapter 12

Quentin Tate was a big man. Darby had always wondered if he'd been born that way, ripping through his poor mother's body and entering the world with a lusty cry. Because everything about Quent was larger than life, from his laugh, to his hands, to the way his voice bellowed when he was telling a story.

"So, I hear you're in charge, girl." Sure enough, Quentin's voice boomed out as he entered The Dory.

She barely looked up. It was after the early morning rush and there was no one else seated inside the café. Everything was in order, her muffins baked, her scones cooling, while a crockpot held warming oatmeal, and a glass jar contained her own special blend of granola. So far, everything had been a hit, and no one had minded the fact that she had priced all the specials just a bit higher than normal.

Quent strolled up and stood with his feet braced apart, hands on his hips, surveying the array of good she had arranged in the glass counter. He looked like the bartender he was, with his shaved head, dark, hard eyes, and biceps so big they could probably crush an elephant. He had his usual five o'clock shadow, even this early, and Darby noticed that there were now a few wisps of gray dusted in.

"So, lassie, you send your father out of town, and you take over the place," Quent said, with what, for him, passed as wit.

"Quent, what a surprise to see you up so early." She said it as sweetly as she could, knowing from experience that the best way to get rid of him was to humor him.

Quentin's Pub was open until last call, and that meant that Quent was not a morning person and didn't usually make an appearance around town until at least noon.

"Everyone's been talking about how Reg's little girl is back in town, baking up a storm. I heard your scones were lighter than air and just thought I'd check them out," he said, taking a seat at one of her tables, pulling the newspaper out from under his arm, and looking like he was more than prepared to settle in for a while.

Quent had shown up in Queensbay half a decade ago, single and unemployed. He'd affected something of an Irish accent when he'd first arrived and took over behind the bar of what had been called the Rusty Nail. He was cryptic on the details of his background, but word was he always seemed to have plenty of cash to throw around.

Soon after, the original owner had sold out to Quent and retired to Florida. Now Quent held court in his own establishment, selling beer, burgers, and clam chowder to the mariners and locals.

"We have plain and cranberry-orange," she said, trying not to let her irritation show. She knew her father sometimes fished with Quent, but Quent's fake chumminess and phony Irish accent grated on her nerves. Not to mention that he was forever making subtle digs at just about everyone.

She knew that Quent had put out a "friendly" offer to buy The Dory more than once, but so far, her dad had said he wasn't ready to sell. She couldn't imagine anything worse than knowing Quent owned The Dory.

"I'll just have a plain one with some butter and a cup of your coffee."

She brought the scone around and set it on a plate in front of Quent, the side of butter in its little dish and a napkin with the flatware wrapped up inside.

"Well isn't this fancy. Seems like you're already putting your own stamp on the place and your Da only gone a couple of days."

She decided to ignore him by focusing on what the weather was doing outside the large plate glass windows. It was going to be a hot day. Yesterday's squall had washed away the humidity for only a little while, and now, even though it was early, the air was hot and wet, surrounding her like a musty blanket. She sighed. She didn't need Quent poking around. Like most bartenders, he had a talent for ferreting out secrets.

"Place could do with a bit of a change. Old Reg seems blind to the fact that there's competition moving in, that the clientele is changing." Quent smiled as he said it, but she still felt a chill run through her.

She didn't like the way he called her father old. Quent himself wasn't that much younger than Reg anyway. Besides, her dad wasn't old. Just set in his ways.

"And this is coming from a man that runs a bar. You couldn't get the smell of stale beer out of there if you tried," she said tartly, even though it wasn't quite true.

With his wad of cash, Quent had cleaned the bar up when he took it over, redoing the floors, painting, buying new furniture, adding TVs, and serving satisfying pub food. All in all, it was a fairly classy place, as far as bars went, and business had been good for him.

"Oh, I try." Quent gave a laugh, and then fixed on her with his hard, dark eyes. "Just wondering how a busy young lawyer like you manages to have a few weeks free. Doesn't that fancy law firm your Da's always talking about need you on a case?" Quent waited, expecting an answer.

She wasn't about to fall into that trap. She had seen it with witnesses on the stand all too often, the need to fill in a silence, to answer a question, to supply more information than was necessary just because a question had been asked. The less you volunteered the harder it was to trip you up.

"I'm between jobs." She let the lie run off her tongue easily. "I'll be starting up again after Labor Day. I saved up quite a bit of vacation time." She took a towel and wiped down a table that was already clean.

"Well, must be nice to have that kind of life. Don't get that working in a restaurant, do ya?" Quent gave her a wink and took a bite of his scone.

In spite of herself, she waited, wanting to know what his reaction was. She watched as he took a bite, saw his eyes open in surprise, and then a smile come over his fierce face.

"Well, just about as good as me old grandma made," Quent said, washing down his scone with a sip of his coffee.

"Glad you enjoyed it," she said absently, her eyes fixed on the figure she could see through the window, making his way straight toward The Dory. It took far less time than she would have thought for him to make it here.

The bell above the door jangled as he entered the room.

"Good morning," Sean said, a trace of a smile curving his lips. "Rumor is you have scones today."

"That she does, laddie," Quent interjected.

She quashed the desire to slap out at him with a towel. Her heart had started hammering the moment she saw Sean, her stomach had jumped doing a happy dance, and her legs felt just the tiniest bit weak. *Sensations, normal reactions to someone I shared a kiss with,* she thought, her rational mind cataloging them, filing them away to be assessed and evaluated at another time. She had to remember that he'd kissed and run, that she didn't, shouldn't even owe him the tiniest bit of interest. But he was here now, looking at her, gauging her reaction. *Just stay cool,* she told herself. *Strong, cool, sexy, confident,* she chanted in her head, turning away from him to buy her some time.

He looked as if he had just arrived from the shower. His golden hair was somewhat tamed, and he was freshly shaven. She could catch the smell of soap and shaving cream on him as he came and stood just a little too close for comfort, setting off more heat in her than a five-alarm fire. She moved out of his way to pick up an empty tea cup and dump it in the service bin. There was no reason for her to be nervous, she reminded herself. Just the fact that they had practically ripped each other's clothes off the night before. Still, it was a surprise to see him standing here, his root-beer-colored eyes fixed on her, watching her, looking like he might just want to eat her up.

Sean tore his eyes away from hers and glanced over at Quent, who was smiling possessively at her. Once again, she fought the urge to snap at him with her towel.

"Don't you have a bar to open up?" she asked, hoping Quent would get the message and leave her alone with Sean.

Quent just smiled. "There's plenty of time. It's best not to start serving alcohol too early in the morning."

Quent then turned his attention to Sean and stuck out a meaty hand. "Quentin Tate, but everyone calls me Quent."

Sean shook it, nodding. "You own the pub?"

"That's me," Quent boomed out. He stood up, took his paper, and folded it neatly under his arm. He glanced between the two of them, his shrewd eyes missing nothing, "Well, lassie, I'll be sure to tell your father that you're carrying on just fine without him. Seems like you missed your talent, taking a law degree instead of going into baking, since your scones are as light as an angel. I'd tell you that you're in the wrong line of work, but I know how proud your dad is of you. Nice of you to help out one last time before your Da sells it."

She froze, the words taking a moment to sink in. "What do you mean, sell it?"

Quent smiled again, and this time there wasn't even a trace of warmth to it. "You haven't heard then? Your father, he's ready to retire, you see, and I've made him a fair offer. Better than fair, seeing how we're fishing buddies. He's all but accepted it and I'm just waiting for him to get back to sign the papers. He was going to take the trip away to think about it, and I bet when he knows what's it like to be able to fish every day, he'll be more than ready."

"But he can't," she said. "It's the family's business. He can't just sell it without talking to the rest of us."

Quent shrugged. "Well, I don't want to get involved in that, but I think your Ma's on board. You know how she's always after him to travel more, do more things besides work. And since you're all set with your own big-time career, doesn't seem like there's much of a discussion to be had, does there?"

Her legs really did feel boneless now, and it was only pride that kept her from sliding into her chair and throwing her head into her hands. Her father selling The Dory? Without even a word to her?

"And a good day to you."

She was dimly aware that Quent was saying his goodbyes, clapping Sean on the back and giving her a smile as he walked out the door.

Chapter 13

"Maybe you should sit down?" Sean didn't like the look on Darby's face. All the color had drained from it, and she looked as if she were going to be sick.

"I'm fine." Darby waved her hand, took a step, and then sank down into one of the chairs, facing the windows.

"Here." He moved quickly, economically, and grabbed a glass and a pitcher of ice water from the counter. He poured a glass for her and all but shoved it into her hands. If he'd had a bottle of brandy, he would have poured her some and made her drink that instead.

"You look as if you've had the rug pulled out from under you," he said, worried when she didn't respond right away.

Darby looked up, and he felt slightly reassured. The green color was gone, and there was a fierce look about her.

"I didn't think my father was really thinking of selling. I thought I had more time."

"Time for what?" He was puzzled. He knew he should have stayed away, if he truly thought that he wasn't good enough for her. But he couldn't, hadn't wanted to. In the cool light of the morning, he had woken up and his first thought had been of her. Not even a series of sprints along the beach or a round of pull-ups and pushups had driven her from his mind.

So he had come up with a plan, a way to make it possible to ease into things with her. However, the thought of taking it slowly was warring with his desire to pull Darby close to him. He reached out a hand across the table, but Darby moved hers away before he could touch her.

Undaunted, he found her hand and pulled it close to him, turning his body toward her so that their knees were touching. He took his other hand and brushed back a strand of hair that was falling across her face. Her green eyes held his, and he thought he detected not fear, but wariness in her eyes.

"Why are you here?" she asked.

"For the scones?" he answered, keeping his voice light.

"If you came to apologize again, don't. I think you've insulted me enough. I thought you wanted that kiss as much as I did. Then you ran away. Was it the thunder? Don't tell me you're afraid of a little thunder. Or is it me? I don't bite—and, well, we certainly know you're not afraid of saying what's on your mind."

"Darby," he started. She tried to pull away from him, but he pulled back, so that she looked at him. "I was trying not to be an ass."

"A what?" she breathed.

"An ass, you know, like you said? I was trying to apologize, and that was it."

"So you didn't follow me home to put the moves on me?" Darby's eyes scrunched together.

"That wasn't the only thing on my mind," he said carefully, wondering how the hell a man was supposed to answer that and live.

He shook his head at the confusion in her voice. "No, I can most definitely assure you that I've been thinking of putting the moves on you since I first saw you. But I was trying to be, you know, a gentleman. I thought I would apologize, let you think about it, and then try and put the moves on you again."

He flashed a smile. "It's just being with you, I guess my timeline got a little compressed. But, for the record, I'm glad it did."

But Darby only nodded, and then seemed to pull herself back into her own thoughts. "Okay," she said, but the frown remained, and he sensed that her mind was moving in another direction.

"Now," he said, "Since I am trying to be a sympathetic example of the male species, do you want to tell me what's on your mind? Because if that guy Quent upset you, I'll—"

"Go punch him out? We know that will only get you in more trouble." She shot him a rueful smile.

In spite of himself, he laughed. "I suppose I could serve him some bad clams, give him a case of food poisoning he'd never forget."

She smiled at him and he felt his heart jump. "But I don't think that's going to solve your problem," he added.

"I don't want my dad to sell The Dory to Quent. I want to work here with him, or if he wants to retire, I'll buy it."

"Sell it to you? Why wouldn't you just take it over from him?" He was puzzled. Most restaurants that were family affairs were handed down from generation to generation, without a question.

Darby shook her head. "My father never wanted me to have anything to do with restaurants. He wanted me to go to school, get good grades, and get into an excellent college. Become a lawyer. You know, make something of myself."

"And?"

"I did all that. Everything he wanted. I became a lawyer because he wanted me to. But I can't do it anymore. I want to cook and bake. I want to make things that make people happy. I don't want to write briefs or threatening letters, or come up with contracts that try to protect every party from every possible thing that could ever possibly happen."

"Your cookies are amazing," he said, savoring the feel of Darby's pulse in her wrist as it beat under his thumb. His own heart was racing, as he thought about the way she had looked at him last night. The connection was there between the two them, something different than he had ever felt before. Sure, there was lust, but something more. He wanted to make this right for her. Whatever it was that was bothering her, he wanted to fix it.

"Lots of people can make good cookies," Darby said. She took her hands back and scrubbed them over her face.

"True, but not all of them want to serve them to the world. Look, if you want to do something different, then you should. It's your life. You can't be happy fitting into other people's idea of who you are," he said, knowing his voice was tinged with bitterness.

Darby cocked her head, searching his face, as if trying to find something.

"You're right," Darby said slowly.

"Sometimes you have to take a chance. Take a leap," he said. He knew they weren't talking about cookies anymore or The Dory.

"A leap," she breathed, and he could feel the way her pulse skittered under her skin.

Somewhere, not too far away, there was the sound of the twinkling bell telling them that someone was coming through the door. Darby shot up, smoothed her apron, and then looked down at him.

"Right." Darby stood up, smiled, and said, "What can I get you?"

He almost answered "you," but realized that she would just brush him off. "Well, how about some coffee and one of those scones?"

"To go?" Darby asked.

"I guess." He waited a beat before adding, "I have an idea, something I would like to test out."

She watched him, an expectant look on her face.

He moved closer and half expected her to rear back from him, but she didn't; she stayed still and watched him.

"I was thinking that you're a nice girl and that since I'm a guy's who trying to be better, that I should just walk away."

"Away?" She breathed.

"But then I couldn't stop thinking about you." *All night*, he almost added and then stopped himself.

"And what were you thinking?" She asked.

Sean swallowed, "That I would like to do just this." And then he leaned in and kissed her. Actually he meant to just let his lips brush hers, to see if the heat, the incredible electricity he had felt yesterday had been for real, or just a product of his imagination.

But once his lips touched hers, they connected and she met him fully. Before he knew it, his arms went around her shoulders and pulled her close to him. He was dimly aware that there were people watching but somehow he didn't quite care.

He was the one who broke it off first and took a step back. Darby stood looking at him, her eyes unreadable.

"I guess you're really not sorry."

She shook her head, giving him a slow, sexy smile that was laced with heat. "I know I should be, but I can't quite stop thinking about you either."

"Well then, Darby Reese, I guess I'll be seeing you around," he said. He smiled and turned, nodded at the couple of teenagers who were staring at him, trying not to laugh, and walked away, knowing that he had left her looking after him. He had passed the test. Yes, he found Darby Reese incredibly attractive, but he would, and could, take things slowly. And he was going to enjoy every moment of it.

Chapter 14

"Was that your stud muffin I saw leaving?" Caitlyn Montgomery was suddenly in front of her, having just finished watching the retreating back of Sean Callahan as he left The Dory.

"Caitlyn, down girl," Darby answered, automatically. She was still trying to process things. One that her father might be selling The Dory, and two, that she had just let Sean Callahan kiss her again.

"So, that's the infamous Sean Callahan?" Caitlyn turned and smirked at Darby. "You're right, probably not my type. But I could so see how he might be yours."

"Please." Darby rolled her eyes, hoping that would throw Caitlyn off the scent.

Caitlyn stepped up to the glass display case. "Scones, brownies, muffins ... my, you've been pretty busy here. Whole town's eagerly waiting for your next yummy treat."

"Thanks," Darby said, waiting patiently while Caitlyn took her time making her selection.

"I met Quent while I was walking here."

"Oh, yeah?" Darby perked up, glad that Caitlyn wasn't asking more about Sean.

"He seemed quite pleased with himself," Caitlyn said, eyeing the brownies. "I'll just take a box of those for the office."

"Isn't he always?" Darby said as she put the brownies in the box. "He told me my dad was going to sell The Dory to him. That it was almost a done deal."

"Does that matter to you?" Caitlyn asked carefully. "I mean, it's not like you've quit your perfectly good job as a lawyer so that your dad will feel sorry for you and let you work at The Dory so you can bake chocolate-caramel brownies for the good people of Queensbay ... Oh, wait, that's it exactly. I can see how selling it to Quent would put a dent in those big plans of yours."

"Shh," Darby said, throwing a glance over her shoulder. For all she knew, Kelly the waitress, or one of the other customers, was listening. News traveled fast in Queensbay and could quickly make its way across the Atlantic to her dad in Italy.

"Ahh, well now, the stakes have been upped. There's a new variable in the mix. I think this calls for a strategic planning session, and food. My house, dinner. We can cook."

"We?" Darby asked doubtfully.

"Okay, I'll supply the wine, you supply dinner, and I'll help."

Darby raised one eyebrow.

Fine," Caitlyn amended. "I'll watch and drink, you cook. Deal?"

"Much safer that way," Darby concurred, handing Caitlyn the box of brownies and an iced coffee.

"I am so excited. I feel like I'm back in high school again, planning on how to get a boy to ask me out. See you tonight."

Darby shook her head as Caitlyn waved and clacked her way out of there in a pair of shoes that probably cost more than what most people made in a month.

Chapter 15

"The review in the newspaper got picked up by one of the area's websites. Reservations have been steadily ticking up. We even had to turn some people away the other weekend." Sean slapped the printout down on the coffee table.

Chase reached for it, glanced at it, and grinned. "Well, just like I thought they would."

Sean and Chase were having their weekly partner meeting over a cold beer and a pizza in Chase's private quarters above the Osprey Arms. Sean was happy that Chase was pleased. Chase had given him a second chance and had given Sean free rein to create his own vision of what the restaurant should be. Sean was glad that he was also able to bring in the profits.

"Thanks for your vote of confidence, but really, this place had nowhere to go but up."

Chase laughed. "You'd be surprised. Some of the old timers have told me that they miss the baskets of fried shrimp."

"And what do you tell them?"

"I tell them to check out your chipotle shrimp cocktail instead."

Sean laughed, feeling comfortable with Chase. Chase wasn't his boss but his partner, and they both had skin in the game. It was a good feeling and Sean was really enjoying the chance to run the restaurant his way.

"Well thanks again, I mean for everything," Sean said. He'd never truly said it before, well, because he was a guy and it was hard for him to say stuff like that.

"Think nothing of it. Listen, I made you an open offer and if it took a while before you had the sense to realize what a great thing you were passing up, well then I guess you were just slower in the brains department than I thought."

Sean decided that he wanted to be serious. "No man, I mean, even after that thing went down with Will Green and my bosses, I just can't believe you had my back."

Chase waved a hand, "Listen, I thought the way they dropped you without giving you a chance to explain wasn't right."

"Probably because I couldn't explain away hitting a guy." Sean caught himself flexing his fist, then stopped himself. "I thought those days were behind me."

"Well, we all make mistakes. Deserve a second chance. Lord knows, I have needed a few of them myself."

Sean looked at Chase. They were about the same age, just over thirty, but Chase had sailed the world, racing sailboats for prize money. He had been smart with his winnings, invested well, and had returned to Queensbay to run the family business when his dad got sick. In just a few short years he had taken a small marine hardware shop and turned it into an upscale mail order company. Then he'd gone on to invest heavily in Queensbay real estate, like the Osprey Arms.

"You'll have to tell me," Sean said.

Chase laughed. "Over something a little stronger than beer. Let's just say if you haven't had a misunderstanding with the authorities of Monaco, you're probably ahead of me."

Sean grinned. "I guess a couple of ball-busting lawyers would have seemed minor league to you."

"All depends on the lawyer. For instance, if you sent over Darby Reese, I just might count myself lucky that I needed some defending." There was a gleam in Chase's eye that Sean recognized as interest.

Sean swallowed. Sometimes it was easy to forget that Queensbay was a small town, just like the one he'd grown up in, where it was only a matter of time before everyone knew your business.

"So I take it you know her?"

Chase nodded. "Sure. In case you haven't figured it out, it's not a big town. We went to school together. She was a couple of years younger, but even so, out of my league. And not about to waste any time with boys like me. I was bit of a wild child. But she was the class president, member of the debate club, captain of the field hockey team. Classic overachiever. And hot too, in a quiet kind of way. But man, when she made cookies for the bake sale, well let's just say there might have been a few fights over who got the last of them."

"But you two never, you know ...?" Sean wasn't sure he wanted to know the answer to the question.

"Dated?" Chase laughed. "Like I said, she was younger and out of my league. I was kind of the guy with a reputation. Reg, her dad, would have kicked my ass if I'd shown an interest in his Darby. He's kind of a big guy. You know, sort of like Bluto from Popeye. Kept a close eye on her."

"Are you trying to tell me to stay away?" Sean didn't like to be told what to do, but he also knew that in high school he'd been the guy slouched in the back of class, marking time until he could be released out into the real world. In high school, and until lately, the Darbys of the world wouldn't have given him a second glance.

"Nah," Chase said easily. "It's just that Darby's always been a bit choosy about who she's gone out with. Always seemed like she was destined for bigger and better things than the rest of us, and last I heard, it seemed like she was well on her way to making them all come true."

Sean tried to make his features look blank. He guessed that it wasn't common knowledge that Darby had been taking cooking classes and was planning on asking her father if she could join the family business. There was a big difference between being a lawyer and running a deli.

Chase watched him and leaned in. "Of course quite a few of us are wondering just how a big deal lawyer was able leave her work behind and come and run The Dory for a couple of weeks."

Sean shrugged. Darby had entrusted him with a secret, and he wasn't about to break the confidence. Besides, if things went as Darby planned, then the cat would be out of the bag soon enough.

"Yeah, it's interesting. Maybe I'll ask her the next time I see her."

Chase leaned back. "So you're planning on a next time."

"A guy can dream, right?" Sean said, knowing he was grinning just thinking about her.

Chapter 16

"I have red and white wine to drink." Caitlyn started talking as soon as she opened the door to Darby. "I didn't know what we're making."

"What we're making?" Darby echoed, as she followed Caitlyn down the polished wood floor of the hallway toward the kitchen.

"You said I could watch. Doesn't that count?" Caitlyn tossed over her shoulder.

"It's not that hard, you know," Darby said, putting her grocery bags down on the granite counter. Caitlyn's mother had redone the kitchen recently, and everything was new and gleaming.

"And don't worry, it's just us. My mom's away at another of her artist retreats, so she won't subject us to any inquisitions about our love lives."

Darby glanced around, eyeing the restaurant-quality appliances. "I don't know why you guys have such a nice kitchen when neither one of you even likes to boil water."

"I know, I know, you're right. But she sold one of her pieces and decided to fund the renovation. I think she thinks if she fixed the kitchen up, it would appeal to buyers."

"You're not thinking of selling the house, are you?" Darby asked, shocked. Caitlyn's house had been in the Montgomery family for generations, built by a sea captain ancestor. It commanded a prime piece of real estate high on one of the bluffs overlooking Queensbay Harbor and Long Island Sound beyond. The house, on the outside, was an appealing example of the Greek Revival style: simple yet regal but with a great porch and high ceilings, wide floorboards, and cozy rooms.

"Not if I can help it," Caitlyn said. "Red?" she asked, holding up a bottle to indicate that the subject was closed.

Darby nodded and accepted the glass Caitlyn handed her.

"Cheers." Caitlyn held up her own glass, and they clinked.

"So, you seem like you've settled in here for a while?" Darby asked carefully, setting out her ingredients. She was going to make them a pasta dish: spicy shrimp and chorizo, dressed with a light tomato cream sauce.

"Yes. I'm enjoying my work at the Randall Group. You know me, as long as I get to be around money all day I'm happy." Darby knew that Caitlyn was only partially joking. Caitlyn had a talent for making money and was a successful financial advisor and investor.

"It's funny. I never thought you'd come back here after what happened." Darby groped for words, letting her hands rest on the cool granite counter. It had been too awful for Caitlyn to deal with, the sudden death of her grandfather, and she'd left for college early, seemingly determined never to set foot in town again.

"Times change. People change," Caitlyn said softly, "and sometimes it feels like there's only one place where you belong."

Darby could understand that. Part of her had never wanted to leave. Not her actual childhood home, since she was more than happy to be living in her own place, but somehow she had always imagined that she'd wind up in Queensbay eventually. The harbor, the town, the way the weather was its own mood. She had loved it since she was little and loved it still. But then again, Queensbay didn't hold the same kind of painful memories for her as it did for Caitlyn.

"You haven't seen him, have you?" Darby lined up her ingredients while Caitlyn stared into her wine glass. She knew Caitlyn would know whom she was referring to.

"Noah? Not in a long time. But then again, he's been busy."

Darby nodded. Noah Randall and Caitlyn had been inseparable in high school. Even watching from the outside, it had been hard to miss the heat between those two. But they'd been young and gone their separate ways. Noah now ran a startup in California and to Darby's knowledge, he hadn't been back to Queensbay either. Darby knew there was a story there, but something about Caitlyn's posture told her it was still off limits.

"But enough about me," Caitlyn said. "It seems like you've been running into Sean Callahan quite a bit around town."

"Where are your cutting boards?" Darby asked, trying to dodge the question. She and Sean ... well, there really wasn't a "them," yet. Just the faint promise of something heady brewing between them.

Caitlyn looked around and pointed vaguely toward one of the cabinets near the oven.

Opening it, Darby was pleasantly surprised to see a range of boards, neatly stacked. She selected one and took out a knife.

"Chef Sean?" Darby asked, trying to keep her voice neutral.

"Or Chef Sexy, as I like to think of him. Tall, blonde, and handsome. With all that charm. I used to watch him on TV and just found myself oozing over him."

"Hands to yourself," Darby said, keeping her voice casual.

"I knew it." Caitlyn smiled. "So you've laid claim to him?"

"It's not like that," Darby said and then set her knife down. Caitlyn would wheedle it out of her eventually. "We kissed." And then had attacked each other like randy teenagers, but Darby decided to keep that part to herself.

"Oh my … and what was it like?" Caitlyn leaned in, ready to hear all of the details.

"Good. Amazing. Just wow. I think if we hadn't been interrupted, things might have gone even further."

"Well, you know, he does have a bit of a reputation," Caitlyn said.

Darby looked and saw that Caitlyn's gray eyes were studying her. "For what?"

"Well not just for yelling at people. Apparently, he even punched someone that worked for him. I just want to make sure he's not the type of guy who uses his fists to settle things."

There was a deadly look in her eye, and Darby wondered just how much more of a story was behind Caitlyn's sudden decision to call off her engagement in London. Darby had only met Michael St. James once and he had seemed a bit too much the perfect picture of an English gentleman. But Caitlyn had appeared happy, so Darby had done what good friends did—kept her mouth shut.

Darby said nothing, just stirred the garlic slices in the heavy skillet she had found.

"So," Caitlyn said, leaning forward in her barstool across the granite countertop, "a 'no comment' usually means a yes."

Darby checked the pot of water she had set to boil. "He's not that type of guy. At least I don't think he is. He told me that he used to be that guy, but he hasn't had a fight in many years. And you know the guy he punched? That was Will Green."

"Will Green … stealer of family recipes and salter of spinach?" Caitlyn said, her voice dripping in mock horror.

"Well, I know violence is never the answer, but if there's one person who ever deserved a fist in the face, it would be Will Green. And it wouldn't surprise me if he started it, pushed Sean into punching him first to make Sean look bad." Darby wondered why she felt the need to defend Sean, then decided she would think more about that later.

"Well," Caitlyn said, "I would say you're a pretty good judge of character, but you did date Will. And just for the record, I never liked him. Just, you know, be careful. Chase told me that Sean was eager to come out here, get a chance to do his own thing, start over. I just hope he's not looking to use Chase as a stepping stone to get back to his former glory."

"Using Chase?" Darby stopped. "Why would he be doing that?"

"Well, apparently no one else wanted to hire him in the city. Chase had already tried to get him to come out here, be a partner in the restaurant a while ago, but Sean said no. Until, of course, he didn't have any other options. Chase is a good guy, so he told Sean the offer still stood."

"Oh." Darby hadn't been quite aware of all of the details of what had happened. The Sean Callahan she had known about had seemed to live for the glory of being in the fast-paced kitchens of restaurants that were more theatrical productions than places to get a good meal. The Osprey Arms was and would never be anything more than a charming small town restaurant.

"I'm sure it's nothing. I mean, he seems like he's settling in. The Osprey's doing great, Chase is happy, and they just got a great review in the paper. So, perhaps Sean's given up the bright lights of the big city for our quieter way of life."

Caitlyn took a sip of her wine, and Darby was aware that her friend was eyeing her.

"Well, look, it's the summer time, and a girl's entitled to have a little fun, especially if a certain Chef Sexy is also looking to have some fun too."

"Amen to that." Caitlyn raised her glass and saluted Darby. A summer fling, really that's all she could expect, right, especially if Sean was thinking of going back to his life in the city. Darby decided not to get ahead of herself. She had other things to think about.

Darby took the skillet, dumped the contents onto a platter, and set it back on the range. She poured some wine into the pan, hoping that Caitlyn would stop talking about Sean.

"So, enough about him. Why are you here?" Caitlyn asked.

"I thought we were going to drink wine and watch bad movies," Darby said.

"Well, we can do that, but I would much rather plan your takeover of The Dory," Caitlyn said.

"Takeover? Caitlyn, I can't just take over my father's restaurant."

"Can't you?"

Darby continued to stir the wine and butter in the pan, watching as they swirled together. Caitlyn's silence forced her into an answer. Sighing, she said, "I don't know."

"Don't know what, Darby? What you want to do with your life?"

"Exactly," Darby said, and she tried to shake the misery out of her voice. "I mean, I should just shut up. I had a good job, a career and yet …"

"All you want to do is bake cookies," Caitlyn finished for her.

"Not quite. It's just that you know the way some girls dream about their weddings, with all the details?"

Caitlyn nodded. "Who hasn't?"

"Well, for me, I would go into The Dory and would make it over in my head. From the time I was a little girl. How the floor would be gleaming wood and the walls would be bright and the whole place would be light and airy. It would be filled with people, sitting with friends, drinking good coffee or hot chocolate, enjoying a little something that would make them, even if it was only temporary, forget about everything else out there."

"There's nothing wrong with that," Caitlyn said. "We're allowed our dreams. That's what makes life exciting."

Darby sighed. This dream had seemed so farfetched she'd never really shared it with anyone. "But that wasn't all. It wasn't enough. Before I knew it, I was dreaming that there would be ten of them, all along the coast. I even came up with a name: The Golden Pear Cafe."

Caitlyn threw back her head and laughed. "And that's what I'm talking about. Go big or go home."

When Darby didn't speak for a moment, Caitlyn asked, "Why do you seem so miserable over it?"

"It seems like it's asking a lot. Here I am, a lawyer. I went to every school on a scholarship, I did everything I was supposed to do, and now I'm throwing it all away to bake cookies."

Caitlyn's face turned serious. "You're dreaming of starting a business. Sure, the product may be cookies, but that's not the point. Stop thinking of yourself as some girl who likes to make cookies trapped inside a lawyer's skin."

"And do what?" Darby asked, fascinated. Caitlyn seemed to have changed before her eyes. She had pushed herself up tall from the counter, and her eyes gleamed with excitement as she brandished her wine glass like a sword from some epic quest.

"Become the cookie queen of New England, the lawyer turned chef, turned entrepreneur, the women who wants to remake the cookie in America—you name it, you claim it. Claim a strong story, and you'll be it. At least that's half the battle. If you want to remake The Dory into the first in a chain of lunch cafes, then go for it. Stop hemming and hawing, and kick some butt. Show your dad what it could be. Give The Dory a complete makeover. Show him your dream and get him to buy into it. That will get his attention."

"It would, wouldn't it? What's that they say: 'It's better to beg for forgiveness than ask permission'?"

"Now you're talking," Caitlyn said, raising her wineglass. Together they clinked glasses, the wine sloshing a bit.

All of a sudden Darby remembered she had food cooking.

"Dinner," she said, turning her attention back to the stove top. Luckily, it was salvageable.

"Hope you didn't ruin it. I haven't had a real meal in weeks."

Darby shook her head and stirred the ingredients in the pan. "Well then, you're in for a treat."

#

Darby shook herself awake and reached for her watch. The luminous numbers glowed faintly. Just about four thirty in the morning. She had taken Caitlyn up on her offer to stay over, both of them agreeing that drinking more wine was a better idea than having to call it a night.

Still, they'd both switched to water before it got too late, snuggling up on the den's couch watching a classic John Cusack movie they'd found on TV. Somewhere along the way, Darby must have fallen asleep and Caitlyn had covered her with another blanket and then disappeared up to her own room.

Darby stretched and then sat up. She was wide awake now and craving coffee. Besides, she had to open The Dory soon, and her mind was racing with ideas, plans for what to do next. There was no question of sneaking in another thirty minutes of sleep.

She gathered up her shoes and the light sweater she'd worn, collected the rest of her things, set up the coffee maker, and wrote Caitlyn a note of thanks before stealing quietly out the door.

Dawn had begun, the sun pushing up above the bluffs in the east, suffusing the sky with a pinkish glow. It was a good time of morning. She breathed in, catching the faint tang of salt water and dried seaweed. A curious blend of smells that meant Queensbay to her. No matter how glorious it had been to wake up in the concrete canyons of Manhattan, there was nothing that could compare to the subtle awakening of the world around the harbor. A gull circled overhead, letting out one loud caw, and a lonely boat, likely that of a fisherman, chugged out across the harbor's channel toward the open water of the Sound.

As she slid behind the wheel of her car, she smiled to herself. The cookie queen, a bakery entrepreneur. That was how she was going to think about herself, how she was going to attack the rest of the day. It was the first day of her new life, her new Golden Pear.

Chapter 17

Darby went in through the front door, pausing to assess the deli. She took in the big glass windows and the slightly chipped paint on the façade. The morning sun was just rising, and she'd have the regulars here before she knew it. Still, she looked. It was a perfect location, right in the middle of downtown, a walk up from the harbor and the marina, nestled amongst the stores and shops that made Main Street a destination.

She pushed open the door, the bell jingling. The floors were cracked and tired linoleum, but that could easily be changed out. The space was large. Her dad kept only a few booths, but if she took those out, there was plenty of room for several more café tables. The glass display counters were fine. The walls were a nondescript beige, but again, nothing a coat of paint and a few pieces of art couldn't revitalize.

She closed her eyes, imagining the place filled with cheerful, upbeat music, couples sharing coffee, young mothers having lunch and gossiping, people breezing in and out to order coffees and soups to go. She could smell cinnamon, vanilla, and spicy chili, and she could even hear the laughter and the happiness.

Taking a deep breath, she decided. Sure, the ideas had been racing through her mind for years, but they had started to take shape after Quentin told her that her dad was ready to sell. And then Caitlyn's pep talk had been the final thing she needed: a call to action. It was time to shake things up, no more doing things the slow and steady way. If her dad wanted to sell The Dory, he didn't need to do it Quentin Tate. He'd have a buyer right in front of him.

She finished her quick survey. Floors redone, a paint job, new furniture and display cabinets, but that was all. She turned and leaned her back against the cool glass. It would be another hot day, and there was a vat of iced coffee that needed to be made, but she took a moment to visualize it once more. She could see the people sitting at the tables, savoring a scone or a brownie, sipping coffee. Mothers and kids during the day. Business lunches, regulars, and tourists all coming in.

Yes, this was what she wanted. And it had been here all along.

Chapter 18

It had been almost two days since she had seen Sean. Not that she was counting, and she'd had plenty to keep her occupied. But even busy with her plans, her mind kept wandering, and she found herself touching her lips as if she could still feel the heat from his kiss.

She sighed. She was beginning to think that the kiss had been a figment of her imagination. At least she had acted cool about it, not falling into his arms and moaning, like she had the first time it had happened.

Maybe she'd been too cool about it, and he had gotten the impression that she wasn't interested. Of course, not being interested was the smart thing to be, right? Sure, he told her that he wasn't the temperamental chef he'd used to be, that he was trying to be a different type of person. But could people really change? She had had enough of temperamental with Will Green.

She wiped clean the counter she had already cleaned and checked the clock. It was the mid-morning lull at The Dory and everything was prepped for the lunch rush. It left a lot of room for her thoughts to race.

Her phone vibrated against her hip, and she pulled it from her pocket. She knew it wouldn't be Sean, of course. She knew that because she had never given him her number. But he was a smart guy, right, he should be able to find it if he wanted to?

Nope, it was her dad, with another one of his reminder texts. Something about checking on the supply of corn starch.

She sighed. She didn't think her father could change. In fact, looking around The Dory, she knew he was immune to it. This place hadn't changed since before her grandmother had died, and now it was looking tired and dated. It did need a total makeover.

Another text buzzed through. This one was from her mom, begging her to tell her dad that everything was okay so that they could go on a tour of Florence.

Sighing, Darby looked at the phone, her mind racing. Carefully, she texted him: *All fine here. Slow day, going to add a fresh coat of paint and new posters, OK?*

She waited, holding her breath. Had she just asked permission to make changes to The Dory? Had she just found a way to put into action everything she had always dreamed of?

The reply wasn't too long in coming. *OK, do it at night so it doesn't smell during the breakfast rush. And don't forget the corn starch.*

Darby smiled, texted back a smiley face, and shoved the phone back in her pocket. She couldn't quite believe it, but she had just gotten permission from her dad to freshen the place up. And that was just the permission she needed to go through with her grand plan. *Maybe change isn't so hard after all*, she thought as she bent down to straighten out some of the baskets in the display counter. There was the tinkle of the bell over the door and she called out, "Just a moment," as she reset the little sign for her caramel truffle brownies.

"Fancy meeting you here." Sean Callahan's voice floated up and she jumped, hitting her head on the inside of the counter.

"It is my deli," she said when she finally came up, resisting the urge to rub the back of her head where she had hit it. The look of amusement in Sean's eye was enough to have her folding her hands across her chest and do her best to stare him down. Two days, she reminded herself. It had been two days since he had kissed her and nearly lifted her straight out of her socks.

"I have the afternoon off tomorrow," he said, grinning at her. "I was thinking, since you're a hometown girl, that perhaps we could go on a drive, that maybe you could show me around a bit."

"Haven't you already been here a couple of months?" she said. "Because this sounds like another one of your pick-up lines. Are you planning on running out of gas on Lover's Lane?"

"Never heard of it," he said quickly and in a deadpan voice. It earned him a smile. "But I've been living in the hotel since I got here and I realized that I haven't really left it, since I was so busy getting everything up and running with the restaurant. But finally, things are where I want them and I feel like I can, actually should, step back a little, see what the team at the restaurant can do without me. So I thought an afternoon off, with you, might be a nice way to test the theory out."

"Are you asking me out on a date?"

He shook his head. "If that's what you want. Or," he amended, before she could answer, "how about we call it me-asking-a-local-to-show-me-around outing. We can sit next to each other, in the car, and talk to each other, get to know one another."

"I already know you," she pointed out, moving down the counter to straighten her jar of homemade granola.

He followed. "True, but I was hoping we could start over. Pretend that all the stuff in the past didn't happen."

"All the stuff?" she asked, moving on to better arrange some napkins. She decided she was happy with this bit of verbal sparring they had going on.

"Well, most of the stuff," he answered, his voice low and throaty.

She looked at him, trying to seem as if she had nothing more pressing on her mind than milk or sugar in her coffee. Finally, she said, "Ok, but not a drive."

"No?"

"You've been here, what, a couple of months. Have you even been on the water?"

He shook his head. "Does it look bad if I say no?"

Darby shook her head. "Well, well, well then, a harbor virgin. We're definitely going to have to fix that. Tomorrow afternoon, then, and I'll play tour guide."

"What can I do?" he managed to ask.

"Prepare to be impressed."

He gave her a smile, and then said, "I think I already am."

Chapter 19

Darby was on her way home, feeling like she was floating on air. She'd gotten her father to agree to changes to The Dory and she and Sean were going on a date—okay, so not a "date" date—together. Things, while not too good to be true, were starting to move along nicely. Perhaps her crazy scheme of quitting her job so that her dad would have to let her work at The Dory hadn't been so crazy after all.

The sun was burning fiercely in the sky and there was just the barest hint of a breeze whispering in from the sea. Perhaps she'd call Caitlyn and see if she wanted to come over and hang out after work. They could look over paint color samples for the interior of The Dory. She was so intent in her thoughts that she almost bumped into him before she saw him, managing to pull herself back just in time, before being bounced back halfway up the sidewalk.

"Jake," she said in surprise, looking up into the familiar face topped with close-cropped blonde hair and light-blue eyes. The face was handsome enough, with well-placed brows and a straight nose. The chin was strong, marred only by a thin white line that was all that remained of a childhood bike accident.

"Darby ..." He looked down at her, his mouth curling into a smile. He pulled her close into him and she managed to turn just in time so that his lips brushed her cheek and not her lips. He still held her by both arms, not letting her go. She finally managed to take a step back, out of his arms, but still he blocked her path.

"I heard you were back in town."

"Just for a bit," Darby said and then smiled. Jake was just the person she needed, if only she could convince him to keep his mouth shut.

"Yeah, your mom said you were helping out while they were away. I'm a bit surprised you were able to get the time off from work." He looked down at her, one eyebrow raised, waiting for an explanation.

"Well, you know, I saved up a lot of vacation," Darby said coolly. She had learned something from being on the debate team. A weak position could be enhanced by strenuously sticking to it.

"Well, I am sure you've earned it. Sounds like you were working hard. But I must say, you're looking good." Jake smiled down at her as his eyes ran up and down her, his gaze appreciative.

"Too bad you already had your chance," she said with a grin as she started to walk. "And you're never going to let me live that down?" Jake sighed as he fell into step beside her.

"Nope," Darby said and then added, "but you might be able to make it up to me. At least a little bit."

"So you'll finally let me take you to dinner?" he offered, his voice hopeful.

Darby shook her head. She had known Jake since forever. Their parents were good friends with each other and they'd been thrown together at countless family gatherings.

He was a few years older and had been the quarterback of the football team. They'd been completely different from each other but once they found a shared passion for superhero movies, they'd been able to get along just fine.

It probably hadn't hurt that Darby had helped to tutor Jake through a rough patch in math, thereby keeping him on the football team his senior year. He'd graduated, gone to play football in college, but after a knee injury he'd come back home to help in the family construction business. Luckily his business skills outlasted his football career and the company had grown significantly in the past few years.

Jake was a good-looking man, Darby thought a bit wistfully. Running his own construction business had helped him keep his high school physique. Her mom was constantly talking about what a "good catch" he was, dropping hints so obvious that Darby had actually started to avoid any sort of family event if she knew Jake would be there. All she felt toward him was the kind of affection you'd feel toward a big bother. It was just that right now she could use some brotherly help.

"I was thinking I could use a little bit of your construction skills." Quickly Darby sketched out what she was thinking. After she was done, Jake just stood looking at her with an open mouth.

"Are you out of your mind? Your dad is going to flip."

"It's just some new paint." Darby said defensively. Maybe she'd been wrong to trust Jake with her plan. "But fine, if you don't want to help me." She started to walk away.

"Whoa there. I didn't say that. It's just, well, you know your dad doesn't like change," Jake said.

Darby turned to look at him. "Did you know he's thinking of selling The Dory to Quentin Tate?"

Jake nodded. "My dad might have mentioned it."

"The Dory is a family business. And I just need to show my dad how special it can be again. Look, if you don't have the time to help me, I am sure I can find someone else to ..."

Jake laughed. "Nice try, Darb, but no way you're going solo on this. Not when I still owe you."

"Thanks Jake," Darby said, sincerity filling her voice.

"Can I get a dinner out of it?" Jake asked hopefully.

Darby shook her head, "Sorry, Jake, I think I might be seeing someone."

Jake sighed. "You and Sean Callahan. Half the village thinks they saw him kissing you out in the middle of the street."

"It wasn't quite the middle of the street," Darby said, since it had been the middle of The Dory.

"Well, whatever. Guess I'm too late again," Jake said, trying for a hangdog look.

Darby shook her head. "You've been too late for years. Besides, you know it would make our parents too happy if we got together."

Jake shook his head. "I can't believe I'm still paying for one little mistake."

"Ha, little mistake my ass," Darby said, feeling elated that Jake had agreed to help her.

Jake stopped her. "There is one little thing ... You know everything in this town needs to get approval from the commission."

Darby nodded. She had already checked the rules. "We're allowed to have the few tables out front, so while the work is going on inside the building, I'll just serve from out there. We'll have to do mostly takeout, but I think I can make it work, since it should only be for a few days."

Jake nodded. "Ok, so you got that covered, but what about that old w ... I mean, Mrs. Sampson. You know she likes to have the final say over everything."

"Just leave her to me," Darby said confidently.

Chapter 20

"We're going in those?" Sean looked at the two brightly colored watercraft bobbing on the water below them.

"Yes, do you have a problem with that?" Darby asked, her voice full of innocence but with a roguish sparkle in her eyes.

"No," he said, trying to think fast. When Darby had said that they were going on a boat, he had envisioned something entirely different than these two slim, insubstantial things that were riding on the blue-green water of Queensbay Harbor. "Canoes are cool," he said.

"They're actually kayaks," Darby said, sitting down on the edge of the dock and taking off her sneakers. She had on a pair of shorts: short shorts, ones that gave him a view of her long, lean legs.

"Oh," he said.

She took off her t-shirt and revealed a light-blue bikini top. Her skin was tan and lightly freckled.

"Shouldn't you have some sunscreen?" he asked, managing to move his tongue. It was just a bikini for goodness sake. After all, he'd seen plenty of girls in them. But Darby's showed off a strong, sculpted back and tight, lean arms.

"Already did." She rummaged in her bag and pulled out a bottle. "But here's mine, if you need it."

"Thanks," he said, catching the container as she tossed it to him.

She saw him assessing her. "I used to row crew in college for a few semesters. You know, those long, skinny boats with the oars? Gives you great muscle tone. I still use a rowing machine for exercise."

He nodded, trying to put his tongue back where it belonged. "Seems like it's working out just fine for you."

"I couldn't really keep up with it."

"What happened? Did you get hurt?"

"No. I always worked, in restaurants, you know, for spending money. And then this place I was working for, the chef left to go to this new place. More upscale, gourmet. We were friends, so he brought me along. It was good experience and better pay. Late nights though. And crew practice was early in the morning."

"So crew had to go?"

She shrugged. "I really wanted to spend a semester abroad in Italy, so I was saving money for that."

"Did you go?" he asked, curious to know, staring down at her.

"Yes, I did. Best four months ever." She tossed her head back and laughed.

"What, the language, the art?" He hadn't been to Italy—yet.

"No, silly. The food!"

He laughed with her. "So what did you do, eat your way around the country?"

"Something like that," she smiled, flipped her sunglasses down onto her eyes. "I took cooking lessons. My first formal ones. I was supposed to be studying Renaissance history but instead I pretty much hung out at the cooking school, bothering the Signora all the time."

"Sounds like something I would have done," he said.

She must have sensed the wistfulness in his voice. "You've never been?"

"To Italy? No. Not yet. I came straight from Indiana to New York and just started going to cooking school and then working. Never seemed like there was any time for all of that fancy stuff. I just kept cooking." And partying and trying to make a name for himself. It had been a relentless whirl, with him and his publicist always looking for the next big thing for him to attach himself to.

"Well, that works too," Darby said, and she swung herself off the side of the dock and landed with catlike grace on the float.

"Your turn," she said, holding up her hand for the bags and the rest of the gear.

He looked at the drop and did his best to match her graceful landing, but the small float dipped under his weight and she was caught off balance and thrown into his arms.

He held her there, a little longer than he had to, enjoying the feel of her sun-warmed skin under his hands, the way she smelled of coffee beans and cinnamon, the gentle bouncing and dipping of the platform beneath them.

The sun sparkled on the water and he could hear the sound of a motor whiz by them, followed by high-pitched laughter. It was summertime, he thought, and it was the first time all season he'd felt like he was having fun. That he was where he belonged.

Darby ran her tongue over her lips, gave him a smile, and pulled back. He couldn't see her eyes behind her sunglasses, but he wondered if they mirrored any of the desire he was feeling for her.

"We better set out, before the tide turns."

"I have no idea what that means," he said.

"Don't worry. I'll take care of you."

"I'm counting on that, sugar."

#

He was doing pretty well, Darby thought, for a guy who'd never really been on the water. He could swim, she had checked on that, but she had made sure they were both wearing life preservers, just in case.

The day's weather was perfect. The breeze was light and shifting, but never enough to make them work against it. She had timed their trip out to the cove so that the rush of the tide in and out of the harbor carried them toward their destination, not pushed them away from it.

One kayak was hers, the other she had borrowed from Chase. They were sporty, lightweight models that sat fairly low on the water, but they cut through the water cleanly and she enjoyed the pull of her shoulder muscles, as she dipped one end of the paddle into the water and then the other.

Sean made up in strength what he lacked in technique and kept pace with her. She had maneuvered them through the thicket of boats that were moored close to the marina until they were hugging the far shore of the harbor. On the one side were bluffs studded with homes that commanded a sweeping view of the harbor. Across from them, across the broad expanse of the harbor, on the far shore was the derelict Queensbay Show House. It had once hosted some big names for summer stock theater, but had long since been closed up.

"Where are we heading?" Sean asked, giving a deep stroke as he pulled up level with her.

"Just a little bit further, I promise," she told him.

She was making for Dyer's Cove, a shallow inlet off the main harbor. The land around it had been donated to the county as part of a nature preserve and the best way to enjoy it was to hike in from the main road or take a small boat like a kayak in. Anything bigger would most likely run aground and since most of the rest of Queensbay seemed hell-bent on enjoying themselves by going as fast as they could on jet skis or motor boats, she was fairly certain they'd be able to have it to themselves.

The opening to the cove came upon them and she scooted in. It was narrow, filled in with sand and rocks and even the rotting planks of an old wooden ship that had been run aground here long ago. The ribs of the hull stood out of the water at high tide and it had been there always, for as long as she could remember, each year, another little bit getting torn away, but so slowly that it seemed as if nothing changed.

They slipped in underneath the trailing leaves of a tree that jutted out over the bank and it was a bit like entering a different world. The sounds of the harbor faded behind them and it was quieter here. The water was flat, as if the breeze that blew and ruffled the water outside couldn't reach.

"Wow," Sean said.

She glanced over and saw that he had stopped paddling and was just gliding, entranced by the sudden peacefulness. "I know. You would hardly even know it's here."

"It's quiet," he said, and though he wasn't shouting, his voice carried over the glasslike water and disturbed a heron, which sailed into the sky, its wings beating the air as if in annoyance.

She led them over to a crescent-shaped, sandy beach. Their kayaks touched ashore at the same time, the hulls gliding out of the water and coming to a stop with a slight thump. She swung herself out of the boat, lifted the bow end, and dragged it up a few feet.

"Why are you doing that?" Sean asked, as he unfolded his long legs from the small compartment of the kayak.

"The tide will turn in about an hour or two and then the water will start to come up and if we're not paying attention, we'll either have to walk home or swim back. And explain to Chase how we lost one of his boats."

Sean laughed. "I guess I see your point."

She pulled out the blanket she had brought and spread it out a little farther up, under the shade of a tree. Sunlight dappled it.

Sean heaved up the small cooler he had packed and threw himself down next to her. She was aware how close he was, the way the fine, light blonde hairs of his arm were almost brushing against hers. If she shifted just a little toward him, they would touch, she knew and she wondered if he would be able to feel the electric current that was racing along under her skin. She hadn't quite thought about what the thought of seeing him in a bathing suit would do to her, though she had a fairly good idea of what the sight of her in a bikini was doing to him.

She stretched out, enjoying the feeling. His dark eyes had stayed steady on her, ratcheting up the heat level between them. He moved and she sat up and jumped away as if he had shocked her. God, she thought, she was as jumpy as that heron around him. To hide her irritation she took a drink from the water bottle she'd brought. The cool liquid slid down her throat and it served to keep her from looking at him.

"Are you hungry or thirsty?" he asked, as he rolled back to one side. He held up a bottle of white wine, still chilled, condensation dripping down. In the other, he had a plate.

"Both. But I don't usually drink in the middle of the day," she said.

"Isn't it five o'clock somewhere?" he offered, with a grin. "Besides, I found a new supplier for the Osprey Arms, and he assures me that the only way to appreciate his artisanal *fromage* is with a crisp white."

"Mick Bonet? From the Westcott Dairy?"

Sean nodded. "I take it that's where the amazing goat cheese came from for your breakfast sandwiches."

"Oh, yes. Mick is quite the salesman. He supplies a few restaurants in the city as well. It's nice that his farm isn't that far from here."

He passed her a cracker already layered with the cheese. She took a bite and let saltiness melt in her mouth. Beside her, she heard the sound of a cork being eased out of the bottle.

"Plastic cups, I'm afraid. Apparently, The Osprey isn't quite prepared for impromptu gourmet picnics."

A moment later he handed her some wine. "Cheers." Sean raised his plastic cup to hers and they clicked them together.

She took a drink, savoring the light crispness of the wine sliding down her throat and wiggled her toes in the sand. A sigh must have escaped her because Sean looked at her.

"Penny for those thoughts?"

She smiled and leaned her head back to the let the sun warm her cheeks. "I was just thinking how I could be trapped inside an office, the only light I got from the fluorescents overhead, the only green from the dusty fake plant shoved in the corner. And here I am, in the middle of the week, in the middle of the afternoon, with my toes in the sand, drinking wine, on a beach."

"When you put it that way, life does sound a lot better around here." Sean rolled onto his back. "I don't see how anyone could be stuck behind a desk all day."

"I know," Darby said, taking another sip of her wine. After just a few sips it was making her feel reckless. "I thought I was going to go crazy, just stuck there, poring over piles and piles of paperwork."

"At least, in a kitchen, you get to move around. It's hard work, but there's a sense of ..."

"Purpose, creativity," Darby finished for him.

"And all that heat ..."

He had turned over, so that they were facing each other, lying side by side. She could feel the space between them closing, the heat between them rising. His eyes were bright in the sun and a light breeze tousled his blonde hair, and she could smell his strong, clean scent of soap and nothing else.

"Passion for food, for ingredients ... ," she almost whispered. His foot touched her—a small tickle of his toes against her—then his hand came up and brushed a lock of hair from her face, then trailed down the length of her arm, slowly, oh so slowly so that her body reacted in slow motion, his touch sending shivers to her core.

Their lips touched and this time she met his, feeling the force between them rise up. She was ready for him, ready for the heat and passion he brought to her. There was nothing tentative in this kiss and there was a sound, a small, low moan that must have been from her as she gave herself into it, melting into him.

Before she knew it, his arms were around her, fisting in her hair, pulling her closer. His mouth left hers to scrape kisses along her neck and she let her head fall back, feeling the primitive need of just wanting him. Above her, the blue of the sky and the green of the leaves jumbled together in a kaleidoscope of color as she closed her eyes and let her senses take over.

She fell back and he moved so that he was on top of her, trailing kisses down her neck. His hand came up and brushed the skin at the base of her neck and her whole body went electric at his touch.

She gasped as his teeth nipped her lips. She shifted under his weight, feeling the need to meet him, and she felt his desire for her. The thought occurred to her that they were on a blanket, out in the open, but her body was too preoccupied with the demands his mouth was making for her to care.

She wrapped his arms around Sean's broad back, feeling the muscles that bunched and moved underneath her hands.

With the suddenness of nature, there was a loud squawk and then the sound of flapping wings again. She almost ignored it, but she heard the shout of a human voice following close on it, and in a swift movement she had pushed Sean away and was sitting up, straightening her bikini top, trying to smooth down her hair, when the hikers came into view.

Sean had shifted over onto his stomach and shot her a look that was part smoldering desire and part amusement. They had been caught just like a couple of teenagers, necking in public.

She nodded politely at the couple, middle-aged, with binoculars around their necks. They were obviously bird watchers, as the husband had already put his glasses up to his eyes and was following the retreating flock.

"Some paté?" Sean said, his eyebrow arched.

She sighed. Her mind was definitely not on food, but it didn't seem as if she'd get to focus on anything else.

Chapter 21

They had finished off their lunch quietly, actually sharing it with the couple who, as it turned out, were staying at the Osprey Arms. Darby had been gracious, giving the couple all the right information they needed to plan a nature walk for the next day.

Sean had watched her carefully, the way her lips were slightly swollen from the kisses he had plied them with. She kept shooting him looks, under lowered eyelashes, so that he felt himself once again grow hard with desire. He even went into the water to cool off, but really because he couldn't stand being so close to her without wanting to touch her, pull her into his arms, and hear her moan his name again.

The couple, Ann and Bob, were in no hurry to leave the cove, and so Darby had looked at her watch and said they had to be off, sending him an arch look that had him thinking about all kinds of possibilities.

They packed up everything, Darby only brushing against him one time, a subtle, seductive touch that had his skin flaming and his heart racing.

"You shouldn't do that," he murmured in her ear.

"Why not?" Her voice dripped innocence.

"Because if you keep doing that to me, I can't be responsible for my actions, no matter who's watching."

Her lips quirked up and it was all he could do not to grab her and kiss her right there, but he was well aware of Ann's interested eyes on them.

"Well, perhaps we better had go back to town and find some-place more secluded."

"Lead the way, sugar."

They paddled back. It felt hotter, and the breeze had died. "It does that toward the evening," Darby said, explaining the lack of wind, as they dipped, switched, and dipped their paddles into the water.

He was enjoying this, the nice steady rhythm, the sounds of the water, the tangy smell of the salt.

"So how is it, city boy?"

"What makes you think I'm a city boy?"

She laughed easily. "The look of fear when I told you we were going in these little things. What did you think—I was going to borrow one of Chase's yachts?"

"Does he have one?"

Darby shook her head. "A nice sleek sailboat, but it's for racing, not pleasure. And I don't think he would lend it to anyone. His brother has a nice little runabout but Jackson's not around, so the boat's not in the water."

"I could get used to this. It's sort of like riding a motorcycle in city traffic. You're small, but fast," Sean said, as a jet ski raced by.

"See, I knew you'd like it. Can't beat being close to the water. Still, next time, we could try one of those." She pointed toward the Jet Ski, and Sean admitted to himself that there was something exhilarating about the idea of speed.

They were also at the marina. Darby managed to land her kayak without a bump and leap gracefully onto the float. She pulled him up and he extricated himself, once again feeling his stomach drop as the float dipped beneath his weight.

The sun was well off to the west, starting its march towards the horizon. She looked so efficient standing there, in her bikini top, tying up lines, taking out gear, that he stopped her, pulled her toward him, and kissed her.

It was a long, slow, gentle kiss and he drew back once and looked at her eyes, searching for an answer. He saw it there, in the need that matched in his own, and he was about to tip back in when there was a loud call from up above.

"Hellooooo!"

"Not again," he said, his teeth gritted.

"Sean, there you are." It was a woman's voice and it was annoyingly familiar. A shadow fell across the float and Darby pushed herself away and looked up, not pleased by what she saw.

"Mandy," Sean said. "I didn't think you'd be coming out here."

"Well, when you stop returning my phone calls, you leave me no choice but to hunt you down."

He turned to Darby, who all of a sudden had made herself very busy with a coil of rope. "Darby, this is Mandy Peyton, my publicist. And Mandy, this Darby Reese ..." He stumbled because he wasn't quite sure how to introduce her. A baker, a lawyer? A friend?

"How nice to meet you," Mandy said, in a voice that even he could tell meant that she could care less about who Darby was.

"And you as well." The ice was plain in Darby's voice.

He sighed and ran a hand through his hair. He wished that Mandy would just disappear, but she showed no sign of going anywhere.

"Sean, I just must talk to you. Surely you won't make me come down there?" Her voice sounded pouty even to his ears.

He looked at the ladder that led from the upper dock to the small float they were on. Mandy, as usual was wearing one of her silky blouses and a black pencil skirt, as well as shoes with heels so high it was a wonder she could walk in them.

"You should go," Darby said, with her back half turned to him. "Don't you have a dinner to cook?"

He ran a hand through his hair, frustration rising in him. He wanted to pull Darby close to him, whisper in her ear that he wanted to see her later but he could tell that such a gesture wouldn't be welcome. "I had a great time. I'll call you."

"Sure, whatever." Darby was already busy again with the boats.

"Sean, yoo hoo, up here—seriously, I have something very interesting to discuss with you."

"Coming." He climbed up the ladder.

Mandy threw her arms around him and tried to kiss him on the lips, but he dodged it and let it slide across his cheek. "Shall we?" she said, slipping her arm through his and leading him up toward the hotel.

Chapter 22

"Look, Mandy, I really can't talk now." He had led Mandy inside the Osprey Arms, wanting to get her out of Darby's sight.

He didn't have anything pressing; in fact, he wanted nothing more than to go find Darby and pick up where they had left off.

"But I came all this way to speak to you," Mandy all but purred.

"I have a restaurant to run. Dinner doesn't cook itself," he reminded her.

"Well, you won't have a fish left to fry if you don't talk to me. So, either spare me five minutes of your time or I stop working my ass off for you." The purring quality had left Mandy's voice, to be replaced by lethal calmness. And a threat.

He recognized it, had seen it in action. He knew that was what made Mandy so effective at her job.

"Fine," he said. "You have five minutes." He gestured toward a cluster of leather chairs in the lobby. Like just about everything else at the Osprey, it had a view of the water from double height windows.

"Are you sure you don't want to go somewhere more private?" Mandy asked, the humming quality back now that she had gotten a concession from him.

There was no way he was going to let Mandy into his room. He had made the mistake of getting involved with Mandy once, when they had first met, before they had even started working together. The romantic nature of their relationship had petered off fairly quickly and by mutual consent, but Mandy was a born flirt and took pleasure in making sure people knew that she was the most important female relationship in his life. Until he'd seen Darby's reaction to Mandy, he'd never minded that before. He would need to explain to Darby that his relationship with Mandy was strictly business.

"Right here is fine," he said, taking a seat so he could keep an eye on the water. Funny, for a guy who'd grown up solidly landlocked in the middle of the country, he was starting to become awfully fond of the water. For one wild moment, his mind flashed back to how Darby had felt in his arms, the way her skin had heated at his touch, the way her eyes had looked into his.

"Earth to Callahan."

Reluctantly, he pulled himself back to the present. "So what brings you out to Queensbay?"

She gave a look around, dismissing the place. He didn't exactly disagree. They had revamped the menu but were still working on the décor.

"You have an offer on the table."

Mandy had disagreed with his partnering with Chase. If it wasn't Manhattan, Mandy thought, it didn't count. What Mandy didn't realize was that Chase had offered him a real-deal partnership. He wouldn't just be the chef; he'd be an owner, too. And if things went well here, which he fully intended that they would, he would have the capital, leverage, and reputation to expand. In Manhattan, this type of opportunity would still be years away.

"I'm committed here," he said.

"This might be worth rethinking that," Mandy said, her voice dripping with persuasiveness.

He waited a moment, and then sighed. "Okay, I'll bite. What is it?" Opportunities had been limited after the incident with Will, so he should be thankful that things were starting to look up, shouldn't he?

"There's a new cable channel. All about food and cooking."

"Isn't there already one of those?" he interrupted.

Mandy shrugged. "Well, this is a new one. Younger, hipper, and all that."

"So I'm interested, why?" He started to rise, impatient. He could hear a rising din from the kitchen and wanted to go find out what the commotion was all about.

"Because they want to you to be the host of your own show."

"My own show?" He sat back down. "What about?"

Mandy paused, flashed him a sideways smile, and said, "It's a cooking competition show."

"Don't they have one of those?" he said, again.

"Well, this is sort of in reverse. You're getting people that have been nominated as the worst chefs, and you're supposed to put them through some sort of tough love boot camp."

"So you mean that I have to go on national TV and be mean? No thanks, Mandy. I thought I was trying to repair my reputation, not solidify it."

"But it films in LA, Los Angeles—you'd get to go to where it's warm."

"It's warm here," he pointed out, getting ready to get up and go and see what was going on.

She put an arm out, pulled him back down. "That's because it's summertime. LA's warm all year round. They'd want you to start right after Labor Day. The producers like your tough guy rep and want to parlay it into a full-time show."

"Isn't there a show like that already?" he asked, starting to get up again. He'd come here to stop being the guy who yelled at people, who was wound so tight he was liable to blow at the slightest provocation. He was here to start over. And he had, more than that, he was building the right kind of reputation.

"But it's your own show." Mandy reached out again, her hand grasping his arm and pulling him back into his seat. "Sure, it's been done before, but that's not the point. We already know the camera loves you. Sure, lots of people around the city saw you on TV, but this will be national, international. Think of this as a steppingstone. Instead of trying to whitewash your reputation as a bad ass, we get to work with it. Trust me—there are a lot more people who are going to want to watch you yell at people than who are going to come here to eat your surf and turf."

"It sounds like a pretty crappy gig," he said, trying to sound firm.

"Does it matter? It's TV, it pays well, and even George Clooney got his start on a bad TV show. How hard could that be?"

"Sometimes it's harder than it looks."

"Look," she said, reaching out and touching his arm, "I know you think this is important, owning your own restaurant, but this is TV, national, and it could be a platform, make you bigger than this a lot faster. I know you came out here because you felt like no one in the city was giving you a chance to be a partner. And because of what happened. But now, with a real TV show, one that plays to your strengths, I think you'd have just about anyone you want knocking at your door."

Sean pulled his arm back, starting to feel like he was playing a broken record. If Mandy didn't believe him, then who would?

"But I'm not that guy anymore. I'm not the guy who solves things by screaming his head off and then punching someone in the face. That was one moment. Sure, I was angry, but he pushed me. No one wants the truth; they just like to think the worst."

"Does it matter what the truth is? Because, trust me, trying to convince anyone in town that wasn't the real you ... pretty much impossible."

"But why?"

Mandy laughed. "Come on, Sean. You may not have been a bad guy, but I don't think anyone ever called you a nice guy or a pleasure to work with. You were a bit arrogant and a hothead."

"But," he floundered. He'd worked in kitchens pretty much all of his life. It was hot, sweaty work, and there was always a lot of yelling. It was the way he had learned, and he had hated it, but when it came to running his own kitchen, he hadn't even attempted to try something different.

"Look, your segments on that late show were great. But you should know that someone took a video of your fight with Will, and, well, it's made the rounds to all the pertinent parties. It pretty much shows you yelling, throwing the first punch, and then the second and third. He didn't even have a chance."

"A video?" he said, his heart sinking.

Mandy looked at him smugly, aware that she had just gained the advantage.

"He didn't try to fight back," he said, remembering how one part of him had thought it odd that Will hadn't had the guts to throw it back at him.

"Yup, a video. It's on the Internet." Mandy whipped out her phone, sighed as she waited for access to the wireless network and then handed the device off to him.

He looked. Someone had added music and some special effects—slow motion, double takes. He looked like some sort of crazed lunatic, and Will ... well, Will looked innocent. No wonder no one would touch him.

"Look, I'm working on getting it taken down, but the damage is already done."

"One mistake," he said, feeling hopeless, handing the phone back.

"Yeah, one mistake, but this opportunity is a way out of here." Mandy waved her hand, her blood red nails making a streak in the air.

"Here?" He looked around. "Did Chase know about the video?"

Mandy shook her head, and then nodded. "I think so."

Chase had still given him a chance; that was all Sean could think about. It was hard seeing the evidence in black or white—or, in this case, full color. But there he had been, beating the crap out of some guy. God, it meant he was no better than his dad. After all these years, after all the distance he'd tried to put between himself and that poor kid from Indiana, here it was, rearing its ugly head.

Feeling a like sick puppy, he snapped his attention back to Mandy. "I'm committed to this," he said. All he could think about was this was where he was supposed to turn things around. Hell, this was the place that had turned things around for him. Without Chase and the Osprey, who knew where he'd be.

"Look, maybe you could find a way to do both. This isn't an opportunity you can just throw away."

He shook his head. "I believe in the power of focus." Even as he said it, he knew that he believed it. He'd been here just a few short months and already he was getting the kind of recognition with the Osprey that had eluded him in Manhattan. Recognition for something real: a reputation for excellent food and amazing service. Not the reputation as the cad about town.

"Fine." She shook her head and crossed her arms. "But I heard Will Green is in the running for the show as well."

He felt his eyes narrow. "Will?"

"Yes." Mandy pretended to be very interested in the hue she'd chosen for her nails.

"That bastard?"

"He's almost as photogenic as you. Plus, he's ruthlessly ambitious, and he's been dating the production assistant."

"He's a sucky chef and a sneak."

"Well then, someone should put him in his place," she suggested, one eyebrow arching up.

"I thought I did by firing him," he said, his anger flaring.

"Punching him out while you did it got you fired and him rehired. So, right now, he's the one with the credibility and you're the one cooking shrimp baskets for the geriatric crowd."

"They're not geriatric," he said automatically, though his thought turned to Bob and Ann. Nice, pleasant, but not young.

"Whatever." Mandy waved a hand.

There was a shout from the kitchen and then a crash. He shot up. "I have to go," he said.

"Just think about it," she called after him.

He waved his arm at her, his mind racing. "I'll be in town for a while," he heard Mandy say. He wasn't sure if that was a threat or a promise.

Chapter 23

Darby took a deep breath. She had made it through lunch rush and now the deli was starting to empty out. Her dad still continued to text her, reminding her of things like where the extra ketchup and napkins were stored. Finally, her mom must have taken the phone away, or likely it was dinner time and he had actually enjoyed his meal enough to stop worrying about how life was going back in Queensbay.

Her back was sore and her feet hurt but it was all a good distraction from thinking about Sean. And Mandy. With her pencil skirt that hugged all her curves and low-cut blouse. Darby went to refill some salt containers. She used to wear pencil skirts and blouses. All right, maybe not as low cut as Mandy's since the woman was going for a kind of sex appeal that was a little too obvious. Did guys really like that?

Maybe that's what Sean liked. Someone obvious. And blonde. Darby sighed. She was never going to be able to compete with that. Besides, she was trying to take it slow. After what had happened with Will, she owed it to herself to keep things light, get to really know Sean before jumping ... where? Into bed with him. Her mind might be telling her to take it slow, but every time he was around, her hormones sang a totally different tune.

She hadn't felt like that since ... when? Never. Sure, there had been other relationships before Will the Manipulative, but nothing like how she felt when she was with Sean. A little dangerous, a little sexy, like she was dancing over a live wire. And that was just from his kisses. They'd barely gotten past first base and she was obsessing over him, wondering what he was doing, wondering if she even had the right to think that there was something developing between the two of them.

The bell above the door rang, yanking Darby back into the here and now.

"I'd like an iced coffee please."

Darby sprung back to life. "Sure thing, Mrs. Sampson." Darby managed a big smile, thinking that this was her lucky day. Mrs.

Sampson was head of the Historic Preservation Committee and did not approve of change. Her family had been part of the community since Queensbay's beginning as a seafaring town, something she never let anyone forget. If you wanted to change a paint color or re-do a sign you had to get her blessing.

Unfortunately, her blessing was usually pretty hard to come by. Mrs. Sampson was one of those people who prided herself on being hard-nosed. She took pleasure in saying no, in reminding people how the character of the village must be preserved at all costs.

Darby was all for preserving character, but when you were told that Dusky Yellow was too yellow a shade to paint your clapboards and to try Eggshell White instead, it was enough to make you want to tear out your hair out and paint your house black out of spite.

Still, Mrs. Sampson's approval counted for everything, so it did pay to be nice to her.

"I wanted to say thank you for sending that tray of cookies down to the Maritime Museum. I barely got to enjoy one myself before they were all gone."

"Oh my pleasure," Darby said, trying to conceal her smile. "I just remembered how much you loved them when I used to make them for the annual bake sale."

She had sent the cookies knowing that Mrs. Sampson's adherence to good manners would ensure she stopped by to say thank you.

"Would you like a pump of mocha in that?" Darby offered with what she hoped was her most charming smile. "On the house, of course."

Mrs. Sampson dithered, back and forth, saying she shouldn't, but in the end the lure of chocolate won out.

"I see it says here that you're going to be closed for a few days due to renovations." Mrs. Sampson pointed to the sign Darby had put up once she started to put her plan into action.

Darby passed Mrs. Sampson her iced mocha, making sure she had wiped off any drips.

"Yes, just some inside work. A fresh coat of paint, really," Darby said, trying to sound nonchalant. "We won't be touching the outside."

Mrs. Sampson pursed her lips and looked around. "Your front door is peeling. And the trim is getting a little dirty. I keep reminding your father that we all need to do our part to keep the village looking spry."

"Oh, I know, but he's awfully stubborn," Darby hedged, wondering where this was going.

"Oh, I do know, dear. Your grandmother was quite the same. But your father is always so generous, sending over bagels and coffee for the Committee's meetings that it hardly seemed fair to bother him about it."

Darby thought for a moment, trying to sense what Mrs. Sampson's angle was. Hoping she wasn't making a mistake, she said, "Well, even though we'll be closed on Wednesday, I am sure I could have the bagels and coffee over to you, no problem."

"Why that would be wonderful dear, I knew you Reeses wouldn't let us down."

Darby smiled, and as Mrs. Sampson made her way to leave, she said, as casually as she could, "I suppose if I'm having the painters in this week for the inside, it might make sense to have them do the outside too? The clapboards are looking a little dingy, now that you mention it."

Mrs. Sampson stopped, looked as if she were considering. "Well, any exterior painting is supposed to be approved by the Committee, and well, that could take a month or two, my dear."

"Hmmm," Darby did her best to look distressed. "Dad will be back by then, and I know he'll just say he'll get to it, and before you know it, another winter will have gone by."

"True," Mrs. Sampson said, slowly. "I suppose I could arrange it with the Committee on Wednesday, get them to make an executive approval decision without all the paperwork. It would be a special case, but I do see your point of striking while the iron is hot."

"Yes, definitely," Darby agreed, shaking her head solemnly.

"And you'll make sure it's white? And the shutters will stay black?"

Darby nodded, fighting the impulse to throw her arms around Mrs. Sampson and hug her.

"Well, then, it seems like we have a deal."

Mrs. Sampson left and Darby heaved a sigh of relief. She had been wondering just how to finagle getting the exterior of the building painted without her father getting involved. He had been ignoring it as a manner of principle, saying that it was his building and that no one else had a right to tell him what color to paint it. But now, with Mrs. Sampson taking care of all the approval, it would be a fait accompli.

Darby smiled. The Golden Pear was starting to become a reality.

Chapter 24

Scrubbing refrigerators was never that fun, but it was tedious enough that it allowed for some thinking. Plus, it kept the noise from the radio and the power saw in the distant background. Work on the newest incarnation of The Dory was going just fine.

Jake had been true to his promise, redeploying himself and a crew to work on The Dory, and things were starting to move along.

All she needed to do was track down some affordable tables and chairs, come up with a new menu, finish designing a logo, order some new signs. She took a breath, trying to calm her racing mind and sort through all the things she needed to accomplish.

She pulled her head out of the metal box. She was almost done. She listened. It was quiet. She checked her watch. Not quite lunch time, but the guys must have knocked off for the mid-morning break. Either that or they were letting something dry and wouldn't be back for hours.

"That smells pretty good."

The voice startled her, so that she almost dropped the jar of pickle chips in her hand. She caught it just in time and took a step back.

"What are you doing here?"

Sean Callahan was back in her kitchen. She hadn't seen him for a few days, not since she'd left him with Mandy. There had been one text, but she had decided to ignore it.

He was in his work uniform, the traditional checked pants of a chef with the neatly buttoned double-breasted uniform, his name, and that of the Osprey Arms, on it. It looked good, sharp, professional. She made a mental note to order one for herself. And maybe for her dad, too.

He was standing by her pot, sniffing it, and staring at her with a question.

"It's a chowder I'm working on."

His ginger beer-colored eyes danced, and she had to turn away to keep herself from being drawn into them. His gaze dropped, and then shifted away abruptly.

She put the pickles down and closed the refrigerator, aware that the cool air had been having a rather obvious effect on a certain part of her anatomy. She crossed her arms over her chest, hoping to distract him, but it was no good. His eyes had dropped for more than an instant before he looked up at her again, a knowing and sexy smile on his face. She decided that it wasn't just the cold from the refrigerator that was making her anatomy spring to life.

"Can I taste?" he asked, politely enough.

She swallowed, knowing there was no way she could say no. "There are some spoons in that drawer," she said, pointing.

With a smile and twinkling eyes, he pulled it open, found a spoon and dipped it into the soup.

She watched as he tasted, rolling it around on his tongue. His eyes closed, and she could see him thinking.

"Tarragon? Bay leaf? A hint of hot sauce?" he asked.

She nodded. He'd nailed all the flavors, but she wasn't about to give away her secret recipe.

"It's good. I might try a little paprika, you know, to mellow it all out." He tossed the spoon in the nearby sink and turned to look at her.

"Thanks for the advice," she said. She decided she could try and uncross her arms now. "It's for the crew. I'm testing it for the new menu." As soon as it was out of her mouth, she didn't know why she had said it. Perhaps having Sean Callahan in her kitchen giving her advice was too big an opportunity to throw away.

There was a pause while he looked at her. "I texted you."

"I've been busy," she said, and let it hang.

He walked across the kitchen, peeked into the main part of the café. "I see. New floors, paint. Seems like you've got something cooking here. More than the soup."

"Maybe," she said, not wanting to give in to her desire to tell him everything.

"Hmm," he said, coming back and leaning against the counter next to her, so close that her shoulder, bare in its tank top, brushed against the skin of his arm. She felt the shock radiate through her, an electric thrill that had her whole body doing a little dance, like she had been jolted by an electric eel.

She looked up, to see if he had noticed, and he was staring down at her, one eyebrow lifted. His golden blonde hair was in its usual tumbled, devil-may-care disarray, which she was finding charmingly sexy.

"Let me guess. It looks like you're fixing the place up. And in a hurry. So, I deduce you want to get it done before your dad's back in town."

"Maybe," she said again, cursing herself for not coming up with anything cleverer.

"And," he said, snaking an arm past her and grabbing a sheet of paper, "this, if my expert eyes aren't mistaken, looks a lot like a menu."

He looked it over. "The Golden Pear. Classy. Soup of the day, French Dip sandwich, a quiche, and of course the cookies. I'll take one of everything," he said, handing the menu back to her.

"What?" she said.

"It looks great. It's a great menu, and, well, I think that people will flock here. And not just for your cookies."

"Really, you think so?" It came out so fast she wasn't aware that she'd been holding her breath, craving his approval.

"Well, you never know until you open, but you've got an established location, a proven track record. And as long as you keep a plain turkey sandwich on the menu for the old-timers, I don't see how you can go wrong."

She rubbed her hands over her face. "Well, my ingredients are a bit more expensive, but I've raised the prices, so theoretically my profit margins should stay the same. I studied my dad's books, and you know, The Dory was doing okay. I mean, he was making money, but you can tell business has slowly been slipping off."

"Probably because he wasn't catering to the new clientele."

She nodded. "That's what I thought. I told him that a year ago, but he just shook his head and said if people didn't like his sandwiches, then they didn't have to come."

Sean smiled, took a step closer. "Got to admire a man who sticks to his guns."

She looked up at him. "I sort of like a guy who can admit he's wrong."

"Nothing like starting over, is there?" His breath fanned her face, and she swallowed, almost reaching to him, but stopping herself.

"You know, Mandy is just who I said she was. She's my publicist. She technically works for me."

"And that's all she ever was?" Darby had to ask the question but wasn't sure she wanted to hear the answer.

"No," Sean said slowly. "I won't lie about that. She and I did date, briefly, a while ago, but that's over. I haven't been with anyone in months, since before I moved here. I don't double-dip, Darby; you need to know that."

"Not even when a model comes walking in our door?" Darby shot back. She didn't know why she was feeling jealous, but she was. It wasn't like she was some virginal high schooler. Everyone had a past, but she had to admit that being with someone whose past relationships had been a little more public was slightly unnerving.

He leaned down, smiled at her, "I have a strict one model at a time policy, sugar."

She didn't say anything, not trusting herself. Suddenly his expression turned solemn as he eyes roamed over her face. "Listen, Darby, I'm serious. A lot of those people you might have seen me with were just photo ops. Things to raise my profile or the other person's. At the end of the night, we all went our separate ways. Mandy orchestrated it all. And to be honest, I do owe her. Without her, I'd probably still be some hick kid from the Midwest chopping vegetables in the kitchen. She really helped launch my career, got me on TV, got me my first big job, and made sure my star was on the rise."

"And now what? Is she looking out for your next job?" She tried to keep the sarcasm out of her voice, but Caitlyn's words about Sean's motivations haunted her. There was no reason a small town chef needed a publicist.

"She did have some business to discuss. But that's all it is with Mandy, business."

She looked at his face, searching but decided, no, needed, to think that he was telling the truth.

Before he could say more, there was the bang of the swinging kitchen door, and Jake was in the kitchen. He didn't seem at all abashed to have caught them like that, but Darby still took a good step back from Sean.

"Oh, man." Jake wiped his hand on his shirt and looked at Sean. "I heard you were in town. I love that piece you do on The Night Show. You know, the Get Laid piece."

Darby's head dropped down, and she all but groaned. She shot a murderous look at Jake, but he seemed immune to it, moving enthusiastically over to Sean, clapping him on his back, and holding out his hand.

"That's not really what it's called, you know," Sean said, hesitating for a moment before he took Jake's hand.

"I know, but I mean, man … that's what it's about, right?"

"Sort of." Sean shifted uncomfortably, as if he didn't want to remember it.

Darby stepped in. "Sean, this is Jake Owen, an old friend. He's a contractor and agreed to bump me to the top of his list."

"Yeah, all it took were some of her cookies." Jake put a friendly arm around Darby, and she fought the impulse to shrug it off. She'd known Jake since they were kids, and he had always been a bit like an overly affectionate puppy, which normally she found endearing. Now it was annoying.

Sean looked between the two of them, his eyes unreadable. "Well, I guess I'll leave you two to it, then. Nice to see you again." Sean left the way he had come, the screen door of the kitchen slamming shut.

Darby untangled herself from Jake's arm. "Why did you have to do that for?" she said, irritated that Sean had walked away.

"What do you mean? Putting my arm around you?" Jake said, his eyebrows wiggling up.

"Yeah, exactly. You pretty much ran him off," she said. It seemed like she and Sean were always just this close to having something happen between the two of them. Maybe it wasn't meant to be.

"Because now he's jealous," Jake said, reaching for the tray of cookies she had set aside.

"And that's good how?"

Jake wiggled his eyebrows again. "You know how little boys are. We always want the things we think we can't have. Right now he's walking away, kicking himself, wondering if he's too late and he's getting all worked up. And in about three seconds, he'll be back."

"What are you talking about?" She rolled her eyes. Jake truly was the annoying big brother she wished she never had.

There was the sound of the door opening, and Sean poked his head in.

"By the way, Darby, it seems like your big plan deserves a celebration. I'm off again tonight. Maybe I could make you dinner? Your place, sevenish?"

She felt her mouth flap open, and then she quickly shut it, throwing on a smile. "That would be great."

"It's a date then." Sean sent Jake a cool nod, and then he was gone again.

Darby turned to Jake, who was smugly eating a cookie. "How did you know?"

"Because it's what I would have done. And, you're welcome. Are we even yet?"

She shook her head. "Not even close."

Jake just shook his head, took his cookie, and headed back into the dining room. "Oh well, it was worth a try."

Chapter 25

"And what are you so happy about?" Chase Sanders strolled into the kitchen of the Osprey Arms, hands stuffed into the pockets of his tailored khakis, a pressed golf shirt on, looking more like a champion sailor than a businessman.

Sean pulled his head out the freezer and glanced over. "Happy?"

"You're humming. And is that a smile? Wow, has hell frozen over? The terrifying Chef Sean is about to do a happy dance."

"So?" Sean shrugged, feeling self-conscious. He hadn't realized he'd been humming. He was just pulling together the things he wanted to take over to Darby's house.

"Well, when you first came here, you were scowling and shouting a lot."

"Shouting?" Sean said.

"Yeah, I mean, it's one way to motivate your team," Chase said, looking around. "The place looks great. Must have had the crew cleaning. And dinner last night was great. Ran into a few people in town and they can't stop talking about the special pasta of the day. And it looks like you have another one cooking."

"Something like that." Sean paused, and then decided he didn't mind sharing, perhaps getting a little intel. "Heading over to Darby Reese's house. I was going to make her dinner, sort of a celebration."

"Ah," Chase said, leaning against the counter, looking completely at ease. "The buzz is out on that. Everyone's talking about the work going on over there. Seems like Darby's pulling a bit of a switcheroo on her dad. Good for her. She's a good lawyer, but I think she's a better baker."

Chase shook his head. "Still, I'd like to be a fly on her wall when her dad comes in and discovers the changes. Reg isn't what you'd call big on changes."

Sean nodded, thinking back to this afternoon. He figured Chase was as good a source as any.

"There was this guy Jake there, looked like he used to be a quarterback."

108

"Jake Owens. You're right, former quarterback, now runs a construction company."

"Yeah," Sean nodded. That would be good old Jake. An athlete and handy with a hammer. "They aren't together, are they?"

"I think Darby is the best person to explain their relationship." There was something that looked suspiciously like amusement in Chase's eyes.

Chase gave Sean a wink, and Sean was about to thank him when he heard the familiar click of heels behind him.

"Mandy." Sean turned, trying to keep his voice bland. He had wanted to escape to Darby's without Mandy being aware of it. True to her word, she had stuck around for a few days, claiming she needed a vacation, sunning herself at the pool in a skimpy bikini, keeping an eye on him, waiting for him to change his mind.

"You look like you're going somewhere," Mandy said. She was wearing her usual outfit, a scoop-necked shirt, fitted pencil skirt, and heels. She lounged against the door jamb and fixed her blue eyes on Sean. He wondered just how much she had heard and decided that he didn't care.

"Mandy, you look lovely." Chase straightened, smiled, and moved in, giving Sean another little wink as he brushed past him. "I was just thinking ... there's a new restaurant in the next town over I wanted to try. People have been raving about it, and I thought I would give the competition a little once-over. I could use your opinion."

Chase was actually holding out his arm to Mandy, and Sean almost had to smother a laugh at the befuddled smile on her face. She desperately wanted to know what he, Sean, was up to, but there was no way she was going to say no to Chase. An opportunity to go out with a successful, good-looking guy like Chase was right up her alley.

With a large smile plastered on her face, she took Chase's arm. "I would love to."

Chase gave Sean a nod and a knowing smile and smoothly led Mandy out of the kitchen.

Sean sagged with relief against the counter. Chase might have been a great sailor, but he wasn't bad as wingman, either.

Chapter 26

Darby was looking through her small closet. It wasn't that her collection of clothes was small, it was just that an old house had a limited amount of space one could devote to clothes and shoes. Still, she had done the best she could. She had work wear, her lawyerly suits with their skirts, all lined up in a row pushed to one side, beneath them the sensible low-heeled pumps she had favored. Then there were her chef clothes. Cooking was a messy business, and she had an impressive collection of ripped and slightly stained t-shirts.

Sean had said it was a date, but that had just been an off-the-cuff comment, right? She had called Caitlyn, asking for advice, but Caitlyn had suggested she wear nothing but an apron and high heels. Darby had hung up after that, realizing she was on her own. Obviously a pinstripe suit was out of the question, as were a stained t-shirt and a pair of khaki shorts.

That left her with a choice between a sun dress from last year and a flowered skirt. She looked at the skirt. The truth was that she didn't know what to wear with it. They were supposed to be cooking, right? So anything white was out of the question. An invitation for disaster. That left the sun dress with the spaghetti straps and the brightly colored pattern.

She snaked it over her head and checked out how she looked. She rooted around in the closet and found a pair of low-heeled sandals. Not fancy, but a definite step up from flip flops. Then she looked at her hair in the mirror. She'd taken a shower, and her hair was damp. It was warm and humid, which meant that her hair would remain curly no matter what she did with it.

A loose ponytail it was. She had a light tan, so she skipped makeup, just adding some mascara and lip gloss. Satisfied that she looked like herself, not too fussy, she went downstairs. Nerves jangling, she waited for Sean.

She had cleaned the house, though it didn't really need it. The first floor consisted of the eat-in kitchen, a living room with a dining nook, and a sort of sun room that she had filled with light wicker furniture, plants, and books. She had repainted everything a light cream color, so that the stained edgework made a nice, crisp contrast.

Her grandmother had liked heavy, dark furniture, but Darby had sold most of it and replaced it with a few good, modern pieces. One or two small area rugs covered the floor, and some photographs— ones Darby had picked up on haunts around the Village—rounded out the decorations.

Since she had been renting the house out, Darby had included few personal touches or knickknacks, but now that she planned on living here full time, she was looking forward to adding more of her to the space but just hadn't gotten around to it. Still, even in its somewhat barren state, there was something soothing about it. It was a restful place, a good place to come home to.

She smoothed the skirt of her dress and popped into the small powder room on the first floor. She checked herself in the mirror, added a bit more lip gloss, and debated about whether or not to put her hair down. Shaking her head, she decided to keep it up in a ponytail. Nothing ruined a meal faster than a stray hair.

She walked out through the living room and into the kitchen, debating whether or not to light candles, but then decided that it would be too much. She didn't want to seem like she had any expectations. After all, this could just be a friendly dinner between two chefs, she reminded herself as she checked on the bottle of crisp white wine she had chilling in the fridge.

She checked for spots on the wine glasses and almost dropped one when she realized her hand was shaking like a leaf. *Breathe*, she told herself. Suddenly the house seemed silent all around her.

Music. She needed music. Rushing to her stereo, she plugged in her music player and fiddled over her playlists. She had them sorted by mood. There was classical—perfect for writing detailed legal briefs, since there were no words, and then there was her list of heavy metal hair bands—great for a row or a gym workout.

There was the playlist she had used with her college roommates while they were getting ready for a night out—upbeat, party music, and then there was the playlist for when they came home—the "Get Lucky" loop, they had dubbed it. *Definitely not that one*, she thought.

She needed something fun and upbeat, but not suggestive. Finally she found what she was looking for and, in relief, pressed play. The familiar music of Train's latest hit flooded over her, and she felt her heart rate slow just a little.

There was the sound of footsteps, the tread heavy on her front porch, and then a cheerful hello. He was here.

#

Sean stepped into the house. He'd been only as far as the front porch, he realized, and he fought down a quiver of excitement. So this was where Darby Reese lived. Ever since he'd been a kid, he'd loved seeing other people's houses. He knew it was because he'd grown up in such a disheveled way that going to someone else's house was the only true glimpse he'd had of what a home was supposed to be.

A quick survey took in Darby. She wore a simple sundress, which dipped just low enough in front to allow his imagination to run a little wild. Her thick, red-brown hair was pulled into a ponytail. Some of it had escaped around her face, and he could see a light smattering of freckles across the bridge of her nose. Her lips looked lush and full, and when she brushed her tongue over them, he felt himself tingle with excitement.

The house wasn't big, and it wasn't what he expected. If Darby's house was a prim and proper Victorian on the outside, then on the inside it was more like some sort of mod girl. The dark wood floors, gleaming white walls, and framed photographs all appealed to Sean. The lines were simple and clean, yet there was nothing sterile about it.

"Nice kitchen," he said, casting an appraising look about it. It was small but well-designed, with plenty of counter space and the perfect triangle of space between the sink, the stove, and a prep area. Top-of-the-line appliances and granite countertops vied with glass-fronted cabinets.

"Thanks." She caught his look and elaborated. "I kind of bartered for it. Remember Jake, the contractor? He wasn't getting paid on some big commercial job, but I wrote a letter or two and took care of things."

"And this was how he thanked you, with a top-of-the-line kitchen?" He felt his blood simmer a little faster at the thought of Darby and Jake. It was an awfully nice way to repay one letter.

She shrugged. "He sent over the labor and got me the materials at cost."

"You must be one heck of a lawyer."

She grinned sheepishly. "Well, I am, but we sort of went to prom together, too."

"Was he trying to win you back?" The words were out of his mouth before he could stop them. He had assumed that she wasn't seeing anyone, but then again, he hadn't really gotten around to asking.

"Not exactly. He was trying to make up for ditching me at the prom to sneak off with another girl."

He nodded, feeling as if a weight had lifted from his chest. "Let me guess? Your best friend?"

Darby shook her head, and he thought he caught a glimpse of amusement in her eyes. "Nope, more like my bitter enemy. I beat her out for class valedictorian, and I don't think she quite forgave me."

"So, this kitchen is his way of saying sorry?"

"In more ways than one. She was a total bitch and dumped him after she made sure my humiliation was complete. He apologized to me."

"And that's it. You shake hands and move on?" He knew disbelief had crept into his voice.

"I never said he was my boyfriend. He was just my prom date. We've been friends since we were in diapers. Jake was the good-looking quarterback, always dating the cheerleader. I was head of the debate team and on the academic team."

"So brains and brawn?" he asked, not quite getting it.

"Jake's a year ahead of me. He's like my big brother. He took me to the prom as a favor. Otherwise, my dad wasn't going to let me go. Reg, that's my dad, is kind of protective. But Jake still ditched me, which was totally not cool. And since I never told his dad, or mine, about what an ass he'd been, he's been trying to make it up to me ever since."

"Excellent negotiating skills, councilor," he said, moving in closer to her. She took a step back, and he realized that she was nervous. He decided that he liked it when she was off balance around him.

"How about a glass of wine?" she asked, her voice breathy.

"Sounds nice," he said. He looked around as she poured the wine and said, "So this is your house."

She was moving around the compact kitchen, but he took a step toward her so there was really nowhere she could go without running into him.

"Yes, my house. My grandmother left it to me."

"Along with her super-secret recipe book?" he asked. He took the glass of wine she offered, their hands brushing. She jumped again as if she had been shocked and then sent him a look that was half embarrassed, half amused. He took a sip of the wine, admiring its clear, cool crispness, and then set it down. He didn't need anything to settle his nerves. He enjoyed the electricity snapping between them, the sense of the promise in the air, as if the very house understood the inevitability of them being together.

"She loved to cook. She took over the deli from her dad and ran it with my grandfather and then my dad for almost fifty years."

"And it's been a town institution ever since?"

"Something like that. Though I don't think she ever meant for it to get frozen in time. Sure, she loved her old recipes, but she was always trying new things out. Somehow, I think my dad was always happier just doing the tried and true. I don't think he ever thought he would wind up running the deli."

"No?" Since he didn't think she would object he wandered over to a small shelf where there were a series of framed photos.

"He went into the Navy and then he was working on boats, crewing on yachts and fishing charters down in Florida and the Caribbean. He just liked to be out on the water, go fishing, that sort of stuff."

He picked up one that was obviously a snapshot of the whole family, from not too long ago, maybe last summer. It was Darby, her mom, a pretty, smiling woman who had Darby's red brown hair and freckles, and the giant bear of a man he'd heard so much about. They were all standing on a dock, the sun setting in the background with Reg holding up his catch of the day.

"And then what happened?"

"My grandfather got sick, my dad came home to help out, and before he knew it, he met my mom, got married, had me, and stayed here."

"So do you think he wants to keep you out of running The Dory because he doesn't want you to settle, the way he had to?"

"Something like that." Darby nodded. "I mean don't get me wrong, he'd do anything for me and for my mom. He'd never say that's why, and maybe he doesn't even realize it, but sometimes, he sneaks out, how he wishes that maybe things had been a little different."

"What about your mom, what's she like?" he asked.

"Well as you can tell, we look a lot alike," Darby said, moving closer to him and pointing at the photo.

"Does she help out with The Dory?"

Darby burst out laughing. "Not a chance. My mom can't even boil water. She's a serious liability in the kitchen. She works as bookkeeper and office manager for a local medical practice. She's actually a whiz with computers."

"Well that's not such a bad skill to have," he said as he put the photograph down. "And now you're going to come along and shake things up?"

"That's the plan." She said it lightly, as if trying to shrug it off.

"This is a tough business. Not only do you need to know what you're doing in the kitchen, you have to know how to run a business, make sense of the numbers, tell people what to do, keep a hundred different details straight in your head. You have to be one-hundred percent sure it's what you want. You have to be ready to burn those bridges behind you because there's no turning back." He knew his tone had grown serious, but he had seen too many try and fail at this business and that was something he knew, no matter what happened between them, that he did not want for her.

"Okay. I think quitting my job counts as burning bridges. Also sinking some money into The Dory to redo it shows I'm serious, right?" Her voice was barely more than a whisper as she looked at him. They were half facing each other, only a few inches apart.

He felt it then, the moment when the air between them tingled and zapped with a charge. The music, which he had barely noticed, changed, and he laughed when a look of pure mortification crossed her face.

"I had no idea that song was on there," she stammered as Marvin Gaye's *Let's Get it on* came on.

"I like it," he said. "I think it sums up what I'm thinking about." He pulled her to him, gently, then, so he could feel her body pressed close to him, the way she felt soft and hard at the same time, and the way it fitted against his. He let his hands slide around from her arms to her back, to pull her closer to him. She didn't fight him, not this time, but she kept her eyes locked on his.

He lowered his lips, and she rose up to meet him. He kissed her, gently at first, but then he wanted more, more from her than he had ever wanted from anyone else. He took her ruthlessly, his hand fisting in her hair, his other holding her close.

Darby rose into him, her breasts pressed against his chest, and he felt her moan, a soundless moan that nevertheless filled him with desire.

He let both his hands roam over her back, and then he brought one round to her front, felt the hard nub of her nipple. He caressed her and was rewarded with another moan, this one low and urgent. He raked his teeth over her long neck, burying himself in her smell of strawberries and oranges.

"I want you," he said, his voice ragged with desire. He pulled away just long enough to look at her, to see the answering look of need in her eyes as she smiled, just a bit shyly. His whole body tensed at that, at her wide, trusting eyes, and he pulled her toward him again.

His strong hands lifted her up, and he practically carried her to the couch in the living before setting her down. His kisses rained down on her, and his stubble-roughened cheek grazed her jawline.

He felt her hesitation and stopped then, dropping down so he was level with her sitting on the couch.

"We can slow things down a bit," he said, his voice low, knowing he needed to keep the pleading out of it. This had to be all her decision, even though it would cut him to the core if she wasn't ready.

#

Darby didn't need to think. She just nodded, and Sean smiled at her. One hand had found the hem of her dress, and it was slowly working its way up her leg, sending delightful shivers up to her core. She felt the heat rush through her, the warm twisting clench between her legs as his fingers found the thin fabric of her panties and pushed them out of the way. A finger, gentle but insistent, found her and stroked her, and she gasped from the sudden fierce pleasure of it.

She opened her eyes and found him watching her, his own eyes a deep, intense brown that pulled her in. It was too much, and when he stroked harder, faster, she threw back her head and moaned, the delight coming hot and fierce, her hand fisting as she rode the wild wave coursing through her.

One hand had dipped below the neckline of her dress, and caught the hard knob of her nipple. He rolled it between his fingers, and she moaned blissfully. She felt the excitement building in her, felt her breath coming in hard, hot gasps as he brought her closer and closer to the edge.

"Yes, yes, Sean," she heard herself moan. His hands moved more rhythmically, more insistently, and she was almost there. She shuddered against him, the tension building, and then he had pushed her dress up and torn off her panties.

She reached for him, snagging his belt with one finger and snaking it off. His shorts dropped, and she could see he was just as ready for her as she was for him. She reached out and touched him, feeling his erection through the thin fabric of his boxers.

"Oh yes," he moaned, and she pulled him closer, peeling off the boxers until he sprung free.

"Now?" he asked, and she could do no more than nod as he prepared to enter her. He moved gently into her, then as the want built within him, he took her with sharp, strong, assured thrusts.

She wrapped her legs around him, pulling him close so that she could feel the exquisite pleasure of each and every thrust. "Oh, yes!" she cried as he took her over the edge. Her body convulsed in spasms of pleasure around him, and she could feel him reach his climax.

There was silence, just the thudding of their hearts. What had happened, she wondered, to the music? Did it matter? Sean, all glorious six foot two of him and his hard, muscled body was lying on her. Their legs and clothes were tumbled and tangled together, and she could feel the rise and fall of his chest.

There, the music had started up again. And it was normal—upbeat, none of the sexy music that had slipped in before. God, what had she been thinking when she added those to the playlist? They'd been total "doing it" songs, and that's just what they had done, with an intensity she'd never felt before. Nothing before this had even come close.

"Say something," she asked him, needing to know if he felt the same way.

"Wow," he answered, and she hazarded a glance at his face. It had all happened so quickly, she didn't quite know what to say. She, Darby Reese, who waited until at least the tenth date or more before going all the way, had just allowed a guy to ravish her—on a couch, no less. She was still wearing most of her clothes, for goodness' sake.

"I am so sorry. I don't know ... I don't understand just what happened. I don't usually ..."

She tried to sit up, but he was too heavy. He looked at her with those twinkling eyes. His blonde hair was even more boyishly mussed than usual, and he looked so hot that she felt that familiar clench between her legs. Why did he have to be so darn adorable?

"Sorry for what, sugar?" He moved up a bit, a lopsided grin on his face. "I would say that was better than the tasting menu at ..."

She felt herself blush, and she looked away.

"Hey," he said, his hand reaching out and holding her chin so she had to stare at him. "I get it. You don't usually jump into bed with a guy you've just met."

"Well, technically, we've known each other a long time," she said.

He groaned. "You had to bring it up. Should I say I'm sorry again? That I'm not the man I used to be?"

She smiled, feeling a delicious need rise in her again. "I like the man you are right now."

#

They made love again, this time in her bed. He took his time with her, his hands assured, his eyes wicked as he explored her body gently, then not so gently pushing her until she felt limp and ragged and thoroughly satisfied.

Dark had fallen, and they lay curled against each other in her room, a light breeze stirring the curtain in her window. Darby lay against him, feeling a sense of contentment she hadn't felt in a long time.

"Well, councilor, that was something else," he said, nuzzling her ear.

Even though she knew he had felt it, too—the deep connection between the two of them—it was a relief to hear him say that, to confirm that this was where they had meant to end up.

"Well, you weren't bad yourself." In fact, it had never been this good with anyone else, but she decided that she might keep that little fact to herself.

"Wait until next time," he whispered.

She turned, looked at him. "Will there be a next time?"

"What do you mean?" A look of puzzlement flashed in his liquid brown eyes.

"I don't know. I'm just wondering if you're here for good, or if you finally got your call back up to the big leagues?"

"What do you mean? Are you still worried about Mandy?"

She managed to shrug one bare shoulder, shivering as he ran his hand lightly over her.

"It's just that I know that the Osprey Arms is your chance to work your way back up to the big leagues. And your publicist showing up—I just figured that maybe your ticket had come up and I guess I want to know if I'm the distraction along the way."

"What do you think I am, some sort of rock star? I'm a guy who boils pasta. I don't just expect that every woman I meet is going to drop her panties for me."

"An interesting way of phrasing things," she said, but she realized that the pounding of her chest was easing and the awful feeling that had reared up in her stomach, tying it into knots, was unraveling.

"I told you, the stories of my past relationships have all been greatly exaggerated. When I'm with someone, I'm with them."

Darby let that settle in, but Sean wasn't done. He flipped her over, so she was lying on top of him, chest to chest. He shook his head. "You know what I don't get?"

"What?" she asked, but she was pretty sure she knew what it was.

"Why you, a lawyer, would give it all up to work in a kitchen. All those years of school, the chance to make a lot of money, be treated with respect, and you want to trade it all for a chance to swing a knife."

"You get a lot of respect," she pointed out.

"Because people are afraid of me. You ... you probably walked in the room and people respected you without you having to say a word."

She shook her head. "You sound like my dad."

"Well, maybe he's on to something. Did he pay for law school? Because I bet he'll be pretty pissed when he gets back and finds out you quit your job."

She realized that Sean wasn't angry, just interested to know what she thought would happen. "Weren't you the one who was saying that I needed to be all in, to burn my bridges if I wanted to succeed?"

"Well, metaphorically speaking—mentally, that is. Plan B has to suck; otherwise, you give up too easily."

"What was your Plan B if this cooking thing didn't work out?" she asked, suddenly curious.

He laughed, a throaty, gravelly laugh. "Stealing cars maybe, working on the road crew, which would have been legit, at least."

"What happened?" she asked, feeling sorry for him.

"My dad wasn't much of one. He had a real temper and liked to drink. Sometimes he would slap me and Mom around. Not badly enough so that anyone would believe us."

She sat up and looked at him, but he kept going.

"Then he had a car accident. He was drunk of course and was killed. We were left alone, with nothing. So I became that kid, you know the one who got into trouble, stole things, and started fights."

"What happened?"

"Well, I tried to rob this restaurant in town, this rib and chicken place, nothing fancy, but it was the most popular place in town."

"And," Darby could hardly stand to hear.

"I got caught. By Mac, the owner. He was a big, tough, son of a bitch. With a temper. Yelled, but funnily enough, that was it. People fell into line."

"So what did he do?" Darby waited with bated breath for the rest of the story. She could imagine Sean, a teenager, alone, rebellious, trying to find his place in the world.

Sean shook his head. "Saved my life. Instead of turning me in, he put me to work. First it was in his garden. He had a big two-acre plot that he grew all these vegetables and herbs on. Said I could work there for a dollar an hour or I could take my chances with juvie court."

"So you did?"

"Mostly. At first I balked at it. Even tried to take Big Mac down, but he showed me.. One punch was all it took to show me that it was a losing battle. Then he took me into an office, poured me some cheap whisky and set me straight."

"How did he do that?"

"Told me I could stop blaming the world for what happened and start behaving like a man and make something of myself. That I had a choice. I needed to stop doing all the dumb shit I was doing and start applying myself."

"And did you?"

"Yeah. He promised he'd give my mom a job if I held up my end of the bargain. And I did, and so did he. I moved from the vegetable garden into the kitchen, doing every one of the dirty, nasty jobs, finally working my way up to a line cook."

"What happened?"

"I loved it. Cooking, that is. Finally I knew what to do with all those vegetables Mac had made me pick. I found my thing. Of course, Mac ran a tough kitchen. He kept everyone in line because we were all just a bit of afraid of him. For him, it was a very effective motivator. When I finally got to run my own kitchen, I guess I just modeled it after Mac's. And well, I was still an angry kid most of the time."

"So Big Mac didn't have a heart of gold?" Darby said, feeling somewhat disappointed.

"Nope. Still runs the restaurant. People are too afraid to quit on him, so he keeps his staff, even though he's a terror to work with. The restaurant is a goldmine. Nothing much to look at, but a nice high profit margin. He did lend me the money to go to culinary school, and by that I mean lend, with interest. There are no free rides with Big Mac."

"Sorry, it sounds like it was tough on you." Darby said.

"It made me tough," Sean said. "But I think that's what drove me all those years. Whatever I could get I would take, always looking for the next big thing."

"What about your mom?"

Sean gave a laugh. "Mac gave her a job as a hostess, and she was pretty good at it too. Finally married one of the customers. A nice, relatively mild-mannered dentist, named Alan. She's retired now and plays Bunco and gardens. She's happy. And the dentist is a nice enough guy."

"Do you ever see them?" Darby asked.

"Big Mac? Nope, not since I walked out of that small town over a decade ago."

She punched him lightly on his arm, "I meant your mom and Alan."

"Ouch," he said, grinning while he rubbed it. "Of course. They came to visit every time I started a new restaurant. And I send my mom gifts on her birthday, Mother's Day, Christmas, and even Valentine's Day. She's my mom and like I said, Alan, the dentist, isn't a bad guy at all. I try to make time for them, but it's been hard the last couple of years. Life's been moving pretty fast."

"So you do have a softer side?"

"Shh, don't tell anyone that," he said, kissing her, and she felt her heart slip as his hands roamed over her, her body already alive and responding to his touch. She had just made love with Sean Callahan, but she was afraid she might be falling in love with the former bad boy who did have a heart of gold.

Chapter 27

"Whatcha doing?" Caitlyn swung in the back door of the restaurant. "Smells like paint."

"That's because they're painting," Darby said from where she was perched on the chair, checking her list.

"Got any chocolate muffins?" Caitlyn asked, as her finger skimmed over the cranberry-orange scones Darby had just taken out of the oven.

"Not yet." Darby crossed some items off her list and added some new ones. The list never got shorter; it just kept changing.

"How did it go last night?"

"What about last night?" Darby hopped down from the chair.

"You know, your date."

"It was just dinner," Darby said, as she went back to the chopping block. The restaurant had been painted the cool cream and glossy white that she wanted. One more day of waiting for it to dry, and then she could start bringing in the furniture, redoing the display cases, and setting out the new menus. She'd had a banner made to cover up The Dory's old sign, deciding that a permanent one could wait just a bit longer. She would love to have her new logo painted on the big plate glass window at the front of the shop, but the sign painter couldn't come before next week, and still she wasn't sure she should go that far. A myriad of details raced through her head until she took a deep breath to calm herself down.

"So, you look like you've been more than kissed," Caitlyn said, as she propped herself up on the counter.

Automatically, Darby waved her off, and Caitlyn slid down with a sigh.

"So, what happened?"

"What are you talking about?" Darby brushed past Caitlyn to put the pan of meatloaf on the refrigerator.

"Hold on." Caitlyn grabbed her arm, stopped her, and stared at her intently. "You have that glow."

"Glow?" Darby broke free and snorted.

"You know, the glow that comes from nocturnal exercise."

"Oh, please," Darby said, as she shoved the pan into the fridge and shut the door. "Nocturnal exercise ... really? Is that the best you can do?"

"Well, I could call it the in-the-mattress mambo, but whatever I call it, all signs point to ..."

"Yes, yes!" Darby cried, covering her ears. If Caitlyn came up with one more phrase, she was going to die from embarrassment.

"You did it," Caitlyn said, her hands clasped together in excitement. "You have to tell me more."

"Aren't you supposed to lecture me, not hound me for details?"

"Umm, were you safe?"

"Of course," Darby said, mortified.

"Well, lecture done. Now you can tell me all the good stuff."

"I am not telling you the details," Darby said.

"Well, was it good?"

"Yes," Darby breathed and slumped against the counter. It had been good, very good.

"Aww, c'mon. I need some of the finer points. You haven't had a relationship since that jerk Will, who you were willing to talk about in excruciating detail, and now—"

"Who said anything about a relationship? It was just dinner, which in fact we never ate, and well ..."

"And it gets better and better," Caitlyn pointed out.

"It just happened. I didn't mean for it to," Darby said, feeling a mix between elation and misery. Reckless. Getting involved with—worse yet, falling for—Sean Callahan was reckless. And she had never been that.

"Well, then, if you didn't, you're a fool," Caitlyn said.

Darby snorted. "Weren't you the one who was telling me to careful? That maybe he's just biding his time here in Queensbay?"

"Yeah, but I already saw him. He must have been walking home from your place and he looked ecstatic, and now you look like you're over the moon, so it must have all been for the best. Though, there seems like a 'but' in there somewhere?"

Darby had been trying not to think about it, the way she had all of a sudden felt her world slip sideways and then steady back to reality. Love. Was that what it was?

"Have you ever been in love, I mean real, honest to goodness love?" she asked suddenly. Caitlyn had been engaged; surely, she must know what it was like. Maybe she could help Darby figure these things out.

Caitlyn's gray eyes grew guarded, her fingers playing with the scone she had picked up from the baking sheet. "The thing about love? It's a tricky little devil."

"You were engaged." Darby let it slip out before she thought about it.

"And I'm not now. I think it's easy to think you're in love," Caitlyn said carefully.

"Does everything feel different, bright, full of promise?"

Caitlyn closed her eyes as if remembering. "Yes, that's exactly how it feels."

Darby paused for a moment, wondering if she had found the answer she had been looking for.

Chapter 28

"Are you checking up on me? You know you don't have to invent an excuse to come down to the marina to see me." A shadow fell across Darby as she moved the bucket around the cockpit of her dad's fishing boat. She looked up into the sun to see Sean standing above her, silhouetted against the sky.

"Hardly. My dad texted me. Wanted me to check the gas line on his boat," Darby said, smiling. "And then I thought I would wash down the decks too."

"I thought I get to see you later tonight, but this is a pleasant surprise. Guess I should ask permission to come aboard or something like that, right?" Sean said, eyeing the boat.

"Guess you should," Darby said, coyly. He looked her over. She was wearing her bikini top and a pair of cutoff jeans and the afternoon sun looked warm on her back. Sean was wearing jeans and one of his t-shirts that seemed molded to him.

"Permission to come aboard, Captain?"

"Permission granted," she said and Sean stepped onto the boat. In a moment he had her in his arms, his mouth covering hers. She reached up and into his kiss, letting her hands twine around his silky blonde hair, loving the way every part of her body seemed to light up at his very touch.

"But there's something you should know," she said when they came up for air.

"And what's that?" he said as he nuzzled her neck.

"The captain's always in charge."

"Hmm," he said, as his teeth nipped her ear, "I think I can live with that."

"Want to take her for a spin?" Darby asked, not bothering to hide the excitement in her voice.

Sean looked at her. "Are you allowed? Won't Big Reg object to you taking out his boat? I told you my days hotwiring cars—or boats—are long gone."

Darby smiled. "Like he's going to object to me remaking his restaurant?"

125

"So is this a case of in for a penny, in for a pound?" Sean asked.

"Something like that," she said, looking at him as if daring him. "You know, I'm not the always good girl you think I am."

"Oh, I think you proved that conclusively the other night. You might look sweet and taste sweet, but I'm pretty sure I've seen your wild side."

Darby almost blushed at that. Her wild side had only come out with Sean. With him her body felt powerful and sexy and, well, it just made the experiences, all of them, that much more exciting.

"So are you in?"

Sean checked his watch. "I have to be back in about an hour."

"Can you stretch it to two?" Darby asked.

"Well, since you're the captain, I guess I have to," Sean said.

"Perfect. Here," she said, going to the steering wheel, "you can cast off."

#

Darby knew just where she wanted to take Sean. Dyer's Cove wasn't the only secluded spot in the harbor. She kept the speed low as she skirted the edge of the mooring field, then as they entered the channel, she pushed down on the throttle, and the boat leaped forward. Sean sat in the seat next to her, sunglasses on, leaning back, enjoying the sun.

"Want to take the wheel?" she asked.

"I suppose I'd better not hit anything with Big Reg's boat." He looked just like a kid who'd been given a free pass to a candy store.

"Nope, that would definitely not be a way to get on his good side," Darby agreed. Sean stood and took the wheel in both hands. Just in case, she stood next to him, one hand near the throttle.

"We can cut to port—that's left to you, landlubber, and head here," she pointed toward a flat, low line of land. He turned the boat and had them headed in the right direction.

"And now you can go faster," she said.

"How fast?"

"Pretty fast, since there's no speed limit in this part of the harbor."

Grinning, he pushed down on the throttle and the boat responded underneath him, charging forward. Sean gave a whoop as the boat surged through the water.

The little spit of land came into view quickly.

"Now we have to go in slow," she said, and Sean eased down on the throttle.

"What do I do now?"

"Just keep going, nice and easy; I'm going to get the anchor ready." Darby went up to the bow of the boat, checked the anchor and line and stood there, ready.

When they were about twenty feet out she told Sean to cut the engine. She dropped the anchor and the boat drifted, and then she felt as the anchor caught, digging into the bottom. She tied the anchor line down and went back into the cockpit.

"Now what?"

"We go ashore."

Sean looked at the distance that separated them from the rocky beach.

"How?"

"We swim, then we wade in. Unless you're afraid of getting wet?"

He shook his head. "Lead the way, sugar."

"I told you not to call me that,' she said, playfully.

"Yeah, but that was before you decided you liked me."

"And I like you now?" she asked, her heart skipping a beat as she looked at him. He gave her a grin and then took her hand.

"I sure hope you do, because I'm beginning to like you." He kissed her hand. "A lot."

Darby didn't want to think too much about what that meant. He liked her, but he said nothing about love. And that, Darby thought, drawing a breath, was a good thing, right? It was too soon to talk about more, to complicate things, even if both her brain and her heart were telling her differently.

"Like me enough to do this?" Darby quickly stripped off her shorts, leaving her in just her bikini. In one graceful move she stood up on the edge of the boat, turned so she was facing Sean, and did a back flip into the cool salty waters of Queensbay Harbor. She sank down into the water and then propelled herself upwards towards the light and the surface.

Sean was still in the boat, looking at her.

"Are you going to come in?" she asked.

He looked down at her and then into the water. "Are you sure that it's safe in there?"

"What are you afraid of? Sharks? Seaweed."

"Are you calling me chicken?"

"Absolutely," she said.

"Well then, I guess if my manhood is in question, I need to prove myself."

He went in headfirst and came up sputtering. "It's cold."

She laughed. "Only at first. It's refreshing. C'mon."

With that she set out toward the shore with steady, strong strokes.

Sean had said he wasn't much of swimmer, but his long arms and legs propelled him forward so that he easily caught up with her.

They hit the sandy bottom of the beach at the same time and she turned over, so she was half in the water and half out, letting the sun and water wash over her. She had guided them around the lee side of the little island, where she knew they would have privacy. Around them, they could still hear the sounds of the harbor but it all seemed far away.

"So what do we do now?" he asked, turning over. She glanced at him with half-lidded eyes. He had shed his t-shirt and just wore his shorts. She allowed herself to admire the ripple of his stomach muscles before answering his question.

"Nothing."

"Nothing? What, we don't explore, or ..."

"You could, but it's really just a little hump of an island. There are a few trees and the birds like to nest here. So if you get too close, they'll dive bomb you."

"So we just sit here?"

"Yup, just sit here, the two of us."

Sean looked around. "Ahh, I see what you mean. So what is this, your private little necking spot?"

Darby shrugged. "Not exactly. I mean, I heard about it when I was in high school, but no one would ever take me here."

"Why not?" Sean asked.

"I don't think any boy was brave enough to date me. My dad has a way of scaring off guys."

"Really." Sean had inched closer to her; she could feel it without looking at him. She relished the heat layered between the two of them.

"So this is some high school dream of yours to make out with a boy on your little lover's beach."

Darby nodded, "Pretty much. Too bad Daddy left me the keys to his boat and went on vacation an ocean away."

Suddenly she was on her back, her head on the sand and he was over her, his body hovering, his lips just inches from her face. "Why, Darby Reese, aren't you the bad girl!"

"Let's just say I'm trying to play by my own rules," she said, as she pulled his face down to hers. His mouth clamped over hers, and he let out a little moan as his arms slid down her shoulders to cup her breasts in his hand. His thumbs scraped against her already taut nipples and she arched her back into him. A knee slid between her legs, gently opening them up as his hand trailed down her bare stomach and ran a line along the top edge of her bikini bottom.

She could feel him, hard and ready for her, as she ran her hands through his hair and down the strong muscles of his back. She ground her hips up to him, already knowing she was ready for him.

"Are you sure we're alone?" he whispered.

"Absolutely sure," she managed to pant as his fingers slid into her bikini, finding and then gently brushing down her mound and into the v of her legs. She was slick and moist and his fingers moved in and out, pushing her, pushing her closer and closer to the edge until she practically sobbed his name.

His head came down and he took one of her nipples in his mouth and she let out a strangled cry as she felt her whole body draw tight with sensation. God, she wanted him; all she could think about was him inside her. She whispered, "Now, now," but the only answer was a throaty chuckle as his mouth found her other nipple and she bucked against him as his fingers pushed her ruthlessly farther and farther.

Her arms tightened close around his shoulders and her body trembled. Then when she thought she could stand it no more, she felt her bathing suit bottom slide off and one of his hands returned between her legs, continuing to push her toward the edge. She saw him quickly remove his own shorts.

She looked up at him and could see that he was more than ready for her. She spread her legs for him and he took the invitation, plunging into her, riding her with quick, assured thrusts that pushed toward the edge and over it. Her head came back as she cried out, and he quickly silenced her with his own mouth as she felt him climax too.

She lay there for a moment, Sean's weight on her. Her eyes were closed, and she opened them slowly. Above was still the cloudless blue sky. Around her was sand and water. A boat motor droned in the far off distance and she could hear her own heavy breathing, mingling with Sean's.

Carefully he rolled over on his back so that he too was looking up at the sky.

"I'm sorry," he said for a moment.

She panicked, wondering what for, what was coming next.

"I think you're going to have sand in some places that will be pretty hard to get out."

She laughed. "I've heard that's one of the perils of sex on the beach, but all in all, I think it was worth it."

"Worth it?' Sean gave a grunt and then rolled over and kissed her. "That was pretty hot, Captain. It's not every day that a guy gets pirated away for a little romantic interlude on the beach."

"The joys of living by the water," Darby murmured as she met his kiss.

#

"You know, you never told me why you decided to quit being a lawyer," he said as they swam back to the boat.

She looked at him. "I did. I told you I didn't want to sit in an office all day. And ever since I was a little girl I loved cooking for people."

He looked at her, one hand hooked on the side of the boat, his legs treading water. "But that wasn't your moment."

"What do you mean by moment?"

He laughed, "You know, the moment when you knew that this was what you wanted to do."

She didn't answer at first, just ducked her head under water. When she came up he was still there, looking at her, not letting her get by without answering.

"I'd been working at my firm about two years. I'd been told I was on the fast track already, that if I put in my time and kept up the good work, I'd probably become a partner. It's sort of like being handed the golden key. Not everyone gets told that, and it means that you get the best assignments, the right mentor. In other words, everyone is looking out for you."

"What happened?"

"I walked into my mentor's office. We were supposed to have our monthly 'check in' lunch and she was at her desk, tears streaming down her face, looking at a picture in a frame on her desk."

"Why?" he asked.

"Apparently some big issue had come up and she had missed her kid's concert. Again. And when I asked her about it, she burst into tears and said that she'd made a huge mistake, that she'd given up her dreams to do something safe, to make her parents proud and that not all the money in the world could compensate for her missing her kid growing up and not writing a book like she wanted to ... It went on and on and it turned out that she was miserable and that her advice to me was that if I ever had any dreams, that I should go for it sooner rather than later."

Sean looked at her. "So what happened to her?"

"She quit," Darby said, pulling herself up into the boat. Sean followed her. "And last I heard she became a teacher at the high school in her home town and was working on writing a novel."

"And what did you do?" Sean asked.

"Enrolled in that class at the Culinary Academy," Darby said, grinning. "Remember that?"

"I keep hoping you'll forget it," Sean said, looking at her closely. "Know that I'm not that person anymore. That a guy can change. Be changed by things that happen."

Darby was about to give him a light answer, make a joke of it, but it seemed he wanted more.

"I never think of it anymore" she admitted, as she pulled him closer for a kiss.

Chapter 29

"And there you are." Mandy's voice floated above and across the open refrigerator door. Sean sighed as he shut it. He had actually thought that Mandy had checked out, but here she was again. He was in the middle of the dinner prep and the last thing he felt like doing was chatting with her.

"I thought I gave you my answer," Sean said.

"Well, I have something that may change your mind," Mandy said, looking at him, arms crossed so that they just managed to push her cleavage to the forefront of her blouse. Sean looked around, caught Kevin, the line cook, ogling her and snapped, "Get back to work."

Mandy shook her head, "I thought you weren't yelling at people anymore?" she said.

"That was speaking firmly," Sean said as he carried the tray of pork ribs over to the counter.

"Well, whatever. Look, they've sweetened the pot," Mandy said, her voice direct.

"What are you talking about?" he asked, his mind thinking ahead to the night's dinner. The Osprey was booked solid and it promised to be a busy night. He was wondering if he had enough of the seafood special to go around.

"The producers. Apparently they really want you. The video that Will made, well it went viral, and now you're an internet hit."

Sean felt a flare of anger and took a deep breath. "I thought you were going to get that taken down."

"Oh, I did, but apparently, not quite soon enough. It turned out better than you might think, since it means you're a hot commodity to them now. Go in, audition for this, and I'll let it be known you're shopping around for a new gig and who knows who will bite? This could be it, the break you've been waiting for."

All around them, the kitchen was warming up, beginning the dance necessary to prepare over a hundred dinners a night. Sean watched his crew, noted how a couple of his line chefs joked and chatted while they worked but still managed to stay focused. The waitresses were looking over the dinner specials, familiarizing themselves with the items. It was beginning to heat up in the kitchen but that's what Sean expected. It was time to get cooking.

"Mandy," he stopped and looked at her. "No way. My place is here. Tell them I'm not interested."

"Look Sean, that was a great tactic, the first time, and it got you what you want, but I don't think it will fly again. This time they'll take a look at someone else."

"What, like Will Green? They can have him, if they want him. No, seriously, Mandy, I've got a business to run."

"But, Sean," she leaned over and grabbed his arm, her talon-like nails digging into him. He took a deep breath, resisting the urge to throw her off.

"Seriously, Mandy, it's time to move on, okay? I'm just not going to do it. Got it?" His voice rose a little, he noted, but no more than was necessary to make his point above the buzz and the hum of the busy kitchen.

"Are you saying you're going to throw your career away over some little tramp? Looks like she's trapped you good, Sean. I made you, don't you know that? You can't walk away from me."

Sean almost saw red, at Mandy's words. He wanted to defend Darby but realized it would only lead to a shouting match. He was about to calmly and rationally explain things to her when there was a loud bellow behind him.

He turned and saw that Kevin and one of the busboys, Sam, were toe-to-toe, eyes narrowed and fists balled. Sean moved quickly, out of instinct, sensing the fight before it actually happened.

"I told you to keep your hands off of her," Kevin shouted, his finger pointing right at the center of Sam's chest. Kevin emphasized each word with a definitive poke in the chest. Sean saw right away that Sam wasn't going to take it.

"She's eighteen, a grownup, able to do whatever she wants," Sam said, his voice taunting.

"Look, guys," Sean started to say, but he was a moment too late. Kevin took a swing at Sam, who ducked easily and grabbed Kevin low around the waist in a grapple. Kevin went staggering back toward a counter loaded with vegetables. Julienned carrots went flying as Kevin hit the counter hard.

Sean could sense all the other people in the kitchen drawing closer toward the action, forming a ring around the two duelers. It needed to be stopped. There wasn't going to be any fighting in his kitchen.

Kevin got back up and Sean could see the rage coursing through him. With a swift movement he stepped in between Kevin and his adversary, but Kevin was quicker than he thought. He already had his fist out and no doubt he meant to catch Sam straight in the jaw but instead it caught Sean in his stomach, a good hard punch that knocked the wind out of him. Sean staggered back, his head hitting something and a blinding pain made everything go black for few seconds. He sensed rather than heard a few shocked screams, but then there was silence.

It took a moment for Sean to shake it off and when he did, Kevin was just standing there, staring at him, a mingled look of fear and horror in his face. Sean turned and saw the same look on Sam's face.

He took a deep breath. "Kevin, go take five; get some fresh air."

Kevin nodded, then murmured, "Yes, Chef." Sean watched as he scooted out the back door.

Sean turned to Sam, who held up his hands. Before Sean could hear any of his stammered excuses, he cut him off.

"Sam, get a broom and a mop and clean this mess up."

There was a pause and then the room seemed to swarm into action, everyone going back to their stations as if nothing had happened. Out of the corner of his eye he saw Mandy slink off. Sean sighed. It was probably for the better. He didn't have anything else to say to her, and right now, the back of his head was throbbing.

"Here." All of a sudden Chase was in front of him, tossing him a bag of frozen peas. "These always seemed to help me when I got a whack in the head."

\#

It took a little while to sort things out. Sean took himself off to the bar area where Chase poured him a drink that Sean decided he didn't need. Sam came in, apologized and then Kevin, after his ten-minute cool-off period, did the same. Sean even made sure they said sorry to each other and watched as the two them went back into the kitchen as if nothing had happened.

"Guess they were fighting over a girl," Chase said, shaking his head.

"Yeah, I think Sam was putting the moves on Kevin's sister. Once Sam assured Kevin he'd treat her right, I think the whole thing was settled. Good thing there wasn't a knock-down brawl." Sean took a deep breath. "I'm just glad no one got hurt. I mean really hurt."

Chase paused for a moment. "Seems like they all have you to thank for that."

"What do you mean?" Sean's head was pounding a little less now. There was a lump on the side of his head, but a small one and it no longer hurt when he took a breath.

"You stepped in, took a hit, didn't hit back—and then told the other guys to cool down. Sounds to me like you're the one who handled the situation pretty nicely."

Sean thought for a moment. Not once had he been tempted to hit back or even yell. His only thought was to make sure that nothing bad happened in his kitchen, that there wouldn't be anything to interfere with the success of his restaurant.

"I guess you're right," he said slowly. "I handled it like a real pro."

"Yes you did. I guess Queensbay isn't such a bad place after all."

Sean smiled, "I can think of a few things I like about it."

Chase gave a laugh. "I'm guessing a certain redhead came to mind. Seems like you too are pretty serious?"

Sean eyed his friend, who was standing behind the bar, arms crossed, rocking back and forth on his heels, as if he hadn't a care in the world, but Sean could see that he was eagerly awaiting the answer.

"A certain redheaded lady friend might have something to do with the recent increase in my satisfaction levels."

"You're only satisfied?" Chase shot him a look. "This is Darby Reese you're talking about. I mean this was a girl who was smart, hot, and could cook. And wouldn't let any of us near her, back in the day. You have to give me a little more."

Sean smiled, feeling a bit like the cat that'd been given a nice big bowl of cream. "Let's just say I find my time with Darby very satisfying." He might have been about to give Chase a little bit more but Darby burst into the room.

"What happened here?"

"And look who's here," Chase said, pretending all of a sudden to be busy with some of the glasses behind the bar.

Sean swiveled around. Darby was there, wearing jean shorts and a pink halter top that showed off her tan shoulders. Her hair was in a ponytail and there was a worried expression on her face.

"I heard there was fight! Is everyone all right? Are you all right?" She took a step closer into the barroom and Sean felt his stomach do a little flip flop. Her top was the color of strawberry ice cream and he had a sudden desire to have a taste of her.

"Nothing to see here," Chase said, moving around from behind the bar. "Sean here was breaking up a fight and happened to get caught in the middle."

Darby looked between the two of them, as if searching for the truth behind the words.

"What did you do?" She turned to look at Sean and he could see that she was bracing herself for bad news.

"Nothing. I mean Chase is right, I stepped in the middle and took a punch to the stomach. Then I fell back and hit my head."

Darby's eyes grew wide at the explanation. "Are you okay? Do you need to see a doctor?" She had moved closer and was looking Sean over, her green eyes filled with concern. Still, her arms stayed locked at her sides.

"No, I'm fine. Just a little bump," Sean explained.

There was a pause and he watched as she swallowed, before she asked her next question. "Then what did you do?"

He took a deep breath, noticing the way Chase had eased himself out from behind the bar and was sneaking away.

"I got up, told one guy to take five and the other to clean up the mess. Didn't even yell."

"You didn't yell?"

Sean shook his head.

"You didn't hit him back?"

Sean shook his head and then called out to Chase, who was almost out the door. "Isn't that right?"

"He's telling the truth, Darby. Handled it like a real professional."

Darby sagged against the bar in relief. "Oh my, I was so worried when I heard the story. Or part of it. It's already making its way around town."

Sean winced. "I am sure it's getting worse with every retelling."

Darby looked up at him and smiled. "Funny thing is though, you're not in it."

Sean straightened up. "Really?"

"Well, they are saying you're the one who broke it up. But that's it. They're all talking about how Kevin's sister is running around with Sam."

Sean looked at her. "So why did you come running down here?"

Darby gave a little shrug. Sean smiled, reached out his arm and snagged Darby's hand, pulling her close to him, so she was snug against him.

"Were you worried about me?" he asked, trying to keep the elation out of his voice.

Darby rested her head against his shoulder. "I might have been."

He ran his hand down her hair, smoothing it, loving the way she felt, nestled against him. He was overcome with a sudden, profound feeling that this was right, that everything was going to be all right.

"That's mighty sweet of you, sugar."

There was a muffled sound of laughter. "I told you not to call me sugar."

Chapter 30

Darby looked around the deli, starting to feel like things were really coming together. The paint was mostly dry, so she had brought in the new tables and chairs she scouted from a local restaurant supply store. Now she was going over her budget and was carefully allocating money out for all the items she wanted.

She'd been saving for years, just about everything she had earned. She'd even given up her apartment months ago, choosing to take a cheap sublet, so that she would have plenty of money in the bank for when she was ready to make the move. Her clothes had all been bought on sale and since she'd worked so much she hadn't had much time for a vacation or, hell, even go to the movies.

But without a doubt, doing it this way, remaking The Dory, was a lot less risky than trying to open a brand new restaurant. The Dory had an established location, with an existing clientele. All she was doing really was changing up the menu. But if her projections were right, she felt that soon there would be room for more than one Golden Pear along the coast. But the most important thing was to get the opening of the first one right.

Her parents had given her so much already; she didn't want The Dory to be just one more thing they handed to her. She wanted to show her dad that not only could she run it—

and run it well—but that she had the cash to make a real offer for the place.

Darby sighed and looked around. She ran through a mental checklist and decided that she'd done all she could for one day. Besides, checking her watch, she realized she needed to run down to Village Hall to drop off some paperwork for a business license for the catering part of her business.

Just in case, she decided, she would bring the clerk a box of cookies, to make sure everything ran smoothly. Not a bribe exactly, so much as a goodwill present. As she rose up and stretched she realized she would relish the chance to get out and see the day.

The afternoon was hot and steamy, the midst of the dog days of summer. But she knew it wouldn't last. Soon, fall would be sweeping through New England, bringing riotous colors and cool days and cool nights without even a hint of humidity. But now, the sun was beating down, and the air was like a wet, warm blanket wrapped around her.

She almost stopped and turned when she saw the other woman heading her way, but then decided that it had to be faced.

"Hello," Darby said.

Mandy looked her up and down, managing to both toss her hair and give a sniff as if Darby didn't smell quite right.

Darby held her ground. She had dealt with Mandy's type often enough—in college, in law school and even in court. They used the superior act to fake you out, make you think that there was something—no matter how small—wrong with you, whether it was the color of your shoes or the bag you were carrying.

The best thing, Darby had learned, was to ignore them.

"Chef Sean had to go to the city; he had some business to take care of."

Darby kept her smile tight. She knew that, because Chef Sean had told her that exact information himself, before he kissed her goodbye.

Mandy pretended to be examining a nail, then her blue eyes lifted, and she gave Darby a baleful stare. "Sean is a very talented guy. The cameras love him. But he needs to be in front of them for that to continue to happen."

Darby tried to keep smiling, but she could feel some of her bravado start to fade. Was that why he had gone to the city? Was he already planning his next move? No, Darby took a deep breath. He would have told her about it, right? They had talked, told each other about themselves—surely he wouldn't be making a decision like that without telling her?

She decided to play it cool. There was no use making an enemy of Mandy, but there was no sense in trying to be friends with her either.

"I wasn't aware that was something he was still interested in doing."

"Oh, but he is. He just seems to be having a hard time recognizing a great opportunity when he sees it. This could be the start of something bigger for him, but only if he stays focused. He can be out of this backwater town in no time if he doesn't let anything distract him."

Darby drew herself up tall. Mandy clearly thought she was the distraction keeping Sean from pursuing his next big step. Suddenly, she wondered just how much of a stake Mandy had in Sean's success. A celebrity chef needed a publicist a lot more than one who just owned a small town restaurant. And a publicist who could claim a big-name client was more likely to get more big-name clients. Mandy must be seething that Sean didn't seem as interested in fame as he used to be.

There was a pause, and Darby was struck by an idea.

"Would you like a cookie? I baked them for the guys at Village Hall, but I have a few extra."

Darby flipped open the box of cookies she'd decided to bring with her, and the look of wariness evaporated from Mandy's face.

"They look really good, but I never eat carbs."

"Oh, they are worth every bit of carbohydrate grams in them," Darby responded. Her cookies were known to turn sworn enemies into best friends, reconcile in-laws, and stave off break-ups.

"How about a half?" Darby said, quickly reaching in and breaking a piece off. She held it up to Mandy, knowing she couldn't refuse.

"Well ..." Mandy accepted the cookie and took a huge bite. Darby was willing to bet that Mandy hadn't had a carb in days, so satisfied was the look on her face.

"Wow, these are really good."

"Thank you. It's my grandmother's recipe. With a few extra touches thrown in."

Mandy looked at her shrewdly, reassessing Darby. "You know, I could use a basket of these sent into the city. Think you could arrange that?"

Darby hesitated for only a moment before she said yes. If she had to hand deliver them herself, she would make sure they got to wherever Mandy wanted to send them.

Whipping out a small pen and pad from her purse, she wrote a note on a piece of paper. "Can you have them there for tomorrow, lunch time?"

"Not a problem," Darby answered.

"Perfect. Be sure to send me the bill," Mandy said, as she gave one last, tight, little smile. Darby watched her walk away, feeling her heart hammering in excitement. Maybe Mandy wanted to send cookies to the TV studio as a thank you. Or to another restaurant. Or any of her big-shot friends. Darby would make sure they were wrapped up nicely and had plenty of business cards. The Golden Pear's first shot at fame.

She looked down at the piece of paper Mandy had shoved in her hand. It took a second to realize what it was. Darby recognized the name. It was a big bakery that was known for picking up on the latest trend, whether it was mini-cupcakes or giant birthday cakes, and stealing it and making it their own.

Mandy was probably hoping they would reverse engineer her cookies or something like that. So much for neutralizing Mandy. Apparently the way to her heart was not through her stomach.

With a sigh, Darby kept walking, hoping that the cookie would end up permanently on Mandy's hips.

Chapter 31

"Hey sugar." Sean came in the back door and had his arms around her before she even knew it. He buried himself deep in the crook of her neck. "Vanilla and cinnamon. Scones? Cookies?"

"Brownies," she said, disentangling herself. Things were moving along nicely with the work in the café. Soon, she'd be able to open officially, though the sign painter said he couldn't fit her in until the end of the week. She had decided that was fine as it was the last item on the to-do list. Serving just from the streets was getting more and more difficult and she was eager to have the restaurant back.

She moved to the refrigerator to pull out some eggs. She'd also had time to think about what Mandy had told her. Was Sean really looking to make his next move? Was she just some sort of distraction for him? It was an unsettling thought since she had already decided that she was in love with him. But she'd known what she was getting into all along, right?

"Hey, what's up?" he said, watching her.

"Nothing's up," she said. Two could play at this game, she decided. If Sean was only using her as a summer fling, well then she certainly wouldn't go and reveal the depth of her own feelings to him.

"How was your trip into the city," she asked, setting the eggs down on the counter.

He shrugged, "You know, I saw a few old friends, talked to some people. Not a big deal."

It was just that, Darby thought, Sean taking a day off, blowing off some steam; she knew she shouldn't read too much into it.

They had moved closer to each other and now he pulled her into his arms and held her tight.

"I missed you," he said.

Her heart skipped a beat. "Missed you too."

"Good. I have to work tonight, but I was thinking maybe I could stop by later? Unless you have any big plans?"

She looked up at him. "You know where the key is," she told him.

"Great. Well, I'll see you later?" He looked down at her, and she nodded. He kissed her once and she melted into it. Finally, reluctantly, he pulled away, dived in for another quick kiss, and then left her sagging against the counter, her thoughts still tumbling along.

Chapter 32

She hadn't exactly been honest with Sean. She did have plans. She picked Caitlyn up after work and headed out along the road that hugged the coast. They dipped up and over hills, a view of the water always in front of them.

The town of Nattick was a good twenty minutes to the west of Queensbay and it was still just a little bit sleepy, but like Queensbay, the signs were all there. Proximity to the water, faster commuter trains, and even the fact that businesses were moving their headquarters out of the city all meant that it was a desirable, yet still affordable, address. And just far enough away from Queensbay to not cannibalize sales.

"So this is it?" Caitlyn said doubtfully, eyeing the building. Darby knew that it didn't look like much from the outside, but for her it was more about location. She'd been glancing through the real estate section of the newspaper when the ad had caught her eye. An empty store front on Nattick's Main Street, not too far from the water. This spot was within walking distance of just about everything in town, so that meant it would be a popular stop. There were also some office buildings not too far away, so she'd get a solid lunch crowd, plus some catering jobs.

The look was similar to The Dory in Queensbay, a nice-sized storefront, big plate glass windows, the building white clapboard with black trim. Classic and classy, even though the paint was peeling and one window had a crack in it.

Darby turned off the engine and hopped out of the car, determined to look through the windows. Behind her, she could hear Caitlyn's door open and then the clack of her high heels as they followed her across the sidewalk.

Darby peered in through the windows, but there wasn't much to see, just the late afternoon sunlight filtering in and illuminating an empty space.

"I think it used to be an antique store," Darby said. "I called and the owner is retiring. But, before that it was a bakery and, supposedly, all the equipment, the ovens, and stuff is down in the basement."

"So if it all works," Caitlyn said.

"It will make startup costs a lot lower," Darby finished for her. The space looked to be about the same size as that of The Dory, which would mean she could set it up along the same basic plan.

"They haven't had anyone interested in the place all summer, so I think there's some room for negotiating the lease price," Darby told Caitlyn, who had taken a step back and was surveying the property.

"It needs a paint job," Caitlyn said.

"And the floors redone, a paint job inside too, tables, chairs, and display cabinets, and of course I'll need additional equipment, but I figured if my projections work out I'll be able to open up a second location by the end of the year."

"Moving a little fast, aren't you?" Caitlyn said but there was a note of admiration in her voice and her gray eyes sparkled in anticipation.

"Maybe, considering that I haven't officially opened as the Golden Pear yet, nor told my dad yet that I've hijacked his restaurant, but already the new menu is drawing in more business and with the higher prices—and profit margins—it looks like revenue and net profits will be up over thirty percent this month."

"Not bad," Caitlyn said, her lips pursed and Darby could already see the wheels turning. Caitlyn was a business genius and that's why Darby wanted her advice.

"How about I look over all your numbers and see if they make sense. You can make me a pizza while you're at it," Caitlyn said magnanimously.

"What if I'm busy?" Darby countered.

"With what, Chef Sexy?" Caitlyn scoffed. "Happen to know he's working tonight, so you're free until he's done and he sneaks into bed with you."

"He doesn't sneak," Darby said.

Caitlyn laughed. "Well now I know he does. Anyway, Joan from The Garden Cottage swears he saw him scurry out of your house the other morning, doing the walk of shame."

"Joan wouldn't know what the walk of shame was," Darby said, trying to retain some last vestige of dignity.

Caitlyn shook her head and looked over at Darby. "You would be surprised at what our parents' generation knows. Joan definitely said 'walk of shame'."

Darby groaned. "Do you think she texted my mom?"

Caitlyn shrugged. "I don't know, but aren't your parents going to be home soon? You've been a busy little bee and you're going to have a lot of explaining to do."

Darby leaned back against the cool glass of the window and rubbed her hands over her face. "I know, I know. Soon there will be no hiding the truth."

Caitlyn snorted. "If you think you're hiding the truth, you're sorely mistaken. The whole town is on to you."

Darby looked at Caitlyn in horror. "What do you mean? Who's been talking? I've kept everything about the name change a secret. Sure, the paint and the tables are there, but no one but you and Sean are supposed to know the whole thing."

Caitlyn shrugged. "No one cares, mind you, since we all know it means you'll be baking us cookies on a regular basis. Besides, I think everyone is waiting to enjoy your dad's reaction. I mean, come on, he's going to blow when he sees what you've done to the place." Caitlyn gave a little laugh as if she were imagining the scene.

Darby slumped further against the glass. "Do you think Quent Tate knows? He's been sniffing around but I haven't told him a thing. I could see him telling my dad. It would be just like him."

Caitlyn shrugged. "I don't know. But in any case, they'll be home in a few days and I bet everything will go over better if you have a nice solid business plan to show them. Let's go work on it; it will be fun."

Darby straightened herself up. "You know, when I decided to do this, it was so I would never have to look at boring documents again."

Caitlyn slung her arm around her friend's shoulder. "Au contraire my good friend, that's where you're wrong. Numbers never lie; so let's go see if we can make your dreams of becoming the cookie queen of New England a reality."

Chapter 33

Darby was locking the door of The Dory, and took a moment just to sag against the doorframe. It had been quite a day.

"Well, lassie, looks like you've been quite the busy little beaver." The sound of Quentin Tate's voice had her back up before his greeting was finished. This was the last thing she needed.

"Quent, always a pleasure to see you," she said, lying through her teeth. All she could think about was getting home and the pleasant thought that Sean might be waiting for her.

"Oh, are you sure about that?" Quent grinned, a smiled that stopped at his lips. His eyes remained hard and curious. She saw that he was trying to peek around her, trying to get a glimpse of what she was doing.

"It's just a paint job, Quentin, surely you can't object to that."

She put the key in her pocket and started to walk down the street. *It will be a pleasant evening*, she thought, one of those glorious wonderful nights that August kicked out at you as the summer wound itself down.

"Well, I don't know. Your Da and I have already agreed on a price. I wouldn't want you to think that any of your improvements will have me rethinking my offer."

Darby shrugged, trying not to let Quentin get to her. He would smell any weakness a mile away.

"Well, I guess that's between you and my dad, right? I just thought the place needed some new paint."

Quentin let out a sound like a muffled snort. "And you painted the front too. Don't think you can try and get someone in to bid against me. It's a fair offer I've given your Da."

"The Dory still belongs to the Reese family," Darby said, hurrying her pace. She could almost see her front gate. Suddenly she found herself spun around and facing the bald, hulking form of Quentin.

"Don't think you'll pull any of your fancy lawyer tricks on me. I know there's no other buyer interested in the deli, so don't think your little redecorating scheme will get me to change the asking price."

Darby almost let herself smile. She had rattled Quentin, which gave her no small pleasure. But even better, he was on the wrong track. He thought she was making the improvements to get another offer, not because of her own plan.

"Like I said, you can discuss it with my dad when he gets back. He's approved all of the changes I've made."

Quentin's eyes narrowed. "Are you sure about that? You know one call to him and I'd bet he'd be real interested in what's going on. You may have everyone else snowed, but I know you're up to something."

They were at her gate. Her hand a little unsteady, Darby opened it and then turned and faced Quentin.

"Like I said, The Dory still belongs to the Reese family. I wouldn't go counting your chickens before they hatch."

Quentin just looked at her, but she decided that she'd said enough. Quickly, she walked up the pathway to her door.

Chapter 34

"I let myself in," Sean's voice called out, and Darby stopped at the front door. She'd texted him that she might be running late and told him to make himself at home. And he had. Over the past week, they had fallen into something of a routine, with him coming to her when he was done with work, spending the night. Then there were those few stolen moments during the day, before he started work and when she finished.

She had finally seen where he lived, in one of the larger rooms in the Osprey Arms, when she had run down to say hello. The temporary nature of it made her feel sorry for him, but he had successfully distracted her thoughts from it with a quick but very intense bout of lovemaking, somewhere in between the lunch rush and dinner prep.

She was glad that tonight was another one of his nights off, and already there were delectable smells wafting from the kitchen. He had put something on the stereo—his own mix, as it was something she didn't recognize.

She took a moment to just melt into the doorframe, suddenly spent. It had been a tough day. Until now, her plans for the Golden Pear had been going along smoothly, but today, things had slowly started to unravel and then had continued to do so with a vengeance. And that was before her run-in with Quent.

Jake had had an emergency at another job and hadn't been able to make it in today. She had decided to formalize herself as a business entity and had set up a business account at the bank and was also looking into a line of credit. And then she had found out that she needed more permits. So she had spent the day arguing, cajoling, and even moving furniture around. But she was close, close enough to feel it. The Golden Pear would have its grand opening in the next day or so—and none too soon, as her parents were due home any day now.

"You look beat." Sean appeared to fill the doorway between the kitchen and the living room.

"I am," she said, even as she felt the jolt of electricity seeing him always elicited. He was wearing a light gray t-shirt that hugged his arm muscles, a pair of flips flops and ... "Is that a bathing suit?" she asked incredulously.

"Yeah," Sean said sheepishly. "Chase insisted he take me sailing."

She let a smile flicker on her face. There had been a strong breeze today, the water outside the harbor flecked with white caps. "What did he you take you out on?" she asked, knowing that Sean, landlubber that he was, didn't quite appreciate boats yet.

"It had a sail." Sean shrugged. "Don't forget, I'm from Indiana—the land-locked part of it. There aren't many boats that you don't have to paddle around there."

"Big or small?" Without realizing it, she had drawn closer to him. He smelled of wind and water and the barest hint of spice. His hair was wind-ruffled, and it looked as if he had gotten a sunburn on his nose.

"Smallish. It tipped over a lot. And it had two of those whatchamacallits—"

"Hulls," Darby guessed.

"Yeah," he said, as she moved closer to him. His eyes widened, and she heard his intake of breath. Gently, she touched his nose.

"Ouch."

"You got some sun. It's a catamaran. That's what he took you out on."

Swallowing hard, he nodded at her.

"I have something for your sunburn. It's actually in the kitchen." She brushed past him, relishing the contact.

"I picked up some fresh fish from some guy at the dock. And then I got some tomatoes, vegetables; I thought we'd just throw it all on the grill."

She smiled at the question in his voice. "Sounds reckless. No recipe. No fancy ingredients?"

"Well, I did bring some stuffed clams from the deep freeze at the restaurant. They're baking in the oven.

"Sounds great," she said, as she plunked herself down on one of the stools.

"Have a glass of wine," he said, pouring a glass of white from a chilled bottle and pushing it toward her.

She took a healthy sip, letting the crisp coolness run down her throat, already feeling some of the weight of the day lift from her.

"Tough day?" he asked as he took up a vegetable peeler and started in on some zucchini.

"Yes," she said, and hesitated.

"Want to tell me about it?"

She hesitated, and then felt it all tumbling out. "I don't know if I'm doing the right thing."

He looked at her, uncertainty in his eyes. "About what? Us?"

"No," she said, hearing the panic in his voice. "Not us." That was the one thing she was sure about.

"Oh, you mean your grand plan about sneaking your father's restaurant from under him and signing a lease on a new location."

"How did you find out about that?" she asked.

"I didn't. You just told me," he said.

Darby shook her head. "I can't believe I fell for that trick."

"I saw the ad circled in the paper, so I guessed you were already thinking big."

"Big." Darby heaved herself onto one of the stools that stood at the counter. "I think I'm going at light speed."

"Just because it's fast doesn't mean it's bad. I've seen your plan. I've seen your work. I've heard your customers talking. I don't think you're moving too fast. I think you've seen a market opportunity, and luckily you have the resources to capitalize on it."

Darby took a deep breath, feeling the tension sink out of her. She hadn't realized how much it meant to her to have Sean believe in her.

"So do you think I can pull this off?"

Sean came to her, took her chin in her hand, and looked her in the eye. "You make it sound like you're pulling some sort of hat trick. Does it really feel that way to you? Doesn't it feel like it's finally all come together and you're going in the right direction?"

She stared into his eyes, almost lost in them, before she nodded. "Thank you. I needed that." And she knew that she did. That she needed him too. They hadn't touched on the future, but she knew that she couldn't imagine one without him. But she put that thought far away, willing herself to enjoy the moment as he shot her that quick, happy grin, his caramel-colored eyes twinkling.

"Any time. Pep talks are free."

"I thought there was no such thing as a free lunch," she answered him.

"You're right, because dinner is going to cost you," he said, pulling her close to him. "I was hoping we could pick up where we left off?"

"From when? The time ... ," she began, lowering her voice to whisper as she described a particularly naughty encounter on the porch. "Or the time when ..."

She heard his sharp intake of breath and felt the rasp of his stubbled chin against her neck.

"Either one would serve," he said, "but how about I show you?"

His mouth clamped over hers, and she felt herself melt into him. Whatever nagging thoughts she had about his intentions dissolved as her body took over her mind, as his hands roamed over her, as she let herself be engulfed by him.

Together, they moved as if in a dance through the house, clothes dissolving around them. She led them up the stairs where, in one fluid moment, he swept her up off her feet and carried her into the bedroom, laying her gently down on the bed. For a moment, he did nothing but stand there, looking down at her, and she could see the look of reverence in his eyes. It swept over him quickly, clouded over by what she recognized as desire.

Slowly, gently, torturously, he lowered himself over her, his eyes searching her face as if looking for an answer. The tension and desire began to build in her until she could stand it no longer. She reached for him, her arms wrapping around his neck to bring him closer, but he stopped her.

"Just let me look at you," he breathed, a hand tracing down the front of her neck, tracing a line down to her breasts. A thumb flicked over her breast, and her nipples tightened in response, her belly clenching with desire.

"Touch me," she whispered, not sure she could be patient. She wanted him, wanted him now, his hands on her, him filling her. His hands cupped her breasts, and she arched up to meet him, a small moan escaping her lips. She saw his smile, the way his eyes lazily traveled up and down. Somewhere along the way, she had lost her shirt, and now, with a quick motion, he removed her bra, her breasts springing free.

He brought his mouth down to one, then to the other, his tongue driving her mad. Slowly she felt his hand travel down the length of her stomach to skim the top of her shorts, and then with another efficient flick, he opened the button on her shorts, and his hand slid down between her legs. She was already damp, ready for him, but his hand just hovered, slowly, patiently caressing her through the thin fabric of her underwear.

She raised her hips and pushed down her shorts. Accepting her invitation, he slid them off and then her panties until she was naked beneath him. He watched her with an intense, dark look as his hands ruthlessly worked her, driving her toward the edge. Her hips pumped up to meet him, and she felt the climax slowly build. She was almost there, but just before she reached it, his hand came away and his mouth traveled down the length of her body.

She heard rather than saw him take off the rest of his clothes, felt his weight suspended over her as her hands clenched the bedspread.

"Please, now, I need you, Sean," she practically sobbed as he slid into her, taking his time, going in deep until she was filled with him. Slowly, he moved, and she moved with him, her own needs forcing her to match him and move against him quickly.

"No, slowly, like this," he breathed, moving with deep thrusts that speared her. She could feel the wave building in her and knew she hadn't much longer. She sobbed his name, and in his answer she could hear that he was ready as well. Together, they rode the wave until they both crested, spent, satisfied.

"Wow, I should make dinner for you more often." He rolled over on his side, his arm snuggling her close. Darby let herself relax, feeling the aches and pains unravel within her as she settled into him.

"I don't think we ever got around to eating dinner." Again.

"There's still time," he said, his lips brushing her neck.

#

Sean woke to an empty bed and sunlight filtering in through the open window. Sunshine, birds signing, even the sound of a boat horn. All he knew was that he was content. Happy—well, not entirely, since the bed next to him was empty. He wanted—no, he *needed* Darby. The realization hit him last night as he had made love to her, slowly, reverently. She didn't have a clue how beautiful she was, how amazing she was to him.

It occurred to him that, all of a sudden, he was thinking about a future. And not one that just included the next dinner he was going to cook, the next restaurant he was going to work in, or the next step in his career. Sure, he'd always thought that one day he would settle down, find the one, and have kids. But that had been in some distant far-off future. And since he'd come to Queensbay, he'd only been thinking about leaving. But that had changed even before he met Darby—the second time.

Here she was, taking the biggest leap of her life by starting her own business, and she wanted to share it with him. She came home and told him about her day, and he told her about his, and he couldn't imagine it any other way. He sat up, throwing off sleep. He wasn't certain just when he'd fallen in love with Darby Reese. Not, perhaps, from the moment he saw her, since that had gone badly, but perhaps from the moment he had stolen her mushrooms. But he knew for certain that he didn't want to have a life that didn't include her.

He found his shorts and checked the clock. With any luck, she would still be here, before she had to start her day.

#

"You're still here." Sean stood there, his hair standing on end. He was wearing only his shorts, and she could see, even in the dim light, the play of his perfect six-pack on his stomach.

"It's early; you should go back to bed," she said to him.

"It's empty," he said and came to sit at the counter. "Are you making coffee?"

"Yes," she answered, turning her back, feeling suddenly shy. She found the glass coffee carafe, then her canister with her beans. Today, there were still a million things that needed to be done at the café—not that she could remember any of them as he sat there, in her kitchen, shirtless, his beautifully defined abs inviting her to feel them, distracting her.

Suddenly, he was there, standing behind her, his arms circling her, and she was slowly turning to face him. He had a light wash of blonde stubble on his face, and his eyes, which had blurred from sleep, were alight now with hunger.

Slowly, he started to kiss her neck, and then he trailed his lips up her cheek to her forehead and back down again.

"What are you doing?" she managed to whisper.

"Kissing you," he breathed, his eyes looking deeper into hers. There was an intensity there, something more than simple lust. She didn't know what it meant, what she should do with it. Last night had been different, like they had shared a deeper connection. Was it possible, she wondered, to be in love after just a few short weeks?

"But I'm making coffee." She said the first thing that came to her mind.

"Coffee can wait. It's lonely up there," he said.

"I have a meeting at nine. I need to shower, get dressed ..." Her voice trailed off.

"There's plenty of time. Especially if we do this." With one swift movement, he swept her up and into his arms.

"Sean, what are you doing?!"

"You said you needed a shower," he said, and with a laugh she let herself be carried off.

Chapter 35

Mandy pulled back. She hadn't thought things had made it that far. But there it was, Sean Callahan nuzzling the neck of that Darby Reese as he walked her to her store. Mandy smoothed down her pencil skirt and fluffed her hair. What did Darby have that she didn't? Chocolate chip cookies? Was that all Sean cared about?

She had discovered Sean Callahan when he'd been green, fresh. She had gotten him his first booking, his first TV spot, on one of the local stations. That in turn had gotten him his first big job. It was her constant work on creating the image of Chef Sexy that had made him who he was. He was her biggest client. People took her calls now because she represented him. They were a symbiotic team. He needed her, and she needed him.

Mandy had known Sean a long time now, and she had seen him date. She even assumed he had taken a few of those kitchen groupies to bed. But she had been patient, knowing that he would tire of them. He always did. He would order a bracelet, almost the same one each time, from a jeweler and gently disengage himself, always throwing himself back into work.

If they didn't take the hint from Sean himself, Mandy usually found a way to make sure they got it, loud and clear. Most of them had moved on gracefully, and Sean was always a free agent again, always telling her that he'd be lost without her.

But not this time—not with Darby. Mandy could see that the girl had her claws in him but good. And Sean was telling her he was committed to this little backwater and dinky restaurant. Sure, he'd gotten a chance to be on national TV, but Mandy had had to beg for that. The calls were going to be few and far between if Sean didn't get his head back in the game. He could have his own TV show, and here he was canoodling with Darby and probably making plans for the future.

No, Mandy thought. Darby Reese would have to be put in her place.

Chapter 36

Darby arose at dawn on the morning of her opening day to clear skies and the sounds of the birds singing. Next to her, Sean lay wrapped up in the sheets, his bare chest rising slowly and steadily with the movement of his breathing. He seemed at peace, his face smoothed out, and his blonde hair curly, tousled. She almost ran a hand through it but resisted. She didn't want to wake him. He had gotten home late after overseeing a busy night at the Osprey. Word was getting out about the new chef and menu, and it meant that they were staying open later.

He had crept in, but she had been sleeping lightly, waiting for him, wanting him. They hadn't talked much, just made love and then both fallen asleep, tangled up in each other.

Sean wasn't a morning person, but that was all right with her. She liked these moments early in the day, when the world was calm and hers alone. It would all change after this. Today was her grand opening. She had told everyone that she was just redecorating, but her new sign, which had been hung and covered with a tarp, was waiting to be unveiled.

Quent had been sniffing around, but she had sworn everyone who knew to super-secret double-ninja secrecy, so while he was suspicious, he couldn't be sure of what was going on. And now she had just a few days until her parents were back, a few days to operate as The Golden Pear, to show her dad just what The Dory could become. If he hated it, he could always go back to his old menu and put the old sign up.

It should be foolproof, she thought, even as she felt her stomach knot and clench and realized that she felt just a little bit nauseous. This was a big leap, and she had the right to feel the jitters as she crept down the hall and into the bathroom.

The thoughts milled through her head as she took a quick shower and dressed. She stopped once, looking at him. He was still asleep, deep asleep, and she decided not to wake him. Gently, she brushed her lips against his forehead and bounded down the steps. She pushed the *on* button on the coffee maker and let herself out.

She went down the street. If she'd been a whistler, she would have been whistling a tune. There was no one on the street, and she liked Queensbay this way. She could see the blue of the harbor, glinting in the rising sun, the seagulls wheeling around. A lone motorboat chugged out, someone getting a head start on a day of fishing, grilling, and relaxing. She sighed. After the summer, maybe on a weekday, she would take the boat out. Maybe she would go fishing with her dad—maybe, just maybe that would placate him. He never could resist a fishing trip with his little girl. She would pack a lunch, let him relax, have a beer, and she could handle the boat for him.

Yes, she thought, making her plans. She looked at the cafe. That was strange. There was a light on. She'd been sure she turned it off the night before. She walked toward the cafe, a feeling of dread coming over her. It couldn't be. The door was unlocked, and she pushed it open.

"Dad."

Her father turned, and she didn't like the way he looked.

"Here, you need to sit down." Hurriedly, she pulled a chair out for him, and he slid into it, like an old man. "Water, here let me get you some." She pulled open the cooler and grabbed a bottle of water. She cracked the top and handed it to her father, but he didn't take it.

His blue eyes looked at her accusingly. "Darby, what have you done?"

"Now Reg, take a deep breath."

Darby stood back, never so glad to see her mother in her life.

"What happened here?" Reg seemed to have found his voice, and he stood up again, moving around.

Without waiting for an answer, he walked around the seating area, peering into corners, poking his head underneath tables, bending down to rap his knuckles on the floor. He shot a look at Darby, and she swallowed. She'd been a good kid, but any time she'd started to step out of line, that was the look he'd given her. Still, she was a grownup now, with a grownup plan and the cash to back it up.

He walked over to the counter, ran his hand down it, and picked up one of the laminated menus. He looked it over and then tossed it back down.

Darby tried not to look at the clock. It would be opening time soon, and she had a ton of things to prep before the early bird regulars started to come in.

Without a look or a word to her, he went behind the counter, through the swinging doors to the kitchen.

Darby looked at her mother, who was wringing her hands. That was not good. "You weren't supposed to be here for another three days," she hissed.

"I know, I know. Your dad just said he couldn't sit around anymore. He got us booked on the red-eye home before we knew it. He wanted to surprise you, and I had no idea he would get up and come straight here. I'm sorry; I would have texted."

Darby shook her head. "It had to happen sometime. I will talk to him. It's all my fault." She turned and headed toward the kitchen, but her mother stopped her and pulled her into a tight embrace. "It's a big change. More than just a coat of paint, Darby."

Darby swallowed, looking around. The deli looked completely different. Not like the old Dory at all.

She was about to stammer out an apology when her mother looked at her, a sparkle in her eye. "Oh dear, it's so beautiful."

Darby felt herself relax. "Thanks, Mom."

Pushing through the doors, she faced her father. "Dad—"

"At least you didn't change the kitchen," he said, running his hands along the counter.

"I'm sorry, but it seemed like the only way."

"Darby—" he said.

She rushed on, "Quent told me you were going to sell it, and you hadn't even discussed it with me, didn't even give me a chance to make an offer, to buy it from you. I thought I had to act fast, show you that I was serious about wanting this. I know you didn't want me to go into the restaurant business, but I'm not happy doing what I'm doing. I want to cook. I love to cook, and I want to do it right here. I thought if I made some changes, you would see I was capable, that I could handle it." She petered out as her father looked at her. "And I figured that a new coat of paint would help the resale value," she finished lamely.

Reg had both his hands on the counter, his head hanging down, and suddenly Darby was ashamed. She had tricked him, taken what was his and changed it, erasing everything that had been his. "I'm sorry, Dad. I guess I went a bit too far."

"The floor, the paint, the menu. The name," he said, shaking his head. "I knew a new owner would do all this, but my own daughter?"

"I know, but I just wanted to show you that I could handle this on my own, that I had a plan."

"But you have a job, a career, even an apartment."

She took a deep breath, getting ready to explain.

There was the sound of a door opening. "Hello, is my egg sandwich ready?"

Sean appeared in the kitchen, and she stiffened, thinking, *Not now, please not now.* She wasn't ready for her dad to meet Sean. But it was too late.

"Excuse me, mister. You're coming in the wrong door." Her dad turned, bristling at the intrusion.

"Sorry." Sean didn't seem flustered at all, and she tried not to remember how she had last seen him, with the sheets wrapped around his naked body. "I thought I was going to be able to catch Darby alone."

"You know her?"

Reg had stood up to his full height, feet spread wide, arms folded across his chest. She swallowed. Her father had managed to scare off just about any potential boyfriend just by pulling his Big Reg act, and it looked like Reg, with that unerring sixth sense fathers had, had immediately sized up Sean.

Before a pissing match could begin, she stepped in. "Dad, this is my ..." Her tongue tried to make the words come, but Sean stuck out his hand.

"Sean Callahan. You must be Reg. Heard a lot about you from Chase and his brother. Great place you have here. Let me tell you, your daughter has a way with flour and sugar that you wouldn't believe."

Reg looked down at Sean's hand and then ran his eyes up and down. "Aren't you on TV or something?" he drawled.

"Only sometimes. I'm Chase Sanders's partner in the Osprey Arms restaurant." Sean didn't back down, and for that, she was grateful.

Grudgingly, Reg shook Sean's hand. "You were saying. About my daughter?"

Sean smiled. "Her chocolate cookies are amazing. And have you tried her breakfast sandwiches? The whole crew at the Osprey Arms swears by them as the perfect cure for a late night, if you know what I mean."

#

She wasn't quite sure how Sean did it, but he had her father out in front sitting down, talking about his trip like they'd known each other for years. She breathed a sigh of relief and closed her eyes.

"Darby!" Caitlyn burst into the kitchen, breathless, her eyes crazed. "I just drove by your parents' house. I think they're home early." She stopped short when she heard the unmistakable roar of Reg's laughter, followed by Aggie's lighter, more fluid tones.

"What—"

"Sean. Don't ask. I just have to get ready. I open in thirty minutes, and today's the big day."

Chapter 37

"It's been quite day, hasn't it?" Her father came up behind her and put his hands on her shoulders.

The Dory—no, The Golden Pear—had been busier than she would have thought possible. It may have been the samples of cookies she passed out along the street, but most people had been persuaded to come in to order something, whether it was one of the new special sandwiches or a cup of her chowder.

"We ran out of stuff," Darby thought aloud, focusing on what hadn't gone right, "and I think I should have priced the specials higher."

"Darby, would you stop?"

"What?" She looked at her dad. She thought that maybe there was a tear in his eye.

"Darby, this place was busier than it's been in years. I took a walk down the street, and they were all talking about us." He took a deep breath. "This has been one of the most amazing days of my life. In a few short weeks, you have turned this place around. I was thinking of selling to Quent because I was tired of running it, tired of watching The Dory get old and tired and slip away, but the truth is that my heart isn't in it anymore, hasn't been for a while."

She turned to look at her father, feeling the emotion welling to the surface. "So, you're not mad anymore?"

"Mad is a relative term. I wish we could have talked about it before, but who knew if I would have listened. It was time for a change. That's what happens when you get old. You get stuck in your ways. Sometimes you need to be yanked out of the rut."

"So, you'll sell me the cafe?"

Reg shook his head. "It's not easy, running a restaurant, a business. I know you love cooking, but there's a whole lot of other stuff that goes into it. I always thought you would have it easy sitting behind a desk in an office."

"But ..." Darby trailed off. Maybe her father hadn't understood at all.

"But you hate it. And you have a genius for food. Ever since you were a little girl. Who am I to deny the world the magic of your chocolate chip cookies?"

Darby felt the relief wash over her. "Thanks."

"And," her father said, "If I know you, you're probably already thinking bigger. That and Caitlyn might have mentioned something. But before you go and open another location, well, make sure you see me first before you hit up the banks. The Dory, or whatever you're going to call it, is still a family business, even if I get to spend a little more time sailing into the sunset."

Darby was speechless, but she pulled her father into a tight hug.

"Aww, now don't get all mushy on me," her dad said, but she could hear the catch in his voice.

Chapter 38

"Mandy, really, I need to get back to work," Sean told her. She had texted him, telling him that she needed to see him, and he had agreed, hoping that they could still be friendly.

"Come, let's take a walk," she said, slipping her arm through his.

He nodded, thinking that it would be better if they stayed in public. She was less likely to yell at him that way. She led the way along the walkway that ran along the water. It was the last weekend of summer, and the crowds were out. Queensbay, for a small town, was hopping.

He looked down at Mandy. Her blonde hair was down and loose, and her lips were dressed in cotton candy pink. They made almost the perfect bow. Her body was long and lean, and she had on a short, backless dress that made it clear she was letting very little get in the way between her skin and the sun.

She'd already collected a fair number of double takes along the way, and he was aware that, with the way she was hanging on him, people might think they were together. That was the last thing he wanted. He had tried to shake her off, but it seemed to make her cling to him even more, so he just stopped, knowing that she would fill him in on her agenda.

At least he was out of the kitchen. Perhaps he'd have a chance to run up and check on Darby. He'd barely had a chance to talk to her this morning, and he was dying to know what her parents had said. Things had seemed tense to him when he'd walked in and, when Reg had recognized him, he'd decided to shamelessly play the celebrity card, especially if it would help Darby.

"Seriously, Mandy, I need to get back to work."

Mandy looked over her shoulder. She seemed nervous, but then a look came over her eyes.

"Sean, this isn't how I wanted to tell you, but you leave me no choice." She cleared her throat. "You're making a mistake. Throwing away everything we've worked for. Without me, you'd be stuck as a line chef in some diner in some hick town. I made you who you were, and now, you're just going to sit back here. You don't get second chances to make it big."

Sean laughed. "Make it big? Is this what this is about, the TV show? Mandy, find me some guest segments that I can do here and there, and I'll be happy. But I'm not dropping everything to run to LA for months to work on some cable show that might or might not make it, especially if it's one where I have to yell all the time. That's not who I want to be."

"Be? You'll be famous; that's what you'll be. Or on your way to it," Mandy said, her voice rising.

"Or I'll just be a joke of myself. I am fine, more than fine here. I own a business, the publishing company wants a cookbook, and the local TV station said they'd love to have me on sometime. And I can do all that from here. I don't need fame to be successful."

"It's because of her." Mandy almost spat out the name. "Darby. You think you love her, the pretty little baker? Well, she's holding you back. Sure, you may be happy right now, but what about in six months, when the only people that recognize you are the librarian and the lady who runs the antique store? You won't have your groupies, you won't have the press, and you won't have me."

"Okay," he said, holding his hands wide. "It's okay because I'll have the things that really matter. A place to call my own, a woman who loves me. A home. Something I never really had. And if that means I'm not as famous as I could be or don't get to show up on late night TV, so be it. I'll make my reputation back the old-fashioned way."

Mandy drew herself up to her full height, and he braced himself for the coming gale. But then the anger seemed to leave her, and she gave a small shrug. "You really mean it."

He nodded. "I love her. I love Darby, and, well, we were meant to be here together. I am truly thankful for all you did, Mandy. You were the best publicist a tough kid from the Midwest could want. But …"

"That's fine," she said, looking at her fingers, pretending disinterest. "I was going to fire you anyway."

"Shouldn't I be firing you?" he said, almost laughing.

"You're a crap client. No offense. I need to find someone else now."

He did laugh then, realizing that it was going to be okay. Mandy was taking it better than he had expected.

"I have no doubt you will. Thank you, again, for everything. It's not you; it's me."

"That's what they all say. Good luck and all that," Mandy said. She started to walk away, and then she turned, threw her arms around him, and kissed him, twining his hair as she pulled his mouth down to hers, hungrily devouring him.

And that's how he felt—like a prey that had been snapped up by a predator. Her tongue was lashing at him, and he could feel her moan and writhe up against him. But there was nothing. Not a reaction. He pulled away, and when she tried to stay closer, he reached up and forcibly removed her arms from around his neck. He settled them down in front of her and took a step back.

"What was that for?"

"Something to remember me by. And you really must love her if you felt nothing."

"I do. I love Darby," he said, feeling his heart fill with the strength of saying those words out loud.

"Well, then, I'll leave you to it," Mandy said, throwing him one last look and turning on her heel. Sean breathed a sigh of relief and all but sagged against a railing.

#

Darby had decided to take a walk, after closing up for the day, to take a moment to savor how everything had worked out. She had sent her dad home, and he went, saying he was eager to go fishing but had one stop he had to make first. She knew he was going to go have a drink with Quent first, to tell him the deal was off.

She wandered down the hill, toward the harbor, hoping to be able to catch Sean on a break. She hadn't seen him since he'd walked into the cafe earlier that morning. After charming her parents, he'd bolted, saying he had something to take care of. Of course, she'd see him later, she knew, but she just wanted to say thank you for how he had come to her rescue.

Then she saw him standing there, out on the boardwalk that overlooked the harbor. Her pace quickened and she was about to call out to him, her heart going into its familiar pounding rhythm whenever she got near to him.

But he wasn't alone. She sighed in annoyance. Mandy was there as well, and she had Sean pulled in close to her, as if she were showing him something. There was the way she rubbed his arm and the fact that he didn't pull back from her. And then Mandy leaned up on her platform sandals, and it looked to her as if Sean leaned down and into her, kissing her.

She didn't wait to see more. She'd seen enough. Had it been going on all along? Or had it just restarted? It was enough. She wasn't going to be played for anyone's fool. So much for his claims of commitment. The sun, which had been shining a few hours earlier, was playing peekaboo with the clouds, and there was a freshening breeze off the water. Suddenly, she felt cold, very cold, and knew she had to get away, anywhere but here.

Chapter 39

The rain had indeed come, and come with a vengeance. Darby looked at the world outside the windows of the cafe. The sky was a sullen, heavy blanket of gray and rain lashed against the glass. Inside, it was still warm and snug and since she hadn't wanted to go home, she was readying the last of the preparations for tomorrow before she headed to her parents for dinner.

She heard the swing of the door in the kitchen and barely looked up. She figured someone had forgotten their umbrella so she didn't even look up as she said, "It's on the back hook."

"Were you expecting someone else?" Sean came in. His eyes were clouded and the tips of his hair danced with raindrops. He had on a light windbreaker, but his khaki shorts were drenched.

"No," she answered, finishing wiping down the counter. She was almost done, and she was ready to leave. Truth be told, she wanted nothing more than to crawl into her own bed, pull the covers up, and stay for about a week. But she couldn't do that anymore. She had responsibilities.

"I came to see how your day went? What happened?" Sean made as if to grab her arm but she danced neatly out his way.

"Don't," she hissed, slapping the cloth down, ready to fight. She shouldn't let him get away with this. Her determination to be an adult about it was warring with her need to cry.

"I can't touch you now? What's going on, sugar?" She could hear the confusion in his voice, couldn't believe he was going to take that tack with her.

"You had your summer fun. Now you can go back to your real life."

"My summer fun?" he asked, his voice dangerously low.

"I know you're a busy man, with lots of opportunities and you should take them. It was great while it lasted, but you and I both have to get on with our lives."

The words cost Darby but she figured this was the easiest way. That way she wouldn't have to accuse him, and he wouldn't have to lie—or worse yet, admit that he had a thing going on with Mandy all along.

After all, Mandy wanted to be with him, in the city, pushing his career. Darby on the other hand, was happier here, in Queensbay. She had learned that the fast-paced life wasn't for her, but she couldn't force anyone else to make that choice. Especially Sean who so obviously wanted something and someone, else.

"You want to get on with your life? What are you talking back?"

"Yes, especially if you have feelings for someone else," Darby said, raising her chin and willing back the tears. She wouldn't give him the satisfaction of seeing her cry for him, wouldn't use that trick to even make him think twice.

"Feelings, what are you talking about?" His brown eyes were dark, angry. Darby was glad there was a counter between them, relishing the distance it put between them.

She turned away. "I saw you and Mandy today. Look, I know there was something between you two once and that it's hard to give that up."

"Me and Mandy ... today?" Sean held up his hands. "Look I don't know what you think you saw ..."

"Stop," Darby said, anger replacing her hurt. "Don't try to lie to me. I won't be played for a fool."

"A fool, is that what you think?"

"Go. Get out of my restaurant." Darby said the words firmly, a horrible weight of finality crashing down around her.

He looked at her, and she couldn't read any emotion in his eyes. "If you can't trust me, Darby, if you don't think ..."

"Get out," she repeated, not giving him a chance to finish.

He gave a short, sharp laugh. "As you wish, sugar."

And then he was gone. Darby sagged against the counter, finally letting the tears flow.

Chapter 40

"We need to shake her out of it." Chase marched into Caitlyn's office, dropping a bag with her lunch on her desk.

"Delivery? Since when did the Osprey start to deliver?" Caitlyn said, looking up from her computer, where some of the numbers were actually starting to swarm in front of her eyes.

"It's your usual from The Golden Pear and we need to talk."

"About what?" Caitlyn was confused.

"Darby and Sean."

"There is no Darby and Sean. They broke up, you know, because he was two-timing with his publicist, Mandy." Caitlyn had heard all about it, more than she wanted to. Darby had been a wreck. It had been a week, and though she went about her business, served her customers, and generally seemed to be holding it all together, underneath she was very close to losing it.

Chase said, "Look, Sean said Mandy kissed him. And then fired him. It wasn't what Darby thought she saw."

Caitlyn looked down at her screen. "It doesn't matter, a cheater is a cheater."

"Are you so jaded by your own bad experience that you can't help out a friend?"

"This isn't about me, Chase. This is about Darby. Her heart's broken. She really had it bad for Sean. I think she thought he was going to settle down, stay here, that he wanted to be part of the community."

Chase ran a hand over his close-cropped hair. "But he does. He is."

"Then where did he go?" Caitlyn asked.

"He had to take care of something in Indiana. With his mom. She's okay, but he needed a few days off. Look, Sean is not going anywhere. He's working on a cookbook featuring recipes from the Osprey Arms and he's just about talked me into opening up a cooking school. The man is not running off with Mandy."

"What about the TV show?" Caitlyn asked, trying not to sound as if she cared. "You know, the one that's supposed to be filming in Los Angeles?"

Chase shook his head and pulled a piece of paper from the pocket of his jacket.

"An announcement in the paper, about the casting of show on a startup food network. As you can see, Sean's name is nowhere in there. The only TV show he's interested in is one on the local network."

Caitlyn's eye narrowed as she scanned the article. She looked up at Chase. "So Mandy got Will Green the job on that TV show."

Chase nodded. "Now do you believe me? Please, you need to help me. Sean's moping around the kitchen looking like somebody killed his puppy. He can't even work up the energy to yell and, worse yet, his cooking's off. One more raw sea bass entree and we'll have to call ourselves Sushi at the Osprey Arms."

Caitlyn looked at Chase for a long moment, deciding she was enjoying see Chase beg, even just the tiniest bit.

"Please, you have to help me. They need to be together. I mean I was just at The Dory. Even Darby's cookies are off. The people of this town shouldn't have to suffer because our two young lovers had a misunderstanding."

Caitlyn knew Chase was only half joking. She felt herself relent just a little. "He's really in love with her?"

"Never saw a guy more head over heels in love with a woman, except for you and Noah."

Caitlyn shot him a look. "Don't go there, okay? Look, Darby's in love with him too, for what it's worth."

"See, we'd be doing a public service, right? Queensbay won't know how to thank us."

Caitlyn looked at Chase fondly. "After all the trouble we caused when we were younger, I guess we do owe the town a good deed."

Chase smiled and sank back in his chair. "Thank you. I knew you would help me. So here's my plan …"

Chapter 41

"I don't understand why you wanted to go to this wine tasting," Darby whined again. "Some of us have to open a restaurant first thing in the morning."

"And I have an investor call at nine. We don't have to stay for long, I promise." Caitlyn pulled her arm.

"Don't you have other friends?" Darby mumbled.

Caitlyn shot her a look. "No, not really. You're all I've got."

Caitlyn had suggested she wear a dress, try to make it look as if she cared, and so she had, a simple wrap with a plunging v-neckline. September was still holding onto the summer, at least during the day, but at night the temperature dropped quickly. She'd thrown a silky wool wrap over her, but she still thought she could see her breath hanging in the air as they made their way down toward the pier and the Osprey Arms.

It would be nice to light a fire, curl up under a throw, pour herself a glass of wine, and watch some mindless TV or flip through the pages of a book that she wouldn't quite follow. Or then there was just listening to some mildly depressing girl music. A little Norah Jones, perhaps.

That was the kind of mood she was in, the kind of mood she had been in. She knew she should shake herself out of it, since Sean had clearly moved on. And that she should too. The cafe was doing great, sales up almost a hundred percent, and already there had been one write-up about them in the paper. More and more people were seeking them out, coming for lunch, making inquiries about a few catering jobs, and she had even agreed to ship some cookies to Ohio as an engagement present. Everything in her life was going better than she had planned. So why did her heart hurt a little more every day?

"Are you sure he's not going to be here?" she asked for the hundredth time. On the one hand, she knew seeing him would be inevitable. After all, Queensbay was a small town. But she'd done a successful job of avoiding him for over a week.

"Yes, Chase assured me he's still away. You're perfectly safe. It's just a glass or two of wine, right?" Caitlyn said, her words sounding forced and too cheery to Darby.

With another sigh she followed her friend into the Osprey Arms.

#

"I thought we were meeting a new winery rep?" Sean said, glancing over at Chase. "I guess he's running a little late," Chase answered, then checked his watch again.

"Do you have someplace else you need to be?" Sean asked, feeling irritable. It was a Monday night, a slow one in the kitchen, but still Sean would much rather be there than here, having to be social, trying to look and sound as if he cared.

"Let's go up, okay, maybe he's already set up," Chase said.

Sean shrugged and nodded, then followed Chase up. The stairs were in the center of the room and as they ascended he could look out through the big plate glass windows. Full dark had fallen and the floodlights were on, illuminating the small lawn area around the docks and then the docks themselves. Boats were still moored there and even further out he could see the twinkling lights of the houses that ringed the bluff lining the harbor.

"Here we go," Chase said, stepping aside. Sean shot him a look, but Chase only took his arm and propelled him into the room. Shrugging, he went in and pulled up short.

"You," he breathed. Darby's back was to him, but he could see the fall of her reddish hair. It was curling in loose waves down her back. She was standing by the window but she turned slowly.

"What are you doing here?" she said and he could hear the surprise in her voice.

"I'm supposed to be meeting a winery distributor." It took him a moment to find the words, to form a sentence. The last time he had seen her, she'd been in shorts and t-shirt, wearing an apron. She'd been about to cry and he had thought she never looked more beautiful. But tonight she was wearing a dress, something that crossed and nipped in at her waist, skimmed her knees, and left just enough skin exposed along the v of her neck line that he could easily imagine getting lost in it.

"I'm supposed to be at some sort of wine tasting, except that the table is set for two." She waved her hand, and he saw that there was indeed a small round table set close to the windows, set as she had said, for two, with a white cloth, two candles, and two glasses of wine.

"Dinner for two," he breathed, thinking about all those times they'd never quite gotten around to dinner.

There was the sound of a crash, then a giggle, and a voice, Caitlyn's called out, "Everything's okay here."

Sean smiled, feeling relief flooding through him. "I think we've been set up."

Darby smiled too, but it was a sad one. "Seems like it."

She looked at him, assessing him, taking in his features. "How have you been?"

"Fine. You?"

"Okay," she answered, looking anything but. The silence stretched between them.

"Look, I need to go," she said, and tried to move past him.

"Darby, please, don't," he begged. "Let me explain."

She took a step back, closed her eyes. "You don't have to. I mean I saw the paper. I saw that Will Green got the show, that Mandy's his publicist."

"Truly, what you saw that day …"

"Was Mandy being Mandy?" She gave him a rueful smile and he felt the first stirrings of hope.

"She does have an interesting way of conducting business."

"I'm sorry," Darby said, giving him a small smile. "I should have believed you, given you the chance to explain. It's just I must have wondered why you wouldn't want her, the show, everything she was offering. It was your chance back, to get everything that you wanted."

Sean shook his head, took a step toward her. When she didn't move away from him, he stepped closer, until his hands touched her arms, and he could look down into her face.

Sean's hands clenched and unclenched. "I really did fire her."

"I know."

"She did kiss me, but I didn't kiss her back. I know I probably should have thrown her into the harbor, but, well, she kind of caught me by surprise. Told me she wanted me to know what I was giving up, what I was throwing away."

"Why, don't you want it? Your big chance?" Her green eyes searched his, searing into them.

"If you had asked me that question a few months ago, I would have said yes. But things change, people change." He brushed the top of her forehead. "Darby Reese, you changed me."

"I changed you?" she asked.

"You did, this town did. For the first time in my life I was happy. I thought maybe it was the restaurant, but now that I lost you, I know it wasn't. I was happy because of you, Darby, because of how I feel when I'm with you, how you make me feel. I'm miserable without you."

His lips brushed down her forehead, and she leaned up, reaching into him.

"I'm pretty miserable without you, Sean Callahan."

"I wanted to stay for you, Darby. You're the first thing that's really mattered to me in years. Besides a business, besides a restaurant. I want to be with you."

"Really," she breathed, and before she knew, she had taken a step and he pulled her toward her and kissed her.

"Really, since I saw you that first morning and I thought you were going to go after me with a chef's knife, you're the only thing that has mattered."

"Are you saying," she said, looking up at him, holding his face in her hands, staring at him.

"I'm saying that I love you Darby, love you with everything I have. I may be a kid from nowhere, but everything I have is yours. I want to be here with you, make a life and a family with you. I love you and I want to marry you."

Her smile came fast and flooded him with joy. "I love you too."

Dimly, behind them, they could hear the pop of a cork and a shouted, "It's about time."

Darby laughed and he pulled her close to him, feeling the way her heart beat in time against him.

"Always and forever," she whispered.

"Always and forever," he echoed.

Rough Harbor - Caitlyn & Noah's Story

Book 2 - The Queensbay Series

Drea Stein

Chapter 1

Caitlyn Montgomery carefully let herself in the side door with the key hidden under the flowerpot. Police tape fluttered along the back of the house, the side that faced the water, but here, under the small overhang, there was nothing, only a chilly October breeze and the more distant sound of the water lapping at the rocky shore.

The house was quiet, the silence of sadness. Dusk was falling outside and it was dim inside, but she resisted turning on the lights. Her footsteps echoed across the polished wood flooring of the hallway as she walked onto the marble tiles of the foyer. She knew it well, had almost grown up here, and had spent many nights here in the recent months, playing chess and sipping whisky with an old man.

The door to Maxwell Randall's study swung silently open. Caitlyn crossed the floor quickly, her sneakered feet sinking into the plush carpet. She came around to Maxwell's desk, an ornate, obnoxious thing meant to look like something a Gilded Age robber baron would have owned.

It was just as he'd left it. Empty. Maxwell hadn't been one for bringing work home, she had discovered. His desk was clear; a simple blotter aligned in the middle, with a phone to the right, a brass lamp to the left. A pad of paper and a can of pens and pencils sat within reach. There was no computer, no planner or desk diary. She supposed if there had been one, the police would have taken it.

Slowly, methodically, she leaned over and began to open the desk drawers, her small flashlight illuminating the usual desk stuff. Nothing of interest in the two large drawers flanking the right side, nor in the drawers on the left. She turned her attention to the middle drawer, the thin one. It stuck a bit, and she felt her heart flutter in anticipation. She knelt down to get a better view, pushing a strand of her brown-black hair behind her ear and squinting in concentration as she carefully slid her hands towards the back of the narrow drawer.

"What are you doing?" Light flooded the room.

Her head jerked up, hitting the side of the drawer as she rose to her feet. Her vision danced as she reached out to touch her head.

"You?" Caitlyn said, surprise radiating through her.

There was a pause. Caitlyn drew herself up to her full height and looked at Noah Randall, all six-foot-one of him, standing in the doorway.

"I didn't think you'd be here." She spoke the truth, saying the first thing that came to mind. *At least not so soon.*

Noah's dark eyes were looking at her, traveling up and down her face and the length of her body. Caitlyn felt herself flushing. There was nothing like being caught red-handed to lose the advantage.

"Maxwell was my father," he finally answered. "Of course I'd be here." He lifted a drink to his lips and swallowed. He was drinking whisky.

"I'm sorry. I know." Caitlyn came around from behind the ornate wooden desk and stood in front of it. Noah had not moved from the doorway, but stood looking at her, surveying her. Beyond him, Caitlyn could see into the foyer where she'd last seen Maxwell alive. She swallowed. It gave her the creeps.

She moved closer to Noah, her natural instinct to reach out, to comfort him, but she held back. It had been a long time, and they hadn't left on the best of terms. Still, he seemed familiar to her, his face thinner, the features sharper.

"Want a drink?" he finally said.

Caitlyn nodded. She didn't really, but she wasn't ready to leave him alone. She hoped he would go out of Maxwell's study, maybe to the living room where Maxwell had kept more booze, but instead he pushed past, into the room, and went to a cabinet on the wall.

Opening it, he pulled out a glass and splashed some of the amber-colored liquid into it.

"You'll have to drink it neat," he said, shoving it into her hand. Their skin touched for an instant, and Caitlyn jumped back from the small jolt.

"Our eternal spark," Noah said with a grim laugh, throwing himself on the couch.

Caitlyn stood, studying him. He looked the same, sort of. He'd been only twenty, she two years younger, when she last saw him, and he'd been lanky, with shaggy brown hair tipped with blond highlights from a summer spent sailing and swimming. His clothes had always seemed too big on him, as if he had been swimming in them, too.

Now, though, ten years later, he'd filled in. His biceps swelled tight against the fabric of his shirt, and his legs looked lean and muscled under his faded jeans. His hair was darker now, but still kissed by the sun. He was a California guy, a software developer turned CEO turned investor, not the East Coast prepster he'd been raised as. He'd always been confident, self-assured, but there was something else now, an aloofness that hadn't been there before.

Still now, with just a hint of stubble on his chin and the dark fitted t-shirt that moved with him, Caitlyn could see that, all in all, Noah Randall had filled out very nicely.

"So?" he began again. "Why are you here?"

"I didn't break in. The key was where it usually was." Caitlyn took a swallow of the whisky, savoring the slow burn down her throat, thankful too that she had something to keep her hands occupied.

She just hasn't counted on him being here, at least not so soon. She thought she would have more time to prepare for seeing him. Now, looking at him, she wondered how she thought she'd ever have enough time. Memories threatened to push in, but she shoved them away, far away, locking them tight. She couldn't afford a trip down memory lane, not now.

"When did you get into town?" she asked instead.

"You can sit, you know. I won't bite." He tossed her a smile and waved his hand at one of the couches.

Caitlyn stepped across the rug and sat at the opposite end of the leather couch. Noah, lounging and looking perfectly at ease, gave a short laugh and looked her over.

"You haven't changed. Much." The last was said bitterly.

Caitlyn said nothing. She hadn't wanted to change. That had been Noah.

"I was in New York already," Noah continued. "The police found my cell phone number among my father's things. I took a car service and got here as soon as I heard."

That's why she hadn't seen a car. She knew she'd only have a small window of time before everyone came swarming in. The funeral was already set for tomorrow. Sam Harris, Maxwell's second in command, had handled the arrangements, no one knowing if Noah would be up for the task.

"You were the one who found him?" Noah's eyes dropped, to stare at his drink, and then lifted back up to hold her gaze.

Caitlyn nodded. "He took me to dinner at the club that night. I drove him home, and… well, when he didn't come to work the next morning, I came to the house. I knocked and knocked and looked in the windows. His car was here. I didn't figure he'd be taking a walk." Maxwell wasn't big on exercise unless it involved a golf club and some cigars.

"And he was just there, at the bottom of the bluff?"

Caitlyn nodded, swallowing against the memory of seeing him, stiff, blue. "I checked him to be sure, and then called 9-1-1." After her initial shock, she'd thought about coming to look in Maxwell's study, but there hadn't been enough time before the police came.

"So, you were the last person to see my father alive?"

The police had asked her the same question. That and others. What did you two discuss? What was Maxwell's frame of mind? Did he often smoke cigars and drink while standing so close to the edge of a rocky incline?

None of your business. He was angry. Actually, yes. A nightcap and a whisky, on one of the big Adirondack chairs overlooking the Sound, the lights of Long Island twinkling in the distance, had been Maxwell's favorite way to end the day, short of a hurricane blowing in. Caitlyn had answered all but the first question truthfully. The police could go to the club and find out that she and Maxwell had been having a heated argument. And that he had a lot to drink, which had been typical behavior lately. And that the club manager wouldn't give the car keys to Maxwell, only to her. But she was guessing they wouldn't.

"You weren't…" Noah looked down at his drink.

Caitlyn glanced up, not comprehending. And then it came to her. "You think Maxwell and I were having a relationship?"

She dissolved into a heap of laughter, shaking so hard that tears were coming out of her eyes. It was the first solid laugh she'd had in days.

"I'm glad you think that's funny. That's another one of the questions the police asked me," Noah said.

Caitlyn stopped laughing and tried to wipe her tears away, surprised to find that they were real tears now. "Maxwell was like a father to me, Noah. We would have dinner together. He was lonely." And so was she. But not lonely enough to have considered Maxwell anything more than a kindly old man. And then there was Noah, the memory of him that they had in common.

"You let him get drunk," Noah said, his eyes accusing. He was facing her, the space between them on the couch narrowing, so she could feel the heat from him, smell his scent - something soapy, fresh and clean.

"I didn't let him do anything. You know that." They both did. Maxwell got what Maxwell wanted. "He'd been drinking a lot," she added.

"Why?" Noah asked, leaning forward so that she couldn't avoid the nearness of him. She felt her stomach clench, her heart skip a beat. A totally normal reaction, she told herself, a remnant of their old attraction.

Caitlyn frowned. "I'm not sure. He seemed upset, depressed about something." She hesitated. It was nothing, really, but she had felt there was something. For weeks she had known there was something wrong. But that night, she had been sure he was about to confide in her, but he'd gotten drunk instead, angrier, evasive even.

"But I'm sure you knew how to make it all better. You always had all of the answers, didn't you?" Again, there was that trace of bitterness in Noah's voice.

Caitlyn shook her head, feeling anger rise in her throat. There had been a time when Noah Randall wouldn't have thought the worst of her.

"I worked for him. I thought we were close, that he trusted me." She said nothing of the promises Maxwell had made.

"Why did you come back? Why now?" Noah glanced meaningfully at her left hand.

Caitlyn slid it away. "I was ready for a change," she said, embarrassed suddenly, though she owed Noah no explanation. She owed him nothing after ten years of silence, of hearing about him only through tidbits on the news, on the Internet. How many times had she wanted to call, to congratulate him, but had stopped, broken off the desire to hear his voice, to know him again? Every time, because she knew he didn't want to hear from her. He had made that perfectly clear the day he'd left Queensbay.

She said no more. She didn't need to go into the gory details of why Michael St. John was a bastard. Especially not to Noah. Why had he known about the engagement in the first place? He couldn't possibly be keeping tabs on her, could he? The thought flooded her with awareness.

Noah nodded. "I see," was all he said. He took another swallow of his drink. She could feel his eyes on her, feel the way they burned through her, the way he looked at her, with … what, desire? Caitlyn looked up. Perhaps it wasn't desire at all but something else entirely - a hard, searing appraisal.

Caitlyn shifted in her seat. She wanted to get back to that desk. Maxwell had been worried about something before he died, and she hadn't been able to get it out of him. Just what sort of mess had he left behind?

"So," Noah said, sliding closer to her. He smelled good, a mix of aftershave with just a hint of the whisky they were drinking. She breathed it in, trying not to let it go to her head. An image of summer flashed back to her, tangy salt air, a faint taste of sweat and that same aftershave. Caitlyn felt a slight shiver crawl up her spine. Fear, longing? A taste of both, she decided, as he leaned in closer.

His brown eyes held her blue ones. And then he smiled, just a few inches from her. His thigh pressed against hers, and she could see every inch of his face, from the strong line of his chin, to the way his nose turned up a bit at the tip, to the flecks of gold in his brown eyes.

Noah turned so that he was almost on top of her, one arm against the back of the couch, the other on the arm of it. She was trapped, and she felt her cheeks flush. Please, she thought, she was a grown woman, not a horny eighteen year-old, but Noah Randall was having the exact same effect on her now as he had then.

"What does little Caitlyn Montgomery want now? What's your angle, Caitlyn? Why'd you leave your big life in London to come back to Queensbay? What did Maxwell promise you this time? You know he wasn't very good at keeping them. Or was that you? It's hard to remember, after all this time, who betrayed me first - my father or my girlfriend."

Caitlyn reared back in shock at the ugly words. "Noah, you don't understand. He really was like a father to me. All these years while you've been off, not talking to him, I was there for him. He helped me with everything. With college, with internships, my first job. I owed him everything."

"And of course, you took what he was willing to give, right, Caitlyn? Why work when you can have it handed to you?" Noah said.

Caitlyn couldn't breathe. Noah's words shook her. He above all knew what she had lost. How she would have given everything back to have her grandfather with her still. But Maxwell had stepped in. He'd needed someone to look out for, and she had needed a father figure.

"We understood each other," Caitlyn whispered, holding Noah's dark gaze. He moved in a fraction closer, so their faces were just inches apart.

"Well, I guess I'm glad he had somebody." Noah leaned back, their connection, their heat broken. "You should go now. It's going to be a long day. You never know what surprises my father will have in store for us tomorrow."

Caitlyn let out a breath. Noah was looking at her, his face closed. She wouldn't be able to keep searching now.

"Yes, I'd better go," she said, putting her glass down. She pushed herself up, and Noah was up with her, facing her again.

"C'mon, aren't you interested? Even just a kiss for old time's sake?" He moved in closer, and Caitlyn pushed him back.

"Noah, you don't mean that. You're upset. Why don't you rest?"

"With you around? I don't think so, Caitlyn. Like I said, you're working an angle - and I intend to find out what it is."

"Go to hell, Noah." Caitlyn turned and walked out of the room. She slammed the door behind her with more satisfaction than she felt.

Chapter 2

Noah watched Caitlyn as she walked out of the room. The door slammed, a muted sound, considering how solid it was. He listened again and heard another door slam, this one towards the back of the house. She would be walking now across the broad lawn with the view of the water, the expanse of Queensbay Harbor stretched out in front of her.

It was a windy evening, blasting straight off the water, and she would be hunched against the wind and the cold until she made it around a slight bend and then, sheltered, she would step onto the wide porch of her own house, a charming solid, early Victorian.

He put his whisky down. On one level, he'd known she'd be around. After all, he'd known that she'd come back and joined Queensbay Capital. But seeing her. He'd thought that it wouldn't have any effect on him, just like seeing Josh, his former party buddy, behind the counter at the Queensbay deli. Just another person from his old hometown whom he encountered, the exchange, familiar, friendly ... brief.

But no, from the minute he had walked in on her, startled her from her search of his father's desk, he'd realized that it wasn't going to be easy. He'd gotten her a drink even though it was far too early, hoping it would calm him, give him some time to think, to gauge how he felt about her.

He'd felt her gaze on him, assessing him, taking the measure of him. Had he grown? Once he'd very much wanted to be all that he could be for her. He'd been a boy, but she made him want to be a man, the best one he could be, just so he would be worthy of the beautiful, confident and capable Caitlyn Montgomery.

She had filled out some, growing another inch or two, her body, clearly visible in her tight-fitting running clothes, lithe. Long legs, dark, almost black, wavy hair, blue eyes and that fair skin. There was still just a smattering of freckles across the bridge of her nose and on her cheeks. He'd seen that much when he'd been close to her on the couch.

186

There had been that moment, an instant when he'd felt intensely everything he'd felt that summer long ago when she'd waltzed into the pool at the club, in nothing but a red bikini. True, she'd barely had any curves then, but she'd still been arresting, every adolescent boy's eyes glued to her and the way she strolled. She'd just come off a semester in France, and she had blossomed, every ounce of awkwardness gone. Caitlyn had been funny, confident and completely sure of herself. It had been over ten years, he thought, and no matter how hard he'd worked to make himself who he was, Caitlyn Montgomery could still ignite that flame of desire.

Not that she'd have felt it. Ice queen. Focused, intense and driven. That was the Caitlyn he knew. And the real question was: just what she was doing back in Queensbay? He hadn't bought that story for an instant, the one where she said Maxwell had been like a father to her.

Maxwell Randall had many skills, chief among them making money, but fatherly instinct was not one of them. Nope, Caitlyn was here for something else entirely. She had a nose for money, and she was probably following it.

Noah looked at the desk. She had thought to find something there. Snuck into the house, sure no one would be here. And why not? Apparently his father hadn't told anyone about what they had agreed to. They'd run out of time. Noah had thought he would have more with his father, but Maxwell's accident had taken that from them. Noah took another swallow of his drink, watching Caitlyn as she faded into the darkness. Then he saw a light flip on at her house. She was home, safe. He found himself breathing easier and then cursed himself. What was he thinking? He had long ago tried to stop thinking and caring about her. And he'd failed then, just as he was failing now.

Chapter 3

Caitlyn had tossed and turned all night, her sleep light and broken. For the first time since she'd been back, every creak and groan of the house sounded loud, like the echo of a gunshot, taunting her. Memories had danced through her head, memories not of her grandfather this time, but of Noah. The first time he had kissed her on the beach - a light, feathery kiss as if he expected her to pull away, when she'd been planning, dreaming about it for weeks. Or the way he had surprised her by asking her to dance at the Fourth of July picnic. Or the time they had taken his father's boat out for a sail.

Dawn came, and she gave up, making herself coffee first and then heading back upstairs to her old bedroom to get dressed. Even though she had been home for almost nine months, something kept her from moving into the master suite. Silly, but not even her mother, after all this time, had wanted to take over that room. It stayed there, vacant, little changed.

The house itself, at least its outer shell, hadn't changed much either. Surprisingly, there hadn't been much money left after her grandfather's death. Sure, there had been his shares in the Queensbay Capital Group, but Maxwell had assumed those. At first the lawyer couldn't explain it, how a man who was supposed to be so good at making money for other people had been spectacularly bad at keeping it for himself.

And then the full scope of the damage Lucas had left behind became apparent, and Caitlyn and her mother had been happy that the house, at least, had been spared. She and her mother had been paid off with modest trust funds. Caitlyn had used most of hers for her education, first at Wellesley, then at the London School of Economics, while her mother had managed to spend hers trying to maintain a "lifestyle."

Now, rising home prices and over-development had made waterfront property of any kind incredibly desirable - and valuable. Her mother had hinted at this often, the desire to sell, since they were equal owners, but Caitlyn had simply said no. She needed to know that this house, with its quirky floor plan, oddly shaped rooms and truly fabulous wraparound porch would always be there for her. If she had to, she would buy her mother out, but it hadn't come to that yet, and Caitlyn wanted to keep her money ready for other things.

Caitlyn shut her window, which looked out over the back lawn and the trees to the flat expanse of the water. The sun was up and bright, the sky blue, but a strong wind chopped the surface of the harbor into a shade of bottle green. Seagulls floated against the sky, holding steady, drifting and then tail diving to the surface.

It had been three days since she found Maxwell's body, the initial shock turning into an efficient numbness. A nice uniformed officer had walked her back up the beach to her own stairs and into her home, telling her gently that she really should keep the door locked. The police hadn't known what to make of Maxwell's death then. Accident or not? She had sat in the study, chilled to the bone and trying to get warm, trying not to think on all the awful possibilities.

Then there had been phone calls from Sam Harris, and she could sense his cool disapproval over the phone, as if this were somehow her fault. But, ever dutiful, he had told her he would take care of things, and she was spared the ordeal of speaking directly to Noah, telling him that his father was dead. No, instead she'd just been caught by him while breaking and entering.

Caitlyn pulled on her dress, a dark charcoal gray sheath in silk. She struggled with the zipper in the back, remembering that, the last time she'd worn it, she'd had someone to help her. Fingers shaking slightly, she knew she didn't want to go to the funeral, but her mother, safely distant in New Mexico, newly detoxed and in love, insisted.

"You must represent the family, Caitlyn," Serena Montgomery had said. The conversation had happened yesterday, before Caitlyn had decided to search Maxwell's desk. Serena was still smoking; Caitlyn could hear her sucking on her cigarette over the phone. There was the bark of a dog in the background, and Caitlyn tried to imagine her mother, tall, very thin, pale-skinned and dark-haired, out there in the desert, baking in the sun like one of her own clay pots. Caitlyn neglected to remind her to wear a hat.

It had been on the tip of Caitlyn's tongue to ask her mother when she had ever cared about representing the family. But that was one of the topics they avoided, one of the many.

"I'll send flowers," her mother had said.

"But it's Maxwell," Caitlyn had answered, as if that said everything.

"And he doesn't deserve flowers? After all, he's given you a job. After everything." Serena didn't like thinking about all of that *unpleasantness*, as she termed it.

Her mother had refused to fly back. "Caitlyn, you know I want to sell the house, cut ties to Queensbay. It was your decision to come back. I won't be pulled there."

Not for Maxwell, not for any of you. Her mother didn't say it, but it was there between them, the truth of their relationship. Her mother was moving on and wanted Caitlyn to as well.

"Yes, Mother," Caitlyn had said and ended the conversation - because, really, what else could she say to that?

Caitlyn pulled on her jacket, smoothed the skirt of her dress, and went to her bureau, running a brush through her hair. Her fingers hovered over the jewelry box, passing lightly, as they always did, over the single, square-cut diamond ring she no longer wore, but that Michael had refused to take back, telling her that they belonged together. Caitlyn selected pearls, for both her ears and her neck. Thus armed, she went out the door and to her first funeral since her grandfather's.

Chapter 4

Caitlyn took a seat in a pew about halfway up the church. It was already close to full, and several rows ahead of her, towards the front, she could see the other mourners from the office. Tommy Anderson, another associate of the firm, was there with his wife. And then there was Deborah, the office manager, and Caitlyn's own assistant, Heather Malloy. There was not enough room for Caitlyn to squeeze in, and in any case, she preferred to be on her own, away from them, the better able to keep her emotions in check.

She had known Maxwell Randall all of her life. He had been her grandfather's business partner and, after her grandfather's death, the sole steward of the Queensbay Capital Group, the money-minders of the quietly rich. He had filled the role of both father and grandfather, and through the years, he had stayed in touch with her, swooping in on her in college and in London when on business - taking her to dinner, remembering her birthday, giving her career advice, perhaps even making sure she got her first job. And when she had called him, told him she was ready to come back, he had made room for her.

But in truth, though he'd always been kind to her, not many had truly loved Maxwell Randall, thought Caitlyn, looking over the somber suits and blank faces. Most were here because it was the right thing to do. He could be difficult to love, as his ex-wives had found out. But for her, he had been there. And still, all she could think about was their unfortunate dinner at the club.

There was a murmur in the church, and Caitlyn looked up. The name moved like a ripple through the crowd, and though she wanted to squeeze to the side, to run and hide, she was right there, in the open, visible. She watched as Noah walked, eyes straight ahead, Sam Harris trailing behind him. He looked every inch the success he was. Gone were the t-shirt and jeans of yesterday, replaced by an expensive, fitted suit. His hair was combed neatly in place, and he looked like what he was - a successful tech entrepreneur who had just sold his first company and was working on his next.

Noah claimed he was taking an early retirement, but the tech and business blogs were frantic with speculation about what venture he'd turn to next. Already there were rumors he was looking for his next big thing, the next technological breakthrough. The gossip pages, though, were having a field day, detailing every party, purchase and happening that newly-minted billionaire Noah Randall attended.

His eye caught hers as he walked to the front of the church, and he gave a barely visible nod. He looked somber, but not as if he had continued to hit the whisky after she had left.

Noah was alone, except for Sam Harris, who was eagerly guiding him up the aisle. What, Caitlyn thought, he'd had no one else to bring with him? He was always being paired with someone, usually a model or actress. Caitlyn ground her teeth. She had promised herself that she would tune Noah out, but that had been harder and harder to do the more he showed up in print and online.

The funeral was appropriately grand. Not many tears were shed, but everyone extolled Maxwell's virtues as a businessman, a philanthropist and a pillar of the community. No one spoke about family. No one mentioned his recent erratic behavior on the golf course, at the yacht club or at the historical society's auction.

Caitlyn waited until most of the people had left and then, trailing behind the crowd, she walked down the aisle, her feet echoing quietly. It was cowardly, but she wished to avoid another face-to-face meeting with Noah, especially under these circumstances. No doubt they would have something to say to each other soon enough, and she could see the strain was getting to him, the awful truth. He looked stretched and tense, ready to snap, she thought.

Sam Harris was waiting for her at the end of the aisle.

"Caitlyn."

"Sam," she said, looking at her boss with wary eyes, trying to suppress the feeling of distaste than ran through her every time Sam came near.

"I'm glad you're here. Are you going back to the house?" he asked, the meaning clear.

Caitlyn shook her head. She had paid her respects to Maxwell, and that was enough, but Sam took her arm and pulled her off to the side so they were standing in a patch of light made scarlet by a stained glass window.

"I wish you would." His grip tightened around her arm, and though she made a point of staring at his hand, his viselike crush didn't relent.

"As a representative of the Queensbay Capital, if for no other reason. Family is very important to this firm, and you're a

Montgomery." His voice was silky, but there was something in his eyes that told her there was no room for argument on this.

"Oh, and today we want to remind people of that fact?" She knew she sounded bitter. Sam had been against bringing her back from the beginning. But Maxwell had taken her side against him, and here she was. Still, she knew to some she was a painful reminder.

Sam smiled thinly. "That's old history, Caitlyn, and people like to see the new generation in action." His gaze turned towards Noah, and Caitlyn could guess the gist of his thinking. Side by side, the members of the next generation of the firm. Given the suddenness of Maxwell's death, it was just about the best thing Sam could get to calm clients who were nervous about their money.

"You know how good you are with the clients. I am sure Maxwell would have wanted it." He smiled, but it didn't reach his eyes.

She knew there was a threat there. Maxwell had been more than happy to throw her name about, telling clients, "This is Caitlyn Montgomery, Lucas Montgomery's granddaughter, but she's like a daughter to me."

He said it without any self-consciousness, avoiding the fact that he had a son of his own to whom he refused to speak, and who refused to speak to him.

Still, Maxwell has always neatly sidestepped the question of the future, even as he made noises about retirement, travelling more. Maxwell had known what she wanted. But all bets were off now.

And Sam ran the firm, at least until Maxwell's will could be sorted out, and the clients that were here today - and there were plenty of them - were looking for assurances, assurances that everything would continue as before, that Maxwell had left behind him a legacy intact.

Sam was pulling rank. If she didn't play nice today, there would be hell to pay tomorrow. Caitlyn took a deep breath and forced herself to think rationally. Her plan did not involve burning any bridges.

All of this went through Caitlyn's mind as Sam looked at her.

She nodded, acknowledging that he had won.

"I'll go."

Chapter 5

Caitlyn went up the front steps this time, getting an eyeful of the Randall house. It was a monstrosity with a water view. Once Lydia Randall, his first wife and Noah's mother, had divorced Maxwell, all restraint had fallen away. Maxwell had many passions - unfortunately, none of them matched. Colors had not mattered to the man at all; neither had the differences between marble, tile and linoleum. He lived at the whim of any decorator who sensed a commission but, typically, he lost interest in their efforts and stopped paying. Even the outside was a mess, a mix of shingles, clapboards and fieldstones, the trim two different shades of blue. Inside, modern sculpture vied with sepia-tinted photographs. It was a grand house, in its oddity, the rooms spacious, filled now with dark-suited mourners and white-coated caterers.

The desire to leave was so strong Caitlyn almost escaped before Sam took a hold of her and propelled her into the living room.

"There are some people I want you to meet," he said, and introduced her to a group of men.

Their faces were uniformly bland, but their stances betrayed their impatience, as if they too would rather be anywhere but here. They perked up when they heard her name, sizing her up, trying to match an image with the name, and Caitlyn, fighting her discomfort, smiled to see if she could disarm them.

"It's wonderful to have the next generation join us. We're preparing for the future," Sam said, his arm curving protectively around her. She resisted the urge to shake it off. Ever since Michael, she had hated to be touched with this level of familiarity and possessiveness.

"Where were you before you joined the firm?" one of them asked, his eyes slightly lecherous behind thick glasses.

"I was with Capital Trust in London."

All of them nodded, but she could tell the name meant nothing to them. It had been a small firm, so she wasn't surprised.

"And what are you doing now, for the firm?" the one with the mustache asked her.

"Primarily client relations, but I was working with Maxwell on investment strategy." She wanted them to know she was good for more than a few lunches and free tickets to the hot new show in town.

"Well, they were the best, Lucas and Max." All of them raised their glasses in a toast, and Sam maneuvered her away.

"There are a few other people I would like you to meet, if you don't mind. Just offer them some reassurance, remind them that you have experience and you're looking forward to a long future with the firm." His voice was low.

"What about Noah?" So far Sam hadn't said a word about him. Noah had been acting more like a playboy than a businessman lately, and Sam was a bit old-fashioned, not quite getting technology companies and some of their sky-high valuations.

Sam looked at her and then scanned the room. Caitlyn followed his glance and saw Noah alone in a corner, his face dark, eyeing everyone with a wary expression. There was a glass in his hand, but he didn't seem to be drinking much, just scanning the crowd.

"What about him?"

"Well, if you want to make such a big deal about me, then people will start to ask about him. After all, he's the celebrity."

"Noah Randall is not a member of the firm. And he's known for spending his money, not saving it. We'll have to let Noah answer those questions on his own, won't we? Just tell people you don't know what his plans are."

Which was the truth. None of them knew how big a part Noah would play in their future. Caitlyn felt her body tighten. Her future could be in his hands; her position at Queensbay Capital was determined by whoever was the boss - which had been Maxwell, was now Sam, and tomorrow, who knew?

Caitlyn looked at Sam, whose poker face wasn't nearly as good as he thought it was. She saw what he was thinking - that Noah wasn't going to inherit the firm. In Sam's mind, there was no way that Maxwell would make such a decision, to leave a company on whom more than a few people relied, in the hands of someone he hadn't spoken to in ten years. No way would he pass over his faithful right-hand man for some newly-minted paper billionaire, someone who had gotten lucky at best and was an irresponsible playboy at worst.

"I see. Thank you, Sam." Caitlyn smiled briefly and moved away, thinking that in all of the years Sam Harris had worked for Maxwell

Randall, he had failed to see the fundamental foundation of the man. For Maxwell, blood really was thicker than water.

Caitlyn looked down at the little woman in front of her. She had to lean down and close in to hear what the woman was saying, since she refused to speak louder than a whisper.

"I remember your grandfather."

Caitlyn smiled, preparing herself. Such a statement did not always mean what was coming next was a good thing.

"He was a good man," she said, the implication being that Maxwell had not been.

Caitlyn figured the woman - Mrs. Smith, Sullivan, or something like that - was close to eighty. She looked scattered and smelled like mothballs and lavender.

"I remember your mother, too." Definitely not a good thing, Caitlyn thought and waited. There was no mention of her father; no one remembered him, not even Caitlyn, who dutifully sent him a card each Christmas. He was an alcoholic drifter who lived on a boat in the Caribbean. The marriage to Serena, Caitlyn's mother, had been just long enough to give Caitlyn legitimacy, which her grandfather then decided to question by having her name changed back to Montgomery.

"I wanted to speak to you, dear. Maxwell wouldn't listen to me, said I was being daft. But you'll listen. Adriana said you would."

Caitlyn stiffened. She didn't know what the woman was talking about, but if Adriana Randolph was involved, it couldn't be a good thing. But a client was a client.

"Of course I'll listen. What can I do for you?" Caitlyn pitched her voice low, soothing, inviting confidence.

"There is something wrong with my account. I tried to get money, and they said it wasn't there. But then it was, and everything was fine."

Caitlyn smiled, her mouth going dry at what the woman was saying.

"Your bank account?" She forced her voice to stay calm.

"No, the firm account."

"I'm sure it was nothing." Caitlyn looked up. There was a noise, a commotion towards the other end of the long room, and she tensed before she realized it was just too-loud laughter.

The woman fixed her watery gaze on her. "I want to show you something."

"I'm not sure now is the best time," Caitlyn said, her eyes scanning the room. She saw Noah standing in the corner. Their eyes caught, and he raised his glass to her in a mock salute. She tried to ignore the queer little flip-flop her stomach did and turned her attention back to the woman tugging at her sleeve.

"Well, if not now, when?" The woman looked up at her, and Caitlyn struggled to remember her name - Sullivan-Smith, that was it.

"Mrs. Sullivan-Smith," Caitlyn began, but was interrupted.

"It's Smith-Sullivan, and I don't know why I bother. I went to Maxwell, and he gave me the same run-around. Well, let me tell you—"

"Tomorrow? I do want to talk to you." Caitlyn looked at the other woman and offered what she hoped was a friendly smile and a reassuring squeeze of her arm. "Call my office, and we'll set up a time to meet." Caitlyn dug into the pocket of her jacket, pulled out her business card and handed it to the woman.

"Hrmph." The woman made a sound, which Caitlyn guessed was one of appeasement. "Very well."

A waiter came by, and Caitlyn lifted a glass off the tray and handed it to Mrs. Smith-Sullivan. "Thank you so much for paying your respects; I know Noah appreciates it."

Mrs. Smith-Sullivan looked over in his direction. "Didn't turn out so bad after all. Must take after his mother's side. If I were you, I wouldn't let that one get away again."

Caitlyn didn't know quite how to respond. Oh, she had thought they were being discreet about their relationship, but apparently not discreet enough. Quite a lot of Queensbay remembered that summer.

"I don't know what you mean." Caitlyn decided ignorance was her best course.

"Oh please, the looks you keep shooting at each other could write a book. You should just go over and talk to him." Mrs. Smith-Sullivan took a sip of her drink and smiled. "And if I were forty years younger..."

"Things are just a little more complicated than that," Caitlyn said, ignoring the way her skin prickled as she knew Noah was still watching her, his eyes burning across the room, finding her, following her. She felt too warm here, and knew that coming had been a mistake. She needed to keep her distance from Noah Randall if she hoped to not make a fool of herself.

She set her drink down on a small side table and found the door. "Excuse me; I need to get some air."

"Suit yourself," Mrs. Smith-Sullivan said.

Chapter 6

Noah stood in the corner, in his father's house, nursing his drink. He had made it through the funeral, and now here he was, back at the house, surrounded by people he did not know, a stranger in his home.

But Caitlyn moved through the crowd as if she belonged, the right mix of sympathy and assurance. What was she doing here? What had his father been thinking? People were circling him, not sure whether to talk to him or leave him alone. He kept the scowl plastered on his face, hoping that would keep some of the insincere well-wishers away.

He followed her with his eyes until she looked his way. She glanced away, and he was satisfied. She couldn't stand to look at him, not after what had happened. What had happened? He had wanted her, and she had said no, she couldn't, didn't want to be with him. Simple as that. His pride had been hurt, and he had called her a tease - a mean thing to do. She'd told him he was being a fool, being reckless. He'd ignored her. They'd both been right, hadn't they, all those years ago?

He saw her put her drink down, eyes darting around the room, and he knew she was going to leave. Before he had a chance to think, he was after her, his long strides overtaking her. He caught her arm just as she was about to leave the room and spun her around so she faced him.

Her cheeks were flushed and her eyes were bright, her hands clutched tightly together. She looked beautiful.

"Where do you think you're going?"

"Out. I need some air." Her breath was coming in short little bursts, and she glanced down at the hand he had wrapped around her arm. Caitlyn's eyes flicked up to meet his, and he saw something, not quite anger, but nervousness, fear in her eyes.

"You look upset," he said, dropping his hand from her arm and noting how some of her tenseness seemed to leave her.

"So do you," she countered quickly. He looked at her more closely. Her face was drawn tight, and there was sadness in her eyes, a sadness he remembered well.

"You really are upset, aren't you?"

She gave a small laugh, and he thought he saw her eyes glisten. "Of course I am. He's dead. And I'm upset. Because I cared for him. And maybe you didn't, so maybe this doesn't bother you."

Noah felt the anger and the sadness well up in him. "He was my father. Of course I care."

"You haven't seen him in ten years. You broke his heart, Noah," she said softly.

He saw red then, almost felt the need to shout. They were drawing attention to themselves; he could feel that every eye was on them. All of a sudden, there was someone next to him, holding his arm.

"Why don't we go outside, get some fresh air?" The voice was smooth, but the hand on his arm was strong. Noah looked over and almost sagged with relief.

"Chase."

"Sorry, buddy, I was in Europe. I flew home as soon as I could."

"I'll go now," Caitlyn said. Noah looked at her. Her tears were threatening to overwhelm her; he could see that now.

He almost told her not to, but Chase got in his way, and he saw Caitlyn go.

Chapter 7

Chase had taken him outside to get some fresh air - and to keep them away from prying eyes.

"Were you two going to get into it right there?" Chase had found them coffee, which Noah found was going down a lot better than the whisky had.

"Did you know she was back?" Noah asked.

Chase Sanders, his oldest friend, looked at him. "Sure, I knew she was back. I live here, she lives here, and we run into each other."

Noah took a sip of his coffee. They were in the back of the house, overlooking the water, on a sheltered part of the terrace. Most of the mourners had left, and the catering crew was cleaning everything up.

"You're not...?" he found himself asking; he had to know.

Chase looked at him, his brows drawn together. "What? You mean, me and Caitlyn?"

"Yeah, you're not, you know, together, since you didn't bother to tell me she was here." Noah tried to keep the jealous note from his voice, but knew he was failing.

"No, we're not together. Though I did buy her a sandwich her first week in town. But we see each other around, say hi. That's it," Chase said.

"So why didn't you tell me she was here?" Noah asked, suddenly needing to know why everyone had wanted to keep that a secret.

"Because I know how you feel about her. Besides, I didn't think you were ever coming back here, so I didn't think it would ever come up."

Noah looked at his friend. Chase had been a champion sailor, and he knew something about keeping a strategy to himself. Still, he had the grace to squirm.

"Look, you're not rational about her. Remember when you found out she was engaged? It took me a week to pull you out of that one. I was waiting for the right time to break it to you."

"It's been months," Noah pointed out. It was warmer today, and in the sunshine it almost felt like the sun he was used to back in California.

"Like I said, I was working up to it. And anyway, your dad seemed happy about it."

Noah looked at his friend. "Happy?"

"Yeah. Look, your dad and I weren't buddy-buddy either, but he seemed pleased when Caitlyn showed up. Kept bringing her places, introducing her around as an old friend of the family."

"If he was so over the moon, why was he drinking so much?" Noah asked. And why had he been so desperate for cash?

Chase shook his head. "I don't know, but that had been happening for a while before she showed up. If anything, her appearance slowed him down for a bit."

Noah put his coffee down on the edge of the railing and scrubbed his hands through his hair. Just what had been going on?

"Do you know why she came back?" he asked.

"I heard from some friends in London, you know, through the grapevine, that it was because her engagement busted up. The guy was a real asshole, from what I saw, and there wasn't room in the same city for the two of them."

"Did he hurt her?" Noah asked, feeling his chest tighten, thinking about the way she had looked at him when he had grabbed her arm.

"Down, boy. Honestly, I don't know. The guy had a temper, I did hear that, but the details of what happened, well, those were pretty hush-hush. I think you should ask her if you're interested," Chase said, a knowing smile playing across his lips.

"Why would she come back here?" Noah asked.

"Because it's a nice place. And it's her home," Chase said lightly. He took a sip of coffee, and they both stared out onto the harbor, taking in how the sun was almost fully set, the way the last colors of fall clung to the trees, and the lone motorboat making its way in from the Sound to the safety of the harbor.

"Home," Noah said, not sure he knew the meaning of the word anymore.

Chapter 8

Caitlyn looked out of the window of her study. It was the coziest room in the house, and she had indulged, building a small fire. The firm had been closed today, in honor of Maxwell's funeral, and though she had her laptop open and was trying to do some work, she couldn't quite focus. She had poured herself a glass of wine and tried to interest herself in a bowl of soup, but she couldn't muster up the appetite. She had her lucky poker chip out, turning it over and over in the palm of her hand while she thought. Or tried not to.

Thank goodness for Chase. He had saved her and Noah from going at it. Caitlyn had promised not to get personal with Noah, not to tell him how much his father had missed him. It would only make Noah feel guilty for something he couldn't change. And she knew how that felt. Guilt for what couldn't be undone. She had felt so guilty after her grandfather's death, she hadn't known which way was up. And she had pushed Noah away, out of anger, anger at herself. But he had left. He hadn't stayed and fought for her. And that had hurt, too.

But now he was back. Seeing him in the flesh, instead of in news articles and Internet stories, only made those memories come roaring back.

Summertime, after the Fourth of July fireworks down at the yacht club. They had slipped away, down to the docks where the club's racing fleet was. They had sheltered under one of the overturned boats, and he had kissed her. Softly at first, then more insistently. She had wanted it, and then had been afraid, nervous, not sure what she was getting into. Her body had said one thing but her mind another. She'd been eighteen, heading off to college, and he'd been between his junior and senior years. They'd been three years apart in school, and he'd never really taken any notice of her before that summer. And she had been so flattered that Noah Randall, the god of Queensbay, would take notice of her, an almost college freshman.

She hadn't wanted to disappoint him, but she had thought then that sex only led to bad outcomes. Her mother had certainly drilled that into her, one of those bad outcomes being an unwanted pregnancy that you were forced to keep. That had been Caitlyn. The other was watching her mother make a fool of herself for one man after another, always giving herself away but never getting much in return.

Not to mention that her grandfather had been almost as adamant about staying away from Noah. She'd never been sure if it had been Noah in particular or boys in general that her grandfather was against. But somehow the fact that it was Noah who had come to pick her up for a date seemed to send him over the edge. And so they had been forced to sneak around, and it had made it that much more exciting.

She had wanted Noah to like her, and he had been patient with her, eager but understanding, only asking that she consider it. And so that night, she had let him go further than ever before, letting him touch her, making her feel things. And then he had stopped. And kissed her gently and told her that there would be tomorrow. That there would always be tomorrow. Noah had made her feel safe and loved, and she knew that if he had asked her again, right then and there, she would have said yes.

The summer had continued like that, all push and pull, full of firsts. Sure, she had kissed a boy before, but it wasn't like it was with Noah. His kisses made her head swim and her heart beat furiously, and all she wanted to do was to be with him, every moment of the day.

And then it had all come crashing to an end. Summer love wasn't meant to last. It filled her head like a song, and she took another sip of her wine, trying to drown out the memories. Being in the same room with him, even one filled with people, even knowing Maxwell was dead, had done nothing to quell her feelings for Noah. He still made her light-headed and her heart beat too fast. But now it also ached, knowing what he had lost, knowing that feeling all too well.

Finally the tears came, and Caitlyn let them silently stream down. She was crying for Maxwell, for Noah, for her grandfather, all that she had lost. She fell asleep like that, curled up in a tight ball, a blanket pulled up over her, sinking into a deep, dreamless sleep.

Chapter 9

Noah Randall stood looking out the window at the view from the lawyer's office. It was of the Queensbay marina, mostly empty at this time of year. The docks, which would be bustling in the summertime with boaters of all types, rolling coolers, stacking lines and tanking up, lay vacant, rocking up and down in the steady waves kicked up by a stiff breeze from the north.

"So, that's it?" he asked.

Gary Burton nodded. "Yes. Your father left you the house, of course."

"How much is it worth?"

Gary pushed back a bit from his desk and steepled his fingers together before replying. Noah waited.

"That's an interesting question."

"What does that mean?' Noah covered the distance to the desk in two quick strides. Gary pushed back a bit, rearing back as if Noah were going to attack him.

"Well, your father had a mortgage on the house."

"What?" Noah said. "But he bought the house outright when I was a kid."

"So he did. When times were good. But he's routinely used it as collateral - it's waterfront, you know, worth quite a bit. He's had to raise money several times throughout the years, and he always used the house to guarantee the loan. Maxwell always paid it off, but I guess this time, he didn't have a chance."

"Why?" Noah asked, sitting, looking interested. Maxwell had lived large, never giving any indication until recently that he needed money.

Gary put his hands on the edge of the desk, grasping it as if for strength. "I don't know why for certain."

"But could you make a guess?" Noah said.

"Don't take this the wrong way," Gary began, "but your father wasn't quite the financial genius he made himself out to be. Between you and me, even though everything always looked good on paper, ever since Lucas Montgomery died, Queensbay Capital seems to boom and bust. Somehow Maxwell always managed to pull it out of the bust, but I think his time was cut short. I believe he was using the equity from the house to cover some bad investments at the company."

Noah leaned back. "So, there's no money, you're telling me? After all those years, my father was, what - basically broke?" Noah let that sink in, and then said, "And that's why he needed my money. Time finally caught up with him." Noah almost laughed, but stopped himself.

Gary cleared his throat. "Broke is a bit of an overstatement." Noah looked at him levelly, and the lawyer swallowed. "Okay, so yes, your father was basically broke, personally."

"Oh, that's rich. You know what he told me when I left for California to start TechSpace?"

Gary shook his head.

Noah did laugh then. "Said the Internet was a fad, good for nothing more than playing games and wasting time. Well, he was right about that. Just didn't know people would pay good money for the chance to do that." Noah took a deep breath. "Okay, so if I want to keep the house, I have to pay the bank. Done. But what about my newest investment? Do I have to go in and start firing people just to keep it afloat?"

Gary shook his head. "There's enough money to keep it going for a while. You don't have to do anything just yet. Actually, the firm appears to be on an upswing again. Given some time, everything will probably play out just right."

Noah was relieved. If his father's wild ways meant that a whole bunch of people were about to lose their jobs, well, that was something Noah wasn't sure he wanted to allow. Now that he could afford to do something about it.

"So, where does this leave me?" Noah brought himself back to the now.

"Well," Gary said, and Noah could tell he was phrasing his words carefully, "I suppose there's no need to check into the Osprey Arms while you're here. You could keep the house, or sell it. Are you eager to get back to California? I know a few real estate agents who would be happy to list it. Surely you weren't planning on running the firm? You never wanted that, did you?"

Noah shook his head in frustration. "I hadn't planned on it, but I'm not going to turn my back on my investment. I have some time to go in and assess things. Does anyone know that he sold it to me?"

Gary shook his head. "I'm not sure; it was a very quiet deal. And since you left pretty much everything in place, I don't think anyone's noticed the change. Were you planning on running it yourself?"

Noah shook his head impatiently. His father had wanted a loan, and Noah had refused. He had made a different offer, and his father, desperate, had taken it.

"I was going to find someone to oversee it and keep an eye on my father. He needed money for a reason, and I wasn't going to let him just run off with mine."

"So, Queensbay Capital is just another company in your portfolio?"

"For now. I suppose that, while I'm here, I'll take a more personal interest. I've been keeping an eye on some of their investment choices, and I have to admit, they have me intrigued."

Gary smiled. "Yes, that would be your old friend Caitlyn Montgomery. She seems to have quite a knack for picking winners, almost the Midas touch, if you will. The two of you should get along well."

Noah shot the man a look. Gary had handled his father's affairs for ages, and from what Noah remembered of the man, he wasn't prone to making jokes. And he didn't seem to be making one now.

Noah chuckled. "This is going to get interesting."

Gary looked up from the papers on his desk, his look questioning.

"You know, she's going to be pretty steamed when she finds out," Noah said, relishing the thought of seeing how Caitlyn took the news.

Chapter 10

Caitlyn sat in her office, twirling in her chair. It was a fairly small office. Maxwell had said he didn't want to upset the team when she first came by giving her one of the bigger ones, and she had accepted that, content to bide her time. After all, she had expected to be sitting in the corner office before long, so a short layover in a space that was a bit larger than a cubicle was no big deal. Still, she had insisted that she be allowed to paint it her own choice of color, a creamy white, and she had filled it with fun art - things she had picked up in London, somewhat funky, kind of avant-garde.

In truth, her own taste was a little more conservative, but she needed to stand out and look different than the leather chairs and wood paneling most people associated with financial management firms. Nothing sent up-and-coming talent away like a place that looked straight out of the men's lounge at a country club. In general, Caitlyn's clients hated to be told what to do by old men in three-piece suits.

So, she'd gone deliberately in the opposite direction. And it had worked. Caitlyn tapped her fingers on the desk as she counted on her hand. Fifteen new clients in eight months. Not a bad track record when she'd had to start over from scratch.

Caitlyn stood and walked over to her window. The view was okay. If you stood on tiptoe and leaned, you could catch a glimpse of Queensbay Harbor, but for the most part, you got a view of the parking lot. Clouds were piling in. It would probably rain later, slicking down the roads and pulling more of the late fall leaves off their branches.

She loved the water at any time of the year. In college, she had been landlocked, and in London, you had the Thames, of course, but it couldn't quite compare to home, to Queensbay. She had missed it, the quiet yet prosperous town, small enough that people knew your name and remembered how you liked your coffee, big enough so that they had good restaurants and decent shopping. They'd even had their own theater at one time, a giant pile of a Victorian folly that had been home to summer stock for a number of years until it had fallen on hard times. Queensbay was small town with a touch of cosmopolitan, and it had the comforting feeling of permanence. The water might be changeable, but Queensbay itself was not.

Caitlyn had thought that the firm wasn't either. At least, that's what her grandfather had told her years ago. It had been founded by his father, the son of a successful merchant, who was descended from a sea captain. Business was business, whether it was investing in a ship to carry cargo from far-off lands or building a portfolio of investments to handle stormy weather. A safe haven in a rough harbor. That had been her grandfather's approach.

And then Maxwell had taken it over and tried to add some swagger to it. He'd been flashier, brasher, a bit of a gambler. She had seen that now that she was closer, had seen some of the records from the past years. Still, Maxwell's gambles always seemed to pay off, hadn't they? And that's what, she thought, had been bothering her. And so she had bothered him, until he had basically told her to mind her own business. In no uncertain terms.

He'd rejected her offer, surprised that she had made it. He hadn't expected her to be ready, and he had neatly dodged it, saying there was still time to sort out the details. It had been a brush-off, she saw that now. And there had been others, slowly but surely. He had been trying to let her down gently. But why?

Caitlyn had thought there would be something, some note, perhaps in his home office. She had meant to be in and out, Caitlyn thought. Why did Noah Randall have to be there at that particular moment? She hadn't found anything, which Caitlyn thought was exactly how it was supposed to be. Maxwell was careful. He wouldn't have put anything like that in writing. What game had he been up to, and why had he changed his mind?

She turned away from the window and sat back down at the desk, restless. Her thoughts were back on Noah. Had Maxwell changed his mind because of him?

Noah had looked good. Too good. Tan, handsome, the way he had filled out his suit and smelled of soap and whisky mingled together. She closed her eyes, breathing, imagining the smell of him.

Caitlyn sighed. Noah Randall was as different from Michael St. John as night and day, but in those few moments with Noah she'd felt more - what? Longing, desire? - than she had in months.

But it was only because of their history together. Their unresolved history. When someone was supposed to have been your first, and it didn't work out, and then he shows up looking all yummy and delicious … and angry … well, a girl couldn't help how she felt, could she?

Caitlyn shook her head and smoothed her dark beige skirt, straightened her blouse. There was a staff meeting in ten minutes, and since she hadn't heard from Maxwell's lawyer, she had a sense of where this was going.

Chapter 11

There was a knock at her door. Startled, she turned and saw Heather Malloy, her assistant. There was a look of worry on her face, and Caitlyn realized she'd barely said hello to the girl.

"Come in," Caitlyn said, and Heather eagerly crossed the beige rug and took a seat, then hesitated. Caitlyn sensed that Heather wanted to ask her something. They had forged a pretty good rapport since Caitlyn had started working there, and Caitlyn hoped Heather felt comfortable enough asking her anything.

"Are we going to get fired?" Heather asked. Caitlyn knew she was trying to save money to move out of her parents' house. Heather was twenty-two, and Caitlyn knew this wasn't her dream job. Her father was a client, and a place had been found for her.

"Probably not. I mean you're not. I might, but they usually start at the top and work their way down."

"Oh good," Heather said, and Caitlyn could see the relief clearly on her face. "I mean, I'm sorry; that's not what I meant." Heather's green eyes looked contrite, and Caitlyn waved away her concern.

"No problem. I understood what you meant."

There was silence, and Caitlyn looked out the window again. Heather didn't seem inclined to move, and Caitlyn didn't mind the company. There was nothing to do but wait right now.

"Is it true?" Heather asked, and Caitlyn turned again.

"Is what true?"

"Did your grandfather used to own the firm? This firm?"

"He did," Caitlyn said cautiously. Heather was probably too young to remember the story or all of the gossip.

"But he's dead, right?"

"Yes." Caitlyn hoped Heather didn't want all of the details.

Everyone knew the story. Lucas Montgomery, scion of Queensbay Capital, investment advisor to the genteel rich, had driven his Lincoln Town Car, not his beloved Mercedes coupe, down to a deserted beach one evening towards the end of the summer. He had shot himself with a gun, no one knowing where he had gotten it, and left a note, saying, "I am sorry. I can't live like this."

"Is what they say true?"

"What do they say, Heather?" Caitlyn countered.

She swallowed. "There's just Deborah; she works at the other end of the office, and she's been here forever. It was just lunchroom gossip; that's all."

Caitlyn sighed and rubbed the bridge of her nose.

"It probably wasn't. Queensbay Capital was started by my great-grandfather. My grandfather was the last Montgomery to run it. He killed himself about ten years ago."

It took effort for her to say the rest. "He had cancer. Inoperable brain cancer. No one knew, and I guess he didn't give himself good odds. So he took fate in his own hands."

"How come you didn't inherit it? You said it was your grandfather's firm."

"Maxwell was a partner. It was a bit complicated. A firm's not like a piece of art or necklace. So, at the end of the day, my mother and I got the lovely house and some other things."

Heather seemed to take this in for a moment. "What about your dad? Wasn't he a partner?"

"My dad wasn't a Montgomery, and my mom had no interest in running it. She never worked a day in her life, at least not in finance. She's an artist and didn't want anything to do with it." Caitlyn was careful to keep the bitterness out of her voice.

"So you're not one of the owners?"

Caitlyn shook her head. "Just an employee."

Heather seemed satisfied, and Caitlyn was glad. She didn't want to relive the memories. The cancer had been the official reason for Lucas's suicide, but there had been other rumors, whispers. Caitlyn didn't like to think about those.

And Maxwell had been amazing, stepping in and stepping up, preserving Queensbay Capital for the new century.

Caitlyn looked at the clock. It was time for their meeting.

"Should we go?"

Chapter 12

Caitlyn entered the conference room just after Heather. It was a large space; still, it was filled to bursting with every employee of the firm. Queensbay Capital was on the top floor of a five-story building. Nothing like the glass-and-steel tower she had worked at in London, but still it reeked of money, quiet old money.

Inside the room, Caitlyn could feel the nervousness rolling off of people. It was in their eyes and in the sweaty armpits of Bob Mancini from the mailroom. Faces reflected in the sheen of the conference room table's shiny surface were worried, ghostly almost. They were all wondering what would become of them.

There was a slight swirl of air as heads turned towards the door. Two men entered, and Caitlyn felt her heart sink, even though she had prepared herself for this. Maxwell the Bastard had struck again. She felt a burn in her throat and just maybe the prick of a hot, angry tear before she got a hold of herself.

Maxwell had used her, she thought, as Sam Harris began to speak. He had salt-and-pepper hair and a perpetual tan. In the summer months, he spent most of his spare time on his boat or hanging out at the yacht club. By October, Caitlyn suspected he had a little help from the bottle.

"Thank you all for joining us. It has been a difficult week for all of us, since Maxwell was such a part of the firm. Some of you may be wondering what will happen now that Maxwell is gone. Well, the good news is that, while nothing stays the same, we can ensure that we will carry on. Maxwell and I worked together for a number of years. In the last few, I began to talk to him about a succession plan. Luckily, he listened to me." Sam took a moment to pause, and Caitlyn looked at him closely. Whatever he was going to say wasn't easy for him.

"Everyone, I would like to introduce you to someone. Many of us here have worked at the firm for years. It's always felt like a family firm, Maxwell like a benevolent uncle guiding the ship."

Caitlyn felt the anger rising in her. Benevolent, her ass. Cheating, deceitful user was more like it.

Sam straightened his tie before continuing. As usual, he wore a suit, gray with pinstripes, and a striped tie, this one alternating navy and red. Caitlyn had seldom seen him wear anything but, not even a subdued paisley. He eschewed French cuff shirts and cufflinks and wore a simple watch with a leather band. The only thing noticeable about him were his dark, dead-fish eyes. They watched everything coldly. Sam Harris had been the man to rein in Maxwell's wilder tendencies, but he did little to inspire anyone to greatness.

"It was a terrible tragedy that Maxwell Randall was taken from us so soon."

Caitlyn scanned the room. The faces had changed from scared and nervous to puzzled. Most were trying to get a better glimpse of the man who stood behind Sam, just out of view.

"In order for our ship to weather these stormy seas in the next few months, we need to present a clear and united front to our customers and the investment community. So, since ownership of Queensbay Capital has passed to Maxwell's son, Noah Randall will be acting as the CEO. By Noah's good graces, I will continue in my present role, overseeing day-to-day operations."

There were a few murmurs around the conference room, and someone started clapping. Soon enough, everyone joined in, including Caitlyn, giving some half-hearted slaps of her hands together. So this was how it was going to be.

"Excuse me, excuse me." Sam Harris raised his arms and called for quiet. "As I said, I would like to introduce you to someone. Noah, why don't you come forward?"

Sam Harris moved out of the way, and Noah stepped forward. Caitlyn looked up and caught his eye. She stared at him for a moment, holding his dark eyes with her own. He had to look away.

"Ladies and gentlemen..." he began. Caitlyn tuned him out, focusing on the small seething little bit of rage within her. Queensbay Capital was supposed to have been hers. Not Noah Randall's, the prodigal son, and certainly not Sam Harris's. It was supposed to have been her legacy, and now it was slipping through her fingers. Again.

Chapter 13

"Can we talk?"

Caitlyn looked up and saw Noah in her doorframe.

"Do I have a choice?" Caitlyn didn't bother to keep the bitterness out of her voice. "You're the boss now, so I suppose you can talk to whomever you want." Caitlyn flipped over some papers on her desk, trying to hide the fact she was shaking with rage, not able to look at Noah. "You know, if you were planning on firing me, you might want to rethink that. My employment contract calls for a rather generous severance package." She looked up when she said it, shooting him a clear, hard look.

"Caitlyn," Noah said with a laugh. He tried not to show that her anger was getting to him. She had always set him off so easily. Nasty boardroom battles, angry investors, nothing could upset him the way a look from Caitlyn did.

"I guess my father didn't share his plans with any of you?" Noah said, trying to keep his calm. Sam Harris had been shocked but had done his best to hide it, to play along like he was happy with the news.

Caitlyn stopped what she was doing and looked at him. Noah had dressed carefully, knowing that he needed to send a message. His suit was perfectly cut, his shirt starched, his cufflinks gleaming. If he now owned a financial company, he was going to look the part.

"No, not this particular plan." Her voice was clipped, but she had stopped shuffling with the papers and stood, ramrod straight, hands clenched tightly at her sides. She looked good in her silk blouse and smooth skirt that managed to hug her curves.

"So, he blindsided you as well?" he said when she stayed quiet.

"It wasn't like that," she started to say, and then stopped. It had been exactly like that, and she didn't need to defend Maxwell anymore, least of all to Noah.

He sat down and placed his hands on the clear surface of her desk. Caitlyn's office was modern to the extreme, including a clear, glass-topped desk supported by simple metal rods.

"I told you he couldn't be trusted," Noah said, his voice softening. His father had opened the lines of communication because he needed money. Not because he wanted to reconcile. Noah accepted that. He had gotten out from under his father's manipulations years ago, but he sensed that Caitlyn was just beginning to shake free from her bonds.

"It must feel nice to be right after all these years," she snapped back.

He was about to say that it didn't, that he didn't want to see her hurt, but he didn't think she would listen.

"Who do you think you are, Noah?" Her voice had dropped to a hiss, and she leaned over the surface of her desk, hands splayed flat at him as she pinned him down with her gaze.

"What do you mean?"

"You were right. All along. You made it. You proved your point. Did you have to come back here and rub it in all our faces? There you go, Noah - you won. You own Queensbay Capital. You outsmarted your father. You outsmarted me. You've paid us all back for not believing in you. What did you do, make him an anonymous offer? Did he even know you were the buyer?"

Noah reared back, shocked by the anger in his eyes.

"Of course he knew. He came to me." Noah could feel his voice rising, and he took a deep breath, willing himself to calm down. He had not come in here to get into a shouting match with Caitlyn. Gary Burton had stressed that Caitlyn was essential to the continued success of the firm, and the last thing he wanted to do was piss her off. At least not too much.

"He came to you?" Caitlyn repeated, and some of the anger seemed to seep out of her. She sank down into her chair and looked at him. "When?"

"About three months ago."

"He called you out of the blue?" Caitlyn asked, her voice more curious than angry. Noah looked at her blue eyes, feeling himself pulled into them. Her hair was shorter than it had been, with layers that framed her face, highlighting her sculpted cheekbones, but it was still a shiny rich black that he had once compared to printer ink. That had been a mistake. It had taken a little charm of a sailboat to add to her bracelet to get him out of that one.

"Do you still have that bracelet?"

"The what?"

"The charm bracelet. The silver one. You used to collect charms for it. I got you one, remember?"

Her eyes went cold. "Vaguely. It was a long time ago."

Noah nodded. "Still, I thought it meant something."

She looked at him, and there was sadness in her eyes. "It all meant something. But it was a long time ago. Too long ago to go back."

He was about to lean in and ask her why when he stopped herself. He remembered what Chase had said about her, about her ex, and decided that Caitlyn's edges were still rough. He didn't need to push, he reminded himself. They had time now, time for him to figure out what made this version of Caitlyn Montgomery tick.

"You're right; it was a long time ago. I was just curious." He saw her take a deep breath, as if steadying herself, and the look was back again. Caitlyn was like the sphinx, a natural poker face. It had been fun to try and rattle her, but ultimately pointless.

"The deal closed about three months ago?" she prompted him, and he had to bite back a smile. This was information she was eager to know, and it wouldn't hurt to make her sweat for it a bit.

"What deal?"

"The one to buy Queensbay Capital," she said, her teeth gritted.

"Yes. My father and I worked out the terms then."

"So, you forced him to sell the company?"

Noah shook his head, trying his best to find the right words that wouldn't give it away. "I didn't force him to do anything, Caitlyn. It was a business deal. Beneficial to both sides. He said that he was getting tired, thinking of retirement."

Caitlyn nodded, and her fingers drummed the table. She bit her lip, once, quickly, and then her face settled back into inscrutability.

"Well, that would explain things," she said, but it was so quiet that he almost missed it.

"But he never told you?" Noah said.

"No one. Was it supposed to be a secret?"

Noah shrugged. It had been a condition of the sale, that no one knew anything had changed, except on paper. Both he and his father had been agreed on that point. Still, he had meant to get more involved, understand the workings of things, but there hadn't been time.

"He just called you out of the blue?" Her voice was tinged with curiosity.

"Not exactly. He had called me about a month earlier."

"Oh." Caitlyn kept her voice flat, but anger flashed in her eyes.

"We talked, worked things out." Noah kept his voice light, wondering if she would believe him. "You're angry, but not surprised," he guessed.

"I didn't realize he was entertaining other offers. Usually you try to play your potential buyers off of each other."

"You offered to buy the company?" Noah tried to keep the surprise out of his voice. Her look was steely.

"Yes."

"But, it cost a lot of money," he said.

It was her turn to give him a smile - a thin, knowing one - and he felt his pulse speed up a bit as he thought that she had only grown more beautiful. If he had thought anything about coming back to Queensbay was going to be easy, he knew now he was mistaken. Nothing about Caitlyn was ever easy, and that was what made her so damn sexy. And made him want her.

"You might be surprised by my resources, Noah Randall. Don't make the mistake of underestimating me."

"Underestimate you? Caitlyn, this was a serious business deal."

"I was aware of that. Noah, you're not the only one who has changed in ten years. It would be smart of you to remember that." She said it so calmly that he felt the anger bubble up in him. She was truly exasperating.

"Fine, then quit. But may I remind you of that non-compete clause in your contract?" he said with pleasure. He saw a look of astonishment cross her face, surprise that he had done his homework.

"I wouldn't give you the satisfaction. If you want me to go, then fire me and pay up. But it will cost you. And more than just money. It's my clients, my picks that are keeping this ship afloat." She spread out her hands in a relaxed gesture.

Noah let her words sink in, and then he said, as calmly as he could, "Well, then I look forward to working together, for a long and profitable future."

She was taken aback, he could see that, not expecting him to give in, and he felt a surge of pleasure at having won this battle. He let a bland smile cross his face. Caitlyn Montgomery had a lot to discover about this Noah Randall. He'd learned a bit about how to tame his impetuous nature and how to keep his business rivals guessing. He was going to enjoy keeping Caitlyn Montgomery off guard, even if he had no intention of keeping their relationship purely professional.

"Fine, I have work to do," she spat out. "So you should go. I am sure you have someplace to be."

She rose, walked around him, allowing him a view of her shapely backside in the tight pencil skirt, and he felt his heart skip a beat and growing excitement in his pants. She opened the door for him, her expression cold. He took his leave, brushing past her on his way out, deliberately letting his shoulder touch hers. She felt it, too - the small thrill of electricity. He saw it in her eyes and heard it in the quick hiss of her breath and the way she quickly jumped back, giving him a wide berth.

"I look forward to working with you, Miss Montgomery," he said as he stepped out in the hall. Heads of assistants and secretaries swiveled towards him.

Caitlyn smiled. Two could play this game. "As do I, Mr. Randall."

Chapter 14

Caitlyn resisted the urge to slam the door after Noah left. Heart pounding, she waited for it to settle down, trying to convince herself that she hadn't just wanted to kiss her boss. Instead she sent out a smile that caused the assistants to put their heads down and get back to work. Only Heather didn't, instead handing her a little pink message slip.

"I held your calls for you," she explained unnecessarily as Caitlyn looked down at the message and sighed. Mrs. Smith-Sullivan had called, and though Caitlyn knew she should call her back soon, she crumpled the paper instead. It would just have to wait.

Retreating to the safety of her desk and sinking into her chair, Caitlyn rubbed her forehead. She felt a headache coming on as she let the implications of her conversation with Noah settle in. He had looked good, better than good, in his custom-made suit. He had looked like the master of the universe the press had proclaimed him to be. Not a whiff of doubt or regret. Caitlyn had known there had been no love lost between Noah and his father, and she still couldn't believe that Maxwell had gone to him instead of her.

She had made it clear that she had a serious offer. Because it would have been a kind of sweet success to know that, after all these years, Queensbay Capital was back in the hands of an actual Montgomery. But Maxwell had made an end run around her, going to the son he had practically disowned and selling him her family's company.

Her heart rate, which had calmed, sped up again the more she thought about Noah. What did he now want with Queensbay? After all, he had sworn never to come back here. And how had she behaved? She had basically pissed off her new boss. Not smart, she told herself.

What had she wanted? Caitlyn sighed, her pen drawing doodles on a pad. Glancing down, she realized she was drawing hearts. Disgusted with herself, she ripped the page off her pad and crumpled it up.

She did not want to be thinking about Noah Randall that way and what it would be like to kiss him. Again.

It was just all the emotions swirling around. There had been a lot of endings lately. Her engagement, her life in London, the death of Maxwell, who had been her mentor. Not to mention all the other emotions Noah's reappearance had brought up: nostalgia, loneliness, anxiety and, even, of course, more than a little bit of lust. There was no way she could deny the last.

It had been months, possibly years, since she had felt like that, remembering the way her stomach flipped and her body trembled. Snatches of that summer came back. Bright, sunny days spent at the beach, or sailing, together, always together. They had been inseparable that summer.

Lust wasn't love, but it was almost the same. She couldn't get caught in that trap again. That was the only thing to do. Caitlyn knew she needed to avoid him. She was not going to get caught up with another man, not going to get caught up in the past, and that certainly meant that she needed to stay away from Noah. They had too much history together.

Resolved, Caitlyn turned her attention back to her desk and the unfinished work that was in front of her. When she had returned to Queensbay Capital, Maxwell had made it clear that she needed to impress him with new investments that would net them a profit and new clients with big bank accounts. It wasn't impossible, but finding clients with a high risk tolerance wasn't easy.

Chapter 15

"Mr. Harris wants to see you." Heather poked her head in the office. "All the account managers have been going in, all morning."

"How do they look when they come out?" Caitlyn asked.

Heather paused, thought about it a moment. "Kind of grim, come to think of it. Are we going to get fired now?" Heather looked nervous again.

"Again, you, probably not," Caitlyn said with a smile. "Me, I'm not so sure about, but no use speculating. I'll just have to see what he says."

Getting ready to go into Sam's office, Caitlyn took a moment to compose herself. She put on her suit jacket and smoothed her hair. Ready as she could be, she went along the corridor and into the small suite that was Sam Harris's domain.

"Caitlyn." Sam smiled and indicated one of the chairs in front of his desk. She took it and sank into a seat that was too big for her. Perching on the edge, she was careful not to look or feel like the little girl who had been called into the principal's office.

"I asked everyone to come in today to talk about the future of the firm and how things stand. As you might imagine, some people view this as a crossroads for the firm. A great deal of the company's mystique was tied up in Maxwell. Without him, we need to very actively work to find a way to continue, to ensure that the mystique does not end with him."

Caitlyn nodded, keeping her face impassive.

Sam hesitated, but she knew what he was going to ask even as the words came out of his mouth.

"I gather the fact that Maxwell sold the firm came as a surprise?"

Caitlyn gave a small nod. She wasn't sure how much Maxwell had shared of her offer to buy him out of the firm.

"Well, I had been working with Maxwell on a similar proposition, but I guess that blood is thicker than experience."

Caitlyn said nothing, knowing that she didn't want to be sharing confidences with this man. There was something in the way his eyes looked at you and through you. Sam Harris had come on board after her grandfather had died. That alone didn't make him a bad person, but he and Caitlyn had disagreed on just about everything. And worse was that Maxwell had always backed him up.

"Not sure how Maxwell left things with you, but I understand that since your grandfather had some connection to the firm, you might feel a bit of a proprietary interest in it." Sam's smile was thin.

Caitlyn gave a slight incline of her head. "I'm sure it's in good hands."

"Well, glad to see you're on board with the changes. Which is a good thing. Noah asked me to take a look at your employment contract. Seems like you and Maxwell had quite the deal. If I fire you for no reason, we owe you a lot of money. If you decide to quit, though, we have you with a non-compete clause for two years. That means no poaching of our clients. Long time to stay out of the business, don't you think?"

Caitlyn said nothing. If Sam thought that two years of no work would hurt her financially, all the better. And there was nothing in there about Caitlyn's ability to find new clients.

"Of course, there is that little incident in London."

Caitlyn shifted in her seat, wondering why Sam was bringing it up, and how he had heard about it. She wondered if somehow Michael's lies had made their way farther than she thought. She didn't like where this was going.

"All hushed up, of course, but people will talk. So it seems like it would be difficult for you to get another job, wouldn't it? But then again, I'm guessing that's why you were so eager to cross over to our side of the pond."

Caitlyn said nothing, feeling her anger seething to the top. How dare he bring that up? It had all been cleared up, she had been absolved of any blame, but there was always the worry of rumors. And rumors, in a business involving money and based on trust, were dangerous.

"You wouldn't dare," she said across the silence.

Sam smiled at her, his even, white teeth gleaming. "Let's just say I have my eye on you, Caitlyn. If you mess up, I can fire you and not pay you a dime. And it would be pretty hard for you to go off on your own. So, it seems like I hold all the cards in this relationship. And that means you better do a good job, a better than good job, got it? I'm watching you, waiting for you to mess up. Are we clear?"

Caitlyn looked at Sam Harris, who leaned back in his chair, a smug grin on his face. He seemed pretty secure in the fact that he had Noah's trust. At least for now.

"Perfectly," she said.

"Good." He smiled again. "As you can see, I have transferred some of your accounts and given you new ones."

He pushed a list towards her. She looked it over. The names were unfamiliar, which meant they were probably low-worth accounts.

"Where's Ryan Fitzhugh?"

Ryan Fitzhugh made commercials for ad agencies, which happened to pay well, if not exactly exalt him in artistic circles. He had a high risk tolerance and enjoyed bragging to his friends about how well his investments did. Caitlyn was proud that she had been able to deliver.

"I transitioned him to Tommy Anderson. I am quite confident he will be able to carry on your good work."

"But he's my client."

"Tsk, tsk," Sam said. "Technically, they're the firm's clients, and if you have a problem with that, well, you know where the door is."

Caitlyn took a deep breath. He wanted a reaction, but she wasn't going to give him the satisfaction of getting one. At least she had kept Johanna.

Johanna Temple had inherited two magazines from her father, both with flagging circulation and laughable ad revenue. In two years, she had managed to turn around one of them by making it the bible of the lady equestrian set. A small but profitable niche. The other one, targeted to amateur tennis players, was also doing well, and Johanna was considering her next acquisition. Caitlyn had helped her and the firm make a nice little profit on the investments.

Since there was really nothing more to say, she tried, with as much dignity as she could muster, to sweep out of his office gracefully.

Chapter 16

Noah pushed open the door to North Coast Outfitters and took a moment to drink it all in. If sailing could have a scent, he supposed that Chase must have bottled it and had it blown in. As it was, Noah was fairly sure that the smell of the store - a combination of clean, fresh air and something almost like sunshine - was deliberate. Chase didn't like to leave anything to chance, especially if he thought it would help him get more sales.

"Can I help you?" A sales clerk, probably still in college, with sun-kissed cheeks and a fresh scrubbed appeal, dressed in trim khakis and a polo shirt, smiled up at him.

"I'm looking for Chase Sanders. I have an appointment."

The girl, light brown hair pulled back in a ponytail, smiled. "I'm Tory, the store manager. Are you Noah?"

He nodded.

"Great, Chase said to keep an eye out for you. He's upstairs, in the office. Why don't I show you there?" Tory led the way through racks of foul weather gear, shirts, and other apparel towards the back of the store and a set of floating stairs that led up to a second floor.

He caught Tory looking at him; she blushed and looked away quickly. "Do you need anything while you're here? We just got in some great new foul weather gear, which is perfect for spring sailing. There's also a new line of sunglasses in, great for minimizing reflections on the water."

Noah almost laughed. Chase had trained his employees well.

"I guess I'm fine, though it would probably take a bit to get used to sailing along the East Coast again. I have - had," he corrected himself, "a boat out in California."

"I know," Tory said. "Sorry, when Chase said that Noah Randall was coming, I knew the name sounded familiar. I mean, he talks about you all the time. I just never thought that you were *the* Noah Randall."

"One and the same." Noah smiled. It took some getting used to, knowing that people had heard of him. Before he had sold his company, he'd just been one of many, a tech entrepreneur in Silicon

Valley. Now with the sale, he had become a bit of a celebrity, and he'd felt the need to keep his guard up, not sure who was interested in him or just his money.

"Noah," Chase's voice boomed as he emerged from a door. One thing could be counted on. Chase had had his back since the fifth grade.

"How's the tycoon doing? Having fun playing hometown hero?"

Chase slapped Noah on the back, a hearty slap that had him catching his breath. "I see you met Tory here. She's my resident computer whiz. Probably wants to ask you a bunch of questions about databases and algorithms."

Noah glanced over at Tory, who was blushing again. "I'm a computer science major, and it's so totally an honor to meet you."

"Really, I just got lucky."

"Oh no, the way you solved that problem of—"

Chase cut in at that moment. "Tory started out as a sales clerk, and now she manages the ecommerce division and will talk about computers all day. Good thing she's also a great sailor, too, or I would have to throw her overboard. All that tech stuff is geek to me."

Noah laughed. Tech stuff might have been geek-speak to Chase, but he'd trusted enough to give Noah money when his father wouldn't, enough to start TechSpace. Chase had never wanted to be part of the company, content to take over the family business, a marine hardware and supply store. In a few short years, Chase had overhauled the place and turned it into the outfitters of choice for the yachting set. With three locations and a thriving online business, Chase was the consummate businessman, always seeking a profit and not nearly as computer illiterate as he made himself sound.

"I know, computers bore you. You'd rather be outside, sails full out, riding the waves."

"Something like that. Still, it's not a good day for sailing, even for me. We're going to head over to the Osprey Arms and get something to eat," Chase said to Tory, who nodded, still looking shyly at Noah.

They were back out of the store, with Chase shaking his head. "Do all the girls look at you like that or just the computer geeks? Thought she was going to ask you to play 'where's my floppy' in the middle of the showroom floor."

Noah sighed as the brisk October air hit them. North Coast Outfitters was located in an old sail loft along the harbor's edge, right next to the Queensbay Marina, and the Osprey Arms, Queensbay's fanciest, and pretty much only, hotel and restaurant.

"Just the computer geeks, unfortunately. Not like the swimsuit models you get to hang out with."

Chase gave another laugh. "They're sporting apparel models, and they're all professionals. It's just another photo shoot on a yacht for them."

"Whatever you say," Noah said, giving his friend a playful shove. It felt good to be out here on the water, hanging out with his old buddy. It was hard to keep up pretensions around someone who knew you when you had braces and Star Wars pajamas.

"Isn't life grand?" Chase said, breathing deep into the air as he stood overlooking the harbor, letting the fall sunlight soak into him. Noah shoved his hands in his coat. He was still wearing one of his father's. If he was going to stay in Queensbay, maybe he should take a look around the store, let Tory talk him into some kind of overpriced jacket he probably didn't need.

A guy who worked at the marina nodded at Chase, who waved a friendly hand in greeting. As he pushed open the door to the Osprey Arms, the front desk clerk, a young man with a blond ponytail, acknowledged them with a friendly, "Hello."

Chase led the way, and when the maître d' appeared, was greeted with a smile and respect.

"Usual table, John."

"Of course, Mr. Sanders." They were led past empty tables towards the back where a wall of glass afforded a sweeping view of the harbor. The wind was kicking up small whitecaps on it, and channel marker buoys bounced up and down. There were no boats out now, though Noah could see that more than a few, including some heavy duty fishing boats, were still moored in the harbor.

They settled in, both ordering iced tea. Chase leaned back and looked at him, a serious expression on his face.

"How are you holding up, Noah?"

Noah felt himself sink into his chair. He and Chase kept in touch through email and phone, but their busy schedules had made it harder and harder to get together in person, and Noah realized that he had missed that.

"Okay. A bit of a shock, despite what you said."

Chase nodded. He had told Noah that Maxwell was acting kind of off.

"I heard about his last night at the club. He was spending a lot of time with Caitlyn." Chase said the name carefully.

"Yes. I guess I'm actually glad for that. That he had someone. But he was still alone, at the end."

"Well, in some way, aren't we all? At least you got a chance to talk to him, you know, open the lines of communication."

Noah snorted. "He wanted money, Chase, and I said no. I guess he was desperate enough to sell it, even to me. And now I get to run it and take on the likes of Caitlyn Montgomery. She is pissed at me. Do you know why?"

"She hates your guts?" Chase said, offhandedly.

"That was a long time ago. Don't you think she could have forgiven me by now?"

Chase's mouth twitched, and his eyes danced. "I don't think girls like to be called teases. Kind of steams them. Oh, and not returning her phone calls. Seems like you were pretty clear you were over her. Maybe she's really good at carrying a grudge."

"A grudge?" Noah said, watching Chase carefully. "How would you know about that?" Chase had told him that he'd had lunch with Caitlyn, but that was it. He felt his hands wrap around the edge of the table, the white cloth bunching up underneath his curled fingers.

"I told you I looked her up in London. But we spend most of our time talking about you. Or we would if she'd admit to it. Sure, she put on a good face, but I don't think she'd quite left that summer behind, and judging from your reaction, neither did you." Chase smiled smugly as he took a sip of his iced tea and picked up the laminated menu.

Noah took a look out the window and watched the water, giving himself a chance to settle down. Chase had said he'd never gone out with Caitlyn, but that didn't mean he hadn't tried. Girls had flocked to him when they were kids, and they still did.

"So you never even tried…?" Noah hesitated. He didn't want to know, but had to. Maybe he was kidding himself, and this was Chase's way of breaking it to him that Caitlyn was taken.

"No, never. I'll be honest. I thought about it, more than once, but she's always kept me at an arm's distance. Besides, like I told you, her ex was a piece of work. You didn't want to look twice at her; otherwise, her ex would be all over you."

A waiter came up to him, and Chase ordered the crab cakes. Noah looked at his menu, impatient to continue the conversation, and picked shrimp scampi, the first thing that jumped out at him.

"What do you mean? About her ex?" He had thought about what Chase had said at the funeral and the way Caitlyn seemed almost jumpy around him.

Chase grimaced. "Real son of a bitch. Sure, he was all old chap this and old chap that, but if he so much as caught you looking at Caitlyn, he'd turn into a real prick, to say nothing of the way he looked at her."

"Look at her, like what?" Noah felt a cold rage settle into him. He'd heard about Caitlyn's engagement; well, he had read about it. Her fiancé Michael was kind of a somebody over there in London, and their coupling had landed them on some gossip pages. He didn't normally read them, but he'd set alerts for her name, so anytime she was mentioned, she had shown up in his inbox.

Chase shrugged. "He seemed like the jealous, possessive type. I wanted to look out for her, but I didn't want to cause her any trouble. So I kinda stopped seeing her in London. But since she's been back, we go to lunch every once in a while. She's thinking of getting a boat, so I've been looking over listings with her."

"Listings?" Noah said.

"She wants to go used, which is a good choice. It's been awhile since she's been out on one, so I think she misses it. It's just the boats for sale section my friend, nothing more."

Their meal came with soup, clam chowder, and the waiter set down a bowl in front of each of them.

Noah ladled a bit of the hot, fragrant soup into his mouth. It was good, a closely guarded recipe - and the restaurant's secret weapon.

"So, is she seeing anyone else?" Noah finally asked.

Chase just shook his head. "What are we, fourteen? Shouldn't you ask her yourself? Seeing as how you're, like, totally not over her?" His voice rose, in an approximation of a cheerleader, Noah guessed.

"I am, like, so over her," Noah replied, doing his best to keep up the act.

"Whatever." Chase got in the last word.

Chapter 17

Caitlyn traded icy smiles with Sam Harris for a few more minutes, and then she made her way back down the hallway to her office. Eyes followed her, but she didn't stop. She meant to say something to Heather, tell her that it would be all right, but she wasn't at her desk. Caitlyn went into her office and sank into her chair, trying to keep her emotions in check. Her phone rang. Caitlyn intended to ignore it, but it kept ringing. The caller ID said "private." It could be, hope against hope, a client - one who wanted her to manage a very large account with total carte blanche, and oh, by the way, knew several other friends and family also looking for a genius of a financial manager.

It hardly ever worked that way, Caitlyn thought, but you needed to try. Straightening up in her chair, she plastered her best smile on her face.

"Hello, this is Caitlyn Montgomery."

"Kit-Cat," Michael St. John said, his voice silky smooth, so English you could smell the tea and crumpets.

She waited - waited for her stomach to flip, her knees to tremble, her mouth to go dry. Nothing. Nothing happened, no reaction of love, or fear, or desire. She felt not one iota of anything for him, beyond the mild irritation that she had to speak to him at all.

"Hello, Michael, I thought I told you I didn't want to speak to you anymore." Her own voice was steady and even, her palms without a trace of nervous sweat. It was a glorious feeling, this sense of freedom, that he no longer had any kind of hold over her, that she would no longer drop everything to be with him, that she would no longer lose herself in an effort to be more pleasing to him. No more would she spend hours wondering how to have dinner with him, spend the day with him, make love to him, all of the things she had worried and fretted over with him. The last thing she had ever been with him was herself.

"Caitlyn." His voice was a reproach, chastising her for not calling. He waited, and when she said nothing, merely shuffled through some papers on her desk, he rushed on.

"I've been wishing to speak with you."

"Well, I suppose I was unlucky enough to pick up. What can I do for you?"

"I was hoping you would come back, Caitlyn." His voice was pitched low, a tone to make her think he was a sensitive soul.

"You know I won't."

"I've fixed things up for you. Everyone understands that it was just a mistake, not even yours - they're all clear on that. I have people ready and waiting to become your clients."

Clever, Caitlyn thought, he was dangling the very thing he had taken from her. And what he thought was her weak spot.

"You know that I won't do that, Michael. I thought I had made it very clear to you." She kept her voice calm, reasonable, as if talking to an angry child. She knew that it would infuriate him. Michael couldn't stand it when people were indifferent to him.

"But you can't possibly be so stubborn, Caitlyn. There's a lot of money involved in this. I know how you like money."

Of course she did. Who didn't? But it wasn't stubbornness this time; it was pride. Michael St. John, a man consumed by his own ego and arrogance, seldom met anyone who didn't come around to his way of thinking. Caitlyn was defying his wishes, and in so doing, she was making herself that much more alluring to him.

"We could work something else out. Find a totally different position for you. I could talk to a few friends. Caitlyn, it doesn't have to be this way." He was actually pleading with her.

Caitlyn pictured him, an ocean away, at his desk in his office, behind glass doors, turned towards the windows, looking out on a London that would be on its way into nightfall. It would be cold and rainy, of course, the weather a virtual guarantee.

He would be sitting there in a crisp white shirt, handmade to fit him precisely. Suspenders, crisscrossed against his back, silk foulard tie with a discreet yet quirky pattern. Wool suit trousers, polished, hand-cobbled wingtips. Blue eyes straining to convey sincerity, blond hair so fair and fine that it fit his head like a golden cap. Manicured hands, Mont Blanc pens on the desk, everything the finest from shops and stores that the general public never knew existed, shops that catered to the last of the dying breed, the gentleman. No one would ever guess at the anger and the cruelty that lay beneath.

That image of him speaking to her, thousands of miles away, moved her not at all. She checked her vital signs where Michael was concerned and found that she was not registering, not even anger.

She was in control, had the upper hand, and though she did not wish to torture him, would never use it in that way, it fortified her to know that she did not weaken in the face of his relentless and wheedling charm.

"Michael, our problems go far beyond a job."

"Or you wouldn't have to work at all, once we were married," he said over her, and she almost laughed.

"What a kind offer, Michael, but as I was saying, we have other problems, as you might recall, and I don't really see any way around those. You chose your path, Michael, and now you need to live with those consequences."

Even as she said it, she doubted that he ever worried about the consequences, unless they were good ones. If they were not, he simply did his utmost to manipulate the situation back to his advantage.

"Caitlyn, what more do I have to say? It was a mistake, and I wish you would forgive me."

She noticed that he did not say he was sorry, and she wondered which mistake he was talking about.

"I can forgive you, Michael," she said, meaning it, "but I can't forget and, quite simply, I can't quite trust you. And I can't live that way."

"Kit-Cat, please." Only he used that nickname, and now she hated it. "Give me another chance; please let me make it up to you. Fly here, and then we'll go to Paris for the weekend, or the Alps to ski. Or someplace warm, instead. Anyplace you wish. Please let me show you that I still care."

Caitlyn almost laughed, but that would have been a mistake. More than most men, Michael believed he possessed special gifts in bed. Like most women, Caitlyn had not found that to be the case, her attraction to Michael having been much deeper and more complicated than that.

"No, Michael, absolutely not. It's over. You made your choice when you decided to sleep with Zoë in our bed. I knew you were a flirt, but you crossed a line. You humiliated me, Michael, and that was the last straw, the last."

"Caitlyn, you made me realize my mistake. Please, how many times do I have to say I'm sorry?"

Just once, she thought, and mean it. To forgive didn't mean to forget. "It won't make a difference. It's over. We're over."

There was a pause, and all of the pleading went out of his voice, replaced with the cold, hard edge she remembered so well. "Don't think you will get away from me so easily, Caitlyn. You were mine, and I am not accustomed to letting what's mine walk away."

"Michael, I was never yours." Caitlyn hung up, the click of the receiver adding to the finality of her words. He was probably calling her a bitch, but she decided she did not care, and this, too, was another step towards freedom for her.

Her breath hitched, and she saw that her hands were shaking. She had lied, those last words. She had let Michael think that she was biddable, too impressed by who he was.

"Are you okay?" Heather looked in the door. Caitlyn glanced up and saw the look of concern on Heather's face. It was obvious that she had been standing there awhile. Heather was young, but not dumb.

"I'm fine."

"Are you sure?" Heather took another step in and stood there, hands twisted together, looking uncertain.

Caitlyn gave a short bark of laughter. "Ever had a bad breakup?"

Heather smiled. "Who hasn't?"

"Right, I guess it's a rite of passage. This one just won't get the hint that it's over." Caitlyn smiled, starting to feel a little less shaky.

"Well, if you want, I can screen all of your calls for a while, you know, if you just tell me who to look out for."

Caitlyn smiled at Heather, who looked less nervous and more than a little excited at the prospect of being useful.

"That would be very helpful." Caitlyn, struck by inspiration, added, "Would you like to grab lunch together? My old friend just took over the deli on Main Street. She's turned into a fun little café. It's about time I stopped by, and my schedule's free. My treat."

Heather beamed. "That would be great."

Caitlyn smiled, feeling better, and watched as Heather went back to her own desk. In the meantime, she tried to push the thoughts of Michael St. John and his threat to the back of her mind.

Chapter 18

Caitlyn had enjoyed her lunch with Heather. The deli had been renamed The Golden Pear. The owner, Darby Reese, was an old friend from high school. They'd fallen out of touch for awhile, but since they had both returned to Queensbay at the same time, they'd become friendly again. Now Darby, a former lawyer had taken over her family's former deli and had turned it into elegant breakfast and lunch place.

Darby was much happier keeping the people of Queensbay supplied with baked goods than she had ever been practicing law. And it didn't hurt that she also found the love of her life with Sean Callahan, the chef at the Osprey Arms.

She and Heather had both ordered salads, and when Darby had sent over a piece of chocolate cake, they had bonded over a mutual love of chocolate and Caitlyn had felt more at ease than she had in a while. It was nice to have a friend again. Heather didn't disguise the fact that she was more interested in fashion than in finance, but that didn't bother Caitlyn as long as she did her job.

After a cup of espresso to banish the carb coma, they had returned to the office, laughing over a shared joke. Caitlyn had just made it back to her desk, ready to look through her email and messages, when Heather rang her.

"You have a call." Heather had been briefed and was screening her calls.

"From who?"

"A Mrs. Biddle."

"Who's Mrs. Biddle?" Caitlyn asked, the name not familiar to her.

"A client. She's threatening to pull her money out of the firm if you don't speak to her."

She told Heather to put Mrs. Biddle through. An irate client, just what she needed to deal with right now.

"Hello?" The voice was too loud, as if the woman were shouting into the phone.

"Yes, hello, this is Caitlyn Montgomery. Is this Mrs. Biddle?"

"Yes, it is, where's Jeffrey?"

"Jeffrey?" Caitlyn asked and then remembered. He had left, a young man whose marginal brainpower was compensated for by superior family connections. He had decided it was time to try his hand at independent film producing. His timely departure had helped create the vacancy for Caitlyn to fill.

"Jeffrey Walsh. I always used to speak to him."

"He's left the company."

"I told them if they changed account managers on me one more time, I would take all of my money and store it under my pillow."

Caitlyn decided the woman was only half-serious, so she took a bit of a risk.

"That would be very unwise, Mrs. Biddle. Your pillow won't pay you any interest."

"You're a good deal smarter than Jeffrey." Caitlyn did not dispute that.

"What can I really do for you, Mrs. Biddle?"

"I need a date for tomorrow night. Jeffrey was always happy to escort me to these events," Mrs. Biddle continued over Caitlyn's astonished pause.

"Yes, but I'm not Jeffrey," Caitlyn said as she dug through the papers on her desk, desperately hoping to find something, anything on Mrs. Biddle. She pulled up a sheet and glanced at it. Her decision was made clearer by the amount of money in the account.

"However, I'm free tomorrow evening." Caitlyn decided she didn't care when or what for.

"Are you? Well, isn't that convenient? It's a reception, a cocktail reception. The press will be there. You can dress appropriately, I assume?"

"I assure you, I can."

"Very well, my car will pick you up at five tomorrow." Somehow, over the course of the conversation, Mrs. Biddle's voice had changed from shaky and tremulous to sure and commanding.

"Yes, Mrs. Biddle, that sounds fine." Caitlyn marked the date down in her calendar and thought about the problem of what to wear.

Chapter 19

Noah stared at the whisky in his glass. He swirled it gently, as if he hoped that he would find the answers he had been looking for in the amber liquid. He should give it up. He knew that drinking never solved the problem. Sure, it might put things in perspective for a little while, but ultimately it wouldn't give him the answers he was searching for.

Whisky hadn't helped his father get out of his current crisis. Or had it? He'd wondered about that - if Maxwell, knowing that the firm was no longer his, had decided that there was no further reason to keep on. Noah hadn't been subtle when he had made the offer to his father. Noah hadn't wanted to be the bigger man, and his father had been in no position to demand it. Noah's money had saved the firm.

And when it was done, had his father thanked him? Not likely. No, his father had told him to stay the hell out of it. However, the simple fact was that Noah could have done anything he wanted. But he stayed away, too pissed at his father to care.

He looked blankly at the painting above the fireplace. It was an abstract, large blocks of color fading out to nothing at the edge. It made no sense to him, but it had probably cost a fortune. That was Maxwell; his father was always spending money on the showy things.

This was where he had walked in on Caitlyn, that first day. She had been looking for something - what, she had never admitted to, he realized belatedly. The whole thing didn't make sense. Why was she back here? She hadn't exactly sworn off Queensbay the way he had, but she had been pretty broken up by Lucas's death - and none too happy that Maxwell had taken over the firm. She had even accused Maxwell of robbing the Montgomery family. So why was she back?

He heaved himself off the couch. He had traded his power suit for jeans and a t-shirt. It was taking some work getting used to the East Coast in late fall, and he was glad for the warmth that brushed his skin as he passed in front of the fire on his way to his father's desk.

Noah looked at the vast expanse of mahogany with its almost-bare top. His father hadn't liked clutter, so anything interesting was likely in the drawers below. Noah began his search.

Chapter 20

He pounded on the door. The Montgomery house rose tall and proud on the bluff overlooking Queensbay Harbor. The original part of the house had been built almost two hundred years ago by a seafaring ancestor, and since then the Montgomery clan had flourished as ship builders, merchants and then as bankers. Each successive generation had added onto the house, so that now it was large and rambling, with some fanciful Victorian touches, painted a creamy white with dark blue shutters. Its constant was a wide, wraparound porch. He was on it now, sheltered from the wind blowing off the water. Still, it was cold out in the dark, and he hadn't thought to bring a coat. There were lights on in the house, so he knew she was home.

"Caitlyn, open up! I need to speak to you."

There was a sound, and he paused. Finally she answered, "Go away."

"Not going to work this time," he told her, remembering how she had said that to him once and he had been fool enough to listen. She'd never let him back in. But this time was different.

He tried the door handle, and it turned.

"Next time try locking the door," he said as he let himself him. She stood in the hall, on the faded runner, hands on her hips. She had changed from the day and was wearing a pair of black sweats, a sweatshirt and bare feet. Her black hair was pulled back in a messy ponytail, and her eyes glowed an electric blue in the light from the wall sconces. Noah felt his pulse quicken as he took her all in. She was lovely to him, but he could tell that she was mad.

"Perhaps I was expecting someone," she said, tilting her head.

He felt his heart stutter and the slightest twinge of jealously. It hadn't occurred to him that she might have someone else. Chase had sworn he had harbored no intentions towards her, but that didn't mean... Noah swallowed. After all, she was the one who had gotten engaged. She had moved on; that's what that meant.

"Then I'll be brief," he said, though he had no intention of leaving anytime soon.

"I suppose you'll want a glass of wine, then?"

She didn't wait for an answer but turned on her heel and walked down the hallway to the kitchen. He walked in and noticed the changes right away. It was lighter than he remembered, less old money and more casual beach house.

She noticed his regard, and said, "Serena," as if that explained it. She picked up the wine she had been drinking. He realized that she never referred to her mother by anything other than her first name. It made sense. Serena had been only seventeen when she'd had Caitlyn and, if truth be told, none too happy about it. Motherhood, in name or actuality, hadn't suited her, and Caitlyn had really been raised by her grandparents, Lucas and Elizabeth.

"I like it," he said, the look appealing to him. It felt more like a home than his father's place.

She didn't respond to that, instead saying, "What do you want?" Her tone made it clear that she was not happy.

"Tell me how it happened," he said, tired of beating around the bush. He had met with the police, and they had given him the official report, but Caitlyn had been there. She had been the last one to see him alive, and the first one to find him.

"Noah, you don't..." she said. Her eyes softened. "It's better that you don't know."

"Would it have been better for you if you never knew about Lucas?" He tossed it back at her, and her eyes went cold again, her mouth set in a firm, straight line. He remembered the way her lips had molded under his once. She'd been young and eager, and it felt like they fit together. They couldn't be together more than a few minutes without wanting to kiss, to touch each other. His skin felt warm, and he felt himself stir with desire.

She dropped her eyes and took a sip of her wine. "That was different. I needed to make sense of what happened."

"Caitlyn, I need to make sense of what happened. You need to tell me; you were there."

She looked at him, her gaze level, considering, and then she began. "We went to dinner at the club. He insisted on driving me, but I realized about halfway through dinner that there was no way he could drive home. So I stopped drinking, which only seemed to make him madder."

Noah nodded. His father didn't like to be told he was drinking too much. It only served to make his temper nastier and the drinks to go down faster.

239

"Our dinner was not pleasant. He was, to be honest, a bit of an asshole that night." Her eyes closed, and her hand gripped the counter, as if she were remembering.

"And," Noah prompted, deciding that he didn't need to know what they had talked about. He had a fairly good idea anyway.

"I drove him home, walked him into the house and left him in the foyer. I left, walked home across the lawn. I watched some TV, sent some emails, had a cup of tea and went to bed. The next morning I got up, went to work. When he wasn't there, I became worried. So I drove back to his house and found him."

She paused, watching him carefully.

"How did you know where to look?" Noah asked.

"I didn't at first. I came into the house, which was unlocked," she said, before he could ask, "and then I searched around. His car was there, so I was reasonably certain he hadn't left. I was upstairs, looking out the window, when I thought of the bluff and the stairs. It had been rather warm that night, and somehow I just knew, just felt."

Noah nodded.

Caitlyn went on, remembering, as if he wasn't even there. "I ran to the edge and looked down. The stairs were broken, like someone had fallen, so I ran back to my house and my stairs. I went down them and looked. I didn't see anything at first, but then I went right to his stairs and saw him."

She paused. He saw her eyes glisten, and she hurriedly swiped a tear from the corner of her eye with the back of her hand.

"I ran over to him, tried to find a pulse, but I didn't. I had my cell phone with me and called the police. I started to shout for help, and one of the neighbors came down and ... well, I don't know; it was kind of a blur," she admitted. She turned and busied herself with straightening the kitchen towels that hung on the handle of the oven.

Noah watched her, the way the low light of the room caught the dark highlights in her hair, the way her blue eyes glittered with unshed tears. He took a deep breath, fighting back the wave of protectiveness, the urge to reach out and touch her that was rising up in him. He still had questions, and she had the answers.

"It must have brought back memories," he said, his tone more harsh than he had meant.

She looked at him, and something between fear and loathing crossed her face.

"I don't think there was anything similar in the two situations." He could tell she was fighting her memories of her grandfather, from the coldness in her eyes, in the way she stood, arms folded, keeping her distance from him.

"The thought crossed my mind." Noah tried to keep his voice level. "Two men, same business, take the easy way out."

"An easy way out?" Caitlyn hissed. "Is that what you think it was for him, for either of them?" She swallowed, as if she were trying to find her control, and it was a moment before she spoke again.

"I know you didn't care anymore, but I did. About my grandfather, Maxwell and the firm. I know it seems trite and silly to you, but it means something to me. My grandfather, he wanted me to be a part of it. He wanted it to be a legacy passed on to me. It was who I was meant to be."

Noah felt his blood burn. There had always been that between the two of them. The firm. A goddamn piece of what? Offices and filing cabinets, tradition and responsibility, and he had wanted none of it - and she had wanted all of it.

"You never told me what you were doing in my father's house the other day." He took a sip of wine. It was heavy, bold with a hint of spice. Caitlyn's eyes watched him over the rim of her glass, her gaze inscrutable. She was an excellent poker player; he remembered that. He and Chase had lost their shirts, figuratively, and once literally, playing with her. He saw nothing in her face that gave anything away.

"I don't see how it's any of your business." She made a move to get up and away from him, but he snaked his arm out and pulled her close to him, so he could look into her eyes.

"Babe, it's all my business now." The term of endearment, which she had once loved, made her nostrils flare and her breath quicken. Firelight danced over her skin, pale, almost ivory-like. He could smell her, a combination of the spicy wine and her own perfume, a heady and overpowering scent.

Caitlyn smelled rich. He was reminded as he had been a long time ago by Lucas, that he was out of her league. Quickly he tamped the thought down and sent silent curses out to the ghost of the old man who haunted him still. Noah had vaulted several leagues ahead, hadn't he?

She dropped her eyes down to his hand on her arm, and he let go. She answered, "I gave your father a letter. A formal proposal for buying Queensbay Capital from him."

She pulled away from him so he could no longer smell her, no longer feel her warmth. God, she was killing him, the look of her, the way she had filled out in all the right places, the way she looked angry. He felt himself grow hard with want, the desire to touch her and kiss her overwhelming him.

"You wanted to buy the firm?" If he'd been twenty again, he would have thrown himself at her to see if she would have him. Still, he was a grown, successful man. He took a deep, cleansing breath and put another step between them, knowing that disbelief showed on his face.

She drew herself up to her full height, five-seven in her bare feet yet still managing to glare at him down her nose.

"I told you that, yet you still sound surprised." Her voice was dangerously quiet, and he knew he should retreat.

"It was a rather expensive purchase." The words were out of his mouth before he realized just how pompous they sounded.

"Then you probably paid too much," she said coolly, lifting her wine glass to her lips and drinking.

"I..." He didn't know what to say to that. He considered the fact that perhaps his father had been playing him after all and that Caitlyn, with her advantage of having worked there, might just have known more than she was letting on.

"I hear that's what paper billionaires like to do ... overspend in certain areas to overcompensate for deficiencies in other areas." Amusement tinged her words, but there was a dangerous glint in her eyes.

"You might be surprised. Care to find out what you've been missing all of these years? I can assure you that all my assets are impressive."

He knew as soon as the rough proposition was out that it had been a mistake. Caitlyn made a move, a sudden, violent move. He wasn't sure if he expected a slap, but it was the warm, red liquid that hit him square in the face. Noah managed a smile and licked his lips slowly, as if savoring every last drop of it.

"Get out," Caitlyn said, her voice quivering with carefully controlled anger.

He swiped a hand over his face, not caring what dropped on the floor. He backed away, his eyes holding hers, until he was in the doorway. Then and only then did he turn his back to her and leave her house.

Chapter 21

She managed to put thoughts of Noah out her mind, although not quite successfully, as she pulled out the mop and cleaned up the mess she had made in her own house. Dramatic moves like that were better done with white wine, or someplace with a cleaning crew, she thought as she mopped up the liquid.

But what he said had bothered her. An accident. Maxwell had stood there, on the bluff night after night - and had never fallen. But that night? His frame of mind had been, what? Angry, mean, nasty. Had he been despondent? There was something wrong with the firm. She had figured that out soon after being there. Yes, she had dug around a bit, saw that things were on shaky ground. She knew he needed money and had offered it. But he had pushed it away, going to Noah.

Had he been so upset, so defeated, he'd given up? Had things been that bad? She'd done her part to bolster things, but was it enough? Had he been hiding more losses from them? Had Noah known, or had Maxwell seen an easy target in his son?

She wrung the mop out and made her way up to bed, her thoughts troubled. Sleep didn't come easily, and her body twisted and turned as she thought about Noah. She had finally given up about two in the morning and found some outdated investor magazines to read down in the study. Those had done the trick, and she had woken, cramped and stiff, but with the light of dawn in the sky.

She was tired and cranky when she went into the office, and it seemed as if everyone else had had a restless night, too. The office was subdued as everyone watched, looking for glimpses of the new boss. She saw him here and there, in Max's office, talking with Sam Harris, pacing, talking on the phone. At one point, she was certain he was staring at her from across the row of cubicles, but he had looked away before she was sure.

She had a plan. If they ignored each other, this just might work. However, she spent so much time making sure that she did, and trying to see whether he was doing the same, that she got little done.

And when four o'clock rolled around, she realized she needed to get a move on if she was going to make it to her "date" tonight.

Caitlyn changed in the bathroom at work. It was rather small and uncomfortable, but she was managing the contortions required to slip into her dress when Heather walked in, looked surprised, and almost walked right back out.

"No, it's all right. Just another minute or two." Caitlyn had traded her work suit for a black dress, which hit just about the knee, with spaghetti straps, a plunging back and just enough of a dip in front to keep it interesting. A gauzy wrap, ill-suited for warding off the fall chill, and shoes with heels up to there helped to compete the look. She wasn't dressed for comfort, but she looked too good to care.

"I thought this wasn't a date?" Heather asked, her green eyes lighting up with interest.

Caitlyn laughed as she put on one of her diamond earrings. "It's not. I mean, Mrs. Biddle didn't sound like my idea of a date."

She had asked Heather to call Mrs. Biddle back to tell her that Caitlyn would meet her at her house at five. She didn't need a ride in a car.

"Adriana Biddle always took Jeffrey to the best places," Heather said wistfully. "I think she knew he wanted to be an actor, so she brought him to all of these movie openings and things like that." Heather rinsed her hands and dried them, giving Caitlyn a friendly but critical once-over.

"Here, I think you should wear it like that," Heather said. She tugged on Caitlyn's dress, and all of a sudden it settled just right. Caitlyn looked in the mirror, pleased by what she saw.

"Which earrings?" She held up one of each pair - one a chandelier drop, the other a cluster of diamonds.

"The drops, I think, younger, and better with the dress."

Caitlyn tried them on, and nodded at the makeup spread out on the counter. "Okay, smoky eye or something low-key?"

Heather looked over the assorted tubes and containers, then opened her own purse. "Smoky, definitely. The look might be a bit edgy, but with your dark hair and light eyes, we really want to play up the contrast."

Caitlyn smiled, enjoying the girl talk. It had been too long since she had gotten dressed up to go anywhere by herself.

"Well, go at it. I know it's not in your pay grade, but I'm sensing I'm in the hands of an expert."

Heather smiled and patted the counter. Caitlyn jumped up and closed her eyes while Heather got to work.

Almost as an afterthought, Caitlyn asked, "Did you say 'Adriana'?" as Heather brushed something over her cheeks.

Heather paused. "Yes, Adrianna Biddle, though Jeffrey only ever called her Mrs. Biddle. I think he was a bit afraid of her, as much as she tried to help him, but she was always pleasant enough on the phone. Why?"

"No reason," Caitlyn said. "I just didn't know her first name. Adriana."

"Yes, it's a pretty name," Heather said, and then, "You're done."

Caitlyn jumped down and turned, looking at herself in the mirror. "Wow," she said. Heather had been an artist, doing something with the materials at hand to create a look that made Caitlyn feel ... sexy.

"I went for the sultry thing. Jeffrey always said that wherever they went there were sure to be some celebrities, and well, I just thought you should bring your A-game. I know we work in finance and your suits are fine, but this..."

"Is taking it to a whole new level." Caitlyn swished her hair a bit. She had always taken time with her looks, but had never thought of herself as a slave to them. Now her dark hair framed a face that showed sculpted cheekbones, dark, dramatic brows and glittering blue eyes. With the drop earrings and black dress, she looked and felt like a panther on the prowl. Perhaps tonight might just be the night to catch something.

"Do you like it?" Heather said nervously.

Caitlyn turned to her. "I love it. I would hug you, but I don't want to ruin your work. I look good. Different but good." Caitlyn gave her hair a little shake. She felt better than good; she felt sleek, sexy and powerful. She hadn't thought that she needed a makeover, but here Heather had made her feel a bit like Cinderella.

Heather smiled back at her in the mirror, as her hands separated and sorted all of the makeup containers.

"Well, happy hunting tonight. Whatever you're after."

Heather left her alone in the bathroom, and Caitlyn had a few moments to herself, to change over from her day purse to her evening purse, while her mind turned over the possibilities. The Adriana she knew hadn't been named Biddle. She had been named Randolph. And she would be ancient, wouldn't she? Then Caitlyn realized, after some quick calculations, she would only be in her late sixties. Not that old. The one and the same? One last look in the mirror had Caitlyn reminding herself that Adriana Biddle, whoever she was, was a big client. Big clients got big treatment.

The drive to Mrs. Biddle's house was familiar, and after a few moments, Caitlyn ignored the directions and the address Heather had written out for her and simply followed her memory. Mrs. Biddle did not live near the water, but in a wooded section of the town that was crisscrossed by small, winding roads, cul-de-sacs and tall, old growth trees. Caitlyn pulled into 127 Meriwether Road a few minutes before five and followed the winding driveway until the house finally appeared, set in a clearing among the trees.

Caitlyn stopped, turned the ignition off and surveyed. It was a large house, built in the late 1930s, white stucco cut across by wood beams that gave it a faintly Tudor appearance, a look helped along by a steeply pitched slate roof, many gables and a rounded tower sprouting from it. Even in the fading light, she could see that the garden was in its winter mode, burlap sacks tied over bushes, the grass faded and waiting for spring.

Lights winked on and off in various rooms of the house, but Caitlyn sensed little life in there. The house seemed empty, windows on the upper floor looking down at her with black, blank pools of glass.

Caitlyn pulled her wrap more tightly around her, picked up her evening bag and started up the well-lit fieldstone walk. She rang the door, and it was a brief moment before an older woman, fiftyish, rather plump in a black skirt and a cream-colored blouse, answered it.

"Miss Montgomery."

Caitlyn nodded and followed the woman in.

"Hello, Marion," Caitlyn said, dredging the woman's name up from her memory.

Marion smiled. "Well, I wasn't sure that you would remember me, child. You have grown."

Caitlyn nodded. Marion had grown older, too, her blonde hair shading towards gray at the roots, her body a little more round.

"You are really quite pretty now, aren't you?"

It wasn't a question that demanded an answer, which was just as well since Caitlyn found herself blushing.

It had been close to twelve years since she had seen Marion, since she had been a guest in this house. Then she had been an awkward adolescent, an unwelcome guest at a grown-up party, the result of her mother having not arrived home when she should have and her grandfather's not wanting to cancel a social commitment. It had happened more than once that summer, and Caitlyn had grown used to spending her time in Marion's kitchen, while the woman made tea and baked gingerbread, endless batches of gingerbread, which Marion must have thought the cure to all of adolescence's ills. All it had done with Caitlyn was put on a few pounds that had disappeared once her mother had returned.

"Adriana is back here. You should be ready to go in just a little while. I called Henry and asked him to come around at a quarter to six."

Caitlyn nodded and stepped into the living room. Adriana Randolph Biddle sat there, on her couch, looking through some papers. She looked up as she heard them enter the room, and Caitlyn stepped forward into the light from one of the lamps.

"My goodness," Adriana said, her half-moon glasses slipping off of her nose, a hand going to her heart.

"Mrs. Biddle," Caitlyn said, her voice tight.

Chapter 22

"Caitlyn. It really is you. After all these years. I can see your grandfather in you, and your mother, too."

They spent a few moments there, standing apart, surveying each other. Caitlyn saw a woman who was closer to seventy than to sixty, her silver hair attractively done so that it looked neither too matronly nor too young. A short, beaded jacket and shoes matched a light gray dress. The body under the dress was pulled up straight, neither too skinny nor too plump. Only the hands, wrinkled and spotted, showed her true age. The face was tight, the product, Caitlyn would have had to guess, of at least one session under the knife.

"Would you like to sit down for a moment and have a drink before we leave?"

Caitlyn hesitated.

"Why are you mad, my dear?"

"I'm not mad," Caitlyn said too quickly. Her adolescent sulk was coming back. Adriana's easy charm had always had that effect on Caitlyn, when in truth, that was one of the things she had most envied about the woman.

"Just sit down and let us talk. Marion, please bring me a sherry. Caitlyn, what will you have?"

"White wine, please." Caitlyn moved from the edge of the living room, the colors deep reds and blues, and sat on the couch. "You should have said something on the phone," Caitlyn told her.

"I didn't want you not to come. I was afraid. Did Jeffrey go off to Hollywood, for real?"

Caitlyn nodded, and Mrs. Biddle made a tsk-tsk sound before she continued, "It just seemed that it would be better to talk to you face-to-face. You were very angry with me the last time we saw each other."

"I was very angry in general," Caitlyn said. She wasn't quite ready to apologize, but she could acknowledge it.

"Are you still angry now?" Mrs. Biddle said.

"I feel a little tricked."

"Not about tonight dear." Adrianna paused, and then asked, "Do you still think about it all the time?"

"Yes, but I am not angry anymore," Caitlyn said.

"I miss your grandfather very much," Mrs. Biddle said.

"So do I," Caitlyn admitted. That much was true, and something that they could agree on.

Marion brought their drinks, and Caitlyn was grateful to have something to hold on to. Mrs. Biddle took a sip of her sherry and placed it on the table, on a coaster apparently kept there for that purpose.

There was silence, and with no crackling fire to break it, Caitlyn was aware of every sound - the clock ticking in the hallway, the creaks of the house settling in around her.

"So," Caitlyn said, "where are we going tonight?"

"To a party my nephew is having."

"Your nephew?" Caitlyn had never heard her talk of any family.

Mrs. Biddle nodded. "My husband, Trip Randolph, died about three years ago."

"I'm very sorry," Caitlyn replied automatically, taking a sip of her wine. It was light and crisp and went down smoothly.

Mrs. Biddle shrugged. "I could pretend to be, but we all know that I would be lying. You shouldn't look so shocked, Caitlyn. You can afford to be more honest as you get older."

"Still, you must have loved him once."

"Once was a long time ago." Adrianna gave a regretful shrug of her shoulders. "However, I found that, to a certain extent, after all of these years, I enjoyed being married. I met Aaron Biddle right after the death of Trip. We were married about a year later."

"Congratulations," Caitlyn said automatically.

Mrs. Biddle shrugged. "Unfortunately, he's in a home now. It's easier on both of us. His memory is failing him. It all happened very quickly, and we just couldn't take care of him here, not just the two of us. He is a good deal older than I am. I always did have a thing for older men, you see."

"I see," Caitlyn said, and she did. Her grandfather had been more than ten years older than Adrianna when they had been together.

"Don't feel sorry for me, Caitlyn. Those are just the facts of my life. I loved your grandfather, very much, but it was never meant to be for the two of us. And so we learn to make do. I was very happy with Aaron, believe it or not - I suppose since I knew that there wasn't someone else out there, waiting for me, anymore."

Caitlyn shifted, uncomfortable. She hadn't thought about the realities of her grandfather's relationship with Adriana Randolph in years. Worse, in fact, was that her teenaged mind couldn't grasp the fact that two people, what she had thought of as old, could actually have been in love. Much less engaged in the actual act.

"And the party we're going to tonight?" she asked, trying to change the subject.

"Yes, my nephew, Tony Biddle - Aaron's nephew, really. Just mine by marriage, but since Aaron never had any children, and neither did I, he's just about become a son to us. Tony is opening a new lounge, restaurant thing in the city, and I said I would go. He said that if I were there, then the press would take notice."

Caitlyn couldn't hide the reaction on her face. Mrs. Biddle, before she had been Mrs. Randolph, had been Adriana Wellington, the daughter of a prominent industrialist, a social figure in her own right, solidified by her marriage to Randolph, a wealthy businessman. Adriana had kept her name in the paper through her philanthropy and dedication to nurturing the careers of starving artists.

A word from Adriana could overnight turn an unknown into a known, the works being collected and sold, the artist fortified by money and notoriety that guaranteed the ability to continue to create.

"I know, dear; he was being kind. The press hasn't taken much notice of me lately, which is fine, and deliberate. Besides, I understand that his openings attract enough big names on their own to keep the press in pictures for days."

"No, that's not what I meant," Caitlyn offered her reassurances. "I am just excited to be going to one of his clubs on its opening night. I've been to the one in London."

"This is his second in New York. Apparently it's even more expensive than the other ones. Have you ever met Tony?"

"Actually, yes. Briefly. He stopped by our table. I was with someone he knew." She didn't bother to mention that the someone had been Michael.

Adrianna looked at her shrewdly. "Tony remembers you. He said you're engaged."

"Yes. I was engaged, but now I am not." Caitlyn forced her voice to stay calm, to take a sip of her wine.

"Oh, really? What a pity," Adriana said blandly.

"Not in this case," Caitlyn countered.

"Better before the wedding than after." Adriana raised her own glass in a toast. "Though I suppose that means you're unattached."

Caitlyn felt a sense of dread. "You're not thinking…"

"Of course I'm thinking," she said. "Old people still think."

"I mean, about Tony or me, or anything like that," Caitlyn said.

Mrs. Biddle, in an uncharacteristic display of maternal instinct, had tried to fix Caitlyn up once, when she was sixteen years old, with the grandson of a friend. It had been a disaster. The boy had been pimply and nasty, but headed for Princeton and eager to grope a girl, any girl, before he left for college. Caitlyn had gotten away as quickly as possible.

"Why would you think that, my dear?" she asked.

Caitlyn was fairly certain that Tony Biddle was not all that interested in women, at least as dates.

"I don't think it would work."

"Of course it wouldn't work. Tony doesn't date girls. I know that."

Caitlyn smiled, feeling relieved. "Well, that's clear then."

"That doesn't mean that there won't be plenty of other eligible young men there. In my mind, the best thing after a breakup is to get right back up on the horse. Don't let your heart get too broken, especially if he's the one that did the breaking."

Mrs. Biddle, at a signal from Marion, rose from her seat.

"Who said he did the breaking?" Caitlyn asked, wondering if it were written all over her face.

"Just a hunch, dear. I am sure it was all mutual, or whatever other phrase people call it these days. And that you're in control of the whole situation. Now, are we ready to go?"

Chapter 23

The trip into Manhattan did not take that long, as the traffic was relatively light. Mrs. Biddle's driver, Henry, took the Lincoln Town Car smoothly over the narrow roads of the Merritt Parkway and through the Cross Bronx Expressway into the city. Horatio's, Tony Biddle's newest creation, was in the mid-twenties on Park Avenue South. Adriana kept up a breezy stream of small talk that Caitlyn was able to reply to while trying to remember everything she could about Tony Biddle.

He had once worked in advertising but had spent most of his time in the city going out. Soon he had tired of his day job and had used his family connections to raise money to start a quirky bistro supper club. The restaurant, small and unknown, had quickly become a success, in part because of Tony's infectious personality.

Important people, or those whose opinions seemed to matter, came for the food and returned for Tony. The success had given him the ability to expand. The original bistro was long gone, but now his clubs dotted New York, London and San Francisco. He had a little empire on his hands, and that was all Caitlyn needed to know.

"We're here now," Caitlyn said and couldn't keep the eagerness out of her voice. A club opening wasn't quite a movie premiere, but there was some of the same atmosphere of anticipation with velvet ropes and security at the door combining to create energy, that buzz of a happening, in the air.

Caitlyn gave Mrs. Biddle her arm, and together they walked up the short carpet to the door. A flash popped in their faces, surprising Caitlyn, but the other woman was prepared.

"Smile, Caitlyn. Jeffrey always did photograph well."

Caitlyn smiled in time for the next flash of light and guided Mrs. Biddle into the crowd.

"Will there be people you know?" Caitlyn asked.

"Of course. You won't have to babysit me all night," Mrs. Biddle said as they moved through the double glass doors into the restaurant proper.

"That wasn't what I meant, Mrs. Biddle."

"I think you should call me Adriana now. Mrs. Biddle sounds so formal." It was on the tip of her tongue to say that was how Caitlyn preferred it, but she didn't. Adriana was a client, after all, no matter how complicated their history.

"Fine, Adriana, may I get you something to drink?"

"Yes, let's have champagne." A waitress, hearing this, swished by, and champagne flutes were delivered to them.

"And now let's see if we can find Tony," Adriana said and moved nimbly through the crowd. Caitlyn smiled. The woman was in her element, surrounded by people, certain and confident, and any thought Caitlyn had had of her as old vanished. Gamely, Caitlyn followed, checking off faces she recognized. There were some actors here, not quite stars, but perhaps soon to be. A few people looked like they might be musicians, and there were quite a few others who looked like they belonged on the business side, as managers, promoters or executives.

Caitlyn was aware of more than a few men's eyes following her through the crowd, and in spite of herself, she felt a warm flush, the automatic response to admiration. It had been a good thing, if only for her ego, to come here and to remember that she could still engage in the game of attraction without becoming too involved. She must remember to thank Heather again, tomorrow.

"There you are," Adriana said and pulled Caitlyn closer.

"Caitlyn Montgomery, this is my nephew, Tony Biddle."

"Hello." It was necessary to shout in order to be heard above the noise of the conversation and the pulsing world beat music.

"It's a pleasure to be here," Caitlyn said. "I've been to Daisies in London, and I loved it."

"Thank you." Tony Biddle was, as she remembered from their one brief encounter, a tall man, almost gauntly thin, tending towards baldness, for which he compensated by keeping his head closely shaved. He wore a slate gray turtleneck sweater and black wool trousers, topped off by a leather jacket and shiny, square-toed shoes. He had very white teeth, a tremendous smile, and his manner was warm and friendly, especially towards Adriana, whom he called Addie.

"And what are you doing here with my aunt?" he asked.

"I work for her at Queensbay Capital."

"Ah, the money people."

"That's right."

"Well, Addie was kind enough to help me with my restaurants."

"Over your uncle's objections, I might add," Adriana said.

"Well, I'm sure he was right. Most restaurants fail." Tony laughed, now able to enjoy the joke.

Lights swirled around them, and people started to dance. Waitresses passed around food and drinks; instead of being dressed in the traditional black and white, they were all stunning young women in red dresses that showed off various levels of décolletage. The whole place had the feeling of being inside a genie's bottle, the high ceilings draped in fabric, the swirl of deep, rich colors.

"But you've managed to beat that record quite nicely," Caitlyn said. "Quite an impressive feat."

"Well, I need new investors for the next one. This time I want to go to Tokyo."

"Have you thought about diversifying your portfolio, expanding your investment base, your access to capital?"

"Not really, but I bet you can help with that," Tony said, following it with a wink to let Caitlyn know that she hadn't gone too far.

"Of course I can. I'll give you a call tomorrow, and we can talk further."

Tony looked over at his aunt, whose eyes were already roving the crowd to see who else she knew. He laughed.

"She's always matchmaking somehow. Sure, give me a call tomorrow, and we'll talk. I'm familiar with your work, as they say. I have friends in London."

Caitlyn smiled, hoping that they weren't good friends, and took an appetizer. It was duck in puff pastry and absolutely amazing.

"Wonderful," she told him, and he smiled.

"There's Carlos Mitchell. I really must speak to him. Come along." Adriana pulled Caitlyn's hand, and they moved off through the crowd to an older man, whose jet black hair was accented by silver streaks at the temples, with a face set off by a craggy nose and wide lips.

He smiled when he saw Adriana, and introductions were made. Caitlyn soon lost interest as the two spoke about people she did not know. All the same, she was excited. She had managed to get a meeting with Tony Biddle. He was established, almost a celebrity and certainly knew a few. If she could sign him as a client, then he could well be a stepping-stone, an entrée into world of the young and rapidly rich. Tonight could be very valuable indeed. There were others here, the managers and the producers who needed her services and had access to the clients with the money.

Caitlyn glanced back at Adriana, who was still engrossed with Carlos. They had been joined by a small crowd, and not all of them old. Knowing she would not be missed, Caitlyn began making the rounds. She felt a surge of exhilaration. The hunt was on.

She was doing well, having latched on to someone she knew slightly, a London theater producer who just happened to be in New York at the moment. She managed to exchange cards with quite a few people before she turned around, startled.

"What are you doing here?" Noah said, his face hard to read in the muted lighting of the club.

"I could ask the same of you," she said to him.

"Well, I was invited." His eyes roamed over her, taking in her dress, lingering where it dipped low over her chest, and then traveled slowly up to her eyes.

"And so was I." So there, she thought, but did not say it.

"You look amazing," he whispered, leaning in, his lips brushing past hers so quickly that it could have been inadvertent, but as they pulled apart, she could still feel the warmth of his breath on her cheek, feel the wave of longing that washed over her. He wore a blue shirt, open necked, and a cashmere blazer. His hair was combed back, and he looked, compared to almost everyone else, very tan and golden in the sweeping lights.

"Don't do that," she said automatically.

"And why not? We're colleagues, aren't we? It was just a friendly gesture. Or can't we even be polite to one another? What do you say? Why don't we let bygones be bygones?" His voice was light, even, and he was smiling at her, but there was something else in his eyes.

"I came here with a client," she said, feeling her face burning from where his lips had been. She had promised herself that, no matter what Noah Randall did, she would keep her distance. There would be no more throwing wine at him.

"Adriana?" he guessed.

"How did you know?"

"I was her back-up date if she couldn't get you," he said, smiling. His hand still held hers, and she pulled it away, aware that they were in a room full of people.

"How strange," Caitlyn said.

"Really? Am I that bad?"

"That's not what I meant. I thought I was her back-up. You came on your own?" Caitlyn asked, desperately wanting the answer to be yes, knowing that even if she didn't want him, she didn't want anyone else to, either. Childish, she chided herself, but she couldn't help it.

"Yes. After all, I'm new in town, and you're the only girl I know on this coast."

"I find that hard to believe."

He was looking down at her, tan, handsome, smug, even. Noah had always been cocky, able to walk in a room, look around and soon command the center of attention. But he was no grandstander. People - well, women, Caitlyn admitted to herself - had always gravitated to him, which was why she'd been like an overeager puppy that summer. Sure, she'd done her best to play it cool, using every trick she'd picked up people-watching in Paris, but inside she'd been a big puddle of grateful happiness that Noah Randall wanted her. Ancient history, she reminded herself, and no reason to fawn over him now.

Before he could answer, Tony Biddle descended upon them with a glass of champagne in his hand. He grabbed Noah in a great hug.

"Everyone loves it. They keep asking me who the fairy godmother on this project is. So many people want to meet you. Come, come." He gestured impatiently.

Noah looked at Caitlyn with a smile as he said, "Seems like I'm a wanted man," and followed Tony through the crowd. Caitlyn was puzzled for a moment before she understood that Tony was referring to Noah's involvement as an investor in the restaurant.

Alone now, she looked around until she spotted a group of women, one of whom she had met earlier. Caitlyn sidled up to them, hoping to join in their conversation.

"That's Noah Randall."

"He's cute."

"He's that software entrepreneur. Heard he just sold his company and made a bundle," another one said.

Caitlyn moved in ever so slightly, receiving tepid nods as she went into information-gathering mode.

"I thought he was from California. He was dating the director's daughter, Lakota Reynolds, but they broke up."

"Oh no, they broke up ages ago. You're thinking of the brunette who was just in that movie that made everyone cry. He went to the premiere with her. Pictures, so cute!"

They mentioned the name of the movie, and Caitlyn remembered hearing about it. Unfortunately, the actress's assets had gotten more attention than the actual movie.

"I hear he's moving back to the East Coast." That was news to Caitlyn. She thought he was here only temporarily while he sorted things out with the firm.

A tall, blonde woman looked at him speculatively.

"I heard he was here for a funeral," another one said.

They all agreed he looked a little sad.

"I think I might go and comfort him." The blonde pursed her lips, considering, and then plunged in.

Caitlyn almost said no and then stopped herself. Noah could speak to whomever he wished, and if this woman was his type - tall, tanned, blonde and with abs that could crush beer cans - then far be it from her to stop it. Caitlyn broke away from the group, watching as Blondie made her move on Noah, disengaged him from whomever he was speaking with and worked him out onto the dance floor. Caitlyn took another glass of champagne and watched as the vigorous dancer moved all over Noah.

He caught her eye once and looked almost as if he were pleading for rescue, but she shrugged. He was a grown man, a CEO, and if he could handle investors, employees and customers, he could surely handle one overbearing woman.

Caitlyn didn't let herself be a wallflower, either. A nice banker, Kevin, who was still in his pinstripes, asked her to dance, and she said yes. After that, there were others, and the time passed until she checked her watch, saw it was nearly midnight and, realizing her feet were killing her, knew it was time to find Adriana.

She found her at a table, sitting with a group of people. "There you are, Caitlyn. You looked like you were having a lovely time out there."

Caitlyn smiled. A few of her dance partners had insisted on getting her business card, but she sincerely hoped none of them would call. Her eyes strayed to Noah. He wasn't dancing anymore, but the blonde was still draped over his arm. They stood at the bar, having a drink while Noah talked, the blonde's gaze fixed on him adoringly.

As if he felt her eyes on him, he turned, looked in her direction and held her stare. He did nothing, made no gesture, just looked at her with such intensity, his jaw set, his face dark, that she felt him burning into her. It was an invitation. Caitlyn knew - she knew that if she just walked over there, the blonde would be history and that Noah would take her, be hers. The full realization of how much she wanted that to happen swamped her, and it took all of her willpower to gather Adriana up and hurry her out the door, forcing herself not to look over her shoulder, lest her resolve break.

Boss, Caitlyn told herself. Rich playboy, she said. She'd already made that mistake in London, and she wasn't going to make it again. Not to mention that he was the boy who had dumped her ten years ago because she wasn't ready. He was all of those things, and still, she wanted to throw her caution, her resolve to the wind, and go and find him.

"You seem to be in quite the hurry to go," Adrianna remarked, her voice placid as Henry brought the car around for them. They were near the entrance with the fresh air pouring in and over her, and Caitlyn felt her body settle down, the hot flame of longing dying off.

She could do this. She just needed to stay out of Noah Randall's orbit. He had to go back to California soon, to his real life. Queensbay, the firm, it had to be nothing more than a distraction for him, a distraction from his desire to build and grow things.

Caitlyn looked over. Adriana was staring at her, a shrewd and knowing look on her face. Caitlyn wasn't certain how much of her and Noah's history the old woman knew about. Certainly the fact they'd been a couple that summer hadn't been a secret.

"You knew he'd be here," Caitlyn said, her voice hoarse.

Adriana shrugged. "Perhaps."

"What are you trying to do?" Caitlyn whispered, hearing the pain, the heartbreak in her own voice. Because that's what it was. Noah had broken her heart when he'd left, when they'd had their last fight, and she hadn't forgotten that pain.

"Maybe I still believe in second chances," Adriana said simply and let herself be helped into the car by Henry. Caitlyn waited a moment and then followed.

Chapter 24

Caitlyn woke the next morning as dawn crested. She lay in her old bedroom, which faced the water, and watched from an angle as the sun rose, pushing light up over the ridge of hills that ringed the harbor. The light appeared from behind the spindly branches of the bare trees, turning them into black lines etched against the very pale sky. Cold air seeped in from the window she'd left cracked open, and she took a deep breath, savoring the fragrance of sand and salt water, mixed in with mud, the smell weakened by the strong fall wind.

In the summer, the whole scent would be stronger, and there would be more to it, perhaps a whiff of gasoline, the smell of barbeque. Instead, this morning she could smell fire, someone burning leaves.

She moved slowly as if testing herself. She did not have a headache, which was a good sign. She hadn't drunk that much last night and was glad of it, since she'd been avoiding her runs along the beach, a normal but silly reaction to finding Maxwell dead upon it. But she shouldn't keep putting it off any longer. She needed to reclaim her beach, from both the dead and the living. Caitlyn pulled on her warm running pants, a turtleneck and a fleece vest.

Setting off from the drive, she took her traditional path, finding her stride a little rough after her time off. She didn't really like the exercise bit, but it was something she had to do, she reminded herself. It got a little better after the first mile, and she started to zone out, focusing only on her breathing and putting one foot in front of the other.

She had to pass Sailor's Rock, but it wasn't until she rounded the bend for the final stretch that she saw him standing there against the sky, hair blowing. She guessed he had made it home last night after all. She looked away quickly, eyes straight ahead of her as she ran towards home. She had as much right to be on the beach as anyone else.

"Caitlyn," he called, the name stretching out with the wind. She debated whether or not to keep going, but he called her name again. She stopped and slowly walked over to him, wishing she were strong enough to keep running, but knowing only that she wanted to go to him. Avoiding him wasn't working when he seemed to be everywhere. She would need to find a better way to keep her distance from him.

Chapter 25

Noah had a feeling she'd be here; in fact, he was waiting for her. He hadn't been quick enough to see her leave, had wondered if she'd left with the guy in the suit, the banker who'd been all over her all night.

She was breathing heavily, beads of sweat across her forehead.

"So, you got home all right?" she asked casually.

"Alone, but no thanks to you," he smiled faintly. He hadn't expected it to be so hard to watch Caitlyn dancing with a parade of bankers, their grabbing hands on Caitlyn's bare skin. He had watched one of them escort her off the dance floor with his hand on the small of her back, skin touching skin. But he couldn't very well make a scene every time Caitlyn danced with someone, so he had paid attention to the blonde, whose name was Jennifer. She had given her number to him, but he threw it away as soon as he left. He'd had enough of women like that. He drove home with the windows open to clear his head.

"You?" he asked, equally as casual.

"Yes, the car took us home to Adriana's, and then I drove back from her place."

"Did you have a good time?" he asked.

"Relatively," she said, though something flashed across her face. "Did you?"

"It was business. A little different than an all-night coding session with a bunch of college-aged kids, but not bad."

"Why didn't you tell me?" she asked.

"About the club?"

She nodded. "And everything. Everyone was all abuzz about you. Software entrepreneur, moving back to the East Coast, investing in things left and right. It sounds like you've been quite the busy boy."

"I've been trying to keep busy," he said. "Tony's a nice guy. I thought since I planned on spending more time here, it would be nice to have a place to go, you know, someplace where everyone knows my name."

"So you decided to open a club? Surely there are better and cheaper ways to find friends. Not that you seem to have much trouble with that."

He looked at her carefully. Could she be jealous? He wondered why that thought would lift his spirits.

"It's none of my business," she said too quickly.

"You know you can't believe everything you read in the papers," he told her.

"Who said I read those kinds of papers?"

Noah smiled. Caitlyn had a weakness for the gossip pages.

"Well, that's good then. I wouldn't want my reputation to proceed me." He actually hoped she hadn't. The press had been all over his relationship with Lakota Reynolds. She had been a nice girl, beautiful of course, but not as talented as she was made out to be. Funny thing was she had known it, which was why her Plan B had been Noah. A rich man's wife. Sure, she promised to be a good one, but Noah didn't want someone who wanted him for his money. Even if she had been honest about it.

"Of course, I am sure you'll get a lot of press about last night."

"Not me. It's Tony's place. I'm just the silent partner. But I'll always get a table. And free appetizers."

She looked at him. "What about a percentage of the profits?"

Noah laughed. "Tony said there wouldn't be any. At least for a year. So I get free apps instead."

"I hope you made a better deal when you sold your company," Caitlyn said. Her eyes were worried.

Noah reached out and took her hand. He felt her wanting to take it back, felt the heat crawling up his skin, and not because she had been running.

"Don't worry; I did. I can afford to work on my passion projects now."

She laughed. "That sounds very Californian of you. Are you sure you want to move back east? I think we're a little more serious-minded here."

Noah took a step closer to her, so that they were almost touching, not just his hand and her arm, but just inches away, face-to-face. He felt his breath quicken as he looked into the deep blue of her eyes, wanting to brush back a curl of the black hair that escaped from her cap, twine it around his fingers, feel its softness.

Her back was against the solid bulk of the rock, and he had her caged by his arms. Her cheeks were flushed, and he could hear the heavy sounds of her breath. He took one hand and slowly undid the zipper of her fleece, exposing an ivory v of skin where her shirt dipped down.

Caitlyn watched him, eyes locked with his. He didn't know what she was thinking, but she wasn't making a move. Noah took that as an invitation and trailed his fingertip against her exposed skin. Just skimming it along, but he saw her eyes flash as she convulsed.

"You were saying something about being serious," he whispered, leaning in over her. Even now she smelled clean, fresh, a hint of apple, maybe something lemony.

"I don't remember..." Her hands went up, running up his arms, tracing the breadth of his shoulders, coming to rest around his neck. She looked at him a moment, invitation in her eyes. Noah went for it, bringing his lips down to meet hers. She rose up to meet him, their lips joining. At first, it was slow and hesitant, but all of a sudden he wanted more, all of her, the part of Caitlyn he'd never gotten. He pushed her up against the rock, raising her up so she was on his level, letting him kiss her, harder now. He could feel her fingers running through his hair and the soft murmur of his name that became a moan.

"Noah..."

And then it became "No, no." He stopped, suddenly jumping away from her. His breath was coming hard and fast, and he could feel himself aroused.

"God, Caitlyn, what are you doing?" he said, running his fingers through his hair. It was chilly this morning, and he suddenly noticed the wind whipping in from the water, the sand dancing in the air.

"What am I doing?" Her eyes flashed and she took a step forward and then back from him, so she was clear to run. "You're the one who..."

"What?" he asked. He was calmer now, watching her. Surely he hadn't been imagining the want in her face, the desire he'd felt.

"It can't be this way."

"What way?" He was puzzled.

"We're not teenagers anymore, Noah. I'm not going to shag you on Sailor's Rock for the whole world to see."

"Oh, so you mean you were considering it?" Noah felt himself getting ready again, but Caitlyn held up her hand.

"We snuck around once. I won't do it again. Noah, you're my boss. Been there, done that." Caitlyn started to back away from him, her feet sinking into the stony sand.

"Who said anything about sneaking around? In case you haven't noticed, there's no one left to sneak around for. But you always were terribly interested in what other people thought," Noah said.

The arrow hit home, and she spun around. "Just because I didn't want to throw our relationship in everyone's face didn't mean I didn't want to be with you."

"You were too afraid to stand up to an old man. You were tease then, and you're a tease now."

Noah didn't know why he was shouting. Last night, when she'd been dancing, it had been all he could do not to step in and break the guy's nose. It had hit him then. No matter what, he still thought of Caitlyn as his girl. And he wanted her, desperately, all over again.

Her face went white, as if he had slapped her, and then it changed. All the anger drained out of it, and he saw only sadness.

"No, Noah. You never understood. He was all I had. He didn't want me fooling around with you, didn't want me making the same mistakes as my mother. I just needed time, and you were pushing too hard, too hard for a commitment I couldn't make. You're the one who thought it was because I didn't love you enough. But you were wrong. It was because I loved you too much."

Caitlyn turned and walked away, feet crunching on the beach. Noah felt like he'd been sucker punched, but he knew that he couldn't go after her.

Chapter 26

Caitlyn was late to work, but only by a few minutes. She kept a smile plastered on her face, but inside she was seething. How dare he accuse her of being a tease again? And the kiss? What had he been thinking? What had she been thinking? It had made her feel, like what? Like a teenager again, like when he used to kiss her in the boathouse, on the eighth green of the golf course, just about anywhere they could sneak away to.

Her grandfather had been so set against the relationship, for so many reasons. One had to be the memory of her mother. Don't let history repeat itself, he'd told her, and Caitlyn had swallowed, trying to see past the implication that she was a mistake. Her grandfather had simply wanted her to wait, to be herself before she became wrapped up in one person.

Caitlyn had known from a young age that boys were only out for one thing. It had been drilled into her by her grandfather. But all of that careful indoctrination had gone out the window when she met Noah. She'd always had her eye on him, even though he was two years older. He'd always been confident, smooth, a guy with a vision, a plan. She had been eighteen, waiting for college to begin, bored with Queensbay, and he had been twenty, primed to quit college and head out to California, ready to get on with his life. She had been just back from Paris and ready for adventure.

She sunk into her chair and just sat there, not even turning on her computer. Why did she still have feelings for him? Ten years later, other men, a whole career, even an engagement, and it was still Noah Randall who made her palms sweat, her heart pump and her breath catch. She could go out with anyone she wanted to, nice, uncomplicated guys who knew nothing about her past, like that banker from last night, Kevin. She should go for it. A nice, normal guy, no complications.

She didn't need Noah Randall, and their history, clouding her brain. Not to mention her present and future. No matter what he said, he was still technically her boss. And dating the boss was stupid, a lesson she had learned from Michael St. John.

Caitlyn shook her head to clear it and booted up her computer. She had work to do, real work. And that's what mattered.

There were a list of messages, some from people she had met last night, one from the persistent Mrs. Smith-Sullivan and two from Michael. Those she crumpled up. She thought she'd made it very clear she didn't want to speak to him again. Mrs. Smith-Sullivan needed to be called back. It could have just been a simple mistake, but the more Caitlyn thought about it, the more it seemed she should dig a little further. But there were things to do first.

Caitlyn called in Heather and handed her the stack of business cards from the previous night.

"If I could, I would give you a raise, but you'll just have to settle for my thanks - the makeover you gave me made sure I was pretty popular last night."

Heather smiled warmly. "I suppose it would be crossing a line if I asked if you got lucky?"

"Hopefully only in landing a few new accounts. Remember, love fades, but money is forever."

"That's not very romantic," Heather pointed out.

Caitlyn laughed, glad she could. "Following my heart has only ever gotten it broken. More than once, so guess what? I'll take a fat bank account any day. So here you go. Can you go through these and send them all our marketing kit? Overnight them and make sure they go out by noon, if you can. I'm going to start making some phone calls, so it would be great if I wasn't disturbed."

"Sure thing, boss."

Caitlyn dialed Mrs. Biddle's number first. Marion answered the phone and said Adriana had gone to visit Mr. Biddle. Caitlyn asked for her favorite champagne and wrote it down. She ordered a gift basket of fruit and champagne from the liquor store and arranged to have it delivered that day, along with a thank-you note.

Caitlyn looked at her watch. It was time to call Tony Biddle. He picked up on the first ring, sounding not the least bit tired, and they chatted, Caitlyn inquiring how the rest of the party had gone.

"Great. Have you seen the papers?"

Caitlyn said she had not.

"I got a mention in the *Daily News*, and there were people from the *Times* and *Bon Ton*. Here's hoping we'll see some pictures next month. Addie was fabulous. She gave a little interview on all of her work over the years, connecting artists and their society patrons."

Caitlyn made a mental note to mention that to Adriana when she spoke to her next, and then artfully, she steered the conversation around to her primary reason for calling.

"I would like to put together a presentation for you, something to show what we can do for you. Would next Tuesday be all right? I can meet you in the city or," Caitlyn could hear him flipping through the pages of an appointment book, "you could come out here."

"I am supposed to see my uncle and Addie." She could hear him musing, thinking.

"How about lunch? Then you can visit them in the afternoon," Caitlyn suggested.

"Perfect."

They set the date, and Caitlyn wrote it down, trying to contain her excitement. She would have a lot of work to do between now and then if she wanted to land Tony Biddle as a client.

Caitlyn returned some other calls and made more appointments, answered questions and was generally well pleased with herself by the time lunch rolled around. In the next two weeks, she had five meetings scheduled with potential clients. If she managed to get half of them - well, hell, if she managed to get Tony Biddle - then she would be well set for the future. Her strategy, developed and honed in London, was showing signs of traveling well.

There was an interoffice package envelope to her. It was silly, since the whole firm only took up one floor, but some people still used them.

"Sorry for how we left things. Let's start over. Will you have dinner with me? Check the box Yes or No."

She almost burst out laughing at that. Worded like a high school note, it was designed to evoke memories of when things were easier between the two of them. Taking her pen, she checked off the "No," put it back in the envelope and gave it to Heather to send back.

Her fingers brushed against her lips gently, as if she could remember it, the burn of his lips against hers.

<< >>

Caitlyn looked up from the papers that were spread all over her desk. She was still putting together Tony's presentation, spending too much time on it. He was coming the next week. She had put everything out of her mind, focusing instead on what she needed to do now.

"Don't forget you have that meeting with Mrs. Smith-Sullivan, the one she insisted on scheduling," Heather told her, her head poking through the open door.

Caitlyn swore. It was this afternoon, and there was no way she was going to be able to make it. "Could you please call and reschedule?"

Caitlyn turned back to the work on her desk, focused on the information in front of her. There was something she was still struggling to understand. From what she could tell, Tony's empire might not be as impressive as the media claimed. His restaurants were always crowded, and they charged a hefty fee for the privilege of being seen there.

However, Tony didn't seem very good at keeping much of that money. He was always borrowing to expand, and he didn't seem to have all that much in other banks or accounts. Of course, she couldn't be sure of this until he allowed them to look deeper, but it was part of her best guess. Tony didn't need any special deals - he needed Finance 101.

Caitlyn stretched. Her grandfather had been a big advocate of Finance 101, a basic common-sense approach. Slow and steady wins the race. Tony needed to pay himself first, diversify into holdings other than houses, cars and boats, and look into safe and boring stocks and bonds.

She put together her plan, even selecting a picture of a fat, happy and self-satisfied tortoise to put on the cover.

Chapter 27

The next few days flew by in a rush of work, and when she finally left the office, she realized it was Friday and she had no plans. She decided to walk along Main Street in the village and see if anything caught her fancy for dinner. She had worked late enough that even the idea of heating up her own dinner held no appeal to her.

She had been working diligently on her accounts, keeping her head down, trying to avoid Noah. Sure, he made excuses to bump into her in the hallway, and once there had even been an awkward moment at the coffee machine until Heather interrupted them. He had left early tonight, and she figured that he was probably heading out to hang with Chase; at least, that's what she hoped. Kevin, from the club opening, had called her twice but had gotten the message after her polite but firm brush-offs.

Distracted by the sight of a chocolate cake in the window of the bakery, Caitlyn didn't see Marion, Mrs. Biddle's housekeeper, who was walking down the street and smiling until she was actually upon her.

"Well, we were just thinking about you," Marion said, by way of hello. "Adriana tried to call you at your office to invite you for dinner."

Caitlyn smiled and stamped her feet for warmth.

"Please come. Adriana could use some company. You don't have any other plans, do you?"

"I couldn't impose." Caitlyn knew she was being silly. Marion lived to feed people.

"Nonsense," Marion said. "She already called your office, but you weren't there. She'll be so happy to see you. We're having my famous pot roast, and my chocolate cake that you used to like so much."

Caitlyn wavered. Marion's pot roast was no joke, a mouth watering, hearty dinner that she remembered from long ago. That, and the fact that all that awaited her at home was a frozen pizza for one, was enough to convince her.

"All right, dinner would be wonderful," Caitlyn accepted, and Marion's smile, if possible, grew wider as Caitlyn offered to carry her bags to the car for her. Marion chatted on, and Caitlyn let the wave of talk wash over her, a welcome relief from her other concerns.

She had been blindsided by Adriana. All careful planning on the woman's part, luring Caitlyn in for a friendly dinner in order to sic the ancient and not quite coherent Mrs. Smith-Sullivan on her.

Mrs. Smith-Sullivan claimed she was being robbed and could prove it. Caitlyn had paid attention, under Adriana's watchful eye, knowing that if she blew her off again, she would hear about it.

It was almost time for the chocolate cake before Mrs. Smith-Sullivan, also known as Sully to her friends, told the story.

"The money was not in my account."

"What do you mean?" Caitlyn had tried to reach for another glass of wine, but Adriana had moved it just out of reach. Caitlyn shot her a look, but Adriana frowned at her. Listening to Sully required concentration.

They were sitting in Adriana's elegant dining room, vaulted ceilings and wallpaper that held a menagerie of delicate birds on it.

"I went to get money from my account, and they said there wasn't enough there. I told them they were mistaken."

"Do you regularly get money from this account?" Caitlyn asked, her attention now engaged.

Sully shook her head and waited as Marion brought in the chocolate cake.

"No. I don't really touch my Queensbay Capital account. I just let it grow and grow. Only this was a special occasion."

"Her grandson got into medical school," Adriana said, by way of explanation.

"And I wanted to give him some money for it," Sully added.

Caitlyn nodded. "Congratulations."

"So I went to get the money, a certified check, and they said there wasn't enough money in the account. I was certain they were mistaken because the account has been doing quite well all of these years. Maxwell had assured me of that and, according to all of my statements, there was no reason why the money shouldn't have been there."

"Okay," Caitlyn said carefully. She hoped it was all just a misunderstanding on Sully's part.

"Well, I called and complained."

"Who did you call?"

"Maxwell himself, of course. I wasn't going to trust that imbecile Jeffrey. He was clearly not up to the task."

Caitlyn didn't disagree with Sully's evaluation of Jeffrey. "And?"

"Well, Maxwell looked into it and said there must have been some mistake."

"Did you get your money?"

"Eventually."

Chapter 28

It wasn't until after Sully had left, to be driven home by Henry, that Adriana really came after her.

"Thank you for coming over here, Caitlyn."

"It's not a problem," Caitlyn said as she took her last sip of coffee.

"Are you sure?"

"What are you asking, Adriana?" Caitlyn looked at her.

"Something that is none of my business. I'm old; it's my right. I am just wondering why you're here with me, instead of someplace else."

Caitlyn put her cup down in her saucer. "There is nothing going on between Noah and me. It was over a long time ago. One chance meeting, if that's what it was, isn't going to change that."

"I see." Adriana looked Caitlyn over carefully, and she braced herself for whatever might come next.

"You know," Adriana said, "I remember when you were younger." Caitlyn looked up, about to say something, but Adriana rushed on. "I remember that summer quite well. Where had you been?"

"I went abroad for a term, in high school. To Paris."

"Yes, I think you needed that time away to fully emerge. I mean, you had changed slowly, but we all needed that time apart to realize how much you had grown, how much of a young lady you had become. It was hard for your grandfather to accept that. You weren't a little girl anymore, and your mother, I believe, was away."

Caitlyn nodded. Her mother had decided to spend part of the summer in an artists' colony in Maine. Once again, it had been just Caitlyn and her grandfather, an arrangement they were used to and perfectly happy with.

"Noah Randall was home from college, deep in it with his father, trying to convince him that he would never be just a banker, trying to get the money to start his company. He came to ask me for advice. Did you know that?"

Caitlyn shook her head. She hadn't known that.

"I told him I didn't understand what it was about - all that computer stuff was never my thing, but I was impressed by the amount of energy and passion he had for it. I still wasn't sure if it would work, but I could see how he deeply he was committed to the idea, so I did manage to find him opportunities to meet people, see people, telling him it had to be a secret. I didn't want to openly come between a father and a son."

Caitlyn wondered where this was leading. She ran her finger over the smooth rim of the coffee cup, looking around Adriana's sitting room.

"I saw a great deal of him that summer, and it was clear to me - I think it was clear to everyone else - that he fell in love with you. Yes, he had known you all of his life, but he described you to me the same way he spoke about his passion for his company. They were all intertwined for him."

"Really?" Caitlyn said, her voice faint. A rush of memories came back to her, but it wasn't the old Noah that she thought of now; it was the new Noah, the one she saw every day at the office, the one she tried to ignore and avoid.

"I saw you as well, and while you were never quite as romantic as he was on the subject, I don't think I have seen two young people so much in love."

"It was a wonderful summer," Caitlyn agreed.

"Your grandfather worried that you might go in the same direction as your mother, even though he thought Noah was a much better choice for you than your father had been for your mother. I told him to trust you, that you weren't your mother."

Caitlyn looked down at the carpet, felt herself blushing. She'd never thought of herself as a prude, but it had been awhile since she had talked to anyone about it.

"I hope I was right?" Adriana asked quietly.

"For the most part. We spent a night together, but nothing happened, at least not that. Noah wanted to, but I said no, that I wasn't ready. Part of me felt if I said yes, I would be letting my grandfather down, even though we were prepared, we would have been safe. We settled for something more innocent."

Caitlyn took a deep breath. This was where it got painful for her. "We also fought that night. He told me he was going to tell his father he was going to drop out of college and head to California with his friends, to start up his company. Instead of being supportive, I told him he would regret disappointing his father. He thought I was being a snob, that I wouldn't like him if he didn't follow the tried and true path. I suppose you could say that killed the mood as much as anything."

"But you didn't go home that night?"

"No. I'd told my grandfather I was staying at a friend's house, so I wound up going there, and then the next morning when I finally did come home, the police were waiting for me."

Adriana was silent for a moment before saying, "I thought that might have been what happened. I saw the two of you at his funeral, but you weren't together anymore. Something had been broken."

"I pushed him away. I felt guilty. If only I hadn't gone out of the house, if only I hadn't been with Noah." Caitlyn, her eyes wet with tears, turned to Adriana. "Why did he have to kill himself? I would have taken care of him."

Adriana answered, her face sad, "He didn't want to be a bother to anyone. He knew your mother wouldn't do the right thing, and he didn't want you to stop your life to take care of him. Especially when he knew that recovery was almost impossible. It was a timing issue for him."

Adriana wasn't looking at Caitlyn, her eyes focused off in the distance, as if she too could reach out and touch those times. "He pushed me away, too, and I let him, let him say it was for the best, that we couldn't go on lying to my husband, the people we loved, setting a bad example. And I let him go."

"And that's it. He didn't want to be a bother to us? To the people who cared most about him?" Caitlyn asked. Her grandfather had left behind a tidy estate, all the loose ends wrapped up. Except for Queensbay Capital. Somehow that had all gone to Maxwell.

"I don't know. I never thought Luke could do such a thing. He was always so full of life."

"There's more to it," Caitlyn said and waited.

"No," Adriana disagreed. "There isn't. Sometimes it just is what it is. Caitlyn, your grandfather loved you. He probably thought that, by ending it how he did, he made it easier for you. I know it's hard for you to understand. It was hard for me, but your grandfather expected you to get on with your life. And you should. Look to the future; think about what you want for yourself. Don't worry about what's right, or what other people think. Do what you want."

Chapter 29

Noah had been watching her for a week. He had fought the childish urge to storm into her office when her note came back marked no and demand a yes. Instead, he'd decided to play it cool. He had listened to her patiently at staff meetings and, oh, so subtly brushed against her in the hall. And then there had been that moment at the coffee maker where she'd taken pity on him and helped him figure out which button to push. She'd had to get close to him, and he could tell she hadn't been oblivious to the feelings between the two of them. And if they hadn't been interrupted, he was sure she would have kissed him.

So when he saw the light on in her office long after the rest of the floor was dark, he paused, considering. It was time to stop playing games. He couldn't stop thinking about her, yet she was doing her best to appear unmoved by him. He walked down to her office and found her, high heels on, black pencil skirt, light gray blouse, pacing as she looked at some papers.

"Are you mad at me?" he asked. She was focused and intent, and his voice made her jump.

She looked up, startled, as if pulling herself back into reality.

"I'm not mad at you," she said, finally, watching him carefully.

"Then what is it? You barely talk to me," he pointed out, taking a step into her office.

"I didn't realize we had anything to talk about."

"Is that why you almost kissed me over the hazelnut cream coffee?" he asked, trying to keep his voice light.

"I think you must be imagining things. And I'm not mad, I'm avoiding you," she said, moving a fraction of an inch away from him. Noah moved closer.

"Why would you want to do that?" He found that his voice had dropped and his tongue was thick, as if it were tied in knots.

"Because we're no good for each other. Because of what happened. Because you're my boss. And that is never a good idea." Her voice too was low, and he felt a ripple of desire twist through him. Chase had been right. He was so not over Caitlyn Montgomery, and this time, he wasn't going to let her get away from him. But then he saw the look in her eyes - not panic, not fear, but sadness, pain, and he pulled back.

"Think of me more as an absentee owner. Sam's the day-to-day guy, and soon you'll barely see me. Besides, isn't sucking up to the new boss what you're supposed to do?" Noah asked, trying to force some lightness into his voice.

It was the wrong thing to say. She whirled on him. "I don't need your charity, Noah Randall. Just because you waltz back in here, after all these years, with enough money to buy anything you want doesn't mean you can." Caitlyn moved away from him, anger lacing her words. "I'm not for sale, Noah. I don't know what you think you heard about me, but I'm not a gold digger. If you think you can come back here and dangle your money in front of me and make me swoon at your feet, you're mistaken. I don't know what you heard about me, but I worked hard for everything I achieved. I did in London, and I will do it here. With or without you, or the firm."

She was quivering with rage. He'd hit a nerve, so he held up his hands and said calmly, reasonably, "Caitlyn, I know you can't be bought. I know you were loyal to my father. I am sorry things didn't work out the way you planned. I know you. You may think I don't care, but I still do. You must have had a plan when you came back here, and I'm guessing that right now you don't know which way you're supposed to turn. I just want to help you, be there for you."

Caitlyn shook her head and asked simply, "Why?"

Noah stood and crossed the room to her, standing close to her, putting his arms on her shoulders. "Because I wasn't there before. I regret that. I want to be your friend."

Caitlyn laughed, but it was bitter. "Friends. We're too complicated to be friends, Noah. And I'm a big girl. I don't need to be protected by anyone."

Noah shook his head, trying to clear away the frustration. Things were always complicated with Caitlyn. But that was what made her so compelling.

"We never tried to just be friends, did we?" His fingers seemed to leap to her without his being conscious of it, his hands twirling a strand of her dark hair. He felt the silky texture, caught the sudden flash in her eyes as her breath caught. "We just raced right onto the horny teenager part, didn't we? Can't we have a do-over?"

"Noah, stop. You're my boss."

Noah leaned in closer, his lips hovering above hers, his arms moving around her, pulling her closer to him, so he could feel his body next to hers, feel the swell of her breasts, see every freckle on her nose.

"So? I'm lots of people's boss," he murmured, letting his lips feather across her cheek. Her eyes opened wide, and he knew that she was feeling, that he had gotten to her.

"Noah…" It was more of a moan than a whisper.

"Shh, I know you're not after my money. Just shut up and let me…"

Kiss you. And he did, their lips touching. Softly at first, so he could taste her, smell her perfume, something spicy, and her shampoo, something fruity. She moved in his arms - not away, but closer - and he took that for an invitation, an invitation that his attentions were wanted.

He deepened his kiss, letting his tongue explore, letting his hands slide from her shoulders down to the v of her neck, skimming lightly over her breasts, feeling the fabric of her bra, then the hard nubs of her nipples, which sprang to attention under his caress.

She moaned, answering his kiss, her hands running through his hair, pulling him towards her as their embrace deepened, grew more passionate, his hands roaming, feeling, possessing her.

Until. "Stop, Noah, stop." She broke free, her head moving away from him, her hands still twined in his hair. She lowered her eyes and leaned against his shoulders.

"What, what is it?" His voice was husky, raspy, and he could feel desire, the sheer wanting of her flowing through him, all the way through him. She felt it, too, and took a step back.

"Noah, you're my boss. This could get me fired. And we barely know each other. I mean now. I just can't get involved right now."

She took another step back, almost all the way across her office, next to the window. Her eyes were shrouded, hurt, and she was biting her lip.

"Is this really about me being your boss … or is it about something else?" he asked, remembering her evasiveness when he asked about her engagement.

"Noah, it's too complicated. There are too many people watching me. I just can't." Sam Harris was watching her. He had made that clear, and even though she was kissing Noah, she couldn't have him stepping in to save her.

He moved closer, and she stepped even farther back, keeping the distance.

"Can't or don't want to?" he asked, demanding the truth.

"Can't ... not sure..." She was breathing heavily.

Noah nodded slowly. He never needed to force himself on a woman. And when he'd left Caitlyn, he'd been, what? A bit of a jerk, feelings hurt, blaming her for not wanting him, when she'd only asked for more time. He'd been young, but she had been even younger, inexperienced, and looking back, he knew he'd been pushing her.

"Fine." He held up his hands, then ran one through his hair. "I understand."

"You do?" she said, surprised.

"Yes, we're adults, professionals. As you said, I'm your boss. It is complicated."

"So that means..." she started to say.

"That I won't try to kiss you again?" Noah walked over to her, stood next to her at the window, but not too close, and let one finger trail along her cheek, watching her eyes darken with desire, with memory. "No, I'll try. But I'll wait until you ask me."

"What makes you think I will?" she said, defiance in her voice.

He smiled and was rewarded when he saw her swallow thickly. "Oh, you will. Because you and I have unfinished business, Caitlyn Montgomery, and I won't be leaving until we sort it out."

He let his hand linger, running it along the edge of her jaw, while she watched him with dark, steamy eyes. "I'll see you around."

Chapter 30

"So it's a straight hand flush?" Heather asked, squinting at her cards. Caitlyn sighed, and Adriana gave something that could only be described as a giggle.

"No, there's a flush, a straight and a straight flush," Caitlyn explained patiently while appraising her own cards.

They were sitting in Adriana's game room, which was unchanged since her first husband. Green baize table, leather chairs, dark paneling, a crackling fire and lots of dark reds and greens. For this game, there was white wine and Cosmos, and potato puffs and veggie dip instead of sandwiches and beer.

Heather had seen Caitlyn's lucky poker chip and said she wanted to learn. A casual mention to Adriana and a full-blown ladies night was created. Marion had promised to feed them if they dealt her in, and Adriana had broken out Trip Randolph's cocktail shaker and his old poker chips. Darby came, too, bringing along her most famous creation, The Golden Pear's chocolate chip cookies. All of them had made her promise to play only for chips, not real money, but Caitlyn was still having a hard time not cleaning the others out.

"A flush is when all of your cards are of the same suit, but not in sequence. All hearts for instance. A straight is when they're all in the same sequence but not the same suit."

"And a straight flush is when they're the same suit and in order," Heather said, taking a sip of her Cosmo. Caitlyn wasn't sure how many of those she'd had, but as her playing was getting worse, rather than better, she suspected it was more than a few. It was fine, since Caitlyn had offered to be the driver and was now sipping club soda rather than something stronger.

There was a pause while Caitlyn watched as Heather reasoned it out. "Isn't that hard to get?"

"Yes," Adriana and Caitlyn said in unison, while Darby giggled and shook her head.

"How do you keep all of this straight, four of a kind, full house, two pair, deuces wild?"

"Practice," Caitlyn said wryly, putting her cards down. Heather did as well and looked at Caitlyn expectedly.

"You should have folded," Caitlyn told her.

Heather sighed and reached out to clutch Adriana's arm. The two had hit it off immediately, when Adriana had admired Heather's vintage Louis Vuitton purse. From there, they had become fast friends, sharing notes on the best places to score fashion deals. Caitlyn had even seen Adriana jot down the name of an online auction site.

"You're our last hope. Please tell me someone can beat her," Heather said.

Adriana smiled, and Caitlyn watched her levelly. Adriana had been playing a good, but not great, game. Caitlyn suspected it had been part of her ploy all along, trying to lull Caitlyn into a false sense of security.

"I believe it's what you call a straight flush," Adriana said mildly, laying her cards on the green baize of the table.

"Wow, doesn't that beat her, what do you call it, four of a kind?" Heather pointed out, taking a big sip of her wine.

"Yes, it does." Adriana could barely contain her glee as she raked the chips towards her.

"Well done," Caitlyn conceded. Sometimes you just couldn't beat the cards.

Adriana looked at her shrewdly as she stacked her chips.

"You let me win."

Caitlyn shrugged and let a trace of a smile ghost across her lips. "If that's what you want to believe."

Darby snorted and said, "Caitlyn never loses."

Adriana said, "Caitlyn was always an excellent card player. Poker, blackjack, hearts, even bridge. Her grandfather loved cards, chess, anything that stretched his brain and seemed like a game."

"Is that who taught you?" Heather asked.

"Yes," Caitlyn said, shuffling the deck. "My mother had no interest in cards, and when my grandfather saw that I did, he taught me everything. Adding stakes - even if they were only pretzels or chocolate chips - only made it more interesting to him."

"Oh, the poker games he, Maxwell and Trip would have," Adriana said, her eyes bright with memories. "They didn't really like each other, but they all ran in the same circle, so a no-holds-barred poker match was really the only way for them to get at each other."

"Did Caitlyn's grandfather always win?" Heather asked, curiosity tingeing her voice. Caitlyn tried to shoot her a warning look, but Heather just raised one blonde eyebrow over a bright green eye and turned her attention back to Adriana.

"No, of course not. They were all good players. There were others that played, too, but really I think Maxwell, Lucas and Trip were the only ones who considered it a blood sport. Maxwell was reckless, a true gambler. He would sometimes be outrageously lucky and win huge, and other times he would lose all night. Lucas and Trip were more careful, considerate." Adriana shook her heard. "It got worse once Trip suspected Lucas and I were having an affair."

Caitlyn, who had just been taking a sip of her drink, choked and almost spit it out. She glanced over at Heather and Darby, who were both looking at Adriana, entranced. Marion threw Caitlyn a sympathetic smile, with a "what can you do about it" kind of look.

"You and Caitlyn's grandfather?" Heather asked. Caitlyn focused on the large oil painting above the fireplace, a tasteful depiction of a three-masted, fully rigged ship riding the cresting waves. She wasn't sure she wanted to hear this, but was fairly certain that Adriana meant for her to.

"Oh yes, I was his mistress. Trip was pretty dreadful and had cheated on me almost from the first. I didn't, not until Lucas. I was good friends with Annabelle, his wife, Caitlyn's grandmother, and of course I would never do that to a friend. Once she died, though, I think Lucas began to look at me in a different light, as they say."

"Why didn't you two get together? Why stay with Trip if he was so awful?" Heather asked, enthralled in the story.

"Divorce wasn't an option. Too expensive. And dangerous. Trip had a bit of a temper, and we had a pre-nup. It made a divorce mutually too expensive for us. I came to the marriage with a good deal of money, you see, more than people imagined. Untangling our assets would have been a nightmare. So he looked the other way for a while."

"For a while?" Heather asked.

Adriana smiled. "Did you know that Caitlyn used to gamble professionally?"

"What?" Neatly diverted, Heather turned her attention back to Caitlyn, who kept shuffling her cards.

"Professionally is a bit of an overstatement."

"Your grandfather was livid when he found out."

"I was running a card game at school," Caitlyn explained, "and the captain of the football team was a sore loser."

"What happened?"

Caitlyn shrugged. "I had to donate most of the money back to the school booster club."

"Most?"

"I managed to keep some of it."

"What did you do with it?"

Caitlyn smiled, remembering. "Gave it to Mikey DiGiovanni. His father owned the pizza place in town. He needed a car to start a delivery business."

"You gave it?"

"It was more of a loan. He paid it back. With interest. And now he owns ten different locations across the state." Caitlyn let the cards play under her hands, the whisper of them oddly soothing.

Adriana looked at her shrewdly. "I'm guessing that wasn't the last time you did something like that."

Caitlyn glanced at Darby, who smiled and said, "Caitlyn knows a good investment when she sees one."

Feeling uncomfortable, Caitlyn decided to change the subject. "A girl has to get her start somewhere. Speaking of that, perhaps we should switch it up, play something we're all good at?"

"Hearts," Marion suggested hopefully.

Caitlyn looked at Heather. "I was thinking something more along the lines of Go Fish."

There was a round of laughter as Caitlyn began to deal the cards.

<<>>

"So, Noah wasn't the captain of the football team, was he?" Heather asked once they were in the car alone together. They had dropped Darby off first, she had to open the café early the next morning.

"I don't really remember," Caitlyn said curtly, hoping she could stop this conversation before it started.

"Really? So, he wasn't the one who turned you in?"

Caitlyn shook her head. "I think Adriana was exaggerating for effect. It wasn't that big of a scandal."

"Really?" Heather shifted in the seat of the car, and Caitlyn could feel her looking at her.

"Well, my grandfather decided to send me away for a year. To a boarding school in France."

"Like a military academy?" Heather said.

"More like an all-girls finishing school. He felt I needed some positive female role models. I only stayed a semester, but it was enough."

"Enough for what?"

"To learn my lesson. I came home, and I wasn't quite as rebellious as before. Before I was the girl with the crazy, man-obsessed mother, no father and the strict grandfather. I spent a lot of time rebelling, you know, black hair, black clothes, big clunky black shoes. And being mad at no one in particular."

"And then was it like *Sabrina* when you came home?" Heather's hand clutched Caitlyn's arm. "I can just see it now; you must have walked into the room or someplace, and everyone there just turned to you and stared? Were you wearing a hat? Designer? Please tell me it was Chanel?"

Caitlyn laughed, navigating one of the twisty backwoods roads as she headed towards Heather's house.

They were in Caitlyn's car, the Mercedes coupe she had inherited from her grandfather. It had been one of his prized possessions, and driving it always made her feel closer to him.

"I don't remember what I wearing, but suffice to say, it probably wasn't head-to-toe black."

Caitlyn was holding back with Heather. It had been a red and white polka dot bikini, and every eye on the pool deck at the club had turned her way. Half of them hadn't recognized her, and she had been absurdly grateful for the overlarge sunglasses that hid her eyes. The walk to her lounge chair had seemed endless, but it had signaled a new beginning for Caitlyn, the realization that she could be who she wanted to be. She was her mother's daughter in name only. She had begun to take pride in being a Montgomery, in being Lucas's granddaughter. She had begun to think of her legacy.

"So, was that when Noah Randall caught sight of you?"

"What are you talking about?" Caitlyn shifted in her seat and let her eyes glance over in Heather's direction.

"Come on, you have to tell me. I mean, it's not like I can't tell there's something going on with you two." Heather's eyes gleamed in the reflection of the dashboard lights.

"What are you talking about?" Caitlyn felt her chest tighten in panic.

"I mean, I heard that you two used to date. In high school. I mean, if my high school boyfriend had turned out to be Noah Randall and I dumped him ... wow, I would have kicked myself."

"I didn't dump him. He dumped me," Caitlyn said tightly. They were getting closer to Heather's house, and she was glad.

"What, he dumped you? Was he crazy? The nerve."

Caitlyn had to smile at the fake outrage in Heather's voice.

"It was a long time ago," Caitlyn said, pulling into the driveway of Heather's house.

"Well, sometimes you just never get over your first," Heather said.

Caitlyn paused, letting the silence sit in the air.

"He wasn't?"

"Long story. He was supposed to be my first, but it just didn't work out that way. Something got in the way." Caitlyn didn't feel like she needed to give Heather the whole story, how Noah had pushed her away when she needed friendship the most. She knew his adolescent male ego hadn't handled the rejection well.

"Intriguing," Heather said. "But I'm sure you two are making up for lost time. The looks you send each other. Half the time I can't tell whether you two want to kill each other or get it on right on the boardroom table."

There was a pause while Heather thought about this. "Tell me you haven't?"

"No," Caitlyn said emphatically, hoping this was the end of the conversation. But Heather wasn't done.

"Are you sure? Because the two of you aren't fooling anyone with that whole 'Miss Montgomery and Mr. Randall' act. I can tell you just want to jump each other's bones."

"We do not," Caitlyn said.

"Oh please." Heather rolled her eyes. "Have you thought maybe that's exactly what you need? You know, get it out of your system, instead of trying to fight it?"

"What do you mean?" Caitlyn said.

"Well, according to you - and I'm not quite sure how this happened - you two were in love, first sweet innocent love and yet you never managed to do the mattress mambo. So here you are, years later, with all these pent-up sexual what-ifs going through your head. And not that you're big on the details, but I know there's a bad breakup in your past, and you probably haven't gotten any since you lived in another country."

Heather paused, and Caitlyn thought she was done, but it was only so she could add, "And there's only one way to answer a 'what-if.'"

"How?" Caitlyn asked, but she was pretty sure she already knew the answer.

"Do it," Heather said in triumph, as if she had just pointed out the most logical thing in the world.

Heather said her good byes and thank yous, and Caitlyn was about to let her go when she stopped her.

"Does anyone else know? Or suspect?"

Heather gave a little laugh as she leaned in through the open door. "Well, the interoffice envelopes are pretty discreet. I don't think anyone else knows you as well as I do."

Caitlyn was about to say something when Heather beat her to it. "Don't worry; your secret is safe with me."

Relieved, Caitlyn nodded, and Heather shut the door and practically skipped her way up the brick walkway to her front door. Caitlyn waited to make sure her friend was in before pulling away and heading to her own bed. It had been good to have a girls' night out, something she hadn't enjoyed since she first moved to London. Once she had met Michael, he had monopolized most of her time and her thoughts. She had kept herself free in case he made last-minute plans, which he often did, but turning down friends so many times had left her with few people to call on when he'd changed plans on her.

But maybe Heather was right. Maybe what she needed was to satisfy that what-if. No strings, no commitment, just an answer to a question that had been out there too long.

Chapter 31

Noah watched her watch him. Something had changed. It was subtle, but now when he looked at her, she looked at him. Long, appraising looks that made him stiff between the legs while his blood rose. This had been going on for days, but still she hadn't said so much as a word to him beyond the usual polite hellos and good mornings. It was driving him insane, and he knew if he didn't get his arms around her, and his lips on her, he would explode. But today was her big day, her meeting with Tony Biddle, and she had come to work looking fierce, intent.

Chapter 32

Caitlyn eyed Tony carefully. He had enjoyed his poached salmon and pasta salad, and seemed to feel at ease in the conference room. Caitlyn had called on Darby and asked her to make lunch. Once Darby had gotten over the nervousness of cooking for one of the nightlife world's celebrities, she had outdone herself. Which was good, Caitlyn thought, because lunch seemed to be the one thing Tony was enjoying the most.

They had chatted and gossiped, and it was going well until Caitlyn started to get down to business. Her plan made sense, and Tony could see that. He was having a little more difficulty in facing the truth.

"I don't know, Caitlyn. It all sounds so difficult," he said. "You make it sound like going on a diet."

"It's not depravation. It's not very exciting, I'll admit, but it works. Was opening your first restaurant sexy and exciting, or was it a lot of hard work, day in and day out, repetitive work until you got things right?"

"True, but..." he said.

"It was all part of a bigger picture for you. I understand that, Tony, and that's what I want to help you with. Once we get the foundation set, you can build whatever you want on top of it. This is a beginning, something to put you on the right course."

"If I tie up all of my free cash in these other things," he glanced down at the paper, "I won't have the money I need to expand."

"Tony, you need to think about your future - protecting the money you have. You could easily become one of those shooting stars, Tony, white-hot in the moment and then tomorrow, gone."

Caitlyn thought for a moment and tried to put it into terms he would understand. "What if someone got food poisoning at one of your restaurants or you got a bad review? Attendance drops, the buzz switches to someplace else and suddenly you don't have the money coming in like you've always expected."

"I've been rich, and I've been poor. Rich is better," Tony said.

Caitlyn nodded. "Exactly." She felt a surge of excitement. He was starting to feel it; he was getting there. She was about to push the papers towards him when there was a knock on the door. Heather poked her head in, looking nervous.

Caitlyn had asked not to be disturbed.

"What is it?"

"It's Sam Harris," Heather told her. "He said he needs to talk to you now." Heather was apologetic. "He's insisting."

Caitlyn went into her office and picked up the phone.

Sam was in Boston on business, and his voice came across the telephone crisp and demanding.

"Caitlyn, I need you to pull up the statements on the Harts." The Harts were an older couple, one of her new clients.

"Why? I'm in a meeting now." She tried to keep the waspish sound out of her voice, but Sam couldn't have picked a worse time to call.

"Who, Tony Biddle?" Sam didn't think Tony was a proper client for the firm. "I'm supposed to meet with Richard Hart, and I just want to be prepared. Pull them up and fax them to me."

He gave a number, and Caitlyn did as she was asked. She gave the task to Heather, and the whole thing took no more than a few minutes. Why Sam couldn't have just asked Heather or his own assistant for it made no sense, but Sam had been keeping close tabs on her, questioning her on big and little things at almost every opportunity. It was beginning to tick her off.

Fuming at the delay, she walked back to the conference room. Tony was standing, the papers piled up neatly in front of him.

He made a show of checking his watch, and said, "I really need to be going."

Caitlyn smiled. If Tony Biddle thought he was going to get out of here without signing the new account paperwork, then he didn't know who he was dealing with.

"Well, I'll only need one more minute," she said, sliding a pen across the table to him.

Chapter 33

The note came through the interoffice envelope. Heather delivered it to her with a wink and craned to see what it said, but Caitlyn shooed her away as she extracted the piece of paper with the neatly typed note. *"Congratulations on your new deal. Will you allow me the pleasure of your company to celebrate?"*

He had signed it with a simple, bold *N* and added a handwritten postscript: *Don't even think about saying no to the boss.* He added only one box, with the word *Yes* underneath it.

Caitlyn considered only a moment before she took her pen, checked the box and slipped the paper back into the envelope and put it in her out box. She knew what she was saying yes to, and anticipation coursed through her. It was a good day to answer what-ifs.

Chapter 34

He had received the envelope back from her, and the little check, with the accompanying scrawl of *XOXO ~ C* made him grin in anticipation. He was getting his second shot with her, and he wasn't going to mess it up this time.

He called Heather, not caring that he wasn't discreet, and asked her what Caitlyn liked to eat. She mentioned The Golden Pear and how Caitlyn had a thing for the molten chocolate cake there.

Noah smiled into the phone. "Perfect." He had no idea what a molten chocolate cake was, but Caitlyn, he knew, was a sucker for chocolate in any of its forms. He called Darby and made arrangements for a complete meal, ready to be picked up at six, with instructions for re-heating included.

Later in the day, he struggled over what to wear and then stopped himself. It was just dinner, he reminded himself, and settled for something casual - dark gray slacks, a white shirt and a soft, midnight blue cashmere sweater. The whole outfit had dutifully been picked out by his personal shopper, who had been hired by his publicist, whose job it was to help him look less like a college kid and more like a CEO. He had scoffed at first, but then appreciated the power being well-dressed had given him in a room full of scruffy programmers, for most of whom not wearing flip flops was a big deal.

He kept checking his watch, waiting for her to arrive, pacing, checking on the dinner, touching things, re-checking his wine selection, fussing over the music he had playing. She wasn't even here, and she was tying him in knots. Noah was more nervous now than he had been facing down a boardroom of venture capitalists.

It was just Caitlyn, he reminded himself. He'd known her practically his whole life, but he'd been a couple of years older, and he hadn't really noticed her until that summer. He'd come home to try to convince his father to invest in his idea, while his buddies lived together out in Silicon Valley, coding. It had been a futile effort, the investment part, but he'd been with Caitlyn, and he hadn't minded his father stonewalling him so much. She had the power, the power to make him feel invincible. And how he had wanted her - to be her first, to be that for her - but it hadn't worked out that way.

He saw headlights flashing through the front windows. She'd driven instead of walking across the lawn. One last check in the mirror. Tonight was a redo. It was time for Caitlyn Montgomery to meet the man she'd let get away.

"May I take your jacket?"

Caitlyn wasn't sure she wanted to surrender the warmth of her coat, but Noah held out his hand, so she shimmied out of it and handed it to him. She felt his eyes slide over her body. She didn't know what she'd been thinking wearing this dress. It was a wrap dress, deep blue with a light pattern on it, and it shimmered when she moved. Plus, it had a v that dipped, but not too low, in just the right place. It had cost a fortune, bought in Paris on a weekend trip. She hadn't had the chance to wear it yet, and now, on its maiden voyage, she knew it was sending out some pretty strong signals. But that was what she had come for, right? She hadn't asked Heather for help with her makeup, instead working off the memory of some of the tips she had given her.

"Shall we have a drink?" Noah's dark eyes were back on her face. She swallowed, realizing that neither one of them were interested in being just friends.

But she nodded, desperately wanting something to keep her hands occupied. Caitlyn followed him into the kitchen, a big, designer one, with gleaming granite counters and top-of-the-line appliances. Everything was new and sparkled. Maxwell had had it redone not too long ago, but even then, he never used it. He was a bachelor, eating out most nights.

"It smells wonderful," she said, and it did.

Noah smiled as he handed her a glass of wine. "I worked all day."

Caitlyn glanced around the immaculate kitchen. "I can see all the hard work that went into it."

"Are you teasing me?" he asked, moving closer to her. A dangerous smile quirked up the corner of his lips.

This time she didn't try to dodge him, but let him get closer to her. His hand went up, but he was holding his wineglass.

"Cheers," he said simply.

She clinked her glass to his, her eyes never leaving his face. Noah put his wine glass down on the counter, sliding it well back from the edge. He leaned in closer, one arm on either side of her so she was trapped, the small of her back against the edge of the counter. She could feel a stool behind her, and she was dimly aware there was music playing and candles lit, flames dancing.

"How was your day?" he asked, his chin brushing against her cheek. She inhaled deeply, smelling his aftershave and his soap, a fresh, clean scent that did nothing to hide the maleness of him. His bulk was on top her now, the front of her dress pressed against him.

"Fine," she managed to answer. "I signed a new client today."

"I heard. Wonderful news." His teeth skimmed across her ear, and then one of his hands went up and brushed back her hair and his lips found the soft, sensitive spot just beneath her earlobe. His breath fanned her ear and pumped her heart. Caitlyn could think of nothing, not any coherent thought, and not any reason she should push him away.

His fingers trailed down her neck and skimmed the v where her breasts met. She shivered, desire licking through her.

"Cold?" he asked, his eyes locking with hers.

"No." She shook her head. "Not cold at all."

He shifted his weight, and one leg slid in between her thighs, and she moaned, already feeling wet with pleasure.

"Caitlyn," he said, his voice hard, raspy, "is this what you want? Tell me now, and I'll stop. I'll let you go." His hand skimmed one breast, then the other, giving a sharp little tug so she became hard under his touch.

She kissed him then, feeling him grow hard between her legs. His hand dropped lower, pulling the skirt of her dress up her thigh, his hands trailing up them until he pressed a thumb against the triangle of silk.

"You never answered me." His hand hovered there, and she felt herself move, almost involuntarily, to get closer, to be in contact with him.

"Yes," she managed to say, her voice hitching as she wrapped her hands around his shoulders, threading her fingers through his hair, bringing him closer to her. She leaned back, and his lips skimmed her neck, sending pulses of arousal through her, while his fingers pushed aside the silk barrier and found their way into her sex, massaging her, gently pressing there until she moaned and writhed with pleasure, feeling the sensations build in her slowly, almost painfully, until she could nearly bear it no longer.

His other hand came around behind her and cupped her, grasping the flesh of her buttocks tightly.

"Yes, what, Caitlyn?" He stopped all motion then, and she was forced to look into his eyes.

Her arousal was intense; she could feel the pressure of his fingers inside, a slow insistent pressure, prolonging the sweet agony and the ecstasy.

"I want this. I want you," she said simply, and he smiled, gripping her harder, pushing her up higher against the counter while his fingers moved more insistently. She was swept away, all feeling, her nerve endings alive, while his lips and teeth trailed kisses down her neck and breasts, nipping at them until they were hard. He whispered to her, encouraging her, his voice, his kisses, his hands sweeping her until she hovered on the edge, poised on the knife of pleasure.

"C'mon, babe, it's good … let it go," he said to her. And she did, the orgasm ripping through her, thoroughly sating her, so when the last shudder had passed, she lay back against the counter, dress tucked up, her panties pulled down low, hands gripping the counter, letting the sensations slowly spill out of her.

Noah looked at her, a smile on his face. He was still between her legs, and she could feel his need for her. She reached for him, grabbed his belt buckle and pulled him closer, one hand starting to unbuckle him.

His smile turned to something dark and simmering. His hand went to stop her, but she loosened the buckle.

"Not here," he said. "Not for our first time." His breath was ragged as he looked at her, and she saw the desire for her in his eyes.

She didn't know if she could make it upstairs, but Noah took the decision out of her hands, pulling her up and to him, so that her legs were wrapped around him as he carried her out of the kitchen and into the hallway, pausing only to lean her against the wall at the bottom of the stairs, pinning her up against it while his tongue ravished her.

"Now," she panted, feeling the desire rise in her.

"Shh," he whispered, starting up the stairs. "We've waited this long… what's a few minutes more?"

She wanted to argue, but her brain wasn't thinking. She was aware of only the sensations racing through her body, the feeling of need that was building. Caitlyn barely noticed what door he opened once they made it up the stairs, only that there was a bed and a lamp on, throwing a soft light. There was some music playing here, too, and he'd set out some candles as well, the flames dancing over the walls, throwing long, lingering shadows.

He dropped her on her back, and she lay there, with him standing over her, looking at her, his eyes devouring her. Noah stripped off his belt, and his trousers dropped. Deftly, he took off his shoes and then turned his attention to her, one hand grabbing her panties, which were snagged around her knees, drawing his hand up her leg, inch by exquisite inch, until she could barely take it, barely hold on. Then he removed her shoes, one by one, tossing them gently on the floor, followed by her panties.

His grin was wolfish as he undid the belt of her dress, letting it fall back against the bed. Caitlyn felt her insides grow liquid once again as his eyes never left her face.

Noah skimmed his fingers over the length of her legs and up her body, coming up to the white lace of her bra. He cupped a hand over her breast, squeezed one gently, then the other, while his other hand deftly undid the snap of her bra and they lifted free.

"You're so beautiful," he said, bringing his mouth down, sucking at her, nipping at her bare, exposed flesh until she felt herself aroused all over again. Sensing her impatience, he let her undo the buttons of his shirt, and she shook it free, sending it over the side of the bed. She reached for his waist, but he stopped her, holding her hand and hovering above her, while he took off his underwear, and he sprung free, ready for her, his eyes impatient.

Noah leaned over her. She circled her arms around his neck, and he hiked her up, her legs wrapping around him. Caitlyn was dimly aware of the cool satin of the bedspread beneath her, but her mind went blank as he entered her, slowly at first, testing her, thrusting slowly, each one pushing her to new heights of pleasure.

His rhythm changed, more insistent as he worked towards his climax, and she matched him thrust for thrust, pleasure for pleasure, until she could take it no longer, and she was pushed over the edge, calling out his name, her hands kneading his back, her head flung backwards. He watched her and then followed, the two of them riding the crest until it exploded over them and everything faded away.

<<>>

Noah looked at her, his beautiful Caitlyn, her pale skin lit by the soft lamplight, her long, lithe body spread out beneath him, her legs and arms entangled around him. He was leaning heavily on her, and knew he should move, get up, get her clothes, a drink, something, but he was spent, too overcome to do anything but admire her. He brushed his hands through her hair, feeling the thudding of her heart against his chest. Her hands were stroking his back, touching his hair, and she was looking at him with a mix of wonder and satisfaction.

He smiled back at her. "Worth the wait?" he asked, hoping against hope that the answer would yes.

Caitlyn nodded. "Yes. Well worth the wait." She said each word slowly, and he felt a wave of relief wash over him, as she asked shyly, "For you?"

"Oh babe," he said, kissing her nose, "you have no idea." She laughed, a simple, happy sound, and he pulled her close to him again, just letting her warmth wash over him. Yes, it had been worth the wait, every minute of those ten years, all he had done to be sure that he was worthy of her.

His Caitlyn.

They talked after that, about nothing in particular and then, when she confessed to be hungry, he found a shirt for her, and she wore that down to the kitchen, where they had their wine and their dinner.

They sat at a small table in the corner of the kitchen. She changed the music to something a little more upbeat.

"Funny, I'm not complaining, but the chocolate cake seems an awful lot like the..."

"Shh." He put a hand to her lips. "Just enjoy the experience."

Caitlyn took his finger, held it to her lips and said, "Oh, I am."

He felt himself growing ready for her again, but he let her finish her cake before he pulled her from the table and led her upstairs.

Chapter 35

Caitlyn had risen, getting up carefully so as not to disturb Noah. He was big, stretched out in the bed, the covers bunched up over him. His arm skimmed the place where she'd been, and he gave a slight sigh. She watched, scarcely breathing, until his hand found the pillow and clutched it to him.

Last night had been amazing, she thought smugly as she found a brush in the bathroom, ran it through her hair and availed herself of some mouthwash. The best sex of her life? Caitlyn looked at herself in the mirror, at her tousled hair, her lips, slightly swollen, as if they'd been kissed too much and too hard.

She had borrowed one of his shirts, a soft blue cotton one that smelled of clean laundry, soap and Noah. She breathed it in, closing her eyes, and when she opened them, looking in the mirror, she saw someone, herself, with a cat-that-ate-the-canary grin. She had answered the what-if.

Yes, she felt great, better than great. If she and Noah had been together when she was eighteen, would she have ever wanted to do anything else, to be with anyone else?

One last look over her shoulder told her Noah was still sound asleep. So she moved quickly, gathering her clothes, dressing herself in the semidarkness. She was almost at the bottom of the stairs, heading towards the door, before she heard his voice.

"Where do you think you're going?" His voice was rough, sleep-thickened, and he was just a shadow in the early morning gloom. Then a light went on, the foyer's chandelier, too bright until he dimmed it.

Caitlyn felt her mouth go dry. "I have to go to work."

"At dawn?" He came down the steps with just his boxers on. She saw the firm outline of his shoulders, his well-muscled arms.

"You weren't running away from me, were you?" he asked, his voice light, but his eyes begging her not to.

She shook her head, letting him wrap his arms around her. "Please don't go," he said, barely whispering.

Caitlyn felt his strength wrap around her, felt his desire for her through the thin film of his shirt. One of his hands dropped, caressing her thigh and then inching up. She trembled at the pleasure it brought, felt her nipples grow hard.

He trailed his lips against the length of her jaw, and she let her shoes drop to the floor again, giving herself up to him. Noah looked at her, one hand still inching up her thigh, drawing closer to the space between her legs, teasing, tantalizing her.

Noah kissed her then, a rough, fierce kiss that seemed to want to possess her, and Caitlyn gave in, arching her back into him, wrapping her own arms around his back and his neck. He hiked her up a bit, driving one of his thighs between her legs, opening her wide and stroking, gently stroking there until she moaned in pleasure.

He started to turn, to carry her to the bedroom, but she shook her head. She couldn't wait.

"Right here," she told him, and he leaned her back against the stairs, one arm grabbing her wrists, holding them there. His eyes watched hers as his hand touched her, and she let herself go, enjoying the feeling, her whole body shuddering, bucking with pleasure. Caitlyn could feel her body slick with sweat, knew that the only thing that mattered was Noah and his hands and what he was doing to her, how he was making her feel.

His fingers kept at their work, and then his head slid down, nudging her legs a little wider until she felt him down there, one hand playing with her breasts, massaging her nipples into little fierce points of pleasure.

She moaned, felt the moment come, savored it and then let herself go, her body shuddering with the explosion of her climax, her head thrown back, her legs open, her whole body heaving.

There was silence, just a moment. "Are you okay?" Noah asked, his face drawing level with hers, a wicked smile on her face.

Caitlyn let all the feelings wash over her and settle for a moment. One of his hands was still casually stroking her inner thigh, the other over her thudding heart.

She smiled. "Your turn," she said, her hand finding him, hard and ready. She stroked, and his eyes widened. Then she brought him to her, guiding him into her, receiving him, giving him as much pleasure as he gave her, his eyes boring into her, and then finally, finally closing in pleasure as he came, too, pouring himself into her.

Chapter 36

Caitlyn watched as he moved down the floor towards her door. He stopped and chatted with people, and they bantered and laughed back. Noah did have a way with people; she did give him that. He was making his way towards her, and she let the knowledge that she'd had him, and he her, spread through her, a warm feeling that left her a little breathless. He leaned casually against the frame of the door, dapper in slacks, a button down and a jacket.

"Hello, Mr. Randall," she said, trying not to smile. "You seem awfully happy today."

He grinned at her. "I had a very interesting meeting last night, Miss Montgomery."

Well aware that the door was open and that their conversation could be overheard by the entire office, she asked, "Business or pleasure?"

"Why, a little bit of both." He took two long strides across the carpet until he was standing in front of her desk, hands resting on the back of one of the chairs.

He looked casual yet commanding, and Caitlyn felt her heart race and her stomach flip as she remembered just how those long, elegant fingers had made her feel the night before.

Noah caught the drift of her gaze, and he flexed his hands while the smile disappeared from his face to be replaced with a harder, more considering look.

"If only you didn't have a wall full of windows, Miss Montgomery, I think I might just be able to show you a little more of that pleasure."

"Oh." Caitlyn felt her stomach turn to jelly and realized she had forgotten to breathe.

"But," he said, standing back up, his voice still low enough that it couldn't be heard out in the hallway, "I was thinking maybe we could just have dinner?"

She swallowed, tried to speak and nodded. "My place or yours?"

"How about yours?"

"Eight o'clock then?" Caitlyn said, well aware that Heather was back at her desk, her chair tilted back, straining to hear every word.

"Delighted. Glad we'll get to talk business, Miss Montgomery," he said, winking at her and turning to go.

"My pleasure, Mr. Randall."

He stopped, looked at her and dropped his voice. "I sure hope it is. See you later."

And with that, he turned and walked out the door.

Heather was up out of her chair and in her office in an instant. "Can I get you anything, a cup of coffee?"

Caitlyn busied herself with her computer screen, pretending to type, trying to keep her head down, trying to let her heart rate return to normal.

"No, I'm fine." Caitlyn thought that would be enough to get Heather to go away, but it wasn't.

"So," Heather hissed, "how was it?"

"I don't know what you're talking about," Caitlyn tried to claim loftily, but Heather just rolled her eyes.

"Oh please, you've been glowing since you walked in here, and Noah looks like he's walking on cloud nine."

Caitlyn glanced around and beckoned Heather closer. She dropped her voice. "Amazing. Better than amazing."

Heather moaned and put a hand to her chest. "Details."

Caitlyn laughed. "No way. But you were right about what-ifs. There's only one way to answer them."

Heather gave her a wicked smile. "Hopefully you'll have to try again just to make sure."

"Out," Caitlyn said playfully, and Heather laughed herself back to her desk.

Chapter 37

"Caitlyn," Sam began. He had called her into his office towards the end of the day. She knew it was designed to throw her off schedule, when she had planned to leave early to get things done before Noah came over.

"I had a disturbing question from the Harts the other day."

"The Harts?" Caitlyn searched her memory and then remembered how Sam had pulled her out of her meeting with Tony to ask for information.

"Yes, apparently they tried to get some money of their account and, well, embarrassingly enough, the check bounced." Sam's eyes were steely behind his glasses.

"Really?" Caitlyn said casually. "Did they recently do another large withdrawal?"

"No. That's just it. According to their statements, there should have been plenty of money in the account. Plenty. But there wasn't."

The panic, unbidden and unjustified, rose up in her. It was a familiar feeling, one she hadn't felt since London, and but like that time, this was overwhelming, threatening her ability to think. But she must. She took a deep breath and schooled her face into a blank mask.

"Of course I rectified the situation, Caitlyn. The Harts have their money now. Perhaps it was just an accounting error. But make no mistake, I will be looking more deeply into this."

Sam sat behind his broad desk, arms crossed. He was smirking, if such a thing were possible, and she knew he was taking pleasure in watching her, waiting for her to squirm.

He leaned forward and dropped his voice. "I heard what happened in London. I don't know how you managed to hush it all up, who you managed to convince with your poor-little-me act, but it won't happen here. I'm on to you, and if I find so much as a penny out of place, Caitlyn, you're done here, and in the business. No one will touch you when I'm done with you."

She fought the urge to rear back. She had known that Sam Harris didn't like her, but this was the first time he'd made a personal

300

attack. And bringing up what had happened in London. It had been buried, rightly so, since she had done nothing wrong. But a rumor, a slightly different spin on events, and she knew how it looked.

"Oh, I assure you, everything is in order." She rose, managing to look down at him with all the resolve she could muster before letting herself out.

Caitlyn walked down the hallway, trying to shed the panic. She thought about what Sully had told her. She'd been busy, too busy thinking about Noah, wanting Noah, to focus on what was important. Her own life. Her own reputation. Michael St. John had nearly destroyed all that she had worked so hard to build. She couldn't let that happen again.

Chapter 38

Even after the meeting with Sam, Caitlyn was home early enough to get dinner started. Unlike Noah, she could cook when she wanted to and had even taken a week-long cooking class in Paris. Tonight, she had planned steaks with a blue cheese sauce, a mixed green salad and some crusty bread she'd picked up from the market. The cooking soothed her, focusing her to think.

But before she did anything else, she went to her room and opened the lid of her jewelry box, the polished wood cover lifting to reveal the red velvet lining. It had once played "Greensleeves," a long time ago, but it was broken, and she'd never gotten around to having it fixed.

She picked up the ring from the bottom of the velvet-lined drawer, where she had tossed it, carelessly almost. She'd kept it only because he insisted she should, a way to remind her, to force her to reconsider. But now she knew for certain there wouldn't be any reconsideration. She didn't need Michael or his promises, the allure of his perfect, well-ordered, elegant life. Deep down, he was a treacherous, cheating bastard. The trouble he had made for her was coming back to haunt her. She didn't need that in her life. It was time to send the ring back.

<<>>

Noah showed up for dinner with a bottle of wine and flowers. He kissed her, a passionate, hot kiss, but through it she heard his stomach growl.

"Are you hungry?"

He nodded sheepishly as she handed him a glass of wine. "I kind of got caught up in things. I forgot to eat."

She pulled him to the kitchen. "Come, we have all night. Let's eat now."

Caitlyn had set the small pine table in the kitchen and had their salads ready to go. The steaks took just a moment, and she watched as Noah nibbled on some of the cheese and olives she had put out as appetizers.

"This is nice," he said.

"What do you mean?" she asked as she put the steaks on.

"Just sitting here, talking."

She looked at him. "What are we talking about?"

"I don't know. How about you? What have you really been up to the last few years?"

She sighed. She knew she needed to tell him, no matter how painful it was. Caitlyn took a sip of her wine, letting it roll off her tongue. "It's nice, the wine."

"I live near Napa, so I know my wines," he said, "and you're avoiding the question."

"I was engaged. To man named Michael St. John. And then I broke it off."

"Why?"

"He just wasn't the right one for me." Caitlyn picked up a knife and put it down, unsure what to do with herself.

"I'm sorry."

She shrugged. "Better before the wedding than after. But I guess I felt a bit lonely."

She didn't, couldn't let her emotions show. "It seemed like a good time to return to the mother country, if you know what I mean," she finished.

Noah nodded.

"And you? Ever married, engaged?"

"You would have heard."

"I'm not sure that I believe that. You seem like you'd be quite a catch." She meant it. She would have thought Noah Randall would have been off the market long ago.

"Internet billionaires are a dime a dozen out there in California. You have to be rich, spout poetry and speak five languages to really stand out," he said, his eyes twinkling.

She laughed. "Ah, the perils of success." She got up and took their steaks off her grill pan and set them on plates, drizzling her sauce over them and adding small heaps of onion straws on top.

"Wow, that looks fancy," he said, as she placed it in front of him.

"I took a week-long cooking class in Paris."

"My very own Julia Child," he said, taking a bite. "Delicious."

"Thanks." She took a bite herself, chewed, swallowed and then asked, "So what have you been doing. I mean, since you sold TechSpace?"

"Well, I took a trip. Six months. Traveled the world, catching waves, eating, drinking, hanging out," he said.

"Then what happened?"

"I woke up one morning, bored."

"I hear that happens to billionaires," she said lightly.

"You'd be surprised. But I met some people on my travels. And I decided that it was time to start something new," Noah told her.

"New?" Caitlyn's eyes had lit up, matching his own enthusiasm.

"Well, not that new. Solar power."

"Solar power?" There was an interested gleam in her eye.

"It's big out west, as you can imagine, and it's catching on in the rest of the country. It's because technology has advanced so that the solar panels are much more efficient."

"Interesting."

"Yes, well, they need someone who's comfortable with technology to help them develop some custom software, the stuff that will help turn your home into its own little power plant. Plus, the fact that I have successfully built a company before doesn't hurt."

Caitlyn smiled. "No, I'm sure it doesn't. It sounds good - good for you and good for the earth. Profits and passion."

"Yes," he agreed, excited. "It is. It's what I've always dreamed of, and now it's happening. All of the hard work, all of the choices are paying off."

"You mean dropping out of college ... heading out west with a few friends and a laptop?"

His decision had created something that had never been fully addressed by them. He had thought she hadn't wanted him to go because she didn't believe in him or, worse yet, because she was a snob - that she wanted him only if he stayed in college, graduated, went to business school, worked at the firm.

"I should have been more supportive of you," Caitlyn told him, putting her fork down and looking at him. "You needed someone to believe in you, and what I said, well, you must have thought that I didn't."

Noah shook his head slowly. "I don't need an apology, Caitlyn. I probably should be giving one to you. I called you a snob, and worse."

"Yes, as I mentioned, I think 'tease' was another one of the insults."

Noah reached out his hand and took hers, holding it tight. "And for that, I am truly sorry. I didn't mean it like that. And I didn't really think about what it might mean to you. About your mother and your grandfather."

"It's not that I didn't want to be with you, Noah. It was just that…"

"You were young. I was older."

"I never felt like you were taking advantage of me," Caitlyn told him, and she hadn't. The Noah then, just as the Noah now, had a way of making her feel wanted, safe.

"Good. It's just … I wanted you, badly. In case you couldn't tell. My pride was wounded."

"That's not what I meant to happen. I just got scared. And then my grandfather…"

He nodded, still holding her hand. "And I was a jerk about that. I felt like I had to leave, that if I didn't go, then the opportunity would pass me by. I could have waited. I'm sure I left you scared, alone."

Caitlyn nodded. "It was difficult, but I got through it."

He kissed her hand gently, tenderly, and looked at her. "And are you scared now?"

She closed her eyes, swallowed. "Not about this." She stood up, and he rose with her. Caitlyn slowly led him out of the kitchen, up the stairs and to her bedroom, kissing him along the way, slowly peeling the clothes off of both of them until they were standing together. She turned to face him, pulling him close to her. He didn't wait for anything more but kissed her deeply, slowly, savoring her, taking his time being gentle with her as they fell together on the bed, exploring each other, loving each other.

Chapter 39

Michael St. John looked at the FedEx package on the desk. It was late in the evening. He was scheduled for dinner in an hour, but he had waited until now to open it. His secretary had signed specially for it. Michael poured himself a drink from the bottle of single malt. Alcohol in private offices was frowned upon, but he didn't care about the rules. He sipped, noticing that he already needed another bottle; he'd replaced it just a few days ago.

He looked at the return address, and his jaw clenched. Throughout the day, he had looked at it, aware of whose it was and what might be inside. She could have sent it straight home, instead of to the office. Several people, including his secretary, might have guessed the contents as well. In that case, it would be all around the office. Caitlyn's final go to hell.

Michael opened the package anyway, and there nestled among protective wrap was the black box. He removed it from the package and flipped open the lid, the hinges stiff and tight. It was there, all fifty thousand quid of it. It glinted in the fluorescent office lights. Almost absently, he moved it around, letting the light catch the stones, creating a rainbow of prisms on the floor, the wall, before he put it aside.

She had included a note. A single cream-colored card, her handwriting, which was beautiful, staring up at him. In no uncertain terms, in black and white, in elegant, cursive script, she told him it was over.

He put the card down and looked at the ring. It wasn't quite over, he thought. Caitlyn Montgomery had another thing coming.

Chapter 40

"Let's see," Heather came in. Her skirt was just this side of professional in a muted leopard print, but the outfit was salvaged by an understated black blouse. "You have two, count 'em, two messages from Mrs. Smith-Sullivan, one message from Johanna Temple and a stack of mail."

Heather placed everything on Caitlyn's desk. She jumped a little, brought back to now.

"Are you okay? You seem a little distracted," Heather said.

Caitlyn shrugged. It was nothing, really - nothing she really wanted to discuss. Things were going along fine, too fine, it seemed. She was making progress uncovering deals, she had potential clients and she and Noah were spending a lot of enjoyable time together. But it all had an air of playacting about it, as if the director would call "cut" soon or the curtain would come crashing down. Perhaps it was the fact that Sam was watching her, literally his eyes following her. She had started to look through her accounts, trying to uncover anything out of the ordinary, but so far, things were looking okay.

"It's nothing."

"It's the time of year," Heather said with authority. "Not quite winter, not quite the holidays and all of the newness of fall has worn off."

Caitlyn looked out her window. It was unremitting gray out there and had been for three days. The sky was gray, the water was gray and everything was whitewashed in gray. It was the kind of non-color you could lose your way in.

"True, I'm sure it's that, so…" Caitlyn thought for a moment, "mannies and peddies after lunch at Sunny Spa?"

"Perfect. I'll call ahead, make sure they hold the space for us. I'll have The Golden Pear make us something to go," Heather planned.

"Perfect." Already Caitlyn could feel her mood lifting.

"Great, and just so you're warned, I plan on pumping you for details."

Caitlyn smiled. Perhaps a little girl talk was what she needed.

<<>>

"So the sex is good," Heather said around her cappuccino.

"Not so loud," Caitlyn hissed. Sunny Spa had an unassuming storefront in a strip mall, but inside the walls were lemon yellow and the vibe was definitely hip. Frothy music beat from hidden speakers, and the staff was young and good-looking. The owner, Randy, had sought Caitlyn's advice about the possibility of taking the concept and opening some more locations, and Caitlyn had been intrigued. She figured that come hell or high water the ladies of Queensbay were not going to skimp on their pampering.

"Well, it's nothing to be ashamed about. You're thirty years old, unattached…"

"Twenty-eight," Caitlyn corrected.

"Almost twenty-nine." Heather liked to needle her about her age. "And there's no reason why you shouldn't be enjoying a healthy sexual relationship with your boss."

"Shh," Caitlyn hissed again.

"It is healthy. I mean, it was worth the ten-year wait, wasn't it?"

Caitlyn closed her eyes as the warm water from the pedicure chair bubbled around her, letting herself drift off into a rush of memories of her and Noah. The way they fit, their bodies moving with each other, the way she had quickly become attuned, once again, to his every mood, and he to hers. They were in sync again, and it was the deepest, most satisfying feeling she'd ever had.

"Very healthy. And very worth the wait," Caitlyn conceded, if only to get Heather to shut up.

And that was the problem, she thought, as Heather went on about her last disastrous date. She and Noah hadn't talked about anything more than the present, which was how Caitlyn wanted it. But she could sense in the way Noah looked at her that he wanted more. He had always wanted more, been the more passionate of the two of them, and now she could feel his eyes watching her, waiting for something that would give him the go-ahead to say more.

Don't rock the boat, was all she could think about. Things were going fine, and after the last year and the blow up with Michael, she didn't need deep and heavy; she needed light and easy.

"Well, it's not a relationship," Caitlyn said quickly in response to something Heather had asked. "We're just dating. You know, seriously dating."

Heather squiggled around in the pedicure chair, and her cat-shaped green eyes pinned Caitlyn down. "Oh, is that what you're calling it these days?"

Her laughter trilled, and Caitlyn closed her eyes, trying to close down any thoughts of the future and instead enjoy the present.

<<>>

Noah found her after lunch. He knocked, came in and shut the door behind him.

"Is everything okay?" she asked.

He shrugged. "This is the right kind of privacy. Anyway, something came up. I have to go to California for a while, not long. And," he watched her carefully, "I thought then I would just go to my mother's in Ohio for Thanksgiving. I'd be back that weekend, at the latest." Noah saw the look of disappointment in her eyes, quickly replaced with one of nonchalance. Still, he was oddly grateful that he got even that.

"Do you have plans for Thanksgiving?" Noah asked her.

She answered quickly. "Of course. Adriana invited me over. She's having a dinner for some friends and assorted family."

"Oh good." He had wanted to ask her to come with him, if not to California, at least to his mother's house for the holiday, but the way she had made plans let him know she didn't want to be asked.

There didn't seem to be too much more to say, and he didn't want to start a fight before he had to leave. She wanted to keep things quiet, simple, she said, but the sneaking around was wearing on him, as was her refusal to talk about anything but the present. Their past, except for jokes, was off limits, and she hadn't so much as asked him how long he planned on staying or what he wanted to do with the firm.

"Have a safe trip," she said, giving him a warm smile. Since he had closed the door and the office was reasonably quiet, he walked the few feet to her desk. She rose as he came to her, and he kissed her, a long, deep, lingering kiss that had her pulling up to her toes, twining her hands around his shoulders and moaning his name.

He broke away, shot her a light grin and said, "Something to remember me, babe. See you in a week."

Noah left before she could think of anything else to say.

Chapter 41

It was after Noah had left and almost the end of the day before Caitlyn picked up her message slips and finally touched base with one of her favorite clients.

"How are the horses?" Johanna treated her horses like her babies, and Caitlyn did her best to remember most of their names.

"Fine, fine," Johanna said, but she offered no more details.

"Well then, what can I do for you?" Caitlyn asked after she had exhausted the weather and what Johanna's plans were for the holidays.

"Look," Johanna hesitated, and Caitlyn felt her pulse quicken like a harbinger of disaster.

"What is it, Johanna? You can be straight with me."

There was another pause, and Caitlyn could hear Johanna take a deep breath before she plunged in.

"I'm going to be moving my accounts elsewhere."

"What?" was all Caitlyn could manage to say. Of all the things Johanna could have said, this was the most unexpected.

"I'm sorry; it's nothing personal. It's just that I feel that my money would be best served somewhere else," Johanna said brusquely, rushing through it, so she could be done with the unpleasant task.

Fear, anger and dread created a curious brew in Caitlyn's stomach as she rushed to her own defense.

"But, Johanna, the firm has given you a great return on your money, and I managed to find the money to finance your growth and buy out your competitors. You wouldn't be where you are today without Queensbay Capital's work."

"I know that." Johanna sounded miserable. "But I just don't feel it's right anymore. "

Suddenly Caitlyn knew. It was the same kind of phone call she had received in London - the ones from her clients, ones who had been happy with her, who had suddenly changed their minds, all without explanation.

"I am sorry to hear that. You said it wasn't personal, but I am wondering, would you feel more comfortable if someone other than myself was handling your money, or is it the firm?"

"Caitlyn, it's just..."

Caitlyn held her tongue. She wasn't going to make this easy for Johanna, not after all the hard work she had done for her.

"I know you have worked so hard, but certain ... things..." Johanna stopped, then added, "I'm sorry." Johanna's voice rose as she seemed to gain back her resolve. "I would like to wind down my account as soon as possible."

"I understand, but I would hate to think that you're making this decision based on some rumors you might have heard."

There was silence on the other end of the line, and Caitlyn knew she had gotten to the heart of the matter.

"Tell me the truth, Caitlyn. Were you fired from your job in London?"

It was Caitlyn's turn to pause. She hadn't been fired, technically. Everything had been murky, and there had been a lot of covering up. She had hoped not to address her time in London by leaving there. Everyone involved had wanted the whole incident to stay buried. Even Michael had enough sense to keep quiet about it, since he'd come off the worst.

"Where did you hear that from?" Caitlyn countered. It was important to know.

Johanna hedged again. "Just some people have been talking."

Caitlyn nearly slammed the phone down on the desk. She couldn't believe this was happening again. When you took care of other people's money, your reputation was essential. And now, again, someone was trying to ruin her.

"And you're going to base a decision this big on something you heard over cocktails?" Caitlyn was desperate. Perhaps having Johanna question her own judgment would get her to rethink her decision.

"I..." She could hear the quaver in Johanna's voice, so Caitlyn went in for the kill.

"Johanna, please. Just give me another two weeks. And then if you're still not comfortable, no questions asked. You can close your account, and you won't ever have to speak to me again."

There was a tense pause between them, and Caitlyn could almost imagine what was going through Johanna's mind.

"One week," Johanna said finally. "I will think about it and let you know in one week."

Caitlyn breathed a sigh of relief. One week. It wasn't what she wanted, but it was something.

"Thank you," Caitlyn said, but Johanna had already hung up.

Caitlyn looked at the phone, trying to steady herself. She had felt the panic rear up and knew it was exactly the wrong response. It was like a game of poker. Someone was trying to bluff her. Someone who knew just enough about what had happened in London to get the rumors started. Someone who wanted her to fold.

She thought about Michael and then dismissed the thought. The two of them were both under strict gag orders not to speak about the incident. He because of what he had done to her, and she because Michael was too powerful. No one had wanted to go against him.

But Sam Harris knew. He had said as much. She propelled herself off of her chair and was almost out of the door before she stopped herself. He hadn't wanted her here from the start. And now he was playing dirty. Maxwell wouldn't have heard a bad word against her. But Noah ... Noah just might.

Caitlyn walked back into her office and shut the door. It was quiet. She needed it, the quiet, the time to think. There was no way she was letting Sam Harris push her out of the way.

Chapter 42

Noah had returned from California after Thanksgiving, and they had picked up where they left off. They had both been invited to Adriana's holiday party, but Caitlyn insisted that they take separate cars, the better to pretend that they were not a couple. He had agreed only after he told her that he intended to meet her and follow her from the house.

"Make sure you wait a moment or two before following me in," she reminded him, as he opened the door for her in front of Adriana's house.

"I don't see why it matters," he said, pulling her towards him, kissing her deeply, running his hands through her hair. "Who cares who knows about us? What's the matter? I'm not good enough for you?" His voice was teasing, but there was an edge to it.

"No, Noah. Of course you're good enough for me. I just want to keep things private for a while longer." Caitlyn didn't want a repeat of what had happened in London.

He looked at her, holding her close on the path. Caitlyn was aware other cars were pulling up, that they were in full view of the wide bay windows, lit up, festooned in ropes of evergreen.

"So, if you're not embarrassed to be seen with me, why won't you be?"

Caitlyn sighed, looking into his eyes. "I told you. I don't want to be that girl."

"What girl? My girl?"

"No, the type of girl people think got ahead by sleeping with the boss."

"As I recall," he said, his head just inches from her lips, "we haven't been doing much sleeping."

Caitlyn stepped away. "My point exactly. Just for now, please, can we just keep it...?"

Noah took a step back, and she could see the flash of wounded pride. "Sure, I get it. We'll keep it light. Whatever you want, Caitlyn, right? Your way, right?" he said, and his tone was bitter.

"Noah!" she said, but he was gone, already walking to the front door, ringing it and walking in, without a backwards glance, leaving Caitlyn to wait a moment or two before following him up the path.

Noah had watched her the whole evening, one half of his mind listening and making small talk, meeting people, discussing business, just as Adriana wanted him to, the other watching her. Caitlyn moved with the crowd here the same way she had at his father's funeral, with graceful self-assurance, her black dress a little less discreet, with a neckline that plunged just enough to keep him looking and a back that was barely there, exposing the smooth ivory of her skin, the fall of her black hair a contrast in ebony.

She smiled, laughed, complimented the wives, made nice with the husbands, deftly turned down offers from the single men, all while discreetly collecting business cards and making friends.

He swallowed more champagne, telling himself that he couldn't do what he wanted to, which was to walk over in the middle of the room and kiss her, possessively and passionately, until no one there was unclear that she was his.

But Caitlyn wasn't, was she? He knew that she wasn't seeing anyone else, but she refused to be seen with him, refused to take their relationship seriously.

"So, you think solar panels are the wave of the future, eh?" Some old gent, in a tux jacket and plaid vest, with a mustache and large tufts of hair jutting from his ears, had cornered him, literally, allowing him to watch Caitlyn's every movement.

With an effort, he turned his attention back to the man. Adriana had whispered that he was rich, always looking for new investments, and loved new technology.

Noah found a way to answer, promising to call the man on Monday to discuss more. Caitlyn had disappeared from the room, towards the solarium, and he needed to catch her, to talk some sense into her. He needed her, wanted her, wanted her to want to be with him, and if she couldn't commit, well, then ... Noah almost stopped, knowing that he couldn't leave her. No, Caitlyn Montgomery was the woman, the only one for him.

"Noah, you okay? Look like you've seen a ghost." Sam Harris was there, a drink in one hand, looking festive with a red tie.

Brought up short, Noah stopped, shaking his head. Caitlyn had been right about one thing. They were being watched. And he was, technically, her boss. It didn't matter to him. He knew that she was one of the smartest people in the room, deserving of everything she had earned, but he could see her point now. Caitlyn had worked hard to make a name for herself based on her own merits. It was exactly what he had wanted to do, why he had left Queensbay, why he had worked so hard to get it right, vowing never to give up, not on his own dream and his desire to prove that he was man enough for Caitlyn Montgomery.

"Sorry, slip of the tongue." Sam laughed, and Noah realized that maybe he'd had a bit too much to drink.

"It's okay, Sam. This house just brings back some memories, you know?"

"Well, I'm glad I caught you. Haven't seen you around the office much, and there was something I needed to talk to you about."

Noah started to excuse himself, but Sam caught his arm, stopping him.

"What is it?"

Sam cleared his throat, and Noah felt the need to tamp down his impatience.

"I've been getting a few calls lately. From clients. They've had some issues with getting money from their accounts. They'll write a check against it, only to get an embarrassing call from the bank saying that the funds weren't available."

Noah felt restless. These were the kinds of details he didn't like to be bothered with. Who cared if the bank was having problems with its accounting software?

"I assume the bank found the money and returned it to them?"

"Well," Sam's voice dropped. "It's not quite as simple as that. The money wasn't actually in their Queensbay Capital accounts. There was less than there should have been. Of course I authorized the firm to cover them, to keep the clients happy."

"Of course," Noah said, but he suddenly had an awful feeling of where this was going.

"Are you saying…?"

Sam's eyes darted around as if he couldn't bring himself to say it. "I don't want to be premature in raising any alarms, but it appears as if the problems began about a year ago. And so far, the amounts are small, on accounts that don't have a lot of activity. I am looking into this, carefully, but I just wanted you to be aware of the possible situation."

"Of course," Noah said. He tried to not look for Caitlyn, not to try to search her out as his first instinct. Sam was watching him carefully, and Noah nodded. "Thanks for the heads up. Please keep me posted."

With a curt nod, Noah excused himself before Sam could say anything more.

Chapter 43

Something was bothering him, she could tell. It was Sunday evening, the day after Adrianna's party, and though they'd been together the whole time since, his mind had been elsewhere.

"I don't understand what you're getting at," he said.

She was having trouble explaining it herself, but more often than not, she felt like Sam Harris was becoming more and more critical of her work. No idea, no proposal she presented met with even the barest hint of approval.

They were sitting on the couch at his house, in the study Noah had taken over from his father. He'd made it his own, papers and folders stacked around, not one, but two laptops set up on the desk.

"I shouldn't be talking to you about this," she said, throwing a pillow at him. He caught it and laughed.

"No, I want to hear about your workday. Tell me." He slid across the couch and picked up one of her bare feet.

"That tickles," she said, but didn't move. All of a sudden, their relationship had slipped into a sort of easiness, something comfortable, like they really had known each other all of their lives. It had taken her by surprise, the way she expected to see him, hear his voice on the phone.

"Sam Harris is acting strangely." She paused and then followed up, "Not strangely. Just different."

Sam was checking up on her constantly, nitpicking everything she did. She was almost certain he was behind the rumors about her, the ones that had Johanna Temple doubting her.

"Maybe he's just being conscientious," Noah suggested, but there was something in the way he said it that made her look more closely at him.

"Maybe." Sam was taking accounts away from her. She had signed two more small ones last week, but he had already reassigned them, telling her that she should focus solely on finding new business.

"So, you think he's giving you a hard time on purpose?"

"No, no, it's not that." That was the last thing she meant to suggest. It was too difficult for her to speak to Noah about work, sounded too much like she was complaining.

"Are you sure you're not just getting too worked up about things? I mean, all you seem to do is work."

"That's not true," Caitlyn said, stung. "I'm right here now, with you."

"You're talking about work now."

"I'm sorry. I guess it's just natural for me." It was out of her mouth before she could stop it. She had meant it had been natural for her to speak about work with Michael. They had talked about work all the time. "Old habits die hard," she said, hoping Noah wouldn't notice.

"It's okay. I know there was a life before me," he said with a smile, but it didn't linger.

"Sorry. Let's talk about something else. How's your new opportunity going?" Noah had been busy with his new company, meeting with people, finalizing plans.

He looked at her. "When are you going to tell me?"

"Tell you what?"

"What really happened? With him. Why all of a sudden you left your life, your perfect life in London, and came back here? I know he cheated on you, but London's a big city. Surely that wasn't the only reason you left."

"You don't really want to know," Caitlyn said, but knew it was because she didn't want to talk about it.

"I think I do. Caitlyn, we spend all of this time together, yet we never seem to talk."

"I thought that was never a problem for men," she said lightly.

"You know what I mean. We never talk about us, about what happened then, or why you're here now."

"We never talk about the future either. Don't you have to go back to California? For a man in demand, you seem strangely able to leave your life behind."

"I can work anywhere I want. I'm not tied to any one place, and I intend to stay here."

They were almost shouting.

"You are?" Caitlyn asked, her voice softening.

"Caitlyn, I don't talk about the future because you don't. You're too busy dealing with the past, which you won't talk about either."

Noah ran a hand through his hair. She had moved away from him as their discussion heated up, and now she watched him carefully.

"Would you want to talk about it?" she asked.

"Yes, I would, because I need to know if you can forget him, before I can talk about the future."

Noah waited, the silence loud, marked by the ticking of a grand-father clock in the hallway. She stared at him, debating, and then she began.

"I got an internship right after college in London. Maxwell asked me if I wanted to work at the firm, and I said no. I didn't want to do that. Anything to avoid coming back here, possibly seeing you. A week later, someone from a bank in London called and said they had 'happened' upon my resume. I am now sure that Maxwell was behind it, helping me out, but I never did find out for sure.

"So I went to London. At first, it was a job in the marketing department of the bank. It wasn't very time-consuming, and I spent a lot of time going out. There was a young woman there, Zoë, who was my age, recently graduated from Cambridge. She was one of those people - you know, old, old money. She was playing around at the bank and spending most of her daddy's money going to clubs and dinners. I went with her most of the time, though I took work seriously, too.

"At the end of the summer, I got a full-time job at the bank, and Zoë didn't. Not that it mattered much. She went to work in publishing and had a lot more fun. We shared a flat together, and I decided to stay on. I liked my job, and because of the people I met through Zoë, I came to the attention of the private banking division. They had a group that worked with very high net worth individuals, figuring out who they were, what they liked and targeting them. Were they interested in becoming art collectors? If so, we had art advisors to guide them through the gallery. If they liked the theatre, we got them seats to opening night, and so on. I became a chaperone to these events."

It had been fun, and she had been good at it. It had all seemed so much simpler back then.

Noah nodded, encouraging her to go on.

"And one time I met Michael, not because he was a client, but because he worked for the same bank. I looked great that night," she said, with a smile. The dress had been amazing.

"I had earned this reputation, the crazy Yankee, a curious mix of working too hard combined with the ability to party. Michael asked me to lunch the next day, and probably because I didn't act all that impressed by him, even laughing at his pretensions, it went on from there. He said I was refreshing. I took it to mean I was naïve, and I spent a great deal of time planning my interactions with him. I hadn't had many boyfriends, really, so…"

She trailed off, glanced up and, seeing she still had his attention, kept going. Noah had been her first real boyfriend, and her last serious relationship before Michael. Sure, in college, she had dated, but after Noah, she'd been determined to keep things light.

"I think that was part of the attraction for him. One thing led to another; he wanted to get married, and I said yes. It all seemed perfect. The accent, the clothes, the convertible roadster, the country house, the dinners, all of the right gestures. It made me feel grand. It made me feel respectable.

"As soon as I said yes, things began to get a little odd. He seemed to get more possessive and more attentive. He would suggest how I should dress, what books I should read, whom I should talk to and about what. But if he thought I was too attentive in talking to someone, especially another man, he would fly off into a rage. Or if it seemed like I wanted to go out with my friends and not him, he would get cold, and withdrawn.

"I spent more time trying to figure out how to keep him happy, in a good mood, than I should have."

She glanced at Noah and saw that he was staring at her, his jaw clenched tightly, his hands balled into fists.

"Did he ever…?" Noah could not say it, didn't want to think what he would do if he had.

"What, hit me? Threaten me?" Caitlyn gave a bitter laugh. "No, Michael was far too clever for that. He used other ways to get at me. Kept me so busy trying to please him that I lost a bit of myself. And then came the final blow. I came back early from a business trip, to surprise him, you see, and I did, in the truest sense of the word - with Zoë, my friend." Caitlyn shook her head, remembering. "I was shocked, but it was good; it brought me to my senses. I was angry, angry at him, but more at myself. For allowing myself to become so caught up with someone, to have spent so much of my time and energy trying to be something for someone else. It reminded me of my mother."

"But that wasn't it?" Noah said, his voice low.

"No, surprisingly enough, he couldn't believe that I wanted to end it. I think that was what stunned him, that we couldn't work it out. He still wanted to marry me, but didn't think that he needed to observe the traditional idea of monogamy. That was a deal breaker for me, and he called me American and provincial."

"Didn't that make you angry?"

Caitlyn laughed. "Angry was an understatement. But I tried to take the high road, not telling people what really happened. He used that to his advantage, so suddenly I seemed like the bad one. What I had thought of as my circle of friends had shrunk considerably. My personal life was in shambles, and I didn't get the promotion I thought would and, well, London didn't look so friendly anymore. No one would touch me, offer me another job."

"So my father called, and suddenly good old Queensbay looked okay," Noah said, connecting the dots.

Caitlyn nodded. "No, I called him. And begged. He always said there was a place for me, but I think that's because he never thought I would take him up on it. But I needed to get away from Michael, so I thought it would be better to get away, to come back, to see what this place held for me."

"Did you ever love him?"

Caitlyn paused for a moment before answering, "I thought I did." She didn't add what she was thinking: *Not the way I thought I loved you.*

"So, I guess you're over him?"

Caitlyn looked at Noah, held his deep brown eyes. "I would say so."

He moved towards her, and she let him kiss away the memories. They still hadn't talked about the future, or about their past, but she knew that could wait.

"You haven't had it easy, have you?" Noah paused, his hands holding her face to his.

"I don't know. Things could be a whole lot worse. Who said life was easy? As long as there is some fun in it."

"We could have some fun now." He skimmed his thumb along her cheek, his smile back, and Caitlyn felt relieved. She wasn't ready for serious. She didn't do serious anymore.

"Yes," she agreed, wrapping her arms around him, "we could."

Chapter 44

They spent that night together, and Noah cooked her breakfast the next morning before sending her to work with a kiss and then surprising her by telling her he had some things to take care of. Since then, Noah had been busy, around, taking her to dinner, always picking her up at the house, respecting her wish that they keep things on the down low, eating at restaurants outside of Queensbay where it was less likely they would be spotted.

He warmed her bed some nights, but he had business meetings in the city, and sometimes he stayed there. It wasn't that she sensed their relationship was cooling off, not at all. It was just getting comfortable, into a rhythm, like she - and he - expected that Noah would be there.

Still, he hadn't brought up the future again, or pushed. Noah was following her lead. Caitlyn was pondering this, missing him, since he had spent the last two days in Boston on a business trip, judging a business plan competition, and wondering just how she and Noah Randall, hot-headed teenage lovers, had settled into this. A couple. A couple that no one knew about with a future they dared not touch. And it was almost Christmas. What did one buy for one's secret billionaire boyfriend?

Caitlyn was looking on the Internet, searching for ideas, when the phone rang. She looked at the caller ID on her phone and sighed. It was Tony. And she didn't really need to deal with Tony right now. It was first thing on Monday morning, and she hadn't finished her coffee. But you couldn't keep your best client waiting. She picked up the phone.

"Hello."

"Caitlyn," Tony's voice bellowed over the receiver.

"Of course, what can I do for you?"

"I need my money."

"Excuse me?" Caitlyn said.

Her stomach did a flip-flop. How come they never called when they were happy? They never congratulated you when you made them money. They only called when something was wrong.

Caitlyn pulled Tony's files. The quarterly statements had been sent out to clients last week and copies delivered to the account managers just before that. Everything looked fine with the accounts.

"What's the problem, Tony?"

"I need the money I sent you."

"What money?" Caitlyn said.

"The million-five I sent you to get involved in the partnership."

"How did you send it?" And what was he talking about?

"I wrote checks. From different accounts, I might add," Tony said.

"And you sent them in the mail, to me?" Caitlyn felt like she was the slow tortoise trying to catch the fast hare.

"Yes, that's what the material you sent me told me to do."

"Who told you that?"

"No, you told me. Your name was on the letter," Tony said.

Caitlyn tried to hide her surprise.

"Don't you know what's going on there?"

"Of course I know, Tony. But you put up the money to invest in a deal - what deal?" she asked, frantically searching her desk, flipping through screens on her computer as if the answer could be there.

"How the hell do I know? I trusted you, so I sent the money. Caitlyn, that's not the problem. I need my original amount back now."

Tony sounded like he was in a panic, and Caitlyn was curious. It didn't sound like the man she knew.

"Is everything okay, Tony?"

She heard him draw in a deep breath. "It's fine, just fine. But I have some unexpected capital needs, and I need the cash back sooner, rather than later."

There was an opportunity to preach, Caitlyn thought, to say something along the lines of "I told you so." She didn't think it would be a good idea and certainly wouldn't endear her to Tony. Of course, it might bear to remind him of the fact once everything had cleared up. It might make him more willing to believe that she really did have his best interests at heart. "Listen, Tony, this doesn't have to be a problem. Let me see what I can do."

"Fine. Sooner would be better." He hung up on her.

Caitlyn looked down at the phone. This bothered her, more because she could have seen it coming. She knew about Tony's financial position. That was why she had advised him on the slow and steady route. But who had sent him paperwork asking him to invest over a million dollars?

Caitlyn found Sam Harris in his office, as usual, staring at his computer.

"Caitlyn? What can I help you with?" He looked up, and Caitlyn was hit with a sudden realization. He reminded her, in certain ways, of Michael. Or perhaps it was just the feeling of revulsion that came over her whenever she thought about either one of them. At least she only had to work with Sam.

"I just got a call from Tony Biddle." She sat down in the chair across from him, staring straight at him.

"So? He's your client."

"Funny, that's what I thought, too. But, apparently someone sent him some deal paperwork asking him for quite a bit of money."

Sam leaned back and crossed his arms. "So, you invited him in on a deal, and he sent in the money. That's the business we're in, Caitlyn. He can't just have it back, you know, not until the investment term is up."

"Yes, well, I never sent him the paperwork."

"Really?" Sam typed something up on his screen and turned it to show her. "This is in the system."

Caitlyn looked at the screen in disbelief. Tony had said he had gotten a letter from her, and here was an electronic copy.

"I never sent that to him. He's not ready for that kind of risk, and he doesn't really have that kind of money to invest. He needs it back." Caitlyn fought the small wave of panic that was settling over her.

Sam laughed a little. "We're not a library, Caitlyn. He can't just have his money back."

"Sure he can. We have the money; we can give it back," Caitlyn said.

"If we gave back money to anyone who changed his mind, then we wouldn't have much of a business, would we? Our business is built upon the assumption that we get to keep the money for a while, to invest it. It's in the paperwork."

"But this was a mistake. He was never supposed to get that paperwork," Caitlyn said, thinking fast. She didn't know how Tony had gotten it. Perhaps Heather had messed up? Still, there would be time enough to figure that out later. Now she needed to focus on keeping Tony a happy client.

Sam lifted his hands and shrugged.

Chapter 45

"You seem to have settled in quite nicely here," Chase said. They were in the boatyard, walking amongst the hulls of boats wrapped in plastic against the coming winter. Chase had wanted to take a look at one for sale, and Noah had agreed to accompany him, more to get out of the office than anything else.

Early December was cold, with the wind rolling in from the water. Noah hunched down into the new coat he'd bought at North Coast Outfitters and wished he'd sprung for a pair of gloves as well.

"Hey, earth to Noah."

Noah looked up quickly. Chase was staring at him, a look of curiosity on his face.

"Sorry, I've just been thinking about things."

"What, your new business or Caitlyn?"

Noah shook his head. His friend knew him too well. "Caitlyn."

"So what's wrong with that?" Chase asked, ducking under a metal brace and around the stern of a boat. He was searching for something by name.

"It seems like she's all I can think about," Noah said, complaining. It was true. He couldn't get the thought of her out of his head, but anytime he tried to talk to her seriously about them, she changed the subject.

"You sound like a teenage girl," Chase said.

"You just wait," Noah shot back. "Your turn will come."

Chase shook his head. "No way, I am a confirmed bachelor. Too many fish in the sea for me to settle on just one, but you're different. You know, like a swan."

"A swan?" Noah wasn't sure he wanted to be compared to a swan.

"Yeah, you know, the big white birds that mate for life. You and Caitlyn are swans. You two are meant for each other, but you're too thick-headed to see it."

"I'm not thick-headed," Noah said, almost hitting his head on the keel of a sailboat as Chase abruptly changed course.

"Well, maybe you're not, since you're the one talking about your feelings with your best friend, but one of you is. If you two screw it up this time, I'm gonna have to knock some sense into both of you." Chase stopped suddenly and tilted his head back. "This is it. The *Windsway*. She's a beauty, don't you think?"

Noah looked up. The yacht was not wrapped in plastic like the others, so he could admire the clean lines and simple design. Chase was right; it was a beautiful boat.

"Owner lost his shirt on some real estate deal. He's selling things off left and right. I already bought his Porsche, and he'd said he'd give me a deal on the boat. Only a year old, never sailed. Sucker," Chase said genially. Noah knew his friend hated it when people bought boats and didn't use them.

"So, what do I do?" Noah said.

Chase looked at him, his mind clearly on the boat and not on Noah's trouble. "Umm, have you ever tried telling her how you feel, really feel?"

Noah waited, and his heart skipped a beat. "I'm afraid I'll lose her if I tell her."

"Well, then you never really had her, did you? You either win or you lose, but you can't keep playing forever."

Chase looked up at the boat. There was a ladder against the side. The breeze had brought with it a light drizzle, and Noah wished for a cup of hot coffee.

"Want to take a look?" Chase's grin was boyish, and Noah couldn't resist his friend's enthusiasm.

"Let's go take a look at your great deal."

As they climbed the ladder, Noah decided to remind his friend, "Ever hear the one about if it's too good to be true, then it probably is…?"

"You're just jealous I found this first…" Chase's voice was muffled. He was already in the cabin of the boat.

Shaking his head, Noah followed his friend.

Chapter 46

It had taken some work, but Caitlyn had finally convinced Sam Harris to send Tony's money back to him. After having to listen to another half-hour of lecturing, Caitlyn had returned to her desk, exhausted. She had won a battle, sure, but she felt like she was losing a war. Sam Harris didn't have any faith in her. That much had been evident.

It would be a good night to go home early, Caitlyn thought, checking her watch, and then realized it wasn't so early. Noah had an unexpected business dinner with some investors in the city, and she was alone. It would be a nice evening to relax, have a glass of wine and look at account statements. She still hadn't had a chance to look at Mrs. Smith-Sullivan's paperwork, and the woman had been calling daily, harassing her.

Caitlyn pulled her coat tightly around her and turned off her office lights. The rest of the floor was empty. It was the holiday season, and no one was staying late. The parking lot was in the back of the building, looking at the brick face with its symmetrical row of windows. It was cold out, the sky already darkening, and the smell of fireplaces was in the air, unmistakably winter. The quaint gas lamps of Queensbay were draped in evergreen garlands and red ribbons, and last Sunday had been the official lighting of the Christmas tree, complete with the Victorian-garbed carolers.

She picked up some supplies in the local market, chatting with the woman behind the counter. It was starting, she thought, to feel like home.

She had set some lights on a timer, and the warm orange glow greeted her as she pulled into the driveway. The house was solid, comforting, and even though it was quiet, she was happy to be home.

Already feeling calmer, she heated up some dinner and poured a glass of wine. She took it all into the study and set out the papers Mrs. Smith-Sullivan had given her. The old girl Sully wasn't that far off, Caitlyn thought, after looking through things and using her calculator. According to her Queensbay Capital statements, there should have been more than enough money for her to write a check to her nephew.

But that wasn't what had happened. It was only after she had needed it and complained that the money showed up in one lump sum. Someone had forgotten to keep up the transfers, though according to Sully they were supposed to be automatic. And if there had been enough money in the firm account, then there was no reason why someone wouldn't have made those transfers.

Caitlyn leaned back and took a sip. It didn't matter; the woman had gotten her money, after all. Of course, it would be interesting to see if it was just a simple administrative error on someone's part. The money was just sitting in Sully's account.

She looked a little deeper and then called Adriana.

"Hello, I'm sorry to bother you," Caitlyn said. She could hear the sounds of some people in the background.

"No bother, it's bridge night."

"I had a favor to ask. I was looking at Sully's account."

"Well, it's about time. She'll be happy to hear that."

"Well, don't say anything yet," Caitlyn warned her, "but I was wondering if you or Sully could give me the names of anyone else with accounts at the firm that might have had this problem."

"Well, I haven't heard anything," Adriana said.

"Well, I was thinking of people like Sully, you know…" Caitlyn hesitated.

"You mean old biddies who don't check their money regularly?"

Caitlyn sighed. "Exactly. I'm sorry; I know there's no right way to say it."

"It's fine, dear. I'll draw a list up tonight. I have a house of old biddies here to help me, and I'll have it to you tomorrow."

"That would be great, but Adriana, don't say what it's for, okay, at least not yet?"

"Are you asking me to lie, Caitlyn?"

"Stretch the truth?" Caitlyn countered.

"Ah, as you know, I am very good at stretching. You'll have it tomorrow. And now I must get back. Who knows what Agatha is doing in my absence?"

"You're a doll, Adriana."

Caitlyn hung up with Adriana and let the apprehension settle. It was nothing more than a hunch she was following, but it could make sense - and explain Max's erratic behavior over the last few months. And why he had decided to sell to Noah.

Noah. Caitlyn thought of him and what this might mean. She had to be careful, had to be sure. Something like this was devastating, as she knew first-hand. But the truth had to come out.

Chapter 47

Noah walked up the hotel corridor slowly. He had agreed to this meeting, but now he wished he hadn't. Still, his curiosity had gotten the better of him, and he felt compelled to find out what the man had to say.

He knocked on the door, and it swung open. Noah found himself face-to-face with Michael St. John.

"Noah Randall?"

Noah nodded and followed Michael's invitation into the suite. The door swung quietly shut behind him, a small breeze of air raising the hair that was growing over his collar.

"May I take your coat?"

Noah handed his overcoat and watched as Michael placed it on a hanger.

"Tea, coffee, a drink?"

They moved over to the living area of the suite, where full-length windows commanded a majestic view of downtown Manhattan.

"I'll have whatever you're having," Noah said. Michael was drinking scotch and soda, and he poured another one and handed it to Noah.

There was a small silence between them, while Noah sipped his drink and studied Caitlyn's ex-fiancé.

Michael St. John was perfect. He looked, spoke and walked like an advertisement. His blond hair was straight and smoothed back. His shirt was thick cotton and perfectly tucked into his wool trousers. Expensive shoes, buffed to a high shine, were on his feet. When he smiled, he showed a whole mouthful of brilliant white teeth. Even now, in his hotel room, he wore a jacket and a tie.

"I don't know what Caitlyn's told you about me."

"Not much," Noah said roughly and then told himself to cool it. There was something about this man that got to him.

"No, probably not. Things ended badly. I suppose you've heard?"

Noah shrugged, not willing to commit.

"Well, I can't say it's an easy story to tell. I'm here as a courtesy, really."

"A courtesy?" Noah said carefully.

"As such. I understand that your father hired Caitlyn after she came home."

Noah nodded.

"Truthfully, I'm a little surprised."

"Why?"

"Well, certainly, you know Caitlyn's background."

"Her background?" Noah tried to sound indifferent.

Michael retreated a little, his chin pulling up and in. "Ah yes, I see. You've heard rumors. Well, she could hardly escape them. Your father gave her the benefit of the doubt, gave her a position, and now you're committed to justifying his decision."

"He's dead."

"Yes, I am terribly sorry. I did hear. My own father remembers him a bit. Apparently they had done some business together at one point or another."

Michael didn't say it, but the implication was clear. A point long before Maxwell had gone off the deep end.

"Thank you." Noah took another sip and waited, sitting back casually on the sofa, legs crossed, trying to look for all the world like nothing this man could say to him would cause any amount of concern.

"As I said, I'm here as a courtesy to you."

"Yes, you said."

Michael leaned in and put his glass down. "Caitlyn Montgomery is not a well woman."

"Excuse me?" Noah stopped mid-swallow.

"I can see that you're surprised. Yes, you see, I knew her quite well once. We were engaged."

"Yes," Noah said through gritted teeth. Stay cool, he told himself, don't let the bastard get a rise out of you.

"You probably heard what that was like as well. It ended badly, no other way to say it. And Caitlyn couldn't handle it. She went, quite literally, crazy. I mean, I always thought she was a little melancholy, a private one, you know. Happy face to the outside world, crying on the inside. The death of her grandfather, she seemed to blame you for."

He paused and looked at Noah.

"Me?" Noah couldn't believe what he was hearing.

"Well, you, your father. It sort of all got jumbled together when she went off on one of her rages. Swearing revenge to her dying day on you."

"Revenge?" Noah was losing his taste for his drink, but he didn't put it down, couldn't let Michael St. John know he was getting to him.

"Yes, went off the deep end at some point, as I said. Went after me." Michael St. John gave a small grunt of laughter. "Well, she seemed to lose it, after that. It was no good. I tried to help, but she seemed to be intent on revenge of some sort. Making me look bad. She used my name to get several clients, and then she stole from them. Almost like she wanted to be caught. And she was, of course. It could have been bad, very bad. But, luckily we were able to help her, as much as we could. She left London, of course. She couldn't stay, not after what happened."

"No. Not after that story made its rounds, I would imagine," Noah managed to say.

"No one would hire her. I tried to help her find a job, but she didn't want help. And then she disappeared. Back to her homeland."

"Why are you telling me all of this?" And why now? Noah wondered.

"This pains me, but I think she may be at it again. I think she's ready to do something that will destroy you. I think it's like a compulsion with her. Doing something like this, so she'll get caught. Maybe she wants the attention. I don't know. I am not a doctor, just a banker, of course."

"Of course," Noah said.

"She's been calling me, leaving messages, sending things to my apartment, my office. I think she wants to get back together. I mean, she's a lovely girl and all, and well, she can be quite a good bit of fun, if you know what I mean."

Noah couldn't help the flush of anger that spread across his face.

"Oh my." Michael St. John leaned back. "I'm sorry. I had no idea. You're, well, you're involved with her."

"No," Noah tried to say and found his voice was gone, "we're not really that involved."

"I see she is developing a pattern. Not only with the money, but also with men. I mean, I'm sorry. I've been hearing some things. I just wanted to give you a little bit of a warning. Common courtesy. It can be so difficult these days to really say anything against anyone."

Noah looked at him. He seemed to be telling the truth. Every inch of his face radiated sincerity.

"I'm afraid," Michael said, his eyes dropping to the glass in his hand, "I still love her. I know it's pointless. But I just want to help her."

"I knew her. I thought I knew her," Noah said. His drink was gone, and Michael poured more.

"Here, to falling under the spell of the lovely Caitlyn Montgomery."

Noah clinked his glass and felt the hot liquid burn down his throat. All he could think about was her and what she hadn't told him. What else was she keeping from him?

Noah waited until he was safely in his own hotel suite, much father downtown than Michael St. John's, before he made the phone call. It was earlier in California, so he caught Ted Waters at his desk.

"I need some help?"

"Of the legal kind? Or something else." Ted was a former employee, ex-military and a brilliant software hacker. He done well with his TechSpace stock and had turned his unique talents to starting a security business. He had specialists in computer hacking, accounting, protection and security. Noah couldn't think of anyone else who would be more perfect for this kind of job.

"Remember how I told you I bought this company awhile back?"

"Sure, I remember, the one on the East Coast. Something happening out there?"

"Yes," Noah said, looking out at the lights of the city below him. "I think there's quite a bit going on there. But first, I need you to run a check on a few names."

Noah rattled them off and gave a few more pieces of information to Ted, who promised to get on it right away.

After hanging up the phone, Noah collapsed in the chair and just stared out the window, wondering if he had done the right thing.

Chapter 48

"I missed you," Caitlyn said and went into Noah's arms as if she belonged there. She still hadn't decided what to tell him about what she had found out the other day. Adriana had given her the names, but so far, Caitlyn hadn't done anything with them. It was cowardly, she knew, but she was afraid of where it would lead her, lead them.

He had come back from the city, and she hadn't seen him at work. But here he was at home, and she had come to him to reassure herself that they were okay. Because all of a sudden, no matter what had happened in the past, what was happening in the present, she wanted him.

"Me, too," he said, hugging her back, but she sensed a hesitation, a reserve.

She looked at him carefully. "What is it?"

He motioned her into the house, back towards the kitchen. It was late afternoon, but he had a fresh pot of coffee on. He poured her a cup of it, finding her cream, one sugar, just as she liked it. All the while, he remained silent, and she felt a corresponding heaviness come down on her.

"You have to tell me what's wrong," she pleaded, needing to know what he was thinking, no matter how much it hurt.

Noah looked at her, his eyes dark, impenetrable. "What really happened?"

"What do you mean?"

"When you left London and your job? Something else happened that you haven't told me. Not just about Michael cheating on you."

She looked at him, feeling her skin redden.

"What is this about?" She thought she could leave that behind. Maxwell had told her not to worry, told her he didn't care.

"It's about you and us, Caitlyn." Noah made as if to reach out and touch her hand, but he drew it back. "About why you really came back. About why you're with me."

"With you? I'm with you because..." Caitlyn trailed off. She couldn't say it, could barely admit it to herself. "Because I like being with you. You make things feel right," she finished.

"And is that it?" he asked, looking at her, waiting. When she said nothing, he shook his head and started to walk away. "I don't know what he did to you, over in London, or what you think Maxwell did to you, but I'm not either one of them. And until you figure that out, maybe, maybe ... just show yourself out, will you? I have work to do."

"Wait." Caitlyn couldn't let him walk away. "There is more to it. But I didn't tell you because I'm embarrassed by it." There, she had said it.

"It can't be that bad, can it? You didn't do anything wrong, did you?"

Caitlyn shook her head and sat down. "I think I might have."

Noah walked back, stood closer to her, but still didn't touch her. "Tell me."

And Caitlyn knew she had to.

"After I found Michael sleeping with my best friend, I was upset. I moved out, into my own place. I was unhappy, upset, angry and basically not much good to anyone. My friends snubbed me, and Michael tried to persuade me to come back. He was quite forceful, threatening even. And when that didn't work, he told lies. He became the injured party, and I became *persona non grata* - not very good when your job is to be out there, mingling, going to parties, getting clients. It seemed that a lot of my good fortune had rested squarely on Michael's shoulders. But I still had a few loyal clients and, well, things did seem to get a little better.

"But then somehow, one of my clients, an older man, ancient really, who couldn't be expected to know what was going on in the gossip pages, sent a check. And supposedly it got misplaced. In the wrong account. His money went missing, and there were some errors in my accounting. He called about it, of course, and the whole thing was taken very seriously. There was an investigation. I couldn't remember getting the check, didn't know what happened to it.

"But my assistant swore she had seen it. She said it came across her desk, I endorsed it and then had it deposited in an account I had control of. I demanded a full investigation."

"What happened?"

"The paper trail led back to Michael. He wasn't very smart about it."

"And what happened to him?" Noah's voice was rough, angry.

Caitlyn shrugged. "Michael's father is a very important man. The whole thing was hushed up, I was cleared of any wrongdoing, and after a little while, everything died down, or at least I thought it did. But the rumors were out there. I could tell that I was going nowhere at the company, or in London. A fresh start seemed the best thing. Maxwell knew that. He saved me."

"So, you didn't come back out of revenge?"

Caitlyn looked at Noah and laughed. "Revenge?"

"Against my father. For stealing the firm, for ruining your life."

Caitlyn put her hand on Noah's arm, and he let her. "No, that's not why I came back." But she couldn't help thinking of what she had learned. Perhaps if she had known then what she knew now?

She looked into Noah's eyes and saw that he was confused. He believed her, but he had his doubts, and how could she blame him? She had been very angry and bitter for a long time, and he didn't know the whole story. She couldn't tell him yet - it would be too much and not quite believable.

"Just hold me," she asked, and he did. He kissed her softly, at first, and then it became more intense. His hands were more insistent, stroking her, finding her sensitive spots, his mouth clamping down on her nipples, pebbling them against his tongue. He pushed her against the counter. His teeth grazed her neck, and his hands lifted up her skirt and pulled her panties down, lifting her up so she was braced against the cold marble. She was ready for him, ready as he touched her and his fingers worked her, steadily, unremittingly to a climax. She came quickly, a burst of need, and then he was inside her.

He was thrusting deeply, holding tight to her, and she clung to him, not wanting to let go, hoping that this would make things right between them, that they could get back to the place where they had been. Somehow she could sense things were unraveling between them, that they could no longer bury the past or not face the future. But she moaned as he emptied into her and tried to focus, just for a little while longer, on the present.

Chapter 49

They had spent the evening together, finally making it to the bedroom. They had made love again, barely speaking a word, simply letting their bodies do the feeling. Still, she could not sleep, and it was close to the middle of the night when Caitlyn dressed and let herself out of the bedroom, leaving a note. She tiptoed across the hall and down the stairs. What she had to do wasn't right, wasn't pleasant, but she needed to know if she and Noah were to have a future together.

She went to the study, to Maxwell's desk. The drawers were unlocked; Noah had already been through them. But found what she wanted easily enough, in the second drawer, the master set of keys to the office and the small index card with Maxwell's personal passwords to the firm's computer system on it. She left the house and went out to the car. It was pitch black; dawn was still far away. She looked up at Noah's window and then got in the car.

She drove down into Queensbay, to the parking lot of the office building. She was only half-dressed. She had on her skirt but no pantyhose and no coat, and it was cold as she hurried across the parking lot and let herself into the building. She used her ID card to let herself in and she took the elevator up to the fifth floor. Only dim emergency lights were on as she opened the doors of the office and made her way towards what was now Noah's office. The key was in there; she felt it.

Caitlyn slipped a key into the door of the office. It took a few tries, but she found the right one and let herself in. It was so perfect in here. Noah hadn't done much to make it his own, and Maxwell's computer was still there. She turned it on, waiting for it to boot up.

She left the office just before dawn and went to her own house to shower and change. She knew she would need to go back into the office, as if everything were still fine, to face what she needed to face, and then she would be free to go. She could put it all in Noah's hands.

As she walked towards her desk, the look on Heather's face said it all. Caitlyn wondered if she should even bother to take off her jacket and then thought it would look bad if she didn't. She thought for a second about how the scene should be played. She needed them to believe she was hiding something, stonewalling them, but that she thought she was innocent. Because she was, and someone knew it.

"Mr. Harris wants to see you," Heather told her. She looked so pained that Caitlyn almost wanted to ask her what was wrong. But she did not, simply smoothed her hands over her jacket and played dumb.

Sam was in his office alone. Caitlyn shut the door behind her and took a seat, not waiting to be invited.

"Caitlyn."

Caitlyn smiled, trying to fake a braveness she did not feel.

"Why were you in the office last night?"

"Excuse me?"

"We have security cameras, you know, and they showed you coming into the office in the very early morning hours."

There weren't security cameras in the office, just in the lobby. Caitlyn swallowed. She hadn't quite thought about that. Still, though, they wouldn't know what she'd been doing once she'd been inside the office.

"I had some work to do."

He looked at her, his blue eyes gazing directly at her. "I find that hard to believe. How did you get in?"

She shrugged. Not much she could say there, without dragging Noah into it.

Sam went on. "Caitlyn, I have been informed that there are some irregularities with your accounts."

"My accounts?" This time, instead of fear, she felt anger. It was happening again.

"Yes. Inconsistent accounting, amounts missing. I am launching a full investigation into it, and until that time, I am suspending you without pay from all firm-related activities."

Caitlyn saw that Sam was trying hard not to gloat. He thought she was done, out of the way, an obstacle removed. So, she let him believe it, protesting her innocence and even letting her eyes water. But he was adamant, would not show her anything. He did not bring up what had happened in London. At the end, she collected herself and her dignity and got up to go.

"Caitlyn."

She turned.

"This looks bad. I thought…" He paused. "It's just that Maxwell trusted you so much."

She looked at him and nodded.

Head held high, she marched out. Eyes followed her out. She took her coat and said nothing to Heather, who just looked at her, a look of despair.

"Don't worry, Heather; it will all be okay," she told her.

"It's not true," Heather burst out. "I told them it couldn't be true."

"I promise. It will turn out all right."

Caitlyn's reassurances seemed to help, and Heather dabbed her tears and gave Caitlyn a big hug before letting her go.

There was a security guard waiting for her at the elevators.

"I need to escort you out, Miss." He was young, and they had once had a friendly relationship. He didn't quite take her arm, but he was uncomfortable. He asked for her badge and then for the keys.

"I don't have the keys."

He looked at her.

"But how did you get in last night?"

She shrugged and gave him the badge. She walked out the door and to her car, driving first to Noah's. He deserved an explanation and what information he needed to figure things out.

Chapter 50

"Listen, boss, I'm sorry to bother you with this." Noah looked up. He had come into the office, after finding that Caitlyn had disappeared. Now Sam Harris stood in his door. Noah fought back his irritation. He didn't need this, not with all that was happening.

"Can it wait?" Noah said, with a wave of his hand.

"I'm afraid not. There have been some new developments with the situation I discussed with you."

Noah frowned. There were a lot of situations, weren't there?

"At the party. The accounts, the irregularities."

"Yes, of course." Noah sat up, apprehension rippling through him. Sam stepped into his office and closed the door.

"Well, there have been a few developments - something serious, at least in terms of the amount of money that's been moving around."

"What are you saying?" Noah asked carefully.

"I think we have a thief. And I think I know who it is." Sam sat back in his chair, concern rippling over his face.

"A thief?"

"Oh, yes, I think your father was aware of the situation, which was why he came to you. The amounts gone ... well, this is big. It could ruin, destroy the whole firm. Everything your father built."

"My father," Noah said, but even to him, his voice sounded far away.

"I know he trusted her, but I think that it was misplaced, very misplaced. These things can be hard to trace, but I do have a friend who works in private banking. In the Caymans."

"Caymans?" Noah swallowed, trying to think fast.

"I think, now that we know where to look, things will become pretty clear. I don't have to tell you that we might be better off keeping this sort of thing quiet, of course, pursue some sort of private action. Last thing we want to do is tip her off. Have her make a run for it, you know?"

Noah looked carefully at Sam Harris, who leaned forward and pushed a single piece of paper towards him. Noah picked it up, glanced at it and nodded.

"You're exactly right. Something needs to be done," he said.

Chapter 51

They were facing each other, like tigers ready to pounce. He looked at her and hated himself. She was close to tears, he thought, dark color suffusing her face, her lower lip unsteady, her whole body twisted and coiled.

"Are you saying you don't believe me?"

He looked at her, reaching for her. "No, of course not, I know it's not true. But there's something going on."

She felt a rush of relief. "Well, it's the right answer, but it took you too long. If you had to think that hard…" Caitlyn picked up her jacket and started to move away from him.

"Don't go. Listen, I had no idea you would take my keys and do something stupid like break into the office." Noah ran his hands through his hair. He'd been proceeding carefully, working with his team of investigators and a lawyer. No matter what, his lawyer had said, they didn't want to spook the perpetrator. They had to catch the crook red-handed.

"Stupid?" Caitlyn shook her head.

"Listen," Noah said. "It's true. There are some problems with your accounts. I've had a team looking into it."

"My accounts. Do you think I would steal?" Caitlyn was angry, her body tight and coiled again.

Noah wanted to reach out and grab her, pull her close to him, but he knew she wouldn't let him.

"No, I don't, but someone is."

She seemed to relax a bit after that. "So, you know about it?"

"Not that much yet. And I don't know who. I haven't even told Sam Harris what's going on. No one can know, yet. We don't want to tip our hand."

"What made you think…?"

Noah sighed and told her about his meeting with Michael. "Hopefully he's well on his way to London. But it got me thinking, about what you told me … Tony Biddle's account. That friend of Adriana's. So I called a security firm. They have lawyers, accountants, everything we need to figure it out."

"But you don't know everything yet?" she asked.

He shook his head. "But I need to ask you for your patience; let this all play out. If the person who's doing this knows we think it's you…"

"He, or she, will do something stupid."

Noah nodded. He could tell she was still mad. "I'm sorry I didn't tell you sooner. These things are delicate." He wanted to pull her to him, tell her it would be all right, that he would make it right for her. He took a step towards her, but she moved back.

"Don't touch me, yet. There's more that you need to know."

Caitlyn took a deep breath, pulled a thick envelope from her bag and threw it onto the counter between the two of them.

"It's all in here, Noah. It will make sense. And I don't care what you do with it. I won't tell anyone, and no one has to know. I think it will be okay now; your money made it so. But I can't be involved anymore. I thought coming back would give me some peace, let me be me again, and well, it seems like I got sucked in just like everyone else did."

"I don't understand what you're saying." His forehead creased, and he looked at the envelope but did not touch it.

"It's all in there," she repeated. "Look at it, and you can decide what to do."

She picked up her bag, and he rose from where he was sitting.

"Are you going?" he asked, and she thought she heard panic lace his voice.

"Caitlyn, don't," he said. He pulled her close, and she let him. He touched his lips to her hair, put his arms around her back and pulled her in.

Finally, she pushed away, gently, then harder.

"No, Noah. No. I thought … I thought I could get away from it, thought I could leave it behind. But I can't. Our choices stick with us. There are always consequences. I wanted to get away from here so much, I went too far away. Now I am not sure I can ever come back." "Caitlyn, where are you going?" She had picked up her coat. "Caitlyn." He felt panic rushing over him. He couldn't let her go. This wasn't what he had meant to happen.

He moved to go after her, but she turned around, just inside the door.

"Noah, if you trust me, let me go."

She let herself out, and he stood there, alone and miserable, not sure what to do. Let me go, she had said. It was what she had said to him years ago, after her grandfather's funeral. He had gone to her, to tell her that he would stay with her, be with her as long as she needed him to. And he had been told to let go, to let her go, to leave for his own life. He had left her then, let her go. And now. He sat down on the bottom step of the stairs, looking around him at this big, empty house that wasn't his.

Believe in me, but let me go. The hell with that, he thought, as he heard her car pull away. Caitlyn Montgomery was not getting away from him. Not this time, not ever again.

Chapter 52

"You don't look so good, my friend." Chase handed him a beer and threw himself down on the couch next to his friend.

"She told me to let her go." Noah took a pull of his beer, found that he didn't really want it and put it on the low coffee table. He had come to Chase's place, the suite of rooms he kept in the Osprey Arms.

"Caitlyn left?" Chase gave a long whistle. "What did you do to her?"

"What makes you think I did something?"

Chase laughed. "Because with you and her, it's usually you who screws it up. Didn't I tell you to go back and say sorry to her? And you didn't. Before I knew it, the two of you were three thousand miles apart and miserable."

"That was a long time ago."

"Exactly," Chase said, taking a sip of his beer. "So, what happened, really?"

Noah ran his hands through his hair and scrubbed them over his face. "There's something wrong at the firm. Money missing, unaccounted for."

He filled his friend in on what he had learned so far from Ted and his investigation and what Sam Harris had told him.

"Oh," Chase said, and there was something in his voice that had Noah looking at him.

"You knew about it."

"No, no way." Chase held up his hands. "But I think Caitlyn did."

"The money is missing from her accounts," Noah said.

Chase laughed. "Well, you don't think she did it, do you?"

"Of course not. And I told her that. But things just don't add up. And, well, the evidence is pretty clear that someone did it."

"And that's why she left, because you didn't believe that it wasn't her?"

Noah looked out the window. Chase had taken rooms that overlooked the marina and the harbor. It was quiet down there, but the tall lamps threw out great pools of light.

"There was something more," Noah said, and told Chase about what Michael St. John had done.

"Well, that sounds like something that bastard would say. He's got a nasty reputation."

"I know." Noah told Chase about the call he had made. "It didn't take them long to find out all the stuff on him. Apparently his family has some deep pockets, so things keep getting covered up, but he's a pompous ass with a mean streak."

"So, you're not taking his word for it that she was out for some sort of vendetta?"

"No," Noah said, "but she didn't really give an explanation. Just handed me this." Noah pulled out the envelope of papers Caitlyn had shoved at him and tossed it to Chase, who neatly caught it.

"Have you looked at it?" he asked.

Noah shook his head. "I haven't had the time."

"Mind if I?" Chase asked, and when Noah nodded his assent, he slipped the sheaf of papers out of the folder.

Noah stood up, unable to sit for any longer. He paced the room, filled with restless, nervous energy, his mind going over what Caitlyn had said to him, what he had said to her, how in a matter of minutes everything they had built up had managed to come undone.

"Noah, I don't think Caitlyn's been entirely honest with you," Chase said, and Noah turned to look at his friend. Chase's expression was serious, and Noah felt his heart skip a beat.

"What is it?" He almost didn't want to know if it were true. Perhaps he could go now, tell her it was okay, no matter what.

"Well, there are two things."

"Okay." Noah wasn't sure where this was going.

"First off, Caitlyn doesn't need anyone's money."

"Well, I know she's not broke, but that house, the car, her clothes, it all has to cost money. And she makes good money, but it does seem like she must spend it as fast as she makes it. Lucas didn't leave her much."

"Noah, Caitlyn doesn't need anyone's money because she's already rich."

"What do you mean, rich?" Noah didn't understand what Chase was trying to say.

"Caitlyn is quite rich. She doesn't like to talk about it, but she was or is part owner of two restaurant chains, two websites, a video production company, a sailing goods company and an Internet start-up that recently went public."

Noah felt his knees grow weak. "What are you saying?" he asked, though he was beginning to have a pretty good idea.

"Caitlyn's been investing in companies since she was a teenager. I guess she took whatever she inherited from Lucas and began investing. Remember how about three years into TechSpace you needed more money? I was dry at that point, and I know you were pretty desperate."

"There was a last-minute private investor who wanted to remain anonymous." Noah remembered it well. He had been on the ropes, about to see everything he had worked for go down in flames. But the infusion of cash had been just what the company needed, and they had been profitable ever since. It hadn't been a loan; it had been an investment, and when TechSpace went public, that chunk of the company had been worth several million dollars.

"She was the anonymous investor?"

Chase nodded. "It wasn't her first or last. Like I said, she's part owner of a pizza restaurant chain, a couple of media sites, and I'm proud to say, of North Coast Outfitters, though I intend to buy her out in a few months."

"But how...?" Noah said and then answered, "Playing cards?"

Chase shrugged. "Caitlyn keeps her secrets. But when you needed money, she was there for you. She didn't think you would accept it from her, or if you did, that you would feel like you owed her, so she kept it quiet."

"And I took it, believing my idea was so brilliant there were people lining up to fund it." Noah thought of something. "How did you know about this?"

"I plied her with too much champagne one night, and let's just say that's when I realized that she was so not over you." Chase watched him with sympathetic eyes. "I know it's not my story to tell, but the two of you keeping secrets from each other is driving me crazy."

"Secrets. I'm not keeping secrets. She's the one who..." Noah ran his hands through his hair. He didn't know what to think, except that, once again, he had doubted her.

"She never asked for anything in return, did she?"

Noah shook his head.

"She just wanted you to be happy, to have your dream."

"I really did screw it up this time," Noah said, the realization crashing down on him. Once again he had let her walk away.

"I think she would be willing to forgive you. After all, she wasn't exactly honest with you."

"What do you mean?" Noah saw that Chase was looking down at the papers he had given him.

"I think she was trying to protect you." Chase rose and handed a few pages to Noah. He looked at them, not sure what he was supposed to see, and then it hit him. Suddenly it all made sense why his father had needed his money so badly.

Chapter 53

Noah looked at Ted Waters. He had taken the red-eye in from California, and though he yawned, he looked well pleased with himself. He was short, stocky and had biceps like Popeye. It had all been simple, especially once Noah had given him the evidence from Caitlyn. It hadn't taken too much work, becoming obvious once you knew where to look - someone who was living above their means. A quick check of financial records had them honing in quickly.

"It looks like he's been skimming for a while now. The red flags are there if you look closely enough. Everything's just a tad too nice. And he and his wife pay for a lot of it in cash. Questions to a few of the local and not-so-local merchants turned that up."

"So, how does it work?"

"Well, we're not entirely sure, since you said you wanted to keep this matter discreet, but just as your associate showed you, it looks like real statements were being diverted to a post office box, then doctored statements were being sent out instead. The doctored statements showed healthy accounts with modest growth, while, in reality, the balances have been drawn down for quite a while." Ted's biceps bulged as he tapped a list of names. "Targets fit the profile, generally senior women, for whom the firm does not present the bulk of their assets. For the most part, they don't take money from the account. If they needed money, your guy just moved it around, so that no one person ever got suspicious."

Noah shook his head, feeling sick. "Do you know where the money's gone?"

"Like I said, some of it was just spent as cash on day-to-day stuff, but we're pretty sure it's been stashed somewhere. Doesn't mean we won't find it, just might take awhile."

"How much?" Noah asked.

"Well, it's been going on for a while," the Ted aid.

"What, like a couple of months?" Noah said, hoping Ted would put his fears to rest.

Ted ran his hand through his light, buzz-cut hair and looked at him and laughed. "More like a couple of years. Try almost a decade."

"What?" Noah's voice went up, and he felt his stomach twist.

"Oh, yeah. For quite a while."

"But, he's only worked here for a couple of years."

"He had a partner," Ted said, and Noah pushed back in the chair as the full implications of this hit him.

Oblivious, Ted went on. "Obviously, the authorities will have to be called in, but you can keep this quiet if you're willing to personally guarantee the money…"

Noah waved his hand in consent. The money meant nothing to him, now that he knew the truth. Was this what Caitlyn had been trying to protect him from? That his father had been stealing all along?

Chapter 54

Caitlyn had left Noah's and gone straight to Adriana's. What she had found on Maxwell's computer indicated that money had been going missing from accounts for a very long time. It wasn't a recent occurrence, and Caitlyn was sure that Adriana knew more than she was letting on.

She pulled her coat more tightly around her. It would snow soon, she was sure. The air was still and heavy, and everything was gray, with a deep silence.

"Caitlyn, what are...?" Marion answered the door.

Caitlyn pushed into the foyer, glad even for the marginal improvement in warmth.

"I need to see her. Is she here?

Marion looked at her, surprised at the grim look on Caitlyn's face.

"She was on her way out."

"This won't keep," Caitlyn said and started to walk down the hallway that led to the library. She hadn't made it far when Adriana, dressed in a buff pants suit, stepped out into the hallway.

"We need to talk," Caitlyn said when she saw her.

Adrianna looked older somehow, less vivacious. But her voice was perfectly even as she nodded and said, "I suppose we must."

Without another word, Caitlyn followed Adriana towards the back room, where the lamps were all on, casting pools of light over the dark wood and crimson tones of the leather chair and wool rug. She took off her coat, and Marion reached out a hand for it.

"Coffee?"

Caitlyn nodded and raised a hand, dismissive and appreciative all at once. Adriana gestured towards a chair, and Caitlyn sat, running her hands through her hair, fighting the urge to shiver.

"Will you light the fire?" Adriana asked, and Caitlyn did, finding the matches in the small box on the mantle, dropping to one knee and watching as the light curled around the edges of the paper and kindling that had already been laid on the hearth. She stayed as close as she could until she could take no more and then sat back in her chair, the two of them catty-corner to each other, flanking the small but bright fire.

Marion brought in coffee before they began to speak, and Caitlyn poured it for them both, adding milk and sugar for herself and eagerly taking advantage of the oatmeal raisin cookies that had been provided.

Now alone, Caitlyn asked, "What really happened?"

Adriana snorted and answered, "I already told you."

"Not all of it."

"First, tell me what you know," Adriana said.

Caitlyn continued, "You wouldn't have agreed to see me so easily, if you didn't think I knew."

"True, but I promised to keep it a secret."

"For how long?"

Adriana moved her shoulder. "Forever, I suppose."

"Does it matter now?" Caitlyn asked.

"No, it probably doesn't. Time has a way of changing things. What seemed so vitally important then ... well, now it seems to have little power to shock or scare. What was once considered damaging, now most likely isn't. So, don't judge us too harshly."

Caitlyn felt her heart sink. It was as she had thought.

"How did you find out?" Adriana said.

"I didn't until now."

"So, you bluffed me," Adriana said, but she didn't seem upset.

"You said it yourself. My grandfather was too full of life to not fight for it. No matter what odds the doctor gave him." Caitlyn said.

"We told some lies." Adriana said simply.

"Why?" Caitlyn spat out the word.

"You know that your grandfather and I had an affair. But what you don't know is that it started almost thirty years ago, and went on and off, while your grandmother was still alive, while I was very much married to Trip Randolph. I am not proud of it, but I cannot deny what we had."

Caitlyn shook her head. "Wasn't she your best friend?"

"I told you I wasn't proud of what happened. But Lucas and I couldn't stay away from each other. Well, you would think that divorce would be easy, especially after your grandmother died. But Trip was another story. As I told Heather, divorce would have been expensive, complicated. And Trip would have gone after Lucas, destroyed him first."

"So, what happened?"

Adriana shook her head. "Lucas broke it off with me, suddenly, a few weeks before the end of the summer. No explanation, and then he was dead. Cancer was the official reason, but then Maxwell came to me. He was worried, panicked. Begged me to help him, told me Lucas would want that."

The pulse in Adriana's cheek moved, and she stared into the fire.

"He had pictures, of me and Lucas. Not a pretty sight in black and white, middle-aged love. You would think that I wouldn't care anymore, that the world knew about me and Lucas, but as I said, I knew Trip would, and would turn his anger to me."

"So?" Caitlyn prompted, though she had an idea where this was going.

"Max blackmailed me. Said he wouldn't go to Trip if I would give him the money he needed to get the firm back on its feet."

"And you did," Caitlyn said.

"Yes, with one provision."

"And that was?"

"Take care of you and your mother. Make sure that you had what you needed in terms of money and education and opportunities."

"I see," Caitlyn said, so much becoming clear. All the internships that had seemed like long shots, mysterious opportunities complete with stipends, had opened for her, chances to go to London, to Europe, to travel, to study abroad. Now she could see the invisible hands that had moved them all, the phone calls, the favors that had been traded and dealt. The currency of guilt, not any sort of adoptive paternal instinct.

Adriana looked at Caitlyn. "All this time, you thought there was something you could have done to stop him? That if you had been there that night, been there for him, it would have made a difference."

"Haven't you thought that, too?" Caitlyn asked.

Adriana nodded. "Yes, of course. But it seemed like Luke had his own plans. I think he thought that Maxwell could make him a fall guy - blame the money problems on him, and it would all work out. I don't think he knew the extent to which Maxwell was in trouble."

Caitlyn wiped away the tears, and Adriana handed her a tissue.

"Do you feel any better?"

"No. Yes." Caitlyn laughed. "Maybe. I guess we won't ever know the whole story." She thought for a moment, and then decided she owed it to Adriana. "Maxwell never stopped, you know. His financial shenanigans."

Adriana leaned back in her seat. "I thought you might have figured that out. That's why you wanted those names, right?"

"It was a pretty simple scheme. Maxwell was making false statements and sending them out to account holders who rarely withdrew money from their accounts. He showed a nice, steady growth of return, and he raided their accounts and moved the money around. If ever they needed it, he just moved it back in. If someone, like Sully, did something unexpected, he claimed an administrative error, and most people were satisfied."

"But?"

"Well, you can only keep that kind of game up for so long. That's why he needed me. At first, he thought I would bring some money to the firm. But I wanted to buy him out. I think he was considering it, until Noah. I think he thought Noah would have been so desperate to mend fences, especially now that he made it, that he would give him the money, no questions asked."

"So, he thought he was going to fix it all again?" Adriana said.

"Boom and bust. I am not sure where all of it is, but I think Maxwell just wasn't very good at making money or keeping it. Sure, there was the house and the club membership, the cars, but as far as I can tell, there's no secret bank account in the Caribbean."

"And Noah?" Adriana asked.

"He knew nothing about it. But I think Sam Harris was in on it, and he's trying to set me up to take the fall." Caitlyn explained what had happened with Sam Harris.

"You don't think Noah thinks that, really?"

Caitlyn felt restless. Noah had said he didn't, but she knew that the evidence, when weighed with her past, would look damaging.

"I don't know. It's complicated." Caitlyn said.

Adriana made a tsk-tsk sound. "I think your generation uses that phrase when they want to avoid the fact that loving another person is difficult. Otherwise, it wouldn't be love. It would be lust."

"And I suppose you know a thing or two about it?"

Adriana drew herself up in her chair. "I do. I loved Trip Randolph for a good while, and then I met your grandfather. Nothing could keep us apart. We knew it was wrong; there was every reason that it wasn't right. And we never made it work. We were too scared, too proud, too complicated. Don't make the same mistake." Her gaze held Caitlyn's. "Do you love Noah?"

"Yes," Caitlyn whispered and felt her heart soar.

"Well, then you need to tell him that."

"But how? I just got fired for stealing money."

"You didn't do it."

"It's hard to prove."

There was a sound, footsteps entering the room. They both looked up.

Chapter 55

"I thought I would find you here." Noah said. There was some-one else with him, and Marion was hovering in the background, wringing her hands.

Adriana looked at Caitlyn, who was just staring open-mouthed at Noah.

"Perhaps some coffee, or tea, Marion."

"Of course," Marion said, obviously thankful to have something to do.

"What are you doing here?" Caitlyn said, feeling her heart thudding in her chest.

"We need to talk," Noah said.

"Is he here to arrest me?" Caitlyn said, her eyes flitting to the man who was standing behind Noah.

"Ted Waters, security expert and investigator. You must be Caitlyn Montgomery. Pleasure to meet you. That was some great work you did, digging that stuff up." Ted moved forward, shook Caitlyn's hand, then Adriana's.

Of all the things Caitlyn had expected to hear, that was not one of them.

"Excuse me?"

Noah came to her, stood before her and held out his hands. She let herself be pulled up and drawn into his embrace, his strong arms coming around her, his lips brushing the top of her hair. She knew that they had an audience, but she didn't care. The only thing that mattered was that he was there.

There was a discreet clearing of a throat, and she smiled at Noah. They could talk later.

"Sam came to me a few weeks ago and said there were some irregularities with some of the accounts." Noah began, as he and Ted sat.

They had gone through two pots of coffee and a plate of cookies before they were done hashing out the details of a plan.

"I don't like it," Noah said again, shaking his head.

"I'll be fine."

"It's the cleanest way," Ted agreed. Caitlyn had come up with the plan herself, but Ted had latched onto it quickly, refining the details, while Adriana had thought it sounded exciting. Only Noah had reservations.

"It could be dangerous," Noah said. "Have you forgotten that my father is dead?"

"The police said it was an accident."

"For lack of any compelling reason to say otherwise. But now…"

"I'll be fine." Caitlyn took a hand and placed it in Noah's. He looked at her, his brown eyes worried, but she leaned forward and kissed him lightly. "Trust me?"

He managed a smile. "You're the best poker player I know."

Chapter 56

"How did you get in here?" Sam Harris looked up in surprise.

Caitlyn dangled a key in front of her. It was almost nine at night, and the offices were deserted, except for his. Only the desk lamp was on, and Sam was mostly in the shadows, surrounded by stacks of paper.

"I have my ways. Going someplace?"

Sam swallowed, then flashed a quick smile. "Perhaps. I never was a big fan of the winter."

"Interesting. I suppose getting rid of me was just so you could buy some time."

Sam shrugged. "I'll be gone soon. They'll sort it all out. I doubt it will stick to you, but it looks pretty bad. Hopefully you won't actually get arrested. Just spend some uncomfortable time explaining your actions."

Caitlyn laughed. "Pretty smart. You're right; no one would believe me, even if I said something. Besides, I am sure there's just enough money sitting in some offshore account to make me look pretty damn guilty."

Sam shrugged. "There might be."

"But just enough right? The rest you have. What did you do? Did you and Maxwell spend it over the years? Or is it all sitting someplace safe for you?"

Sam Harris gave a bitter laugh. "The fool wanted to stop. After all these years, he wanted to stop. We've never been caught, but all of a sudden you come back and Maxwell feels guilty."

"So, what did you do, go for the big score? Is that why Maxwell needed his son's money?"

Sam shrugged. "Things have been in place for a while. Maxwell just wasn't aware of it. But you asked too many questions. So he looked deeper. Found out I wanted more than a new car every year. I wanted the big one - the score that would set me up for life."

"So you took it ... and you were going to let Maxwell swing for it?"

Sam laughed. "Not like it hadn't happened before."

He came around the desk, and Caitlyn tensed, but saw that his hands were just at his sides.

"So, what will it take, Caitlyn?"

"For what?"

"Six hours."

"Six hours of what?"

"Your silence. You cover my tracks for six hours, and I'll make it worth your while. You will walk away a very rich woman. All you have to do is not tell anyone you saw me tonight. By tomorrow, I'll be long gone. You can protest your innocence all you want. I am sure they'll figure it out, too, but by then I'll have disappeared."

"You think you can buy me off?"

"Sure. That's what happened in London, right? Your fingers got a little sticky? Everyone has a price, don't they? That house, your lifestyle. All must cost a pretty penny. I know what we paid you, and it doesn't add up. That's why you were the perfect target. Not to mention all those pesky rumors from across the pond."

Sam Harris was actually leaning against the front of his desk now, his arms crossed, looking perfectly at ease.

"I guess we can't run from our pasts, no matter how hard we try."

"Well said. So, do we have a deal?" Sam's eyes flashed in triumph.

Caitlyn hesitated. She knew that she had enough, that Noah and Ted were waiting, listening to what was going on through the little recording device Ted had strapped on her. She had only to say the word, and it would be over. But there was something she needed to know.

"Maxwell ... did you?"

Sam smiled a thin, chilling smile. "Maxwell's time was up. When the game's up, the game's up."

Caitlyn didn't have time to say any more. Noah pushed into the office then, almost knocking her over in his haste to reach Sam.

Noah had just enough time to throw one punch before a police officer intervened. It landed square on Sam's jaw with a sickening crunch.

Ted pulled Noah off. The office was suddenly filled with people, and Caitlyn found herself pushed to the side. But it was only a moment before Noah found her and pulled her to him.

Chapter 57

Noah sent Caitlyn home. She looked exhausted, and though he knew she wanted to be there for him, it was better for her sake to wait it out, let the investigators do their job. Sam was taken into custody, and Noah heard just enough to know that Sam was willing to cut a deal. He'd tell them where the rest of the money was, where he had hid it, in return for not being charged in Maxwell's death, which he claimed had been an accident, despite what he had said to Caitlyn.

Noah was ready to go find her after that, when found himself standing in the doorway of her office. Everything was still here, as she had left it. This was where she belonged, he thought. There was a movement, and he turned and saw her assistant, Heather, behind him. She had a strange look on her face, a cross between puzzlement and disgust.

Chapter 58

For Caitlyn, the realization had come on her drive along Shore Road. It was over. She was in love with Noah, and none of it mattered. None of the stupid messed-up things that his father or her grandfather had done mattered. What mattered was the now. A fresh start. Together, in the open. Nothing bad was going to happen to her, to them. They were ready for each other. She only needed to go home, wait for him.

Now, as she opened the door of her house, she sensed someone was there.

"Have a drink with me?"

Caitlyn stopped. Michael St. John stood and smiled at her.

"What are you doing here?" She took a step backwards, one hand on the edge of the door into her living room, the other holding her keys, claw-like, as if they would serve some useful purpose, as a weapon perhaps.

"Really, Caitlyn, you should care more about where you keep your spare key hidden." He dangled something in front of him, a key on a red ribbon. Silently, she swore to herself. Yes, she had remembered to lock the doors, but she hadn't removed the key to the back door from its hiding place under the fourth flagstone.

"You need to leave here this instant," she told him, trying to command a bravery she didn't feel.

He smiled at her, a small, gentle smile.

"Please. Let us just talk for a while. I don't mean to hurt you. I don't bite, Caitlyn. I really don't."

"Forgive me if I find that hard to believe." She still had not moved into the house. Her house, she reminded herself. He had no right to treat it as if it were his own. She took a step across her threshold, into her living room.

"Here, have a drink?" he offered again, handing her a glass of champagne.

She took it automatically. Michael had set up here. A bottle of champagne, chilling in a bucket, two flutes, a blanket spread out in front of the fire. A wave of nausea hit her, and she almost put the champagne down.

"You can't possibly think…?"

"What?" He looked over at the blanket in front of the fire. "That you would be so kind? No, Caitlyn, that's not why I am here. Please, just sit for a moment. Have a drink with me, and let me explain things."

"Explain what?"

"You'll have to sit, my dear."

Caitlyn hesitated. The house was silent, though the wind outside creaked through its porous skin. She could feel a cold draft snake around her ankles. The fire crackled and flickered, and a candle cast shadows in the far corners. Michael St. John. She looked at him, waiting for that pop, that singing, the physical reaction that had hit her every time he was near. Nothing. Relief flooded her. Not the sound of his voice, or his physical presence, nothing could make her feel. She smiled.

"Sure. I'll have a drink with you." You bastard, she answered silently.

He didn't touch her, just sat next to her on the couch.

"To," he started, raising his glass, "new beginnings."

"New beginnings?"

"For both of us. Without each other."

She looked at him. His blue eyes were soft, gentle. This was the man she remembered, the quiet look, the assurance, the man who had made her laugh. But she couldn't let herself forget how quickly it could all turn to displeasure, rage even. He was changeable and possibly dangerous.

"All right."

She took a sip. She wanted food, a glass of cold water, not alcohol. She needed to call Noah. Needed to speak to him, tell him how she felt.

Michael took a sip and looked at her.

"You're still beautiful, you know. I won't get over that."

She smiled, feeling uneasy. "You still haven't told me why you're here."

Michael picked up the bottle, a napkin wrapped around it to catch the drops of condensation. He filled up his glass and held out the bottle for hers. She took another sip and let him pour her more.

"Thank you."

"I wanted to thank you."

"For what?"

"For making me, as they say, see the light. I owe you an apology, Caitlyn, a big one."

"You do?"

"Yes, you know I do. I maligned you, ruined your career and tried every underhanded way to get you back."

"You did," Caitlyn said, waiting. Michael refilled her glass even though she had barely taken a sip. The champagne was not sitting well on her empty stomach, and already she felt a bit light-headed.

"You see, I thought I owned you, Caitlyn, and with every other woman, I have. They were nothing to me, the ones I could have so easily. But you were different, untouchable, even when you let me make love to you. I wanted you all the more."

Her stomach was queasy, a pit of nausea, and she wished only for him to be gone.

"And then you didn't want me anymore. Anything I could do to get you back, I tried so hard. But you wouldn't play. But you know about that. You see, you're a dangerous woman, Caitlyn."

He leaned in over her as she moved out of his way.

"You know my secret, don't you? I thought you'd made a promise. A bargain is a bargain, Caitlyn. But you meant to break that trust, didn't you?"

"What are you talking about?" She didn't like the way his eyes looked, hard as glass, empty.

"You sent the ring back, my dear. That's when I knew. Knew that you loved someone else. You couldn't be trusted anymore. You're dangerous." His finger traced against her jaw line, and she felt it, thick, like a heavy blow.

And then she realized she was in trouble.

Chapter 59

Noah felt cleaner, clearer than he had in a long time. His lawyer had cautioned him that Sam's words might mean nothing in court, and that they might never know what had really happened that night. Noah didn't think he needed to. Whether his father had fallen or jumped, he knew enough already. And the past wasn't what was important now. He had a future to look forward to. No more lies, no more secrets between them.

"What are you still doing here?"

Heather Malloy was standing in the corridor looking at him, a puzzled look on her face.

"What do you mean?" Tomorrow they would have to tell the firm something about Sam Harris, but for now it could stay quiet.

"I thought you wanted to make up with Caitlyn."

"What are you talking about?" He was surprised when Heather walked towards him.

"Look, I know I work for her, and you, and that I'm not supposed to know about you two, but who are we kidding here? She's more like a friend than a boss to me, and after what you did, and that other creep did, and the way she looked today, do you have to be such a jerk? What is it with you rich guys? Do you think that just because you have big bank accounts that you can treat women any way you want?"

Before Noah could get a word in edgewise, Heather went on, without pausing for a breath, her green eyes sparking and her finger pointing.

"Caitlyn is one of the best, most generous, honest people I know, and if you think..."

"I know," he said, simply holding up his hands in surrender.

His statement had the desired effect. The wind seemed to go out beneath her sails. "Oh."

"I'm going to find her now, to see if I can convince her that I'm good enough for her."

"Why did you come back here? I already told you, she's probably been home for an hour or so."

"What are you talking about?" Noah felt the first tickling of unease ripple through him. He's sent her home ages ago.

"You called a couple of hours ago, said you needed to see her. I felt bad for you, so I told you where she was, that she would be at home by now."

"I never spoke to you."

"Yes, you did. I mean, I thought you did. I mean, the connection was bad, and I didn't recognize the number, but I..."

Apprehension had turned to fear, and Noah felt his stomach plunge.

"Where did you tell him she was going to be?"

Heather looked scared, too, but she answered, "Home, Caitlyn should be home by now, I would think. Is everything okay? I mean, did I do the right thing?"

Heather looked distraught, but Noah barely paused on his way out the door. "It's okay. You didn't do anything wrong."

Chapter 60

Noah had leapt into his car, one hand dialing her number, but the phone rang and rang, going to voicemail. He hesitated for just a moment at the intersection and then turned towards the water. Her house first, he thought. She would go back there, hunker down, if she were upset.

He pushed the car, faster and faster, hugging the curvy road. He screeched around the corner, almost clipping another sedan that came towards him, but yanked over just in time. The other driver's horn echoed in his ear.

God, Noah thought, if he was too late ... if Michael St. John tried to hurt her... Noah felt his blood rise and a film of red come over his eyes. Calm, he needed to stay calm. He didn't know for sure that Michael St. John would even be there. Or that the man was crazy. Obsessed with Caitlyn, certainly. Possessive, no doubt. But would he hurt her?

Focus, Noah told himself, pushing the speedometer up, faster and faster. Hopefully he would find her curled up in front of the fire, a glass of wine or tea in her hand. Angry, but he could overcome that, he thought. He'd just have to tell her how he felt about her, how he had always felt about her. How she was the last thing he thought of at night, the first thing all morning and how now, and even over the past ten years, he had been constantly asking himself, "What would Caitlyn think of this?"

Noah topped a small rise and saw the turn-off for her drive. No, there was no way he was going to lose her again.

There were just a few lights on, and her car was there. He felt relief wash over him as he whipped into the drive and jumped from the car, calling her name. Noah ran up the steps of the porch. The curtains were drawn in the sitting room, and he went to the front door and pounded.

Chapter 61

"Sounds like the cavalry is here after all," Michael said, his voice mocking. "I was so hoping we wouldn't be disturbed. Now I want you to tell him to go away, so we can keep talking."

"Why would I do that?" Caitlyn lifted her chin high.

"Because I have this." Michael very casually pulled a small gun out of his pocket and pointed it towards her.

Caitlyn kept her eyes on the gun that glinted dully in his hand, while her heart leapt with fear and joy. Noah had come for her. Even now she could hear his footsteps on the porch, his frantic cries.

"What are you going to do with me, Michael?" Caitlyn knew she shouldn't push him, aware that his mood could turn on a dime, but she wanted to give Noah time.

"That, I will tell you later," he said, the whisper sending shivers down her spine. "I told you I just wanted to talk, talk some sense into you. So, tell lover boy to go away."

"And if I don't?"

"We wouldn't want any accidents, would we?"

There was a pounding on the front door, and she could hear him calling for her. Michael pushed her out into the hallway.

"Tell him."

She swallowed hard, trying to find her voice, wondering just where she had underestimated Michael St. John's anger towards her. But she had to keep Noah safe.

"Noah, go away. I don't want to see you." She forced the words from her throat.

"Caitlyn, please, let me in," he called to her.

Caitlyn hesitated, and Michael twisted the gun in her side as a reminder.

"I can't," Caitlyn all but sobbed. "Go away. I don't want you. I don't want to see you."

There was a pause. She could hear his heavy breathing, and hoped that he would go away. Caitlyn's heart beat raggedly. She needed to know Noah was safe. She could handle Michael - all he needed was to be reasoned with - but she wasn't sure that Michael wouldn't hurt Noah. And that, she couldn't have.

"If that's the way you want it." She heard Noah's voice, heard the pain and anguish, and then there were sounds of footsteps trailing away.

She felt her heart stop, stutter as she realized that he was leaving, then squared her shoulders. She had saved him; that was all that mattered. She would find a way to apologize later, when she had calmed Michael down.

"Can you put the gun down now? I'll talk to you."

Michael's pale blue eyes followed her as she led him back to the living room. She didn't like the dead look in them. There were fire tools in there, Caitlyn thought, maybe something she could use to defend herself if it came to that.

"Let's have another drink. We'll talk it out." It was the voice she would have used to placate a small child. It worked with Michael when he was being unreasonable or when he was working himself up into a rage.

Chapter 62

Noah backed away, even got in his car and drove away. He stopped up the road, pulled out his cell phone and called reinforcements. He had heard the fear in Caitlyn's voice, even though she had tried to hide it. She was in there, and he was sure she wasn't alone. There was no way he was going to leave her until she had told him to go away to his face. And even then, he wouldn't leave. There would be no more of that.

The moon was out, a half moon, with enough light that he could move quickly though the line of trees towards the back of her house. The kitchen door was locked. He checked under the flagstone where the key was supposed to be and cursed.

He looked at the panes of glass in the kitchen door. It was old, not as old as the house, but the glass in it was single pane. It would break easily. He could only hope that it wouldn't make too much noise.

Noah took off his jacket, wrapped it around his fist and smashed. The first time nothing happened, so he hit it again harder. Nothing. The third time and his anger did it. The glass cracked and one piece, large enough, fell. There was a mat right by the door, and he heard only a dull thud as it landed there.

Pleased, he reached his arm in and unlocked the door, swinging it slowly open as he moved as soundlessly as he could into the house. There was the murmur of voices, and he followed them.

Chapter 63

He heard Caitlyn's voice, calm, steady, as if she were talking to a child. Through the dark, he walked out of the kitchen and into the back hall, heading for the living room. He approached the doorway slowly, inching his head around.

Michael had his back towards him, but Caitlyn was facing him. Her eyes narrowed only momentarily before she brought them back to focus on Michael. He was pacing, walking the room and waving something. Noah hazarded another glance and saw that his first impression was right. He had a gun.

He saw the fear and worry in Caitlyn's eyes and knew that she had only been trying to keep him safe.

Noah looked around. He needed something heavy. Something to smash down on Michael's head, preferably. He found a vase on the small table in the hallway where Caitlyn dumped her mail and keys. White with a blue pattern, it was probably an antique, but he hoped that Lucas Montgomery would forgive him.

Caitlyn was ready for him. She was looking at Michael intently, even reaching out her arms towards him when Noah came in. Then the vase was above Michael's head, and Noah swung it down with enough force that it shattered.

Michael turned, stunned but not quite down for the count. He still had the gun, and Noah went for it. He and Michael were grappling for it, and he sensed a blur of motion in the background.

The force of Noah's leap had knocked them both to the floor, and they were on the rug, rolling around, wrestling, trying to reach the gun. Michael was enraged, screaming obscenities, but Noah was on top of him, just about to get him when Caitlyn struck. The poker from the fireplace connected with Michael's arm with a sickening thud, and the gun went flying.

Caitlyn leaped and picked it up. Her hand was unsteady as she pointed it at Michael.

"It's over."

Chapter 64

The police came soon after, and then came the lawyers. Caitlyn sat on her couch as the crowds milled about her. She wasn't sure what would happen to Michael since he wasn't a citizen and the gun had turned out not to be loaded. All the fight had seemed to go out of him. He sat in the kitchen a broken man. He had finally gotten the message.

Noah was all about, taking care of things, and now she could sense the crowd thinning out. They would be alone soon.

He came with a cup of tea, milky and sugary, and handed it to her.

Noah sat down beside her and pulled her tight to him. "I'm sorry," he began. "I never would have sent you home if I thought..."

"You don't have to say it. You came for me." That was all that mattered to her.

"Of course I came for you. I love you, Caitlyn," he told her as she snuggled deep into the comfort of his arms.

She stilled, knowing he was waiting for her answer. She sat up so that their knees were touching, so she could look into his eyes, run her hand along the smooth, strong plane of his cheek.

"I love you, too. From the first time I let you kiss me on the beach under the fireworks to the moment you cracked a seventeenth-century antique on a crazy man's head for me."

She hoped that would be enough.

"Do we have any more secrets, Caitlyn?"

She sighed. "You mean beyond your father was a blackmailer and a crook? And my grandfather was adulterer who lost other people's money?"

He considered it. "Yes, beyond that."

"I didn't really forget my towel that day at the pool. I knew you would be there."

"So, you staged the whole thing?"

"The whole thing."

"I guess I can deal with those," he said, a light note of teasing in his voice as his mouth grazed her cheek.

"And I cheated at poker that one time," she said.

"You mean the time we played strip poker," he asked, and she nodded, her eyes closed as he nuzzled the smooth curve of her chin.

"The only time, I swear."

He had her mouth then and kissed her long and deeply.

"And I invested in your company and never told you about it."

"I heard about that. And I thank you."

"You do?" Caitlyn looked at him, surprised.

"You kept my dream alive. I could never be mad about that."

"So, you can live with all that?" she asked, feeling hope swell inside of her. She had Noah, and that was all she needed.

"I guess I can live with all that. On one condition." He brushed his lips along her cheek again.

"What?" she moaned, her mouth searching out his lips again. He held her, stopped her.

"Are you going to run from me again?" he asked.

"Run from you?"

"I mean ... Caitlyn, I love you, and I want to be with you. In every way possible. I want you to come back to the firm, as the managing partner, fifty-fifty. But," he stopped her before she could interrupt, "I want to be more than a business deal to you."

He looked down at her hand. Her fingers, long and delicate, twined around his own.

He pulled the box from his pocket, popped it open and let the simple round diamond set on a gold band speak for him. "I got this from my mother at Thanksgiving. It was her grandmother's."

She was looking down at his hand, at the ring, which glittered and shimmered in the flames from the fire.

"Caitlyn Montgomery, I love you. I fell in love with you that summer long ago, and it broke my heart when we left each other. When I came back, I knew that I would see you, and I was prepared to not feel anything, but I couldn't. The moment I saw you in my house, I knew. I knew that there was never anyone but you for me. And I almost lost you again, but never again will I let that happen. Will you be my wife, my better half, my partner?"

She looked at him, at the crooked smile, at the love that was in his eyes, and she felt the answer in her own heart.

"Of course," she said, "but I have one condition, too."

He held the ring out for a second and waited.

"What?"

"That we don't wait too long to make it official."

He smiled. "How about we start off the New Year right?"

The Ivy House - Phoebe & Chase's Story

Book 3 - The Queensbay Series

Drea Stein

Chapter 1

Phoebe Ryan could feel the real estate agent eyeing her as she surveyed the house. "It has charm," Sandy Miller said. "Perhaps if you added a fresh coat of paint, cleaned out the backyard…"

"Hmm." Phoebe just made a noise, wishing the woman would be quiet and let her think. She was still bleary-eyed from the time difference. She had left Los Angeles yesterday morning, landed in New York, hit the lawyer's office, rented a car, and finally found her way just after dark to the Connecticut shore. She had checked in at the Osprey Arms, the only hotel in town, and after a surprisingly delicious salad and a glass of wine, had curled up on the big four-poster bed and cried herself to sleep.

Now, less than twenty-four hours after she'd left California, she was getting her first view of it. Ivy House was a short walk up from town, at the end of a little lane that jutted off from the main road, commanding a prime piece of property on a bluff overlooking Queensbay Harbor.

Phoebe breathed in deeply. She could smell the fresh tang of salt, see the white caps that flecked the blue-green surface of the water, hear the gulls cawing as they wheeled around the clear sky. It was beautiful, and she could already see herself here, watching the boats come and go, enjoying the sunset while sipping a glass of wine. At least that's how she had imagined it back in Los Angeles.

But if Queensbay Harbor and town were New England charm personified, Ivy House was not. It was the eyesore, the black sheep in the town's collective spic-and-span family. It was Victorian in style, seeming taller than it was wide, with a steep slate-covered roof, pointed gables on either side, and a tall, thin square tower topped with the classic widow's walk. A deep porch wrapped around the front, and a black iron picket fence separated the house from the street.

Paint peeled, the porch sagged, shingles were missing. Weeds choked the front yard, and the iron fence was rusted through. The flagstone path was uneven and while there had once been an extensive garden, now everything was wildly overgrown. The plant that had given the house its name covered one side almost completely, even the windows. Everything about it screamed genteel decay and Phoebe took a moment to ruminate about the prospect of fully renovating the place. It wasn't as she had imagined it. But then, things seldom were.

Phoebe had only glanced toward the side yard, but she could see stuff. Some old wicker furniture, perhaps a refrigerator, plastic jugs, maybe even a beer keg. It was hard to imagine the late, great Savannah Ryan having anything to do with this place. The thought of her grandmother threatened a fresh onslaught of tears, but Phoebe forced them away.

"The major appliances are all there," Sandy said and then corrected herself, "I think."

"Electricity? Water, heat?" Phoebe asked. If she focused on the details, the little things, she could avoid thinking about the big things. She closed her eyes briefly, ready to sense the possibilities. That was her gift, a vivid imagination, a mind that saw things in pictures, one that could turn those pictures into reality. She envisioned the house as Savannah had described it to her, as it had been, when the sun set across the expanse of the harbor and the backyard, with the sloping lawn leading to the sandy bluff.

"You'll have to have all the utilities switched to your name, but I have the numbers for you to call. Shouldn't take more than twenty-four hours for it all to come on once you do," the agent assured her.

Phoebe nodded, ready to walk up and into the house. She put a foot on the first step to the porch, tested it with her weight, and was pleased to find that it was solid. Good bones, she thought. All the house needed was some TLC.

"Here are the keys," Sandy said, dropping them in Phoebe's outstretched hand. Phoebe closed her hands over them tightly, afraid perhaps that it wasn't true, that the house wasn't hers.

"I did a walk-through after the tenants left and there are some scrapes and scuffs and a hole in the wall. They left it broom clean, though, if you want, I can give you the name of a local cleaning service I use. In my opinion, you'd be better off gutting the place first."

"Gutting it?" Phoebe tried to keep the horror out of her voice. How could you consider destroying a masterpiece like this? The house was living history and she could already feel herself falling in love. Visions of fairy lights in the trees, the setting sun, a table set up outside, and some friends to share it with. Still, she shouldn't get too attached yet. Her home, her life was three-thousand miles away. Imagination couldn't always overcome reality.

"Oh, well," Sandy blinked, then resettled her oversized sunglasses more firmly on top of her head. "I mean, you'll see. As I said, everything's perfectly sound, but things haven't been updated in a while."

Phoebe smiled. All the better, she thought. So many people ruined old houses by trying to update them too much, trying to drag them kicking and screaming into the modern world, while not respecting their expert craftsmanship and clean, simple lines.

"I like old houses," Phoebe said. "They have character." In California, old was a relative term, but here she was dealing with a jewel built in the nineteenth century, before planes, cars—electricity, even. It would need to be respected, cherished. And more so because it had belonged to Savannah.

Sandy was about to say something when her phone rang. Holding up a finger, she checked the screen and then excused herself to take the call.

Relieved to be alone, Phoebe moved up the porch, imagining how it would look with some fine old wicker rockers, instead of those hideous, rusty folding chairs. She stood in front of the door. It was the original: a fine wood-paneled door, painted a bright blue. Cheerful, but to her trained eye, a little too bold. Something softer, duskier would suit. She tried to peer through the sidelights on either side, but they too were original and the glass, wavy from age, made it difficult to see inside.

She put the key in the lock and turned. The lock was stiff from disuse, but she wiggled until finally it opened. Perhaps there wasn't much cause to lock your door here and that thought pleased Phoebe immensely, who lived in the city and always made sure to triple-lock the door.

Swinging slowly back, the door opened with a scream on its hinges, a slow, protracted squeal. It was a sunny day, but as Sandy had mentioned, there was no electricity and the sun only just touched the interior.

Phoebe took a step in, smelling mustiness and dampness, the scent of a closed-up house. Her eyes poked through the gloom and she was finally able to see.

"Oh, my…" she said out loud.

"I told you." Sandy had come up behind her, her phone call done. "In my business, it's what we call a tear down."

Chapter 2

The agent left and Phoebe let herself have a full-blown moment of panic. She managed to breathe despite the filthy atmosphere and explored the rest of the house. She took the sight of the inside in stride, telling herself it was what she should have expected. After all, considering the way Savannah had handled her affairs, it was a miracle there was anything left for Phoebe at all. And this was more than she could have hope for, she decided, as she reminded herself of the house's basic sturdiness.

Unfortunately, despite what Sandy had said, the house had been subjected to a number of redos throughout the decade, the latest of which had left lots of linoleum, probably covering the original, wide plank-wood floors; peeling wallpaper; and mirrors, lots of mirrors.

The paint colors throughout were faded or jarring or both, as though the rooms had been painted by someone color-blind or using the clearance colors from the local home improvement store. Definitely both, Phoebe thought as she opened the door to a smallish room, the dining room perhaps, and took another look.

The rest of the house wasn't much better—it was dusty and dirty, and the tenants had left piles of things, from old bedding to stacks of newspapers, in various places. A few of the windowpanes were broken and had been covered up with pieces of cardboard.

Finally, she found herself outside in the backyard, taking in the view. There was a flagstone terrace out here, with a fire pit, ringed by a low rock wall, perfect for enjoying cool spring nights and watching the water. A strong breeze blew through the trees and she wandered down to the edge of the bluff. A picket fence ran along it, and there was a set of stairs going down to the beach. She looked over it. Apparently, this was the only thing the tenants had decided keep in good repair, the beach access, because here and there were pieces of new wood on the stairwell. This was what Sandy had meant when she said it was a million-dollar view.

Carefully, she made her way down to the beach, stopping when she got to the bottom. The shore was a mix of sand and rock, and there was a large driftwood log pulled up around what looked like the remains of a fire. She sat on the log and breathed in, the smell of the charred wood assailing her senses.

The sun was getting warm and she needed to think, figure out what to do next. The water, the sand, and the sun were working their magic. Already, less than a day out of the city and she felt calm, rested. The sadness of Savannah's death, the stress of dealing with her estate, and that big looming question—*What do I do now?*— seemed to fade away. Phoebe took a deep breath, her grandmother's words coming back to her: *Enjoy the moment.* All that mattered was that it was sunny and she was enjoying the view.

She tried not to think about the wreck that was looming, both figuratively and literally, above her head. Ivy House was a disaster. It would take a small fortune to fix it up, that much was clear, and Phoebe didn't know if she had it in her. Either physically or financially.

The agent had already dropped hints. Despite its decrepit condition, it would attract some serious buyer interest. Just because of its "historical significance." Phoebe had almost burst out laughing at that one. A torrid love affair wasn't exactly world peace. Savannah and Leland had been more infamous than famous, but that still didn't stop legions of people from obsessing over them. All the more now since they were both dead.

But Phoebe was a Hollywood girl. She knew that the public's obsession with the life of movie stars was never quite rational. Any little thing, be it a prop or a costume piece, could be fought over by a serious collector. And now, if now, the chance to own the actual house that had been the love nest for the "Romance of the Century" became available, Phoebe knew she'd have more offers on her hands than she could handle.

Phoebe was still taking it in. She had thought that Savannah had sold the house years ago after Leland's death. Instead, she had kept it, renting it out year after year. Despite the fact that Savannah could have used the money, she had not sold the house. She had left it, mostly intact, for Phoebe. What had Savannah been thinking, leaving Phoebe with a wreck of a house three-thousand miles away from her home?

I'll just have to figure it out as I go, Phoebe thought to herself, her natural optimism returning as she trekked back up the steps. There was always a way to salvage a disaster.

Chapter 3

That was strange. Phoebe was sure she had closed the back door to the house behind her, but here it was, open again. Tamping down a wave of panic, since this was charming Queensbay and not the big city after all, Phoebe pushed open the door a little wider. It was probably one of the former tenants, maybe with an extra key, coming back for something they left behind. Hadn't she seen an old stuffed animal—a teddy bear or maybe a bunny rabbit—in one of the rooms upstairs? Couldn't leave Floppy behind now, could you?

"Hello," she called. Her first attempt was weak, so she cleared her throat and called out again, "Hello, is someone there?"

She heard the floorboard creaking and looking up at the ceiling, she could see the floor sag as feet made their way across.

"You don't look like you're from the electric company," she said, keeping close to the door just in case.

Feet, shod in Converse sneakers, and legs, in jeans, emerged down the steps, followed by a large brass belt buckle, a blue windbreaker, and finally, a head.

Phoebe watched as the man crystallized into view. A pair of sunglasses, aviator-style, hung in the v of the t-shirt that poked up through the collar of his jacket. The man loomed, Phoebe thought, as he reached the bottom step and casually supported himself by putting one hand on the wall, the other crooked at his side.

"Lovely place you've got here," he said in a smooth voice that sent shivers shooting through her, despite the sarcasm.

He was taller than Phoebe by several inches, even in her high-heeled boots, which put him at well over six feet, and she could see that his arms were muscular underneath his jacket. He wore a smile though and Phoebe didn't feel threatened so much as aware, hyperaware of his presence.

He was every inch a male and was assessing her, conducting a slow survey, starting with her face, running down the length of her body, and back up to her face. He stopped there, his gaze lingered, narrowing, and then a slow grin spread over his face.

Phoebe could only guess that he liked what he saw because he rocked forward a bit on his feet and leaned in.

She found herself pinned to the wall by a set of the darkest blue eyes she had ever seen. They were set in a tan face, a face that obviously spent a good deal of time outside. His hair was black, an inky, undiluted black. Dark brows slashed across a wide forehead, which ran down to a straight nose and then tapered to full lips and a charming cleft chin.

"It needs some work," Phoebe admitted, because it was true and the only thing she could think of saying. Witty responses had never been her thing, especially when faced with a grin like that—cocksure and confident—which had a strange, tingling warmth spreading over her. She'd never had such a physical reaction to the very presence of a man before.

He touched the wall with the palm of his fist, and she could hear the plaster gently falling down behind it.

"Please stop wrecking my house," she said, feeling her heart pump a little faster.

"That was just a light touch." He took a step closer and she almost wanted to rear back.

"You need to leave right now," she said, trying to hold firm. She had felt an instantaneous shock of attraction and knew that she needed to get rid of him.

"Sorry, the door was open. I thought I heard someone crying for help, so I just let myself in. Wanted to make sure you hadn't fallen through the floor or something like that." His tone was light, joking.

He laughed then, and the grin came quickly and he looked almost mischievous. "It was probably just the cry of a seagull. Were you down by the beach?" He took a step forward and Phoebe felt the need to step back, but she stopped herself, holding her ground.

She shifted the leather bag she was holding from one hand to the other and almost back again before she stopped herself. What had Savannah said? It is the small gestures that give you away. It was her way of saying *never let them see you sweat.*

Because this guy was making Phoebe sweat. Not nervously, as in he wasn't a creep or causing her to wonder why she was alone in an empty house with him, but more along the lines of how she couldn't stop herself from looking at his beautiful face, or the way, even in the jacket, she could see how his waist tapered in and then how his long, powerful legs were encased in his jeans. She hadn't been this aware of a guy in a long time and the feeling was totally disconcerting.

He moved closer and she caught the scent of him. Something woodsy and spicy, just a hint of soap, nothing too overpowering. God, she was a twenty-eight-year-old woman, not some teenager, and already she could feel her heart start to flutter.

His eyes glinted down at her and Phoebe wished that she had closed the top button of her blouse, but to do anything now except meet him head on would betray the way he was making her feel.

"Can I help you with something?" She lifted her chin and met his eyes boldly, the way Savannah had told her to. Phoebe had never been much for channeling her inner femme fatale; still, the man had the grace to look a little ashamed that he had been caught staring.

"You just remind me of someone. Not sure who. Do you get that a lot?"

Phoebe smiled, but her back stiffened. It was a question she got so often that it annoyed her. Too bad, because before he had gone for the obvious line, she had felt that spark of interest on her part, her vivid imagination working overtime, wondering just how his wide, sensual lips might feel brushing against hers.

"Not really," she demurred, while cursing the Ryan genes that showed so plainly in her face.

"Are you sure?" he said, snapping his fingers. "Because I swear, you remind me of someone. Let me see, someone famous. A model?"

Phoebe managed to arch an eyebrow. She had a swimmer's body, moderately tall, wide shoulders and slim all over, but she'd never been mistaken for a model before.

"Nah, not quite tall enough, though those shoes make your legs go on forever," the guy said, his eyes twinkling. He was smiling so outrageously that Phoebe almost didn't mind that she was being blatantly hit upon. Perhaps his recognition of her had been fake, a cheesy come-on. Maybe he had no idea. "A singer?"

"Tone-deaf," Phoebe countered.

"Too bad—you'd look pretty bad-ass up on stage." Somehow, the guy had moved closer to her, invading her space and yet, Phoebe didn't mind at all. He had lines around his eyes, as if he squinted too much in the sun, and his hands, one of which was splayed on the wall, like his clothes, were not those of a man who spent all of his time inside.

He snapped his fingers. "The stage. That's it. You're an actress. Theater? TV. A cop show. I can see you arresting the bad guys."

Phoebe shook her head, feeling the smile that was lighting up her face and the buzz in her body as she decided to play along.

"Medical drama?" He tried again.

"Hate the sight of blood."

"You're sure I don't know you from somewhere?" The guy leaned over her, his eyes looking into hers. Thoughts, none of them coherent, raced around Phoebe's head and she was aware that it was warm, very warm in the house, where before it had been cool, almost too cool.

"No, I'm nobody," Phoebe said and managed to take a deep breath, almost willing that to be true.

"I don't believe that for a second, miss." He leaned in close to her and his voice dropped to a dangerous whisper. "With a face like that, you're surely someone."

Phoebe didn't know what to say to that and she didn't have to. Her phone beeped and, eager to break the intense connection between herself and this man, she pulled it out of her bag and saw that there was a text from Sandy, the real estate agent.

Have interest from buyer, heavy hitter, wants to see house ASAP.

Phoebe cleared the text in frustration. She thought she had been very clear. She wasn't ready to entertain any offers for Ivy House yet. But some people were rude and didn't take no for an answer. Phoebe looked up. The guy, this "heavy hitter," apparently hadn't gotten the message because he was already looking around the place as if he were measuring how well his flat-screen TV would look above the fireplace in the living room.

Phoebe texted back, *"Not interested...send away..."*

Fast and furious came the text message back: *"Too late, he's already on his way..."*

Phoebe gritted her teeth in frustration. *"Fine, I will take care of him."*

She put the phone away just as it started ringing. It was Sandy, but Phoebe decided to ignore her. She wasn't interested in hearing the woman try to save her own commission.

"Excuse me, sir." Phoebe found him in the back room, the one she had already imagined would be perfect as the studio study, looking out the full wall of windows.

"Quite a view," he said with an easy gesture, seemingly unembarrassed at having been caught roaming around the house.

"I'm sorry, I think there's been a misunderstanding. The house is not for sale," Phoebe said, drawing herself up to her full height.

The man looked over at her, a lazy smile on his face. "Is that so? It's a prime piece of property. I've had my eye on it for a while. The old owner never would give me the time of day, though, no matter what I offered."

"Well, guess this isn't your lucky day either because I have no intention of selling," Phoebe said. It wasn't exactly true. Last night, she'd had every intention of glancing the place over, getting a price from the real estate agent, and heading back to the city. But now…she'd already imagined sipping wine on the terrace.

She heard the ping, but before she could reach for her own phone, she saw the man take his out of a pocket. The conversation was brief, but Phoebe was almost certain Sandy, the real estate agent, was on the other end of it.

He hung up, looked at Phoebe, a sharp, appraising look.

"Well, I guess I was mistaken. But you know what they say: the harder you work, the luckier you get."

Phoebe stiffened. The real estate agent's meaning had been clear. Waterfront property in Queensbay was a highly sought-after commodity. There would be plenty of people who would be willing to take it off her hands, even in this economy, so there was no reason she needed to be grateful to the guy for being the first.

She drew herself up. "Ivy House is not for sale. I have no intention of being taken advantage of just because I'm not from around here."

He only smiled again at her huffy tone, unperturbed by it.

"Trust me, I would never try to take advantage of a lady. I will be happy to offer a fair price for a fair bit of property."

Phoebe looked into his eyes. So he was only interested in the property, not the house. She guessed he couldn't see the house for what it was—a diamond in the rough. Did he not know? Or was he playing it cool?

He pulled something from his pocket, a white envelope, and held it out to her.

She looked at it, puzzled.

"I know I'm supposed to go through the real estate agent, but sometimes I find it easier to just deal with the other party directly."

"What is that?" Phoebe said, trying to keep her voice level.

"A very generous and more than fair offer for the property." He said, still holding it out towards her. She crossed her arms, feeling childish, but refusing to give in even an inch.

"I told you that Ivy House isn't for sale."

He cocked his head to one side and put the envelope back in his pocket, a wise move Phoebe thought.

"You keep calling this place Ivy House. I haven't heard it being called that in years."

"It's what my grandmother called it," Phoebe said. Savannah could only be persuaded to talk about Ivy House and Leland after a glass or two of wine and even then, it was a tricky subject.

His mouth dropped open and a look that Phoebe didn't understand crossed his face.

Chapter 4

"You're Savannah's granddaughter," he said, as if everything came together.

"Who did you think I was?" Phoebe asked with real curiosity. In Los Angeles, the recognition was almost immediate mostly because people there knew their celebrities, even the older ones.

"Well, I told you, you looked like someone. I didn't realize Savannah still owned the property, that's all. I've been sending offer letters to a lawyer in New York the past couple of years and getting pretty strong nos."

"So you thought you'd take your chance with the new girl in town," Phoebe said, wondering just how outraged she should feel.

"I always like to make newcomers feel welcome." He had inched closer and the cocky grin was back.

Warning signals chimed in Phoebe's head. She was in no condition to have anything to do with a man like this. He was all male and obviously a huge flirt. Definitely not what she needed right now.

"Well, very thoughtful of you, but like I said, the house is not for sale and I have some work to do."

He looked around again at the dusty floor and the empty room.

"I'm sure you do. Still, I think you should consider my offer. I'd be happy to take the house off your hands, as is. You wouldn't have to do a thing to it. You could be back on a plane and back to your life by tomorrow."

"Listen, Mr..." Phoebe realized that she had never gotten his name.

"Please call me Chase. All my friends do," he said with another one of his grins. Phoebe had the feeling that Chase was the kind of guy with plenty of friends. And she had no intention of becoming one of them.

"Why are you so interested in the place?" she asked.

For the first time, she saw that he hesitated, his feet doing a little dance. "Let's just say the property has always spoken to me."

Phoebe looked at him. With the broad shoulders and the constant grin, Phoebe didn't think Chase looked like the kind of guy that let anything but tall blondes speak to him, but she supposed you never could tell. But that wasn't her problem. Ivy House had also spoken to her, and she wasn't about to let the legacy Savannah had left her go so easily.

"Well," he said after a moment, when he realized that Phoebe wasn't going to say anything else, "it was nice to meet you, miss..."

It was her turn to hesitate, though she supposed it didn't matter. All he needed was the internet. He could find out anything else he wanted to on the internet.

"Phoebe Ryan." She couldn't be invisible, not if she expected to spend any amount of time in Queensbay. Word was bound to get out.

"Well, it's nice to meet you. And I'm sorry for your loss." She gave a quick nod. It had been almost six weeks since Savannah had died, but it was the sympathy from strangers that still got her. She managed to blink away the tears that were forming.

"Here, please take the envelope. Like I said, it's a good offer. More than fair and, well, you'll be getting more of them, so I just want to make sure that you have mine."

"Listen, I told you," Phoebe started, her anger quickly replacing her tears.

"I know, Ivy House isn't for sale," Chase said, his face serious now. "But just in case."

He practically shoved it into her hand and she had no choice but to accept it. She gritted her teeth as she took it, their hands brushing, and she felt an unfamiliar thrill of electricity run through her at his touch. Chase must have felt it too because he looked at her and time seemed to halt for a moment, and then Phoebe became hyperaware of everything around her. The small settling sounds of the house, the chirps of the birds outside, the gentle sway of the branches.

Then the moment broke because he picked up her hand, brought it gently to his lips, and said, "Perhaps you'll come around. Until we meet again."

He dropped her hand finally and brushed past her on his way out the door. She heard the fluttering sound of more plaster falling as he walked down the hallway. Reluctantly, she trailed after him and watched him as he strolled with his hands stuck in his pockets, whistling as he made his way out the front door, down the steps, out onto the path, and through the rickety gate. He turned once, gave a wave, and then kept walking. Phoebe watched him go and then found herself leaning against the wall, hearing the whisper of dust as it fell down behind her.

She had no intention of selling Ivy House, at least not anytime soon, but she couldn't get the wild thoughts out of her head, thoughts of how it would have felt if she had stretched upwards a little farther and let her lips brush against Chase's face and feel his perfectly-formed lips upon hers.

Chapter 5

"Hi there." Phoebe turned to see a woman standing on her porch.

"Sorry, I didn't want to intrude. I'm Lynn Masters. I live next door." Lynn was shorter than Phoebe by a couple of inches, with long, wavy brown hair and dark chocolate-colored eyes. She was wearing blue hospital scrubs and had a welcoming smile on her face.

"Hi. Phoebe Ryan," Phoebe said, stuffing Chase's envelope into her pocket. How long she had been standing there, in the hallway, dazed, with the front door wide open, she didn't know.

"Are you related?"

"Excuse me?" Phoebe braced herself. Her brush with anonymity was truly over, she supposed.

"Your last name. Were you really related to Savannah Ryan?" Lynn asked, excitement sparking in her eyes.

"Yes. I'm her granddaughter." Phoebe said, stepping onto the porch. The sun was out in full force and the porch was warmer— much warmer—than the inside of the house, and Phoebe realized it felt nice.

"Wow, that is so cool. My parents moved here about two years ago. My mom was so excited when the real estate agent told her that Savannah Ryan lived here, she nearly had a cow, but of course once we moved in, she realized that it didn't mean Savannah still lived here."

Phoebe gave a small smile. Lynn was chatty and, apparently, a fan, or at least her mom was. Once people found out the relationship, they usually pumped Phoebe for information. Over the years, Phoebe had learned to keep quiet about the family connection with Savannah if she didn't want total strangers asking her bizarrely private questions, like if Savannah really spent all day in pink silk pajamas.

"Looks like you have your work cut out for you," Lynn said and Phoebe forced her attention back to her.

"What?"

"This house. It's such a great-looking place, but the last couple of tenants were a little crazy. College kids. Threw some great parties though."

"Oh." Phoebe looked around, remembering the condition of the property. "Yeah, it will probably take a while to clean it up."

"Did you know Savannah well? Oh gosh, where are my manners. I am so sorry for your loss. I just couldn't believe it when I read about her death."

"Thank you." Phoebe had to smile at Lynn's openness and lack of pretense. Lynn's face radiated sincerity, and instead of feeling the onslaught of tears, Phoebe was able to summon up a bit of lightness.

"Well, she was well over eighty." All the years of cigarettes and champagne had finally caught up with Savannah. And in the end, it had been time for Savannah to let go.

"Well, it's nice to know that the house will still be in the family. Are you going to be moving here alone?" Lynn shook her head, her brown hair moving with her.

Phoebe gave a noncommittal shrug. She didn't know what she was going to be doing. The next couple of months stretched wide open in front of her, but the truth was that except for this wreck of a house and her room at the Osprey Arms, she had nowhere else to be. But she didn't need to explain that to anyone, did she?

"Oh. Well, like I said, it would be cool if someone young moved in. Queensbay's pretty and all that, but it's not exactly a big city."

"So you live next door?" Phoebe asked, glad the subject had veered away from her family.

"Yes, I'm finishing my last year of residency. Pediatrics," Lynn said, waving a hand to explain the scrubs, "So I'm living with my parents to save money. Plus, I'm rarely home, so it doesn't make much sense to have my own place. And," Lynn dropped her voice, "my mom is a great cook."

Phoebe smiled at the conspiratorial tone.

"Which is one of the reasons why I'm here. When my mom heard that there was someone closer to my age moving in, well, she wanted to make sure I invited you over for dinner."

As an afterthought, Lynn added, "...if you don't mind, that is. Like I said, she's a really good cook. And she's not as meddling as I might have suggested."

Phoebe was disarmed by Lynn's friendliness. Phoebe was happy being on her own and she had envisioned a quiet few days in a new place to get her head on straight. It was on the tip of her tongue to say no, but Lynn's open smile and friendly manner had her changing her mind.

"That would be nice," Phoebe agreed. The thought of a home-cooked meal suddenly sounded very enticing.

"Great," Lynn said. "I have to run out to work now, but how about six tomorrow night? My mom's making something Italian, is that OK?"

"Sounds great," Phoebe nodded. She would bring a bottle of red, she decided, as a thank you.

Lynn stole a glance around Phoebe and into the house. "Good luck with the place. Everyone's excited that someone's taking an interest in it, after all these years. Not that all renters are bad, but I think it's time this place had someone who really cared about it." Lynn put her hand on one of the columns of the porch and, as if on cue, a part of it fell off and bounced on the porch.

"Oh, dear," Lynn started to reach down to pick up the piece of rotted wood.

Phoebe laughed. "Don't bother. I am sure it won't be the last thing that falls down around here."

"Well, I guess it's good you have a sense of humor about the whole thing."

They shared a laugh and Phoebe said goodbye to her new neighbor. Lynn squeezed through an opening in the bushes and a moment or two later, Phoebe saw a car drive past, with a hand waving out the window.

Not trusting the rusty chairs and wanting to enjoy the sunshine, Phoebe plopped herself down on the porch step, drawing her knees up so her chin rested on them, thinking. The house was both more and less than she had bargained for.

She remembered it from when she had been young and visited. Everything about the place and the town had seemed magical from a little kid's perspective. But now the house seemed smaller and dingier and it needed a lot of work. Savannah, though, had loved it so—must have—to keep it all these years, without letting on that she still owned it.

Phoebe sighed. She knew why Savannah had left it to her. Phoebe's parents had been Hollywood types too—her father an up-and-coming director, her mother a soon-to-not-be struggling actress—when they died in a car crash. Savannah had taken her in, her only living relative, but Savannah had never been the maternal type. Ivy House had been a part of Savannah's history, her happiest times. A place where Savannah had believed that anything was possible, until it wasn't.

The reasonable, solid, practical thing to do would be to sell Ivy House. Phoebe had built her own life a whole country away, in Los Angeles, and if her prospects there were somewhat in flux, it made more sense to stay there than to think about moving her whole life here. Her practical, reasonable half pulled the envelope Chase had given her from her pocket, because selling Ivy House, even to someone who only wanted it for the view, was the smart thing to do. She didn't belong here. This was Savannah's history, not hers.

A picture of Savannah from long ago flashed into her mind, when Phoebe had been little, her red-gold hair in pigtails. She had been whispering to Savannah about how the house was magical. And Savannah had been in full, solemn agreement and had made her promise not to tell anyone else. Their secret.

Phoebe sighed again. Just what had Savannah gotten her into?

Chapter 6

Chase Sanders spun around aimlessly in his office chair. He was supposed to be looking over quarterly reports and making some decisions on what to include in the new product line, which, at this point, was looking pretty dismal. But he couldn't concentrate. Not even the sight of the stiff breeze kicking up whitecaps on the harbor could distract him from thinking about her. The blond at Ivy House. Phoebe Ryan. He should have known the minute he'd seen her, but he had acted like a fool, making all sorts of inane remarks that had probably sounded like cheesy come-ons, which, in a way, had been just that.

The sight of her, it was a bit like staring at a ghost. Except he'd had an entirely different reaction between his legs than fear. Nope, no doubt about it. Phoebe Ryan was almost as much of a looker as her grandmother had been in her day.

Still, that was all it was—a fully physical reaction to her. Her red-blond hair, the splay of freckles over her nose, the light blue eyes, the long, strong body. The way she had glanced at him coolly, obviously put out by his presence, but keeping her cool. She'd been wary, wondering what his game was. But he hadn't told her anything beyond the fact that he was interested in the house.

He had at least remembered to offer his condolences, which were sincere. He didn't hold anything against Savannah. In fact, his entire family just ignored the whole thing. Sort of pretended that Leland had never existed. His grandmother had even remarried, so Chase hadn't realized that Grandpa Sal was really just a stepgrandpa. And with a different last name than Leland, Chase had gone through most of his life without giving his connection, however tenuous, with Leland another thought.

Well, she'd probably figure it out soon enough, and then the game would be up. Well, the game would be up as soon as she would look at his card. If she ever did. She seemed adamant about not wanting to sell the house, which meant that the Historical Commission would be up in arms. They were naturally distrustful of outsiders, and a blond Californian had them all in a dither. They were afraid the new owner was going for a tear down. So, Chase had valiantly decided to play the white knight and rescue Ivy House from the West Coaster who didn't know a gable from a cupola.

It hadn't worked quite as smoothly as he hoped. Phoebe had seemed a bit stuck-up, not melting into his charm. Chase, with some satisfaction, had yet to find a red-blooded female who didn't give in to it. But Phoebe had just kept looking at him like he had two heads. He was trying to concentrate on paperwork, but all he could do was shuffle around the documents so incoherently and roughly that he knocked over his paperweight, which hit the floor like his jaw had when he first glimpsed Phoebe Ryan.

"That's a way to make a mess," Noah Randall said as he walked into Chase's office, "and not much else. What's eating you?"

Chase felt sheepish as he looked at his oldest friend. "It's nothing."

Noah, tall, slim, with light brown hair, laughed. "Sounds like girl trouble to me. What's her name? Beth, Bethany?"

"Ha." Chase gave a halfhearted laugh as Noah threw himself into one of the chairs on the other side of his desk. "It was Bethany and we broke up six months ago." Chase got up and picked up the paperweight, a solid glass orb with a replica of the schooner *America*, the winner of the first America's Cup.

Noah shook his head. "That long? Wasn't she some sort of model?"

"Wasn't my type," Chase answered curtly.

Noah shot his friend a look. Bethany had been a swimwear model and Chase had met her at a photo shoot for the spring catalog. "I didn't know there was a girl who wasn't your type."

"Well, let's just say she seemed to be more interested in what I could do for her than in my sparkling personality."

"Wow, sounds like you're maturing. Good thing since you're turning thirty in another couple of months and all that," Noah said with a laugh.

"Very funny," Chase said, managing to keep the sarcasm to a low boil.

"Are we going to spend all of lunch talking about your love life?" Noah asked, one foot swinging casually off the side of his chair.

Chase gave a half smile. Noah was his oldest friend, and they'd been through a lot of things together, including girls.

Chase shook his head. "There's nothing to tell." Once he had grown tired of Bethany, who, like most of the other women he'd dated, seemed more interested in his wallet than him, he'd decided to take a break. It had been refreshing—six months of not worrying about what someone else thought—but a man had needs. And right now, there was a certain blond up on the hill who was occupying more than her fair share of his brain space.

No wonder she had looked at him down her nose. He was dressed like a dockhand. He should have put on a suit and tie, the kind that he kept for meetings, but he'd been so excited when the agent had told him that Ivy House might be available that he rushed up there, sure that fate was handing him his chance.

"I keep telling you: dating models and actresses isn't the key to lasting happiness," Noah said, shaking his head, bringing Chase back to his present predicament.

"Just because you're married now doesn't mean you're the expert," Chase shot back.

Noah gave a small laugh. "Isn't that the truth? I've known Caitlyn just about all my life and been married to her for over a year, and she still surprises me."

Chase took a long appraising look at his old friend. The surprises must have been good ones because Noah looked happy, at ease. Of course, it was easy to be that way when you were a successful tech entrepreneur, had reconnected with the love of your life, and were expecting a baby.

"Congrats, by the way, for real. I haven't seen you since you guys announced the news," Chase said.

He meant it too. He and Noah had grown up in Queensbay together, thick as thieves as kids. Noah had lived in the big house on the bluffs high above the harbor, while Chase, his brother, and parents lived down in town, near the marina.

Noah and Chase had learned to sail on the harbor at the Yacht Club and had hated each other at first sight. That had led to a game of chicken, in boats, which resulted in one boat sunk and the other one in dry dock for weeks. To help pay for the damages and learn a better way of handling their feelings towards each other, their dads made them work at the marina, scrubbing down boats and pumping gas. Since that hadn't helped their relationship, they decided to settle things the old-fashioned way—with a race. Chase had beaten the pants off Noah, and Noah, always one to use brains over brawn, shook his hand and offered to be his crew for the Club's Junior Cup. They'd won that year and every year thereafter.

Since then, they'd been inseparable on the water and off, he and Noah making a powerful team. After high school, Noah had headed to college for a couple of years and then dropped out to go to Silicon Valley, California. Chase, too, had gone to college, but spent most of his time with the sailing team, and finally, after a few semesters, the lure of sailing in the big leagues caught up with him.

Chase had focused on racing, on winning, driven by the money it made him. He'd been doing just fine and hadn't thought much about it when Noah, turned down by his own father, had asked for a loan. Chase and his brother Jackson had scraped together everything they had, and Noah had given them a bunch of papers in return.

And then his dad had gotten sick, and with his brother still in college, Chase had to come home. The family business had needed help and Chase assumed the helm. He'd discovered that the papers that Noah had given him meant he was a part owner of Noah's company and that had been all he needed, besides his own winnings, to take the family's boating supply store, North Coast Outfitters, and grow it into an upscale catalog, a chain of stores, and a website catering to the yachting crowd. The success and the hard work it had taken left him with no regrets about giving up his racing career. Sure, a chance at the America's Cup was probably out of the question now, but he had a good life, and his father, while not in perfect health, was doing OK.

Chase had his own membership at the Queensbay Yacht Club, a forty-foot sloop in a slip at the marina, which he now owned to boot, and he was the hometown boy made good. There was just one thing missing to make his dream complete.

"Thank you. Caitlyn's been down with morning sickness for the past three months, but she says it's easing up. Either that or she can't stand being cooped up anymore. Watch out, I'm sure she's planning some sort of party soon." Noah ran a hand through his hair.

Chase had nothing to say for a moment, lost again in thoughts of Phoebe and her downright refusal to sell the house to him. Well, she hadn't been subjected to a full-on campaign of his persuasive powers yet, had she?

"Hey there, Earth to Chase." Noah was looking at him curiously. "OK, from what I can see, your business is doing great, so that means that something else must be bothering you. If it's not a lady, what is it?"

Chase grimaced and ran a hand through his hair. "It's the house. Ivy House. Would you believe it that Savannah Ryan owned it all these years and left it to her granddaughter?"

Noah shook his head. "I don't get why you're so fascinated with that house. You would think the fact that your grandfather once shacked up there with a movie star would make it off-limits for you."

"Very funny. That's history. And who cares about that?" Chase pointed out. It had been a scandal over fifty years ago, and because of its tragic ending, it still got dragged up now and then on some entertainment shows. "That house, with the tower, the gables, and the view...Do you know how often these waterfront properties come up for sale? And with that size lot? I've wanted it ever since I could remember."

"OK," Noah said, nodding, playing along, "So you said the owner is Savannah Ryan? I thought she sold the place years ago."

Chase shook his head. "Guess not. That's why all of my offers must have gotten rejected. I guess she didn't have any kind feelings towards the family. But she's dead, and now someone new owns it."

"You know if you want to tear down the house, the Historical Commission is going to have a fit," Noah told him.

"Well, that won't be a problem since the new owner swears she isn't selling." Chase didn't defend the house. He had no intention of tearing it down, but he didn't want to seem too sentimental. Truth was, after poking around there a bit today, he realized that Ivy House wasn't so bad. Of course, it wasn't as big as some of the newer bluff homes, but it was big enough, with its distinctive tower and widow's walk. And it was perched high above the harbor, a guardian overlooking the town and the marina. And he had always loved it, imagined himself owning it from the days when he'd been looking up at it from the water below. Ivy House had been a commanding presence in his life even before he realized the family connection.

"Weren't the last tenants pretty rough on it?" Noah said.

Chase nodded. "Yup, and the new owner, Savannah's grand-daughter, is from California. No way she's going to commit to fixing this place up, not if she wants to get back home anytime soon. Or, worse yet, I bet she wants to build some modern box-type thing with a thousand windows."

Chase focused on one of the photos he'd hung in his office. North Coast Outfitters had grown so fast because of who he was, or at least the image he'd played up. It was a picture they'd used in last year's catalog: Chase at the helm of a sleek racing yacht, the seas foaming and looking rough around him. He could remember the feel of power, the sheer strength of the boat beneath him, the sense of rightness. He'd always felt the same way about Ivy House, the way it watched over the village with a quiet dignity, even as its condition took a turn for the worse.

"Savannah Ryan has a granddaughter?" Noah said with a low whistle. "Now *that* I find hard to believe."

"Well, believe it because here she is."

He turned his laptop around to show Noah. He'd been doing a little internet research on Phoebe.

Noah's eyebrows shot up in appreciation. "Wow, so that's Savannah Ryan's granddaughter. Nice to know sometimes the apple doesn't fall far from the tree."

Noah pursed his lips as he thought through things. "Wait a second. Isn't there a problem? Since her grandmother and your grandfather were married, does that mean you two are related? That could be a little weird."

Chase shot his friend a withering look. "We're not related. Leland left my mom behind when he ran off with Savannah Ryan, and she already had a kid. So, there's no weirdness there and no blood relations. I guess we're like stepcousins or something."

Noah laughed. "Weird, no, but trust me, the media would eat it up. If they got wind that the two of you were even talking. And that Phoebe was living in *that* house. I can see the headlines now." Noah held up his hands as he intoned, "The Romance of the Century, Part Two."

"I'm not interested in her. Just the house." Chase groped for words. There had been an unmistakable spark between them, but she had stayed curiously immune to his teasing, to his flirting. Phoebe Ryan was a cool customer, and well, dammit, if he didn't like a challenge, which had to be the reason why the thought of her kept distracting him.

"Well, that should be fine then. She probably has to head back to Los Angeles soon though. That is sort of your type, isn't it? Someone who isn't looking for any sort of long-term commitment?" Noah said.

"We will see," Chase paused. "She flat out told me she wasn't interested in selling the house. Her house, she called it." Maybe that was what was bothering him, the fact that Phoebe had never even seen the house Chase had loved since he was a kid and was now getting all possessive about it.

Noah smiled. "Well, hearing 'no' never seemed to stop you before. Let me know what I can do to help."

Chase shook his head. "Well, I'm not sure she's put it together, who I am, you know, since Leland had a different last name and all that.

"That's a good thing, isn't it? Kind of awkward, right? Savannah and Leland came to a bad end. Not something I would want to bring up in casual conversation."

Chase pulled the computer back to him, looking at the picture of Phoebe Ryan. He had done a basic internet search on her and was surprised by the amount of information that came back. First off was the website for her company, Ivy Lane Designs. Apparently, she was some sort of designer.

And then there were a bunch of image results and press releases.

"Isn't that guy on some TV show?" Noah said, pointing to one of the pictures. Chase looked at the headline.

"Yeah, some cop show. Looks like he and Phoebe are an item."

Noah pulled the computer back to him. "Hmm, Caitlyn likes that show. She says it's because of the acting, but I swear, that guy always seems to be taking his shirt off."

"Lucky for Phoebe," Chase muttered. The guy's name was Garrett McGraw and he looked like the standard actor type: tall, dirty blond hair, artful stubble. He and Phoebe looked good together, Chase thought.

"Well, if she has that to go home to, maybe she won't be so eager to stick around. Come on, it could be a good thing."

Chase shot his friend a look, but Noah was busy scrolling through something on the computer screen.

"You know, once word gets out that Ivy House belonged to Savannah Ryan, the price will go up." Noah looked up.

Chase smiled, thinking about the envelope he had given her. "That's why I've made her an offer she can't refuse."

Chapter 7

Phoebe stared at the envelope. It had been delivered by a courier service from the lawyer's office in New York. She had opened the package and first read the typed note from Savannah's lawyer, the one who had informed her about Ivy House.

Dear Ms. Ryan, your grandmother asked that you get this letter after you had a chance to visit Ivy House. As I understand you have done this, I am now releasing the letter to you.

The letter wasn't dated, but it couldn't have been too recent because Savannah's script was firm and legible, before her body had been ravaged by the cancer.

My Dear Phoebe,

If you're getting this, it means I'm gone. I don't know how much will be left, but I have ensured that I have one thing to leave you. Ivy House. I found it hard to live there after Leland's death, and after your parents died, it seemed cruel to move you away from the only home you had ever known. But Ivy House was always special to me. It always seemed to have a touch of magic about it. I am told it needs some repairs. And probably some love and care after all these years. Leland Harper was very special to me, and the time we spent at Ivy House was some of the best, though all too brief, years of my life. How it ended with Leland was a tragedy, a twist of fate.

Ours was a passionate affair and our love burned brightly. I do not know if it would have lasted, but he was the love of my life, even though the press had the world believe otherwise.

I know that I have not always been the best mother or grandmother. To be an artist requires a bit of selfishness, I always felt, especially an actress. You belong to your fans and it's hard to be everything to someone else, especially a child. I didn't always do right by your father, but he turned out fine—better than fine. My only regret is that he too was taken from this world too soon.

And he and your mother did just fine by you, giving me the most precious gift. I know you haven't always enjoyed the life you had to lead with me, and, to be frank, I am not sure it suited you. But you did the best you could with it and that is all anyone asks.

So now, when I can bear to part with it, I give you Ivy House. It was a safe port for me and Leland when times were rough. I hope you may find it to be your own safe haven and a place of happiness and magic. While I was there, I found out who I was...I hope it holds the same promise for you.

Phoebe dropped the letter onto the desk. She was in her room in the Osprey Arms. It was a decent size, with a nice view, and the feeling it was supposed to encourage was one of colonial charm, but the mix of toile and floral fabric was a bit overdone and dated.

She flopped down in the wingback armchair and looked out the window. It was a sunny day. Gulls wheeled in the sky and there were boats leaving the marina heading out for a day on the water.

I give you Ivy House... How very Savannah, Phoebe thought. *I hear it needs a little work...* Also very Savannah-like, Phoebe thought, to give something that wasn't quite fit for gifting. Savannah had left her with many obligations.

Phoebe looked at her phone. The story had hit the papers just as she was getting ready to leave Los Angeles. She didn't want to endure the pity of all her friends. But there it was, in black and white: *"Savannah Ryan Dies Broke..."* was the most succinct. After Savannah died, Phoebe had faced a mountain of paperwork and bills, which the Los Angeles lawyers had summed up for her nicely: sell everything or come up with a mountain of cash to keep it.

While Phoebe wasn't broke herself, Savannah, what with her illness and the nursing home costs, had depleted all her savings quickly. She had already moved out of the house in Malibu and had been living in an apartment. It was on a lease, but the landlord had been happy to let Phoebe out of the contract. That had left furniture and clothes, most of which Phoebe had put into storage, and the rest she had arranged with a dealer friend to sell.

At the end of the day, there had been just enough to cover Savannah's final expenses with a bit left over. So much for the remains of a long career spent entertaining the masses. Savannah had never been interested in anything other than making movies. She had never attached her name to any product or cause. And for the last decade or so, she hadn't been working.

Phoebe glanced over the story. It had the basic details down right, and it included a notice about the sale of some of Savannah's furniture at the gallery. But that was just a sentence or two. The author of the piece had decided to fill the story with some salacious details, rehashing all the details of Savannah Ryan's life: her scandalous child out of wedlock and then her determined wooing of Leland Harper, a married man quite a bit older than her, and their stormy and passionate marriage, which had resulted in his messy divorce and a relationship that kept the media hopping.

She sighed and kept reading. Savannah and Leland's relationship, always heated, turned almost violent, with Leland drinking and accusing Savannah of hooking up with her costars. Before things could get really ugly, Leland had died in a plane crash. Sympathy swung in Savannah's favor, as she became a tragic figure, the lover left bereft, and her career had slowly revived.

Savannah had had a fortune, both from Leland's money and her own work, but she had let it all slip away. Worse, though, was that she had spent Phoebe's inheritance too. Her parents had died in a car crash on the way home from an awards ceremony. Phoebe had been only eight when it happened and Savannah had been awarded custody, moving from Queensbay back to Hollywood, trying to be a mother, while also trying to revive her career.

Phoebe hated the papers. She'd managed to stay out of them and, after a while, so had Savannah. But she'd known enough people, friends and acquaintances, who were hounded by them; the merest indiscretion fodder for endless days of stories, the loss of privacy unbearable.

Phoebe looked at the other envelope on the small side table. Chase had given it to her the day before. He had said it was an offer for the property. As if that was all Ivy House could be.

Her practical side warred with her outrage. And then she thought about what Savannah had done. She had left her a dilapidated house requiring immeasurable investments of time, money, and energy.

She reached for the envelope. It was a simple white one and she slid open the flap, giving herself a nasty paper cut in the process. Strike two against him, Phoebe thought, as she stuck her finger in her mouth, trying to soothe the pain away.

A single sheet of paper fell out. It was a heavy bond and there was a simple, solid dark blue type on the letterhead. But her eyes glossed over that as they fixed on the number. Sure, there were a bunch of words surrounding it, outlining terms and details, but it was the number that got her attention.

"Holy shit," she mouthed and looked again to make sure she wasn't mistaken. Sandy, the real estate agent, had been right. It really was a million-dollar view. More than a million dollars.

She read over the terms and saw they were simple. The offer was for the house and lot, as-is conditions, no questions asked. All cash, possession to be taken as soon as possible. Phoebe knew that if she accepted this offer, she could be on her way back to Los Angeles and her life within a day or two.

Tempting. Yes, very tempting. She had left Los Angeles at loose ends, and while it didn't mean she needed to get back there right away, she didn't think her absence would make getting her life back together any easier. With that kind of money, she wouldn't have to go back to Los Angeles with her hat in hand, wouldn't have to rely on Dean to sort things out for her. She could be independent, really independent for once, be able to work for herself and not rely on the whims of clients.

She took another look at the letterhead. *Chase Sanders.* The name niggled at her, like the face of someone you saw in a crowd, but couldn't place. Perhaps she needed to do a little more research on this guy.

Chapter 8

Phoebe made her way through the lobby of the Osprey Arms. Like her room, it was elegant in a bland sort of way, with reproduction antiques and a rug that that did nothing for the place except hide the dirt. The effect was a sort of cheap imitation of what elegance should be. It could be so much more.

She was more intent on checking her bag, making sure she had remembered her pencils, her sketchbook, and her laptop, than in noticing her surroundings, which is why she was so startled when she connected with a wall.

"Ouch," she said and then looked up. It wasn't a wall at all, which made sense, since she had been quite sure she'd been walking in the middle of the lobby. Now the contents of her bag, including her sketchbook, were scattered across the floor.

"You," she said. It was Chase. "Chase Sanders," she corrected herself. He was standing there, looming above her.

"You weren't looking where you were going," he said, but she could see that he was more amused than angry. No, she decided quickly. He wasn't just amused. He was openly laughing at her. Not surprising, since she was so startled that she had popped back about three feet upon coming in contact with him. He was a lot more solid than he looked and a definite lurker.

"Do you always stand in the middle of hotel lobbies?" Phoebe snapped back, knowing that it wasn't much of a comeback. She had to look up at him and wished she were wearing higher heels. The Chase of jeans and a windbreaker were gone. This Chase had on tailored slacks, a white button-down, and a dark blue sweater. The expensive sunglasses hung in the v of his sweater and she wondered if he ever went anywhere without them.

He shrugged, the laughter gone, but the amusement still in his eyes. The preppy outfit couldn't hide the broad shoulders and well-developed biceps, even more apparent because he was standing with his arms crossed.

"Here, let me help you with that." And before she could tell him to leave her alone, he was on the floor, casually gathering her things up.

It was too much. She had told herself that she would be calm about the whole thing, but, really, this was too much.

"I don't know who you think you are," she said, finally, as he stood with her sketchpad and some pencils in his hand.

"And what sort of scheme you're trying to run." She felt emboldened and crossed the distance between them. Her finger found his chest and she jabbed it into him, hoping to make her point perfectly clear. "You must be up to something. And just to make it clear, Ivy House is not for sale."

A puzzled look crossed his face. "Is that what you think the offer was? Some sort of scheme?" He stepped back a little from her poking finger. Phoebe noticed that the guy behind the desk—blond, with a stubby little ponytail and one small gold earring—was paying close attention to them, while pretending to do anything but.

"Yes, that's what I think it is exactly." Phoebe felt herself beginning to get worked up. Why else would he have offered so much money for a decrepit house? He was trying to bribe her. That had to be it. Get her to sell and move out and leave Ivy House to the fate of the wrecking ball.

"I don't think when one is set out to scheme against someone, they make such a generous offer," Chase said, his voice mild even as he stopped her pointing finger from stabbing him in the chest again. He held her hand for what seemed like a minute too long, and Phoebe was distracted by the thought of how nice and big it felt wrapped around her own. And then she realized she was close enough to smell him and that he smelled good. Fresh soap and some sort of spicy aftershave.

She swallowed. There had been a point somewhere in there. Ah, yes, Chase Sanders was a conniving bastard with a too-sexy-for-words smile. Phoebe drew herself up to her full height. She had fallen for the sexy smile once too often, but this time she was forewarned. If he thought he could try and sneak Ivy House away from her, then he was surely mistaken.

"I don't know if you think you can steal Ivy House away from me, or what you're planning on doing with it, but I'm no fool. I've done my research. I know what it's worth and trying to sneak in and steal it from under me is a dirty, underhanded trick."

"I take it then that you didn't look at the offer. Because if you had, you would be aware that I offered more than what it was worth."

Chase released her hand and gave her back her pencils. She took them and shoved them in her bag. He still had her sketchpad, and it was with alarm that she watched him start to flip through the pages.

"What are you doing?" Phoebe knew her voice had risen and also knew that the guy at the reception desk was no longer pretending not to notice what was going on in the middle of his lobby. No, he was avidly staring at the both of them.

Chase looked up at her face and then back down at the pad. He had stopped at one of her latest designs, something she had come up with on the plane. Phoebe held out her hand, feeling her face start to grow red. Finally, after what seemed like forever, he handed the sketchbook back to her. She dropped it into her shoulder bag, relief flooding through her now that it was safely back in her possession.

"I assure you, Ms. Ryan, I wasn't trying to steal or sneak anything from you." Chase was smiling again, easy and confident as his blue eyes roamed over her face. Phoebe was aware that her foot was starting to tap impatiently. This encounter wasn't going quite as she had imagined it.

"I'm sorry. I didn't mean to deceive you. I was simply making a fair offer for the house," he said smoothly, and Phoebe took a deep breath.

"I meant what I said; I am interested. It's a great piece of property and ones like those don't come on the market very often."

"Well, I think you might be surprised to find out that you can't just charm your way into everything." Phoebe had done a little more research. Chase's offer had been good, but there was always room to negotiate. That wasn't what Phoebe intended, but she needed to know where she stood.

Chase smiled a slow, lazy smile, and Phoebe felt her stomach do a little flip-flop. Chase was not handsome, at least not in the pretty-boy Hollywood way she was used to. But he had as much presence as any movie star, and it was hard to keep her mind focused when he turned his dark blue eyes on her.

"Oh, you're right. I don't expect charm to work in this case. I figured it was going to take some cold, hard cash to get what I wanted. What do you say? I know I'm breaking one of the first rules of deal making, but that was just my first offer. Care to hear my second?"

There was something almost casually obscene about the way he made the remark, and Phoebe felt herself taking a step away.

"Really, I…" She spun on her heel and walked over to where the guy with the blond ponytail was sitting behind the reception counter. Jim, his nametag read, all of a sudden seemed to be very busy with his computer.

"Excuse me." Phoebe thumped her hand on the scratched wooden surface of the desk. Jim looked up, an embarrassed smile on his face.

"Can I help you miss?" He asked, sounding like he was anything but eager to do so.

"This man," Phoebe did a half-turn and pointed to where Chase was standing, arms folded, rocking slightly on his heels, a very amused expression on his face, "is bothering me. I am a guest at this hotel and I demand…"

Before she could continue, Chase spoke up. "It's quite alright. Sorry to bother you, Ms. Ryan. I'll be going now. But please, think about what I said."

The smirk was back on his face and so were his sunglasses, and if Phoebe wasn't mistaken, she was almost certain his shoulders were shaking ever so slightly as he walked out the swinging double doors and onto the wide porch.

Phoebe turned back to look at Jim, who seemed to be having some sort of choking fit. His face was bright red and when she asked if he was OK, he waved his hand and managed to cough out, "Fine, just fine."

She left after that, satisfied that she had made her point to the lurking and looming Chase Sanders. Ivy House would not be for sale to him. Savannah did not want her to sell it, at least not to someone who probably only wanted it for the view.

Phoebe started out across the village, taking Hill Road, aptly named because it snaked up the high bluffs that circled the harbor. A mix of colonial and late Victorian houses lined the road, and as she got to the top, it flattened out and little lanes jutted off, leading to the water's edge. Ivy Lane was just a half mile up from Queensbay, but it was a steep hike, and she was just a little bit winded when she made it to the front gate.

Ivy House stood there, starkly white against a bluer-than-blue spring sky. It had beckoned to her since yesterday. All of last night she had dreamt of it, strange dreams that had played out like one of Savannah's black-and-white movies. Looking at the house now, the images came back to her. Savannah had appeared, dressed in a simple flowing dress, an elegant blonde. Stepping into the frame had been an older, distinguished man, Leland Harper, dark haired, white suited.

Savannah and Leland's affair and marriage had been so passionate that books had been written and even a miniseries had been based on it. Phoebe's grandmother hardly ever talked about Leland, so Phoebe had done what any kid would do. She'd gone to the internet, watched the miniseries—filled with B-list actors—read the books, and tried to imagine what it had been like.

Savannah and Leland had decided that the best way to quell the uproar was to appear normal. So, they had stayed in Queensbay, Leland's hometown, and had tried to live like normal people for a while, as normal as a movie star and millionaire could be. The happily-ever-after hadn't lasted, of course. They were too close to Leland's ex-wife, who wouldn't leave them alone, and Savannah couldn't be kept from acting.

No one knew if it would have lasted since Leland had died in an airplane crash, making the story tragic and epic. Still, from the dreamy look Savannah got on her face whenever she talked about Leland and Queensbay, Phoebe knew that Ivy House had been a special place.

Now looking at the house, Phoebe tried to sense the magic Savannah had written about in her letter. The house was beautiful, at least if you looked past the cosmetic blemishes. The white tower that shot up lent the house a quirky sense of possibility. Magic, though? Phoebe looked around at the overgrown garden, the rusted fence, and the broken flagstones. She closed her eyes, breathed in the scent of the water, and let the movie play again in her mind.

Ivy House was gleaming white, the sky blue, the water bluer. Seagulls wheeled in the sky and a light wind rustled the oaks. Foxgloves and lupine bloomed, and the fence was a gleaming black. There was the sound of laughter and the porch invited you to sit. The door was painted Phoebe's favorite color, a slate blue, and the brass knocker shone.

Smiling, Phoebe opened her eyes. Perhaps this was it, what she needed. Maybe Savannah had truly meant to give her something that needed to be put back together again. She could restore Ivy House, whether for herself or to sell it; maybe that didn't matter. But it would be a project, real, honest work while she sorted out her life. It was the perfect reason to disappear from her old life for a while. And if she decided to sell it, she could be choosy, sell it to someone who didn't want to tear it down, someone who would respect it.

Chapter 9

She tried to push away the thought of Chase Sanders laughing at her as she spent the day at Ivy House, starting to make a plan of what needed to be done. She looked down at one point at her to-do lists and saw that she had drawn his face. And not just once, but several times. She had drawn him once with his eyebrow quirked up, another one with the beginnings of a smirk, and finally one that focused on his shoulders. She sighed and drew bad-guy, villain-type mustaches on all of them, hoping it would get the thought of him out of her mind.

Halfway through the day, her creative energy had taken a turn, and Phoebe abandoned the plans and the numbered lists, grabbing her sketchpad and drawing, designs coming easily to her. She felt that her creative energy was sapped while she was trying to care for Savannah, and she had given up designing everything after the incident with CallieSue Owens. But now, on Ivy House's stone terrace, with the light breeze ruffling her hair and the gentle lap of the waves in the background, she felt absorbed, and a plan, one that included the house and her dream, began to take shape.

Phoebe had been so caught up, she'd looked up in surprise when Lynn found her, sitting on the low stone wall, sketching the way the setting sun purpled the sky. It was just a way to capture the colors around her, the way everything seemed so bright and vibrant.

"Ready for dinner?" Lynn had asked cheerfully, and Phoebe realized she was. She hadn't eaten since breakfast and the idea of a home-cooked meal was definitely appealing. Gathering all her stuff, she shoved it into her bag, jumped up and stretched.

"Do you ever get tired of it?" she asked Lynn as they both looked over the bluff and toward the water.

Lynn sighed. "No, not really. I know that I'll have to move out soon and I'll miss it, but maybe someday I'll find my way back here."

Phoebe had lived close to an ocean all her life, but there was something soothing and calm about this harbor, the way the bluffs were like arms encircling you in a hug, the simple beauty of lights twinkling in the windows of the houses that ringed the shore. It was comforting, she decided, as she and Lynn walked through a break in the privet hedge that separated the houses.

Phoebe was welcomed into the Masters' home as if she'd grown up there. As promised, Mrs. Masters, who was a doctor as well, was an excellent cook. She was also a huge Savannah fan. Mrs. Masters was just as open and friendly as Lynn and the pasta fra diavolo was so good that Phoebe decided she didn't mind supplying all the information Mrs. Masters was after.

Lynn's father, also a doctor and chief of the local hospital, drifted off to watch a baseball game right around the time Phoebe started to give details about Savannah's eating habits. It was after the mixed-berry pie à la mode that Lynn had to put a stop to all of her mom's questioning and declared that she and Phoebe were going out on their own.

"These margaritas are delicious," Phoebe said, taking a sip. She and Lynn were down in the village at a place called Augie's. It was different from the Osprey Arms, with a younger, more fun crowd. There were a few families finishing up their dinner, but mostly it was couples and singles, groups of people at tables, some people milling about by a pool table. There was even a jukebox; someone popped in a new song, and people were starting to dance.

"It feels so good to get out," Lynn said, her dark hair curling around her delicate face. They were leaned up against the bar, so she was swaying to the music and sipping her drink.

"It must be tough, all the hours you put in," Phoebe said, also feeling herself starting to sway to the music. It was a nice atmosphere, totally low-key, but fun, and even though she was stuffed from Mrs. Masters' meal, she was eyeing the potato skins someone had ordered a few chairs down.

"Well, at least there's a light at the end of the tunnel. One more year and I'll be a real doctor. I am so excited. It's been a long slog. College, medical school, then residency. But it will all be worth it," Lynn said. Phoebe thought she detected a note of wistfulness in Lynn's voice.

"What do you think you want to do?" Phoebe asked. She had known a few doctors in Los Angeles, mostly plastic surgeons or dermatologists. Not bad people, but they were always working an angle once they found out who she was, trying to see if Savannah would be interested in endorsing them. One guy had even gone so far as to promise Phoebe some "free work" if she could get Savannah to recommend him.

"Well, my dad knows a few people who would be happy to bring me into their practice. Or I could get a job at the hospital. Since he's the chief of staff there, it might be a little weird though, you know, like everyone would think I only got the job because of him."

Phoebe shook her head. "In Los Angeles, it's all about who you know. No one would think twice of using any connection they could to get ahead. My last boyfriend was an actor." She thought briefly of Garrett and the way photographers had always seemed to be around when they went on dates. "And it turned out he was all about my connection to Savannah."

"Sounds like you were burned by someone." Lynn looked at her. "Come on, spill. If you tell me about yours, I will tell you about mine. Can't be worse than someone who got turned on by 'playing doctor.'"

"Dumped me about a week after Savannah's funeral."

"What?" Lynn said, her voice disbelieving. "That creep. What reason did he give you?"

"It was him, not me, you know. The same old stuff. I realized I had just about outlived my usefulness, especially since he had just gotten cast on a new show. And I had this rule: no dating actors. I thought I had learned my lesson, but Garrett was so charming, I just couldn't resist."

Lynn's nose crinkled. "Do you mean Garrett McGraw, the one who's going to be on the new medical show?"

Phoebe looked at her glass. It was almost empty. There was a group of guys, late twenties, early thirties, casually dressed. One of them tried to catch their eye. Phoebe sent a quick smile and then turned to Lynn. Somehow, a blond cutie in a fleece wasn't doing it for her tonight, not when she had spent the afternoon drawing pictures of a dark haired, blue-eyed lurker.

Phoebe shook her head. "He's the one. I thought he was different. We actually went to high school together and, believe you me, he was not that cute back then. So when he showed up looking all yummy and delicious, fresh off that other show, I thought I was being the shallow one, you know, giving him a second chance."

"But let me guess, he was just using you?" Lynn said, her eyes wide and knowing.

"He wanted to impress Savannah. Turns out, he wanted her to make a few phone calls to some producers, which I guess she did. She never could resist a cute face. Or tight abs. And before I know it, he goes from having a few bit parts in a TV show to being cast as the charming yet deep doctor on the most anticipated show of the season, 'Mercy.'" Phoebe shook her head and looked into her drink. She had managed to finish her entire margarita.

"Well, if it makes you feel better, real doctors hate those shows. Everything's always so dramatic and over-the-top. And trust me, none of us look that good in scrubs," Lynn said.

"Thanks, but I don't think that makes me feel better."

"So did you ever act?" Lynn asked.

"No way. Not for me. Let's just say I am definitely a behind-the-scenes girl. I worked as a set designer for a while and then as a graphic designer and then a designer. Pillows, fabrics, and things. I have my own company, but I mainly do consulting work."

"Would I have bought any of your stuff?" Lynn asked, and Phoebe could tell she was curious.

"Sort of," Phoebe answered.

"Sounds like another story."

Phoebe sighed. Not even tequila could make this story better. "I told a client that she had the taste of a hillbilly."

"A client?" Lynn was puzzled.

"I was hired by a certain celebrity, one with her own cooking show, to help her develop a line of dinnerware. She and I had different ideas on what things should look like," Phoebe said simply. The taste of that defeat was still far more bitter than what had happened with Garrett. She had gotten what she asked for when she dated an actor. But the breakup of her professional relationship had come out of left field.

It had hurt when CallieSue Owens hadn't bowed to Phoebe's far superior design sensibilities. And that manufacturing company, the one paying Phoebe's fee, had chosen CallieSue's white-trash design sensibilities over her own.

"You don't mean CallieSue..." Lynn started to guess.

"Shh. No one is supposed to know she's not designing it herself. But yeah, I mixed it up with a gal from Texas and guess what?"

"What?" Lynn asked.

"You really don't want to mess with Texas," Phoebe said.

Lynn hooted with laughter. The blond guy in the fleece was starting to make his way over to them, and Phoebe decided she didn't care if he came over or not. Perhaps a preppy guy in fleece was just what she needed to block the thoughts of Chase out of her mind.

"Did you get another job?" Lynn asked.

"No, not at the moment. I am clientless." Phoebe only hesitated for a moment. CallieSue Owens had made sure of that. Phoebe had underestimated the amount of pull the woman had and, now, no other celebrity would touch her. Dean, CallieSue's agent and a friend of Phoebe's, was trying to smooth things over, but she was pretty sure that it was a long shot.

"Then what were those sketches I saw you working on?" Lynn asked.

Phoebe hesitated. She had, in between consulting gigs, been working on her own designs, her own lines. It had been sort of a sideline, the pillows, but the designs had started to take off around Los Angeles. Someone she knew, an interior designer, had used a few in a client's home, and that home had made it into a style magazine and Phoebe had gotten credit. She had a website, of course, and before she knew it, people were trying to order pillows from it.

So far, Phoebe had done everything through phone and email, but now that she had no other commitments, she was thinking that perhaps it was time to get serious about it, about her own line of home goods. Still, the decision was so new that it felt weird talking about it out loud. But if there was one person who would certainly not judge her, it was Lynn.But if anyone was certain not to judge her, it was Lynn.

"No, I've been working on a business idea. I think I was getting tired of coming up with all these great ideas and having other people take the credit for it. Quitting my job, taking care of Savannah, coming here—it all feels like maybe it's a part of a journey, some journey to find what I really want to do with my life." Phoebe stopped.

"Well, Queensbay is about as small and real as it gets. Not that we don't have our little society here. There's the Garden Club and the Yacht Club—Friday night barbeques, not to be missed..." Lynn gave a laugh. The guy in the fleece, joined by a friend in a ball cap, was edging closer.

"I guess it wouldn't be such a bad place to try and blend in," Phoebe said, twirling the stem of her oversized margarita glass. She realized that she was really considering the thought. Sure, Ivy House needed work to make it fit for habitation, but not that much. After the renovation, she could keep working on it while living there and running her business.

"You totally could. It would be great. And in the summer, the place really picks up. Plenty of guys with absolutely no ambition of becoming actors. You could go incognito."

Augie's was filling up, the energy rising. Phoebe could feel the tequila in the margarita starting to loosen her up. It would be nice to be somewhere. Put down roots, start over, far away from the too-bright sun of Los Angeles. Savannah had always said Ivy House was magical. Maybe it just needed a little love to bring the magic back.

"I could do it," Phoebe said, emboldened by the liquor. "I can fix up Ivy House and live there. Why not? I'm twenty-eight years old, I have some money in the bank. I don't have to be anywhere I don't want to be."

Lynn threw her head back and laughed. "You go girl."

They clinked their glasses. "And here's to dating people who have no idea who we are," Lynn said.

"Here, here. No real names and no real professions tonight!" Phoebe agreed, already feeling the smile starting to curve up her lips.

Chapter 10

Phoebe woke up with a throbbing headache, cursing the curtains that had been left open. Sunlight, bright and harsh, streamed into her room. The margaritas. She and Lynn had had more than a few, and then they had walked back to the Osprey Arms, after collecting more than a few phone numbers, all of which they had dumped in the trash can. Lynn had crashed on the couch in Phoebe's room, and sometime in the morning, while Phoebe was still sleeping, had left to get ready for work.

She'd left a note, scrawled on the pad from the desk: "*Take two and call me later. Lynn.*" A packet of headache medicine was on top of the note, and Phoebe decided that she must have just been subjected to some sort of doctor humor.

She had dreamed of Ivy House last night. It had been a full, richly layered dream, startlingly vivid to her, fueled no doubt by the alcohol. But it had seemed so real, and in it, Ivy House had been perfect. Gleaming wood floors, comfortable couches, color, and light. And there had been laughter drifting through the house. This time, there had been no Savannah. In fact, everything about the dream had been modern, very present day. It had felt right.

Phoebe looked at herself in the mirror. She felt much better now and she sent a silent shout of thanks to Lynn and her medicine. Time to decide what to wear. She tried to open the windows to see what the temperature was, but the paint was so thick that they were effectively sealed shut. She tried applying some force, but that only made her head hurt, so she flopped down in the little wing chair that looked out over the docks and picked up her phone.

She checked the weather first. Another perfect spring day here on the East Coast. Jean capris, she decided, and her pink-and-white-striped Oxford shirt. A pair of canvas sneakers. She still had some cleaning to do at the house, so she'd pull her hair back in a ponytail. And she had a nice lightweight fleece in case it was cooler up there.

That decided, she glanced through her emails. She'd set an alert to go off whenever her name or Savannah's came up on the Internet. The phone had been buzzing all morning, as more papers picked up on the sad state of Savannah's financial affairs. Her phone buzzed with texts and calls, none of which she answered. They were from friends and colleagues asking if she was OK. It would have been nice, except she could sense the avid curiosity. They were all wondering what it felt like to be poor.

Her phone rang at that moment. She almost didn't answer it, but the temptation was too much, and she glanced down to see who it was.

"Dean," she said, feeling a smile form on her face. Dean was one of her closest friends, the kind of guy who was always there for her. They had met in college when Phoebe had signed on to design the sets for the theater department's production of "Anything Goes." Dean had been in the chorus and they'd formed an instant bond, poking fun at the self-important lead, sharing the same taste for bad action movies, and a love of ice-cream shakes.

After college, Dean had realized he couldn't handle the amount of rejection and poverty it took to be an actor, so he had started working at a talent agency. His good looks coupled with a killer business sense had him quickly rising up the ranks. He'd been responsible for a lot of Phoebe's more interesting and lucrative gigs, whether they were set designs or movie posters, and since he was CallieSue's agent, it was he who had suggested they work together on CallieSue's own line of country chic placemats, tablecloths, and other things.

Too bad CallieSue couldn't see the chic through the forest of tackiness she lived in. But even though CallieSue was Dean's biggest client, he had fought hard for Phoebe, so hard that Phoebe had to quit before Dean could ruin his own career trying to help hers.

"Phoebs, I saw the article, are you OK?" His voice radiated concern even over the phone. It was early on the West Coast, but she knew Dean rarely slept more than a few hours a night. He was seemingly married to his job, always dealing with clients, crises, and other issues. Phoebe knew he was angling for a big promotion.

"I'm fine. It's nothing." Phoebe tried to brush his concern off. He'd been a great friend for her the past few months as Savannah's decline became apparent, checking in on her, sending over takeout, sending flowers, and even his own housekeeper when Phoebe needed help sorting through Savannah's stuff. Still, she had come all this way so that the news from Los Angeles wouldn't bother her, so that she could have time to think, to be herself.

"So are you really out there, in the middle of nowhere? Sure I can't convince you to come back to the Los Angeles? Tinseltown misses you."

Phoebe tensed. After Savannah's death, Dean had told her that he would find a way for her to get her job back, that he could smooth things over with CallieSue, but she had resisted, asking for more time to sort things out. He hadn't thrown a fit, but it seemed like they had come dangerously close to having a moment, to him telling her how he "really felt" that she had panicked and started talking about her need for a strawberry shake. Emotional honesty averted, they had been able to part as friends.

"Dean," she said carefully since she didn't want anything to change between them. She looked out at the water because she found the view, the sky blue with only a few wisps of milky white clouds, and the surface of the harbor cobalt, flecked by the tiniest of white caps, calming.

"I know, I know. You're on a leave of absence from your life. I get it, but let me know if you get bored and want to come back. CallieSue is busy terrorizing someone else and I'm pretty sure she has forgotten about you. I wouldn't be lying if I told you I already have some other opportunities brewing for you. Maybe another movie set, a big-name director. It can be just like old times."

Phoebe smiled wanly into the phone. That was the problem. She hadn't been happy with old times and always working on someone else's vision, and Savannah's death had only brought that into focus.

Sensing her hesitation, he hurried on. "Well, whatever it is, I'm here for you, Phoebs. You know that, right?"

Phoebe took a moment to picture Dean's face. He was fair, blond, with green eyes and high, sculpted cheekbones. He was a good-looking man, gym-fit, with a nervous energy and driven ambition. She had seen him be both charming, with clients, and ruthless, when it came to winning a deal.

"I know that." Phoebe closed her eyes.

All the time they had known each other, they had never managed to both be single at the same time, so the question of getting together had never come up. But now it was out there. Dean was a great guy and, unlike Garrett and a string of others she had dated, didn't need anything from her. But she wasn't sure that was enough.

After a few more words of support from Dean, she clicked off and leaned back again, closing her eyes, trying to soothe her troubles away. Could three-thousand miles really change her life? There was little for her in California. To focus on taking care of Savannah, she had even given up her apartment, putting most of her things in storage, and ever since she'd sold Savannah's house, she'd been couch surfing. She had no house, no job, and perhaps no future.

Savannah's words came unbidden to her: *We make our own destinies.* If anyone could truly believe a saying like that, it would have been Savannah, who'd been sublime at reinventing herself. From the girl next door to an ingénue to a stately matron, Savannah had played every role and then some.

Phoebe took a deep breath. Perhaps she was where she was supposed to be. She was free. For once in her life, she had no ties. She had money in the bank and a roof over her head. *Count your blessings,* Savannah's voice whispered to Phoebe and she laughed.

Phoebe checked the email on her phone. There was only one email from a reporter asking for a comment on the state of Savannah's affairs. She ignored it. It would be better if that story died out.

Right now, she needed to focus on her legacy and her future.

Chapter 11

The fall line was bothering him. Or it wasn't, which was part of the problem. It was boring. North Coast Outfitters was growing fast and that was good, but perhaps there were only so many ways to make a raincoat look sexy.

Chase slowed his steps as he headed up Main Street towards The Golden Pear. They had the best chocolate-chip cookies in town, and he had promised his staff that he would spring for a box of them at the next meeting. It was too nice a day to be cooped up inside, and he had welcomed the chance to walk up towards the restaurant. But it wasn't the smell of cookies that had him slowing down.

It was the sight of her. He hadn't seen Phoebe in a few days, ever since she had literally run into him in the lobby of the hotel, though he'd done his best to keep an eye out for her. Short of walking up to Ivy House, where she had made it clear he wasn't welcome, he hadn't quite figured out a way to run into her again.

But his luck, as it usually did, was holding. He could see her, but only from behind, through the large plate glass window of The Garden Cottage, Queensbay's furniture and knickknack shop. Joan Altieri, who owned the place, was a friend of his mother's, so it only took Chase a second to come up with a plausible reason for wandering in there. The chocolate-chip cookies would have to wait.

A bell tinkled overhead as he pushed his way into the store. The Garden Cottage had a nice collection of stuff. Lots of things for the garden, of course, and then the usual doodads—candles, candlestick holders, dishes, glasses, plaques, centerpieces, and the like. It was the kind of place women loved and men only stepped in under duress or if they were shopping for a present. His mother's birthday wasn't too far away, and this time, instead of remembering at the last minute, he could kill two birds with one stone: find something for his mother and bump into the perfectly delectable Phoebe Ryan again.

He gave a little wave and a nod to Joan, letting her know that she shouldn't interrupt what she was doing to bother with him. Chase scanned the shelves, desperately trying to think of how his mother had decorated her new place in Florida, seeing if there was anything that she would like, all the while trying to inch closer to Phoebe.

Phoebe hadn't noticed his arrival yet, since she was so intent on what she was showing to Joan.

"Barrel stitched. All hand done. I have some great seamstresses working for me. And this size is available in five different fabric options."

Chase moved through the wine lovers section and angled himself so he had a good view of what Phoebe was holding up. Rectangular, plump. A pillow he surmised. He watched as she dropped the pillow down on the counter and held up her phone to Joan to show her something.

"And you said these have appeared in *Pacific Living*?" Joan asked, but even Chase could hear the doubt in her voice. Joan was not really a risk taker when it came to stocking her inventory. He'd often thought the store would play better with a slightly fresher sensibility. It was definitely the place to buy your mother or grandmother a gift. No man would ever think of buying his wife or girlfriend something from here.

He came up close enough so he could peer over Phoebe's shoulder. There were five or so pillows laid out on the glass counter and they were fun and bright. A nice pop of color against the muted palette of The Garden Cottage.

"Well, they're certainly bright," Joan said. She was chewing on the end of the earpiece of her glasses and Chase knew that was never a good sign.

"You know, I was thinking that's exactly what my mom needs for her new place." Chase emerged out of the shadows and was rewarded with a huge smile from Joan and a frown from Phoebe.

"Well, they're certainly beachy." Joan agreed, perching her glasses on her nose and running her fingers along the fabric of an azure blue-and-white-striped pillow.

"They're inspired by coastal living," Phoebe said. "West or East Coast." She offered Joan a smile after deliberately turning her back on Chase.

"Well, the summer season is coming up," Joan mused.

"And I'll take two for my mom," Chase said, already reaching into his pocket for his credit card.

Joan looked flustered at that response, and Chase knew that she and Phoebe hadn't quite talked terms.

"Well, I'd be happy to give you the standard wholesale price," Phoebe jumped in quickly and pushed a piece of paper towards Joan, who glanced down and smiled.

"And perhaps," Phoebe finished up smoothly, "you can take a few more on consignment. Showcase them for a few weeks, and when they sell, you can pay me then. You seem quite trustworthy."

"Oh, she is," Chase said, putting his credit card down on the counter. "Why don't you ring me up and I'll pick them up on my way back from the bakery."

Joan flashed him a brilliant smile, and he realized he'd probably been a bit foolish not to ask the price, but hey, he was trying to impress the girl. He hazarded a glance at Phoebe, who was looking at him coolly, arms crossed, chin up slightly. Apparently becoming a customer hadn't changed her mind about him.

Phoebe was pleased with what she had managed to accomplish. It was a small accomplishment, of course, just a few pillows, but Joan had certainly seemed a lot friendlier towards her once Chase had appeared on the scene.

A shadow fell across her path and she looked up. He was standing there or, rather, leaning against the front of one of the shops, waiting as if he had nothing to do but to worry about the large white box he held.

Phoebe swallowed, not sure whether she should follow her nose, which was currently fixated on the smell emanating from the box, or focus on the smug look on Chase's face as he looked down at her from behind his sunglasses.

"You're welcome," he said, his grin turning positively cocky.

"What for?" she said, tucking her sample book back into her bag, trying to feign indifference, though she knew exactly what she should say thank you for.

"Are you always this unfriendly towards your customers?" he asked.

Phoebe pursed her lips. No she wasn't. When someone bought one of her designs, she prided herself on saying thank you. But somehow, the words were having a hard time coming where Chase was concerned.

"Thank you," she managed to say, turning and starting to walk. With catlike grace, Chase was up from the wall and following her. Her nose twitched and she couldn't help but glance at the box he held.

"The Golden Pear's chocolate-chip cookies. Best on the planet," he said, his tone sober.

She stopped. "You're serious?"

"I never joke about these chocolate-chip cookies. The recipe is some old family secret and is guarded better than the gold in Fort Knox here," he said and easily peeled open the box. The aroma of baked goods was overpowering and Phoebe swallowed her desire.

"Try this." Chase held out a cookie.

"No way. That thing is huge. It's practically the size of my head."

He looked down and shrugged. "Half the time they're the size of my head. But that never stops anyone. Trust me."

Chase had pushed his sunglasses back up on his head and she could see the teasing look in his eyes. Good sense and fear of death by chocolate warred against the goddess of hedonism as she took the cookie.

She took a bite, aware that Chase was watching her intently. She chewed, swallowed, and took another bite.

"Oh, wow," she said, around a mouthful of sinfully velvet chocolate and smooth dough. "That really is good."

She took another couple of bites, letting the chocolate chunks sit on her tongue and melt. Phoebe was aware of something. She opened her eyes and saw Chase staring at her with a heated look. She was aware that she had let every nuance of how the cookie was affecting her show on her face. Hurriedly, she swallowed, took a deep breath, and tried to compose herself.

"I told you so," he said, smiling. Phoebe barely listened to him. Here she was in the middle of the street eating an entire chocolate-chip cookie. There was pretty much no way Chase was going to get this back from her.

"Sinfully good," she muttered, letting her tongue find another bit of chocolate to melt away in her mouth. A couple, strolling hand in hand, walked past them, the woman giving Phoebe a strange look.

Phoebe glanced up at Chase. He was leaning in again, watching her, and there was the unmistakable air of amusement about him.

Self-conscious, she looked down. She'd eaten more than half the cookie, which wasn't a surprise since she'd skipped breakfast this morning. Too keyed up about the sales call, she'd only had coffee.

"What?" she asked, feeling shy all of a sudden. It was not like her to take cookies from someone she barely knew. Especially someone she'd recently been yelling at.

"You have a little bit of chocolate there," he said. She licked her lips, trying to find it, and Chase straightened up, his eyes on her.

"Not quite there," he said. "A little farther up, towards the corner." She found it and it was gone, but she saw that Chase's eyes had lost their amused spark and that he was now looking at her entirely differently.

"What?" Phoebe took another bite.

"Just a bit there," he said and reached in, his finger hovering near her cheek before it gently made contact. It was a feather-light touch, but it made her insides sit up and take notice. Her stomach clenched and rolled, and the two of them were frozen for a moment, looking at each other.

"Excuse me," a voice broke in and Chase's hand was gone from her cheek. Phoebe's stomach seemed to right itself, but not without leaving her feeling a bit dizzy. Too much coffee, she thought, even as the voice kept talking.

"I was wondering from where you got that cookie." It was the woman who had just walked past with a look of disdain on her face, and now she and her husband were standing there, looking at them, the woman's mouth slightly open, the man sending Chase a knowing look.

"It looks amazing," the woman added.

Chase recovered first. "From The Golden Pear, one block up. Make a left onto High Street."

"Best I've ever had," Phoebe said and then wished she had kept her mouth shut.

The couple left, and she and Chase were alone again. He had taken a step back and was no longer leaning, and his sunglasses had slipped down from his head and she could no longer see his eyes. It was hard to read him, and then his mouth quirked up in its typical smile.

"I guess I'll be seeing you," he said.

"I guess so," Phoebe agreed, though she didn't know why. Unless he needed more pillows. Still, she wasn't in the right frame of mind to disagree with him.

He backed away a few paces before he turned and walked in the direction of the harbor. Phoebe stood there, the remains of the cookie still in her hand, unabashedly enjoying Chase's rear view.

Head turning, he caught her looking at him and flashed her a grin. She was almost certain that he threw her a wink behind his sunglasses. And then he turned and was on his way.

Phoebe leaned against the cool brick of the building. It was a shady and ideal place for her to just stand still. Her brain was a puddle of mud. And her stomach was flip-flopping again, probably from the giant cookie she had eaten. Right, that was it. It had nothing to do with the way Chase Sanders kept showing up when she least expected it. And doing her favors. Phoebe shook her head, trying not to get too worked up. In Los Angeles, nobody did favors for nothing. Chase's help had to come with a price.

Chase did his best to keep his cool as he made his way back down towards the marina and his office. He'd only meant to give Phoebe a helping hand with the pillows. He stopped, almost started back, and then thought better of it. Joan still had his credit card and his pillows, but he knew they'd be safe. He'd go by later and pick them up when he was sure that Phoebe would no longer be anywhere in the vicinity.

One glance of her eating that cookie had been enough. The cookies were famous enough around Queensbay. Heck, even Noah swore by them when he needed to get out of the doghouse, but Chase wasn't sure he'd ever seen someone, well, a woman, get so much pleasure out of a cookie. It was like...no, he wouldn't—couldn't—go there. Already he was having too much trouble concentrating without any more thoughts of Phoebe Ryan breaking into his head.

Chapter 12

Phoebe retreated to Ivy House. She had discarded the rest of the cookie and was now eating an apple while she doodled. The internet had been set up in the house, and Lynn had let her borrow a couple of sawhorses and a large piece of plywood from her father's garage. It was serving as a temporary desk and that was just what Phoebe needed.

Joan Altieri had called just after lunch, while Phoebe was busy scrubbing kitchen cabinets. A customer had seen the pillows Chase had bought and wanted some just like it. Did she have more?

Phoebe took a deep breath, lied, and said yes. There was no way she was going to say no to another sale. As soon as she got off the phone with Joan, she called up her workshop in California.

Angela, the manager there, was nice, but always fretting, and Phoebe had to stop herself from screaming with frustration. That would only make Angela fret more and delay the process of her getting any more pillows. Finally, Angela admitted that they did have some stock in the warehouse space that Phoebe rented from them, and that she could send out some pillows by tomorrow morning.

Triumphant, Phoebe fist-pumped and got off the phone before Angela could change her mind. Walking over to her computer, she tapped on the keyboard until her website came up. She sighed. It was a piece of crap. Well, not exactly. It looked good, with beautiful pictures of her designs and even a pretty good headshot of her on it, one that she had bartered for. A duvet cover captured her in a slightly sexy, somewhat just-woke-up kind of look. Phoebe's only quibble was that her resemblance to Savannah was too evident. Dean had suggested that she mention her relationship to Savannah in her bio, but Phoebe had balked. She wanted people to buy her products because they liked the design, not because she was related to someone famous. Dean had smiled at her and shook his head at her naiveté.

But Phoebe wasn't being naive. She knew that putting the Savannah relationship out there could only help her, but it still didn't sit well with her. Savannah too had thought her silly not to make use of her fame, but Phoebe knew that she had also admired her determination to make it based on talent.

Nope, the problem with the site, Phoebe thought, was that it was hard for people to order something from it. Sure, they could email her with inquiries, but there was no way for people to add things to a shopping cart, pay with a credit card, all of that stuff everyone else seemed to have. Something would have to be done about it.

"You look like you're on cloud nine," Lynn said, appearing in her doorway. "I did knock, but you didn't hear me."

"Sorry." Phoebe stood up and stretched. Work and pillows had been a nice distraction from Chase Sanders and his chocolate-chip cookie. "I was on the phone."

"No problem. So you got the internet up?" Lynn asked, nodding at her computer, and before Phoebe could say anything else, she continued. "By the way, my futon from college is just sitting in the basement. It's not much, but my mom wants to lend it to you if you'd like, until you get a real bed. That's if you're serious about not wanting to stay at the Osprey Arms. She also told me to tell you that you're more than welcome to the guest bedroom."

Phoebe looked up. "That would be great. The futon, I mean. I don't suppose we could move it ourselves."

Lynn smiled and her dark ponytail bounced as she held up her arms, muscle-man style. "With these guns, we can move anything we want."

Phoebe laughed, but she knew Lynn was serious. She'd already received a lecture from Lynn on the importance of weight training and been subjected to a rundown of just how much Lynn could bench press.

"Well, sounds good." Phoebe would be happy to move out of the Osprey Arms. The view at Ivy House was better and it was, for the moment, free.

"Whatcha looking at?" Lynn said, coming around to the computer.

"Oh," Phoebe said, her mind going back to the morning with Chase. "I sold some of my pillows to The Garden Cottage. You know, that shop in town."

Lynn nodded. "Sure do, my mom loves that place. My brother calls the owner around Mother's Day, gives her a spending limit, and tells her to pick something out and wrap it up. Looks like a champ every year."

Phoebe laughed. She'd only seen pictures of Kyle, but knew he had a job that kept him traveling a lot.

"Well, tell him this year, he wants to order a Phoebe Ryan original."

"Will do. Is that your website?"

Phoebe nodded. Lynn was looking at the picture of her.

"The resemblance is really uncanny when you look like that." Lynn was looking at the picture of her. The dress was a lot sexier than she would normally wear, and Dean had made her get her hair and makeup done before the shoot. Normally, Phoebe was a lip-gloss-only type of girl.

"I know. But luckily, I don't wear stilettos and plunging neck-lines. Hard to be creative when you're uncomfortable. At least it is for me. But," Phoebe said, thinking maybe Lynn could help her, "I do need some help with the website. I need to put a shopping cart in and be able to accept credit cards and the like. Do you know anyone around here who could help me with that?"

Lynn looked up, lips pursed, and then she snapped her fingers. "Yeah I do. Tory. She's some sort of computer whiz. She helped out with the website for the clinic, and she works for Chase Sanders."

"Chase?" Phoebe said, trying to keep her voice neutral, but Lynn picked up on it immediately.

"You know him? Well, I mean, of course you know him, you must."

"What do you mean?" Phoebe asked, a moment of panic coming to her as she thought about the cookie on the street. It had been good and she had been into it, but really, people couldn't be drawing conclusions, could they?

"Well, you're kind of almost related." Lynn saw the look on Phoebe's face and backpedaled. "Well, not really."

"What are you talking about?"

Lynn looked at her, confused. "You mean you really don't know who Chase Sanders is?"

"He's some guy who wants to buy this house. And he bought pillows from me. And gave me a chocolate-chip cookie." Which was so good, Phoebe thought, that she had to lean against a wall to catch her breath.

"And that's all you know about him?"

"Well, he's cocky and arrogant..." Phoebe added, remembering how Chase's finger had brushed against her cheek in search of an errant piece of chocolate.

"And a total player." Lynn nodded. "Pretty much everyone agrees on that score. But that's not all."

Phoebe shook her head in ignorance.

"Here, let me." Lynn pulled the computer to her, typed in something, and stood back. Phoebe stared down at the image on the screen.

"Why am I looking at a picture of Savannah Ryan and Leland…" Phoebe trailed off, not believing what her eyes were telling her.

"Can you see the resemblance now?" Lynn asked.

"What…How…" Phoebe sat down on the rusted folding chair.

"Chase Sanders is Leland Harper's grandson. You know, from his daughter from his first marriage. She married a Sanders."

"And he lives here in Queensbay?"

"Yes…has lived here his whole life, I heard. I guess his grandmother remarried and stayed here. You mean you never saw how much he looked like Leland?"

Phoebe shook her head. "Savannah didn't keep many pictures. At least not the ones that were out. She didn't like to be reminded of him. Too painful."

It took a moment for it to all sink in. Chase Sanders, he of the ridiculously high offer for Ivy House, he of the pillow buying, chocolate-chip-dispensing charm was Leland Harper's grandson. And he had known all along.

It took about a moment for the shock of it all to wear off and be replaced by searing hot anger.

Outrage propelled Phoebe out of the house, down the hill, and towards the marina. She brought herself up short at the top of the marina's docks, her eyes scanning for dark hair and sunglasses.

"Can I help you, miss?" She looked up. A boy, blondish hair, an earring in one ear, and a polo shirt embroidered with the words "Queensbay Marina" was looking at her.

"Chase Sanders," she barked.

He glanced her over, then decided that she was harmless, and pointed down to one of the long narrow docks.

"The *Windsway*, berth eighty-nine."

"Thank you," Phoebe managed to say.

A hand touched her arm, and Lynn pulled her around.

"Phoebe, are you sure you should be doing this?" Lynn's brown eyes were round with concern.

"Oh, I am sure," Phoebe said, starting down the ramp. The dock bobbed as she stepped on it, and it took a moment for her to catch her footing.

The slips were all numbered, and she walked carefully along. Lynn followed her, calling out suggestions. "You know, maybe you should phone him first."

"What, and give him a chance to come up with some story?" Phoebe said. They were at slip eighty, and she practically jogged the rest of the way to his boat, drawing up short when she came to it. Now that she was here, she wasn't quite sure what to do next. She could hear voices coming from inside the boat. It was a sailboat—long, sleek, with a white hull and a blue sunshade over half of the cockpit. The chrome gleamed and the wood shone. Lines were neatly coiled around cleats and winches.

There was the sound of laughter, high, girlish, and then a lower, deeper, answering chuckle.

She hadn't expected him to have company.

Lynn came up beside Phoebe and looked at her. Phoebe knew there was no turning back.

"Chase Sanders."

"Try again," Lynn suggested. "Louder. Let him know how riled up you are."

Lynn seemed to be enjoying this way too much.

"Chase Sanders, I need to talk to you." Phoebe called and this time her voice was loud and true.

There were sounds of rustling and then a head popped up, one with long, light brown hair, the color of caramel, followed by eyes of the same color, and then came the rest of the body, goldenly tanned, dressed in a pink polo shirt and straight-leg khakis.

The girl, who looked like she could have been a college student, swung her eyes between Lynn and Phoebe, gave a nod to Lynn, and then stuck her head down from where she had come.

"Chase, there's someone here to see you."

Another bit of rustling and Chase appeared.

"What?" His hair was mussed, and he had a finger in his mouth, as if he'd hurt it.

"Oh, thank God, a doctor," he said when he saw Lynn. He pulled his hand up and they saw blood flowing freely.

Lynn went into doctor mode, and Phoebe was left on the side-lines.

After a brief examination, during which Lynn told the other girl to get the first aid kit, Lynn pronounced Chase fine.

"Just keep it clean and a bandage on it for a day."

"I don't need a tetanus shot?" Chase asked. He was sitting in the cockpit, looking like he was used to women hovering about him. Phoebe had stayed on the dock, arms crossed, kicking at it harmlessly with her toe.

"I don't know," Lynn said, cleaning up the supplies from the medical kit and handing it back to the girl. "When was the last time you had one?"

"Not a clue."

Lynn snorted. "How rusty a nail?"

The other girl rolled her head. "It was a paper cut. Chase was pushing papers and I was trying to calibrate his radar system."

"I think it was a splinter." Chase said, his eyes turning puppy-dog round, but Lynn was unmoved.

"A paper cut is more likely."

Phoebe looked up and caught Chase gazing at her, his blue eyes filled with interest. She turned and paced another length of the boat.

"Look, I gotta get back to the office, Chase. I have a call with the West Coast over online promotions."

"Great, Tory, thanks for trying to fix the radar system."

"Trying?" the girl, Tory, Phoebe supposed it was, tossed her caramel-color hair as she easily landed on the dock. "It's fixed. You can bring me a mocchachino later. See you, Lynn."

The girl shot a smile at Chase and Lynn, gave a nod and a wave to Phoebe, and walked back towards land without another look.

Lynn glanced uneasily between Chase and Phoebe. "I think the clinic just buzzed me. I'll catch you later."

She too jumped lightly on the dock and made a discreet "call me" gesture before leaving.

Phoebe drew up near the little step stool that Chase had set up to make it easier to get on board the boat.

"Glad you came by. Tory's a genius with computers, but I think the sight of blood makes her faint." Chase smiled at her, as if nothing out of the ordinary was happening.

Phoebe said nothing, trying to fight the trembling that had come over her.

"You know you're supposed to ask permission to come aboard?" Chase said, the know-it-all grin back.

"I don't think I need to ask anything of you," Phoebe said. Her tone almost wiped the smirk off Chase's face.

"How dare you?" she began and found that she was trembling.

"Whoa, what did I do?" He stood up and the boat moved with him. Phoebe thought better about climbing aboard as he crossed the space of the cockpit and was now standing at the railing looking over her. She didn't need to be in a confined space with him.

"It's more like what you didn't do."

"What are you talking about?" He sounded genuinely surprised.

"How could you have not told me?" Phoebe found that she had gone from angry to upset and her voice showed it. If Savannah had been here, she would have known how to play to the scene. But she wasn't. Instead, Phoebe was facing Chase Sanders, Leland Harper's grandson.

"Told you…You mean you didn't know?"

"Of course I didn't know. You're Leland Harper's grandson."

"So?" Chase said, and he jumped lightly onto the dock. It moved gently underneath them, and a seagull that had been posed on a piling took flight into the warm blue sky.

He was there, right in front of her, standing too close to her. She took a step back and found that her way was blocked, that there was something, a large pole, behind her. To step around would make it obvious that she was trying to get away from him, and she wasn't going to give him the satisfaction of knowing that.

"Don't you think you might have mentioned it?"

Chase shrugged. He didn't have his sunglasses on, and she could see just how blue his eyes were, the sapphire of them surrounded by little lines that fanned out from the corners.

"I guess I was waiting for the right time. Besides, it's a bit of an awkward way to open a conversation, don't you think?"

Phoebe didn't say anything, so he continued. "Anyway, what does it matter?"

"Matter?" Phoebe knew her voice sounded shrill even to her own ears. "Matter. Why do you want the house? Some sort of evil vendetta?"

"Vendetta?" Chase looked puzzled. "What are you talking about? It's a house…"

He didn't get any further than that.

"I know what you Harpers are capable of. And if you think you can drive me out of town, make me miserable, just like you did to Savannah, you have another thing coming."

"What...Make you miserable...Your grandmother was the home wrecker."

"Home wrecker?" Phoebe fought for control. "She was an amazing actress, an American legend."

"God," Chase rolled his eyes. His nonchalant grin had been replaced by something more like annoyance. "You're starting to sound like those crappy Hollywood tribute programs, 'Savannah Ryan, the golden child, blah, blah...'"

"Well, at least she wasn't some dried-up prune of a woman who hounded her ex-husband when he wouldn't take her back."

"Oh, please, like you would know. What is that, the Savannah Ryan Hollywood version of the story?"

They were yelling at each other full on. Phoebe realized that more than a few people had popped their heads out of boats and were looking at them with open interest.

Chase was also very close to her, so close that she could see the way the blue of his eyes was pierced by lighter flecks. They were like pools of water, great, deep, inviting pools of water, and she felt hot all of a sudden, even though the day wasn't that warm, and she was in the shade of the boat.

Now it was Chase's turn to point his finger and, though he kept it from touching her, it wagged annoyingly in her face.

"You might think you can come here, all high and mighty, Ms. Hollywood, but not everyone in this town wants to see that house torn down."

"Torn down?" she said, puzzled, not quite sure where this conversation was going.

"It's practically a piece of history, and maybe all you people from California want new and shiny and modern, but here in Queensbay, in my town..."

"Your town?"

"My town, that's right, we believe in preserving history, not destroying it."

"I don't want to destroy it..." Before Phoebe was able to go any further, there was the sound of pounding feet and an anxious voice.

"Chase." Phoebe looked over Chase's shoulder. It was that girl again, Tory, with the caramel-colored hair.

"Not now, Tory," Chase said without turning.

"Ahh, I think you're going to want to come. There's an issue down in Florida."

"Take care of it," Chase said, but he turned to look.

Phoebe saw that Tory was wringing her hands and looked genuinely distressed.

He turned back to Phoebe. "This," he said, "isn't over." He spun around and walked up the dock, Tory talking to him urgently. The surface under Phoebe swayed a little and she leaned back into the piling. What had just happened?

"Do people think I want to tear down Ivy House?" Phoebe asked Lynn. They were sharing a bottle of wine Lynn had brought over, along with cheese and crackers, sitting on the low stone wall that marked the border of the terrace.

"Well," Lynn said.

"Come on, tell me."

"I guess the thought was that you were some big Hollywood hotshot. What would you want with some big old pile like this?" Lynn trailed off.

"You look guilty," Phoebe said. Lynn had brought along some chair cushions, but still the ledge was not the most comfortable thing in the world. There was an old garden bench tucked under a tree. It was rickety, but with a little work, it would be serviceable. Maybe that should be one of her first projects.

"Who me?" Lynn popped a cracker with a wedge of cheese on it into her mouth.

"Is that why you were so friendly to me? What, did the Historical Commission send you up to make sure I wasn't going to tear the place down and put up some ultra-modern white box?"

Lynn shook her head. "No, of course not. Well, not exactly. But they did ask me what I thought. And I told them you didn't plan on it. Sorry, I didn't mean to be a gossip, but seriously, you do not want these old biddies on your case. Look, it's your house and if that's what you want to do..."

Phoebe shifted as a pointy bit of stone was jabbing her in the thing. "So why does Chase Sanders think that's what I'm going to do?"

Lynn considered for a moment and then a smile spread across her face.

"What is it?" Phoebe knew Lynn was onto something.

"Didn't you say that Chase offered an obscene amount of money for the house?"

"Yeah, I thought he wanted the view," Phoebe said.

"No way. He loves the house. Totally thinks the family connection is cool. I mean, at least that's how I heard him talk about it at one of the Yacht Club things."

"So he's serious about wanting the house. He doesn't want to tear it down as part of some sort of revenge fantasy against Savannah?"

Lynn shook her head. "No, but there is someone who benefits if you sell this place. More so if she has an eager buyer who thinks you might need a ridiculous offer to be persuaded to part with it?"

Phoebe almost smiled too. "Ahh, a little negotiating ploy by the real estate agent." The sun was setting, sending soft rays of light out along the water. The harbor was calm, almost glasslike, which seemed to happen often at dusk. It was quiet and peaceful, and soon the lights in the houses sitting on the bluffs would start to wink on. Most of the boats were safely back in port for the night, and the only real sound was the gentle bell tolling on one of the channel markers.

"Well, both of them will be very sorry. I'm certainly not going to be tearing this place down." Phoebe turned to look at the house behind her. She had taken Lynn up on her offer of the futon. By tomorrow night, she would have moved in enough at Ivy House to give up her room at the Osprey Arms.

"And what about Chase Sanders?" Lynn asked, taking a sip of her wine, her brown eyes twinkling above the rim.

"What about him?" Phoebe tried to forget the way his blue eyes had flashed at her, raising her body heat through the roof. "I think Queensbay is big enough for the two of us. And if I don't intend to tear the house down, I don't suppose the natives, including those old biddies, will have anything to complain about, will they?"

"Not likely," Lynn said, and Phoebe decided to ignore the doubt she heard in her voice.

Chapter 13

Chase sat in the meeting, listening to the bickering going on between the creative director, his PR director, Tory, and assorted staff. It was one of the few things he hated about running a company. Decision by committee. As North Coast Outfitters had grown, he hadn't been able to keep a finger in every pie. Too many locations, too many moving parts. He'd had to do what he did best—be a captain and manage his crew. But right now, his crew was getting on his nerves, and he wished he could make them walk the plank, metaphorically speaking, that is.

The windows of the conference room had a good view of town. He'd been able to watch Phoebe make her way off the docks and head up the road back, he presumed, to Ivy House. She had been angry and had been yelling at him, her eyes bright, the color high in her cheeks. Phoebe had looked lovely and he had wanted to kiss her. There, he had admitted it.

But his meetings with her never quite played out the way he thought. He'd offended her at the first, had her angry at the second, almost won her back at the third, and now she was all riled up again. So what if he was Leland Harper's grandson. The man, except for passing on some DNA, had been a blip on the screen as far as his family was concerned. At least the ones now. He knew Grandmother had never quite forgiven Savannah for stealing her husband. But that was history.

Now they tossed the story around like it was a joke, a legend, history, but of the more colorful sort. Every family had some of that, right?

Chase shook his head. He'd made the offer on Ivy House because his mother had called, saying what a shame it would be if the new owner, an out-of-towner, came and tore down a local landmark. And then Joan Altieri had clucked over the same thing, and before he knew it, Mrs. Sampson, the head of the Queensbay Historical Commission, had ambushed him on his way to get coffee and said the same thing. And then Sandy Miller, real estate agent extraordinaire, had swooped in and told him, for a price, he could have the best view in town.

So much for a done deal. Phoebe Ryan was having none of him.

He sighed and turned his attention to the pictures in front of him.

"The preview emails received a dismal click-through rate," Tory was saying. "I just don't think anyone was very excited about the new designs."

"I know, I know." His creative director looked annoyed. "Look, this is the first time we've ever attempted to branch out beyond our core of sailing and sporting goods. Maybe we need to start over? These designers are great with raincoats, but," she gestured at the portfolio in front of them, "I don't think they're getting it."

Even Sam Waterstone, the PR director, the one who always had an idea on how to make something look fun or sexy or useful or all three, was shaking his head.

"Not getting it?" Chase repeated, looking at the images. Nope, they were certainly not getting it. Everything was blah, boring, and definitely not hip. They needed something fresher, lighter, younger.

Suddenly, Chase felt instinct take over. "I have an idea." He leaned back in his chair, feeling victory within grasp. He knew just the person who could help them.

Chapter 14

The note came the next morning with a large bunch of flowers, creamy white lilies. Looked like Chase had written the note himself, she thought. Thick black marker, simple printed letters.

I think we got off on the wrong foot. Do over? The Osprey Arms, seven o'clock, tonight.

Phoebe held the note, remembering the last time she had seen Chase, his blue eyes flashing, his legs spread apart, hands on his hip, looking for all the world like he was the captain of a ship about to face the maelstrom. Did she want to see him again? Phoebe placed the flowers on the edge of her desk, looking at them.

Of course, she wanted to see him. Her whole body was practically itching with desire at the thought of seeing him, the thought of looking into his eyes, watching his lopsided grin staring down at her, the thought of running her hands through his too-long black hair. She could pretty well imagine the silky feel of it.

Phoebe sighed deeply, inhaling the light, fresh smell of the lilies. Yes, she was going to go. There was no way she could stay away; both her interest and her curiosity were aroused. Chase Sanders, Leland Harper's grandson. A link, however tenuous, to Savannah.

<<>>

Phoebe awoke with a start. She checked her watch. She had worked all day at the house, both on her website and on cleaning the kitchen. It was dirty, hot, and exhausting work. Another day or so and she would be ready to move in, but for now she was happy with the clean bathroom and soft bed at the Osprey Arms. It had been so inviting that when she had come back, she had intended only to close her eyes for a moment, but she'd fallen fast asleep, and now she realized with a rush of panic that she had only a half hour to get ready.

A quick shower and only a few minutes to figure out what to wear. It certainly wasn't a date, so anything with too suggestive a neckline or too low a back was out. But would looking too casual send the wrong message?

Finally, she had decided to keep it simple, a pair of dark wash blue jeans that stretched nicely over all the right places and a purple v-neck sweater. No heels, since she was tall enough already, but a pair of ballet flats and scarf tied at her neck pulled it all together. It was her go-to outfit, she supposed, simple, with the sweater highlighting her eyes.

She felt flushed and slightly embarrassed when she entered the darkened room. It was closer to seven thirty than seven, and as a rule, she didn't like to keep people waiting. The bar at the Osprey Arms was mildly crowded for a Thursday night. There was a couple leaning in towards one another, heads close, hands intertwined. There was also a group of older men, in khakis and sweaters, white-haired with red cheeks, so Phoebe figured they had probably come in from a round of golf.

And there he was, in the far corner, with an empty stool next to him. He saw her and one hand went up. She swallowed. She worked her way down the bar, nodding at the bartender.

Chase stood up when she turned the corner, his hand held out.

She stopped and looked at it.

"What are you doing?"

He smiled, but this time it was genuine, an almost friendly grin. "Like I said, starting over. See, I'm Chase Sanders. Nice to meet you."

Her eyebrows arched up, but she decided to play along, "How nice to meet you, Mr. Sanders. I'm Phoebe Ryan."

"Please call me Chase."

"Thank you." Phoebe let herself be guided into the high chair at the bar, the wide palm of his hand splayed across her back, creating an instant contact burn with her skin, right through the thin cashmere wool of her sweater. No flushing, she ordered herself, glad the dim lighting in the bar would offer her some camouflage for the way her body was reacting to him.

"What will you have?" Chase asked, catching the bartender's attention.

"A white wine, please."

Chase ordered a wine for her and a pint for himself. She was surprised at that, but decided to say nothing. At least he wasn't pretentious in his choice of beverage.

"So…" Phoebe said during the uncomfortable silence that had settled between them after their drinks were delivered.

"To new beginnings," he said, raising his glass in a toast. She smiled. She could agree to that.

Phoebe took a sip of her wine. It was cool and crisp and was probably from a better bottle than whatever the house wine was. She glanced at Chase again. His hand was wrapped around his pint glass and she could see the fine light-colored hair on his tan knuckles. It was not a hand that looked like it stayed inside all day pushing papers around. For a brief instant, she remembered how it had felt on her back, large, warm, almost possessive, as he had guided her onto the bar chair, and she let herself imagine just what else it might be capable of.

"First off, I was sincere when I offered my condolences about your grandmother. Whatever else she was, she was certainly a talented actress," he said.

Phoebe scanned his face, trying to see if there was a hint of sarcasm. She saw none, so she smiled. "Thank you. But did you know, from the first meeting, who I was?" Phoebe asked, curious.

He shook his head. "No, not until you said something. I mean, I was sincere too. You did look familiar. Of course, I realize that it was the family resemblance that had me thinking you were someone."

"Thank you, I guess."

Chase smiled, showing a set of nice, straight white teeth. She felt her skin warm under his gaze. "You're welcome. It was a compliment, however backward it might have seemed."

"It's just I was hoping to be somewhat anonymous, you know, here. Thought it might be possible. To just be myself."

"Yes, of course," he raised his glass again. "Though I think your cover might be blown. The real estate agent is pretty much buzzing with excitement. Apparently she was a big fan."

Phoebe smiled. "There aren't many who weren't. I'm told it makes the house more valuable."

Chase gave her that cocky grin, and she felt her heart bump against her ribcage. "So I would have gathered. Though some may say that it didn't play host to the happiest of couples."

Phoebe smiled. "Happy is probably too mild a word. They were wild for each other, a burning passion. And then it all went downhill. Is that why you're interested in the house, because your grandfather lived there?"

"Leland Harper wasn't my grandfather," Chase said. Phoebe was about to disagree when he continued. "At least not in any way that mattered. When he left, my grandmother apparently never spoke his name again. She remarried Sal, who ran the marina here, and she was very happy. Happier than she was with Leland. So happy she waited her ex and Savannah out, and Queensbay was her town until she died about ten years ago."

Phoebe did the math. Savannah had been much younger than Leland, so the timing made sense. "So, no hard feelings?" Phoebe asked, curiously.

"Do you want me to blame you for something your grandmother did? I assume you didn't have anything to do with it."

Phoebe shook her head. "No. Savannah did what Savannah wanted."

Chase laughed. "I gathered that. Supposedly, Leland was a bit like that too. Perhaps the two of them were perfect for each other."

She liked the way he laughed and had to look down into her wine to fight the warm clench in her stomach.

"And the house?"

"Always loved it. There always seemed to be some sort of mystery about it, but of course, no one in my family would ever talk about it. It took me a while to figure out the history behind it and then I just kept my interest in it to myself."

"It is a great house," Phoebe agreed, thinking of the vision she'd had earlier, it perfectly restored, filled with light and laughter. The feeling of happiness had been so real.

"So you don't want to tear it down?"

"No." Chase looked truly shocked by the idea. There was a pause and then he asked, "You?"

"No. Savannah said it was a magical place. I just didn't know it was such a dump. Or how much work it would take to restore it. I'm not about to tear it down."

"Does that mean you're going to fix it up, live in it?" Chase asked.

Phoebe smiled, hoping she wasn't giving too much away. "I'm definitely going to fix up. As you mentioned, I'm not from around here, and I'm not quite sure I'm up for the East Coast winters."

He shrugged, grinned. "They can have their charm, when the harbor's rimmed with ice and the trees sparkle against the winter sky."

"You sound like a poet."

"I'm a sailor. I notice the weather." There was a pause while they studied each other, and then Chase said, "If fixing it up becomes too much or you get too cold, you know the house would be safe with me."

Phoebe shuddered. "You'll probably want to put in a black leather couch and a giant TV."

Chase laughed. "And what's so wrong with a TV?"

"Fine if it's for screening black-and-white classics. But if it's for watching every game being played, then you might as well be in some place where you're not paying for the view."

"Noted. I'll make sure the couch isn't black."

Then, because her senses were raised and she was aware that she had been feeling too much at ease, too much under the spell of his charm, she asked, "It's awfully presumptuous of you to think you might get a crack at decorating it. Do you always get what you want?"

He looked at her, his eyes dark, smoky in the dim light. There wasn't a hint of a smile as he answered. "Always."

Phoebe swallowed, wondering how one simple word could have her hot, her body tingling with excitement down to her core.

She didn't know what to say next, the art of small talk escaping her as she tried to get her emotions under control, since his closeness was making her feel too hot, too aware of everything going on around her.

"So what brings you to Queensbay? Besides a free house?" Chase asked. He said it casually, his eyes actually on the flat screen showing a baseball game, but she sensed he was deeply curious about the answer.

"You said it yourself," Phoebe replied.

"I did?" He looked at her now, and she felt the force of his presence wash over her. He had, she decided, a very commanding one.

"New beginnings. It seems like it's the perfect time in my life to start over to make a change. I don't have any family, anyone waiting for me in Los Angeles, so I thought it might be time for a change. Savannah claimed the house was magical."

"Magical?" Chase asked, and she looked closely to see if she was making fun of her.

"Well, perhaps not magical, as in witchy magic. But I think for the first time in her life, Sarah Jane Ryan felt like she belonged."

"Sarah Jane?"

"Her given birth name. Legally changed it to Savannah when she was of age. I never did find out why. But Savannah grew up in a small town, in the middle of nowhere, where no one believed in dreams. And to her, Ivy House was the embodiment of every dream she'd ever had, even if it only lasted for a while. Ivy House meant that your dreams could come true."

Chase nodded, but he didn't say anything and was watching her intently. She felt a surge of heat wash over her under his scrutiny.

"It's just a house," he said, a faint trace of amusement evident in the way his lip curled up.

"It wasn't for Savannah and Leland."

At that, Chase tossed his head back and laughed; then he lowered it and looked down at her. "I don't think there was anything magical about them."

Phoebe let the hint of a smile ghost across her face. "Well maybe you only heard one side of the story. Savannah always said Leland was the love of her life and they were happiest here. They were out of the limelight; they could be themselves."

"Savannah was an actress. Was she never not acting?"

Phoebe could feel herself smiling at the memories. Chase had a point. Savannah never did anything by halves. Even sitting by the pool was a production. She would be in a sexy two-piece, with some gauzy swim dress thrown on, with a huge hat and big glasses to hide her face and keep it sun-free. Still, there were times, like when she made a big bowl of popcorn and they sat down to watch a movie, that Savannah had been herself. Just a woman, almost a grandmother. There was something sublime in it, to be in the presence of a legend, yet have her be relatively down-to-earth.

"Savannah knew that most of the time, there was someone watching her. And she was right. Makes it hard to be yourself. But she could sometimes be just herself with me. And that's when you could get the real story."

"Didn't stop her from hooking up with just about everyone under the sun," Chase pointed out.

"Well, she always said you couldn't kiss a ghost."

Chase smiled at that, a genuine smile, and Phoebe felt her stomach do a quick flip-flop. She was finding it very easy to forget that this was a guy who admitted he wanted something from her.

"Guess there's something to that," he said, taking another long sip of his beer.

Two menus had appeared in front of them, but Phoebe didn't touch hers. She wasn't sure it was a good idea to stick around with him. She was pretty certain that Chase Sanders didn't do things just to be a nice guy. He wanted something from her.

"So when are you most like yourself?" he asked.

"What do you mean?"

"When you're not being the ice queen?"

"Ice queen?" Phoebe realized her mouth was set in a firm line. *Relax,* she told herself, *don't let him get to you.*

"Yeah, when you're not all pissed about someone trying to buy your house. Or being possibly, sort of related to you. What do you like to do for fun?" Chase stood there, a big grin on his face as he watched her try to make sense of that.

"I thought you said we were trying to start over?" Phoebe stammered.

"We are. I want to get to know you. I want to get to know what makes Phoebe Ryan tick." He leaned in as he said it and casually brushed her cheek with his hand as he tucked a strand of hair that had fallen out of place back behind her ear. His touch was electric and Phoebe felt her skin burning. She looked up at Chase, who was no longer smiling at her, but looking at her speculatively.

She leaned back in her chair, aware that all of a sudden the taproom of the Osprey Arms was feeling crowded and warm. Chase gave her another smile, this one wolfish, as he looked at her with interest.

The heat, the intensity she had felt before, she hadn't just been imagining it.

"Me, I like to sail," Chase said slowly.

"Sail?" Phoebe managed to croak out. That would explain the expensive sunglasses and the way he was tan, even in the early spring in the Northeast.

"You know, a boat, with sails." Chase had moved in closer so that he was almost whispering in her ear. The side of his face touched hers, his skin rough and charged against hers.

"Do you like the water?" he asked.

"I was a swimmer in high school," Phoebe managed to stammer out.

"I kind of prefer to be on top of the water." He had taken a step back, and she felt the pressure of the air around her lessen, felt able to breathe again.

"Is that what you do all day, sail?" Phoebe managed to ask.

He smiled. "Not exactly. Of course, I still have the boat. She's a fine little sloop, pretty fast."

"So you're sleeping down at the marina?" Phoebe tried to imagine Chase crammed into the small cabin of his boat. Perhaps he swung a hammock up on deck and the thought almost made her giggle.

Chase nodded, a smile playing on his lips. "Sometimes. It's refreshing to be out on the water, even when you're docked."

There was an angry shout and a cheer from along the bar. It was mostly men, a cluster of young and old, mostly professionals, in button-downs and work slacks. Just about everyone's attention was focused on the baseball game, and Phoebe figured that they were a group of mixed fans.

Phoebe realized that she and Chase had slid closer to each other, to hear better in the bar that was growing more crowded and becoming louder by the minute. She was sure she felt his knee pressing into the side of her thigh. When she looked up at him, she saw he had a lazy smile on his face.

She pushed herself away. Chase was an attractive guy, maybe a little too brawny for her. Unfairly, she compared him to Dean, who was lean, ripped, but could carry off skinny jeans if he had to. One of Chase's thighs would barely fit into Dean's jacket.

"Want another?" Chase nodded towards Phoebe's glass. She looked down, realizing it was more than half empty. She'd been drinking fast, probably because she was nervous. Chase's pint was almost gone.

"I really shouldn't..."

"But you will," Chase said, waving his hand, and the bartender appeared almost instantly.

"Hey Paulie, we'll have another round."

"Sure thing, boss." Paulie flashed a quick smile and was gone.

"Boss?"

Chase shrugged. "I'm sort of a regular."

"Will you and the lady want something to eat?" Paulie had returned with their drinks.

Phoebe was about to protest that it wasn't a date, when Chase spoke up. "We'll have a plate of the calamari and salad to start."

"I thought this was just drinks," Phoebe pointed out, annoyed that he had ordered for her.

Chase shrugged. "Shouldn't drink on an empty stomach. Besides, their calamari is amazing. There's a pretty amazing chef here. Unless, you don't like squid?"

"Is it fried?" Phoebe asked.

"Of course."

"Fine, I'm in. But this isn't a date."

"Who said it was? Maybe you have a boyfriend. Maybe I have a girlfriend." He said it casually enough, but she could see that he was waiting for the answer.

"I'm not involved with anyone at the moment." Phoebe thought of Garrett and wished she hadn't. And then she thought of Dean. Good old reliable Dean, who was always trying to help her and her career. He had told her he would always be there, but she needed to ignore that if she was going to figure out what she wanted to do with her life.

"Even better," Chase said and she felt the pressure of his hand along the back of her chair, as he smiled roguishly down at her. Roguishly…where had that even come from? Who did that? It was almost predatory, as if he were sizing her up, seeing how she would taste. Phoebe felt her body tingle with attraction, a rush of heat between her legs, while her brain screamed *no, no, no.* So, she followed her brain and moved her shoulders around to give him the hands-off message, while her hands tightened around the stem of the wine glass.

"Besides swimming and making pillows, what else do you do?" Chase asked, his arm steadily in place. Phoebe stopped trying to shrug it off, realizing that he was too solidly built for her to get him to move it.

"I'm a designer. For a while, I worked with at Shelby Hill, the furniture catalog, and then I went freelance. I've designed movie sets, posters, then I did a lot of work for Doran Industries."

Chase nodded. "You mean the people who take a celebrity's name and slap it on a bunch of stuff and sell it in the big-box stores."

Phoebe smiled thinly. She didn't think that's how CallieSue Owens would like to describe her newest business venture, but that was pretty much what it was.

"Pretty much."

"But not anymore?" he asked.

"No, I stopped when Savannah got really sick, to help look after her. And now, there seems to be a lot of loose ends to wrap up, so I am not sure what I am going to do." Phoebe had her plan, but she wasn't quite ready to share it with Chase at the moment.

"That was nice of you. Hard for someone your age to give up her social life and career for a dying relative."

Phoebe gave a thin smile. "Savannah raised me. We were all each other had. It wasn't hard at all to take care of her."

"I'm sensing a 'but' there," Chase said, his dark eyes holding a connection to hers. Something warned her not to give too much away, but the way he was looking at her, his attention fully on her, compelled her to be honest.

"There's no 'but.'" Phoebe thought about all she had found when sorting through Savannah's affairs. And then she shrugged. It didn't really matter, so she told him.

"Well, after I was around, I started to take a closer look at things. Her papers, bills. I wasn't snooping, at least not at first. She needed someone to handle all of that stuff."

"Of course," Chase nodded in encouragement.

"I should have stepped in a lot sooner."

"Really?"

"Savannah was pretty good at making money, but sucked at holding onto it. She managed to spend just about all of hers."

"What did you do?"

Phoebe laughed at the memory. Savannah had been in bed then, in and out of it, the cancer moving quickly through her body. Phoebe had been so angry with her, she had wanted an explanation, but in the end, she had chickened out. Or didn't want to hear the truth.

"I realized that there wasn't much to be done about it. But at least she left me one thing."

"I'm sorry," Chase said. "I know it's probably not what you expected, the house I mean."

Phoebe almost felt the sting of tears against her eyes. How had he known what to say?

"Sorry." Phoebe dashed a quick hand against her eyes and then took a deep breath. "I'm not usually like this. I can't talk about them, my parents and Savannah, without breaking down in tears."

"My parents died in a car crash," she said to his unspoken question, "a long time ago."

"Were they actors too?"

"Yes. Well, my dad was a director and my mom, an actress. Their careers were just starting to take off when they died. My mom didn't really have any family, so that left Savannah."

"It sounds tough, being alone like that," he said, his dark blue eyes holding hers. Once again, she was hyperaware of everything around them.

Phoebe took a deep breath, determined to move away from her own story. "OK, so that's me. What about you?"

"Me? Well, let's see. I grew up in Queensbay, close to the water, with my parents and my brother. They're retired now and live in Florida. My brother's still around the area, but travels a lot, so we don't get to hang out much.

"Sounds nice, normal."

"Pretty normal," he said with an easy smile, and Phoebe knew he was waiting for her to ask him what he did.

"I learned to sail right here. Spent some time as a sail bum and then came home to take over the family business. We sell boat stuff to boat people."

"Perfect job for a guy like you."

Chase smiled. "What can I say, I'm a simple guy."

"I don't buy that for a second," Phoebe said.

Chase gave a shrug as if to say "no biggie," but Phoebe thought there was a lot more behind those last words than he was letting on. Maybe she had misjudged him earlier. And it made him undeniably sexier.

"So you said you were working. Are you or aren't you?"

"What do you mean?" Phoebe said.

"You said you were, then weren't…which is it, working or not?"

Phoebe stared down into her drink. Exactly the territory she didn't want to veer into right now.

"I'm taking a break. To think things over."

"What sort of things?" he pressed.

"You know, what to do with my life now that I am well and truly on my own."

Phoebe didn't know why she told him. Perhaps it was the two glasses of wine, or the calamari, which she hadn't touched, so intent had she been on their conversation.

"Well, as you saw, when I was in The Garden Cottage, I've been designing my own things, housewares."

"What are housewares, exactly? Plates?" Phoebe felt her eyes narrow as she looked him over carefully. A trace of a smile ghosted across his lips.

"Plates, pillows, curtains, sheets…"

"Sheets?" The full lips definitely curved up. "I like sheets. Better than plates," Chase said, his voice dipping low, along with his head as he almost breathed the suggestion into her ear.

Phoebe forced herself to take a sip of the cool wine. Never had talking about sheets affected her in quite this way, she thought. Somehow, just that one word carried a whole lot of weight to it.

She squared her shoulders one more time, this time quickly and with enough force that Chase's arm fell off the back of her chair. Feeling the weight lifted freed her, and she let a small smile of triumph grace her features.

"So you design things and, what, sell them?" He had taken her flinging his arm off the chair as a challenge because he had moved in even closer so that all she could smell was him. Nothing else but his clean scent, a combination of something spicy and fresh, almost windblown.

Phoebe smiled. "That would be the point."

"You know my boat has beds, except we call them bunks..." he trailed off as he looked at her face.

Phoebe flushed. Chase was so close to her, almost as if they were the only two people in the whole bar. Everything about him oozed sex and suggestion, and she knew that if she let herself, she would be swept up into him, let his big, strong hands pull her towards him, let them roam over her. Thoughts of just where that might lead had her coming to her senses. He was someone who wanted something from her, no matter how rakish his grin or how much she wanted to kiss him.

With every ounce of self-control she could muster, she pushed her wine glass away from her. "This, whatever this is, is over." She was off the bar chair in a flash, only stopping to say something to Paulie, the bartender.

"We're finished here. You can just add it to my room tab."

With that gesture, and hoping Chase didn't take it upon himself to order a steak dinner, Phoebe stalked up to her room, fumbled with her key, and got herself in. She half-expected Chase to follow her, but when he didn't, she was torn between being relieved and disappointed. Still, she made sure the door was double-locked as she threw herself down on the bed, eyes open, staring at the ceiling, willing her body to calm down.

Why was her heart racing? When she closed her eyes, why could she only see his face, close up, dark, intense eyes, searching into her? God, she had pretty much bared her soul to him after one glass of wine. She could talk about her family, but she almost never did, and certainly not with some guy she had just met.

She rolled over and pulled out the card Chase had given her from his purse. She almost snorted.

Slowly, as the wine settled in her stomach and her heart slowed, she thought that perhaps Chase Sanders, as the president of a major sporting goods company, really had been talking about the bunks in his boat and actual sheets for them. Perhaps she had just blown a chance for a design deal with a major catalog.

Sighing, Phoebe rolled over and reached for the drawer in the bedside table where she had stashed a candy bar. Chocolate, caramel, nuts, nougat. It had all the important food groups and would count for dinner, since there was no way she was going down to the dining room again and risk running into Chase Sanders.

Chapter 15

It took Chase another beer before he worked out just why Phoebe had walked out on him. When he did, he hooted in laughter and slapped the bar top so hard Paulie looked over at him. Chase waved him away and continued to eat his steak. Phoebe Ryan had thought he was coming on to her, not trying to make a business proposition. And she'd been offended.

An interesting reaction, Chase thought, as he speared a piece of asparagus. The steak, potatoes, and asparagus were excellent, mostly because he'd seen fit to bring in a top chef from the city. Sean Callahan had helped put the restaurant on the map, and Chase savored every bite of his five-star meal.

Still, he wasn't used to women saying no to him. For the most part, when he beckoned, even if it was with a crook of his finger, they came running. True, most of them hadn't engaged his interest for long, and none of them had half the mystique of Phoebe Ryan, who seemed to have inherited her grandmother's trick of appearing both aloof and alluring at the same time.

He speared a thick-cut steak fry as he watched the home-team batter knock out a home run. Phoebe Ryan had another thing coming if she thought she could get rid of him so easily. Chase wanted her talent, and now, dammit, if he didn't want Phoebe Ryan along with it.

Chapter 16

"You're making some good progress."

Lynn Masters appeared in the front hallway of Ivy House, startling Phoebe, who jumped and then turned. She smiled when she saw who it was. Lynn was wearing scrubs again, and Phoebe wondered if she ever took them off.

Phoebe wiped a hand across her forehead, drawing away some of the sweat that had accumulated. It was surprisingly warm for spring and she was feeling her exertion in the way her clothes were sticking to her, damp with sweat.

"Thanks." Phoebe looked around. She had made good progress. All of the big stuff was in the driveway, waiting for a rubbish removal company to come and haul it all away. She had scrubbed, swept, and mopped most of the first floor.

"This room isn't so bad." Lynn pointed at the large space that Phoebe had decided would be the living room.

"I think if I redo the floors and paint, we're golden. The kitchen is another story, but I'm having a new fridge delivered in a couple of days. In the meantime, I have some iced tea on ice. Want some?"

Lynn nodded and Phoebe led her towards the kitchen. Here, she had already cleaned, and as much as possible, the space gleamed. Phoebe had hit the village supermarket, which was geared towards boaters, and had purchased a Styrofoam cooler, ice, drinks, a sandwich, and some snacks. Paper plates, cups, napkins, and plastic utensils were set out on the wooden table that she had decided to keep. Already, she was imagining the kitchen painted a warm cream, with new curtains, new appliances, and the cracked linoleum removed to reveal something wonderful, like the wide-board wood flooring beneath.

"I found this on my mom's bookshelf." Lynn thumped something on the table and Phoebe looked over from where she was pouring.

"I haven't seen that in ages," Phoebe said, glancing at the cover of the book Lynn had brought. It was Savannah's autobiography.

"I would have thought you had an autographed copy." Lynn said, taking the paper cup Phoebe handed her.

"No way. The critics panned it and it wasn't exactly a best seller. I am not sure they ever printed that many to begin with. I think it was just another flop that Savannah decided to ignore.

"Oh, well, my mom loved it. Read it over and over again. As if you couldn't tell."

"Really?" Phoebe took her paper cup and pulled out the other chair, sitting across from Lynn. "What for?"

"The good parts." Lynn dropped her voice. "Full disclosure. I went through a Savannah Ryan phase too—I mean my mom made me watch all the movies, so I actually read the book too and wow. That's all I've got to say."

"You mean she talked about that?" Phoebe dropped her voice too. Suddenly the thought of her grandmother doing that was grossing her out.

"Well, not in detail. But I could read between the lines. That's probably why she didn't want you to read it. It seemed like she bedded half of Hollywood before she took on the East Coast blue bloods."

Phoebe reached across the table and pulled the book towards her. As Lynn had promised, it was dog-eared and worn, the paper cover faded. She looked at the face of her grandmother staring up at her from the cover. It had been a long time since Savannah Ryan had looked like that.

"You really do look a bit like her, you know," Lynn said.

Phoebe looked up and almost pushed the book away. "Oh, I don't know. I think I have more of my mom in me." She tried to keep her voice casual. Red-blond hair, blue eyes, the same sort of cheekbones. Sure, there were similarities, but Savannah Ryan had been breathtaking, with emerald-green eyes and a voluptuous figure, a true crowd-stopping beauty. She had been every inch a movie star.

"Besides, looks aren't everything. They didn't exactly guarantee her happiness," Phoebe pointed out. Her grandmother had died alone, leaving behind a string of lovers, but no one besides Phoebe to share her love with. When all you had were looks, it was hard to deal well with the passage of time.

"Well, I wouldn't mind being compared to her every now and then." Lynn laughed, a full, hearty laugh that echoed through the relative emptiness of the house.

"Like when she played Helen in that movie about Troy?" Phoebe asked.

"Or when she was the gangster bad girl. Now that was hot."

Phoebe smiled and though she wasn't sure why she said it, she did. "I have the jacket."

"You mean the leather one with the buckles." Lynn's eyes went round and she reached out and gripped Phoebe's hand.

"Please?"

Phoebe laughed. "It's in storage, but I promise, as soon as I can, I'll get it. You can try it on and play cops and robbers."

"You're amazing. That would be so cool. And to show you how grateful I am, how about you come over later and we can hang out? My parents are heading out for the weekend and we'd have the house to ourselves. You can stay in the spare bedroom, check out of the hotel? I mean, I don't think you're quite ready to move in here, even with my futon."

"A slumber party?" Phoebe asked, laughing.

"Come on, you're never too old for them. Trust me, it will be fun. My mom will even leave something for us to eat."

"Deal." Mrs. Masters really was a great cook.

Phoebe flipped to the center section of the book where there were photographs on thick paper. She leafed through them until she found the ones she was looking for. Savannah and Leland Harper. Phoebe scrutinized the pictures carefully. Now that she knew what to look for, she could see Chase in Leland. Leland had been a good deal older than Chase was now when he had married Savannah, but still you could see physical similarities, in the height, the dark hair, and the strong cheekbones, between the two men.

"So, I had drinks with Chase last night," Phoebe said, trying to keep her voice casual.

Lynn looked up, her eyes narrowing. "Just drinks?"

"Why do you sound so surprised?"

Lynn shrugged. "I don't know. When I last saw the two of you, I found it hard to believe that you could sit down and have anything as civilized as a drink with him. Though there's not many around here who wouldn't have a drink with him. He's kind of a local celebrity."

"Celebrity?" Phoebe asked.

"Yeah, I mean for Queensbay. He's some sort of champion sailor in Europe. Grew up here, sailing with Noah Randall."

"Noah Randall, the tech entrepreneur?" Phoebe swallowed. Noah had made a boatload of money selling his company and had showed up on the Hollywood scene for a while. Phoebe figured everyone was trying to get him to invest in movies, but apparently, he'd had the good sense not to.

"Yeah. Noah's from Queensbay too. He lives here with his wife, Caitlyn. Noah and Chase go way back. Anyway, Chase sailed for a while, and then he came back to help his dad run the family business. Basically, it was ship's chandlery down by the marina. Anyway, Chase jazzed it up and before you knew it, they were sending out catalogs and had a website. You know, North Coast Outfitters. They sell fancy boat stuff to rich people."

"I see," Phoebe said, though she had figured most of that out last night.

"Yeah, he's super-yummy. Oh, and supposedly, he loaned Noah the money to start his company."

"What?" Phoebe said.

"Oh, yeah." Lynn nodded.

That explained a few more things. Probably owns the restaurant too, now that Phoebe thought about the way the bartender had called him boss.

"Do you know what else he is?" Phoebe asked.

"Batman?" Lynn joked. "Or Bruce Wayne?"

Phoebe laughed. "No, a total horndog. He tried to come on to me."

Lynn's mouth dropped open. "Shut the front door. No way."

"Way." Phoebe flopped down on one of the folding chairs. She really needed to get some furniture in here. There were a few things in storage in California that she had managed to salvage from the estate, but perhaps an actual shopping trip was in order.

"Whoa. So you're crushing on Leland Harper's grandson. It's like the romance of the century all over again." Lynn's eyes were alight and her hands were clutched to her chest.

"Don't go all romantic. I am not crushing on him. It was just a drink. One," Phoebe said, though she recalled it had been two. And they had spent most of the time head to head, baring their souls. Or, rather, she had provided him with a great deal of information.

"So a drink with Queensbay's resident hottie. I am sooo jealous. I mean, not really, since he's kind of a player."

"A player?" Phoebe asked.

"Oh, yeah. He's a really generous guy, shows up at all the benefits around town, which my dad goes to since he's chief at the hospital and my mom makes me go to since she figures I'll meet an eligible guy there, but he always, and I mean always, has a different girl on his arm. And they are all lookers. I think he actually brings the models from his catalog."

"The foul-weather gear ones?" Phoebe asked, hopefully.

"Nope, definitely the swimsuit ones."

"Oh. Well, anyway, it wasn't a date. It was…" She paused. What had it been? A date? A question about business? A "Hey, how about we get to know each other since our grandparents shagged each other" meeting?

"It is so totally romance of the century, part two."

Phoebe shook her head. "Please, I think it was more like the scandal of the century, and I'm not quite sure it's something that should be repeated."

"But all that passion. I mean Chase is so hot, way hotter than Leland. I mean Leland was kind of an old fogey when he and Savannah hooked up. Never quite sure what she saw in him."

Phoebe rolled her eyes. "It was probably the money. Savannah was excellent at self-preservation. Remember, she had a young child to support." Phoebe couldn't remember her dad talking much about his childhood, at least not anything serious. Fun, light stories about living with a movie-star mom, but he'd never known who his real father was and barely remembered Leland, his "stepfather."

"Well, Chase has got it all: looks and money. So are you going to sleep with him?" Lynn pulled up another chair, the metal feet scraping across the word floor. Phoebe winced, but realized it didn't matter. The floors needed to be redone.

"Sleep with him? Why would I want to sleep with him? He, along with the rest of the village, was trying to buy my house because they think I am some sort of West Coast harpy who wants to tear this place down and build some sort of modernist white box."

Lynn waved her hand. "Don't worry, I put my mom on it. She'll let everyone know that you're planning to restore the house to its former glory. Watch out: the ladies from the Historical Commission will be over here with old pictures and banana bread in about two days."

"Thanks, I think." Phoebe didn't really care for banana bread.

"So you don't want to sleep with him?" Lynn's voice was coy.

Phoebe sighed. "What I am saying is that he clearly wants something from me. I don't think it would be a good thing if I got involved, again, with someone who doesn't want me—only something from me. Besides, I barely know him. I'm not actually a 'buy me a drink and I'll go to bed with you' kind of girl."

"You know, there's no harm in trying it out. And just think of what the papers would say." Lynn's eyes went dreamy. "The fans would love it. It might be good for your business, you know."

Phoebe reached out and grabbed Lynn's hand. "No way. Don't even go there. If a reporter ever found out that Chase and I had even talked. Ugh. It may seem cool to be in the paper, but really, it's not. I left Los Angeles to get away from all that."

"OK," Lynn said, and Phoebe saw that her friend's eyes mirrored her own seriousness. "Mum's the word. But if you do sleep with him, I need all of the details, please."

"Lynn!"

"What," Lynn said laughing, "I'm a sleep-deprived resident who works at a children's clinic. All I see are moms and married dads. I need some vicarious thrills. Please."

Phoebe just laughed.

Chapter 17

"And just what do you think you're doing?"

Phoebe almost lost her balance, waved her arms, and then finally managed to hop off the rusty folding chair and land with a thump on the floorboards. They gave a little beneath her weight, and she swore as she felt the whole house shake.

Chase Sanders darkened the doorway, hands on his hips, filling the space, such that he was a silhouette against the light blue of the sky.

Phoebe stood, her balance regained and looked at him. It was hard to make out his features, but she was sure that there was the unmistakable curl of lips. Laughing. Chase Sanders was trying not to laugh at her again.

She kept looking at him and he lost the battle, erupting into a full-bellied laugh that Phoebe might have been tempted to join in with if she hadn't been the object of it.

"I was changing a light bulb." She tried to keep the prim tone out of her voice, but knew she hadn't quite succeeded.

"The light's out? Are you sure you shouldn't have had the electricity turned on first?" He took a step in and Phoebe could see that he had dispensed with the business attire and just wore jeans and a dark gray v-neck sweater that fitted him tightly, allowing a display of his chest. *Definitely impressive,* Phoebe thought.

"I did." And Phoebe had. She didn't mention that she had cable and internet. Really, it was none of his business.

Chase flipped a switch by the door, and behind him, the light on the porch went on and off.

"See. It works. But this," she pointed to the chandelier above her head, "doesn't. There were some light bulbs in the kitchen."

He moved in closer and she could finally see him now that he wasn't framed in the glare from outside. Chase pushed his sunglasses back on top of his head and reached out.

Phoebe reared back, but his hand gently touched her hair, pulled back in a ponytail.

"Cobweb," he said, and she could feel the warmth of his fingers brush along her scalp, sending a tingle down the back of her neck.

There was an easy smile as he cleared the cobweb away and shook his hand to rid himself of it.

"Thanks," Phoebe managed to mumble, not sure why him being here should suddenly make her feel like a kid on the first day of school; an odd mixture of fear, anticipation, and heightened senses.

"Let me." He held his hand out again and Phoebe followed his gaze to the light bulb she held in her hand. Wordlessly, she gave it to him, and he walked over to the fixture, reached up, and, barely standing on his toes, screwed it in.

"Old houses," he said. "Ceilings are never that high."

"It makes it cozy," Phoebe said automatically, feeling the need to defend her cottage.

"Or claustrophobic." He smiled at her. "Give it a try now."

It took her a moment to understand what he said, lost as she was in the deep, gravelly sound of his voice. Little kid, indeed. She was more like a teenager on her first date. Or like the wallflower who gets asked to the dance by the star football player.

Phoebe shook her head as she reached for a light switch on the wall. The wallflower and the football star were the stuff of movies—Carrie, for one—and she wasn't supposed to be thinking about men. She was supposed to be thinking about her new life.

The light blinked on and the hallway was flooded with light.

"A little too bright, but you can always switch it out with a lower-watt bulb when you're ready," Chase said, picking up the rusted chair and folding it. It squeaked, but collapsed under his capable hands.

"Where does this go?"

"Back in the kitchen, I suppose." Phoebe waved in that direction. She had no intention of keeping the chair, but right now, there weren't too many seating options available.

Chase walked down the hallway and Phoebe followed. He smelled like soap and fresh air, a hint of cologne, but nothing overpowering.

"So, what are you here for?" Phoebe didn't feel like waiting any longer, and truth was, she'd be happy to get rid of Chase sooner rather than later.

"I think you misunderstood me last night," he said, his dark blue eyes dancing as he looked down at her. She was wearing sneakers, and again she was aware of the height disadvantage that they put her at.

"Oh, I don't think so. I thought your meaning was quite clear."

He laughed. "I don't know, what's that they say… Sometimes, a sheet is just a sheet."

"Somehow, I doubt that where you're concerned," she shot back, thinking about what Lynn had told her. Phoebe had no need to get involved with players. She had learned that lesson already.

"Well, perhaps we can address that question later?" He let that hang there and, to her surprise, Phoebe felt herself considering it, thinking about just what it might be like to find out just what kind of sheets Chase Sanders had on that boat of his. She felt warmer all over, warmer than the day warranted.

"Sit, please. I want to talk to you." Chase's eyes were serious now, his mood changing suddenly.

"I'm quite capable of listening while standing up." Phoebe refused to be lured in by Chase's physical presence. Though the chair and the table were small, tiny compared to him, he still managed to look at ease, totally, utterly at ease.

"Fine. Doesn't matter to me. I just thought you might be interested in a business proposition."

Phoebe felt her body tense.

"What kind of proposition?"

"Not sheets exactly," he said, shooting her another smile. "But you had me interested enough to go and do a little research. I really liked your pillows, and my mom loved them. And so did half the staff at the store. And Joan Altieri told me the ladies of Queensbay are going crazy over the rest of your stock. I thought when you said you were a designer, you meant you went shopping with your friends and told them what to buy."

Phoebe reared up a bit. She had built Ivy Lane up slowly over the years, spending every spare minute on it. It was not some hobby.

"Just because I'm small doesn't mean I'm not serious."

Chase held up a quieting hand. "Everyone starts somewhere. Believe me, North Coast Outfitters was one crappy little shop in Queensbay when I took it over. I know you're small, but that doesn't mean you're not talented. Do you want to keep giving away your talent to talentless celebrities of the month, or do you want to share it with the world, on your own terms?"

Phoebe shot him a look. "How dare you come here and try and tell me my business. First my house and now my work?"

"That's not what I meant. I have a real deal for you, if you'll just calm down and let me talk."

Phoebe took a deep breath. Some of her friends in Los Angeles, Dean included, had been dismissive of her efforts, saying they were a distraction. What he had meant is that they were a distraction from what he thought was her real job working with his clients. She had a feeling he hadn't been happy about the success she had started to enjoy on her own. Now, part of coming here was proving to him that Ivy Lane was more than just a distraction.

"Fine. Talk." She held out her hand, in what she hoped was an accommodating gesture towards him.

"Well, I really liked the designs. At least on the site. Don't tell me you're sewing the pillows yourself, are you?" he asked.

She shook her head. "No, of course not. I create the design, get the fabric made and then I have a small workshop that sews the pillows for me. Then, they go to a warehouse, which handles all the shipping for me. I have a part-time assistant, a college student, who oversees it all for me."

"Smart. Leaves you plenty of time to create. And I guess market."

Phoebe shrugged. She hadn't done much in the way of marketing her designs. She'd had some luck there since she'd given some of her pillows as a housewarming present to a friend. The pillows then caught the eye of an interior designer, and soon, Phoebe's pillows had started to pop up all over Los Angeles. But she knew she needed to do more. Going to shops like the Garden Cottage was a first step, but she would need hundreds more like it, across the country, if she wanted to make this a real business. Or one big customer with lots of shops, she thought, beginning to get an idea of where Chase was going.

"It's great stuff, but I was wondering... The website barely has your name on it. Why aren't you playing up the Hollywood angle?" There was real curiosity in his voice.

Phoebe looked down to the floor. "I wanted it to be successful on its own, not because I have a famous name."

Chase nodded. "OK, I get it. But you shouldn't hold yourself back like that."

"It's not up for discussion," Phoebe said sharply, drawing in a deep breath. Business deal or not, Chase could walk right out of here if he thought she was going to buckle on this.

"OK, so noted." He smiled to show that he wasn't put off by her tone. "Here's the deal."

Phoebe crossed her arms, interested in spite of her personal misgivings towards Chase. She had managed to do a little research on Chase Sanders. North Coast Outfitters was the real thing, a multimillion-dollar business with high-end customers, expanding every day. Getting North Coast Outfitters behind her would help her launch her fledging business much faster than she could ever do on her own.

"What kind of deal?"

"Well, I thought perhaps you could do some new designs, pillows, a little California cool, a little old-Hollywood-glamour type of thing, and we market them to our customer base. You make the design, do the samples and I'll take it from there. We'll offer them as a limited-edition set, promote the hell out of them and then see what happens. If my customers like the pillows, then we can try other things."

He was excited, she could tell, as the ideas were flowing out of him. She knew that his attention wasn't on her exactly, but it was still exhilarating to be swept up in his enthusiasm. For a moment, she could see it all mapped out—a limited-edition set of work for North Coast Outfitters, make her name known, then get herself into the pages of magazines. Her business would grow from there, and a Phoebe Ryan design would mean something simple, elegant, yet fun. Good taste for the next generation. Pillows, tablecloths, plates…and, yes, someday, even sheets.

"What's in it for you?" she asked, returning to reality. Nobody did anyone a favor like this without expecting some return. "You can't bribe me. I'm not selling the house, you know," Phoebe said, her defenses rising.

Chase smiled at her and took a step closer. "I know. You made your position very clear. Ivy House isn't for sale. I respect that. Especially since you're not planning on tearing it down. At least that's the word on the street." He gave her a small knowing smile, as if they shared a secret.

"But you know, I was able to take a marine hardware store in a sleepy little town in Connecticut and turn it into a successful online business."

Phoebe swallowed, suddenly lost again in Chase's sapphire-colored eyes, centered on the intent look on his face. Gone was the exuberance and in its place was a look of focus, of concentration.

Phoebe remembered briefly that here was a man who had sailed through the edge of a hurricane to win a race. She supposed he wasn't a man to give in lightly or to second-guess himself.

"It's because I have a talent for knowing what people want and like. Me, I couldn't sew a pillow or come up with a design for one if you had a gun to my head. But I can spot when someone else has created something that people want. If you sign a deal with North Coast Outfitters, I will handle all those pesky details that you artistic types hate. You won't have to deal with suppliers or vendors or whether your name gets in the paper or if the shipment from the factory is late. I take care of all of that for you, so you can do what you do best."

"What's that?" Phoebe breathed.

"Create things." He was close to her now, so close that her vision was filled with him, with his dark, slightly unruly hair, his tan skin, the stubble on his face. She could sense his lips hovering near hers, and for a brief moment, just an instant, she had to close her eyes, break the connection between the two of them.

When she opened them, she found that he was watching her, a step back now, hands shoved into his pockets, one eyebrow raised.

"What do you think, do we have a deal?"

Phoebe hesitated only a moment before she nodded.

Chase smiled, looking highly pleased with himself. He stuck out a hand and she took it, their skin brushing, a bolt of electricity shooting through her. He held it just a bit longer than necessary, looking at her, a lazy, sexy grin spreading over his face.

"I'll have my lawyer send over some papers."

Chapter 18

"So, she took the deal," Noah said.

"She took the deal." Chase took a sip of his beer. Chase had wandered over to Noah's house after work, and now the two of them were holed up in the large garage behind it.

"Do you boys need anything else? I have to go out now." Caitlyn came in and Chase watched as his friend's whole face lit up.

"No, I think we're good. We have beer and a boat. What more could we want?" Noah said, giving his wife a kiss as he pulled her close, his hand touching her still-flat belly.

Chase watched, wanting to turn away, but didn't. Noah was so damn happy, married and soon to be a father that it was enough to make any other guy sick. Except that's not what Chase was feeling. Not envy, for while Caitlyn was beautiful and accomplished, Chase knew he wasn't jealous for her. Just of what she and Noah had together.

"Be careful, please. Let me know when you get there?" he whispered.

Caitlyn laughed. "It's just a few miles away. How much trouble can I get in? It's just dinner."

"Call," Noah said, his eyes narrowing, his voice serious.

"I'll call. Of course. There's some stuff in the fridge for dinner if you boys get hungry. Just be careful using those power tools." She waved once more and let herself out and they heard the sound of her car leaving the driveway.

"Hey, Daddy, wipe the drool off," Chase said to his best friend.

Noah just shook his head. "Wait until it happens to you. Won't know what hit you."

"That will be the day," Chase said, but an image of Phoebe flashed through his mind as he said it. He could still feel the way the electricity had shot through him at her touch. He had hurried away from her, not because he wanted to, but because he so badly wanted not to.

"So you have a deal with the cool and collected Phoebe Ryan. What's next?"

Chase checked his watch. "Well, my attorney's drawing up some paperwork, and my marketing director is through the roof. Would think Phoebe was a movie star herself, she's such a Savannah fan. Coming up with all sorts of ways to market the collection. So we'll see. With any luck, we'll be able to have it ready for the next catalog."

"So you think this will help you get the house?" Noah asked, pulling back the tarp on the oddly shaped thing in front of them.

"The house?" It took a moment for Chase to figure out what his friend was talking about.

"Yeah, isn't this why you're wining and dining her? So you can get her house? At least that's what you said the other day." Noah's eyes, shrewd, looked up at him.

"Sure, the house. I figure she'll be so excited, she'll have the place cleaned up and head back to Los Angeles in a couple of weeks. She'll be the next big design star, and she'll be so thankful to me that she'll sell me the house. No agent's fee or anything."

The words came out easily, but Chase knew he had stopped thinking about the house or even his business deal sometime during drinks with her. She had been refreshingly candid about her life during their dinner. And, of course, there was the way she looked at him. He couldn't quite get that out of his mind. She had wanted him to kiss her, he was almost sure of that. There had been that moment in the hall of Ivy House.

Chase shook his head, trying to clear his thoughts, but he couldn't. Her red-gold hair in a messy ponytail; her wide, sensual lips; her long, thin fingers—artist's fingers. He had felt his body hunger for her and knew that something would need to be done about that. Especially if she was the least bit willing. Oh, yes, if Phoebe Ryan gave him that kind of opportunity, he just might take it.

"Well, just be careful. I don't want to see it all backfire on you." And with that, Noah pulled back the tarp to reveal a boat. It was all wood, the paint chipped and peeling, the varnish bubbling, and there was a large hole in the bottom.

"Wow. It's a beauty," Chase said, running his hands along the gunwale.

"I know. A Herreshoff America eighteen. Limited edition. Classic, yet easy to maneuver."

"And this is your next great idea?" Chase asked. Since Noah had sold his tech company, he'd been working head down on his next one, something to do with a new clean energy source. Noah was cagey on the whole subject, but Chase had told him that there was a blank check waiting for him when he was ready for investors.

"Hey, it's a wind-powered vehicle. Perfectly environmentally friendly."

Chase looked at his friend, staring him down until Noah came out with the truth.

"I wanted to do it for the baby. You know, his first boat."

"Do you even know it's a boy?" Chase asked.

"No and it doesn't matter, right? Girl or boy, it's never too early to get them out on the water."

Chase laughed. "I think they need to be able to walk first. But you're right, it's a beauty. It will be perfect when it's restored."

Chapter 19

Phoebe took a step into the shop. It was more than a shop, she supposed. North Coast Outfitters occupied prime real estate along the waterfront of Queensbay Harbor, adjacent to the Osprey Arms, and an easy place to stop for boaters and general tourists. She figured if she were going to make a deal with the devil, then she should get a better feel for him. Plus, she had some concerns over the terms of the contract, and it seemed more expedient to deal with Chase directly than go back and forth using lawyers, hers in Los Angeles and Chase's in New York. After all, the two of them were in the same town.

Large black-and-white posters hung on the walls of the shop, pictures of people sailing in boats, sunning themselves, generally enjoying the good life. She took a closer look at one of the pictures and saw that, sure enough, it was Chase, at the helm of a large sailboat, standing on the deck like a modern-day pirate, winds filled, water foaming at the bow. She swallowed. He even looked sexy in black and white, his dark hair blown by the wind, his eyes hidden behind sunglasses, his hands large and capable at the wheel. She swallowed, suddenly thinking that it might be better to just send her comments to the lawyer.

She heard it then, a trilling happy laugh, and a stunning woman with dark hair stepped into view. Chase walked next to her, one arm around her shoulder. He said something to her, and she looked up at him and laughed again. Phoebe tensed. He hadn't said he was single when she had given him the chance, but he hadn't claimed to be dating anyone either. Had she mistaken the vibes she'd been getting from him all along?

Phoebe almost turned, ready to hurry back to Ivy House, when she was spotted.

"Phoebe." Chase's voice was sexy, still tinged with the laughter he had been sharing with the woman on his arm.

Without bothering to disentangle himself, he walked over to Phoebe. The woman under his arm glanced up at him and then over at Phoebe.

"Hello, I'm Caitlyn Randall." She held out a hand and Phoebe couldn't quite miss the way the light caught the enormous diamond on her hand. Phoebe felt herself stiffen and plastered what she hoped was a cool and professional smile on her face as she shook the other woman's hand.

"Forgive me. Caitlyn, this is Phoebe Ryan, the new owner of Ivy House."

Caitlyn's eyes lit up and she glanced at Phoebe, speculation in her eyes. "Ivy House, you mean that beautiful old house just up from town? The one with the tower?"

"Yes, I suppose that would be the one."

"Phoebe recently inherited it from her grandmother, Savannah Ryan."

"Oh." Interest lit up in Caitlyn's eyes and Phoebe braced herself.

Instead of the usual questions, Caitlyn's look turned serious. "I am so sorry for your loss. I loved your grandmother's movies. All of them."

"Thank you," Phoebe managed to say, knowing she sounded stuffy, but she couldn't help it. So, this was Chase's type, this East Coast preppy looker. Caitlyn wore a simple wrap dress with knee-high boots and carried an understated leather bag. She looked like she would be equally at home on the deck of a boat in a retro two-piece or riding out on top of some great Charger, leading the hounds in snuffing out their quarry.

Phoebe thought she should have dressed better. What seemed to pass for California chic seemed hopelessly casual here. The morning had promised warmth today, so she had put on a pair of cut-off jeans and a flowing printed blouse and let her hair fall down loose, held back by her sunglasses.

"Well, good luck. Chase says you're planning on doing some renovations before you sell. I can't tell you how excited he is, he's been dreaming of Ivy House…"

"Caitlyn, surely you need to get back to work," Chase broke in smoothly. Caitlyn shot him a surprised look.

"Yes, the market waits for no woman," she said and glanced over at Phoebe and then back to Chase.

"Be sure to say hi to Noah. Tell him I have those parts he wanted."

"I will. And you make sure you keep my little surprise to yourself. His birthday's coming up and I want him to truly be delighted."

"My lips are sealed."

Caitlyn turned to Phoebe again. "It was wonderful to meet you. Perhaps if you're going to be in town for a while, I can convince you and Chase to come over for drinks. Noah hates to drink alone."

"I'm sure that would be wonderful," Phoebe said, puzzled by the comment.

"Chase, I'll let you explain. Do you have a card, Phoebe? That way I can be sure to track you down. I find men are terrible with details like that."

Before Phoebe had quite realized what had happened, she had exchanged cards with Caitlyn Randall.

"Noah as in Noah Randall?" she asked. She remembered now what Lynn had told her and realized she had just come in contact with one-half of a power couple.

"The very same. We go way back," Chase explained, as if it were the most natural thing in the world, and Phoebe saw that it was for him. She smiled. Perhaps it was like having a tableful of Hollywood legends over for Thanksgiving.

When she had told Chase she had some questions about the contract, he had quickly ushered her out of the store and across the street to a set of offices above a modern row of shops. People were busy working, and they paid them little mind, except to say hi to Chase as she followed him down the open floor plan and into his own office.

"Coffee, tea?"

"Coffee would be great," she said. He pressed a button on his phone and ordered it.

"So you go way back with Caitlyn and Noah Randall?" she asked.

"Noah and Caitlyn live up along the east bank of the harbor. Caitlyn loves to entertain, so you better watch out. You will be getting a call from her. Oh, and she's a financial advisor, so she's likely to make sure that you're getting the proper rate of return on your investments, and you can totally trust her. She's like some sort of uber-mother hen."

"I still don't get the drinking-alone thing," Phoebe said.

"She's expecting. About three months along."

"Looks great." Phoebe felt her heart rate return to normal. So, the glow that hovered about Caitlyn had not been due to Chase's grin.

Chase gave a shrug and a smile. "Hey, when I knew him, he was just a computer geek who liked playing video games. Who knew where it would lead him."

Phoebe shot another look at Chase.

"What? Think I'm not refined enough for the likes of Noah Randall?"

"No, not at all. But you do seem a bit like the odd couple," Phoebe said. There was a knock on the door and an older woman with reddish hair and freckles brought in a tray with a pot of coffee, cups, milk, and sugar. She set it down, reminded Chase he had a meeting, and left with a brisk, efficient nod in Phoebe's direction.

"We were an odd couple," Chase said, pouring her some coffee and then a cup for himself. "At first, but we both loved to sail. But I was better. So, Noah used me to win the Junior Cup at the Yacht Club."

Phoebe frowned. "What did you get out of the deal?"

Chase shrugged. "You'd be surprised."

"What does that mean?"

"It means Noah and I have been business partners for a long time. I invested in some software, and he invested in some hardware." Chase made an encompassing gesture and Phoebe nodded.

"Smart."

"And some luck. You never know where a friendship is going to lead you."

Chase's voice had dropped an octave and his grin was wolfish. "Caitlyn and Noah dated each other back when they were teenagers. I've known both of them a long time."

Something about the easy way he said it made Phoebe jealous all over again. Chase seemed to be suggesting he had known both of them—in different ways—for a very long time. They had been very comfortable together. But then she remembered the look in Caitlyn's eyes when she had said her husband's name.

"Well, it's nice to have old friends." She kept the wistfulness out of her voice, glancing around the office as she did so. It was spare, a modern place or, she realized as she studied it, more like a ship's cabin with lots of polished wood and discreet storage space. It was masculine without being overpowering. Unassuming, yet powerful and completely confident, much like Chase himself.

"So, you had some questions?" Chase's eyes sparkled, the sunlight from the expansive windows catching them. His eyes were a deep, deep blue and she felt herself drawn into them, and then remembered why she had decided to track him down in the first place.

"Yes. I thought it would be easier to talk face-to-face instead of going through lawyers."

"Quite right," he said, taking a sip of his coffee.

"Well, I'm fine with just about everything but this part." She handed him over a copy of the contract with the section highlighted.

He glanced it over and then looked over at her, amusement on his lips. "You're saying that we can use your name, but not Savannah's? Is there a problem with her?"

Phoebe shook her head, wiping her hands on her shorts. This was where she could have used some of Savannah's acting skill. A scene played out, Savannah done up as a gangster moll, staring down some scary mob boss as she negotiated for the life of her lover. Or maybe it had been for her brother. There had been so many movies, it was hard to keep them all straight.

"No problem with her. But I would just prefer to make a go of it on my name alone. I have no problem with the catalog or press releases talking about me, but I would prefer not to have my relationship with her mentioned."

"I thought you were close to her."

Phoebe swallowed. "I was. And that's why it would be nice to know people liked my work on its own merit. Not because of some old screen legend."

"So no trading on famous relatives." Chase took out a pen, crossed out a few lines of text, and put his initials next to it.

"Anything else?" he asked. There was a buzz on his phone. His eyes held her and the buzz was insistent. He pressed a button and his assistant's voice filtered through. "Your next appointment is here."

"That's all," Phoebe said. She knew she should go. They both had things to do, but something about his eyes pinned her in her seat and she felt a warmth spread over her, starting between her legs and crawling up over her body. She'd never had this reaction to a man just from his look. The question was what to do about it.

"Well, then I guess we have a deal."

Phoebe smiled. "I suppose so."

"Well, here's to a profitable friendship," he said. His eyes held hers and his intercom rang again.

She got up, pulling her bag with her.

"Thanks for stopping by. Next time, I'll give you the grand tour."

"That would be lovely," Phoebe said, feeling awkward. "I guess I'll be hearing from you."

"Consider the deal done. I guess you better get to work. Are you going to be heading back to California to get started? I have to get out to the stores there soon. I am sure I could look you up?"

Phoebe remembered what Caitlyn had started to say about the house, so she smiled, chin drawn up, and channeled her best Savannah look.

"You know, one of the best things about a job like mine is that I take inspiration wherever I can find it."

Chase had moved around the desk and they were standing close to one another. She could see the way his lips curled up in amusement, and she could feel in her stomach the way his low voice unnerved her.

"Are you feeling inspired?" he asked, his voice dangerously low.

"As it so happens, I have always found that being by the water fills me with a lot of energy."

He looked at her, a slow grin spreading over his face and she felt her body respond to him, heat licking through her as he took her hand to shake it and then brought it up to skim against his lips.

"Just creative energy?" he murmured.

"You can have my designs, but you can't have me," she responded.

"Are you sure about that? I told you: I always get what I want."

She was stunned into silence for a moment, until the door opened, and the redheaded lady bustled in.

"Looks like that's my cue to go," she managed to stammer out, knowing she needed to get out and away from him.

Chapter 20

"Is that a hard hat?" Phoebe stopped in surprise, looking at what Chase had in his hands.

"Yes, it is. Safety first." Phoebe looked up quickly to see if he meant anything by that. There it was, just that sexy-as-hell Chase Sanders grin.

"But it's pink," Phoebe said.

"Well, it is for a girl." Chase said. He took a step forward and she saw that he was dressed casually in faded jeans and a v-neck t-shirt that clung to his chest and abdomen, which showed off how flat his stomach was and the nice taper up to his broad shoulders. *Stop thinking about his shoulders,* she reminded herself.

"A girl?" Phoebe turned her attention back to the hard hat that Chase was still proffering. "Excuse me... For a lady," he corrected himself.

"A lady." Phoebe put down her bag on the scarred wood floor and took the helmet from Chase.

"You said the other day you were going to fix the old lady up, so I thought I'd give you a little housewarming present. And see if you needed a hand."

"You can fix houses?" Phoebe heard the doubt creeping into her voice. She glanced around the room. Chase had found her in her studio, the light flooding in from the bank of windows. She had picked up some paint samples at the local hardware store, and there were large squares of them on the wall so she could decide between Café au Lait and Creamy Blond.

"No, but I know people around here who can. I would be happy to recommend some names to you. All good guys."

Phoebe nodded. She had wondered if she'd have to resort to looking through Yellow Pages to find the names of plumbers and electricians, and the thought had filled her with dread. Taking a recommendation from someone was a much better move. Still, it was a lot of interest on Chase's part for a house he professed to have no interest in.

"Do you treat all of your business acquaintances this way?" she asked, trying to keep her voice light. Right now, the room had one wall of built-in shelves, with cabinets on the bottom. She examined the hard hat more closely.

"I told you, we're partners now. Hopefully, very profitable ones," he countered.

Phoebe hefted the hard hat. It was heavier than she expected. "They really make pink ones?"

Chase laughed. "Not many. It's a special order, but I know a guy in the business."

"I'm sure you do." Phoebe took a sip of her coffee, still looking at the helmet. She wasn't sure what to do with it. Just how much demolition did Chase think the house needed?"

"You don't think I'm going to need it, do you?" she asked, trying to see if he had an opinion.

"You never know," Chase answered, still grinning.

"But…" Phoebe felt her mouth go dry. She thought about some new paint and curtains, but not any actual demolition.

Chase took a step closer to her and held out his hand. She wasn't sure what he wanted, but then he reached out for her coffee cup. Mesmerized, she let him take it from her and watched as he took a sip, her eyes locked on his, his on hers. Slowly, he handed the cup back to her.

"Thanks. I needed that. Look, I happen to have spent a few summers working construction. Thought maybe I could help you do a walk-through, get a sense of what needs to be done now, what can wait."

Phoebe felt herself swallowing hard, trying to forget the way his hand, warmed from the coffee cup, had burned against her skin and made her stomach do a flip.

"But we're not going to be breaking anything, are we?" Phoebe asked, surprised to find her voice was low, throaty.

"Not unless you want to."

Phoebe nodded. There was no reason for him to be holding her hand, but it had felt good. She decided not to dwell on it.

They wound up in the room she had decided would be the master bedroom. The floors were hardwood and she knew that they could be beautiful again.

"I know a guy who does floors. I asked him to swing by later, to take a look around, give you an estimate. They should be done all at once, upstairs, downstairs. That way, you can move in. You can always do your painting later."

Phoebe nodded. "It would be good if I could at least get a bed in here by the end of the week." Phoebe felt it, the slow burn of a flush. Somehow saying the word "bed" in front of Chase made her feel self-conscious. He had dropped her hand by this time, but was still standing close to her, and she couldn't get over the feeling of being on edge, like she had drunk five espressos in a row and the caffeine was buzzing through her in overdrive.

"Really? I didn't know you were in such a hurry to get set up. Is someone waiting for it?"

It took her a moment to figure out what Chase meant.

"I…" she stuttered, cursing her fair skin, feeling the blush crawl up her cheeks and to the roots of her hair.

"So you're just eager to get moved in?" he said, his eyes laughing at her.

"I'd rather not spend that much more time in the hotel. The Osprey Arms is fine, but I hadn't figured on making it a permanent home."

"I like that one." He had come up behind her, and pointed to the middle shade of blue on the paint chip Phoebe was holding. "I'm sure I could arrange a deal for you, since you're practically living there."

"Don't tell me… You know the manager." Phoebe said, the memory of the way he had seemed so comfortable at the Osprey Arms coming back to her.

Chase shrugged. "Maybe I do."

"Well, thank you, but I already did." The shade Chase liked was deeper than she would have gone for, but it was bold too. "I'm a grown woman; I can take care myself. I happen to have plenty of experience negotiating for myself."

"I am sure you can come down hard on them when you want." She could feel him, his bulk and heat behind, and the way his breath whispered in her ear and tickled her hair, which was up in a ponytail. She fought to control the shiver that ran down her spine and the little delicious flame of heat that flicked below her stomach, between her legs. Desperately wanting to put some distance between herself and Chase, she almost took a step away, but she couldn't; she was trapped there, loving the feeling of him close to her.

"I manage to get what I want most of the time," she managed to say in a husky voice.

"I can imagine." She turned slightly to face him so that her eyes were almost level with his chin. One of his arms was still around her and she could smell him, a mix of soap and spicy aftershave, melding together in a heady combination that made her knees feel just slightly wobbly.

His hand grasped her wrist and pulled her closer to him. She met his eyes, could see that they were dark, liquid, as if consumed by something. His nostrils flared and he leaned in, smelling her hair.

"You smell amazing," he said, his voice a hoarse, ragged whisper. She felt any last inhibitions melt away, and she wasn't quite sure who moved first so that they were facing each other and she was encircled in the strong span of his arms.

It seemed as if time stood still, and Phoebe was aware of everything, from the fresh breath of air that wafted in from the window that was propped open to the sound of a bird singing and the whisper of the new green leaves in the trees. And then she heard the sound of her own heart beating and could hear Chase's ragged breath as his gaze roamed over her, taking her in, his blue eyes dark.

"What was that?" They sprang apart, and Phoebe's eyes traveled up to the ceiling. Dust trickled down and the hanging light fixture swung slightly. Her heart was thumping, and she had clutched her hands to her chest, no longer in the strong confines of Chase's arms.

It came again, another crash and then a scurrying sound. Chase's head was cocked up and he watched the ceiling. A slow smile came over his face.

"Squirrels, a raccoon maybe, in the attic."

"Yuck." Phoebe wasn't crazy about animals. Sure, dogs were fine and cats OK, but anything else...especially in her house, was just too off-putting to think about. Somehow, she hadn't thought about that aspect of living in the country when she'd been dreaming of Ivy House.

"Where are the stairs?" Chase asked. He was still looking up, completely oblivious to her, and it was with supreme disappointment that she realized he was not going to kiss her after all.

"Stairs?"

"To the attic." There was a touch of impatience in his voice. "They could be getting away."

"You're going to go up there?"

"Sure. How else are we going to get rid of them?" he said.

Call an exterminator, Phoebe thought, but didn't voice it. "What about rabies?" she said instead.

476

"I'm not going to catch them. I just need to find out where they're coming in from. And then we can set traps and get them out."

"Kill them?" All of a sudden, Phoebe didn't relish the thought of killing innocent animals. After all, in their minds, they had been there first.

"No, of course not. We'll set special no-kill traps, catch them and then release them. But we need to find out how they're getting in so they don't get right back in. So, the stairs?" he said again, his impatience marked with a smile.

Phoebe thought for a moment. "In the hallway."

She led the way out of the bedroom towards the door that led to a closet. It was big for one, an odd-shaped room above the stairs, and it had a round window in it. "Up there."

There was a trap door in the ceiling, with a rope hanging from it.

"You might want to stand back," Chase said.

"Are you sure we shouldn't call someone?" Phoebe asked. Chase had pulled a small flashlight from his pocket and was already pulling on the rope. It was stuck and he handed the flashlight to Phoebe as he put both hands on the rope, tugging hard.

With a squeak and a groan, the door came free and a cloud of dust fell down. Chase was quick, and he sidestepped the dust storm easily, pushing Phoebe out of the way so she was spared the worst of it. Still, grime swirled in the air, and she could feel it settling in her hair.

There was a ladder folded up against the underside of the door and Chase reached up and swung it down. It gave another protesting squeak and then there was silence. In agreement, the two of them paused and listened. The rustling had stopped, Phoebe noted with relief.

Chase put his foot on the bottom rung, tested his weight, turned, took the flashlight from Phoebe, and shot her a wink.

"If I'm not back in five, call in the cavalry."

Phoebe was about to protest, but then she remembered it was just an attic. She watched his amazingly cute backside disappear into the gloom above. There was a pause, silence and she half-expected to hear a scream; she could feel the tension erupting in her.

"Hey, Phoebe, you're going to want to see this."

Chapter 21

Phoebe put her foot up on the ladder and then stopped. "What is it?"

Chase chuckled. "Don't worry, this isn't going to bite you."

Somewhat reassured, Phoebe started up the ladder, entering the low enclosed space.

"Wow." Phoebe emerged into the dim light of the attic. It ran the whole length of the house, unfinished, rough wood, with nails sticking through the sloped roof.

"Watch your head," Chase said over his shoulder. He was ahead of her, his flashlight moving this way and that, illuminating an attic full of...stuff. Boxes, trunks, battered suitcases, coat racks filled with clothes, even an old dressmaker's dummy.

"The mother lode," Phoebe whispered. There were dormers along the length of the roofline, and the small leaded panes of glass provided some more light. Through it all, swarms of dust filtered and danced, caught in the sunlight.

"Is this her stuff?" Chase turned, the flashlight almost catching Phoebe full in the face before he lowered it.

"Savannah's?" Phoebe walked over to a stack of boxes. In magic marker, the words, *"Mystic Moon,"* were written. It was the name of one of her movies. Phoebe ran a hand along a dress hanging on one of the coat racks. It had once been white, but now it was creamy, yellowed with age.

"She wore this in *Scott's Peak,*" Phoebe said. "And these boxes all have the names of different movies on them. Her movies. So, yeah, I would say this is all of her stuff."

"A whole career," Chase said. Phoebe looked up at him. He had an almost reverent look on his face as he scanned the collection.

"You're a fan," Phoebe said, the realization hitting her suddenly.

"What?" The flashlight jumped and Chase caught a hold of it, before he turned to look at her.

"You, you're a fan of the late great Savannah Ryan," Phoebe said, a teasing note creeping into her voice.

Chase smiled, with a slow cat-that-ate-the-canary grin, and said, "Of course I'm a fan of her work. Savannah Ryan made sex sexy back when I was a kid. I think there was only one movie where she took her clothes off, but even as a kid, you could see the sex appeal oozing through the screen. I saw every one of them. Even the bad ones. And she made some real lousy ones." Chase shook his head.

"Those were to pay the bills. She had expensive tastes and money poured like sand through her hands," Phoebe explained.

"So Savannah Ryan really didn't have a heart of gold?" Chase said.

"She was complicated," Phoebe said, and it was a relief to admit it, even to Chase, who had probably believed it all along. She realized Chase had moved close to her so that there were only a few inches between his chest and her, and once again, she could feel the heat, the palpable pocket of warmth between them, like a current of live electricity snaking through them.

"You were saying?" Chase asked, and Phoebe remembered that she had been saying something.

"About a heart of gold..." Chase prompted. They were close again, just as they had been before in the master bedroom, the space between them just a fraction of an inch. She turned her head up so that their lips were almost ready to touch. Her heart skipped a beat and her breath hitched, knowing how badly she did want this—want Chase Sanders to kiss her—even though it was wrong on so many levels.

But for the life of her, she could not think of a good reason why she should pull away when his lips brushed hers. She moved into him, and his arms came around her, crushing her close to him, his lips finding hers, his hands strong and warm against her back.

Phoebe lifted her arms, her hands finding the back of his neck, brushing up to find his thick, dark hair, while his lips crushed against hers, exploring, inviting. A sound escaped, a moan, which she might have been embarrassed about if she hadn't been enjoying herself so thoroughly, all her senses engaged, feelings and need coursing through her.

Her lips parted, an invitation, and he took it, his tongue explor-ing, his teeth nibbling her lips, while his hands pulled her tighter and closer into him so she was possessed, so she couldn't have moved even if she wanted to. His tongue took hers and his arms brought her closer, and she slid into him, one leg in between his so she could feel his desire, hot and hard for her.

Phoebe lost all rational thought as his hands cupped her backside and then one came around to skim the edge of her waistband. Then, it was gone and his hand found her left breast, his fingers pulling gently at her nipple, which sprang to attention at his touch. His mouth moved down her neck, while one arm braced her back and she arched into him as his lips and teeth slid slowly down her neck, to the v of her t-shirt and then nipped lightly at her nipple, which puckered and pebbled under him.

She felt her knees go weak and a flash of heat and wetness between her legs. Chase stopped for a moment, his eyes darting wildly around, and then his hands picked her up and she was on something hard, a steamer trunk, while he kept kissing her, and she could feel that he was just as aroused as she was.

He looked at her for a moment, his gaze intense, lust darkening his eyes. She couldn't say anything, but just nodded at him to keep going. Not waiting for more, he kissed her again, and she rose up to meet him, as his hands traveled down the length of her shirt.

Chase pushed up the thin fabric of her shirt and found the sensitive skin. Hot hands brushed against her and she moaned again, arching into him, wanting him, wanting more.

Phoebe couldn't remember how long this went on because there was another crash and then a shout, loud and hearty.

"Chase, where are you?"

She sprang away from him, but his arms still held her, and he looked down at her, his eyes hazy with want and she felt her lips stinging from his attack.

"And that would be my floor guy." His voice was hoarse, ragged.

"Floor guy?" Phoebe repeated, glad he still had his arms around her, since her knees were shaky.

"This isn't over," Chase said, his voice a low, sexy whisper, and Phoebe almost felt herself sway so that Chase straightened her, brushed a finger along her jawline, before shouting to the intruder below.

"Up here. I'll be down in a sec." Chase took a moment to gain control of himself, while Phoebe sat up, straightened her shirt, and tried to fix her hair.

He turned and started down the ladder.

"Are you coming?"

Phoebe shook her head, hoping that it would shake the lust out of it. It did, but barely.

"I'll be down in a minute. I just want to look around some more."

He threw her a smile and said, "Take the flashlight. We'll just be talking shop."

She watched as his head disappeared down the ladder and then let herself sag against a stack of boxes marked *Trafalgar Square* while she let her heartbeat return to normal. She closed her eyes. She had almost just had wanton sex with Chase Sanders on a steamer trunk belonging to her grandmother. What had she been thinking? And she had wanted it, desperately wanted what Chase had started. Or had she started it? Oh God, Phoebe thought, what was she thinking?

Chapter 22

Phoebe tasted a handful of popcorn kernels, deciding it needed just a bit more salt.

"Are you ready yet?" Lynn's voice echoed from the other room where a gigantic flat-screen TV was set up, the DVD player primed with a string of old Savannah Ryan movies.

"Just a minute." Phoebe added the salt and carried the popcorn into the family room. With Lynn's parents away, they had the house to themselves and were set up for another girls' night in.

It had been four days since Chase had come to Ivy House and found her. He had left soon after Jake, the floor guy, showed up. Jake was good to his word and promised her "the friend of a friend's" discount. What's more, he could start immediately. Until then, Lynn had offered a place to crash. Within the week, Phoebe would be able to live in Ivy House while fixing it up, and it was starting to dawn on Phoebe that this was it. The rest of her life was starting to unfold before her. It was unsettling and so the comfort of spending some time with a girlfriend, in a real house, was strangely appealing.

"Wine and popcorn. Who could have thought of a better combination?" Lynn said, grabbing a handful and taking a sip of the wine. She had traded her scrubs for a pair of cotton pajama pants and a faded sweatshirt. With her dark hair up in a ponytail and her glasses on, she looked more like a college student than a resident just a year or so out from being a doctor.

"I know, genius." Phoebe agreed. The Masters' family room was comfortable: a two-story space with a fireplace, overstuffed leather couches, and plenty of blankets to curl up with. Family pictures, including plenty of Lynn and her brother Kyle, decorated the shelves along with books and a few knickknacks, keeping the room simple and uncluttered.

"So which one are we going to watch fist?" Lynn held up two DVD cases.

"*Mystic Moon*, definitely," Phoebe said. "I think that one is my all-time favorite."

"Oh, good. Mine too." Lynn got up, popped it into the DVD player and flopped back down.

"I just love the costumes in this one. And Roger Dailey was such a hottie."

"She slept with him, you know? Before Leland, of course." Phoebe couldn't resist.

Lynn turned to her, her brown eyes big. "Really. That's so cool. I mean that you know all this stuff. It's like sitting here with Leonard Maltin, or that guy who runs the Actor's Studio and getting the blow-by-blow account.

Phoebe smiled. Even though Lynn was two years younger than she was, Phoebe was already feeling like she had made a true friend, something that had proved a bit elusive in her harried life in Los Angeles. Sure, she had colleagues and girls she went out with, but it seemed like there was always an undercurrent of competition with them. Whose design was going to get picked, which guy at the bar would take an interest in them, who had gotten the best purse or designer shoes.

At first, it had been exciting to be part of such a whirlwind and it had seemed to feed her creativity, but Phoebe had come to feel that it was more draining than energizing, and she'd felt that her inspiration had begun to suffer because of it.

"Well, you wouldn't believe what I found then."

Lynn's nose twitched while she thought about it. "The hat she wore in *Ghost Ship*."

Phoebe smiled as she explained what she and Chase had found in the attic of Ivy House.

"Wow, oh wow," Lynn breathed. "Do you realize how cool that is? Cool and valuable."

"Valuable?" Phoebe tensed a little.

"Yeah, to movie buffs. Not to be morbid, but since Savannah died, the online auction sites have been going crazy with her stuff—you know, autographs, movie posters. But there isn't much of it out there."

"Probably because she kept it all in that attic," Phoebe said.

"Well, I bet it's filled with cool stuff. Let me know if you want any help going through it."

Phoebe nodded. She hadn't thought much about the attic because she'd been busy working on her designs for North Coast Outfitters. And not to mention the fact that every time her phone rang or an email popped up, she had hoped it was something from him. Not a word from him, not unless you counted the crews of workmen he kept sending her way. Someone to haul the junk, the floors, even a lawn guy. Still, there hadn't been any presence of Chase himself for days.

"My favorite part," Lynn breathed a few moments later as Savannah Ryan and Roger Dailey kissed for the first time onscreen. Actually, the scene that had made it into the movie had been their tenth take. Savannah had confessed that she'd kept messing it up because she enjoyed the way he kissed. It had been before Leland Harper, if Phoebe remembered correctly, and Savannah had made a practice of sleeping with all of her costars.

"Chase kissed me." Phoebe didn't know why she said it. Perhaps it was the glass of wine she had already finished or watching the kiss on the screen that forced her to say aloud what she had been remembering for days. The bruising passion of Chase and his lips on her.

"What!" Lynn took the remote, paused the movie, so that Savannah and Rodger were frozen mid-kiss, and looked at her.

"Umm, why didn't you lead with that? So amazing. Is he a good kisser? I mean, he must be. He's just sex on a stick, isn't he?"

"Yeah," Phoebe sighed. She looked into her wine glass. There was no denying it. The kiss had been hot. Even now, at the memory of it, her whole body tingled, reliving the surge of electricity and lust that had shot through her while she was in his arms. She'd barely been able to think, glad that he had left her, but disappointed when he had finally gone.

"So it was amazing. Are you going to do it again?" Lynn was looking at her eagerly, her nose scrunched up, her face happy.

"I don't know. It's complicated." How do you explain the fact that kissing Chase was a bit like reliving someone else's history?

"What's so complicated? You think he's hot, he thinks you're hot. Shouldn't you just get together, you know, do the horizontal mambo?"

"Lynn." Phoebe threw a pillow at her, felling the flush crawl up her skin.

Lynn caught it neatly. "Ahh, I get it. You're not the type."

"What type?"

"You know, the casual, hot-sex type. And he probably is. I mean he's gorgeous, rich, has a boat. And not to mention all the women he's been linked with. Arm candy, every one of them."

"I know." Phoebe had come to that very same conclusion herself, after flipping through several websites devoted to the East Coast's social bigwigs. Chase Sanders had been a regular, a sailor with a girl in every port…or a different one for every occasion. He was a player plain and simple, and Phoebe, after being used for her personal connections all of her life, had no intention of becoming someone's arm candy again. No matter how delicious he might be.

"Still," Lynn continued, "there's always room for a fling. You know, the once-in-a-lifetime fling before you find Mr. Right."

"What makes you think there's a Mr. Right?" Phoebe asked.

Lynn smiled, looking completely self-assured. "Because there is. Everyone has a Mr. Right. Maybe you've just been dating the wrong guys, but you, especially, Phoebe, will find Mr. Right."

"You're such a hopeless romantic," Phoebe said, thinking that love was too complicated. Perhaps arrangements, with chemistry were a better way to go. Still, even casual flings took too much energy, energy that could be better put into her work and career.

"Love makes the world go around. Or at least hot sex keeps it rolling. You should totally go for it. You're not dating anyone. What do you have to lose?"

Everything, Phoebe wanted to say. Lynn had her pegged. There was nothing casual about her and from the moment she had seen Chase, she'd been attracted to him, with just a look from him sending her body into somersaults. And since he had flown out of Ivy House so fast that he'd barely said goodbye, she didn't even know if the kiss had meant anything to him at all.

"I don't even know if he meant anything by it," Phoebe said.

Lynn rolled her eyes. "Girl, you always know." With that, she resumed the DVD player, and Savannah and Roger Dailey's passionate embrace was interrupted by the sound of a gunshot.

Chapter 23

It was the Queensbay annual flea market and the bargain hunters, dealers, and junk sellers were out in full force. The sun was shining, with just a few of those super-white, cotton-candy clouds darting across a perfectly blue sky. A band was playing, there was the smell of coffee and grills going, families with kids dashed around, and groups of girlfriends prowled the tables.

Chase had bided his time after leaving Ivy House the other day. The force of what he felt for Phoebe, what he wanted to do to her, had him holding back, seeing if it was just some sort of madness, some sort of weird reaction to kissing the granddaughter of the woman who had been his first crush.

Perhaps there was some sort of residual lust build-up in the house, because all Chase had wanted to do was pull Phoebe to him and kiss her, run his hands over her long, lithe body, feel what he could do, how far out of control he could push her. Because that would be it. He had wanted to throw her down on that old steamer trunk, break through her air of studied casualness, and find what had to be a red-blooded woman below it.

But he sensed that while it might have solved a momentary itch, Phoebe was a more complicated woman. She didn't trust him yet, and until he could prove that he wanted her, just her, she wouldn't be ready for what he had in mind.

So, he had done his research. It wasn't hard to figure out that she would be here. It was one of the town's biggest events, held on the stretch of grass and parking lots near the town dock and marina.

Chase saw Phoebe first, catching a glimpse of the red-gold hair, standing tall in the crowds. A smile creased over his face before he could stop it, and then he wondered what madness had him so happy to see her, a woman who'd not too long ago called him an arrogant son-of-a-bitch. Perhaps it was the way the sun caught the highlights in her hair or the way her cheekbones cut across her sculpted her face or the happiness that danced in her eyes.

He knew it well. "What are you after?" He slipped up behind her and put a hand on her elbow. She jumped in surprise, turned to him, and felt a tingle of anticipation at the changing expressions on her face. Surprise, delight and then the well-schooled look of indifference.

"What do you mean?" She tried to move back, but he was enjoying the feel of her, the way her body was pulled taut, full of tension, but not necessarily directed at him. No, her attention was elsewhere. He hazarded a look over his shoulder to see which table she was focused on.

"Don't look," she hissed, her blue eyes going dark, as she grabbed to spin him around in the opposite direction. He felt his skin go afire at her touch and an answering reaction between his legs. *If the woman had any idea how much she turned him on,* Chase thought, *she wouldn't be grabbing him like that in public.*

"Ahh, I knew it. So what are you after?" Chase looked over his shoulder again and watched sheer panic light up her eyes.

"Stop, you'll give it away." Her voice had dropped to an urgent whisper.

"I will, if you tell me what you're after," Chase said, pulling her closer to him, laying her arm on top of his.

"Owl salt-and-pepper shakers."

"Owls?" Chase was confused, but was enjoying the sensation of having her close to him. She was so intent on her prize that she seemed not to have noticed how close they were, the way she was letting him lean into her so that he could see the clear blue of her eyes, count the freckles on the bridge of her nose, and take in those full, wide lips, lips that he desperately wanted to kiss again.

Her eyes widened and she stiffened. "Oh, no, you don't." Her breath had become slightly ragged and she was leaning away from him.

"Don't what?" Chase feigned innocence.

"I know what you're trying to do."

"And just what am I trying to do?" Chase countered.

"You're trying to mesmerize me with your big hulking presence." Her eyes flitted around. "Damn," she said.

"What is it?" Chase asked with amusement.

"That old biddy is looking at my salt-and-pepper shakers."

"Your salt-and-pepper shakers? The owls?" Chase said.

"Yes, the owls. They're ceramic and in prime condition."

"And let me guess: they're only a dollar each and you're worried someone else is going to steal the deal of a century."

"They're five dollars apiece," she answered loftily.

"Oh, my," Chase said with mock horror.

Phoebe made a face. "You just don't get it."

"I'm willing to be enlightened."

"Owls are going to be big next season. Those are perfect. The perfect inspiration pieces," she said.

Chase did hazard a glance over his shoulder now, and saw the pair of owls, only a few inches tall, gaudily painted in tangerine, brown, and that peculiar avocado green from the seventies. There was an older woman, gray-haired, dressed in tan polyester pants, a white cotton blouse, and a visor, poking around the other items on the table, but he could tell it was just for show. Like Phoebe, she wanted the owls.

"I think I can take care of this." He spun on his heel and sauntered over to the table, ignoring Phoebe's cry of protest.

Chase smiled at the redheaded woman who was behind the table. He asked about an old beer sign, effectively blocking out the gray-haired woman who started to hover anxiously.

He examined the sign, made a big show of it, and then made his offer. The redheaded woman pretended not to be interested, so Chase took off his sunglasses, flashed a smile, and sealed the deal. He half-expected the lady in the visor to cry foul, but she just sniffed and wandered off.

Chase promised to come back for the sign and took his other package, walked over to Phoebe and handed her a bag with two objects wrapped up like miniature mummies in tissue paper.

"What's this?" she said, suspiciously.

"You can thank me later," Chase said, laying his arm across her shoulder.

Phoebe brought the bag up, poked around, and said, "You didn't."

"I did."

"How did you do it? I mean, what did you do? Pay full price for them?" Phoebe's voice carried a tone of disapproval.

"I simply made her an offer she couldn't refuse. The owls were part of the package deal."

"What package deal?"

"I got a great new beer sign for my man cave—and you have a pair of tacky owl salt-and-pepper shakers."

"They're not tacky!" Phoebe started to protest. And then she laughed. "OK, so, they're a little tacky. But you wait and see. Owls will be huge next season. How much do I owe you?"

He was seduced by the sound of her laughter. It was genuine, unaffected, and directed at him. He felt his heart soar and wondered how he could convince her to kiss him again.

"Like I said, these were part of the package deal. They're on me. Anything else you got your eye on? I'm a master negotiator."

"Yes, I've had some experience with that." He expected her to go cold on him again and wished he hadn't reminded her of how they met.

Instead, she smiled up at him, a flirtatious slant to her eyes. "There's an interesting vase three rows over, with a couple of ladies circling."

"Is it overpriced?" Chase asked.

"Absolutely," Phoebe said, her eyes crinkling up at the corners. She'd let him keep his arm over her shoulder for a while and Chase wanted nothing more than to snuggle her in closer to him, feel the heat of her body connect with his, brush his lips along the side of her face. He needed to stop thinking like that, he told himself. Otherwise, he would embarrass both of them in a very public place.

Still, he had her here, carefree and relaxed, and he wasn't going to lose that advantage. It was time to shake up Phoebe Ryan's expectations of him.

"Lead the way."

<<>>

Phoebe was painfully aware of the way the sun caught the lightened hairs on Chase's forearm as he shifted the gears of the Porsche. His presence overtook the car and she cast a quick glance at his profile. It was just about perfect, with a straight nose and strong chin, and when he threw her a quick look, one eyebrow quirking up as he accelerated up the hill, she felt her breath catch.

They had spent the entire day at the Queensbay antique fair and flea market, and true to his promise, he had negotiated deals for everything Phoebe wanted. It had become a game between the two of them, with Phoebe picking something outrageous and obviously coveted by more than one shopper. Each time, Chase had managed to get what she wanted, usually for half the price. Sure, he often wound up with something else, like a barstool to go along with his vintage beer sign, but Phoebe had gotten everything she'd had her eye on.

She had insisted on treating him to hot dogs and root beer, and now, with the trunk stuffed full of stuff—at least with what could fit—they were heading back to Lynn's house.

Phoebe knew that she shouldn't have let him drive her home, but Lynn, with whom she'd gone to the fair, had been paged into work early, and Chase had promised to make sure Phoebe would get home safely. He'd let his hand linger on Phoebe's back just a moment too long and her mind had gone blank, while her stomach tightened; she didn't have it in her to argue.

Now, when he looked at her, his sunglasses dipping just low enough so she could feel his gaze sweep over her, she felt everything tighten and a rush of excitement. His hand shifted gears and brushed along the side of her leg. Lust shot through her and she shifted in her seat, but not before she caught his triumphant smile.

Phoebe looked out the window at the green trees and houses flashing by. Suddenly, the air in the car had become too hot, too still, so she cranked the window open a little, breathing in a deep breath of fresh air, trying to clear her head.

Too soon, or not soon enough, he had pulled into the crushed shell drive of Lynn's house. The sun was starting to set, and she could see it cast its sparkling trail along the harbor in the distance. Before she could do it herself, Chase was out of the car and opening her door.

He held out a hand and pulled her up. She sprung up with such force that she wound up close to him. Deftly reaching behind her, he shut the door. Still, his arms were around her and his face was very close to hers.

"Thank you," she managed to whisper. She could see the stubble on his face and the way his eyes darkened when he looked at her. "I had a nice time," she managed to stammer.

"A nice time?" he said with mock hurt. "Two of those whatchamacallem—topiary urns—for fifty bucks and you call that a nice time?"

She smiled and he caught her chin with his hand. She closed her eyes, overwhelmed, and when she opened them, she saw that he was looking at her intensely, his eyes searching, pinning her down.

Phoebe couldn't—wouldn't—let this happen. Chase was dangerous for her. She wanted him too much. And lust was never as simple as it was made out to be. Today, though, had been fun. It had only shown that he considered business, even if it was bargain hunting at a flea market, a blood sport. And that was all she was to him. Something to acquire.

He moved in and Phoebe felt the warm, smooth metal of the car beneath the small of her back. His chest was so close to her, she could feel the heat of it, sense the solid wall of muscle that was beneath his shirt.

Chase moved in closer, his lips hovering above hers. Before she could say anything, his lips trailed along her jaw and she felt her knees weaken. How could he make her feel this helpless, this wanted with just the lightest touch?

His leg nudged in between hers and she felt the strong, smooth strength of them, felt his arousal, and his lips found hers and she opened herself up to his kiss. Her hands came up to his neck and pulled him into her.

She didn't know if they stayed that way for a minute or five or fifty. She only knew that their mouths and tongues explored each other, each nibble and kiss and reaction matched the other's, until Phoebe felt as if she were melting, that if she did not have his warm, strong hands all over her, she would combust. Then, she felt something else.

Something that purred and then vibrated, then rang and pierced their consciousness. Swearing, Chase pushed back from her, dug in his jacket until he found his phone. Not taking his eyes off her, he answered it with a terse "Yes."

Phoebe waited for her heartbeat to slow, for her heart to find its way back into her chest, for her knees to stiffen up. She looked down at the ground to find time to recover, let her hands smooth her ponytail back into place, all the while feeling her breathing grow more regular.

Chase put the phone back in her pocket.

"I have to go. Something's come up." He was looking at her intently, his eyes roaming over her like he wanted to possess her.

Quickly, he walked to the trunk, popped it, and took out the bags with her purchases. He placed them carefully on the side of the drive, and then he strode over to her, pulled her to him, and kissed her again, a hard, passionate, bruising kiss.

"Interrupted again, Phoebe. But I will be back. And don't try to tell me you don't want this any less than I do."

And with that he flashed his playboy grin, slung himself into the car and was off, the tires sending up a small trail of dust that settled slowly back to the ground.

Phoebe managed to make it to the first step of the porch before she collapsed on it, her mind spinning. What was she thinking, letting him kiss her like that? Again. Once she could understand, but she couldn't make a habit of kissing Chase Sanders. Of course, it was just lust, had to be.

Phoebe took a deep breath and heard the cry of a hawk, saw it circling overhead, looking for its dinner. Savannah had told her, warned her that men would use her, try to use Phoebe to get to Savannah. But Savannah was gone. And here was Chase Sanders, using all of his playboy charm on her, getting her to relax and like him, winning her over with five-dollar salt-and-pepper shakers, charming her pants off or trying to at least.

She leaned her head against the column of the porch railing, sighing. Because just a few minutes ago, she would have given a damn about history and been perfectly ready to have her pants—and just about everything else—charmed right off her.

Chapter 24

Chase had to take care of a manufacturing problem. It meant most of the night on the phone with a factory thousands of miles away. He'd had to head back into the office and when he was done, it was too late for him to head back to Ivy House, so he went right up to his own apartment at the hotel, a suite of rooms he'd fashioned into a bachelor pad when he'd bought the marina and the Osprey Arms. He had a long bank of windows overlooking the docks, and room service whenever he wanted. Even though it was late, he was too keyed up to sleep, so he poured himself a glass of single malt and sipped it while he sat in the dark and took in the view of the water.

He hadn't been able to stop thinking about her. Even when he was yelling and cajoling, his mind had slipped into wild fantasies. Not just of kissing of her, but of much more. Just how would her long, lean body look without one of her little v-neck sweaters? Or how her red-gold hair would spill across a pillow, or the way her supple legs would wrap around him as he rode her into wild release.

Or the way her eyes had flashed when she had laughed at him today, challenging him to track down ever more ridiculous items. The trouble he had gone to for a pair of pink-and-white-striped napkin rings. And it had all been a pleasure. Phoebe had been relaxed, her guard down, not eyeing him with distrust or keeping her distance.

He had been able to, for a moment, see the world the way she saw it, as a canvas of color and form, a palette of inspiration. She had been able to clearly explain to him how some of the things would influence her and how others just spoke to her, and she had enjoyed the hunt, the seeking of offbeat beauty, talking with all of the different dealers, learning where things had come from.

Chase shook his head. He wanted her; of that, there was no doubt. He had felt something the moment he'd walked into the house and there had been that odd feeling of recognition. True, she had looked a lot like Savannah Ryan that day, but she was as far from a movie star as could be. Phoebe was a jeans-and-sweater type of girl, who craved pretty, but not necessarily glamorous things. She could find a use for anything; even turn an ugly duckling into a swan.

He let himself breathe deeply, imagining the smell of her shampoo, the floral and citrus scent mixing with her distinctive aroma. What he wouldn't give to have her here with him right now.

Easy tiger, he told himself. He'd started out on the wrong foot with her and she was as prickly as a cactus. But still, if she thought to deny her attraction to him, she was crazy. She was a terrible liar and couldn't bluff worth a damn. She wanted him just as much as he wanted her. Chase glanced at his watch. The sun would be up soon and he hadn't slept.

He had a few things to do before he was ready for his next meeting with Phoebe Ryan.

Chapter 25

Phoebe awoke from a pleasant dream. It took her a moment to orient herself. And then she blushed. She had been having one of those dreams. Her face and body felt warm, suffused with blood, and there was an ache between her legs. It came back to her in bits and pieces, the dream, flashes of a dark head and blue eyes, the almost real feeling of his lips on hers, his hands stroking her, arousing her.

She pulled the covers up and buried her face into them. *Oh God,* she thought, *I am turning into a horny teenager.* The idea that an imaginary Chase Sanders, with his arrogant grin and big sexy hands, could have done that to her was just too much.

Before she could think more about it, her phone buzzed. Reaching for it, she tamped down disappointment when she recognized the number.

"Dean," Phoebe said, hoping the embarrassment didn't come across in her voice.

"Well, it seems like you have been a busy little bee," he said. It was cheerful, but Phoebe detected an undercurrent of disapproval.

"Oh," she said, grasping for words. She had left the window up and cool morning air filtered in, bringing her heart rate back to normal. The wild dream of last night receded.

"You saw the press release?" Phoebe had allowed Chase and his team to issue one. A brief notice that North Coast Outfitters and Ivy Lane Designs were collaborating on a new collection. Luckily, no one would pick up on the connection between her and Chase. But still it was out there, a flag in the sand, so to speak, that Phoebe was declaring for herself.

"Yes, I wish you had told me. I would have been happy to negotiate on your behalf," Dean said smoothly. Phoebe heard the clink of china and realized that Dean was already up, fully up, even though it was still very early on the West Coast.

"Well, thanks for the thought, but I did OK," Phoebe said. The terms had seemed fair enough; but then, she hadn't really asked for more, pushed, seen how much Chase was willing to give her. Dean was like a shark; he would never have acted that way on behalf of his client.

"Glad to hear. It's a good thing," he said, "I suppose. I am still working on wearing CallieSue down and knowing that you've moved on might be just the thing to make her want you back."

"Dean," Phoebe began. In truth, she hadn't thought once about losing the job to work on CallieSue's new line of country accessories and home goods. She had been too focused on and excited about her own business and designs to think about anyone else's.

"I know, I know, you said to leave it be. I wasn't sure that heading out there was such a good idea, but who knew you would sign a business deal." He laughed again, but Phoebe had the sense he was dodging the point. Dean was probably sitting in his ultra-modern apartment, high up, with a commanding view of the city.

"Well, I think it's good for me. The house is wonderful," Phoebe hedged. It still needed a lot of work, but she was getting there. "And I've been feeling really creative, full of energy." Inspired, though Phoebe didn't say that.

"Well, I just want you to be careful, my dear. I checked a bit on the company you've signed on with. I hope you aren't dealing directly with the president, a Chase Sanders. He seems to have quite the reputation for himself."

Phoebe felt herself bristle at the implied warning. "He's not anything like the papers make him out to be..." she began, and then realized that she didn't know him that well at all.

"Ahh, so it was a personal deal," Dean said. "Listen, Phoebs, you know I am just looking out for you. I don't want you to get taken advantage of again." He said it gently, kindly and Phoebe felt her irritation slip away. Dean really did look after her; he always had.

"I know, I know," Phoebe acknowledged. "And it's just business, nothing like it was with Garrett. I mean, I have nothing to offer him besides my pillows."

There was a pause on the other end of the phone and Phoebe waited, hoping that Dean wouldn't say anything that would make it awkward between the two of them.

"Well, I am sure you know what you're doing. And, well, now that you have a new job, I'm sure you'll be back here soon working again."

Phoebe laughed with him, not having the heart to tell him that she wasn't sure whether she was going back. She could work wherever she wanted to, at least for a while, and the thought of not hopping on a plane and heading back to Los Angeles was becoming more and more appealing.

<<>>

Her morning, after the phone call with Dean, went well. At least she meant it to, having every intention to focus on work. She'd made a great start on the collection for North Coast Outfitters, but she was fiddling with the first designs, doing her best to get them perfect. Memorable. Unforgettable.

"Don't be alarmed." Jake, the floor guy, popped up in front of her, a bacon-and-egg sandwich in one hand and the other hand clutched around a steaming cup of coffee. Phoebe was so startled she almost dropped the empty mug of coffee that she had been on her way to refill.

"Is there a problem?" Phoebe asked. Chase strolled in right behind Jake, hands stuffed in the pocket of his jeans, looking totally at ease in a leather jacket. He had on his expensive sunglasses, which he removed as his dark eyes gazed around the place.

"We're almost done," Jake said to Phoebe's unanswered question. "I know it still looks bad, but this is a messy job. I need another two days for the upstairs. And then you can really start to move in."

One more night. Lynn's mother had offered her the guest bedroom on a permanent basis while the floors were being done, but so far, she'd been able to stay in the house. Jake, since he was Chase's floor guy, was giving her a deal, which meant he worked on her house in between his other jobs.

"It looks beautiful." Chase gestured towards the living room. Phoebe had picked the darker stain. The wood had been restored beautifully and the floors gleamed, looking sharp and clean. Unfortunately, it only made the paint look more dingy. Phoebe wanted to take her time picking colors, and this way she could live in the house and restore it at the same time.

"Really, it does," Phoebe agreed. She supposed another night at the Masters' home was a small price to pay for perfect hardwood floors.

"Great." Jake took another bite of his sandwich and spoke around a mouthful. "Why don't the two of you get out of here so we can finish up?"

Phoebe couldn't help herself, gazing up the stairs, to the landing, and the attic piled high with the remnants of Savannah's life.

"Don't even think about," Jake said, watching her gaze. "You can't walk up there."

Phoebe laughed and held up her hands in mock surrender. "OK, I get it. I'll get out."

She thanked Jake and walked out the door into a beautiful spring day. She sensed Chase's presence behind her, but did not turn.

"So, fancy going for a sail?"

"A what?" Phoebe turned and looked at Chase. He was making a habit of just showing up and she could see he was serious, completely serious.

"A sail. You said you liked boats. Mine happens to be at the marina, and it's a beautiful spring day, with a nice breeze. There's a deli that will make us some nice sandwiches, a couple of sodas, maybe a glass of wine?"

"Are you sure this isn't just a chance for me to check out your sheets?"

Chase smiled, and she felt heat shoot through her. "As I was trying to tell you that night, I think there's a gap in the market. Boat sheets are boring, bland. And you, I mean, your designs seem anything but."

"So it's another business meeting?" Phoebe challenged.

"We boaters like to call it a pleasure cruise." He was joking, a cheesy-looking leer on his face. He topped it off with a wink and Phoebe had to laugh. But she felt her breath hitch and flame of desire lick through her as she gave serious consideration to the fact that she would be alone on a boat with him.

"Is it going to rain?" The sky was clear, but she could see a sort of haze settling over the harbor.

"Not until much later. Right now, it's a great day out." He'd pushed back his sunglasses so she could see his eyes gazing down at her, and she knew he wanted her to say yes. Phoebe hesitated for a moment, her brain screaming at her to say no, that she should go find someplace to hunker down, open up her laptop, do some work, but her body was sizzling with electricity, the thrill of being near Chase, of wanting to be near him.

"Fine. But I get to steer," Phoebe said.

Chapter 26

She had run upstairs to pack a bag and then dropped it off at the Masters' house, briefly telling Mrs. Masters where she was going.

"A sail. Isn't it supposed to rain?" Mrs. Masters said, glancing at the sky and then back towards Chase who had walked in with Phoebe.

"Oh, I think it will hold off. We should be fine," Chase said and then shifted uncomfortably from foot to foot. Mrs. Masters was giving him that look, the look moms used to give him when he came to pick up their daughters.

Phoebe came downstairs wearing khaki shorts and a collared shirt tied at the waist. A fleece was thrown over her shoulders and she had a pair of sunglasses and her camera.

"We'll be back later," Chase said, trying not to be obvious in noticing the way Phoebe's shorts showed off just about every inch of her long, tan, golden California legs.

He saw Mrs. Masters give him a look, so with one eyebrow raised and a smile, he turned on all of his charm.

"I promise I'll have her back in one piece, before sundown," Chase said, pulling his eyes away from Phoebe's thighs.

His charm worked. Mrs. Masters gave them some cookies and shooed them off. Chase drove them back down to the marina, where he ordered some food from the small deli near the docks. His boat was well stocked with water, soft drinks, and, as promised, wine and beer.

Chase wanted to put his arm around Phoebe and tell her that he wouldn't bite. Not unless she asked him to. But she seemed intent on keeping a distance between them, as if their kisses had never happened. Still, he felt a faint stirring of hope when he caught her looking at him speculatively from underneath her lashes while pretending to browse through the postcard rack in the marina office.

Perhaps she wasn't as cool as he thought. Ice queen was the thought that had come to mind when he'd first met her, but after their kiss, he'd had to rearrange his thinking. She had been more like a fire demon, the way she had moved into him, arousing all of his senses, the way he had wanted the kiss to last forever, how he wanted to run his hands over her body, touch her, feel her. Each time, all rational thought had fled from his mind. Well, he'd had a few of them, like how he could get her alone and under him in a house without a lick of furniture and a pile of old boxes.

"Find anything?" Chase asked, his business taken care of.

She held up a picture of a large building that looked out over the water, a huge Victorian building, covered in lacy white trim, looking a bit like a wedding cake.

"The Queensbay Show House," Chase said, a small smile ghosting across his lips.

"Savannah used to perform there in the summer. I think that was when her agent was trying to revive her career."

Chase raised his eyebrows as he took the postcard for a moment.

"I know. It didn't really work. She never did have the best singing voice."

"Did you ever see her perform in one of her shows?"

Phoebe nodded, her blue eyes sparkling. "Not here—in Los Angeles. Still, it was a bit like magic. My nanny took me, but I got to go backstage where everyone was getting ready, see all these half-dressed actors sitting there, putting on their makeup. It's old and huge and bright and dark, all at the same time, and it was possibly the most exciting place in the whole world for a little girl."

Chase felt his heart tug. She had been lighthearted and free during the flea market, but she hadn't talked about her past. He realized he liked it when Phoebe let her guard down, when she actually talked about herself. He could almost see the little girl she had been, watching the chaos and excitement that was backstage.

"I bet you had your best dress on."

Phoebe laughed. "And I got to eat M&Ms and drink a Coke during intermission. It was a little slice of heaven."

"Well, then, let's go."

"What do you mean? It's been closed for years," Phoebe said.

"I meant we could sail past it. It will have to do, but there's a great little cove past there that we can tuck into and have our lunch."

Phoebe put the postcard back. "Sounds good."

Phoebe might have been more comfortable as a swimmer than a sailor, but she knew how to handle herself on a boat. He watched as she hopped lightly aboard.

"Do you want me to stow this for you?" she said, pointing at the canvas bag packed full with their lunch.

"That would be great," he told her and got busy readying the boat for cast-off. They would motor out of the marina area and out into the wide expanse of Queensbay Harbor. The wind was coming off the land, so they would have a nice clear run up to the Queensbay Show House and then make the trip into Pine Cove. The cove was a decent-sized inlet off the Sound, deep enough for them to be able to go in, nice and protected from the wind and waves, anchor, maybe even take the little dinghy to shore and wade along the sandy shoreline.

When everything was safely stowed below, she hopped onto the dock, untied the mooring lines, and elegantly jumped back aboard. He powered up his engine and his forty-foot sailing cruiser moved away from the slip. Chase guided it out into the channel and towards open water, loving the feeling of the wind ruffling his hair, the smell of the tangy salt water assailing his nostrils.

"Don't worry, I'll let you take the wheel when I set the sails," he told Phoebe, but she merely nodded.

It was warming up and the pale pink of her shirt showed off the light tan of her skin. She looked content, sitting back on the cockpit seat, her head turned up to catch the sun.

It took more than a few minutes motoring slowly to make it out to open water. He gave the wheel to Phoebe, told her which direction to point the boat in, and got his sail up. In a moment, it snapped, caught the wind and the boat picked up speed.

Chase came back down in the cockpit and stood next to her. He felt her tense as he put an arm out to help her correct her course. When she had it, he cut the engine and there was that moment of pure, glorious quiet, the only sound a whisper of wind, and the smooth swish of water beneath the bow.

<<>>

Phoebe watched him move around the boat, capable and confident. He looked as good in a pair of rolled-up khakis and polo shirt as he did in his jeans and t-shirt, and she found herself focusing on the pull of his muscles beneath the fabric of his shirt.

He touched her and her body tensed, but it was only a hand on hers, to help her point the boat in the right direction, and as soon as he did, she felt the boat leap to life below her, surge forward on the power of the wind.

Now he was sitting down, stretched out, hands behind his head.

"Aren't you going to watch where we're going?"

"No, that's what you're here for," he said with a smile.

"But I could hit something."

He shrugged. "It's the middle of the week, early in the season. I bet we have the water all to ourselves."

Phoebe looked around. The harbor was quiet, its high banks covered in a blanket of leafy trees, the sun sparkling and dancing on its surface.

"I guess we'll be safe."

"Just don't get too close to shore." Chase settled in and for all the world looked like he was going to nap.

Phoebe watched him for a moment and then nudged him. "Not fair. I didn't know you were going to make me do all the work."

"Work? You call this work?"

Phoebe sighed, looking at the harbor, at the houses nestled among the trees, at a bird, a hawk probably, flying overhead.

"No, this isn't work at all," she agreed.

"Told you nothing beats a sail for fixing what ails you." Chase sat up now and looked around. He scooted over and came and stood behind her, one arm coming around and touching hers. "A bit to the starboard," he said.

She had lost track of their course. She was supposed to be heading for the wedding cake. That's how she had always thought of the Queensbay Show House, a giant white wedding cake perched on the edge of the bank.

"I see it."

Chase was still behind her, close—too close—when he asked, "If you loved going to the theater, how come you never wanted to be an actress?"

"You mean like Savannah?"

"Exactly. You have the name, the face, and I am sure she would have opened the doors for you."

Phoebe swallowed, surprised that the memory could still pain her after all these years. Chase moved so he could see her.

"What is it? Tell me."

Lips pursed together, Phoebe shook her head.

"That bad?" he guessed.

"Worse," Phoebe admitted and then found herself smiling. "I was in first grade. We were doing a play, "Goldilocks and the Three Bears." I got to be Goldilocks, of course."

"Of course."

"Well, it wasn't just the hair. The teacher had figured out that Savannah was my grandmother and I think she held out the hope that if I got the lead, Savannah would deign to come."

"Did she?" Chase asked.

"Of course she did." Phoebe closed her eyes as the memory replayed itself.

"And..."

"I got stage fright, forgot my lines, and knocked down one of the walls of the Bears' house. Who knew Goldilocks was a comedy?"

"That sounds pretty bad. But you were just a kid."

"And I knew I wasn't cut out for it. And Savannah knew too. You know what she said?"

Chase shook his head.

Phoebe's voice changed, becoming richer, more ironic. "Don't worry, dear, the theater will survive quite nicely without you."

"Ouch," Chase said, but he was smiling, his teeth white against the tanned skin of his face.

"Well, it was the best thing that could have happened to me. I never had delusions of making it as an actress. Savannah helped me find my other talents. She was very encouraging that way. She's the one who kept sending me art supplies and books, even bought me my first computer so I could use a graphics program." Phoebe's voice had dropped back into her own.

"So, she wasn't the prima donna the press made her out to be?" Chase's voice was low, a dangerous growl, but she could sense the humor in it.

"Well, like I said, she was more like an Auntie Mame than an Auntie Bess, but I guess she did her best."

Surprised, Phoebe found her eyes tearing up. She'd been so focused on taking care of Savannah, of sorting through things, that she had put her memories of Savannah far away.

"I always thought she was more like a fairy godmother than a grandmother. I could never call her Grandma. She made me call her Aunt Savannah. I mean, she was absent and forgetful, but then she could be generous to a fault.

"And now?" Chase asked.

"I miss her, but she was so sick at the end. Cancer. But I feel like in some respects, I never really knew what made her tick. She was an actress to the end, playing a role, keeping her secrets."

Chase laughed. "Well, everyone has those. Do you know that my grandmother didn't love Leland?"

"Well, of course she didn't."

"No, I mean before he ran away with Savannah. She thought she loved him, but they didn't love the same things. Leland liked the big life. My grandmother was more of a small-town girl."

"So?" Phoebe didn't know where this was going. So far, they had avoided the fact that their grandparents had been lovers.

"Well, let's just say Leland wasn't leaving a happy marriage behind. Or perhaps that Savannah didn't have to do much to get him to come."

"You know, Savannah always said he was the love of her life. It wasn't easy, but I think they were really, deeply in love. Passionate and stormy, but it was more than just an affair."

"And is that what you think love should be?' Chase asked, his eyes dark as he looked at her.

Phoebe shook her head. "No. I think that's the kind of love that doesn't survive. It consumes people, makes them resent each other. Savannah was a passionate person, but she could be passionate about many things. I think she could claim Leland was the love of her life because she didn't have to spend the rest of her life with him."

She glanced away, out over the water, swallowing before she continued. "My parents loved each other and I don't remember stormy at all. They seemed happy. Like my mom would smile when my dad came home early and my dad's face lit up when he saw her. They could count on each other. I think that's what love is."

"So no dark and stormy for you?" Chase's voice was dangerously low, and Phoebe looked at him for a long moment before she replied.

"I think dark and stormy could have its place, for a while."

Chase gave her his lopsided smile. "Good to know."

He'd taken off his sunglasses and his eyes were boring into her, laying her bare, and Phoebe felt a shiver run through her. She never should have told him so much and wished he wouldn't look at her that way. It made not thinking about that kiss all the more difficult.

"There she is." They sailed past the Queensbay Show House, which almost looked like it were about to pitch into the water. There was a large hand-lettered banner across the front, which read "Save the Show House."

"Guess it's fallen on some hard times."

"Yeah." Chase's hand was on her shoulder and he squeezed it. It was a simple, friendly gesture, but her body didn't respond that way. She wanted to move away, but here she was trapped in a boat, with not a lot of room to hide.

The Show House slipped behind him and Chase took over the wheel. He handled the boat through the channel out into the Sound, gliding past a long pile of rocks that guarded the entrance. Chase headed east, and they sailed along the wide-open water for a while, until he turned again towards the shore. He switched on the motor and she took the wheel as he dropped the sail. He came back and maneuvered them into a narrow passageway that opened up into a wide-open cove, ringed by marsh and trees. It was beautiful, Phoebe thought, and peaceful. A few houses ringed the shoreline, but it was quiet. She savored the calm, trying to drink it in, wash way the nerves she was feeling every time Chase's arm brushed against hers.

"They put this all together pretty quickly for you," Phoebe said. They were eating lunch, an array of bread, cheeses, and sandwiches set out before them. Chase had appeared with a bottle of cold white wine, and Phoebe accepted a glass, as much to settle her nerves as anything else.

"Nothing beats a sail and a picnic lunch. Hard to do it, though."

"Why?"

Chase shrugged. "Work, life. You get older, busier, seems like it gets harder and harder to take a couple of days off to go sailing."

"What about your girlfriends?"

"Girlfriends?" One of Chase's eyebrows quirked up.

"You know, the ones you're always photographed with?" Phoebe asked pointedly.

"Ahh. Well, those. Somehow, I never seem to meet any who actually like to go sailing. They all say they do, but they think I mean on a motor boat. Once they realize that you have to do some work and that the cabin on any boat can be a bit cramped and that it's not all that glamorous, they always seem to get out of sailing."

"Guess you've been seeing the wrong ladies."

"If that was your way of asking if I am seeing someone right now, the answer is no. And, you, of all people, should know that the media has a way of exaggerating things."

"So you're not quite the playboy you've been made out to be."

Chase shrugged. "Let's just say those pictures are pretty much the whole story. I go out, I get photographed, and then my companion and I part ways, the press to the benefit of the both of us, but no further strings attached."

Embarrassed and relieved at the same time, Phoebe looked out at the water. She saw something swimming, a little head poking above the water, leaving a v-shaped wake. Once it got closer, she saw that it was a turtle. The little guy swam right past them, not even sparing them a glance.

"Ah, hell." She looked up and saw that Chase was looking at the sky. The clouds they had noticed before had rolled in, piling up with dark gray underbellies.

"Is it going to rain?" The words were barely out of her mouth when one large, fat raindrop fell into the cockpit.

"Here, get this stuff below," Chase said. "I'll take care of the sail."

Phoebe felt the wind getting kicky too, tossing the trees that ringed the cove, the light undersides of the leaves dancing in the wind.

She gathered up their lunch and brought it down to the table in the cabin below. She dashed back up, grabbed the bottle of wine and their water, and pulled down the hatch as soon as the rain began in earnest, a great sheet of soaking water.

Phoebe stood in the small galley, setting up their lunch again on the small table, while the boat rocked beneath her. Rain lashed against the portholes and she saw Chase's feet flash by. Then, there was a movement and he was in the cabin with her, big and wet. He was soaked to the skin.

"Ahh, you saved the wine. Nothing to do but to ride this out. I thought we had a bit longer, but the faster it comes, the faster it will pass by, I suppose. There might be some thunder and lightning, but I think we'll be safe here."

"I'm not worried," Phoebe said, though the boat gave a bit of a lurch, and she thought she heard a boom of thunder in the distance.

"Good. I'm going to find a dry shirt." He pushed past her towards the rear cabin, where the main bunk was. He didn't close the door and she could see him rummaging for a shirt, and then she got a glance of him as he crossed both arms over his back and hiked the shirt up. Muscles rippled in synchronicity, and she had a full glimpse of his flat stomach and the muscles that ringed it.

Phoebe felt her breath hitch and a tingle of lust shoot through her. No, she hadn't forgotten just how hot Chase was; she just thought that she wouldn't have to confront the shirtless proof of it.

Rain slammed against the porthole and then he was there, crowding into the small galley space. He reached behind her and poured a little more wine into their glasses. He was so close that she could feel the heat rising off him, smell his rain-slicked skin.

"We'll be OK," he said.

"I'm fine," she answered automatically, but she wasn't. Her heart was racing and her skin felt too warm. She half-turned, but found he had her trapped. She would have to push past him—touch him—if she wanted to get to the relatively open space of the cabin. Still, it was all so small, there was really no place to escape him.

"You're shaking," he said, his voice dangerously low, and she felt the reaction between her legs, aware she was thoroughly aroused by him. She made a study of him, taking in the dark, too long hair, his thick eyebrows, one of which had a faint scar under it; the tanned skin with the shadow of a beard on it and the way his shoulders stretched the fabric of his worn t-shirt.

"What are you nervous about?" he asked, and his hand moved closer to her. His hands were still on his hips, but now he moved them to either side of her, truly trapping her. She looked into his eyes and saw an answering need to her own in them. She had to look down and away, and her body shifted so she was against him, feeling his strong, lean legs brush against her thighs, and then the evidence that he was just as aroused as she was.

"This is a bad idea," she said, automatically. His hand came up and stroked the side of her cheek, and she shivered at his touch.

"It doesn't have to be." One finger caught her under the chin and lifted it up so he could look at her.

"You're beautiful," he said, his breath hoarse and he pressed in closer to her. She rose up to meet him and their mouths met. She found his lips and they took and tasted her, while one of his arms circled her and pulled her close. Phoebe moved her own arms up and around his shoulders, finding his neck and pulling in to him, the need to be close to him filling her desperately.

"Chase," she murmured.

"Tell me to stop now," he pulled back a moment and looked at her, his eyes deep, dark, filled with want, "while I can, and I will. I'll go up on deck and get us back to shore. Or…"

Want and need were coursing through her, and she could feel her desire for him rising in her. She shook her head and said, "Don't stop. We have a storm to ride out."

He spoke no more, but his mouth assaulted her, his tongue taking, testing, teasing, while one hand traveled down her neck, skimming her skin, until it found her breast. He cupped it, teasing her nipple, which responded to his touch, puckering beneath it, growing to fullness. Phoebe felt herself give a small moan and heard Chase's satisfied chuckle. Slowly, leisurely, his hand traveled over to her other breast, and he brought that one to arousal.

She kissed him harder, feeling him grow hard against her as his hand traveled down her shirt, to her waistband. His hand was as warm as fire on the bare flesh of her stomach. One of his knees pushed into her legs, spreading her open. His strong arms lifted her up so that she was balanced on the edge of the counter. He pushed in between her and slid a hand down inside her shorts, finding heat and her wetness. Phoebe moaned for him and wrapped her legs tightly around him.

She heard a small crash, realizing it was just the sound of a knife falling into the galley sink.

With a practiced, swift movement, Chase put both hands under her, pulling her close to him. She wrapped her legs around him and he pulled her back from the counter. In a few short strides, he had her in the cabin, throwing her gently down on the bunk.

Above her, she could see rain bubbling and dripping down the clear hatch cover, see that the world outside was gray. Inside, though, in the dim light, all she could see and smell was Chase, the mix of his soap and aftershave, as he pushed her back on the berth. He stood above her, and he took off his t-shirt, revealing the solid-muscled chest she had only glimpsed before. She sat up and ran one hand over his chest, the slight dusting of dark hair, tracing it down to the waistband of his pants.

Chase stopped her, took her hand and kissed it, then nibbled on her fingers. "Take off your shirt," he said, and Phoebe, after the merest hesitation, peeled it off.

Before she could cover herself, he stopped her. "Let me look." She felt emboldened under his scrutiny, and she reached behind her and unclasped her bra, throwing it off to the side.

Chase smiled at her and his hands skimmed across her breasts, bringing them to life, her nipples tightening further under his touch. His other hand found her shorts, and he undid them, pulling them off her, taking his time. Well, her body ached for him.

He was above her, knees on either side of her, dark and handsome. He caressed her breasts, kneading them so that her back arched. Her hands came up to reach for him, and he took them, pulled them over her head, pinioned her there, while his mouth found one nipple, then the other. One hand trailed down her body, finding the thin scrap of fabric between her legs. He moved there, and Phoebe knew he could feel her heat, her need. Slowly, teasing, he brought his hand inside her, and she bucked with pleasure.

He touched her then, finding her spot, while his mouth ravaged her body. His fingers kept pushing her to the peak, a wave building and building until she was there, her body writhing and twisting underneath him, his weight pinning her, until she reached it, reached the crest and let it wash over her.

She opened her eyes, saw him watching her, his hands lightly stroking her. She saw that he was ready for her, his pants straining. Phoebe sat up, her hair spilling across her shoulders and pulled him towards her, opening his zipper, pulling down his underwear, until he burst free.

She stroked him and his eyelids fluttered as he bent down to kiss her, his knees spreading her apart. His hands moved over her, bringing her back to arousal, as he slid himself into her, testing, gently, as she pulled him towards her, and he thrust into her, the two of them rocking together, the boat bobbing in the waves underneath them as he brought her again to the edge, their rhythm driving them both to the edge. This time Phoebe kept her eyes open, as Chase's eyes gazed into hers, as they both went closer and closer. Her hands wrapped around his back and when he came, she went with him, both of them tumbling down the sweet sea of pleasure.

Chapter 27

Chase opened his eyes. He was on his back, staring up at the roof of *Windsway*'s cabin. Phoebe was half next to him, half on top of him, tangled around him. He could smell the flowery scent of her shampoo, the slightly spicy whiff of her perfume. She moved and one of her breasts grazed against his chest, and he felt himself grow hard again.

He ran a hand through her hair, while his other hand trailed down her back. She shivered against him, the movement sending waves of desire over him.

"Wow, babe," he said, and she turned to him, so he could see her eyes, which looked more green than blue in the light. Above them, he could see that the skylight was less wet and that the dark gray seemed to be giving way to a lighter sky.

Her hand lay on his stomach and he could feel it sliding, stroking.

"So that was good?" He thought he detected a note of satisfaction in her voice.

"Good doesn't quite do it justice," he said and was rewarded with a pleased smile. His heart jumped a little at that, and he realized that the thought that he had made her happy, made her feel pleasure, made him happy. It was a new sensation for him. No one had ever complained about his lovemaking. In fact, with most women, he was more concerned about how much he enjoyed himself. But he had a need to please Phoebe, to drink in every bit of her long, lean body, feel her move and cry out with pleasure underneath him, know that it was all because of him.

"The boat's not moving as much," Phoebe observed.

Chase squinted through the porthole. "Looks like the storm is passing by. We may even see some sun." The water was calmer now, and the *Windsway* barely moved beneath them.

"I guess that means we could go home now," she said. Her hands were still roaming over his stomach and then they dipped a little lower, and he felt himself ready again, ready to have her, this time to take her slowly, lazily, to watch her carefully, to see her enjoy every minute of it.

"We still have a few hours of daylight left," he said, pulling her on top of him. He kissed her and she returned it, her hair falling down in a gold curtain around him. He rose up and pulled her closer to him, his hands teasing her breasts, lightly pulling her nipples until she threw back her head in pleasure, arching and bowing her back as he slid lower down, finding her sex again, urging her on, higher and higher, until she was almost at her peak. Then he slid into her, holding him tight to her, and thrust into her, watching her eyes fill with pleasure and heat.

She arched her back and grabbed his head. His lips raked down her neck and to her nipple, and he teased it and pulled it tight in his teeth as she called out his name in pleasure. Resting his hands on her hips, he held her tight as she rode him to the crest of a powerful orgasm. He waited and watched until he sensed she was near, could feel her closing like a hot velvet fist around him, see in her eyes as she came. Then, as she crested, he allowed himself to come, following her over the edge until she sagged into him, spent, and he fell back, dazed.

Chapter 28

Dark was falling as they motored into the Queensbay Marina. The weather had broken, treating Chase and Phoebe to a magnificent sunset, the sun streaking the sky above the water a rainbow of purples and reds. They had fallen into a comfortable silence after they had finally decided it was time to return, Chase giving her directions as she guided the boat, while he took care of the sails and coiled lines.

Phoebe loved the feel of the wind ruffling her hair, the way her body felt relaxed, sated. The sex had been some of the best she'd ever had—nope, make that the best she'd ever had—and when Chase came down to stand next to her, one of his strong hands settling on her to help her steer the boat, she sunk into him, loving the feel of him, the presence of him comforting her.

They docked the boat together, with help from a friendly deck-hand, and as Chase checked the lines, they heard a voice calling them.

"There you are," Lynn said as she came up to them. "Nice boat."

Something in her smile had Phoebe guessing that Lynn had a pretty fair idea of what they had been up to. Luckily, dusk was settling and it hid the flush that was spreading across her cheeks.

"My mom sent me down," Lynn said, apologetically. "She wanted me to invite you both to dinner. I texted, but with the storm and everything, you know, she got a little concerned. Typical mom."

Phoebe wouldn't know, but she wasn't upset. It was strangely nice to be worried about, even if she had been in capable hands. She sent a look to Chase and he answered with one of his own.

"So, dinner?" Lynn turned to Chase. "The Randalls are coming."

Chase looked at her, then laughed. "Noah's coming?"

"Yes. Noah and his wife are big donors to the hospital and the clinic, so my parents wanted to thank them. When Noah heard Phoebe was staying with us, he wanted to make sure you were back in time for dinner."

"I'm sure he did," Chase said drily.

"I don't know," Phoebe said, hesitating, feeling nervous. She wasn't sure she was ready.

"My mom promised to be good," Lynn whispered.

Chase jumped down lightly on the dock. "A home-cooked meal. Sounds great." He held out a hand for Phoebe and she looked at him. He was standing there in his khakis and a fresh polo shirt, looking perfectly relaxed, like he hadn't just spent the afternoon doing that with her.

With Lynn grinning at her and Chase offering her his hand, Phoebe had no choice but to take it.

Chapter 29

Dinner was surprisingly normal. They'd pulled into the Masters' house and Chase took a beer from Lynn's father. The two men sat on the back deck overlooking the water, talking boats and sports.

Phoebe had run up to her room to change and freshen up, trying desperately to get the "I've just had the most amazing sex of my life" look off her. Her lips were swollen and her cheeks reddened from where his stubble had roughened them, and when she looked in the mirror, all she could think about was them, naked and twisting.

She splashed water on her face, changed into a sundress, sandals, and a sweater and ran down to help in the kitchen. Lynn shot her a look and there was a knowing smile on Mrs. Masters' lips, but neither one of them said anything as they brought drinks and appetizers outside.

The Randalls had arrived by then. Noah was almost as tall as Chase, but with light brown hair. Caitlyn gave Phoebe a hug, explaining to Noah that they had run into each other in town. She was wearing a sundress and Phoebe could see that she was glowing, whether from her condition or the way Noah's gaze lingered over her, she couldn't tell.

Chase introduced them and Phoebe could feel Noah appraising her with his eyes, while one arm held his wife close. Apparently, she passed because he smiled and shook her hand easily. The sun was setting, turning the water into liquid gold, and a light wind rustled the tall trees in the Masters' yard. It was a great view and Lynn had snuck in and changed the playlist on the radio to something fun and upbeat.

Chase made room for Phoebe to sit next to him and she did. His arm lay casually across the back of the settee as they made conversation.

"So," Caitlyn said, sipping a club soda, "how are you enjoying our little town of Queensbay?"

Chase's knee brushed against her, and Phoebe had to fight to keep her attention on Caitlyn. "It's very relaxing," she answered.

"Glad to hear it. Chase said you've started work on the house. How is that going?" Phoebe nodded. "Yes, that's the plan, at least."

514

Phoebe wasn't quite sure what else to say, since she didn't know what she planned to do with it.

"Hey, Phoebe," Lynn said, sitting on the arm of one of the wicker couches, "the clinic is running a kid fair soon to raise money. Think you could run the art booth for them, you know, since you're creative and all that?"

"It's for a great cause," Caitlyn said, her hand unconsciously rubbing her belly. "Noah's agreed to be in the dunk tank."

"That I've got to see," Chase said, punching his old friend's arm.

"Only if we take turns," Noah said.

"Hey, Chase, maybe North Coast Outfitters could donate some things, to use as raffle prizes? It is for a good cause." Lynn said hopefully.

"Lynn, you're hopeless," her mother said, as she passed around a plate of hors d'oeuvres, but Phoebe could tell she wasn't upset by her daughter's forthright comment.

Chase laughed. "Well, if Phoebe's in for being creative, I suppose I'm in for some dough. Just don't make me finger-paint." There was the general sound of laughter, and Dr. Masters reappeared with fresh beers for the guys and more white wine for Lynn and Phoebe.

Phoebe caught the look that had passed between Caitlyn and Lynn, plus Caitlyn's knowing wink, and knew that one of the goals of the dinner had been to get her and Chase to agree to help out with the fair. She guessed that Lynn knew it wouldn't hurt to have the granddaughter of Savannah Ryan running a booth. The girl was relentless when it came to protecting and guarding her clinic, she had to give her that. At least it was for a cause Phoebe could get behind.

The rest of the evening passed quickly, with steaks and salad eaten al fresco, laughter, and good conversation. Noah and Chase even told a few stories from their days at school, which had even Dr. Masters roaring with laughter. Phoebe felt alive, a warm glow suffusing her, from the good food and the company.

She saw the way Lynn's parents looked at each other with affection and the way Noah was overly solicitous of Caitlyn and her comfort. There was no fiery passion here, just warmth and love. For a moment, Phoebe's heart constricted and she knew this was what she wanted, more evenings like this, sitting out by the water, surrounded by friends and family.

She hazarded a glance at Chase, saw him laughing at something his friend said and wondered if he could ever want the same thing. He wasn't a settling-down type and was cynical about love. Would he want to be sitting with her here, a year from now, hanging out on Ivy House's own terrace, listening to music, laughing with friends, or would she already be old news to him, another one in his long string of flings? Though he had made it sound like he wasn't as bad as everyone thought.

He caught her looking at him, and he flashed the smile, the one that made her toes curl and her stomach clench. She held his gaze and she could feel herself frown, the sadness growing on her face. Before she could dwell on that anymore, Lynn pulled her into a movie trivia game against her mother and Caitlyn.

"That was awesome," Lynn said at the end of the game. Phoebe had won hands down, easily beating Lynn's mother, who was shaking her head in disbelief.

"I've never beaten her," Lynn said. "Not once."

Caitlyn laughed, but Phoebe could see that she looked tired. Noah wandered over at that moment.

"I think it's time I took my wife home." Noah thanked the Masters and then turned to Chase. "You heading back to the village?"

"Yes, in a moment," he said. He too thanked the Masters, told Lynn to give him a call about the kid's fair, and then turned to Phoebe. They stood awkwardly. She was aware that everyone seemed to have drifted off to give them some privacy, but Phoebe kept her distance.

"I had a nice time," she said, her voice even. He looked at her, a strange smile playing on his lips. He glanced over her shoulder and then took a step towards her. When she began to move back, he pulled her into his arms and covered her mouth with his for a hot kiss. He broke away and whispered in her ear, "I feel like a teenager saying good night to my prom date."

His head gestured and Phoebe turned. Mrs. Masters was hovering, her motherly instincts kicking into overdrive.

"Not at my prom," Phoebe whispered. "I was eighteen and a legal adult and no one cared what I did or who I did it with."

"Does that mean you'll come back to my boat with me?" Chase asked.

Phoebe took a step back, remembering what she had felt earlier. She and Chase had an undeniable attraction, which they had officially satisfied. And that was it. It had to be. They couldn't possibly want the same things. She had to be careful here; otherwise, she would get hurt.

"Not tonight," Phoebe said.

"You're sure you don't want to see where this takes us?" Chase said, his look smoldering into her.

Phoebe jerked her head in the direction of the Masters' house.

Chase glanced over her shoulder and Phoebe could all but feel Mrs. Masters' concerned gaze boring into her. "Perhaps tonight is not the best night for it." He agreed, and she felt a rush of disappointment.

"I could always sneak out after they've gone to bed," she said as she leaned up into him, "...come meet you."

"Tempting as that may be, I don't think you'll get far. Until next time?"

His lips brushed quickly and fiercely against hers and he was gone, disappearing into the dark of the night, towards the street, his car, and the short drive to the marina.

Chapter 30

Chase could kick himself. He tossed and turned in his bed, thinking how easy it would have been to go back and wait for Phoebe to slip out of the house. She was a grown woman and he was a grown man. Neither of them were teenagers, but he knew that Dr. Masters wouldn't go for it. He barely let his own daughter out of his sight, and he wasn't going to let Phoebe go wandering off either.

She had seemed happy tonight. A bit skittish at first, sitting there with his friends and with Lynn, but later she had begun to relax. He wondered if she could be happy away from her life in Hollywood. Queensbay wasn't exactly a backwater, but glittering parties and palm trees weren't a part of their repertoire. Would dinners at the Yacht Club and afternoon sails be enough for her?

Chase wondered why he was worried about that. This afternoon had been intense, more than intense; it had been the best sex of his life. He wasn't a choir boy, by any means, but he'd certainly been pickier than he'd let people believe when it came to actually getting into bed with a woman. Sure, the image of a playboy suited him and his company: a sailor with a girl at every port. The image had been created a long time ago to help him get endorsements for his sailing career and it had seemed to work when he took over North Coast Outfitters.

But it meant he generally met a certain kind of woman. Tall, athletic, gorgeous, but usually with an agenda, one that included using him to help themselves. Phoebe was the first whose arm he'd had to practically twist to take his help. And she was making it difficult by not allowing him to use her connection to Savannah. Still, he could understand her desire to make it on her own.

Chase tossed the covers off and got out of bed. He wasn't going to sleep anyway. Pulling on a pair of jeans, he walked into the living room and threw himself on the couch, where he could look out and see the water. The lights of the marina were dimmed now, and boats bobbed peacefully in their slips. It was calm, quiet, and well ordered, and when he had come here as a kid to work in his dad's store, he had dreamed of this. Of looking over it all and wanting it, wanting it to be his. And now he had it. But it just wasn't enough anymore.

He scrubbed his hands through his hair. It was almost morning: time for him to get up, maybe take a run, work out some of these kinks.

Truth was, it wasn't enough anymore because he wanted something more. Sure, he thought it had been the house, but once he had seen her, all of a sudden, it had been her. He wanted Phoebe Ryan, in his bed, but now he wasn't ready to let her go.

As the sun rose, its rosy fingers painting streaks in the gray dawn sky, he smiled. He had a plan. Every good sailor needed a course, a strategy to get from A to B, to win the race. And if there was one thing he was good at, it was taking his time and working a plan.

Chapter 31

"Sorry about dinner last night," Lynn said, shaking her head. "Would you believe me if I told you it was Caitlyn's idea?"

Phoebe pushed the coffee table out of the way and kicked the rug so that it unspooled across the sheen of her newly refinished floor.

"Really? I hadn't guessed."

Lynn scowled at her sarcasm. "Yes, she wanted to get to know you a little better. And get you and Chase to help out with the fair. She's great, but a little relentless when it comes to making things happen. Not that I'm not grateful, since the clinic needs every penny it can get, but, well, I wouldn't want to say no to her."

"Glad I didn't," Phoebe said, and she was. She was happy to help.

"Nice rug," Lynn said, "but I don't know why you want to put all the furniture down when you still have to paint."

"Not all the furniture." Phoebe pushed back a strand of hair that had escaped from her ponytail. "Just enough so I can live here and move out of your spare bedroom. Besides, it's good to live in a house for a while before deciding on the paint. You need to see how the light plays in the room."

Lynn laughed. "Well, when I finally move out of my parents' house and into my own place, promise me you'll give me some decorating advice. I spend all of my time in baby-blue scrubs and around vomit-green walls. I'll need all the help I can get."

"Color is easy," Phoebe said absently, her mind drifting.

"I don't suppose you found any lost treasures up in the attic?"

"I've barely had time to go through it." Phoebe had been busy working on the designs for North Coast Outfitters and handling the existing orders for business.

"There's no time like the present." Lynn jumped up.

"What are you talking about?"

"Please, I'm totally dying for a chance to poke around Savannah's old stuff."

Phoebe hesitated for a moment. It was her stuff to poke through if she wanted. She'd been avoiding it, unsure if she was ready for what she was going to find. Phoebe took one look at the expression on her friend's face. It was so eager.

"Get ready for some dust," she warned her as they made their way up the stairs and to the attic.

"Wow, Savannah really was a packrat," Lynn said, as she moved a stack of old clippings aside. "Look, a bra." Lynn held up a black lacy number.

"Ugh. That must have been from a movie. I don't think she would have kept it otherwise."

"Yeah, but which one? There's nothing in here that says which one."

Phoebe walked over, looked at the bra, then looked at the stack of clippings. "See, these are all reviews of *The Black Orchid*. It was a throwback to film noir. The bra was probably a part of it."

Lynn closed her eyes, "Oh, yes, now I remember. Wasn't she the fallen lady with the heart of gold?"

"Something like that. So, I guess the black bra was an integral part of the costume."

"You know, sewing up knife wounds may not seem that glamorous, but at the end of the day, I'm glad I don't have to sit around in my underwear in front of a million people," Lynn said.

Phoebe shook her head. "Never seemed to faze Savannah. And she could pick up any object in her apartment and tell you what movie it was from, who her costar was, whether it was a hit or a flop."

They were quiet for another minute, before Lynn asked her.

"Are you going to tell me about it or make me use my imagination?"

Phoebe groaned. "Was it that obvious?"

Lynn nodded. "Absolutely. If I hadn't fallen asleep so early last night, I would have gotten it out of you then. So..."

Phoebe couldn't help the smile that stretched across her face. "It was pretty unbelievable." Just the memory had a smile flooding across her face and heat spreading across her body.

"Wow. And you let him walk off last night? You didn't go back for seconds."

"I think it would have been thirds. Or fourths," Phoebe said, failing to keep the smugness out of her voice.

"Argh, you're killing me. Not really. Keep talking, just because I work crazy hours and barely have time for a shower, let alone a date. I need my vicarious thrills."

"Like I said, it was pretty unbelievable. But somehow I don't think your mom was too keen on me slipping away with him for a night of steamy sex on his boat."

Lynn rolled her eyes. "Yeah, moms can be like that, even when they're not your own." As if realizing what she said, Lynn's face contorted. "Man, I am so sorry. I shouldn't be complaining about my mom…"

"…when I don't have one," Phoebe finished for her lightly, trying to put Lynn back at ease. "Don't worry about saying the wrong thing. You shouldn't be sorry for having a mother, even though she sometimes annoys you, just because I don't. That's life."

"Wow, you sound so serene about it," Lynn said.

Phoebe laughed. "Therapy. I had a lot of it after they died. And then one day, I realized I had to keep on living and so did other people. And it's sort of nice to know someone's looking after me. I think it probably kept me from making a mistake."

Lynn snorted. "What sort of mistake is Chase Sanders?"

Phoebe didn't know what to say. Sex with Chase had rocked her world. It had never been like that with anyone else, the physical sensations. But there was more. More to him and to the sex. She was afraid she was getting entangled.

"It's funny," Phoebe said. "All my life, guys have been into me because I was related to Savannah Ryan. Struggling actors, wannabe playwrights, even my old boss—they all thought there was something more to me because I was related to someone famous."

Lynn sat on an old steamer trunk. "OK, so I get it. You had your own weird version of groupies. But what does that have to do with Chase?"

Phoebe looked at her and there it was like a sucker-punch in the gut as she said it aloud. "I think Chase might be the same way."

"What do you mean? He doesn't seem that way."

"Associating with the Ryan name would be great for his business. I told him I didn't want Savannah's name mentioned, at least until everyone can judge my work for what it is, but I know he thinks I'm being foolish. I don't think he can resist the allure of the romance of the century—the modern-day version—at least from a marketing perspective."

Lynn looked at her, so Phoebe pulled out her phone.

"My friend sent this to me," she said, as she called up the headline. "Déjà vu—Ryan Revives Famous Love Nest." It's short on details, but it talks about how I inherited the house and am intent on bringing it back to its former glory. It goes into Leland and Savannah."

Lynn took the phone from Phoebe and scanned through the article. "So?" she asked.

Phoebe took her phone back and glanced at the article. "It might only be a matter of time before someone makes the connection between this house and the fact that Leland Harper's grandson lives in this town. And then it will be romance of the century, part two."

"And you think that's a bad thing?" Lynn asked.

Phoebe shook her head. "It would be if Chase was behind it. I told him that I didn't want to be known as Savannah Ryan's granddaughter anymore. I have to stand on my own two feet, on my own talent."

"Surely you don't think?" Lynn asked.

Phoebe shrugged. She hadn't had a chance to ask. And besides, Chase had promised he wouldn't, but perhaps he couldn't be trusted.

"For what it's worth, it totally seems like he's into you," Lynn said carefully, taking a sip from her water bottle.

Phoebe leaned back against a box. "I don't know. Maybe." She looked at the picture again. She wondered how the press had gotten onto her efforts to restore Ivy House? And would this be the last of it? The story did mention Ivy Lane's website. She'd already seen a jump in orders today. Perhaps, it would be good for business to play up this angle.

Lynn shook her head. "I don't know, but I think the way he keeps showing up here, finding you at the flea market, buying all of that stuff...I think he wants to be with you. Phoebe Ryan—you—not anyone else."

Phoebe wanted to believe her friend, she really did.

Chapter 32

Chase found her, after dark, in the attic. Phoebe looked up, startled, hearing the tramp of steps and then was reassured when she heard his voice calling up the stairs. She had forgotten to lock the door again, and there was Chase's head popping up into the opening of the attic.

She had turned on the light and plugged in one of the lamps that was lying around, so she hadn't noticed it growing dark outside. Phoebe was annoyed that so much time had passed—she had meant to see what the light looked like in the living room around dusk. She felt herself filled with nervous anticipation when Chase fully emerged into the attic.

"You've been busy," he said, by way of a greeting.

She looked at him, standing there with his hands shoved in his pockets, rocking back and forth on his feet, looking like his usual cocky, assured self.

"I brought dinner. Chinese, I guessed," he said, still smiling, "Since you didn't bother to answer your phone or reply to my texts."

She shrugged. "Chinese is fine," she answered coolly.

"What are you doing?" he asked, one eyebrow arching up.

She had to swallow to bring her body under control. Had she really thought that just once with him would be enough? That she could respond to him calmly, rationally.

"Just sorting through some old things. Savannah left a treasure trove of stuff here."

He came over closer to her and she could smell him, his warm dusky scent.

"Is that a photo album?"

He took it from her. "You do look a lot like her, you know."

Phoebe nodded. "My poor mom. She was dark, but my dad was light. I got all of the Ryan genes. Whenever I was with Savannah, people thought I was her daughter. She liked that better than being called a grandmother. Always concerned with what people thought."

"Is that why you're against using her name?" he asked.

"Savannah lived and died by what the public thought of her. She was obsessed with it. She let them paint her as a home wrecker, a bitch—a slut, even—if she thought it would keep them interested. She was always the actress, never herself, because she was always playing a part."

Phoebe looked up at Chase, who was holding her tight in his arms. "I don't want to do that. I don't want to be someone's publicity piece or be used to sell something. I want to be myself. The papers will take anything and turn it around. You'll say it doesn't matter, but if it starts to make you money, you feed into it, you let it happen because you think it's for some greater good. And what's more, people believe it. The most outrageous things, they'll believe, and then you start to buy into it."

"If they want a show, give it to them."

"Exactly," Phoebe said, looking down. Her hands were dirty and she probably had dust smudges on her face. "But I don't want to be the show."

"Hey," he said, catching her chin in his hand, "what's bringing all this on?"

"I told you I'm not an actress, Chase. I'm Phoebe, not Savannah. I'm not some sexy blond bombshell with a smart mouth and a plucky sense of courage."

He smiled. "I like you just the way you are. Sure, I liked Savannah's movies, but unlike all those Hollywood types, I can separate fact from fiction, and, Phoebe, I know the real deal when I see it, when I feel it."

"No," she said in frustration, "I'm just a private person. I don't like being used." She pulled out her phone and showed him the article from earlier, about her and Ivy House.

He glanced at it and shrugged. "It didn't come from me."

"That's it." Phoebe felt a flash of anger. "How can I be sure I'm not being used? You told me yourself that you do things all the time for publicity's sake."

"Used? You think I'm using you to further my business?" His voice rose a bit, and he put both hands on her shoulders and pulled her close to him.

"You're the one who drew up the contract," Phoebe pointed out, her voice sounding breathy even to herself.

"And I changed it. Before we had sex. So, I wasn't using you then. Or would you like me to tell you that I am using you?"

Phoebe gasped as his lips brushed against her hair, nipped at her earlobe. "For your body, that is, 'cause, babe, you have one hell of a body. And your hair. I can't forget your hair. Or your lips," he had whispered. "I know I am definitely using you for your lips."

Phoebe felt her body respond to his words, the heat starting between her legs and spreading throughout her. It was just one article, one of the minor gossip sites, easy to forget.

"I guess being used isn't so bad," she said as his lips brushed along her jaw.

"Feel free to use me back. Whenever you want. Because what happened yesterday was pretty good, better than good. I would hate to see all that go to waste because you're afraid I'm after your famous name or your house."

"You're not after the house?" Phoebe managed to breathe. "Or my name?"

"Babe, I thought you knew what I'm after," he said, pulling her into him, nudging her legs apart as he pushed his leg in between them. She tightened over him, feeling heat lick through her.

His hands slid around her shoulders.

"Then we should give them something to talk about, don't you think? Give them a real show, ride this little thing to the end," she said, wanting it, wanting him.

Unbidden, Phoebe wrapped her arms around Chase, and he pulled her close, his hands fisting in her hair.

"I missed you," he said when he came up for air, and his sapphire eyes held her, turning her into liquid on the inside.

"I was right here," she told him, and then words and thoughts left her as his hands found the tender flesh of her breasts through the thin fabric of her t-shirt. She responded to him as he touched and tugged and pulled.

"Do you have a bed yet?"

"Second floor," she managed to breathe out, as his hands cupped her bottom and he swung her around.

Suddenly, she found her feet leaving the floor as he lifted her up and over his shoulder. In a flash, he was down the attic ladder, and she had a vision of her hallway swirling before her as he found the right door. They were in the bedroom now, where all she had was her bed, a dresser, and boxes.

Chase had found the master bedroom with ease, the only door on the second floor with light spilling out of it. He nudged the door open with his foot and headed for the bed, just a lumpy futon. He lowered Phoebe onto the comforter and stepped back. She reached for him, but he stepped out of the way, surprising her.

He let his eyes roam over her, from the way her red-gold hair spilled over the pillows, the way he could see her nipples ready for him underneath the thin fabric of her t-shirt, to the way her jean-clad legs seemed to stretch on for miles.

Her blue eyes were bright, alight with desire and her hands reached for him again. He took them, held them, holding and kissing her long, elegant fingers one by one.

"We have no need to rush this time," he told her.

"I thought you had dinner waiting?" she teased.

"I plan on feasting right now," he said as his hand circled her belly button and brought on a shiver of pleasure. Chase wanted to take his time with her, and savor every moan, shiver, and bit of pleasure he could give her.

"Last time, it was fun."

"Fun?" Phoebe sat up, ready to be offended.

"Fun. But I don't think I got to take my time, really figure out what makes you tick." His hand brushed in between her thighs, and even through the thick fabric of her jeans, he felt her body respond.

"That works," Phoebe managed to say, as his hand hooked the waistband of her pants, and he pulled her towards him. She tried to reach for him again, but he moved out of the way.

She sat up and he lifted her shirt off and tossed it on the floor. His hands cupped the lacy fabric of her bra and he brushed his hands over them. Phoebe's back arched and Chase unhooked her bra, tossing it to the side. Her breasts sprung free and he lowered his mouth to feast on them, feeling her come alive beneath them. Her hands held him close, and he started on the button of her jeans.

He took a moment, breaking free, and peeled them off one leg at a time, until she was naked except for her lacy cream underwear. He touched there, felt the evidence of her arousal, and peeled those off too. She was naked before him and he stroked her, watching as her head fell back and her hips rose to meet him.

Phoebe had never felt so wanton, so full of desire. So far, Chase had used nothing but his mouth and his hands on her, but her whole body was alight, tingling from his touch. Her hips angled up to him, as he stroked her sex, while his other hand brought her nipples to attention and his mouth ravaged hers, his stubbled skin brushing against the sensitive surface of her cheek.

Her fingers found the buttons of his shirt and she managed undo them, and she let her hands roam along his back, his chest, and his flat abdomen, and then she dipped below, found that he was aroused, hard for her, but still he kept up his assault, demanding that she do nothing but let herself be taken, and she did, riding the waves of pleasure until he slipped inside her and she wrapped her legs, pulling him deep inside of her, clenching around him, matching his rhythm as she moaned his name and he answered with hers. Then, she tumbled down into darkness, her body releasing as she felt his release wash over her.

Phoebe lay still, very still. Chase was on top of her, a dead weight that did not seem to want to move. His arm was on her stomach and she gently tried to wiggle free.

"Sorry," he said and rolled over to the side, pulling her close to him. His hand stroked her hair and his mouth nibbled on her shoulder.

"I suppose that was worth the wait," Phoebe said after a moment, after her heart stopped thudding quite so fast and the blood had receded from her ears.

His arms encircled her, pulling her in tight and close and, for a moment, Phoebe felt that she could stay like this forever, in the circle of his arms, happy and satisfied.

"It was for me," he said, his teeth nipping at her ear.

Chapter 33

They got cold. And hungry. Night had fallen and the breeze from the open window had become downright cold. She felt herself shiver, and Chase got up, pulled the throw from the bottom of the bed over her, and started dressing. Her heart sank at the thought of him leaving, but she tried to keep her face from showing it.

He only buttoned two buttons and pulled his jeans up, leaving the top undone.

"Where are you going?" she asked.

"I heard your stomach growl."

"Did not," she started to say, just as it did so again.

One eyebrow went up.

"I'll bring it up here," he said. Phoebe looked around. Her comforter was a custom silk one that she'd designed herself and had shipped to her. As romantic as eating in bed sounded, she couldn't bear the thought of anything happening to it.

"Oh, no you won't." She pulled the blanket around her and swung her legs out of bed, hunting for her clothes. "No eating in bed."

"Doesn't that depend on the menu?" he said, pulling her to him. She wasn't sure that they would make it downstairs, but then her stomach growled and he let her go.

"I'll go set everything up," he said and bounded from the room. Phoebe watched him go. The expression on his face was like that of a very happy puppy.

She took more than a moment, running a quick shower and finding a pair of casual linen pants, a fresh t-shirt, and sweater to wrap herself in. The hot water sluiced over her, and she tried to clear her head. It means nothing, she told herself. She shouldn't let herself get too wrapped up in him. It couldn't be permanent. Not for him, and that was what she wanted. Sooner or later, someone was going to get hurt. But for now, she told herself, just enjoy the moment.

When she went downstairs, she found that Chase had made himself useful. He'd moved the kitchen table into the dining room and found candles. He'd opened a bottle of wine and set it out amid the takeout cartons.

"I didn't know what you liked, so I got a little of everything," he said, appearing in the soft candlelight. Music was playing, probably Coldplay, and even without a rug or curtains or a fresh paint job, all of a sudden, it felt right, Phoebe thought; it felt like home. Her breath hitched and her heart lurched. Home. It was what she had been trying to find for a long time.

Chase held out the chair for her and she glided into it. "We have moo shu, lo mein, chicken, and broccoli…"

Phoebe went for the moo shu, while Chase seemed to be happy with a lot of everything. It took a while before he brought up the attic.

"I thought you'd be busy arranging furniture."

"So did I. Lynn wanted to poke around Savannah's things and so we did."

"Did you find anything interesting?" Chase asked.

Phoebe shrugged. "Nothing too out of the ordinary. Just those old photo albums."

"Savannah's?"

"And some from my parents, from before I was born. I didn't really know where they went. Haven't thought about them in a long time. The pictures, I mean. It was weird seeing them."

"Why?" Chase asked.

Phoebe thought for a moment before she answered. "They were so happy. And in love. With each other. I remember it and seeing the pictures brought it all back to me."

"I'm sorry," Chase said, but it was more a question.

"Don't be. It made me happy. Sad too, but happy. Happy that they had that. It was so different from what Savannah and Leland had."

Chase's chopsticks paused midway between his plate and his mouth. "What do you mean?"

"My parents had a steady type of love. I don't remember them ever really arguing. Their relationship was even, steady. But then I think about Savannah and Leland."

"What about them?" Chase's eyes were dark in the candlelight, intently looking at her. Phoebe didn't know why she pressed on, but she had to.

"Their love was intense. Leland gave up a lot to be with her. Savannah even gave up her career for a while. It burned so hot, their love, it consumed them. He was jealous of her acting, but she couldn't not do it. In the end, they loved each other still, but they were at each other's throats. At least that's what all the stories said. It was like they were so on fire for each other, it burned them out."

It hung in the air between them. Chase looked at her for a long time, before he took her hand and gently pulled her towards him, up from the table, into his arms. She looked at him for a long time, staring at his face, and finally he stood up and she did too. She led him up the stairs and into her bedroom.

Chapter 34

Chase stayed the night. He had offered to go back to his apartment, but Phoebe had simply thrown him a look and pulled him towards her. She didn't want him to go, liking the warmth and strength of him. He didn't seem to mind, wrapping himself around her.

It was the weekend and they stayed together the whole time. He helped her move things from the shed into the house and watched as she rearranged. They went shopping for groceries, making themselves pasta. He lamented the lack of a TV, but she made it worth his while.

Monday morning came around and Chase had to go back to work. She sent him away with a bang and the house felt strangely empty without him, but she was ready to start getting to work. She had a contract to fulfill after all. There were also some phone calls and emails from Dean asking her when she was coming back. There were emails from her workshop asking if they should purchase more materials to keep up with the new orders. Her landlord was asking if she wanted out of her lease since he had another interested party.

While she had spent the last couple of weeks in a sexual fog precipitated by Chase, life was going on around her. Decisions needed to be made, decisions that had nothing to do with Chase Sanders and more about how she wanted to live her life. Did she want to run her business from Los Angeles? Her whole life had been there. She had never meant to make her stop in Queensbay permanent, had she? There was nothing to say that she and Chase couldn't keep their relationship going, for a while at least, cross-country. And besides, as Chase said, they were just riding this thing out, seeing where it took them.

So what to do? Phoebe sat in the room at the back of the house, her own little studio. In Los Angeles, she'd never had this much space and it was glorious to be able to walk, to pace, to think as she worked. She had seen pictures of it in the photo album. It had been fitted out like a country gentleman's study, with leather-bound books and dark wood. Now it was white, with gleaming floors and a row of windows that looked out over the backyard and the harbor. Phoebe had come to love this room and her ability to watch the light as it moved over the water.

Her new desk had come, and she and Chase had assembled it, laughing as they tried to figure out the instructions. It was huge, with plenty of room to spread out, and she sat at it now, letting her mind wander, just drawing. When she was done, she looked at what she had created: a pattern of concentric rings in bright pop-art colors. She smiled and pulled her laptop towards her. Ivy Lane was doing well, the mention of her restoring the house driving a lot of traffic to the site.

Things were starting to take off for her and it was time to get really serious. Perhaps, it was time to give Caitlyn Randall a call. She was, by all accounts, a financial advisor and a whiz with money.

The days passed. Both she and Chase were busy with work, including a quick business trip down to Florida for Chase. He was gone only a few days, but when he arrived, he had sauntered in, taking her to bed almost immediately. Then, he was gone until the weekend. The weather was beautiful and they took another sail, threw steaks on the grill, and shared a bottle of wine with Lynn and her parents.

Weeks went by and she and Chase slipped into a pattern. He would stay with her all weekend and then head down to work. They spent most of their time together at Ivy House, but she went to his apartment once, above the Osprey Arms.

"Why do you live here?" she asked. Room service had delivered some fried calamari, and they were eating it on the small balcony attached to his suite.

"I like to keep an eye on things," he said, dropping his eyes as he squeezed lemon on his plate.

"Eye on what? Surely, you get to see enough boats during the day from your office. You have a water view there."

He said nothing and slowly she put it together. "You own this. The marina, the hotel?"

"Yes. I own it. I have a manager, but it's a part of my holdings."

"So you're building up quite the little empire," she said. It made sense how the bartender had called him "boss" and the way her hotel bill had been suspiciously low.

"Sort of. I'm not bad at organizing things, figuring out how to give customers what they want, whether it's a new piece of foul-weather gear or a great place to bring their families for a summer cruise or to a hotel with a great view."

"Are you partners with Noah?"

Chase shook his head. "On some of the things. I was one of his first investors when he started his company. Then, over the years, I leveraged that to invest in some other things. Sometimes Noah joins in, sometimes my brother does, sometimes I do it alone. My brother, Jackson, he's working in New York now, but he comes out on weekends in the summer to sail and hang out. Hopefully you'll meet him?"

The question hung in the air. They hadn't talked much about the future and Phoebe didn't know if she wanted to.

"That would be nice," she said absently. She took a sip of wine as someone blew a foghorn, a signal for the launch to come pick them up.

"Do you always treat your investments like this?"

"Like what?" he asked.

"Wine and dine them?"

"Sometimes, I go out for business dinners," he said carefully, his fork hovering in midair. "I take a personal interest in all of my affairs."

"Affairs?" Phoebe didn't know why she was pushing. Everything was going well. She had been designing like mad, and Chase's own house design team was a dream to work with. He'd even sent Tory over to redo her website and now the orders were coming in, several a day. But her work for the collection was almost done. In another week or so, there would be no real reason to stay in Queensbay.

"I meant business affairs. In the most traditional sense," he said, humor lighting up his eyes.

She had begun to think that she could build her business from anywhere. She'd been ducking Dean's calls, knowing that if she told him what she was thinking, he would try anything to convince her to come back to Los Angeles. He'd been calling and texting almost daily since she had mentioned the deal with Chase.

She was starting to build a life on her own terms, but she wanted to be more than an investment to Chase, something he would hand off to be managed when she had fulfilled her end of the deal. So far, he'd given no indication that it was anything but smooth sailing, but then again, he hadn't asked lately if she were planning on staying or going.

"You're not jealous I discovered that new sweater designer in England, are you? I like her stuff, but I told you, she's an old salt dog, almost fifty, with a Scotsman for a husband. I feel like he's going to run me through with his bagpipes if I even so much as look at his wife."

Phoebe laughed. When Chase had told her that he was going to England for a few days, she had wondered what she would do if all his designers were given the same treatment as her. They had never talked about the status of their relationship as easily as they had slipped into it. She realized that she had just assumed Chase was a one-woman-at-a-time type of guy, but she had no proof.

"Hey, that's not jealousy I see, is it? Imagine, the fair-haired California babe being worried about some lady who knits sweaters in the dark and cold."

"Well, when you put it that way, but surely there must be others. You seem to have quite a stable of talent you're developing."

Chase shrugged, but his eyes were serious. "That's part of what makes North Coast Outfitters successful. Luxury and high-quality goods you can't get everywhere. It takes time and attention to do that."

"I know," Phoebe said. She felt restless. They were supposed to be meeting up with Noah and Caitlyn to listen to some live music at Augie's—Lynn, too, if she got done with her rounds—but there was something that was making her edgy.

"You don't think I'm stepping out on you, do you?" Chase asked, his voice low.

"No. I don't know." She was standing by the railing now, looking over at the bustle of the harbor below. The sun was starting to set and boats were streaming in to get settled for the night, couples were walking about arm in arm and kids raced up and down, playing or enjoying ice cream. It was a happy scene, full of life and Phoebe glanced up. Ivy House was just visible, its tall tower poking up among the trees that were now fully covered in their summer coats. Even from here, she could see that the house needed painting, one of those big-ticket items she had decided to put off. Still, it was there, a landmark, looking down over charming Queensbay, watching the town, protecting it.

Did she want to be part of this life? She could work from anywhere, she knew that, whether it was Queensbay or Los Angeles or some other place she'd never been to. But would she want to stay in Queensbay, in Ivy House, if Chase wasn't part of her life? She looked over at him. He was sitting there, his big frame at ease in the comfortable chair.

"Phoebe, I haven't been with anyone else since I met you...since before I met you and, more importantly, I haven't thought about anyone else. I know my PR department has tried to paint a different picture of me, but like I told you, that was just for show."

"Was?"

"Every sailor needs to find a home port," Chase said. He held out a hand and she took it, and he pulled her onto his lap, cradling her there.

He didn't say it, she noticed. He didn't say the words that she wanted to hear. Only promised her that he was being faithful for now. Phoebe swallowed hard and leaned her head into his shirt, feeling the steady beating rhythm of his heart. She had her answer. She was in love with Chase Sanders, a man who saw her as another one of his business investments. Savannah had warned her about giving her heart away too freely. But she hadn't ever, not to Dean, not to anyone. Chase had her, if he wanted her, but he'd never said he wanted the same things from her, from life, as she did.

"Are you OK?" he whispered into her hair. All of a sudden, she felt sick, her heart pounding, her stomach churning.

"No, you know, I think maybe I better sit this night out."

"What?" He pulled away from her, searching her face.

"No big deal, I'll just walk back to the house. You go, I know you were looking forward to seeing the band. So don't change your plans on account of me."

"But, let me drive you at least."

Phoebe shook her head, resolute. "No, I think the fresh air would be good."

"I'll walk you home. Do you want anything, soup or something? You barely ate anything."

"No, I'll be fine. You'll be late if you walk me home and, besides, if I don't feel better, I know a doctor or two."

She gave him no more time to think, but was already opening the sliding door into his living room, finding her purse, slipping into her shoes. He trailed after her, clearly puzzled, one hand running through his hair.

"Are you sure?"

She leaned over, gave him a quick peck on the cheek. "I just need some sleep, some rest. Listen, I don't want to get you or especially Caitlyn sick."

"I'll call you later." His voice trailed down the hallway after her as she moved quickly to the stairs, intent on getting out of there as quickly as possible.

The rest of the hotel passed in a blur and she emerged onto the sidewalk, breathing the fresh air, feeling the thudding of her heart in her ears. She was in love with a man who wasn't capable of it. How could she have let this happen?

Chapter 35

It took Chase a moment to spot her amidst the throng of kids surrounding her. She was at a booth and apparently making some sort of giant sculpture out of newspaper strips applied to a tower of blown-up party balloons. Paper-mache, Chase remembered from an art class long ago.

Her hair was pulled back in a sleek ponytail, and she was layering strips of soggy newspaper as the kids called out suggestions to her. She had a whole crowd of them enthralled or rolling on the floor with laughter. Phoebe looked beautiful, relaxed, unconcerned and in her element. Any of the shyness or the iciness he had seen was gone, focused as she was on creating and working with the kids.

She lifted one of them up, a little boy with shaggy blond hair and blue eyes, so he could slap a piece of newspaper strip on what was rapidly becoming some sort of not-so-scary monster. Overjoyed, the little boy clapped his hands, and as Phoebe set him down, she ruffled his hair.

Chase's heart clenched. It was at that moment that the sun emerged from the clouds and a shaft of sunlight shot down; Phoebe was momentarily suffused with light, and Chase felt the ground shift beneath him as his whole being attuned to her. He couldn't stop staring at her, feeling that this was finally the moment, the moment when he felt his world shift, the planets align, and stars shine brightly.

Phoebe was his everything. He always thought that love was something he wouldn't experience. It seemed like something for other people. He wasn't that type of guy. He was a wanderer, an adventurer. Women, in his mind, were wonderful creatures. They smelled good, they were fun to be with and most of them made him happy, at least for a short while.

But none of them, until Phoebe, had ever been able to make him feel alive. Sure, he'd had an adrenaline rush from steering a fifty-foot boat along in rough seas or from the thrill of concluding a business deal, but this was something different. Something inexplicable and heart changing.

"She's a natural." Chase was jolted out of his reverie by Lynn.

"What?" It took a moment for Chase to come back to reality.

"With the kids. Have you ever seen a dozen five-year-olds sit still for this long? And the monster was all her idea. Anyway, thanks for hooking us up with a tent guy. The fair benefits the clinic, so every penny saved is more for them. Thanks so much."

"My pleasure," Chase managed to mumble, his attention back on Phoebe. A natural. A creative, talented, beautiful, sexy woman.

Phoebe finally saw him, gave him a curt nod, and then her attention was caught by a little girl tugging on her hand.

Phoebe bent down to listen as the little girl whispered a suggestion that they make pointy teeth for the monster, but her mind was elsewhere. She wondered how long Chase had been there watching her. But now, he was there, giving her a look, something different from the usual steamy ones he threw her way. This one had been intense. It had been the look of a drowning man, who had just realized that the last ship had passed him by. But before she had time to dwell on it, the kids took up the chant of "pointy teeth, pointy teeth," and she was drawn back into the real world.

Phoebe packed up the last of the art materials into a large plastic bin. Her feet hurt and she was tired, but energized.

"That was a lot of fun," she told Lynn as they broke down the card table. Chase had disappeared after a while, and she hadn't seen him again.

"Thank you so much. It was our best year ever, so I hope that means that the clinic will be able to get some new equipment."

"Well, I'm glad you talked me into it," Phoebe said, taking a moment to stretch.

"Let me help you with those." Chase appeared beside them, a smile on his face. Phoebe looked at him, searching for the look he had given her earlier. He took her scrutiny in, but gave away nothing as they continued to clean up. They packed things away and it wasn't until he was walking her to the car that he whispered in her ear, "Let's go home tonight, just the two of us."

She didn't need to ask where he meant by home, but the thrill that shot through her, as he took her hand in his, wasn't lust; it was something entirely different, and she knew that as much as she had pretended that this was a casual affair, it no longer was.

Chapter 36

The moon was full and it came in through the window, suffusing the room with light. Phoebe sparkled like silver and he brought her to him, kissing her gently, sweetly. Slowly, he undressed her, reverently addressing her body with his mouth, feasting slowly and fully on her. Something had changed for him and he wanted to savor her. So far, whenever he had been with her, it had been wild and passionate, the ice queen with the fire dragon underneath. But tonight, now, he wanted to savor every minute of her. When she tried to rush him, he just shook his head and held her hands, letting his fingers brush over her, gently teasing and testing, watching her as the pressure built, knowing she was practically begging for release. Still, he decided to torment her a little more, taking his time as his hands roamed over her, as she writhed and moaned with pleasure.

Finally, she sat up and pulled him to her. "Now," she whispered, and when he smiled, she said, "Please, I need you."

He was undone then and he pushed himself into her slowly, feeling her hot wetness close around him, hiding him tight. He pulled in and out slowly, and as her hips rose up to meet him, he moved faster and she matched his rhythm. Thrust for thrust, they moved together in a slow, steady beat, pushing them higher and higher towards the edge. They reached it together and he gave one more moan and dove into her fully, and he watched as her eyes filled with pleasure. He held back no longer and followed her over the edge.

Afterwards, they lay together, and she fell asleep beside him, curled around him and, for once, he hadn't been thinking of the best way to disentangle himself without waking the woman next to him and making his escape.

No, instead, all he wanted to do was pull her closer to him, breathe in the scent of her hair, feel the rise and fall of her chest underneath his hands. He had stayed that way, unable to sleep, trying to understand just why he felt this way about a woman whom he'd only known a short time. This was totally different from what he had felt about the other women he'd let into his life.

Now he lay awake in the early hours of the morning, listening to the sway of the branches outside the window, hearing the sound of a warning buoy gently toll in the distance. He'd understood what she said about love. His own parents were reasonably happy, but he'd never given much thought to what he wanted. He had been too focused on winning at sailing and building his business to get entangled emotionally.

None of his other girlfriends had stayed long, and he'd grown tired of them long before he found some way to set them free gently or they'd wised-up and gotten out. Phoebe wasn't fragile or a delicate flower. She didn't need to be protected. She was self-contained. Talented.

Phoebe hadn't held back on him tonight. He'd finally had all of her; she'd given freely. He didn't want to let that go. That realization made him pull her tighter to him, causing him to kiss her hair, trace a finger down her bare back, relieved to see the way she murmured and turned, arched towards him.

Chase wasn't sure whether he'd ever have enough of her, the way her red-gold hair blew in the wind or her blue eyes sparkled when she found something she thought was beautiful or interesting or the way her nose scrunched up and her freckles blended together when she concentrated. He knew that he'd bought his way into her life. She wouldn't have stayed if he hadn't offered her a job.

He fought against that thought as he kissed the nape of her neck, running his hand along her spine, cupping her buttocks to him, until she turned, her eyes awake, her mouth reaching for him. Chase wrapped himself around her, nudged her legs gently open, and pushed all thoughts of tomorrow away for the moment.

Chapter 37

Chase rolled the living room rug up to the legs of the couch and draped a drop cloth over it all.

"What are you doing?" Phoebe said, appearing in the doorway. She had slept later than she had meant to and woken to an empty bed and the smell of coffee. She had brushed her teeth, but skipped the shower. Her phone had been lying on the table next to her and she flipped through it. That's when she had seen it.

"You said you're ready to paint in here."

"You're painting?"

He looked at her. She had wrapped her robe tightly around her as if that could be her armor against him and the world.

"Is there something wrong with that?"

She forced herself to keep calm. "I take it you haven't checked your phone today."

He shot her a smile. "I was otherwise occupied." He took a step towards her.

She held up her hand. "Don't."

Concern creased his face as he looked around. His phone was on the shelf and he walked over, flipped it on, and scanned it.

"Phoebe," he looked up.

She shook her head. "This has your fingerprints all over it, Chase. How else would they have known where to get those photos! God, I'm practically naked in one of them."

"You're in a bikini. A really hot bikini, I might add," Chase said.

Phoebe fought down the tears that had threatened to overtake her. The press had gotten a hold of their relationship and their business partnership. It was personal and detailed, rehashing everything about Savannah and Leland, Phoebe's parents, Ivy House, and the deal she and Chase had struck.

There were half a dozen pictures of them kissing, holding hands, and sunbathing on Chase's boat. There were even pictures of Savannah and Leland and the whole history.

"This is the kind of publicity money can't buy." Phoebe shook her head. "Sure beats dating the odd model for this kind of press. I hope you're happy."

Anger darkened Chase's face and his eyes turned almost black. "You think I did this?"

"Who else? Who else would know this stuff? Where to find us, or all of these details about Savannah and my parents? They even have my favorite ice cream. I told you no press and you let them into our lives. Into this. I thought we had…"

Phoebe broke off before she embarrassed herself. Chase had never promised her anything more than a good time. Light and sweet. And she should have never expected more from him. But somewhere along the line, she opened herself up to him, thinking that maybe there could be something more between them.

"Look, Phoebe."

"Save it. I asked one thing of you…that this would be private…"

"I'm sorry, I had…" Chase looked contrite, she would give him that.

Phoebe shook her head. "All my life, people have wanted to be with me, get close to me because of my family. They didn't care that I collect salt shakers or that I love mint chocolate chip ice cream or that I'm ticklish. They never cared about me, only what I could do for them."

"I'm sorry." He was angry now. "Look, I'll talk to my PR guy, straighten it out. Listen, babe." He walked over to her and rubbed her arm. "I'll take care of it. It will be fine."

Phoebe swallowed hard and closed her eyes. She couldn't look at him. "Don't, please don't. Just go. I can't do this."

"Phoebe!" Chase looked at her, but she turned and pointed towards the door.

"Fine." He came closer to her. "I'll give you some time to think it over."

Chapter 38

Chase felt no better after yelling at his PR director. Sam Waterstone had sworn the story hadn't been entirely his doing. It was too good an opportunity to pass up, and Chase had never objected before when a picture of him and a date showed up online or in the papers. So, Sam had given in and now the media had it, and they loved the parallel between Chase and Phoebe and Leland and Savannah. In fact, all of America loved the parallel, from what Chase could see.

Chase refused all requests for an interview, which he knew might only make the story grow faster. But he didn't know what else to do. He knew if he said anything, his words would be twisted, and the media would make his relationship with Phoebe into a big deal. He didn't want her getting the wrong idea. He didn't want her to think he was in it just for the benefit to his bottom line.

Chase swung around in his office chair, thinking about Phoebe. The way she had looked at him, a look full of betrayal. She had told him how much she hated being used because of her connection with Savannah. How she wanted to make a name for herself, on her own. And now it seemed as if he was doing just that for his business because sales had gone up fifty percent since the story broke, and Chase knew that this was the kind of exposure that would cost millions of dollars to buy. And here he had it because of a few pictures of him and Phoebe kissing.

He looked again at those. Someone had gotten them with a long-range lens, a picture of a heated embrace, in front of Ivy House. And then, of course, the reporter had dug up another picture of Leland and Savannah in almost the same pose, in almost the exact same place. Chase hadn't wanted to read the comments section, but he did and stopped when he saw red. Had people no sense of decency? He wanted to punch some of these guys for what they were saying about Phoebe. It was complimentary, but lewd. Didn't they know she was taken?

But was she? She had all but kicked him out this morning. And all he had wanted to do was help her paint. Or let other people do it while he took her for another sail. There was a side creek he had wanted to explore, and he thought he could convince her to enjoy a lazy afternoon of sun and other things.

Would she let him back in? Could he convince her that this hadn't been his doing? Or that it was to her benefit? Every story mentioned her designs and she would have to benefit from all the press too. Chase checked his phone. He had left her half a dozen messages, but she hadn't returned any of them. Anymore messages and he would be considered a stalker. He got up. Sitting in his office wasn't doing any good. He needed to go fix things.

Chapter 39

"I saw Chase," Lynn said as she opened another box. Phoebe's things had started to arrive from California and Lynn was helping her unpack. "He stopped by the clinic; we had a thank you ceremony for all the sponsors."

It had been almost a week since the story broke and she had been hounded by calls from reporters. She had refused them all, even unplugging her phone and letting everything on her cell go to voicemail. Besides, she'd been too busy trying to fill all the new orders that were coming in. The story had been good for business, just as Chase had said it would be.

Phoebe stiffened and then said nonchalantly, "He was one of the sponsors, so it was nice of him to come."

Lynn looked at her in the fading light. "I don't think he was there to check up on his donation."

Phoebe shrugged, trying to show that she didn't care. Why, then, did she want to cry all of a sudden?

"I think you should talk to him."

"What?"

"He looked upset."

Phoebe snorted. "He's upset because his little ploy backfired. He knew..." Phoebe stopped herself.

"Look, I know you think he was using you because of Savannah and maybe that's how it started, but I don't think that's the way it is. You didn't see the look on his face."

Phoebe swallowed.

"Lynn, I just can't. I don't think I can trust him again."

Lynn was about to say something else, but there was a knock on the door. Phoebe looked up, her heart jumping.

"Are you expecting anyone?" Lynn asked. Phoebe shook her head tightly, but she knew, even as she walked to the door, that Chase wouldn't have knocked.

"Dean."

"Phoebe, there you are." Standing on her porch was Dean Grant.

546

"Dean." She gave him a hug, feeling a small surge of pleasure. All of a sudden, it felt nice to see an old friend.

Dean gave her his typical European greeting, a kiss on each cheek, before holding her at arm's length.

"The salt air seems to agree with you," Dean said. He was impeccably dressed, as always, in a light jacket, matching trousers, a robin's-egg blue shirt, with a paisley pocket square that complemented everything.

Phoebe was glad that the dusk hid her flush. She knew that Dean was lying. If anything, the recent turmoil with Chase had left her with some sleepless nights.

"Dean, this is my friend Lynn Masters."

"Pleased to meet you," Dean said politely, but all his attention was on Phoebe.

"You haven't returned any of my phone calls. And..." he lowered his voice, with a glance at Lynn, "I need to speak with you."

Phoebe sighed. She didn't know if Dean was being dramatic, but she hadn't returned his phone calls either, which, he supposed, was why she needed to be tracked down.

"OK," Phoebe said. Dean hesitated.

"You know what, why don't I just clean up this stuff for you," Lynn said. "You two can just run along."

Dean flashed a smile of perfectly white teeth. "An excellent idea. How about dinner, Phoebe? There's this cute little place up the road, the Osprey Arms? Do you know it?"

Did she ever, but Phoebe just nodded. She wasn't exactly dressed for dinner, but it was Dean and not a date, so she supposed that in a few minutes, she could make herself presentable.

Dean had waited for her patiently at the house while she cleaned herself up, and then they walked down to the Osprey Arms together. For a moment she panicked, but then calmed down. She was pretty certain she wouldn't run into Chase because he mostly ate in his room. And so what if she did?

"So, Chase Sanders?" Dean looked at her over his scotch, his gaze unreadable.

Phoebe didn't really want to talk about her involvement with Chase, so she took a sip of her wine instead.

"Last I heard, you thought the man was the devil incarnate," Dean pointed out, but his voice didn't hold any bit of lightness.

"Things change," Phoebe hedged.

"They do. I leave you alone for a couple of weeks, and I find you're reliving the romance of the century. In every way?"

Phoebe decided to ignore that question. She didn't want him to get the wrong idea, but there was no use denying the fact that there was something downright date-like about the corner table and the low lights of the Osprey Arms' formal dining room.

Phoebe smiled at that. "It's like you said: the fresh air, springtime. It does something to a girl."

"Well, I hope that your designing is going well?"

"I've been working on some designs," Phoebe hedged.

"You know, I've been talking with CallieSue. She's very intrigued now..." Dean said.

"Is that what you wanted to talk to me about? I told you I wasn't interested in working with her." Phoebe felt her blood began to heat. CallieSue had probably gotten "intrigued" with her as soon as all the press hit. She wasn't some no-name designer now. She was a bit of a celebrity herself.

"Just a moment." Dean held up a calming hand.

"I don't think CallieSue has developed a better sense of style in the last couple of weeks." The waiter arrived with their first course: a salad for her and soup for Dean.

He took a look at the bowl, sniffed and shrugged, as if resigned to indifferent food since he was outside of a city.

"Not bad," he proclaimed, and she had to wait as he had added a pinch of pepper and had another spoonful. He took another spoonful, and she could tell that he was actually enjoying himself. In the meantime, she pushed the leaves of what she was sure was organic, locally grown, lettuce around her plate as she waited for Dean to get to the point.

"Be that as it may, I think she's more inclined to listen to your ideas now." Dean stopped and put his hand out and covered hers. She was surprised by his gesture.

"Phoebe, I care about you. You know that I have only ever had your best interests at heart."

"What are you talking about?" Phoebe felt her heart race a bit in her chest.

"Well, it's not just CallieSue who is interested."

Something in Phoebe stirred. She knew that this was why Dean was here. He had something bigger to tell her.

Dean smiled, as if reading her mind. "Listen, I know you must miss your life in Los Angeles and here's the perfect chance. You won't have to ride the Savannah coattails—you'll be your own woman. I know how important that is to you; I realize that now."

Phoebe was flabbergasted. "Dean, that's the nicest thing you've ever said to me."

"Really, it's just the truth," Dean said with a smile, his spoon hovering over his soup.

"So who is it?" Phoebe said, even more overwhelmed. It was more than she could have hoped for, more than she should have expected.

Dean leaned in and whispered the name. Phoebe looked at him, aware that her mouth had dropped.

"But that's huge…she's already…she goes by one name."

Dean smiled, enjoying her reaction.

"Why me?" Phoebe managed to whisper.

"Why?" Dean threw back his head and laughed. "Because you're talented." His hand reached across the table and touched hers. She fought the urge to pull it back from him, and his smile was more than just a smile, seductive almost. "How many times have I told you that?"

"All the time." Phoebe managed to remove her hand and dropped it into her lap. Her heart was beating fast. "So, back to Los Angeles?" It was a tremendous opportunity, one she would have killed for even just a few weeks ago.

"Yes. She's based there, so she would definitely expect you to be there, plus she's going on tour in a month, and I think you can expect a fair amount of traveling as well, so you two can continue to work together." Dean scraped up the last bit of soup and looked at her.

"Oh, you're worried about, what, the house here. I am sure you could get a good price for it. It's a waterfront property, right? Or I suppose you could keep it as a vacation retreat, fly back a couple of times a year."

Phoebe thought longingly of her dark-stained floors, newly finished and gleaming, a rug thrown casually over them, just begging to welcome some furniture, and Ivy House, begging to welcome happiness and life back into it.

"Only a couple of times a year?" Phoebe asked.

"Well, of course. Look, it's a big job, and I need to know that you're all in with me on this before I go back to her. It would mean a lot of money, prestige. You could do anything you want. Maybe a TV show and certainly a full line of housewares sold at a major store.

The sky's the limit. Already, the press is buzzing about the possibility."

"Dean, that's so generous of you." Phoebe was at a loss for words, for not only had she thought of Ivy House but also had a fleeting thought of Chase. If she went back to Los Angeles, would she see him again? Would he miss her as much as she would miss him?

Savannah's words came ringing back to her: *Never rearrange your life for a man...*

Smiling, Phoebe reached out and took Dean's hand. "You'll let me think on it for a few days?"

Dean smiled and brought her hand to his mouth for a quick friendly kiss. "I knew you'd come around."

Chapter 40

Phoebe was daydreaming. Or thinking. She had started out the day productively enough, working on designs, but it was too lovely a day to be inside. So, she had wandered out to putter in the backyard and plant some of the annuals she had bought in her new flower pots.

She sat on the stone step of the terrace, with the view of the harbor spread out below her, the sky a cloudless blue. Everything was peaceful, but her mind was whirling with the offer Dean had made her. After Savannah had died, it seemed like the last thing she wanted to do: go back and work for someone else. But now, here was an opportunity to work with a huge name, an international presence. A collaboration, Dean had said, with her name linked. Even more so than her North Coast Outfitters deal, it would jumpstart her business.

She had told Dean she had a contract with Chase, and Dean had only smiled. "I am sure we can arrange something mutually satisfactory to both parties to get you free and clear. And back on a plane to Los Angeles. She wants to get started pronto."

Phoebe knew she needed to speak to Chase directly. See if he even cared that she would be backing out of their deal. At this point, he probably wouldn't, would he? His phone calls and texts had started to tail off.

Well, she had been the one to tell him to go, so she had no one to thank but herself. The gossip pages hadn't slowed down one bit, and she was pretty sure that a photographer was stalking her. Instead, the papers kept going over Leland and Savannah's affair and marriage, and drawing parallels to her and Chase.

Well, she had known what she was getting into, right? Chase had all but told her that he was a player. That this was a no-strings-attached, heated affair, a giving into feelings—of lust—which they couldn't ignore. But somewhere along the line, it had changed for her. Love. She wasn't a lust type of girl. Sure, just the thought of Chase's wolfish smile, deep-blue eyes, and dark tousled hair made her knees weak and panties wet, but it wasn't enough. It wasn't enough to keep her going. She wanted a life, a real life, with someone she loved and who loved her.

Maybe it didn't have to be the house and white picket fence— goodness knows, Los Angeles wouldn't be that. But perhaps it meant that she could find someone who wanted the same things she did: a committed relationship, a family. And what had Chase told her? *Let's just have a good time babe and see where it takes us.*

Well, it had taken her too far. She couldn't sleep in her bed without being woken up by thoughts of Chase and memories of how they had been together. A hot flash of desire and loss seared through her, and she closed her eyes to clear out the memories. Maybe she needed a fresh start. Coming back to the past, to the place where she thought love lived, maybe she was kidding herself. It was just a house, not a piece of magic. She couldn't get her parents back and maybe she couldn't be happy here without Chase. Already too many bad memories.

Chapter 41

Footsteps crunching on the gravel path shook her out of her melancholy thoughts.

"When were you going to tell me?" Chase came upon her suddenly. Phoebe reared back. She had been planting primroses in the empty planters that flanked the steps of the stone terrace.

"Tell you what?"

"Your new deal." Chase tried to keep the anger out of his voice, but he saw her flinch.

"How did you…"

"You don't think I read the business papers, the websites. Everyone's all abuzz that the brilliant Phoebe Ryan is designing a collection with Serena, the hottest international pop and movie star. I thought you were over that, Phoebe. I thought you had committed to your own designs."

He pulled out his phone and showed her. Phoebe gasped. She had had no idea. There was a picture of her and Dean having dinner at the Osprey Arms, drinking champagne and the headline, "Phoebe Ryan makes a new conquest." She couldn't bear to read the rest.

"It's not…"

Chase cut across her. "I understand. You're a California girl, right. You can take the girl out of Hollywood, but you can't take the Hollywood out of the girl. You're putting your career first. Just like Savannah. I suppose this was a fun little game for you while you and your gentleman friend cooked up a way to make a big story out of it."

Now she rose up, truly angry. "You're the one who told me it was no strings attached. You're the one who said, 'Hey, babe, let's enjoy the moment'. And if I recall, it was your PR director who cooked up the 'Romance of the Century, Part Two' story. You're the one who said our relationship was good for business."

Chase froze, his own words thrown back at him. "I…"

"Look, I gave you your designs and you can use them however you want. You've already made sure the world knows exactly who I am, so feel free to say whatever you have to sell more of them. Our business deal has run its course."

"It wasn't about the deal..." Chase said. She could see him fighting to keep calm and she felt her wall coming up, the one she retreated behind when she needed to avoid hurt.

"What was I supposed to do, Chase? You made it clear that you were just in it for a good time. I need to think about my career. This is the opportunity of a lifetime, in case you haven't noticed."

Chase ran his hands through his hair. "I thought this..." and he gestured all around him, "meant something to you. What about your own designs, your work for North Coast Outfitters? Us?"

"It's just a house. A house that needs a lot of work. I need to keep moving forward."

"And going with him is that?" Chase asked, his voice quiet, his face hard.

"This opportunity isn't about that," Phoebe corrected him. It wasn't about Dean.

"Well, then." Chase looked at her, his eyes dark and hooded. "I guess I'll wish you good luck." She could hear his voice catch, but he pushed through.

Phoebe felt her eyes glitter with sudden tears, but she stood firm, quiet.

"Thank you. I guess I'll be seeing you."

Chase laughed bitterly and swallowed, giving her one long last look before he turned and walked away.

Phoebe watched him, not knowing if she had made the worst mistake of her life. How had it come to this? She knew that if he just turned around once, she would be undone; she would go to him, pull him to her, and beg him to forgive her, to take her right there, take whatever she had to offer. Even if it was a lust-only, no-strings-attached kind of a deal.

Phoebe just sat on the rough stone step, the cold seeping through her jeans and into her body. The sun was setting and still she sat, letting the world go dark around her. That's how she felt about her whole world. It hadn't been ideal, how Chase had found out about Dean's offer, but he hadn't even let her discuss it with him, let her see how it might all work out. Because there was nothing left to work out. She thought what they had meant something. But then he had thrown it all in her face. What did she think that Playboy of the Month, Chase Sanders, was going to settle down with her in a small house overlooking the water and watch while she sewed pillows? That he would ever want to settle down, make a home, make a family? And with her, of all people?

What had she been thinking? That she could undo Savannah's mistakes? That somehow the Savannah-Leland history could be rewritten? It never would have worked out, she told herself. But if that were the case, then why did she feel like this? She'd made no final decision. She'd only be toying with the idea of going back to Los Angeles.

Truth was that she hadn't felt the kind of peace she'd felt in Queensbay in a long time. Ivy House had been a magical place to her and it still was. How could she leave it? But what choice did she have?

Phoebe let her eyes travel over the sweeping expanse of the harbor, down its broad length, across the darkening shadows of its hills. The water had steeped into her, even in such a short time. It had allowed her to find her creativity again, to find her playfulness, to find more purpose. Or had it all been Chase? He'd never made any promises to her. In fact, he had been more than upfront about what he had wanted from her.

"Phoebe? Are you OK?" Lynn's voice called out, and she could hear footsteps coming around the path.

Phoebe looked at her and wiped her face.

"What happened?" Lynn came to her, a stethoscope still around her neck, in her scrubs with cartoon characters.

"The bastard, what did he do?" She wrapped her arms around Phoebe and hugged her close.

"It's over," Phoebe managed to say before letting the tears come.

Chapter 42

"Don't you have someplace better to be?" Noah looked at him. Chase had wandered back to Noah's house and was now in the barn, sipping a beer as he watched his friend sand down the bubbled varnish on the little skiff.

"Work was a little slow," Chase said and shrugged when he caught Noah's disbelieving stare.

"I'm the president of a multimillion-dollar company, and I can take the afternoon off and visit an old friend when I want to."

"Did you just call me old?"

"That's not what I meant." Chase scrubbed his hands through his hair. He hadn't been able to sleep or think straight since his last conversation with Phoebe. It had gone even worse than the one before that. And she had thrown his words back in his face.

"Do you think I'm afraid of commitment?" he asked.

Noah looked startled and then he said carefully, "I think that in the past, you've been the type of guy who was offered a lot of options and hadn't felt that any of them were right at the time."

"You make it sound like a business deal," Chase said.

"You look like hell," Noah said affably. Chase knew he should have been irritated, but it was hard to ignore the truth.

"It's Phoebe."

Noah paused his sanding to take a swig of his own beer. "Thought it might be. What did you do this time?"

"Why do you think it was me?" Chase said. "Maybe it was her."

Noah just looked at him.

"What?"

"Seems to me that she's the kind of girl who wants someone who's all in," Noah said after a moment.

"What do you mean, 'all in'?"

"Well, seems to me that she's fixing up that house, trying to put down roots, and she wants to share it with someone—but really share it with someone. Not just a stranger passing through the night warming her sheets. Only thing casual about her is her decorating sense."

"So, she's looking for someone to be all in?" Chase still wasn't sure what Noah was talking about.

"She's looking for a commitment. Maybe it's marriage, maybe it's not. Never can tell these days, but she's in love with you."

"How do you know?"

"Let's just say I know how it feels to be in love with someone and not be sure how they feel about you. And to tell you the truth, you have the same look about you."

"But she's ready to close up everything here and move to Los Angeles, and she didn't even tell me. She doesn't want me. She's putting her career ahead of me."

"Did you ever give her any reason not to?" Noah said. "Didn't she get mad at you about the newspaper articles first? Did you ever give her any reason not to think that you weren't just using her for your business?"

"She knows I would never do that," Chase said sharply.

Noah shook his head. "Does she?"

"But why would she go back to him?" Chase was sure that it was this Dean Grant who was pushing her to go back to Los Angeles.

"Well, at least she's getting something in return from him, right? What were you offering her? Or, more importantly, did you ever tell her what you were offering her? Remember, my friend: men and women speak different languages. You think you're showing her how you feel, but she wants to hear it."

"That's it? That's your great advice?" Chase was angry. "We're great together. How could she not know?"

Noah shook his head. "See, different languages. You're showing her when you need to come out and tell her. All in, my friend, all in."

Chase thought about that. It was true. She'd never really said that she wanted to go back to California—just that it was a great opportunity. And he never asked her to stay. Or worse yet, he never asked her if she wanted to make it work. He had just assumed that she would be willing to take whatever he gave her.

"She wants me. All of me," Chase said with some amazement. Women had wanted him before, but they had usually wanted his money or his lifestyle or some combination of both. In return, they had been willing to warm his bed, but not one of them had really wanted all of him. They had wanted to catch him.

"I think you're finally getting it. I don't think she bought into any of this romance-of-the-century stuff you cooked up."

"I didn't cook it up," Chase began, but then stopped. He certainly hadn't prevented it, figuring it was good for both of them. But she hadn't wanted any of that either.

"I mean, do you think that stuff is true? This whole crazy love thing? Savannah and Leland...that wasn't love, was it? It was just self-destructive lust, right?"

Noah smiled, a dreamy one, as he sanded down the wood on the boat. "Love takes many different forms, my friend, and when it comes to you, you shouldn't fight it. Always seemed to me like your grandfather and Savannah Ryan were all in."

Chase stood there glowering as he thought about it.

Noah laughed and continued with his sanding as he asked, "So, what are you going to do?"

Chapter 43

"Phoebe Ryan?" Phoebe answered her phone, only half paying attention. She was thinking of packing, trying to sort through the things she might want to take with her and the things that could go into storage. She had already contacted the real estate agent about the possibility of renting Ivy House out again and someone at an auction house about making a full catalog of Savannah's stuff. The money could go to charity, Phoebe thought.

"This is Robin Smyth from *Hot Style*." Phoebe perked up. *Hot Style* was one of her favorite reads, filled with all sorts of up-and-coming designers and products.

"I wanted to discuss featuring your line of pillows and accessories in an upcoming issue and on our website and TV segments. Your work recently came to our attention, and I think it would be a great fit in our next issue."

Phoebe stopped what she was doing, trying to breathe. "You want to feature me?"

"Yes, we just love your stuff. Plus, I heard you're restoring an old house. And that it belonged to Savannah Ryan. Listen, I was such a huge fan and was so sad when I heard your grandmother passed away. I just think that since you do such great stuff and if we can tie it in with her work, well, then it would be like the artistic torch is being passed from one generation to the next—even if the medium is different. What do you say, are you interested?"

Phoebe smiled and she could almost hear Savannah's raspy voice saying, "You finally got your big break."

"I don't suppose this has anything to do with all the rumors going around now, does it?"

There was a pause. "Well, to tell you the truth, I got a call from at least four other designers who told me that they just had meetings with Serena about working on a collection together."

"Oh," Phoebe said.

"I guess her agent and manager are really shopping around. I am sure it would be a great opportunity for you, but I really like your stuff, even without someone else's name attached to it." Robin emphasized the word "your," and Phoebe felt her heart beat a little faster.

"Plus, I am a sucker for cute little Victorian house with water views."

Phoebe laughed. "Apparently, I am too. So, no matter what happens with the Serena deal, you want to feature me?"

She could hear Robin shuffling some papers. "Yes. And between you and me," she said, dropping her voice, "I hear she's a total nightmare to work with. And a total attention hog. Listen, it's your business, but something similar happened with her clothing line. She went to ten different design teams before she found one that she stuck with, and they have a total non-disclosure agreement. They can't tell anyone who they work for. And worse yet, they can't put out anything of their own."

Phoebe let that all sink in.

"Great. Now," Robin continued, "I'm not promising anything, but many of the new designers and companies we feature, they see quite a jump in their business. Are you prepared to handle that?"

Phoebe looked around the study and her big workspace. Her sketches were spread out on it. She had been sorting through them, deciding whether any of them were worth keeping. There was a decision to be made here.

"I'm ready to handle it," Phoebe said.

<<>>

Lynn had come over with a bottle of champagne when she heard the news. "I am so excited for you."

Phoebe was nervous, but she could feel the adrenaline and the champagne kicking in. Excitement. Purpose. There was a chance that nothing would come of it, but she had to be true to herself.

"I think, maybe, I'm being manipulated." She told Lynn what she had learned from Robin Smyth.

"I don't think Chase would do that," Lynn began.

Phoebe shook her head. She had done a little more research after getting off the phone and realized that Robin had been right. Supposedly, Serena was not known for sharing credit for design ideas. And once Phoebe had looked a little more closely at the press release about her collaboration with Serena, she saw that the language was intentionally vague about how committed Serena was to Phoebe.

"Not Chase."

It took Lynn only a moment to put it together. "Oh, you think Dean is trying to get you away from here and Chase. I knew he was the villain."

Phoebe rolled her eyes at Lynn's dramatics. "Not a villain. Just being pretty aggressive in pursuing me. I think he's doing what an agent does, spinning the media to make the situation work to his advantage."

"So, you're not going to get me backstage passes to a Serena concert?"

Phoebe shrugged. "Maybe, maybe not. I still know a few people. But I don't think I'm going to be working with her. It's my life, my terms this time."

"This means that you're not leaving?" Lynn's face broke into a smile.

"No, I'm not leaving," Phoebe assured her, knowing in that moment that she really did belong here, that she wanted to be here, to give this a real try.

"I'm glad. I would've missed you," Lynn said, and, impulsively, Phoebe hugged her.

"This means more margarita nights at Augie's."

"I can handle it if you can," Lynn said.

Phoebe took a sip of her champagne, savoring the bubbles. She would need to tell Dean her official decision. But not now. For now, she just wanted to savor the moment.

"Imagine, a major magazine wants to do an article on me..." Phoebe said, feeling her toes tingling.

"So cool. And you don't care that they're going to mention Savannah?" Lynn asked.

Phoebe shook her head. She had thought about this too. "It finally feels right. Like the editor said, an artistic torch being passed from one generation to the next. I think Savannah would have been proud. And happy."

"Have you told anyone else?"

"I haven't talked to Dean yet." Phoebe shook her head. She wanted to keep him out of this opportunity.

"That's not who I meant," Lynn countered.

Phoebe turned to face her. "It doesn't matter if I stay or go. Chase and I want different things. I want to settle down and, well, I don't think he's the type."

"Did you ever tell him that's what you wanted?" Lynn said, taking a sip of her champagne.

They had nearly polished off the bottle of champagne and were digging into a bag of potato chips when Phoebe got the text.

"Ugh, it's Dean. He wants to see me. I guess he wants his answer."

"Can't you text him back?" Lynn suggested, licking the salt off a chip before eating it.

"No. I think a part of him wants to make sure I'm back in Los Angeles. Unless I can explain it to his face that I plan on turning down this amazing opportunity and why, he'll think I'm delusional."

"Are you rational?" Lynn asked, gesturing to the half-empty bottle of champagne.

"I poured you more," Phoebe said with a snicker.

"Ahh, no wonder I feel all floaty and wonderful. I'll hold down the fort while you're gone. Have you got a TV yet?"

Laughing, Phoebe tossed her the remote. She texted Dean back and ran upstairs, changing into a sundress and a pair of high-heeled sandals. Using her sunglasses as a headband, she fluffed her hair, grabbed her bag, and was ready.

Chapter 44

Chase kept pounding on the door. Finally, he heard footsteps and when it opened, he almost barreled in, but stopped.

"Where is she?" he demanded.

"Hello to you too," Lynn said. She was wearing jeans and a t-shirt, not her scrubs, and her hair was in a messy ponytail. He could hear the sound of the TV in the background, and he saw a flash of the screen and almost did a double take until he realized that it was Savannah and Leland on the big screen and not Phoebe and himself.

"Lynn?"

"She had to meet someone. You really upset her, you know. How could you? You know that's the one thing she hates, being used because of who she is."

"I wasn't using her," he said, the panic rising. "Where is she? Who is she meeting?" he demanded again, dread hitting him hard.

"Why is that any of your business? She said your deal is over. She did what she was supposed to, and whether she stays or goes has nothing to do with you."

"She's staying?" Hope filled him.

"Yeah, but not because of you. In spite of you. It's all over the TV now—all the entertainment shows are replaying all these programs on Savannah and Leland. Phoebe's all over the place, the poor little Hollywood girl. She never wanted anyone's pity, you know."

"I know. Listen, Lynn, I didn't leak the story. At least not on purpose."

"Fine, I believe you, and I bet she does too."

"Then, what's the problem?" Chase could hear the frustration in his own voice.

Lynn rolled her eyes. "You've got to tell her, you big dummy. Tell her how you feel."

Chase tried to tamp down his impatience. Lynn was obviously buzzing and he needed her to focus.

"Where is she?"

"Who, what? Oh, she went to go talk to Dean. About the job offer. Down at the hotel."

Chase felt his stomach flip. No way he trusted that guy. Sure, Phoebe had said he was a true-blue friend, but Chase had a feeling there was more to the story, at least on Dean's side.

Chapter 45

"Couldn't we go someplace more private?" Dean took her arm and tried to guide her away from the dock.

She took a deep bracing breath of air and decided. It was almost fully dark now, and the lights along the dock were coming on, one by one. Music from the Osprey Arms' outdoor terrace drifted over, and the air was warm, a hint of summer to come.

"This is fine." All of a sudden, Phoebe didn't feel like being in a more private place with Dean. Public was good enough for her.

"I need to say I think you're making a big mistake." Dean stepped up to her and pulled her up to him, his light eyes searching hers.

"He's not good enough for you, Phoebe. I'm the one who was there for you. I want you to share everything with me. With your name and talent and my help, there's no saying where you could go."

He lowered his lips to hers and pulled her in tight. He tried to kiss her, but Phoebe jerked back, putting a hand out against Dean's chest, holding him off.

"I know you did it," she said. "You leaked the story about the collaboration with Serena. Is it even true? Does she want to work with me?" Anger crept into her voice.

His hazel eyes were confused. "But you're making a mistake. He's not good enough for you, and all of that romance-of-the-century stuff was complete crap. He can't love you, not the way I do."

"As opposed to what you're doing?" Phoebe said coldly.

"Phoebe, please." Dean pulled her close again and she knew he was going for another kiss. His eyes were intent, serious, but the look in them quickly turned to surprise when he fell back. All of a sudden, the dock was crowded.

"Chase, don't." Phoebe was too late.

Chase had already spun Dean around. "Get your hands off my girl!"

"Your girl…" Dean turned back to look at Phoebe. "See, Phoebe, I had to save you from yourself. Is this why you're giving up the opportunity of a lifetime. For this buffoon?"

"What did you call me?" Chase's eyes narrowed.

"Phoebe, I am so sorry." Lynn followed closely behind Chase. "He wanted to know where you were."

Phoebe looked around. Chase and Dean were squaring off against each other, both of them in some sort of fighting stance. She swallowed hard. Dean worked out quite a bit at the gym and was a black belt in karate. But Chase had the more muscular build, like that of a street fighter.

"I can't believe you think you can step in and ruin her life. She's throwing it all away."

"What are you saying, I'm not good enough for her?" Chase's voice was dangerously low. "Do you think you're better for her than me? How dare you try to get between us?"

Phoebe felt the tension rise. She was about to step in between the two of them. She wasn't sure who said what or who went for the other first, but she saw Chase's arm shoot out and Dean staggered back, into Phoebe. She teetered, started to lose her balance, and reached out to grab one of the pilings to steady herself.

"Oh, no," she heard Lynn say, and then Phoebe felt herself falling, heading for the murky waters of Queensbay Harbor.

It was cold, Phoebe thought, as she hit the water and began sinking. The shock had her hesitating a moment before she was ready to kick herself back up to the top. All of a sudden, there was something around her waist, pulling her up, up towards the fading light of the surface.

"Are you crazy?" Chase yelled when they hit the surface. Phoebe gasped in breaths of air, unable to answer. The water was cold and she was shivering. A crowd had gathered and there were flashlights being shone their way.

"Come this way, there's a ladder," someone called. Phoebe coughed, realizing she had swallowed more salty water than she had thought. Chase's arm was still around her as he towed her against the current and towards the walkway.

Strong hands lifted her up. Phoebe looked around. Dean was sitting, holding his nose, while Lynn hovered over him. Someone had a first aid kit and she had broken out an ice pack. She glanced up, gave the thumbs-up sign.

Phoebe felt Chase's presence behind her. "Does someone have a blanket?" he called out and, in a moment, she felt something draped over her. The police were there and so were the paramedics.

"I'm fine. I'm fine." Phoebe waved them away.

Everyone was looking at her, at them. "I can swim, you know." She pulled the blanket more tightly around her and started walking off the dock.

Lynn stood up, but she waved her away. Phoebe stopped in front of Dean, who looked up at her, an ice pack on his nose.

"Dean, I'm really not going back to California. I don't want the job and I don't want you. And that has nothing to do with him." She nodded towards Chase. "I'm staying to pursue my business. And you and me, we're done."

Dean stood up. A lock of his blond hair fell across his eye, and he tried his best to work his charm as he stuck out his hand. "It's my loss. But good luck, I guess. When you change your mind…"

She ignored his outstretched hand. "I'll know who not to call." And with that she kept walking.

Chapter 46

Chase found her by following the wet footsteps across the front porch, through the front door, which she hadn't locked, down the hall and to the terrace. She had lit a fire in the fire pit and changed, though she was still wrapped in a blanket, sitting on the new outdoor couch she'd had delivered.

It had taken him a good hour to straighten things out with the police. Luckily, Dean, like Chase, hadn't wanted to make a big deal out of it, so they shook hands, Chase with his stomach aching from Dean's nicely placed roundhouse kick, and Dean with a shiner that made him look more like a biker than a preppy Hollywood type.

She was drinking tea, wrapped in a soft blanket, staring out at the water. The sun was well down below the horizon, but the last streaks of purple-pink suffused the indigo sky.

"I'm sorry," he said, deciding to lead with an apology.

Her face didn't turn. He could see her exquisite profile, the long straight nose, the way the fire picked up the red-gold highlights in her hair.

"Why did you come today?"

"I came because I thought you were going to Los Angeles with him, for him," Chase said, and felt his hands clench and then unclench.

"Dean?" She had turned now, surprise lifting her voice.

"Yes. I thought you were going to walk out of my life and I was crazy. Crazy that I would lose you."

He came around the couch and dropped down in front of her.

"What are you doing?" she asked.

Chase took her hands in his. They were still cold and her hair was still damp, probably from her shower. She smelled like her flower-and-citrus shampoo.

"Phoebe Ryan, I love you. I love you because you're you. Stubborn, caring, loving despite never being loved, because you're talented and creative. Because I can't think straight when you're around. Because when your blue eyes look at me, I would do anything for you."

"You did jump into the water after me. I was on the swim team or didn't you remember?"

"Shh." He put a finger to her lips. "No sarcasm. I am trying to tell you something here."

She shook her head, lifted her chin. "Then just say it, Chase Sanders."

He smiled. "Phoebe, I love you. Every single thing about you. From your fuzzy slippers, to your silly salt-and-pepper shaker collection, to the way you look in the morning when the sunlight hits your hair on the pillow, to the way your skin smells in the rain. I love you and I want to spend the rest of my life with you. I love you because you're you. And no one else. Will you marry me?"

Chase looked at her, barely breathing. Slowly, excruciatingly, she reached up with her hands and brought his face close to her. She laid a gentle kiss on his lips and breathed the word, "Yes."

They sat there on the couch, entangled in the blanket, watching the dying embers of the fire. It was fully dark now and frogs had grown loud around them.

"So, about this house," he started to say.

"Oh, no you don't."

"I was thinking that we might need to expand it, just a little bit. You know, so you have a proper studio and there's plenty of room for the kids to run around. That's if you want to stay here. If not, I am sure we could find something else."

Phoebe's mouth shushed him with a row of kisses along his cheek.

"We can't leave Ivy House. It's magical."

"Romance of this century," he agreed, as his mouth caught hers and kissed her.

Chasing a Chance - Lynn & Jackson's Story

Book 4 - The Queensbay Series

Drea Stein

Chapter 1

Lynn Masters stood with sore feet and the beginnings of a knot in her back, looking over the patient board and saw with more than a bit of satisfaction that it was just about clear. If the clinic managed to avoid an outbreak of the flu, the common cold, or even a minor trauma, it could mean an early night for her. Sighing at the thought, she debated whether she wanted a cup of the gunk they called coffee or if she could make it through to closing time without another shot of caffeine.

After this shift, she was off duty for three days and her thoughts were excited as the prospect of a break stretched in front of her: empty days with nothing to do, the first real break she'd had in weeks. As far as pediatric residents went, she was senior enough to be at the top of the food chain, in terms of schedule but still, someone else had always called in sick or they'd been short-handed and she'd kept saying yes to working overtime. So now she was well and truly due for some time off and she planned on enjoying every last minute of it.

Skipping the coffee, she made her way down the hallway toward the front desk to start updating her charts. The Queensbay Sailors' Clinic, which had started life in the nineteenth century as a home for destitute sailors, had entered the twenty-first as a facility to provide cost-effective medical services, mostly to women and children. It tried hard, it really did, to be bright and cheerful, despite the dilapidated air about the place. Over the years, it had been housed in a small house, an old church, and other various spots around town, but now was in a building which someone had told her had once been a sail maker's loft. It was a big and spacious, but it hadn't been well-taken care of over the years.

The clinic took up the entire first floor. The second floor was mostly empty, except for a resident psychic who kept sporadic office hours. Her clients climbed up a set of rickety iron steps attached to the outside of the building to have their fortune told. Many of them headed straight down to the clinic, right after their psychic readings, where invariably Lynn would find something wrong with them.

Curious, Lynn had stopped by to see Madame Robireux once, to ask her how she knew there was something physical ailing her clients, but Madame, in true soothsayer's fashion had only waved her heavily ringed hands over a crystal ball and given an enigmatic shrug and started talking about auras. The psychic had offered to read Lynn's own aura, but she had declined, deciding that if was something wrong, she preferred to discover it the old-fashioned way.

In truth, the whole building had the air of an aging woman of the night, with great bones, the last vestiges of beauty not quite gone, but with a general sagginess, as if the whole thing was ready to slide in on itself.

The chairs in the waiting room were hard and uncomfortable and the tables in the exam room were old and the vinyl covers were cracking.

To counteract this, the staff and volunteers had made the inside of the clinic cheery enough, with murals painted on the walls, depicting scenes of oceans and jungles and even a more fanciful one, showing unicorns and fairies in a forest. The kids loved all of them, always stopping to search for their favorite fish or animal each time they came.

And Lynn loved it too. She had poured her heart and soul into her time here at the clinic, helping to raise money for it, donating her own time, and taking pride in watching her patients—kids—grow. She had even started a special program for some of her higher risk ones. Called Healthy Kids Now, she focused on getting her youngest patients exercising and eating better. Sure, everyone knew the basics—eat better, move more—but putting it into practice was harder, even if the parents were on board. Everyone was busy so Lynn had worked to make the program as simple and as easy to use as possible. The successful results were starting to roll in and she'd even received some attention from the medical community. She'd had half a dozen requests to write or speak about it to other clinics and doctors and was trying to field them all.

Lynn strolled the halls, well-being and contentment flowing through her. Sure she might have a bad case of sore feet, but there was nowhere else she would rather be. As she approached the front desk, she saw that the main receptionist, Lori, and her friend Sue, one of the nurses, were there, head bent down, deep in discussion.

"Can you believe it?" Lynn listened with only half an ear, finding the screen on the computer where she needed to sign in; she began inputting information. The two women had worked in the clinic together for years and were best friends. They were always gossiping about something or the other, whether it was what some celebrity had been wearing or who was beating whom on some reality show. Seldom was it of any true concern to Lynn. There had been a time when she might have been interested in all of that, but the last years of medical school and her residency had left little time to keep up on current events, of any kind. Besides she was more of a classic film kind of girl.

"We have a month," Lori hissed to Sue.

"And where are we going to go?" Sue sounded angry. "I've been here for eight years, and just like that they're going to…"

The two of them hushed when they noticed Lynn and in the silence she plainly read guilt.

"What? Is there something wrong with me?" Lynn did a quick scan. She was wearing scrubs and her white doctor's coat. She'd only had one vomiter today, and she had managed to sidestep the projectile launch. Lunch had been turkey on rye, no mustard or mayonnaise, so she knew she hadn't been messy there.

"Is it my hair?" she asked, touching the long ponytail she kept her wavy, dark locks in.

The two women just shook their heads. "You look fine, girl-friend. So fine you better go find a boyfriend."

Lynn shook her head. The two women were always razzing her about her love life, or lack thereof. Being a med student didn't leave a lot of time for dating. Of course, now that she was just about the real deal, a full doctor, the women had told she was a catch. They had even threatened to start setting her up on blind dates, just like her mother, if she didn't start going out on her own. It was just that she knew herself. Her relationships had always ended badly and she was in a good place right now, so why mess with it?

"Nice try, ladies. Fess up. What were you really talking about?" Lynn leaned in and dropped her voice. She knew that Sue and Lori loved to gossip not just about showbiz but what was happening in real life. They were a true treasure trove of information and couldn't keep anything to themselves if they had something really juicy to share.

"Well…" Sue matched Lynn's low tone and threw a glance over her shoulder, "you didn't hear it from us, but word on the street is that the clinic is closing at the end of the month."

"Closing." Lynn's mouth dropped open and her it felt like the bottom of her stomach dropped out.

"Shhh!" Lori and Sue said at the same time, and Lynn muttered a sorry.

"Aren't they always saying that?" Lynn kept her voice down. The Queensbay Sailors' Clinic was a town institution, but it generally ran on a shoestring budget and for as long as Lynn had worked there, there were always threats in that it was one month away from closing its doors forever. Still, she had planned on it being around and had even accepted a permanent position once her residency was done. She had never thought she'd be out of a job so soon.

"But this time it's for real. Mr. Petersen's finally selling and the new landlord wants to turn this place into a day spa. We need to find new space within the month or it's lights out."

"A day spa!" Lynn was too incensed to keep her voice down and Sue gave her another angry look as she shushed her.

"You heard us, girl. This place is going bye-bye to make way for a day spa."

"What do you mean bye-bye? Can't we just move to another location?"

Lori shrugged. "Mr. Petersen hasn't raised the rent on us in years. It would be difficult to find another location like this. And even so, that would take time. The lease is up at the end of the month. That doesn't leave long for the Director to find us another place and get it up and running."

"But that's not right!" Lynn said, feeling her anger rising. The clinic served an important need here in town. It couldn't just go away. And then there was the question of her paycheck. And the new apartment she had just signed a lease on. And her Healthy Kids Now program she was planning on expanding. She felt her head began to throb and her heart beat a little faster. This was so not good. It couldn't be that everything she had worked for the past ten years was going to evaporate in a matter of weeks.

"You tell us! Oh, look. Now she's getting angry; but I don't know what's that going to do," Sue said, shaking her short, fluffy red hair.

Lori laughed bitterly. "Don't go thinking this is like some patient of yours you can go and fix, Lynn. You'd be better off spending your time looking for another job."

Lynn pulled herself out of her own sense of injustice and looked at the two of them. "What are you going to do?"

Lori shrugged and looked at them over her half-moon glasses. "I've got a standing job offer to run my cousin's dental practice. Offered me a thirty percent raise."

Sue nodded. "I've got a lead in on a job at the hospital. Night shift, at least at first, but still it pays better."

"But..." Lynn looked at them. The two ladies didn't appear too concerned, only resigned. "The clinic is an institution, right? It's been here since the town was first founded. Are you going to let over hundred years of history go down the tubes without a protest?"

The two other women looked at her, then at each other, and Sue said, "When you put it that way...I guess so."

Lynn fisted her hands and said, "I'm not going down without a fight."

Sue and Lori exchanged looks as Lynn gathered her stuff and propelled herself out the door.

Lori pulled down her reading glasses and her eyes followed Lynn's exit. It was her best look, the one she used when she was going to pronounce something she felt was important. "Lordy. Think that Mr. Petersen knows enough to get out of the way when she's a coming?"

Sue shook her head as she watched Lynn's retreating back, "No way, she's tiny..."

"But mighty," Lori finished for her.

Chapter 2

Jackson Sanders dressed carefully, his mind going over the upcoming meeting. It was something he had learned playing baseball. Visualizing the play, imagining the outcome to virtually will it to happen. Petersen was playing hardball, blustering; but that was only to save face. Jackson was fairly certain the deal would go in his favor.

Jackson smoothed his tie, ran a hand over his hair, and looked out the window. The water, as always, had a calming effect on him, which was part of the reason why he had decided to return to Queensbay. Europe had been nice, Hong Kong bustling, Qatar sandy, New York alive, but now with this opportunity, he knew he was meant to be here. Finally, again.

He glanced away from the sparkling waters of Queensbay Harbor and scanned the screen of his laptop. As usual, his email inbox was overflowing. There were emails from Chase, his brother, who was on a sourcing trip in the Far East, with his fiancée Phoebe, concerning the prep for planned renovations to the Osprey Arms marina and hotel.

Then there was the email from the board of the local university confirming his meeting with them next week. Plus, emails from the project manager who had replaced him on the job in London, asking for his advice on how to handle some upcoming cost overruns.

Then there was the missive from Petersen, telling him to meet him today with his balls on, ready to deal. Jackson was paraphrasing of course, Petersen wasn't happy about selling the building and it was showing. And who could blame him? It had been in his family for years, but Petersen was on the ropes and needed the cash.

There was a ding, and Jackson looked at the new email. He winced when he saw the sender. Helen. He'd been careful, over the years, to only get involved with women who understood the deal. He was a serial monogamist, true while in a relationship, but he had no intention of falling in love or settling down. He had once, but he had almost suffocated, almost lost himself; and he didn't want that to happen again.

Most of the ladies in his life had understood it and taken what he could give them. It had led to several satisfactory liaisons throughout the world. He had thought that Helen, the latest on the list, had understood his position before they began their affair, but as he read the email, he saw that she wasn't quite as accepting about the way things had ended as she had led him to believe.

Jackson kept reading, blinked, and was slightly shocked when he got to the sign off. The coolly proper Helen Sellers had told him to go to hell. He smothered down a wave of guilt. She had known the score when she had gotten involved. Jackson Sanders wasn't the marrying type, no matter how eligible the lady.

He hit delete, since there was no use brooding on it, but he ran a hand through his blonde hair, then smoothed it back. He had always kept it short, as a true executive would. He'd been young to get so promoted so fast, and he had realized that dressing in expensive suits when everyone else his age was embracing corporate casual made him look more mature. The grizzled old veterans, who recognized a power suit when they saw one, had automatically given him more respect since he had showed them some.

He had never made any promises to Helen he hadn't intended to keep. In fact, he had promised her little, beyond some enjoyable time together. Dinners, companionship, an escort for the host of social functions she had enjoyed attending, and the checkbook to support it. Of course, he had shared her bed and she had been an enthusiastic, eager partner, but at the end of the day, he had realized that she fully intended to become Mrs. Jackson Sanders, convinced that she would be the one to change his mind about marriage and settling down. Just like all the rest of them, she'd been bound for disappointment.

Grabbing a bottle of mineral water, he opened the sliding door and stepped out onto the balcony of the apartment. It was a perfect fall day, mid-September, with a sunny, bright blue sky, unmarked by even a single cloud. A few boats skimmed about on the harbor and he could see a bustle of people in and out of the Osprey Arms Hotel's main entrance below.

He was in an annex to the main building of the hotel he owned in partnership with his brother Chase. They had bought it over a year ago and were slowly putting their plans for upgrades into action. The first had been the restaurant, which had been known for baskets of fried shrimp and limp French fries. Chase had brought in a world-class chef, Sean Callahan, and he had transformed it into an upscale steak and seafood destination that had half the coast clamoring for a reservation on the weekend.

Next up had been this building, at least the top floor, which had been chopped up into apartments. Seeing the potential for some steady income, to offset the seasonality of the hotel—summer was the high season, the cold, damp New England winter, not so much—they had decided to keep them as rental units. All it had taken were some simple renovations, like new paint and kitchen appliances, to leave them with a block of one and two bedrooms to rent.

In a few weeks, they would start the full-scale work to the guestrooms and the public spaces of the hotel itself, plus a freshening up of the first floor of the annex, which they intended to turn into retail space. The Osprey Arms was the anchor of downtown Queensbay and before he and Chase had purchased it, it had fallen on hard times. But now they had a plan in place to restore it to its former glory, to make it a centerpiece of the town and hopefully a true destination for people all over the region.

For now, Jackson was enjoying the fruits of his brother's plans, staying in one of those renovated top-floor apartments. Since Jackson only needed a temporary space, he had selected a one bedroom. It had a compact layout but still had everything he needed, from a decent-sized galley kitchen, to a well-equipped living space, complete with flat screen TV and, of course, the view.

He breathed in. The salty tang of Queensbay Harbor rose up, brought up by the light autumn breeze that danced around. He closed his eyes and the memories came flooding back. The first time he had taken Ashley to the beach. The moon-filled night he had convinced her to go skinny-dipping. The clambake the evening they'd announced their engagement. His hand gripped the iron railing and he opened the eyes. Sunlight flooded his vision and almost immediately, she was gone—the fleeting vision of Ashley carried away by the same breeze that tossed a seagull around.

He knew it would be hard, but he also knew that running no longer helped. If it had, he would have stayed away, and been ready to discuss tuxedo choices and wedding venues with a woman like Helen, instead of standing here, looking over the town he called home but had rarely seen in the past five years.

No, he'd finally realized that the only way to let Ashley go was to come back. To make peace with her memory, so he could get back the life he had wanted before that night. In truth, he had never meant to leave Queensbay, certainly never meant to stay away so long. But in the aftermath of the accident he couldn't stay, couldn't face the whispers, the looks—curious, pitying, but most of all accusing—that had followed him. It was even harder when he knew that it was based on a lie. But the lie was the secret he had sworn to keep. He just hoped enough time had passed to take the edge off the townspeople's curiosity. Curiosity he could survive. He just hoped with the passage of time and the absence of Ashley's parents that all he would get would be the curiosity.

The alarm on his phone beeped, signaling that the meeting with Petersen was near. Time to get his game face on.

Chapter 3

"What do you mean you're not going to do anything about it?" Lynn was balanced on the edge of her chair, which took up almost the entire space in front of Sadie Walker's desk. Lynn had rushed out of the clinic, filled with righteous passion and had then taken a deep breath, thought about her options and decided talking to Sadie first was the best course of action.

"Don't you think if I could, I would?" There was a weariness in Sadie's voice that Lynn had heard before but there was also a sharp edge to it, as if she wanted the conversation to be done.

Lynn took a deep breath. She knew that Sadie, as the director of the clinic did her best in a hopeless job. The clinic was essentially non-profit, providing affordable medical care to those who really needed it—and some who didn't. It was run on a shoestring, a budget that was met by a paltry endowment left over from its original benefactors, constant fundraising efforts, and whatever other money Sadie could scrounge together. It was under the official auspices of the local hospital but was more often than not treated like the forgotten child in the attic. Certainly they devoted little money to it, which Lynn thought was a deliberate move, probably hoping that the clinic would run into a crisis like this so they could swoop in and officially take it over.

But that would mean ousting the current board of directors, a tough crew of old biddies who took their jobs quite seriously, and probably moving the clinic to the hospital itself, which wasn't as close to the town, or on a bus line, making it difficult for patients to who didn't drive to get to them. Now, being right here was the best option for the clinic.

When Lynn had accepted the job here, she hadn't taken it for the money. There would be plenty of time to go out and make that later, and thanks to a small inheritance from her grandmother, who had a passion for buying and holding blue-chip stocks, she'd been able to pay for medical school, with a bit left over. No, the clinic had become her personal *raison d'etre* and even more so now that she'd been working on her Healthy Kids Now campaign. She just couldn't watch all of that slip away, not without doing something.

"The Petersen family has been in Queensbay a long time, and the space has been leased to us at below market rates for years. But he has to sell, and the new owner isn't interested in keeping us on. Apparently, kicking us out is a condition of the deal."

"But without the clinic, all these patients will have over an hour's ride to the next one. Or they'll have to go the emergency room at the hospital—and that's unnecessary and expensive."

"I know, Lynn, you're right. But unless you can come up with some alternative plan, then I really don't see what we can do. It's been a good fight, but it's been a battle, almost each and every day. I know how committed you are, but you don't have any idea of the day-to-day realities of running an operation like this. Look, don't worry, about your residency. I know the hospital will find a way for you to finish it out."

Sadie didn't say anything about the job Lynn had accepted at the clinic once her residency was done. That, Lynn knew, was surely in doubt. Right now, though, that was the least of her concerns. It was the clinic itself she was determined to save.

Sadie was a rumpled-looking middle-aged woman with frizzy hair that had once been red, but now, thanks to out-of-the-box hair dye, was closer to orange. She wore glasses that were attached to her by a long chain strung with beads. Her clothing style could only be described as eclectic, usually leggings, chunky heeled boots, with drapey tops thrown over that camouflaged her true shape.

Sadie's heart was in the right place, Lynn knew, but with her trained eye she could see the Sadie was tired. Dark circles pouched under her eyes, and she had put on her eyeliner crooked. Her hands moved restlessly, squeezing and releasing a rubber band ball as if that would help mitigate the stress.

"Lynn, I've worked here for fifteen years, and trust me, if there was a way to change this decision I would find it."

"But hasn't Mr. Petersen threatened to close us down in the past?"

"About every six months, but he can never get a new tenant in." Sadie shrugged her shoulders.

"That's because this place is a dump," Lynn said. As if to punctuate the observation there was the sound of a slamming door somewhere out in the hallway, and the building shook from the reverberation while a small piece of plaster, dislodged from the flaky ceiling, tumbled down, leaving a vapor trail of dust.

The carpet was an indeterminate mix of gray and beige, with suspicious stains dotting across it like polka dots. The walls in the office were a dirty white, scuffed and grimed by handprints and other bodily fluids. Sadie's door sat unsteadily on its hinges and the framed prints of garden scenes, set in cheap frames, did nothing to alleviate the gloom.

"Well, apparently this time, he's selling the place and the new owner has the money to fix it up."

"Why wouldn't Petersen do that himself?" Lynn asked. She wasn't an experienced real estate investor, but it seemed that if the building had belonged to the Petersen family for decades, it was probably already paid for and keeping it as a rental property was a better way of managing the investment.

Sadie shrugged, looked around and said, "Word is Petersen is about to go through a very nasty divorce and he's going to need the money."

"Why?" She'd met Duane Petersen once and he was middle-aged with thinning hair, the beginnings of a belly and a droopy air. His wife, on the other hand, was aerobics class-thin, pretty in that way, and had a highhanded way about her.

"Supposedly," Sadie dropped her voice as if about to impart a state secret, and Lynn wondered if Lori or Sue had been her source, "Duane's mixing it up with his secretary and he wants to get all the liquid cash he can stashed away before Mrs. Petersen comes after it."

"Oh." Lynn sank back in her chair, suddenly feeling overcome. It did not sound like a promising situation. "And it's the new owner who wants to put in the spa client?"

Sadie nodded as she too slumped back into her chair, the air of defeat clearly visible around her.

"That's the story."

"And you're sure it's true?" Lynn asked.

Sadie laughed, but without any humor. "Of course not. That information about Petersen and his secretary came straight from the two little birdies at the front desk, if you know what I mean."

"That doesn't necessarily mean a thing then." Lynn straightened up, rallying.

"Since Petersen sent a letter effectively terminating the lease, I would say it does."

"Doesn't he have to give us any warning?"

Sadie shook her head. "When Petersen stopped making repairs about two years ago, I refused to sign a long-term lease, instead going month to month. I even made like I was visiting other spaces, to see if I could bluff him into thinking we were leaving."

"And did you find any place?" Lynn asked hopefully. It would be a pain to move the clinic, but she considered that a minor obstacle that could be overcome with a couple of strong backs, boxes, and lots of packing tapes.

Sadie sighed, the corners of her mouth turning down. "Not for what we're willing to pay. But I think the hospital might be willing to give us some space, incorporate us into their facility."

"But they're not on the bus line and are thirty minutes away, at least. It's going to be hard for a lot of regulars to make it there."

"I know, I know. But like I said, it might be our only option."

Lynn nodded. At least Sadie had tried, she thought, glancing around. The problem was that even though the building wasn't on the water, it wasn't far from the center of town. You could still walk into the restaurants and pubs, and it might make a nice location for apartments or even a small office building. Or a fancy medical spa, Lynn supposed.

Lynn wasn't quite sure what to say next, only knowing that she wasn't quite ready to sink into the gloom along with Sadie. It just wasn't in her nature. There had to be a way. She loved working at the clinic, much more so than if she had been in a private practice. The patients here were grateful, relieved to know for the most part, that their problems were fixable, whether it was with a prescription, a bandage, or even some common sense. Of course, it didn't always work out that way, but that was the nature of medicine. Lynn wasn't a god. She was a human with a vast amount of knowledge and skills—growing every day—that she could apply to solve many problems. But not all of them.

This, however, wasn't one of those medical cases where the odds were not good. This was a real world, human being, financial, fixable problem.

There was a commotion and then the receptionist was yelling, "Doctor! We need a doctor…!" There was a scrum of voices and she heard a child crying, then the soothing voice of someone saying, "It will be ok, it's ok…"

Lynn launched herself out of her chair, adrenaline pumping. It might just be a kid with a sore throat, or a broken arm, but still she was a doctor and this was her job. Petersen would just have to wait a bit longer.

Chapter 4

Jackson looked at his watch and stopped pacing, and took a seat. He had made it to Petersen's real estate management company with plenty of time to spare for his four o'clock meeting. All the paperwork was in his attaché case, the terms reviewed and reworked meticulously. Petersen thought he was going to pull one over on him, but Jackson's intel was solid. Petersen was in the midst of a sticky situation between the current Mrs. Petersen and a future one, and he needed cash.

That Petersen needed some was evident in the shabby appearance of the waiting room. It might have been nice once, but the carpet was an indistinct gray, highlighted here and there by a darker patch, obviously some sort of stain. The wall had been papered in a pale cream, but there were scuff marks where chairs had rested against them, and the edges were starting to peel. A water stain decorated the corner of the ceiling and the furniture was vinyl and plastic and patched with pieces of plastic tape.

Yup, Petersen needed some cash—which Jackson happened to have, and plenty of it. Unlike many other buyers, he could offer an all-cash deal, without any bank financing needed. The deal could close within a few days and Petersen could do hell all with the money.

Petersen was late and it was irritating Jackson. Actually, it was infuriating him, but he told himself he was merely annoyed, because once you let emotions get hold of you during a business negotiation, you were done for. Besides, he knew he wanted this piece of property a little too badly. In fact, Petersen had offered him the pick of his portfolio, but Jackson had narrowed in on this one. Not for sentimental reasons, but he was pretty sure that since Petersen hadn't wanted to part with it, it was the best one to have.

There was a banging on the door and he saw the blur of a face pressed against the glass doors and the sight of long, dark curly hair. The door swung open and Jackson watched as a slim brunette walked over to the girl at the desk and asked to see Mr. Petersen. Her voice was clear, crisp, and authoritative.

Annabel, who had said she was the 'fill-in' receptionist, gave the same weary, disinterested reply that she had given Jackson, that Petersen was out and she didn't know when he'd be back.

The girl huffed and stamped her foot. She looked around and he saw she was attractive, pretty even, except that her face was twisted up in a frown and her brown eyes snapped with irritation and annoyance. Jackson smothered a smile. Apparently, Petersen being out was really cooking her goose too and she wasn't afraid to show it. She was older than he had first thought, late twenties, but with a youthful, energetic look to her.

Her hair was pulled back in a ponytail leaving a curly mass that swayed down her back and few stray tendrils had escaped, framing her face. She crossed her arms, chewed her lip, and tapped her foot. Expensive sneakers were on her feet, a riot of neon colors. She wore no makeup but she didn't need it. Liquid brown eyes were snapping with impatience.

And, Jackson thought, swallowing, there was something that looked suspiciously like blood splotched across the right side of her light blue scrubs.

"You're not Petersen, are you?" She had all but thrown herself into the worn plastic and metal chair next to him, since in the small waiting room, there weren't many options.

"No, I'm waiting for him too," Jackson said as he shifted slightly in his chair, feeling as if he needed to put some space between him and this bundle of energy. The woman gave him a quick once over and he braced himself.

"Do I know you? You look kind of familiar, you know?" Her eyes squinted as she took a long, careful look at him. He dreaded what she was going to say next, but then she snapped her fingers in triumph.

"I know you. You're Chase's brother, aren't you?" Her voice was firm and she spoke with a slightly flat accent, almost as if she were from the mid-west.

Jackson straightened, relieved and annoyed at the same time. He loved his brother, but it was tiresome to always be known because of that.

"Jax, right? The one who roams all over the place and barely comes home?"

"Jackson," he corrected her. Her mouth twitched up at the formality, and he wondered if she was laughing at him.

"I'm Lynn. Phoebe's friend?"

He gave a nod, his mind still working. Phoebe was his brother's new fiancée. He had met her exactly once on a quick London layover. She had seemed lovely, the perfect fit for his brother, but they hadn't had time to chat much before everyone had gone their separate ways.

"Of course," Jackson said, hoping that was vague enough. He was surprised. Phoebe was a California golden girl and he had trouble seeing what his elegant, fabric-designing future sister in law would have in common with this bundle of scrubs and stains.

"We used to live next to each other," Lynn offered. "I mean Phoebe and I. Before I moved to my own place. She still lives next to my parents."

Jackson gave another quick smile and then hoped that Lynn would be quiet. And still. Her fingers were tapping a beat on the arm of her chair and her leg; one sneakered foot crossed over the other was bouncing up and down.

He shifted in his chair again, wondering if he could ask her to stop moving. He was trying to rehearse the strategy he was going to use with Petersen one more time and she was definitely a distraction.

"Do you know when Petersen will be back?" Lynn twisted in the small chair and fixed him with chocolate brown eyes.

It took a moment to gather his thoughts before he could respond. Her eyes seemed to draw him in and he noticed that there was the slightest smattering of freckles across the bridge of her nose.

"I had an appointment scheduled to start twenty minutes ago," Jackson found himself saying, though he didn't know why. Any longer, and he would have to get up and go, force Petersen to call him. Waiting on the other man would leave him in a position of weakness. Right now, for some reason, he couldn't quite force himself to get out of the chair.

"Oh, I only need a moment of his time," Lynn said and there was a grimness in her tone.

"Then I am sure you won't mind waiting."

"Hmm," she said and fell silent, but only for a moment until both hands started to tap a steady tattoo on the side of the chair.

Jackson picked up one of the magazines. It was something glossy about people he didn't recognize and didn't care about, and he flipped through the pages mindlessly, trying to distract himself from the ball of nervous energy on his right.

"Do you mind?" he finally said.

"Do I mind? What?"

He gestured toward her tapping fingers.

"Oh, sorry," she said and her hands stilled. But it seemed that only made her brain more active, because she said, "Do you know what I do mind? I mind that when a little kid falls out of a tree and breaks his arm because the babysitter was texting on her phone. She doesn't hear the kid screaming for an hour, and then waits even longer to bring him in. And that's not to mention the bloody nose. That thing was a bleeder...Was too afraid to go to the ER at the hospital, and besides it was too far; she doesn't drive, they had to take the bus. What are people like that going to do when the clinic gets closed down...?"

She kept going, cataloging a list of injuries and other disasters. She hadn't drawn a breath once, Jackson thought, fascinated, watching her lips move. He had long since stopped listening to the actual words, too enthralled by her passion to pay attention to the subject of her tirade.

The glass door opened and looking like he had all the time in the world, in strolled Duane Petersen. He stopped short when he saw Jackson, who rose as the older man entered. Beside him, Lynn had fallen silent, but he could feel her vibrating with energy and intent next to him.

Chapter 5

Finally. Lynn thought, her mouth shutting and her eyes narrowing. She could barely remember why she had been wound up, but Jax, no Jackson, he wanted to be called, hadn't said one word, had just watched her with his icy blue eyes, his face impenetrable. Not once had he agreed with her, or shown any sign about what he thought of the injustice. Perhaps he thought cracking a smile would ruin the perfection of the blond hair, straight nose, and strong jaw.

Get a grip, she thought. She shouldn't be thinking about his beautiful white teeth, or his strong jaw, or his nicely sculpted cheekbones. It was only because it had been, what, like forever, since she had a date. Or even given a thought to a guy. Probably because she rarely came into contact with them. Nope, specializing in pediatrics meant she met a lot of cute kids and their moms. Just because she was in the middle of a dry spell, didn't mean she needed to lose her focus just because of a pretty face. It was Petersen she was here to deal with, and he had just walked in. And luckily his appearance didn't set her pulse racing.

"Just a moment, Mr. Petersen. I need to talk to you. It's about the Sailors' Clinic. I heard you're kicking us out of our space at the end of the month."

She jumped to her feet and spoke before Jackson was even fully standing. It was rude to interrupt, but she was on a mission.

Petersen, who looked as if he had just finished up a two-martini lunch, and if Lynn's nose was working right, smelled like it too, held up a hand.

"Well now, little lady, that's not my problem anymore. This here is the man you want to talk to, your new landlord. He told me it was a condition of the sale." He said it affably but there was a gleam in his eye that had Lynn thinking the joke was on her.

Lynn turned on her heel. Jackson looked at her and gave a thin smile which showed off his perfectly straight teeth.

"What?"

"Yup, I am just about to sell that property to Jax Sanders over here. Told me he'd only take it if it were an empty building." Next to her, she all but felt Jackson flinch at being called his nickname. Duane Petersen gave a sly little smile and Lynn suspected that he knew exactly which of Jackson's buttons to push.

Lynn swallowed, feeling her heart sink. "You're the new owner," she said turning to Jackson.

Jackson Sanders looked at his watch again. "If Mr. Petersen will be so good as to sign those papers, then yes, I guess I will be."

Lynn's heart sank. She remembered what Chase had said about his brother, that he was all business. Why, Jackson hadn't even come home for Phoebe's engagement party, or if Lynn remembered correctly, been seen in Queensbay in years—too busy chasing his career all across the world.

Compassion and doing the right thing would be a hard sell with him, Lynn realized as she looked him over, in his tailored business suit, his face carefully neutral as if not one bit of what Lynn had told him about the importance of the clinic to the community had made it through that wall of armor. Well, she had always enjoyed a challenge.

Mr. Petersen gave a laugh, one that wasn't all that hearty. "Who would have believed it? Chase's baby brother, all grown up and trying to wheel and deal with the big boys? Can't believe you're back in town, but I guess time heals all wounds."

Lynn heard the edge in Petersen's voice and she saw Jackson bristle as Petersen gave him a slap on the back. It was designed to look like a friendly gesture, but the sound of it was too loud, as if Petersen had intended for it to hurt.

"Mr. Petersen, I have other business to attend to, so if we're done," Jackson turned back to Lynn and gave another of his tight smiles, clearly telling her to get out of the way.

"Oh, we're hardly done here, Jax," she said, making sure she put all of the emphasis on his name. She saw his mouth twist in a grimace, and strangely satisfied, she turned to go. With as much grace as she could muster, she walked herself out of the office. Unfortunately, she missed the fact that the wall was not all door. She just about smacked her face into the gold-colored 'N' in Petersen before she caught herself, stopped, and found the door.

There was the sound of heavy silence behind her and then she was almost certain that she heard the beginning of Duane Petersen's slightly tipsy giggle.

Chapter 6

She had decided to work off her anger and humiliation of how the meeting with Petersen and Jackson had ended by doing a hill run. Getting hot and sweaty had a way of taking her mind off things, and if this was the only kind of release available to her, then so be it. Wearing a fleece, running pants and a reflective vest, since dusk was already falling, she set off from the boardwalk in front of the harbor and headed up the streets to the hilly bluffs that encircled the water.

She jogged past the byways of the village proper, a mix of stores and houses close into the center of town that gradually gave way to single-family residences as she got further out. She passed by Darby Callahan's house, the owner of her favorite deli, The Golden Pear, and then she was pushing herself up higher and higher, taking a zig-zagging way up to the Heights, the neighborhood that sat on the east side of Queensbay.

For the most part, homes were a mix of styles, mostly colonials and Victorians, harking back to the days when Queensbay had been a true maritime town, its main industries shipbuilding, fishing, and whaling, with a few more contemporary homes thrown in. The jumble of styles was strangely harmonious, rather than jarring. She'd grown up in Colorado, where everything was open, new, and big. Queensbay was quaint and charming with none of the ruggedness of the western landscape. Everything here was snug and cozy. Sure there were a few sorry-looking worn-down buildings, but those were the exception. Queensbay had the air, ha—with the exception of the clinic—of a lady of a certain age getting a subtle facelift and undergoing a makeover.

She made it up into the Heights, where her parents lived in a sturdy Craftsman style home that was all solid and snug, with fireplaces and solid wood details and a spectacular kitchen, since her mother prided herself on being a gourmet cook. She passed their house, saw most of the lights were off, and figured that they were still out, maybe working late at the hospital or lab; or perhaps they had stopped and had dinner out. Next to that was her friend Phoebe's house, a beautiful, rambling white cottage, where she lived and ran her business.

Phoebe lived with Chase, her fiancé, who was Jackson's brother. Lynn discretely kept her eye peeled as she jogged past it. Maybe Jackson was staying there while Phoebe and Chase were out of town. If she just happened to run into him, then she just might have the chance to talk to him again about the clinic. And this time she would be prepared: cool, calm, and collected.

She sucked in a deep breath of air. Too bad she wasn't known for being calm and collected unless there was a medical emergency. Well, she would just have to channel her favorite movie star of all time, the late, great Savannah Ryan. The woman had known how to play every type, except for scattered and disheveled. That was just how Lynn must have appeared to Jackson in her dirty scrubs and passionate attitude this afternoon.

The Ivy House was dark as she ran by. Her second chance to talk with Jackson would have to wait, she thought, as she headed down the hill and home.

Lights were glowing in the houses and buildings as she passed them and the fall day was turning rapidly into a cool, crisp evening. Already she could smell the scent of wood smoke in the air, as the people of Queensbay lit their fireplaces, welcoming the change of seasons.

She came down finally to the relatively flat stretch of road in front of the harbor and slowed to a walk, allowing her body to cool down. She was breathing heavily, trying to fill her lungs with oxygen, and her thighs burned as she climbed the steps to her top-floor apartment.

Her back was slicked with sweat underneath her running shirt and she was thankful to enter the cool air of her home. She went into her bedroom, stripped off her sweaty workout clothes, dropped them in a pile with her dirty scrubs, and hopped into the shower.

The hot water came in a torrent over her as she scrubbed herself with the soap. She thought about shaving her legs, but decided against it, figuring that she had the next few days off and since she had nothing more planned than to crash on the couch with a glass of wine and some home decorating magazines, it probably wasn't necessary.

She wrapped herself in a warm, plush towel and threw herself down on the bed. The duvet cover was a housewarming gift from Phoebe, a celebration of the fact that Lynn had finally gotten her own place. Of course, she'd lived on her own—in dorms, student apartments—but when she had accepted the residency in Queensbay, where her parents had moved to, it seemed smart to save some money by living with them.

But now that she had—or about to be *did have*, she corrected herself—a real job, she had decided it was time to move out on her own. Her parents had wanted her to stay, of course. Her mom was a great cook and doing laundry didn't require hoarding quarters. Still, it was time for her to move on, to live like a grownup.

Here she was in her first real place, a neat little one bedroom on the third floor of the Osprey Arms annex. It was newly renovated and smelled of fresh wood and paint. So far, Lynn had the whole floor to herself. Chase had said he would be getting other tenants in eventually but he was happy to have her in here first.

Lynn suspected she'd gotten a friend and family discount on the rent, since it was fairly affordable for someone working at a non-profit, but when she had asked about it, Chase had laughed and told her just not to throw any crazy parties. And there, she thought, was the difference between the two brothers. Chase was thoughtful and generous and Jackson was a hard-ass, with his cold blue eyes, too blond hair and chiseled cheekbones. There was something about the way he stood; his fancy business suits that told her Jackson took himself way too seriously.

Stick up his ass, she thought and was about to think of a few other apt descriptors when her phone vibrated. Sighing, she roused herself, hoping it wasn't work calling her in for an emergency, and reached for it. With a groan, she pulled the phone towards her and saw it was a text from her mother.

Don't forget about your date with Nate…it's all arranged for you to meet him at Salsa Salsa.

Lynn groaned again. She had forgotten about being set up on a blind date by her mother. Why had she agreed to this? Oh right, so that it could be a disaster and she could prove her mother wrong and hopefully get her off her back about her love life. She just didn't understand why it was so important to everyone else that she date. Her mother said she was too picky, but Lynn preferred to think of it as being patient. Besides, she'd never felt that urgent need to couple up just for the sake of it. Her life had been so filled, so full of pressure that inevitably anyone she did date either complained of how busy she was; or if he was a doctor too was just as consumed and distracted by his career as she was by hers.

Lynn texted back *long shift today, feeling tired, may need to cancel...*

It was about half a second before the phone ring. She didn't need to look at the caller ID to know who it was.

"Oh no, you don't," Regina Masters said without preamble.

"Don't what? I'm tired," Lynn said. And she was. She was tired from her run, tired of thinking about the clinic closing, and worst of all, she was tired of seeing the smug look on Jackson Sanders' face as she had almost smashed through a glass door pop into her mind. She'd had enough humiliation for one day and a blind date at a mediocre Mexican restaurant could only be the icing on the cake.

"So, you're a doctor: you're always tired. You said you had a few days off. Why not spend a few hours of it going out with a nice young man?" Her mother's tone was reasonable, just like the dependable, methodical clinical researcher Regina was.

"Mom." Lynn knew her voice contained the beginnings of a teenaged-like whine. Her mother was meddling, which she seldom did, which made it all the more worrisome.

"Don't 'Mom' me. Look, you've barely had a date since college. And even those didn't sound very romantic. Hand holding a boy while his high school sweetheart dumps him and takes him back is not my idea of a relationship. Or how about the one who had the mother issues? I mean you keep going out with all these guys with so much baggage. It's no wonder they exhaust you."

Lynn frowned. She had confessed the sorry state of her love life to her mom in a fit of self-pity.

"I know, Mom. That's why I stopped dating. You know, so I could focus on finishing school, my residency, becoming a doctor. You're the one who told me I had a 'fixer up' mentality."

Her mother sighed. "You do tend to see the best in people, and that's just one of the things that's so wonderful about you. But you do keep picking boys that seem to need a lot of attention. But this one isn't like that. He's good looking, has a great job."

"And why did his last relationship end?" Lynn shot back.

"His mother said that the girl had to move back home to take care of her sick father, reconnected with her ex-boyfriend, and got knocked up."

"So he's probably still into her," Lynn pointed out.

"The point is not to get into a relationship, Lynn."

"It's not? Are you sure you're a mother?"

Regina Masters laughed. "You need to practice going on a date. I do not think Nate is the one, but he can afford to pay for dinner."

"At a taco place."

"Accountants are frugal. It's not a bad thing. Talk, have a drink, listen to what he says, pretend to be interested or don't; and at the end of the night you can walk away, but at least you'll have had some practice."

"So you want me to intentionally lead him on?"

"You know, Lynn, your father and I are very happy, but it wasn't like he swept me off my feet. Or that we looked across a crowded room and saw each other. I had to kiss a lot of frogs before I met your father, but that also meant I knew exactly what I was looking for."

"Mom, that's just it. I am finally settled, with a somewhat predictable schedule. For the past ten years I've been busting my ass to become a doctor, and now I am one. Why can't I just enjoy it, instead of getting all carried away with finding a guy?"

"Practice, dear. Besides, you deserve to be treated special, and that's what dates are. Everyone is nice and on their best behavior."

Lynn sighed. She loved her mother, but they were two different people. Her mom's idea of a good time was a four-course gourmet dinner and a game of Scrabble. Lynn's not so much.

"Sounds boring. How do you know this guy is so great?"

It was her mother's turn to sigh. "Look, you're right. I don't know if Nate is great or not, but he sounds normal. And for you, I think that's a step in the right direction. Besides, you haven't met anyone else here, have you?"

The hopeful question hung in the air. Lynn didn't answer immediately, wondering why her mind suddenly flitted to Jackson Sanders and the way he had looked in a suit that must have cost as much as a minor surgical operation. Lynn ran a hand over her face. What was she thinking? And she had barged in there in dirty scrubs. He probably hadn't given her a second thought, unless it was as part of a story he told over a glass of expensive wine to his cronies in the boardroom.

She took a deep breath. Maybe her mother was right. Perhaps she should go out and have some fun. Not that she needed someone to pay for her dinner, but the thought was sort of charming in an old-fashioned way. No one had bought her dinner since Joe, the one with the mother issues, and that had been on his meal plan in the campus dining hall. A nice dinner, a glass of wine, and maybe some conversation that wouldn't resolve around medical specialties all of a sudden didn't sound like such a bad idea. And how bad could this Nate be?

"He's not a doctor?" she asked, checking.

"No, he does something with computers," her mother assured her.

"Fine, I'll go on my date with Nate."

There was as audible sigh of relief from her mother. "Oh thank goodness. I think you'll have fun. And I promise you won't be embarrassed to be seen with him."

"That's the best you can promise?" Lynn asked, wondering if she really needed to go back into the shower and shave her legs.

"Just, don't wear your scrubs, ok? Something besides running shoes? And no fleece. One hundred percent natural fibers, ok?" her mother said before she hung up.

Lynn flopped back on the bed, staring up at her perfectly white ceiling, giving herself a moment to breathe through the panic that was coursing through her. A date. She hadn't been on one of those for years. Sure, guys had tried, but she'd always been able to say that she was too busy. The few times she had decided to give it a whirl, they had been predictable. Dinner at some budget-friendly place, the inevitable talk about work, a tangle over the bill, ultimately deciding to split it, then an awkward kiss with the predictable expectation of "we're students, we don't have much time, why not just get on with it?"

She hadn't succumbed—ok, maybe once, to a particularly charming and buff surgical intern, but he had an ego the size of the Rockies and she hadn't been too disappointed when their relation-ship lost its fizzle.

But Nate was not a doctor. He was a full-fledged grownup with a job. According to her mother. And Nate's mother. Mothers who had met while getting their hair done and decided that their children just had to meet. Too bad mothers were such lousy judges of characters.

She sighed. At least her mom's heart was in the right place. Her parents were madly in love and thought everyone around them should be as well. And if that was taking too damn long, well then, her mother wasn't above stepping in and helping out. If her older brother, Kyle, had been around, instead of halfway across the country, Lynn knew her mother would be giving him the same treatment. But it was a lot harder to fix someone up on a blind date remotely. So Lynn was the de facto winner of the maternal dating game.

Back to the shower, Lynn decided, knowing it was hopeless. If she actually shaved her legs it would practically guarantee no one besides herself would get anywhere near them tonight. But she was a doctor—being prepared was second nature.

Chapter 7

Jackson sat down at the polished oak bar of the Osprey Arms and had the bartender pour him a celebratory Scotch.

"Cheers," Jackson said as he raised his glass, toasting himself in the long mirror that ran the length of the wall behind the bar. Paulie, the bartender, was placidly wiping down glasses and only nodded. He was a much better listener than talker, which was why he as good at his job.

"Good day?" A questioning voice came from behind him.

"Jake!" Jackson swiveled in the barstool and took in his old friend. Jake Owen had been a star athlete at Queensbay Harbor High and now owned a thriving construction business. He had close-cropped brown hair, a summer tan, and a slightly wary expression on his face as if he couldn't quite believe what he was saying.

"It's been a long time. What, three years?" Jackson offered, by way of apology as Jake stood there, hands thrust in the pockets of his barn coat. Not a hint of a smile lightened his face. Jackson took a breath. He had known no part of this would be easy but he had thought that Jake, of all people, might be inclined to cut him some slack.

"Five years, Mr. Jet Setter," Jake corrected him, his hands still stuck in the pockets of his jacket. He rocked back on his feet, as if assessing the situation.

"Can I buy you a drink to make up for it?" Jackson offered, hoping Jake would say yes instead of turning around and walking out. He probably deserved that, but still he needed to make some amends, and Jake was one of the first on his list.

"Only a fool would say no to a free drink," Jake said, hiking himself up on a barstool. "I'll have the Macallan twenty-year-old, neat," he told Paulie.

Jackson raised an eyebrow. That would set him back a pretty penny. "I see your tastes have matured a bit."

"Only when someone else is buying," Jake said with just a hint of acrimony.

Jackson knew he should flat out apologize, get all of the gooey emotional stuff out of the way, but he was a guy and Jake was his oldest friend, and he just couldn't bring himself to say the words.

Paulie poured the drink and slid it over to Jake, who took, raised it and said, "It's good to see you."

"And you," Jackson acknowledged, and the two of them drank. There was silence and Jake stared straight ahead at the row of liquor bottles lining the wall behind the bar. Behind them was a quiet swell of conversation as the diners at the table ate their meals. Jackson waited, knowing Jake was making a decision.

"I hear you've been busy," Jake said, finally, as if no time had passed, and Jackson relaxed a bit. He'd been forgiven, at least enough so they could have a conversation.

"Yes, I've kept myself busy. I got placed in jobs all over the world, so I've been living in hotels or rental apartments. Couple of months here, a couple there, once a whole year almost in Dubai. I was in New York recently, except for the past couple of weeks when I had to go back to the desert."

Jake nodded, but his question was pointed. "You back for good now?"

"Yes," Jackson said. "I'm back. I hear you're going to be starting the renovations on the hotel soon."

"Didn't know you were going to be helping out," Jake said and there was an edge to his voice.

"Only if you need me, which I'm sure you won't," Jackson said. Jake and Chase had been working together for a while and Jackson hadn't really thought how his showing up would look to Jake.

"I see," Jake said unenthusiastically.

Jackson knew he should say more, tell Jake the real reason he was back in town, but he was afraid his friend would think he was crazy. It was a bit of a hare-brained idea, but then again he was tired of playing it safe.

Jake took another sip of his drink but kept quiet. Ok, so Jackson hadn't expected it to be just like old times. Or maybe he had. But here was Jake, playing it close to the vest.

"I hear you did a great job fixing up my grandmother's house."

"It will be done in another week, or so, then you can have a real estate agent come in and take a look, get a value on it. Should go for a lot, waterfront and all that. A little modern for most people, but I'm sure you'll still find a buyer," Jake said, giving him a sideways glance.

Jackson nodded. He had worked with closely with the architect on the house plans; to make sure it came out just the way he wanted it to. He'd had Chase handle the constructions details with Jake, because he figured that Jake wouldn't have taken the job if he'd known it was for him.

"Chase said you cut a deal on the work, but really that's not necessary."

Jake held up a hand. "I did it for Chase, not you. We do a lot of business together."

"Well, thanks. I actually might have a new project for you if you're interested," Jackson said casually.

"I'm not flying off to Hong Kong, or Dubai, or wherever you're shipping off to next." Jake's voice had a trace of bitterness.

"Nope, this one is local," Jackson assured him and waited.

"I might be interested," Jake said slowly, and Jackson could see the telltale gleam of curiosity in his friend's eye.

"It's the old Sail Makers' building."

"You mean Duane Petersen's property, the one with the clinic in it?" Jake's forehead creased in a frown. He twisted so he was facing Jackson, one booted knee propped up on the rung of the barstool. Jackson felt a wash of relief. Jake was a sucker for the old buildings around Queensbay, devoted to bringing them back to life. Jackson knew his real dream was to restore the old Queensbay Show House, a derelict hulk of a building that had once housed a theater.

"That's the one. I think the building will be perfect for what I have in mind, I'd love to turn it into an open concept office space, something high end." Jackson nodded, his fingers drumming on the table in excitement. A new project always got him going and since he intended this one to be personal, it was doubly so.

"Are you going to keep the clinic there?"

Jackson frowned, surprised that it had come up a second time that day. "I wasn't planning on it. Doesn't exactly fit in with the vision I had for the place. I was thinking retail on the first floor, maybe a restaurant, offices above, or possibly even apartments."

Jake gave a laugh and then took another sip of his single malt. "Then that could be an issue."

Jackson shifted in his seat uneasily. He thought about the little spitfire who had been in Petersen's office today. Lynn had been her name. She had a fire in her eye and an intense energy, especially on the subject of the clinic. Memories of their encounter had kept popping up all afternoon, even as he went about sealing the deal with Petersen and handling the paperwork.

"How so?"

"Did you look over the building before you bought it? Word is the town council has wanted to condemn the property for a while, since Petersen hasn't dropped a dime into it for years. But they don't, just so the clinic will stay open."

"I would think the clinic would welcome the chance to get out of there and find some more modern space."

Jake gave a quick laugh and shook his head. "I don't think they can afford to find anything better."

"I thought the clinic had an endowment, funding, that all the whole biddies in town were behind it," Jackson said.

"Tough economy, plus the old biddies are like that - old. Sure, they've gotten some money from a few of the local big donors, but it's really just a bandage over the open wound. Talk is the hospital wants to take it over, in which case they would probably have the money they need to stay, even if you raised the rent."

"Well, times change, don't they," Jackson said, finishing most of his drink. He didn't like to think that his plans wouldn't work out. He'd just assumed that the clinic would be willing to move, but now, based on what Jake was telling him, that wasn't necessarily the case. If they wouldn't go quietly, he'd just have to make them.

"Not everyone in Queensbay likes to forget the past," Jake said, and Jackson knew it was a deliberate jab at him.

"I didn't forget you. I just…"

"We were supposed to go into business together, Jackson. You were going to be the brains of the operation and I was going to be the brawn."

"You've done just fine for yourself," Jackson pointed out.

"No thanks to you." Jake's voice rose and Jackson was aware that Paulie, at the far end of the bar, had paused what he was doing and was standing at the ready, poised to intervene if things got heated.

"Look, I had a plan, everything mapped out. And then she…and then she's dead." Jackson found himself stumbling over the words, but kept going. "And you know what, I couldn't handle it. I couldn't be here anymore. No one wanted me here anymore."

Jackson was aware that he had stood up, pushed off his barstool and was in a tensed, ready position as if for a fight.

But Jake's quarterback bulk stayed right on the barstool while he eyed him. "That's not true. I was there for you."

Jackson ran a hand over his face. He couldn't explain it to anyone, couldn't quite explain just how much Ashley's death had cost him.

"But I get it."

"You do?" Jackson asked, not trusting the hope that was creeping in.

"Yeah. You said it. You admitted that you went off the rails after Ashley died. I get it, I would have too. But dude, you just picked up and ran—didn't talk to us, any of us, for years. We knew her too, you know. We were all friends. Not all of us blamed you for what happened, you know. Or we didn't care. We wanted to stand by you."

"Thanks," Jackson said, quietly, taking a deep breath. Yup, this was going to be harder than he thought, but better to get the subject of Ashley over with sooner than later. "I just couldn't, the memories..." He stopped. He was done lying, he had to tell himself. Ashley would always be a part of the past, but she couldn't take away his future anymore.

"I understand. And I'm glad you're back, whatever the reason." Jake clapped him awkwardly on the shoulder and Jackson decided he didn't need to say anymore, and that if it wasn't quite the truth, at least it wasn't a lie.

Jackson nodded. "Thanks." And then to change the subject, "So you think I'm going to have problems with the clinic? The director, Sadie, seemed very understanding about the whole thing." Or, if not understanding at least she didn't seem too upset. Perhaps she was imagining a nice retirement.

Jake laughed. "It's not Sadie you have to worry about. It's Lynn."

"You mean a brunette ball of energy about this big?" Jackson held his hand out about chest high.

"That would be her. Lynn Masters. She works there, has for a while, and it's become her pet project. I don't think she's going to take the closing lying down."

Jackson thought back to the woman he had met. Her brown, intense eyes, the way she had stared him down, even though she was half his size. Even her clumsy exit had been saved by the fluid way her body moved, dodging the glass wall and finding the door at the last minute. Jackson had never given much thought to how a woman would look in scrubs, but he had to admit Lynn had worn them well.

He shook his head. Maybe she would calm down, accept the news gracefully. If she was worried about losing her job, perhaps he could find a way to help her with that, call on some connections. She'd said she was friends with Chase and Phoebe, so there had to be a way to make this turn out right for her. Yes, he thought, all he needed was to make sure Lynn was taken care of and she would be no problem. Most women were fine like that.

Jake was gazing at him, a speculative look on her face. "She's a nice girl, you know..."

Jackson shook his head. "Don't even go there."

"It's been five years, my friend."

Jackson looked deep into the amber liquid in his glass. "That's what my mom says, as if it matters. I didn't come back here to get into a relationship. I managed to dodge them over seven continents so I think I'm safe in Queensbay. After all, nobody in this town would touch me with a ten-foot pole."

Jake shook his head. "Maybe. Of course, some people do have long memories. But you have a thick skin, right?"

Jackson felt his stomach sink. He had wanted to think that time would have made it easier, maybe even had people forgetting about it, but now Jake was warning him that might not be the case.

"Thanks for the notice. I'll be sure to put on my elephant hide when I go out there."

Jake nodded and pursed his lips. "There will be talk, you know. Some people have long memories, but I think if you just try to be nice, you know."

"I can be nice," Jackson said, surprised.

"Sure you can be, but most people remember you as an arrogant prick with a fast car, a baseball scholarship, and *fuck you* attitude."

"And as a murderer." Jackson pushed his drink away.

"Police said it was an accident," Jake said.

Jackson nodded. It had been one giant accident—his relationship with Ashley and the car crash had only been the icing on the cake.

"Try telling that to the Morans," Jackson said.

"Doesn't matter; just keep your head up high," Jake said.

"And that's the best bit of advice you can give me?"

Jake shrugged. "Yup. I don't have much else. I'm a single guy, working construction who still uses my old bedroom as an office."

Jackson laughed, knowing that Jake's humble act was mostly that. Queensbay Construction was doing a fine business since Jake had officially taken over the family business.

"Single? You mean Darby Reese turned you down again?" Jackson said, referring to Jake's old prom date.

"Turned me down? She went and married another man. She and Sean Callahan are going to have a baby any day now." Jake shook his head but Jackson could tell he was genuinely happy for the couple.

"Who knows, maybe there's a fish in the sea for you? We are, after all, on a harbor." Jackson raised his own glass in a toast.

Jake gave him a lopsided smile and they tapped glasses.

"What about you? Ever thought of, you know...?"

"What, girls? Dating?"

Jake nodded.

Jackson gave a bitter laugh, thinking of Helen's last email to him. "I have dated. Even had as you might call them, relationships; but I'm just not the marrying type."

Jake laughed. "Funny, and I always thought you'd be the first to settle down."

Jackson shook his head, "Let's just say I don't believe in happy endings anymore."

Jake nodded, took a sip of his drink, and Jackson did the same, wondering why all of sudden an image of Lynn Masters flashed through his head. He gave a shake, as if to clear the thought from him. Getting involved, caring, was the last thing he needed right now.

Chapter 8

Lynn was nursing her disappointment over a glass of red wine at Quent's Pub, absorbing the cocoon-like feeling of the very British atmosphere. Quent had an accent that could only be described as vaguely British but was an avowed anglophile when it came to décor. His pub looked like it could have stepped out of a small town on the rugged Scottish coast, with its burnished wood bar, cozy red leather booths, dark green walls and dartboards. He kept the theme going with a menu of pub food, songs from the British invasion on the playlist and a full range of beers from across the pond.

As cozy as it was in here, with a small fire going and the low hum of conversation, Lynn was just about ready to go when she saw Tory Somers walk into the pub with what looked like the entire North Coast Outfitters softball team. They were loud and boisterous, but she managed to catch the other girl's eye and Tory came over.

"Did you win?" Lynn asked. She and Tory had met when she's agreed to donate her time to redo the clinic's website and they had managed to squeeze in a few social outings like coffee and a few runs together into their busy schedules. Tory was head of technology at North Coast Outfitters, the local clothing and accessories business owned by Chase Sanders.

"Yup, beat Queensbay Construction two to one." Tory had light brown hair that was always a perfectly streaked blond, summer or winter, so Lynn had to guess most of it was artifice.

"Good for you." Lynn knew that the rivalry between North Coast Outfitters and Queensbay Construction was good natured but intense.

"Yup, it means that drinks are on them tonight," Tory said with a smile, and then she turned her attention to Lynn. "Killer boots, by the way. But aren't they a bit much for a drink at the pub? And if you're trying to pick up men, might I suggest online dating over hooking up with a barfly from the local dive?"

"This ain't no dive," Quentin, the owner of the aforementioned dive, stood before them, shaved head glistening, arms folded across his chest allowing the massive biceps in his arms to ripple. "It's a fine family establishment."

"Yeah, we've heard it all before," Tory waved Quent's objections away. "We'll have two pitchers, please."

Quent laughed. "And whose tab is this going on—yours on the other team's?"

Tory flashed a smile. "Not ours. Their star slugger didn't show up. Made it that much easier for us to bury them."

Quent let out a rumble, which for him, passed as a laugh.

"And get my friend here another glass of whatever she's having."

Lynn was about to protest, but decided that it didn't matter. After all, she was trying to drown her sorrows.

"Why the fancy duds?" Tory asked, leaning over the back of the barstool, taking in Lynn's dark jeans and v-neck silk blouse.

"I had a date," Lynn said before she realized it. She had vowed to keep her date with Nate to herself.

"What, you on a date? Do I get to meet him? Is he in the bathroom?"

"No, we said goodbye at the restaurant. I came home and decided that it was too nice a night to go home and drink by myself."

Tory shot a look around at the empty barstools surrounding Lynn. "I don't mean to bring my over precise computer developer brain to the situation, but you are, in reality, alone."

"No," Lynn corrected her, "not to bring my overly literal medical mind to the table, but there were twelve other people before two softball teams came in. Technically, I'm surrounded by people, and therefore I am not drinking alone."

"It was that bad, huh?" Tory said in sympathy, taking a seat on one of the barstools.

Lynn took another sip of her wine and looked over when she felt the pull of Tory's intense gaze on her.

"Oh no you don't. Look you can't drop a bomb like that and then go back to calmly drinking your wine like you were making small talk about the weather."

"It wasn't that bad," Lynn started to say, and then in spite of herself, she laughed. "Ok, so he took me to Salsa Salsa."

"You mean the newest version of Augie's?"

Lynn nodded and Tory laughed. "That place changes menus and cuisines every six months."

Lynn laughed too, since Tory was right. Augie's, located a bit off the main street and therefore out the way of the casual stroller by, struggled with an identity crisis. Greek, Italian, French cuisines, had all been tried—the one constant a killer margarita recipe. Finally, the owner, Augusta, had given in and gone for a Tex-Mex theme. Unfortunately, the margaritas were still the best thing on the menu.

"That's the one."

"I hope the margarita went down smoothly."

"It sure made listening to his stories about his Civil War figurines and his job a lot more interesting. He's an accountant. My mom thought he was in computers, but apparently that's his older brother."

"So?" Tory said. "My dad's an accountant and a cool guy. Too old for you but still, he's cool."

"His hobbies include memorizing vice presidential candidates. Did you know that John Quincy Adams used to swim naked every day in the river?"

"Ok, umm gross," Tory said as Quent slid two frothy pitchers of beer toward her, with a stack of glasses. "I guess there won't be a second date?"

Lynn shook her head. "Let's just say, the date with Nate was the icing on the cake of a very bad day." Nate didn't have anything wrong with him. He was good looking and he paid for dinner, calculating the tip in his head to exactly eighteen and a half percent. And most of his vice presidential trivia had been interesting. It was just that he didn't do anything for her. Lynn took a deep breath and twirled her wineglass in her fingers. She really didn't need it, had just wanted to be with some company in a familiar setting.

"How could it be any worse?" Tory asked as she gathered the pitchers and cups to her.

"Well, the clinic's closing," Lynn said.

"Closing? For real this time?" Tory's caramel-colored eyes were wide with concern.

"Yes, and it's all because your boss's brother has decided that a medical spa is more important than a clinic to the people of Queensbay."

"My boss's brother...Who? Oh, you mean Jackson Sanders? What does he have to do with it? Last I heard he was Dubai or New York, or something like that.

"Well, apparently he's here, all six foot two of him, and he's bought the building from Duane Petersen."

"Hmm," Tory said thoughtfully. "So the international playboy has gotten tired of the traveling lifestyle and come home to roost. I guess traveling the world worked out well for him. I wouldn't have thought he'd come here and buy a building. Especially that one. It looks like it's about to fall down. Wonder if he knew that."

"Well, he did buy it and apparently he's a rich enough jerk that he thinks he can do anything he wants, and that includes having a better class of tenants. Why does everything have to get gentrified? I mean a medical spa? Do they call it that just because the people who work there wear white coats? It's an oxymoron, that's what it is. I mean, Jackson Sanders can take his snooty attitude and five thousand dollar-suits and go jump in the harbor for all I care."

"You sound pretty worked up, but it sounds like Jackson. He's not exactly in touch with his soft side." Tory trailed off and Lynn looked at her sharply.

"Do you know Jackson?"

An awkward half smile flitted across Tory's face. "Not exactly. I mean, it's more like I know of him."

"Why, does his ice prince reputation precede him?" Lynn couldn't help asking, knowing that she was dipping into the gossip arena. She had been dwelling on her encounter with Jackson all afternoon and evening, even while eating dinner. Nate had brown eyes, while Jackson had blue ones. Nate's nose was slightly bulbous, while Jackson's had been sharp and perfectly straight. All she could think about was the way his light blue eyes had regarded her coolly, as if she were no more than an unwelcome distraction, distracting her from Nate and his facts about the vice presidents.

As a doctor, Lynn was used to being viewed in a variety of ways, from an angel of mercy to the harbinger of bad news. But never had she felt so inconsequential. It had gnawed away at her all day.

"No," Tory said. Lynn waited.

"No...so what happened? Did his puppy get run over when he was a little kid and that's his excuse for his bad behavior today?"

Tory shrugged, clearly not comfortable with the topic. "Something like that, but worse."

Slightly taken aback and shamed at her own flippancy, she stammered out a "Sorry...I didn't...What could be worse?"

"No, it's cool. Look, it was a while ago but his fiancée died. Like right before the wedding and well, she was from around here and they were kind of the hometown couple, and after it happened, Jackson just kind of left town and that was it. I mean, don't get me wrong, Jackson's not like Chase at all. He was always pretty cocky, kind of a jerk, in fact. But I guess you know, his fiancée dying, that really hit him hard, so he left. He kept in touch with his family of course, but from what I gathered, he was working and traveling all over the world, trying to forget her and what happened."

"Wow, heavy stuff," Lynn said digesting it all, trying to put together the picture of Jackson and his business-like demeanor with that of a grief-stricken fiancé.

"Yup," Tory agreed.

There was a silence, and from behind them they heard a shout, then some laughter. The pub was beginning to liven up and she saw Tory glance back at the table of thirsty softball players she'd left behind.

"You should join us. Just one beer?"

"I do have tomorrow off," Lynn said. Suddenly, sitting at a table full of people her own age sounded like a very good idea. After learning about Jackson's past, she felt even more like she needed a distraction to put the thought of him, and his baggage train, out of her mind.

"And," Tory said, with a smile, "someone else is buying."

Chapter 9

The moon was up and almost full, casting a silvery trail along the calm surface of the harbor. It was getting late but Lynn still felt drawn to the water and decided a quick detour down to the boardwalk along the edge of Queensbay Harbor was in order. She'd grown up out west, among the plains and the mountains and had never thought she was a water girl until she came to Queensbay.

She'd left the bar and the softball players after another beer, ok, maybe two beers, but she felt fine, knowing the walk home along the quaint streets of Queensbay would help clear her head. She gazed down at the water into the ripples of silvered moonlight. She shivered, wishing she had thought to bring a coat. The heat of the day evaporated quickly now and the nights were markedly chillier, but the view was still breathtaking.

It had been fun to hang out with people near to her own age. Everyone had been friendly and the talk had been about normal things. No Civil War strategy rehashes or politics—historical or otherwise. She might even have agreed to join one of the teams, but of that she wasn't quite certain.

Cold now, she headed for her building and started the climb up the stairs, tottering a bit in her high heeled boots. She knew she should think about getting to bed, but in truth she wasn't tired. Her long nights as a resident, plus her own natural temperament had made sleep a luxury for so long she just didn't need as much as other people. Instead, she was restless, unsettled.

Maybe it was the full moon. After all, there was a known correlation between a full moon and a spike in emergency room visits. For whatever reason, people seemed just a little bit crazier when the moon was at full strength.

She didn't feel crazy exactly, maybe a bit morose. After all, she'd just had a lousy date and was about to lose her job. That was a blow, but she was more worried about what would happen with her Healthy Kids Now program. She had made so much progress with it in the past few months, really started to help a lot of kids, that she didn't want to see it all end.

She got to the top and was surprised to see the light was out on the landing, and because of the way the building was situated it was dark on the balcony that ran in front of the apartments. She wasn't afraid, but the light of the moon was a dim gray wash here and it was hard to see.

She fumbled in her purse for her keys and dropped them, of course. With a sigh, she bent down to retrieve them, her eyes trying to grow accustomed to the darkness. One of her high heels caught in the groove between the long deck boards and she wobbled, trying to catch herself when she crashed into something behind her. Her head hit something hard and before she could help herself, a curse slipped out, as if that could lessen the pain.

Fighting the impulse to just lay back and rest, she started to struggle to her feet when the world gave way behind her.

Chapter 10

"What are you doing?"

There was an angry voice and all of sudden she was blinded by a bright light. It took a moment for things to make sense, and when they did, she realized that Jackson Sanders was looming above her, and that the top half of her had somehow managed to find its way inside the door, while her legs, her boots, and keys were very much stuck outside in the cold dark moonlight.

In vain, she struggled to get up, using her arms and her thigh muscles in an attempt to propel herself forward. She almost had it when she felt, rather than saw, something swoop down. Within a moment she had been hauled upright, Jackson Sander's arm holding her steady. It was warm against her bare skin, a lick of fire in the cold night air.

His blond hair was slightly less combed than before, and his dress shirt was untucked and hanging out over his suit trousers. He was barefoot and she judged, after bringing her eyes back up to his face, seriously pissed.

"What am I doing? What are you doing?" Lynn managed to stammer, taking a step back. The high heel of her boot however, was still caught, and she would have stumbled but for his arm, which kept her standing. Drawing a deep breath, she put a hand up on the doorjamb and bent down, and pulled on her heel, releasing her foot. At least now she wasn't stuck, but even in her heels she was still much shorter than he was, and she was now at the disadvantage of looking up into Jackson's smug smile.

"I asked first," he said, his voice so dangerously low it sent a shiver up her back. She remembered what Tory had told her, about Jackson's past, and she wondered what if the icy façade really did hide a grieving man or if enough time had passed that this had become his true nature.

"I live here," she managed to stammer. She had a quick look around, making sure she really did recognize her door.

A not very nice smile came over Jackson's face as his eyes, full of insolence, traveling up and down her, taking in the black leather boots, her tight jeans and the filmy silk blouse that had slid proactively, and with unfortunate timing, off one of her shoulders, baring it to the cool night air. She saw his eyes drawn to the low cut V above her breasts just before they slid up to her face.

He stopped there, one eyebrow raised, a faintly amused expression playing on his lips. She felt her cheeks start to flame. The outfit had seemed like a good idea when she had gone out with Nate. In fact, he could hardly keep her eyes off of her, but his gaze was nothing like Jackson's cool appraisal and the effect it was having on her body.

"Live here? Is that really the best you can come up with?" He leaned against his doorjamb now, arms crossed over his chest. Dimly, behind her, Lynn was aware of some shouts and calls from the street below. It was probably some of the softball team on their way home after their final round of drinks at Quent's.

"What do you mean?" Lynn sputtered, anger rapidly taking over her embarrassment. His blue eyes were like ice chips in that face. A face with beautiful, well-chiseled cheekbones. A mouth with wide, somewhat, full lips. If she'd been feeling romantic and Jackson was being less surly, she might have called it generous. But then she remembered there was nothing generous about him.

"I mean, if you wanted to see me again, you could have called me, made an appointment. I would have been happy to fit you into my schedule during normal business hours. I assure you, you won't get very far trying out your tricks on me."

"My tricks?" Lynn felt as if her head was going to explode, not quite able to piece together what Jackson was saying to her. And then it all came together.

"You think I'm here to what…" Lynn fumbled for the words, "seduce you, proposition you? Because you want to close the clinic?"

Any sympathy she might have felt for him, because of what Tory had told her about his fiancée, evaporated.

The pompous look faded slightly from Jackson's face.

Lynn's anger launched her forward, so that the toe of her booted toe was touching Jackson's bare one.

"Well, I…" Jackson now seemed to be having trouble speaking.

"I've heard about you. Do you think that just because you're some sort of international playboy you can come into this town and throw your money and looks around and just have everyone bow down to you?"

Jackson's eyes widened in surprise and he held his hands up, as if only just now realizing his mistake.

But Lynn wasn't done, not by a long shot. "Listen, mister. I pay your brother good money to rent the apartment…" Lynn leaned back to check, "next to this one. I am sorry that I disturbed you, but the light is out on the porch and I dropped my keys. I had no idea you were staying here, and if I did I certainly wouldn't have bumped into your door."

"What? You're renting here? Chase said nothing was rented." Jackson seemed to have regained some of his composure and the smooth mask slid back onto his features as his arms closed, folded over themselves.

"You think I'm selling you a story? Seeing as how I'm friends with Phoebe, he let me in early. So there."

Lynn could have kicked herself. Seriously, she was spending way too much time with kids, if that was the best parting shot she could come with. She might as well have called him a booger nose and be done with it.

With as much dignity as she could muster, she turned on her heel and this time, it would have been a graceful exit, except she still didn't have her keys. She looked around and saw them, shining brightly in the light spilling from Jackson's door, resting in the soil of a potted plant. She scooped them up, remembering to bend from the knees so he wouldn't get the satisfaction of seeing her ass in the air.

She didn't, couldn't turn around to see if Jackson was still watching, but as there was still a puddle of light spilling from his doorway she had to assume he had watched every moment of her miserable performance. Trying to keep her hands from shaking, she managed to insert the key into the lock of her door, twisted it quickly and thrust herself into the safety of the dark space.

After a moment, she thought she heard the sound of a door closing shut and she saw, through the small crack at the bottom of the door, the puddle of light disappear.

Chapter 11

Jackson went back to the couch where he had his papers spread out, his laptop open, and a beer he didn't need growing warm. He had been running the numbers on his business plan one more time. He looked at the computer but everything merged together. He threw down his pencil and leaned back, running his hands through his hair.

He had officially made a mess of that, he thought. Looking back, he supposed that Chase had mentioned that one of the other apartments in the Annex was rented. The porch light was out, something he had noticed himself, had even made a note to tell the maintenance staff about it; and with it out, it might even be possible to mix the doors up, since no one had gotten around to putting numbers on them yet.

But, honestly, what was he supposed to have thought? There was the girl, the woman, he supposed, that he'd seen earlier in the day, dressed in dirty scrubs. And then all of a sudden she had shown up, with her rich, silky hair piled high on her head, with some stray locks falling down, framing those dark, chocolate brown eyes and the round, slightly freckled face. And then there had been those long, tall boots with heels so high that she maybe, almost might have reached his shoulder. And the jeans, which had molded to her body so that he nothing was left to his imagination. And then her shirt had slipped, giving him a glimpse of one, gorgeously tanned shoulder.

She didn't seem like the type who went for sexy lingerie, but at that moment he would have given quite a bit to find out, just one little peek. Despite his resolve, despite reminding himself that he had sworn off women, especially ones who seemed to want something from him, the thought of Lynn Masters in nothing but her bra and underwear, with her dark hair piled sexily around her shoulders, flashed through his head and had his heart pumping.

Just as abruptly, he shut the thought down and took a sip of his lukewarm beer. Jackson got up and wandered to the window. Chase had kept this apartment specifically for friends and family. It was decorated in a sleek, spare style that fitted a place that was meant to be for transients. The couch was comfortable but not too inviting. The kitchen counter boasted a toaster and a one-cup coffee maker. Throughout, everything was done in shades of neutral with an occasional nautical shade of blue as contrast.

It was efficient and effective, and Jackson didn't really need any more than that now. The work on his house was almost done, and he was eager to move in, to be in a real home. This apartment, as nice as it was, reminded him of all the temporary housing he'd lived in overseas and across the country. Just inviting enough to lull one into thinking it was homelike, but always lacking anything resembling warmth.

Jackson wandered over to the refrigerator, opened it, then closed it, knowing he wasn't really hungry, since he and Jake had sat together talking over steaks at the Osprey. He was just restless.

Was he crazy thinking maybe she'd come to talk to him? Pleading hadn't worked this afternoon, so maybe she thought that a more overt method of persuasion would tip the scales in her favor? What kind of man did she think he was?

But then, how could she have any idea where he lived? And she did finally let herself into her own apartment. With a key. But dressed like that, she looked like she was dressed for something...like a date. The thought bothered him, and then he remembered with a half-smile that if she'd come home alone, it couldn't have been much of a date.

He decided not to dwell on that, but instead look ahead. Tomorrow was the first day of the rest of his future, and he needed to be prepared for that. He didn't have time to worry about Lynn and the clinic. Besides, that decision was already made. If they didn't have the money for the new lease, that was their problem.

Chapter 12

"You mean to tell me you fell into his door?" Tory asked, putting a chunk of blueberry muffin into her mouth. Lynn watched fascinated. Tory seemed able to eat an ungodly amount of carbs and still stay in good shape. Must be genetics, Lynn thought, but her doctor's training knew that wasn't simply the case. Tory loved to run and had already finished two half-marathons this year.

They were sitting at The Golden Pear Café. Lynn had decided to come in for granola and coffee and had bumped into Tory. The café, with its clean nautical theme, punctuated by white bead board walls, topped by blue paint and black and white pictures of sailboats, was a popular destination for breakfast and lunch. It always smelled heavenly, like a mixture of chocolate, cinnamon, and vanilla; and right now, most of the small round tables were occupied as moms met for coffee, retirees complained about the local news, and Tory and Lynn chatted.

"Pretty much." Lynn shook her head. "It was another disaster."

"And he thought you were there to…"

"Use my feminine wiles to get him to not close the clinic."

"You were dressed to kill, so yeah I guess if I was the typical red-blooded guy and some girl like you knocked on my door in the middle of the night I might have thought just about every one of my fantasies had come true. Next time, try wearing your white doctor's coat with nothing on underneath—that might work better."

"Tory!" Lynn said shaking her head. "That's not what I had in mind."

"Sure, of course you didn't," Tory said, her voice brimming with false sincerity.

Darby Callahan, the owner of the café, came up to them, her pregnant stomach leading the way. She held up a carafe of coffee and asked, "Can I get you guys anything else?"

"She needs another shot," Tory said. "And I'll take a box of chocolate chip cookies for the office."

"Long night, making rounds?" Darby asked as she poured their coffee.

"Bad date," Tory answered for Lynn.

"Oh," Darby winced in sympathy. "I don't mind missing out on those." Darby was married to Sean Callahan, the chef at the Osprey Arms. Together they were working on expanding The Golden Pear into another location, and had opened another high-end restaurant. All while Darby was due with their first child.

Lynn waved her hand. "Yeah, yeah, all you happily married people just rub it in our faces."

Darby laughed and rubbed her stomach. Her face winced, and seeing it Lynn stopped and asked, "How are you feeling? Are you sure you should be on your feet?"

Darby laughed. "My doctor says I'm fine. Sure glad the heat of the summer is over. Only a few more weeks to go. Can't wait to meet the little bean." She touched her stomach again and waddled gracefully to the counter to box up the cookies Tory had ordered.

Lynn smiled. Darby and Sean hadn't wanted to know whether they were having a boy or girl, and now most of Queensbay was locked in a fierce betting pool over it. Odds were split evenly, but Lynn knew Darby was convinced she was having a boy.

"Is it me, or does it seem like everyone is coupling up?" Lynn leaned back and looked out the window with a sigh. She'd looked out the window, noting that the leaves on some of the trees were just starting to change from their summer green to their autumnal shades of dusky yellow and burnt orange.

She'd been in Queensbay for a while now, and with the passing of each season she found something more to love. In the summer it was all about being outside, hitting the water, grilling. Winter was about settling in, keeping the wild winter storms at bay. Spring of course, was about the promise of warmer days, watching the harbor come to life around you. Autumn meant festivals and snuggling in, decorating pumpkins, and asking kids what they wanted to be for Halloween. She loved it all.

"Nope, it's not your imagination." Tory said. "Half the guys on the softball team are all shacked up and head home to their honeys. I thought it would be a great way to find a boyfriend, but so far, no luck. Seems like it's harder and harder to find a good man around here."

Lynn's face twisted in a frown as her mind turned to Jackson Sanders. He was not a good man. First he'd been rude, then he'd been arrogant, and then, most likely, he'd been laughing at her. Her last encounter with him had been the icing on the cake. Or rather the straw that broke the camel's back. Not to mention that he was probably still mourning a dead fiancée. Maybe that was why he had come back to Queensbay, to be closer to her in spirit. The thought turned her melancholy.

"I guess we could swear off men forever?" Lynn suggested, hopeful. After all, it wouldn't be so hard; it would almost be like making it official, her current state of aloneness.

Tory looked at her as if she had another head growing out of her shoulders.

"Uh-uh and no way…I am still on the hunt, even if you seem intent on staying out of the game. Man, you must have really been burned. I saw you dump the numbers those guys gave you last night. What about Nate? Are you going to give him a second chance? Maybe he'll grow on you?"

"I don't think so," Lynn had already had two texts from Nate, seeing if she was around anytime soon. She had claimed a busy work schedule and hoped that would be enough for him to get the picture, without having to actually tell him she wasn't interested.

Still, what Tory had said stung a little, and she felt the need to defend herself.

"It's not that I was burned," she said, but stopped herself. "I mean not that badly."

"What happened?"

"Well, it wasn't so much that it was anything in particular. It was sort of a series of events, and I just decided I might be better off, you know, taking a break."

"Who were they?"

"Well there was Ben, who was trying to get over his ex-girlfriend. And there was Joe, who had mother issues, and there was Ryan, I think was gay and trying to use me to persuade his grandmother otherwise. And there was Grant."

"What did he want?"

"To play doctor with me." Lynn shuddered at the memory. "You'd be surprised how many guys have wanted to do that."

"No, not really. But let me guess. Ben got back together with his girlfriend, Joe still lives with his mom, Ryan's grandmother died and he didn't have to pretend anymore, and Grant plays footsie with a hot nurse."

"How do you do that?" Lynn shook her head. "I have what my mom calls a 'fix-it' complex."

Tory nodded. "Oh, you mean the kind where you date guys who have something wrong with them and you think you can fix them, and then you're terribly surprised when they don't want to change."

"Yes. Why, do you have it?"

Tory shook her head. "Nah, I go in with low expectations."

"What?" Lynn said, shocked.

"Except, you know, in bed."

"You mean you go out with guys not expecting it to go any-where?"

"Well, it doesn't mean I jump into bed on the first date, or with every guy I meet, but I figure the chance of, you know, any guy I meet being the one is statistically impossible, even if, you know, there is the one, which again is highly improbable. So I just look to enjoy myself."

"But to just give up on everything else?"

"I'm not giving up, if it happens, great; if not, well then every-thing is a lot less complicated. And I'm happier."

Lynn said nothing, thinking over this.

Tory's eyes narrowed as she pursed her lips. "Out of curiosity, just how long has it been since you've, you know, gotten some action?"

Lynn paled. "Grant was the first year of my residency."

"Whoa!" Tory slumped back in her chair and looked at Lynn with disbelief. "That would be like what, months? Years?"

"Years," Lynn admitted morosely.

Tory shook her head. "Well, there's your problem. Maybe instead of looking for romance under the full moon, or a guy with issues, you should just go for the great sex. After all, you have to start somewhere."

"I think after last night's disaster of a date, I'd be better off being alone," Lynn said, but her insides sank at the prospect. Unfortunately, now that her hormones at least entertained the idea of getting lucky, it would be pretty hard to shut them off.

Tory shook her head in disagreement. "Oh no, you don't get to give up that easy. I think there's hope for you. Besides, work is getting predictable. I need a new project."

"I am not a project," Lynn huffed.

"Nope. you're not. You're great the way you are. But getting you laid is one."

Lynn shook her head, and Tory laughed. "Don't worry. Next time we'll do a double date. This way when one of them starts reciting the kings of England or something like that we can figure out an escape plan."

"It's a deal," Lynn said after only a moment's hesitation. Tory insisted on shaking on it and Lynn wondered just what she had gotten herself into.

Chapter 13

Lynn flipped over the chart, and then stacked it at the nurse's station. It was almost lunchtime, she thought, checking her watch, though there was no need for that since her stomach growled as well, clearly telling her it was time for a sandwich. She usually brought her lunch but today she hadn't planned that far ahead. Luckily, it was a nice day out, the patient load was manageable, and there should be more than enough time for her to run out and grab something.

She pulled on her cozy fleece and was out the door, debating whether or not she should take her car in order to save time or walk into town for the fresh air and exercise. Fresh air and exercise were about to win out when out of the corner of her eye she saw the side door of the building swing open and a familiar figure step out.

"I need to speak you," she said, going right up to Jackson. He was dressed again in a suit, and Lynn wondered if he ever took it off. Everything about him screamed expensive, from the crisp white French cuffs that shot through the dark charcoal pinstripe jacket to the discrete yet elegant print on his tie. His blond hair was neatly combed in place and his blue eyes were their usual icy blue.

He carried a simple leather suitcase, and if he seemed embarrassed to see her, he hid it well. Remembering that he had been the one who'd made an ass of himself, and that she was clearly the wronged party, helped her maintain her sense of outrage.

"You?" It wasn't exactly a question, more an intonation of mild surprise.

"Yes, me. I work here, remember?"

"Of course." Jackson shifted from one foot to another and actually checked his watch.

"Am I keeping you from something?" she asked in what she hoped was a sardonic tone. How dare he try to blow her off?

"In fact, I do have an appointment."

"Of course," Lynn said, and Jackson started to walk. She decided to follow. Time was, after all, of the essence. "Then I'll be brief."

A sound which may have been a stifled laugh came from him. Determined, she ignored it. There was a lot more at stake here than her wounded pride. She just needed to remember that she was a grownup too, a smart, savvy career woman.

"Did you know that last year the clinic saw over two thousand patients and prevented about five hundred unnecessary trips to the emergency room? As you might imagine, a trip to the emergency room is quite costly, but a lot of people without access to a regular doctor head there first. However, a place like the clinic you're going to shut down offers affordable medical care for those without a regular doctor and also cuts down on those emergency room visits, thereby saving everyone time and money."

Lynn glanced back at Jackson. She had decided that turning her case into a numbers game would be the right way to go. After all, if he was all business then he might be persuaded more by hard facts and statistics than an impassioned plea. His face was set, unreadable, but she saw him working his jaw.

She was walking as quickly as she could but his long legs were eating up the distance to the small parking lot where his car must be parked. Still, she managed to throw in a few more selling points about the importance of the clinic to the town. Unfortunately, all too soon they were at a car. It was a sedan, not a sports car, like she had expected, but a luxury model nonetheless. Next to it, her well-worn Subaru with its roof racks looked like the vehicle of a modern-day hippie. She made a mental note, telling herself that it might be time to take off some of the bumper stickers on her car.

"Well then, Miss Masters…"

"Technically, it's Doctor," Lynn corrected him. Usually she didn't care about a thing like titles. Half the time her patients assumed she was a candy striper, since she had what most of them nicely called a baby face. But with Jackson, she had a feeling that titles mattered.

"Well then, Doctor. I am sorry to say that this is really a straight-forward business deal. Mr. Petersen has to sell the building to handle some cash flow issues. I am sure you can find another location."

"Not for what we pay in rent! Not to mention the location is ideal," Lynn burst out as Jackson reached for the handle of his car door.

They were almost toe to toe, and Lynn realized that Jackson, despite the fact that she had never seen him with a real smile, was handsome, if you went for the perfect hair, the white teeth, straight nose, and sculpted cheekbones type of thing. Lynn usually didn't she told herself, but right now, standing this close to him, she was starting to forget the reasons why she liked her men a little rougher around the edges.

They both reached for the door at the same time, Lynn to stop him from going, he to open it. She realized what she was doing and pulled back, her hand brushing against his arm. No, it wasn't quite a spark, she thought. More like a chill. Yes. Definitely a chill, she thought, looking into his frosty eyes. It couldn't possibly be her hormones talking. Jackson Sanders was so definitely not her type. And shouldn't be her type. From what Tory had told her, he had some serious issues, the kind that probably couldn't be fixed easily. And she was not supposed to be in the doctor mode where her love—make that her *sex*—life was concerned.

"And that is exactly the problem. Petersen was too soft, never raising the rents. On most of his properties. And now he's paying the price. Look, I don't make the rules."

"You just break them," Lynn said, wondering how she had, even for a moment, thought that Jackson was the least bit attractive.

"No, actually I like to think I play by them. It's a game you see. And I play to win."

"Good luck with that, especially seeing as how when you win just about everyone else loses." Lynn knew she sounded like a kid in the midst of a temper tantrum.

"Always a pleasure," Jackson said, wrenching the door open, the expression on his face showing it was anything but.

Chapter 14

Jackson's appointment could wait. In truth, he was interviewing a graphic designer and she had suggested lunch. He wondered if she asked for a lunch meeting with all of her potential clients or if it was something she only did with unattached male ones.

He shook his head as he drove. He needed to stop being so cynical about people's motives. It was a business lunch, a chance to get out and meet people. Standard operating procedure in the professional world. When had he become so jaded? He almost laughed at that. The answer was right there. It had been Ashley's death that had made him realize there were no happy endings.

His car seemed to have a mind of its own as it took him to the spot. He could have turned around, deliberately gone the other way, but he didn't, letting the car drive almost automatically to the faintly marked turnoff.

He turned the car into the small clearing and stopped. Ahead of him lay a rough path, almost too narrow to be called a road. If he had a 4x4 or a truck, he would have plowed through, but it wasn't worth the risk of getting stuck in his sedan.

He got out, shut the door, and was amazed by the quiet. Or as quiet as it could be with the sound of birdsong, the wind whispering in the trees, and the distant but steady beat of the breakers against the rocks.

It was overgrown, but you could clearly see the imprint of the path that wound its way under the canopy of trees and bushes. There was an empty beer bottle tossed to the side, along with a shoe, just one. Evidence that some people still knew about it.

He took a deep breath, wondering why he had come. To say goodbye? Or to say hello. He supposed most people would have gone to her grave to do that, but here he was, at Deadman's Bend—his and Ashley's own private version of Lover's Lane.

Carefully, he pushed aside a prickly bramble and continued along. The tall grass was matted down, but not worn bare. The trail was lightly used, he supposed, which was just as it should be. Who knew what stories the kids of Queensbay had spun about this place after Ashley had died?

Sunlight dappled through the branches and lit the way. Already he could see a round circle of blue ahead of him. He walked straight on until the tunnel of woods opened up and he stood on a bluff, high above the Sound. He could see far to the east from here, almost out to the ocean and across all the way to Long Island. It was a clear, brilliant fall day, the sun warm on his face.

Much like the last time he had been here. Ashley had asked him to meet her. It was the weekend, and he was home from his job in the city, staying with his brother. She was home too, of course, since she had gotten a position coaching at the junior high. He should have been suspicious, wondering why she was free on a fall weekend afternoon when she should have been at a game.

He had met her, again not thinking there was anything odd in the fact that she hadn't wanted to drive together. All the signs had been there, but he had been blind, hadn't he? He had grabbed a bottle of wine, some glasses, and a blanket, thinking that perhaps they might spend a lazy afternoon together. Because both of their schedules were so busy, time together had been hard to come by and he had been hungry for her.

She had already said yes to his marriage proposal, and though he had been nervous, determined to make sure everything about the event went perfectly, he hadn't doubted her ultimate answer. They were meant to be. And they had a plan. He would work in the city for a year, maybe two at the most, getting the experience he wanted, and then he would come back to Queensbay and go into business with Jake.

He and Ash would get married and they'd have kids. Not too soon, of course, since he wanted to enjoy being just with her, but he definitely wanted a family. Evenings on the boat, fishing, swimming, barbequing. Everything had been mapped out. He couldn't have been happier. But then she had talked about different things, wanting to travel, to have adventures. And he had changed his dreams; they had started to make different plans, her plans. And he thought she was happy again.

Then he had seen her, waiting there, in jeans and shirt, standing on the edge of the bluff, too close, like she always did, risking everything. Her long blond hair danced in the wind and he wanted to call her to him; but he enjoyed her beauty, savoring every line of her tall, powerful body, just watching her, wondering how such a wild and untamable creature could be his.

Because Ash had been that. She had turned down every boy in Queensbay High when they asked her for a date, until he had finally screwed up the courage and asked her, the day after the baseball team had won the state championships. He had been riding high on his MVP status and thought the world owed him. So he had tested his luck that day and asked her out.

It seemed too good to be true; and it was. He'd been too blind to see that Ashley was using him to make another guy jealous. Maybe that's because he had fallen for her, hard. But she had finally succumbed to his unwavering love. They became inseparable. Ashley became his world, and she needed him because, while she might have appeared like she had it all together on the outside, on the inside she needed him. Needed him to take care of her, to assure her he loved her, to keep her from doing wild things. It had become his mission to keep her safe, to talk her out of her wild, unpredictable moods.

Now, of course, he realized what Ashley had been doing. Creating dramatic situations so that she was the center of them and then demanding attention, energy from everyone, just to fuel her own ego. He'd just been the only one stupid enough to buy into it for as long as he had.

He had known it deep down, recognized it, even as he enabled it because in spite of it all, she was still his Ashley. He hoped that once they were married she would feel safe and secure, that she wouldn't need to be so wild. But even when she turned to him, he still didn't know, didn't understand the expression on her face.

She told him the engagement was off and that she had no intention of living in a small town for the rest of her life, to be saddled with kids, to be stuck with him. She told him she wanted to see places, travel, have adventures.

At first he had begged, told her they could hold off on getting married, that they didn't need to live in Queensbay, that they could do whatever she wanted. Even as he said those words to her, he hated himself for it. And then she delivered the deathblow: she threw Tucker Wolff in his face. Tucker had been the reason she'd said yes to Jackson all the years ago. She had wanted to make him jealous. Jackson had long ago stopped counting Tucker as a threat. As he and Ashley had moved on and upward, through school and college, making plans, Tucker had stayed behind in Queensbay, gaining a reputation as the town bad boy.

Apparently, while Jackson hadn't thought about Tucker in years, Ashley had. More than thought about him apparently. And that was all it had taken. He told her to keep the ring, and walked away, angry, pride hurt but with an overwhelming sense of relief. Ashley had set him free.

Jackson brought himself back to the present, found himself standing on the edge of the cliff, looking down to the rocky beach below. He swallowed and took a step back. He was used to heights— if you helped build skyscrapers you had to be—but there was no sense in tempting fate by standing on the crumbling edge of a sandy bluff.

The last time he had spoken to her in person had been here. A seagull wheeled and turned on the current above him. A light chop rippled the surface of the Sound. He swallowed. He was here and he felt what…nothing. Not her presence. She didn't haunt this place for him.

No, it was just the wind, the water, the ground. A beautiful place, one of his favorites. But she did not haunt him and he was glad. If he was going to stay in Queensbay, he needed it to be his town. Not theirs. He swallowed, taking a deep cleansing breath of the salt air.

"I forgive you Ashley," he said and the words came out aloud. He hadn't said it before. He'd been so angry with her. Because even after death, just when he thought he was free, she had reached back and pulled him into her drama. He'd done the right thing by Ashley and her family, let them take their grief and anger out on him. He hadn't thought that his decision, what had seemed so noble at the time, would turn the whole town against him. He thought if he kept the breakup quiet, kept what had really happened the night of the accident to himself, that the Morans would be spared embarrassment and pain. He would have to play the grieving fiancé for a while but then it would be over. He would be free. It just hadn't worked out that way.

He couldn't complain. Life had been good to him, professionally, financially, and he had learned an important life lesson early. Ashley had taught him one thing he wouldn't ever forget. Love was a trap. You got so consumed, lost in it, you were bound to lose yourself. So no, in some respects everyone was right. Jackson Sanders wouldn't fall in love again; but not because of Ashley, but because he was smart enough to know that love wasn't enough.

Chapter 15

Lynn took a sip of her coffee, letting the hot liquid slide down her throat. She had to be at work in just moments, but really there was nothing like a cup of Darby's coffee, even if she had to take it in a to-go cup. She decided she wanted it with just a touch more cream so she stopped at the milk and sugar station, took the lid off, and topped off her cup until the liquid turned into a frothy caramel color. She inhaled, the scent of fresh coffee and sweet, rich baked goods filling her nostrils. Darby should think about bottling it, the scent of The Golden Pear, and selling it.

She heard the door open, but didn't look up, but she felt the air in the room change as the general hum of conversation died down. Curious, she turned and looked. Jackson Sanders, in a business suit, polished shoes, and even more polished shoes, stood at the glass countertop carefully perusing the selection of pastries while just about every other person in the café stared at him, in utter silence.

As if sensing the attention directed at him, Jackson slowly turned around. His eyes were hooded and his expression grim. He stood though, with his feet spread wide apart, his arms at his side. All Lynn could think was that it was a fighting stance.

Jackson's eyes scanned the tables, looking at each and every person, nodding at some people, who stony-faced, didn't nod back. His eyes flicked up once to take in Lynn, and there was just the barest hint of recognition there and then he kept up his survey of the room.

The girl behind the counter, not Darby, was fresh-faced and young and stood in silence too, but hers was born out of uncertainty, just as Lynn's was. Just what in the hell was going on? Did everyone think Jackson was a cad for shutting down the clinic? Tory had said he'd had a reputation as a hard ass, an arrogant prick, but seriously, the public silent treatment—that was just weird.

Lynn swallowed, and she was moving before she had even thought about it, to stand next to Jackson, and pointing to something, anything in the case, "The croissants are delicious," she said, even though she hadn't had one. She was making an educated guess, everything was good here, but there was no way she could let Jackson stand in silence and not do anything.

He smiled, a half smile, rueful, and he gave her a curt nod. She could see his body was rigid with tension.

The door from the kitchen swung open and Darby herself appeared, the white apron straining across her belly. Her green eyes roved, quickly taking the measure of the situation.

"Jackson, how nice to see you. What can I get you?" Darby nudged the sales girl, who seemed to spring to life, blinking and holding up her tongs, ready to take the order.

Darby's eyes slid to Lynn and she gave a small, almost imperceptible nod. Behind them, the noise level slowly ratcheted up, though there were more than a few whispers and smothered exclamations. Beside her, Jackson's stiff demeanor relaxed fractionally and he inclined his head in Lynn's direction.

There was something in his eyes, something that made them look less icy and hard, and she accepted his silent thanks with a small nod of her own. She knew she should go now, that there was no reason to stay and that any longer and she was risking being late, very late to work.

"This doesn't change anything. I still think you shouldn't close the clinic down," she said as a parting shot. Jackson's eyes narrowed and seemed about to say something, but Lynn decided that it was as good a last word as she was going to get, and this time, as she spun on her heel to make an exit, nothing got in her way.

Outside, in the sun and the light breeze that was blowing off the harbor, she shrugged her shoulders; and sparing one more glance into the café, she headed off to work, while it was still there, wondering what in the hell that had been all about.

Chapter 16

"You're not so bad at this for a football player," Jackson told Jake.

Jake and Jackson were at the batting cages at Queensbay's newest sports complex. It was a huge, almost warehouse-like space that held almost every kind of sporting activity known to man, woman or child, including indoor soccer fields, batting cages, a rock-climbing wheel, a full gym, a yoga studio and even a laser tag arena for the kids.

Jackson had asked Jake if they could talk, and instead of suggesting coffee or lunch, Jake had said baseball. Jackson was happy to agree, and now he found himself facing balls being shot out at him at sixty miles an hour. It had taken a few rounds to get used to the feeling, but swinging the bat felt good, as good as it had felt in high school.

"Hey, I'm the star batter on the company softball team," Jake defended himself as he whacked another one.

"Aren't you the one who pays the team's salaries?" Jackson pointed out.

"They're still happy I'm playing."

It was Jackson's turn and he stepped up to the plate, readying his stance.

"You didn't ask me here to compliment me on my baseball skills, did you?" Jake said as he watched Jackson.

"No, not quite," Jackson admitted as his bat connected with the ball with a satisfying crack.

"Are you going to tell me why you're finally back in town? I mean, besides buying up even more property in Queensbay. I wish you'd leave some for the rest of us."

Jackson tensed. "I guess you spoke to Darby?"

Jake nodded. "I might have stopped by for a cup of coffee. Did the whole place really go silent?"

Jackson nodded. "I half expected them to start to chant something in a creepy whisper. It was eerie. No one said anything, I mean until…"

He stopped himself. What Lynn had done had been unexpected. And kind. Or maybe just ignorant. Maybe she had no idea why the whole town could hate him. She was a relative newcomer to town. Maybe the story of him and Ashley hadn't made it onto her radar yet. Of course, it was only a matter of time.

"Yeah, I heard Darby gave everyone a talking to after you left," Jake said.

Jackson swallowed. He'd have to thank Darby too. She'd been friendly with Ashley, but not once had she ever laid blame at his doorstep for what had happened, either then or now.

"I did have something I wanted to run by you," he said, deciding to change the subject.

"Ok. I'll listen." Jake, said promptly, being a good friend and not pushing the subject.

Jackson tensed. The idea was crazy, but it was important to him, something that he had realized as he built bigger and bigger buildings in places farther and farther away. He had often wondered why anyone would want to live in such places, had thought about all of the resources that were used to build them. And he knew there had to be a smarter, better way to do things. And that's what he wanted to do: build something that wasn't the tallest or the biggest; instead, he wanted to focus on something smarter, something that didn't rob the future to build it now.

"Green building."

Jake looked at him like he was crazy. "This is New England, Jax, not the tropics. People here go for more muted colors. You know, lots of whites, cream maybe."

"Not a green colored building. Green. As in environmentally friendly building practices. Solar power specifically. I think there's an opportunity here to help communities become more energy efficient."

Jake scratched his head. "This isn't the desert either. I know it's been a while since you weathered a New England winter, but for more than three months out of the year, we don't always get our fair share of the sun."

"It's a common misconception that you need year-round sun in order to use solar energy. In reality, solar panels are viable in just about any climate. Of course, they might not power your home or office building all year long, day in and day out, but even just a few solar panels can have a big impact. Or, even better than the roof of a house, let's say you have a big space, say like the roof of the parking garage at the mall…now there's space that just sits, useless old concrete. Why not turn it into a giant battery?"

Jake's arms were folded but he was leaning in and his eyes were narrowed, a sure sign he was interested. "You know, I've noticed a lot more of my customers asking about renewable and recycled materials when we're doing a job. I've even taken a couple of classes on green building so I can talk to clients better."

"It's a growing market opportunity—you can do good and make money at the same time. Don't you like the sound of that?"

Jake's eyes narrowed, in a considering look. "Of course I do. But what's in it for me?"

Jackson hefted the bat on his shoulder. "I figured I would be the sales and marketing guy. I have the deal with the manufacturer all lined up. But I don't have a crew ready to do the installs. But you might."

"So you want me to go into partnership with you—in this town?"

Jackson swallowed. This was the hard part. Years ago, that had been there plan; but then Ashley's death had made that impossible. Any association with Jackson might have sunk Jake. Jake had never said that, of course, but he must have known it.

"I know it's a lot to ask. I thought maybe it wouldn't be a big deal, but you were right, people in this town have a long memory."

"And I say screw them. I know one of the reasons you left was because you didn't want me to feel like I had to go into business with you. But I didn't care then and I don't now."

Jackson smiled in relief, felt his mood beginning to lighten. The reception he'd gotten at The Golden Pear had been much harsher than he expected. He'd been worried that Jake, being a smart businessman, would make the smart, businesslike decision and tell Jackson to go take a hike.

"I figured, I'll be out there, getting the word out, closing the deals, and then your construction crew can come in do the actual install. I can set them up with training and everything else you need. We can work out all the financial details as needed."

Jake nodded slowly, but Jackson knew he had him. Sure he could have gone through with his plan without Jake, but somehow it seemed right that they would do it together.

"Sounds like you have it all planned out. Got anyone willing to pay you for it?"

Jackson shrugged. "First client will be the Osprey Arms Hotel, of course. I convinced Chase to build in a solar powered roof. I figured that will make a powerful statement and be good advertising. Plus I hear the university is thinking of breaking ground on a new science and technology center."

Jake dropped his voice. "That's supposed to be hush-hush. But everyone knows, and all the construction companies are trying to get a piece of it. It's a big job. Why would they consider you?"

Jake's tone was friendly, curious, and Jackson felt the tension in his shoulders ease. Jake may not have officially said yes, but he was on board.

"I have an in. Not a guaranteed one, but the project manager is someone I know, used to work with. The university is apparently very open to the renewable energy idea and this guy has put in a good word for me, good enough so that I've scored a meeting with the planning board next week. But it sure would help my case if I could tell them I was a real company with installation capabilities and not just one man in a suit."

"Guess reports of your international playboy status were greatly exaggerated. You must have actually been learning something out there," Jake said, a smile creasing his tanned face.

"So you're in?"

Jake nodded. "I'm in. But as you said, it's a long shot." He paused and Jackson waited. "What if it doesn't pan out? Are you just going to pick up and go again? Because I won't give you a third chance."

Jackson shook his head, knowing that Jake meant what he said. "I knew it wasn't going to be easy, but I will stick it out here, no matter what it takes, no matter how hard it is. It's my town too."

"I can count on you?" Jake said, and Jackson knew all that was implied in that simple question.

"You can count on me."

Jake smiled and said, "Well shit and hot damn! How do we get started?"

Jackson let out the breath he didn't know he was holding. "I had a lawyer draw up some paperwork, about forming a partnership. I'll have him send it over for you to look at."

"Alrighty then. There's just one more thing. What are we going to name it?"

"Sanders and Owen Construction?"

Jake smiled, "I don't know, Owen-Sanders sounds more official, don't you think?"

Jackson laughed and almost could have hugged Jake through the mesh of the batting cage.

"We'll flip a coin, ok?"

Jake stuck his hand out and Jackson came outside the cage and shook it.

"Of course, now all you have to do is figure out how to convince the clinic to go quietly and you should be all set."

"I don't have to convince them of anything. I have the paperwork that says they have to be out," Jackson said stubbornly. If he wasn't going to back down in the face of town gossip, he wasn't going to back down on a business deal either. He had to be strong on both fronts if this was going to work out.

Jake shook his head and was about to say something when both their sets eyes were drawn to someone just entering the building.

Jackson watched as an all-too-familiar figure, striding with purpose and a bounce in her step, brunette ponytail swinging behind, passed them without seeing them and headed into the long corridor that separated the batting cages from the rest of the gym.

Jake gave him an enquiring look. "Speak of the devil. Perhaps you should see if you're more convincing this time around. Maybe the clinic will go quietly."

"No way," Jackson said, trying to keep the panic out of his voice. He didn't need another run in with Lynn Masters, especially not today. Every time he saw her, he came off looking like a heel. Jackson had never flinched in a business negotiation. His projects always came in on time and on budget. If he needed to be a hard ass, then so be it. It was one of the reasons why he'd been so successful so quickly. He had to remember that there was nothing personal in this. The building was his to do with as he damned well pleased, and he didn't need to be swayed by a bleeding heart doctor. And he didn't owe her anything for what she'd done at The Golden Pear.

All of that flashed through his mind before he realized just what Jake had in mind.

"Don't even think about it," he warned his friend.

But Jake just smiled and called out, "Hey, Lynn. How ya doing?"

Lynn, because it really was her, stopped, hesitated as if with indecision, then turned slowly around. She looked over at them and Jackson knew that she had seen them when she first walked in and had been doing her best to ignore them.

Now she looked at them both and finally said, in what Jackson knew was a deliberately cool voice, "Hello, Jake."

To Jackson, she only nodded before turning and heading in her original direction.

"Wow, you must really have pissed her off. I've never seen her not say hello to someone. Usually she's handing out hugs and lollipops as well," Jake said, his voice showing his amusement.

"Glad you're having some fun at my expense," Jackson said as he quelled the urge to slug his friend with the bat; instead, hefted it and stepped into the batting cage. His one thought was that perhaps Lynn had heard the story and realized she'd taken the wrong side the other day. No wonder she had looked right through him.

"Don't worry, the fun's just begun," Jake said with a laugh, and after a moment, Jackson joined in. It was good to be back home, even if his re-entry plans were not running quite as smoothly as he had hoped.

Chapter 17

"Phoebe!" Lynn cried out, opening the door to her apartment and wrapping her friend in a hug. "When did you get back?"

"A couple of hours ago," Phoebe said, her voice muffled by Lynn's arms. "Wow, I think you got stronger."

"Sorry, I didn't mean to swarm you. It's just that I missed you," Lynn said and realized that she had. Phoebe looked good, relaxed, and rested, with her summer tan still in place and her long blond hair pulled back in a loose chignon. She moved further into Lynn's apartment, an elegant vision in a flowing, floaty linen top paired with a long, clingy skirt.

"I missed you too. I have presents, so pour me a glass of wine," Phoebe said.

Lynn smiled, all of a sudden feeling less tired. The whispers were flying furiously at the clinic about the imminent closing and one nurse had already announced her resignation, saying she had found another job. Lynn had thought a workout at the gym after work would make her feel better, but seeing Jackson had only put her in a sour frame of mind.

Phoebe took a look around and tsk-tsked. "Wow, I'd like to say I love what you've done with the place, but I don't think anything's changed. Except maybe that mountain of magazines has grown."

"You were only gone three weeks. I'm busy," Lynn said. "But," and it was hard to keep the note of pride out of her voice, "I did what you said. I've been buying all those magazines about houses and marking the things I like, you know to help me find out my personal style."

So far, Lynn had only invested in a couch, low slung, slightly modern, in a neutral gray color, her a mattress and bed frame, a TV, and a couple of stools for the bar. Her clothes fit easily into the walk-in closet, so she hadn't even bought a dresser yet. The apartment was a basic white on white theme and while she knew a little color would be a good idea, she was enjoying the clean, clutter-free lines of it. For her, less was definitely more, but she wouldn't object to some pictures, bookshelves, and a knickknack or two.

Phoebe cocked an eyebrow at her and her eyes twinkled as she walked over to the pile of pages Lynn had torn out. She flipped through them, and Lynn waited in silence, finally deciding since it was her house that she could take off her grimy sneakers and shed the top layer of her workout clothes. She walked into her bedroom, dumped her clothes in the laundry hamper and found her favorite slippers, soft and lined with lamb's wool, put them on, and then threw on a clean t-shirt.

As she returned, Phoebe looked up and said, "Your style is kind of all over the place."

Lynn sighed. "I know. I can't decide if I like modern, or beachy, or country cottage. There's nothing ugly in those magazines, which I guess is kind of the point."

Phoebe pursed her lips. "You're definitely not country cottage. You're too simple for that."

"Excuse me," Lynn said as she went over to one of her cabinets and pulled out two juice glasses. She hadn't gotten around to finishing all of her shopping yet.

"I mean your personal style, your method of being, is simple. You care too much about and for other people to really focus on things. But it's not like you're Zen-like about it. You have too much energy and passion for that. But I don't ever see you collecting a bunch of things for the sake of it."

Lynn frowned, but she could see what Phoebe was saying. "I guess I'm more into experiences than things. You know, a great hike or good climb. An exciting vacation. A great run. A ski slope. Those memories get me more jazzed than any one thing."

Phoebe nodded, pondering. "You like old movies and books, but I don't see you as a collector of those since you have everything on your e-reader. You're a health nut, too, so you have all of that sports equipment."

Lynn laughed. "In my case, for the hiking and climbing, it's called gear. And like you suggested, I left most of it at my parents since I don't have a lot of storage space."

"Hmm," Phoebe said as she took the glass of wine Lynn handed her. She picked up the collection of magazine sheets and Lynn watched as she flipped through them again, deftly sorting them into separate stacks.

"What are you doing?" Lynn asked.

"You'll see. How's your new project at the clinic?" Phoebe asked.

Lynn sighed. "I think it's DOA. So much for making a differ-ence." Phoebe had cheered her on through every stage of Healthy Kids Now, even encouraging Lynn to think up some sort of catchy nickname. Lynn didn't know if the name was catchy, but it had certainly made it more real to put a title to it.

"What do you mean? I think it's a great idea. Childhood health and wellness is such an important issue. I thought you had all the support you needed." Phoebe's wide blue eyes were clouded with concern.

"I did. That's not the problem. The problem is the clinic may not be around much longer."

Phoebe looked up from her sorting. "What are you talking about?"

"Two words," Lynn said. "Jackson Sanders."

"The elusive, ruthless, and enigmatic Jackson," Phoebe said. "Not even his own brother can explain him to me. Do tell."

So Lynn told and Phoebe nodded along.

"Chase told me about what happened to Jackson's fiancée," Phoebe said. "I guess it really tore him up. Chase isn't one to talk about things like that, but I can sense that Jackson's never really been the same since then."

Lynn took a moment to wonder what the old Jackson could have been like. Happy, carefree, a shorts and flip-flop-wearing beach bum? Somehow she didn't quite buy it. Jackson looked as if he'd been born in one of those expensive suits.

"Are you sure he won't change his mind? I mean, I know Jack-son's not the friendliest person but shutting down the clinic, that's cold."

Lynn could only shrug in answer.

They had moved to the couch and were sitting facing each other, knees drawn up, bare feet tucked underneath. Despite the subject matter, Lynn was glad that Phoebe was home, here to speak with.

"What will you do?" Phoebe asked.

"I guess find another job," Lynn said, though in truth she wasn't so worried about that. There would probably be a space at the hospital, at least initially, and there were usually openings in private practices. But it was the loss of the opportunity to pioneer her Healthy Kids Now program that was gnawing at her.

She'd made a lot of progress already, collected a lot of data and worked one on one with dozens of kids. And she was starting to make a difference. Already some of her kids had lost weight, taken up a sport, started to do better in school. And best of all, they all felt great about themselves, filled with pride that they could make a difference in their own lives. But without the clinic she didn't know how she would keep the program going.

"What are you more upset about?" Phoebe asked after a moment.

"What do you mean?"

"The loss of the clinic or the fact that you won't get to work with all those kids?"

Lynn didn't hesitate. "The kids. I mean the clinic is great, but there are other places people can go for care. The hospital for one, or some of the other clinics in the area. A lot of them are in newer buildings, with better facilities."

"So maybe you're focusing on the wrong thing, if it's not the clinic that matters most to you," Phoebe suggested.

"And maybe you're taking his side because he's going to be your brother-in-law?" Lynn suggested, but without any anger.

"I don't feel there are sides here; but in any case, it doesn't seem to me like Jackson would care what I think. I have a feeling Jackson does what Jackson wants. But you," Phoebe fixed Lynn with a steady gaze, "surely, if you wanted to you could figure something out. You're a resourceful, successful, savvy woman."

Lynn sighed. "So I keep telling myself."

"What does that mean?" Phoebe laughed.

"I can't seem to have a successful date, my apartment looks like a dorm room, and every time I'm in front of Jackson I wind up looking like an idiot." The last part was out of her mouth before she could stop herself.

Phoebe's eyebrows rose and she sent Lynn a knowing look. "Interesting. I've never known you to care about how you appear to other people. Usually, you're not above strong-arming them into helping you with whatever cause you're working on."

"Apparently, Jackson is immune to strong-arming," Lynn muttered, deciding that she definitely wasn't ready to admit to Phoebe that she found her future brother-in-law attractive. A jerk, true, but an attractive one.

Phoebe reached out and patted Lynn's knee. "Well, there's one thing I can help you with. And that's your apartment. Here..." She picked up a sheaf of magazine pages. "I separated them into three different styles I think you'll like. All you need to do is pick the one you like best and then we can go shopping."

"Ok. I guess one out of three isn't bad," Lynn said, deciding that shopping might be just the thing to distract her from thinking about the way Jackson's shoulders looked in a pinstripe suit.

Chapter 18

"What the hell is going on in here?" Jackson looked up from the plans he had spread out on the desk to see his brother Chase, holding a six-pack and standing in the doorway of the top floor of Jackson's new building.

"And it's good to see you too," Jackson said, tossing down his pencil.

"Come here, little brother. You, back in Queensbay. I've been waiting years for this. Each summer I'd hope that you would come back, that we'd take the boat out for a spin. But each time, September would come around and we never get our sail in."

Chase, his big brother, grabbed him in a giant bear hug. Chase was shorter by a hair but more solidly built, a point he could never help but emphasize whenever he got the chance. Jackson relaxed, let Chase get his hug in, and then breathed again when his brother let him go.

"There was the time we met up in Norway and sailed the fjords. That was pretty spectacular," Jackson pointed out, though it had been cold enough to freeze the pickled herrings.

"True, but even here it's not too late. We still have a few good weeks of boating weather left," Chase said, his eyes flashing with eagerness. Jackson shook his head, knew that if Chase had the chance he'd be out on his boat all year round.

"We'll see. We have a lot to get started on," Jackson pointed out.

Chase held up his hand. "That stuff can wait. I still can't believe you're here on home soil."

"Don't get all misty eyed. Did you and Phoebe have a nice trip?"

"Couldn't have been better. Almost convinced her to elope with me on the shores of a beach in Indonesia, but I figured Mom and Dad would kill me. And Phoebe didn't want to disappoint all of her friends. We're planning something for the spring, maybe at the hotel, maybe at The Ivy House. Depends on how many people we invite."

"Don't you mean 'you,' not 'we?'" Jackson said. His brother collected friends the way other people collected lint in their pockets.

If Chase was going to throw a party, there was a good chance he'd invite the whole town.

Chase rubbed his short, dark hair and looked a little sheepish. "Should I be blamed for wanting everyone to see how great she is?"

Jackson shook his head. Phoebe was smart, talented, and beautiful. And she happened to be the granddaughter of Savannah Ryan, a famous movie actress who had once had an affair with Jackson and Chase's grandfather. It had been quite the scandal a generation ago and hadn't exactly ended happily. But Chase and Phoebe had somehow managed to defy the odds and seemed truly happy. It made Jackson wonder if sometimes fate really did smile on some people.

"I would feel the same way if I were you."

"You know you'll be my best man. You and Noah, of course. I figured the women get to have all those bridesmaids, so I can have my brother and my best friend up there with me."

Jackson shook his head. "I can't believe you of all people are settling down. I mean, if anyone would have said to me that you would find *the one*, I wouldn't have believed it."

Chase laughed. "It's like role reversal. I'm the guy looking to settle down, and from what I hear you've been dating your way across the seven continents."

There was a pause. "Hell, I didn't mean it that way, Jax. I know if what happened to Ash..." Chase trailed off and Jackson waved his hand. Chase had been there for him, tried to get him to talk about it, but after being shot down so many times, usually knew better than to say anything about it.

"Hey, it's the past. Besides, I couldn't let you have all the fun. And now that you're off the market, just means there's more left for me."

Chase laughed with him. The lie slipped off of Jackson's tongue easily enough, but he could see Chase wasn't quite satisfied. Truth was he envied Chase, just as he knew that he couldn't go down the same path. Jackson knew he could never love like that again, never get so caught up in someone else that he forgot himself. Nope, he'd leave love to the stronger men of the world.

"I like what you've done with the place," Chase said, pointing to the hole in the wall.

"I decided I was ready start on the remodel," Jackson said and hoped that Chase wouldn't ask him more about his thoughts on relationships. In truth, after seeing Lynn at the gym, he had had felt the need to destroy something and decided that now was as good a time as any to start on the demolition part of his planned remodel.

"I can see that," Chase said, setting down the beer on the large piece of plywood set across two sawhorses, which was currently serving as a desk, worktable, and everything else in the place. An old boom box sat in the corner next to a large, super bright light. The radio was on the local classic rock station.

"I'll take one of those," Jackson told Chase, gesturing toward the six-pack. Without saying anything, Chase popped the tops off of two bottles and passed one over.

"You know, Jake could send a crew over here to do this for you."

"Feels good to take a swing at it." He looked over at the wall which was partially down.

"Hell yeah," Chase said, putting down his bottle and picking up the sledgehammer, hefting it in his hands. "Just tell me where."

Jackson indicated a stretch of the thin dividing wall he had started on, and Chase lifted the hammer, readied his stance, and swung a blow. There was a satisfying crunch as the thin materials crumbled against the onslaught.

Chase took a few more whacks and then stopped, looking at him. "So what is this all about? Why now? You stay away for years and now you're back?"

Jackson said nothing, just glanced down at the plans he had spread on his makeshift desk.

"I heard the Morans are selling their house, moving. Is that it? Is it because her parents won't be here anymore? You know they almost got divorced, but I hear they're giving it another chance and want a fresh start."

"I did hear that," Jackson acknowledged. "Mom told me. You know, even though she doesn't live in town anymore, she still manages to keep up on what's happening." Jackson ran a hand over his hair. "And maybe that was some of it. But finally, it was just time to come back."

Chase looked at him. "I always thought there was something you didn't tell me. I know you weren't there that night, cause you were crashed on the couch in the basement. You got that phone call and you left. And then you asked me to not say anything."

"I never asked you to lie for me," Jackson said.

"I would have," Chase shot back.

Jackson knew. He nodded.

"You weren't there, were you? With her when she died?"

Jackson didn't say anything, but he should have known Chase would have guessed the truth, or close enough to it.

"I was at the hospital," Jackson said, clinging to the one bit of truth among the lies.

"But there was no way you were driving that car, was there?"

When Jackson said nothing, Chase just shook his head, "Man, she sucked you into her drama one last time didn't she?"

Jackson knew his brother had never been a fan of Ashley, but after Jackson had kicked his ass over it one too many times, Chase had learned to keep his opinions to himself.

Jackson felt his pulse speed up, "You can't..."

"I can. She's dead but even when she was alive, Ashley Moran had her claws into you so deep and your head spinning you didn't know which way was up. I've known you all my life and I know what you were like before she walked into your life when you were sixteen. She said jump and you said how high."

Jackson didn't say anything, couldn't because it had been true. He had fallen under Ashley's spell until the very end, until faced with a truth not even he could ignore. Still, a promise was a promise.

"Well, now she's gone. I'm here—back, because I wanted to be, I'm ready to start over."

"Are you? Don't get me wrong. I want you here, more than anything. I just want to make sure you're not going to disappear on me, ok?"

"I told you, I'm here," Jackson said, one last time and knew it was true. He wouldn't let anything drive him away from his home again.

Chase, too, seemed relieved. "Well then, why don't we get started on getting you a real place to work." He hefted the sledgehammer again and aimed at the wall. Before he swung though, he turned and looked at Jackson. "By the way, why are you so eager to kick the clinic out? And aren't you letting the psychic stay? Seems like your priorities are all wrong."

Jackson gritted his teeth. He had made his decision and to back down now would only make him look weak. The clinic would have to go if only to prove that he, Jackson Sanders, was a force to be reckoned with, not just Chase's baby brother.

"My building, my rules," Jackson said.

Chase shrugged. "Sure whatever you say. Though you know the clinic serves an important function providing important care..."

646

Jackson wondered just how many people the good Dr. Lynn Masters had given that speech to. His brother seemed to have it memorized.

"She's gotten to you too?"

"What, who? Lynn?" Chase smiled. "Quite the little spitfire, isn't she? Have you met her? You're staying next door to her, you know."

Jackson took the sledgehammer from his brother's hand, spread his feet, and swung. The walls trembled and a large hole bloomed from the impact. He handed the sledgehammer back to his brother, went over to the radio, and cranked up the volume.

Chase smiled but got the picture. The subject of Lynn Masters was officially closed, at least for now.

Chapter 19

"Thank you for meeting me." Lynn didn't know why she suddenly felt shy but she did as Caitlyn Montgomery Randall, looking luminous after having given birth just a few weeks ago, strode forward and shook Lynn's hand. Caitlyn was wearing a stylish dress and heels, and Lynn wished that she'd had something more dazzling to wear. She had scrounged together a pair of black slacks, a silk blouse with a small stain that she hoped wasn't noticeable, and her one pair of serviceable pumps for this meeting, trying for what she hoped was a grownup, 'I'm a professional' trust me look.

"My pleasure. I was delighted when you called. It's never too early to start planning for the future. But come, let's go to the conference room so we can talk."

The offices of Queensbay Capital were in a four-story building set back on the hillside that led out of town, one that looked ordinary enough from the outside. However, once you stepped off the elevator and onto the main floor, Lynn could feel the energy.

The whole office was light and bright, not what Lynn expected from an investment firm where people took money seriously. She had thought there would be lots of dark wood and old men in suits. Instead, most of the staff seemed on the younger side, and though there were plenty of suits, there was nothing stodgy about them. Colorful art, many of them waterscapes with a modernist touch, lined the wall, and instead of old-fashioned polished mahogany desks, they were all light blond wood or glass and metal contraptions.

There were tablets and sleek computers and there was just enough bustle going around in the air to make the place seem vibrant and electric.

Caitlyn, not slowing down at all, led her into a glass-walled conference room where a bank of windows commanded a distant view of the harbor.

"Thank you for seeing me on such short notice."

"Always a pleasure, Lynn. I hear that you took a permanent job at the clinic. How wonderful."

Caitlyn Montgomery Randall was a few years older than Lynn and had grown up in Queensbay. She was married to Noah Randall, a technology entrepreneur, who had also grown up in town. Now, she ran a successful investment firm, while her husband advised other start-ups. They'd just had a beautiful baby boy, Lucas, and they lived in a beautiful house on one of the bluffs that ringed the harbor. Lynn had been there once for a cocktail party, a fundraiser for the hospital. You could have hated them for their obvious happiness and good fortune, but you wouldn't. They were generous to a fault, and Caitlyn was vivacious and striking so that you couldn't help but be drawn into her orbit.

"Thank you." Lynn felt a moment of guilt. Caitlyn had offered to help Lynn get started investing when she was ready and Lynn had used that as a pretext for this meeting. Still, that wasn't the reason Lynn had come, instead hoping that Caitlyn's reputation as a philanthropist might serve her instead.

"I imagine this isn't quite a social call or a let's set up an IRA account type of visit." Caitlyn looked at her shrewdly, one eyebrow raised above her luminous gray eyes.

"Not exactly." Lynn felt a sense of relief that she wouldn't have to beat around the bush. "I am so sorry to bother you, but I couldn't think of anyone else who might be able to help. See, we're also under a time crunch. At the clinic, I mean; and I need your advice."

"What sort of time crunch?" Caitlyn asked.

"The landlord wants us out."

"Duane Peterson is kicking you out?" Her voice was filled with surprise.

"It's the new landlord. Jackson Sanders."

Caitlyn's face registered surprise. "He bought the building?" Her face turned serious. "I hadn't heard that."

"I think it was the first thing he did when he got here. I think Chase is pretty surprised too."

"Aren't we all," Caitlyn said in a low voice, almost to herself. Lynn wondered if Caitlyn's bewilderment had something to do with what Tory had told her about Jackson's fiancée.

She looked up, shaken out of her thoughts. "But I don't see how I can help with that."

"It's your advice I need. See, it's not so much the clinic I am worried about. I'm sure we're already looking for some new space, but it's about my program—Healthy Kids Now."

Caitlyn nodded. "I remember you mentioning it."

"I wanted to formalize it, set it up as a real program, not a business necessarily but maybe more like a charity. I have some money to start up with, and now that I've had some success, I want to put together a real plan that can be used by other clinics and hospitals in the area."

"Sounds impressive."

"It's a start. Really, it's not so hard, knowing what to do. I mean the information is out there, but there's almost too much of it. I found when I started to give my patients—the kids and their parents—some simple guidelines, like just one or two behaviors to modify at a time, there was a much higher success rate than berating them on all the things they were doing wrong. Soon I was seeing more active, healthier kids. I was sort of just trying it out at the clinic, but I want it to be independent of it, so if the clinic closes all of the work I've done isn't for nothing."

Lynn realized she had been sitting on the edge of her chair, so excited to talk about her ideas that she couldn't relax.

"You sound like you have this all thought out," Caitlyn said.

Lynn leaned back a little in the comfortable leather chair, trying to appear professional. "Thought is just about all I've done." It had been Phoebe who had inspired her to take this next step, and together they had decided that Caitlyn was the perfect place to start.

Caitlyn leaned forward. "I like it. I think you're on to something. Of course, there would be some start-up costs, even if, as you said, you want to incorporate it as charity. Nothing too substantial, but you will need to make it official, and you'll need a lawyer. Don't worry, I know someone who will be very reasonable. I also know a woman who started a non-profit to make school lunches healthier. I'll give you her name too so you can chat. She'll have a lot more practical advice than I can give you. And of course, you'll want to set up some banking accounts."

"I have the money." Lynn said, thinking of what her grandmother had left her. It wasn't much but it would probably be enough to get the project under way. And if Lynn had to move in with her parents to make ends meet, well then that's just what she would have to do, until she found another job.

"I know you do, after all you do let us manage it. But while I admire your desire to build this on your own, I think you may have more success if you reach out to others for support. And becoming an official entity will be a step in the right direction. It will make everything more official, but it will also make sure the rest of the world takes you seriously."

Lynn leaned forward in her chair. She had known that coming to Caitlyn would be a good idea. The woman knew everyone, or so it seemed. Inspired, Lynn asked for a pen and a piece of paper and started to make some notes so she wouldn't miss anything. For the first time in days, she began to feel a glimmer of hope. Maybe something good could come out of this situation.

Chapter 20

Lynn walked past the batting cages, trying to make it seem like she couldn't care less who was there. Overall, though, she was in too good of a mood, riding high off her strategy meeting with Caitlyn, to let the thought of running into Jackson Sanders bother her.

Still, there was no harm in being prepared for a rogue sighting, since it seemed to be happening quite frequently. Especially if she was going to do a workout that would leave her sweaty, she wanted to ready. Ready for what? She sighed. Jackson had made it clear that he thought she was a nuisance in scrubs. Smelly workout clothes wouldn't help her case either. Too bad Queensbay was only big enough for one health club. And there was no way she was going to let the fear of Jackson seeing her hot and sweaty keep her out of it. Especially since hitting the gym seemed to be the only action that was happening lately.

Somehow the twin thoughts of Jackson and hot and sweaty made her stomach do a flip-flop, and she had a brief, intense image of naked bodies twisting together. She wondered what he would look like out of his work suit. She'd hadn't caught more than a glimpse of him when he's been here with Jake, only that his shoulders had seemed broader than she remembered and the muscles in his arm had all but rippled when she had turned to catch him swinging the bat. She shut down her hormones with a groan. Really, you would think there was one only one thing she thought about.

Swallowing, she told herself to stop thinking that way, but still she breathed a sigh of relief when she saw no tall, lanky blondes at the batting cage; only some middle-aged dads and their kids. She planned on a good, long workout and didn't want to be disturbed.

She went to the locker room, changed, and headed out onto the main floor of the gym, to the rock-climbing wall, which in her opinion, was the place's best feature. She fairly tingled in excitement looking up at it now, noting the pattern of the toe and handholds. She had climbed it a hundred times, but that didn't mean she could be lazy about planning her route.

"Hey, Lynn. Haven't seen you in a while." Bode Weller, one of the gym's personal trainers, came over and gave her a hug. He had longish brown hair, bleached blond at the tips, brown eyes, and a body like a Greek Adonis. She let herself enjoy the hug for a moment, feeling his muscles squeeze around her like a python, and then gently pushed him away.

"Bode, how have you been?"

"Great," he said. "Even better now that I've seen you." He gave her a puppy-dog sad look from underneath his eyes.

"Oh please! Like you even noticed I was gone." She shook her head. Bode was one of the more popular trainers at the gym and had a regular parade of women, young and old, salivating over him. Lynn herself had looked at him quite a few times as well, but that was all. Bode was a little too relaxed and easy going for her to think of him seriously. And he was a notorious flirt, but she knew that she had no problem allowing him to practice his charm on her.

Unbidden, she found herself doing a little comparison of Jackson to Bode. He probably wasn't as bulky or a ripped as Bode, but there had been the hint of decent musculature underneath that nicely tailored suit. Of course, he was pretty tall, so that meant that any weight he did carry would be nice and evenly distributed, probably leaving him long and lean like a cat. She gave a mental shrug to clear the image of Jackson from her mind. She was here to focus, and to climb.

"Here, let me get that harness rigged up for you."

Lynn was perfectly capable of doing it herself but she let Bode check her equipment, smiling a little as his hands lingered in all the right places. After all, he was only doing his job.

"All set here," Bode said.

"Thanks," Lynn said, going up to the rock wall and locating her first hand grip. She'd been delighted to find that a gym with a large indoor rock-climbing wall was opening up near Queensbay. She'd been one of the charter members, figuring that if she couldn't go out and climb the real thing, this was almost as good.

Focused, determined, Lynn started her climb. She didn't try to do it fast; rather, she took her time, letting her mind both wander and focus. One part of her concentrated on the different handholds and footholds while the other half ruminated the other issues facing her.

Even though it looked like The Healthy Kids Now program might take off on its own, she was still left with the problem of the clinic closing. So far, Sadie had made no progress on finding a new place for them to go. Time was counting down and somehow she had managed to tick off the only person who might be able to help the situation. Jackson Sanders.

It was his eyes that gave her hope, she thought. Sure, most of the time they were indecipherable, like a cat's, but occasionally she thought she saw flashes of...what? Hurt, compassion? Maybe, but Jackson always seemed alert, tightly wound like a leopard or a lion. Waiting to pounce.

Lynn almost had to laugh at that. There was no one who would ever accuse her of being catlike. Or waiting to pounce. She was more like a puppy in that regard. Ready to play, ready for action.

She was almost halfway up the wall when she became aware that there was someone else on it with her. She could hear Bode coaching the climber from below, but she could also sense a presence, fast approaching.

It wasn't long before a hand, large and well formed, at the end of a long arm, appeared at her side. In a moment, the rest of the climber came into view and she swiveled her head to see who it was.

The surprise caused her to falter, and it was only when the large hand reached out and steadied her that she was able to catch her balance.

"Are you ok?" Jackson asked her.

It took another moment before her mouth and brain connected and started to work together again.

"What are you doing here?"

He looked at her from underneath his helmet. Yup, definitely the blue eyes of a predator, Lynn thought.

"I believe it's called climbing," he said, his leg pushing him up and propelling him forward so he was able to climb ahead of her.

"Is this your first time?" she asked. She would not have pegged Jackson as an outdoorsy type.

"No, not quite. But don't tell the instructor. He seems intent on giving me directions I don't need."

Lynn frowned. Bode generally knew what he was doing; and if he thought that Jackson needed instructions, then he probably did.

"I didn't figure you for a climber," Lynn said, looking up. She pulled herself up so she was more evenly matched with Jackson. *It's not a race,* she told herself, but it didn't seem quite fair he had come out of nowhere to pass her by.

"I hear it's excellent exercise," Jackson said, looking up and around for his next grip. Lynn watched his technique. It wasn't very refined but it got the job done. His big frame made it easy for him to find a foot or handhold and then it was just a matter of sheer strength for him to pull himself up.

She looked at him, could see how his back muscles bunched and tightened under his fitted t-shirt, the way his long, muscular legs moved with the rest of the body. Well, whatever he was doing for exercise, it was working nicely, Lynn thought, since there was nothing wrong with his body, especially the view from below and behind.

"You don't climb for real, I mean outdoors?" Lynn asked, picking up her pace. The top half of the wall was trickier than the bottom half, with the grips more spaced out. She used her knowledge of it to pull ahead of Jackson, watching as his hands searched for a good position.

"You mean on real rocks? Not since I was a kid," he said, his voice holding just the hint of breathlessness.

"You should try it sometime, might loosen you up."

He gave a snort. "Does that mean you climb trees too?"

"Only when something's chasing me," she said, sending him a proud grin as she passed him and made her way to the top.

A rueful look flickered over his face, but he kept going, pulling himself up to the top more slowly.

Lynn looked around, surveying the space and catching her breath. Ok, so it wasn't anything like what she had climbed back in Colorado, but it wasn't so bad. And the Mountain State had never had a view quite like Jackson Sanders in it, either.

"Hey, guys. Time to come down; I've got some people waiting," Bode called from below. Lynn nodded and readied herself for the rappel down. Sure, there was no way this could compete with the real thing, but it was still no small thrill to let yourself leap out into the air, the only thing keeping you from free falling your harness and a piece of rope.

With a little whoop, she shoved off, relished the speed and then slowed herself down to a more respectable, rule-abiding pace.

"Nice work out." Bode caught her and then set her upright, his hands moving over her just a little as he set her upright.

Jackson landed neatly next to her, glancing between her and Bode. Lynn decided that she didn't mind the way Bode let his hand rest on her shoulder, not when she saw how Jackson was looking at them. Maybe this was the way to pierce Jackson's ice demeanor.

"Not bad for a first timer," Bode said offhandedly to Jackson. Lynn could feel Bode drawing up tight beside her, his arm still possessively around her. She nearly sidestepped but just to keep watching Jackson's reaction, she stayed where she was.

Jackson only said, "I'm a quick learner."

"Your form and technique could be a little better," Bode said quickly. "Maybe we'll just have another go at it, and then I'll critique you."

Lynn looked between the two men and decided she had better make herself scarce. "I'm just going to go over and use the weight room. Thanks, Bode."

"No problem." Bode shot her a smile and then said, "I was thinking maybe we could grab a beer together. My buddies and I usually hit Quent's Pub around eight?"

Lynn tried not to care if Jackson overheard this exchange or not. Bode had been bugging her to go out for a 'beer' for a while, but she'd always found some excuse, usually work related, to say no. But now her hours were more regular, so there really wasn't any reason she couldn't, shouldn't go out. If she told her mom she was going on a date voluntarily, then she'd be less likely to set her up on another blind one. She was fairly certain she could drag Tory along so she'd have backup. After all, Tory had told her stop over-thinking her relationships, and Bode had never struck her as much of a thinker. Maybe he was just what she needed. And there was the fact that Jackson was standing there, watching, as if he actually cared what she had to say.

"Sounds good," Lynn said, and glanced over at Jackson, and just caught the look that flitted across his face. Was he angry? Jealous? Whatever it was, he certainly wasn't indifferent.

She tried to hide her smile, and knew good manners needed her to say something. "I'll bring my friend Tory along, so Jackson, if you're not doing anything, maybe you'd like to join us?"

His blue eyes raked over her, took in Bode standing next to her, arms crossed.

"I have other plans, thank you," he said coldly.

Lynn nodded, but felt what? A small shiver of disappointment. Still, she turned to look at Bode, with his surfer-length brownish-blonde hair, bulging biceps, and pecs that practically danced on their own and decided that there could be worse ways to spend an evening than in the company of the very well-toned and defined Bode Weller.

"Well then, catch you later, Bode," she said as casually as she could, and walked away. She didn't dare look back, but she was certain she could feel two sets of eyes staring at her as she crossed the gym floor toward the weight room.

Chapter 21

Jackson didn't know why he disliked Bode almost on sight. Certainly it wasn't because he was jealous of the easy way he had gotten Lynn to agree to go out with him. Or the way Lynn had clearly been staring, ogling Bode in his sleeveless shirt and workout pants. But he just didn't like the guy.

He hadn't planned on running into her; at least, that hadn't been his primary goal in coming here. Sure, he knew that this was the only gym in town. The thought had crossed his mind that maybe, when he decided to go for a workout, there was an off chance he might bump into her. The thought bothered him, but he hadn't tried to stay away either. It was just that he wasn't supposed to care about her one way or the other. And yet he couldn't deny that he had been strangely gratified when he'd seen her walking in and stopping at the front desk. His eyes had followed her to the locker room and then before he realized what he doing, he had sweet-talked the receptionist into booking him onto the wall at the same time as Lynn.

He still didn't know why he had done it. The right thing to do was to stay away. He hadn't come back into town to start dating. Especially not his brother's fiancée's best friend. That would definitely be against his no-strings policy. And Lynn didn't even like him. She, who seemed to welcome the rest of the world with open arms, looked at him like he was one step above medical waste. He shouldn't need to work at this, he had a thousand other things to occupy his time.

Now, after listening to Bode gave him a lecture about climbing wall safety, Jackson was doing his usual gym routine, running, lifting some weights. He had kept an eye on Lynn while she did her own workout, seen her use some free weights, then do pushups and pull-ups, her toned little body moving effortlessly through the exercises. She was slicked with a bit of sweat, and her workout clothes, while not tight, clung closely enough to her curves so that he couldn't help wondering what she would look like without them on.

He watched as she disappeared into the locker room, presumably done for the day. Off to her date with that muscle head Bode.

He tried to put the thought of her out of his head as he finished up his workout. He headed over toward the water cooler to get a drink and then hit the showers, when he heard Bode's voice from inside one of the gym offices.

"Dude, climber chick is going out with me tonight."

Jackson froze, listening.

"What, you mean Lynn, the hot little doctor? She agreed to go out with you?" The other voice was raised in disbelief.

"Yeah, finally. She's going to meet me at Quent's tonight. Said she's bringing a friend; want to ride shotgun?"

Jackson thought it sounded like Bode couldn't quite hide the triumph in his tone.

"Think her friend is as smokin' as she is?"

The other guy's voice was eager and Jackson clenched his hands in anger.

"Of course. Hot chicks run in packs. But look, Lynn's mine—you get what you get."

"Fine, but man, I still don't know how you got that sweet piece of ass to say yes to you."

He heard Bode laugh. "Who could resist me?"

"She's probably only interested in you for your body."

Bode laughed again. "What do you think I want her for? An interesting conversation over wine and cheese? I'm just hoping she'll want to play doctor with me."

There was a bout of loud laughter, and Jackson swallowed the impulse to shove open the door of the office and take a swing at Bode.

He heard a sound and turned, trying his best to look like he was casually strolling away, clenching and unclenching his hands, trying to work off some of his anger, when Bode came up behind him, clapped him on the back and said, "Not a bad day for a beginner, dude. You know we're running a special here, fifty percent off your first month of training. I'd be happy to set you up with the paperwork."

Jackson let his anger settle down. It wouldn't do any good to take a punch at Bode. At least not yet. But there was no way he was going to let a guy like Bode prey upon an unsuspecting girl like Lynn. With her big brown eyes, that curly hair, and passionate personality, she was an easy mark for guys like him.

Barely sparing a smile for Bode, he disentangled himself, promising to stop by later, and made his way to the locker room, mulling over his options. Perhaps he might just stop by Quent's tonight after all.

Chapter 22

"What made you decide all of a sudden you wanted to go on a date?" Tory asked. They were at Lynn's apartment, getting ready to meet Bode and his friend.

Lynn was looking through her paltry selection of tops, trying to decide what to wear. She had lived the last eight years in scrubs and was slowly realizing that her wardrobe had suffered for it. She couldn't wear a repeat of her date with Nate. Hence the emergency call to Tory, who seemed to have perfected the casual chic look, for some fashion advice.

"What do you think about this one?" Lynn asked, holding up one of her favorites, a scoop neck, tunic-length top in a dark red.

"Hmm," Tory said getting up from the bed and coming over to Lynn's closet. "You didn't answer the question."

Lynn shrugged. What was the real reason that she had volunteered to go on a date? Was it to keep her mom off her back? Or had she only said yes to the date with Bode because Jackson had been standing there and she had the sudden, crazy impulse to see if she could get a reaction out of him? But that had backfired. Jackson had seemed to have cared less that she was going.

And why should he? He was what? The clinic's landlord. And a mean one at that. He seemed to have no room in his heart other than what was best for the bottom line. What did she hope to gain by talking to him so more? Just more of those icy, cold stares that sent shivers down her back. And there had been plenty of those today.

All she knew was that whenever she had looked up from her workout, he had been looking at her. He looked away of course, thinking he hadn't been caught, but she had been totally aware of him the whole time.

"Earth to Lynn...Since you agreed to go on a date, did you decide to take my advice? Does this mean you think Bode is really hot, or have you just decided that it's been so long something's going to rust shut if it doesn't get used?"

"Rust shut?" Lynn asked. "You know that isn't physically possible."

"I wasn't being literal," Tory said with a wave of her hand.

"Well it's not literally or metaphorically possible for it, as you call it, to rust shut." Lynn shuddered at the image, but she had to admit that Tory had a point. It had been a while and her hormones seemed to be in overdrive. She had thought it was because she had finally reached a place in her life, professionally, where things were going well. And that meant that the other part of her body wanted in on the action, even if the reason things were going so well was that she had neglected her hormones.

But now everything was turmoil and her hormones hadn't gotten the message that there was a much bigger crisis going on than their lack of activity.

"It's really been, like years? How have gone so long?"

"Med school is pretty demanding," Lynn said.

"It must not have been very good," Tory said casually as she plucked a blouse off a hanger, looked at it, and discarded it on the growing heap of clothes on the floor.

"What?"

"The sex, silly."

"It was ok," Lynn defended her experience.

Tory smiled. "Ahh, that's the problem."

"What do you mean?"

"Honey, sex isn't supposed to be ok, it's supposed to be good." Tory pulled out the syllable in the last word and gave Lynn a knowing look. "You need to up your expectations," she continued.

"And what should my expectations be?" Lynn asked.

"Great sex. That's it. Nothing else. Don't expect more than that, especially from someone like Bode, who let's admit, doesn't seem like much more than a pretty face, and you'll be fine. Probably better than fine. You just need to get laid, without all that other crap about hearts and flowers and moonlight walks into forever."

Lynn blinked. "That doesn't sound very romantic."

Tory shook her head. "That's the point. You need to start with baby steps, you know, personal pleasure, and then you can move onto romance. At some point."

"But..."

"Look, did you find Nate attractive, envision yourself doing the horizontal mambo with him?"

Lynn shook her head.

"Good, so you cut him loose right?"

661

Lynn nodded. It had taken some dodging and excuses about her crazy schedule, but Nate had finally stopped texting her.

"And Bode's easy on the eyes, right?"

"True," Lynn agreed.

"Well, unless you have someone else in mind?" Tory said, with a wicked smile on her face.

"What?" Lynn found her face flaming. How did Tory do that?

"Nothing, just working out a hunch," Tory said, her voice innocent, as she held up a sweater, considering.

"This isn't some game," Lynn said.

Tory smiled, her caramel colored eyes dancing, "Oh yes it is. And now it's time to play. Wear this one, with that skirt, and these boots and let's see if you can score a goal, slugger." She tossed the outfit on the bed and smiled.

"You're mixing your sports metaphors," Lynn said. She looked at the outfit Troy had picked out. Simple, casual and the v-neck sweater would show just a hint of cleavage. Maybe Tory was right. Not everything, especially guys, needed to be a matter of life or death. Maybe she just needed to enjoy the ride.

Chapter 23

Bode was waiting for them, and as promised, he'd brought a friend. Bode looked good, Lynn thought: a little more polished than he usually did at the gym. Tonight, he wore a pair of dark jeans and a charcoal-gray t-shirt that seemed like it had been poured on. She stopped and took a moment to drink in the perfection that was Bode Weller's pectoral region. His brownish-blond hair was slightly tousled and his dark brown eyes looked her over appreciatively as he pulled out a barstool for her.

Lynn introduced Tory to Bode, and Bode introduced them to his friend Greg and there was hand shaking and hellos all round. And then silence, except for the backdrop of music. Classic INXS was playing and there were more than a few people singing along.

"Been a while since I heard this song," Lynn said, looking to break the quiet.

"Yeah, well, it's Aussie night and Quent is running a special on beer from Down Under. Can I get you one?" Bode said, smiling at her.

Lynn nodded, and Bode went to go fetch the drinks. Tory and Greg eyed each other, and then Tory suggested they try a game of pool. Greg seemed thankful for something to do and Lynn was left alone.

She scanned the pub. There was a baseball game on one TV, football on another, and soccer on the third. None of them were big games, and no one was paying that much attention.

"Here's your beer. It's an Australian micro-brew, one that Quent swears by," Bode said, returning with two bottles of beer and a bowl of nuts.

He slid onto one of the barstools at their little table and she immediately found that somehow the stool had moved much closer than before. Bode's knee was touching hers and she pulled back just a little. Maybe she hadn't been on a date in a while, but she thought they should have at least one beer before he tried for close physical contact.

Undaunted, he leaned his head in. "It's a nice change to see you here, outside of the gym. You look good there, but you look pretty hot outside of it."

"Yeah, it's good to get out," Lynn said, fighting the impulse to lean back. Her pulse was racing but it wasn't her hormones talking. She didn't know what was wrong with her. Bode was nothing like Nate, the Civil War, vice presidential-loving accountant, who'd left her with nothing but the desire to run away screaming in boredom.

Nope, Bode was almost the exact opposite, and while Nate had been scrupulously polite about touching her, Bode was going in the total opposite direction.

She felt a hand brush casually against her thigh and she moved away. Bode sent her a lazy smile and she turned the talk to where he liked to go on vacation. They talked about other things and Lynn decided that except for an interest spending time at the gym, they didn't have much in common. It didn't seem to deter Bode though, as he kept reaching out, trying to close the distance between them, while she just as carefully tried to maintain it.

Finally, she decided she needed a break and excused herself to use the restroom. She was washing her hands and thinking through ways of politely breaking off the evening. First, she would need to give the signal to Tory, which was too bad, since she genuinely seemed to be enjoying herself with Bode's friend, Greg. Still, Tory was her wingman and that was the nature of the job.

She took a deep breath, counted to ten, and told herself she could do this. It was part of being a grownup, part of dating, being able to play the game right, let someone down so that they got the picture but weren't left with hurt feelings. How had Tory phrased it? "It's not you, it's me..." Time for a graceful exit speech, she supposed.

Lynn came out of the bathroom and headed briskly down the hallway into the main room of the bar. Out of her peripheral vision she caught a glimpse of something. She stopped just before she hit it, but still managed to connect with something cold and slightly wet.

"What are you doing here?" she asked, looking up.

Jackson stood there, looking down at her, a slight frown on his face, one hand holding a beer bottle away from her. There was a foamy head at the top, probably from the impact Lynn had had with it.

"Here, let me get you a napkin," Lynn said. She reached over to the bar, where there was a pile of small square, white napkins neatly stacked. She swiped a bunch and started to pat down Jackson's sleeve.

"Don't worry about it," he said, moving a little out of her reach. He was wearing a crisp white button down, a pair of dark wool slacks and dress shoes.

"I thought you had other plans," Lynn said, feeling silly holding the bunch of slightly damp napkins in her hand. She looked around and then set them down on the bar. She hazarded a look around. Unlike The Golden Pear, no one here seemed to take notice of Jackson and he seemed, relaxed even confident, with none of the tenseness that had radiated through his body the other day.

She knew she should get back to Bode, but her curiosity at finding Jackson here was getting the better of her.

"I did, but they fell through. I didn't feel like sitting at home, so I thought I would come out and watch the game."

"The game?" Lynn asked.

He pointed towards the baseball game.

"You like baseball?" Lynn asked, knowing her voice sound more surprised than was polite.

"Like, love it, used to play it."

"Really?" Lynn said, considering. So that explained the batting cage. She took a step back, assessing him. Sure, he was taller and lankier than a lot of baseball players and certainly a lot fitter than most of them, but she could see it now, a cap pulled low on his head, his eyes roving over the infield, assessing each player's position, just waiting for one of them to make the wrong move.

"Not since college, of course, but, yes I play it."

She nodded and was about to start back to the table where she'd been sitting with Bode, whose back was to her, intently looking at something on his phone.

"You seem shocked," he said, taking a sip of beer, his blue eyes watching her carefully over the rim of the bottle.

She shrugged, not wanting to admit that she had been giving him that much thought. "You didn't strike me as a guy who played a sport."

"I'm also a black belt in Taekwondo."

"Oh," Lynn said, trying not to sound impressed. So maybe she did need to rethink her assessment of Jackson Sanders. Not quite the priss she'd thought.

"How many sports do you play?" he asked.

"Soccer, for a team sport. But I grew up out west, so I ski, climb, hike, and bike."

"That's an impressive list. You sound quite active." Jackson said.

She looked at him quickly, wondering if he was being sarcastic, but he merely looked down at her. He seemed a little more at ease, a little more human now that he had ditched the full business suit. He looked almost cute, Lynn decided and then tamped down that feeling. He was evil. Ok, so maybe evil was overdoing it, but he was not a nice guy. She wasn't about to just forgive him for his decision to close the clinic because he decided to smile at her. She was a stronger woman than that.

"I like the outdoors. And climbing things. Trees, rocks, hills, that sort of stuff. Was that really your first time on a rock wall?" Lynn asked, curious to know.

He looked at her and the faintest of smiles ghosted across his lips. "Second, if you count the time when I was ten at Boy Scout camp."

"Really? You were pretty good."

"Thanks, but I was just following you."

The compliment threw her off guard. She wasn't expecting him to be nice and it was destroying the image she had of him.

"I should go, get back to Bode," she said, suddenly knowing she needed to pull herself away.

"I thought you said this was a group thing?" he said, his voice casual.

"Umm, sure it is. I mean Tory's over there with Bode's friend Greg, playing pool, but I guess it's ok, I mean, yeah sure, come on over." She knew she was stammering, but somehow Tory's quick guide on dating hadn't covered this scenario.

"I was just teasing. Go, enjoy your date. I am sure Bode's quite the interesting fellow."

"*You have no idea,*" Lynn almost shot back, then before she could say anything, she turned and walked away, knowing that her face was flaming.

Bode had swiveled around and watched her coming.

"What's he doing here?" There was a querulous tone in his voice. Lynn stopped, surprised to realize that Bode and Jackson were eyeing each other like a pair of roosters in a chicken coop.

Lynn threw one look over her shoulder. Jackson was watching her, and when he caught Bode's eye, raised his beer bottle in a mock salute. Bode stared back at him and finally gave the barest of nods.

She watched the whole thing like it was some sort of surreal show, not sure what to make of the testosterone pissing match going on.

"He said he came to watch the game. His plans fell through," Lynn said, hopping up on the barstool. She looked. Bode had gotten her another drink, but she was sure she didn't want it. She was ready to go, before Bode and Jackson's visual sparring turned into something worse. Her brother, Kyle, had once explained that sometimes guys just didn't like each other, that it was just a guy thing, and that when that was the case you could never tell what would happen. It had never made sense to Lynn until she was in the middle of it.

"Really?" Bode shot Jackson another look, this one dark and dangerous, and Lynn put out her hand on his arm to calm him.

"It's a small town. Not too many places to grab a beer and watch the game if you don't feel like being on your own."

"Guess not." Bode gave a smile and seemed to shrug Jackson off. Lynn was glad but she was also wondering just how she could get Tory's attention and bring her back over so she could find a way to leave. She could feel a headache beginning to loom and suddenly she wanted nothing more than to go home, to her nice new bed in her nice new apartment, and go to sleep.

"Well, where were we?" Bode said and he leaned in closer. Lynn was pretty sure they had been talking about hiking in the Catskill Mountains of upstate New York, but Bode seemed to think they had gotten much farther than that.

His hand was sliding up her leg, inside the skirt that she was wearing. The shock of it had her frozen. His other arm snaked around her shoulders as he drew her in for a kiss. For a moment she didn't quite get what was happening and then when she did realize it, she wondered why she didn't like it.

She pushed hard on his chest with her hands, managed to say, "Bode, I think maybe you should stop."

He pulled back for a moment and shot a look of disbelief at her. "Stop? If you didn't want it, why did you come out with me? C'mon, not like we have a lot in common, except we both got good bodies and I would sure like to find out what yours feels like. I've been watching your ass climb that rock wall for weeks now and I'm ready to get my hands on it."

Lynn was too shocked to say anything, and Bode must have taken that as an opportunity because he went in for another kiss, his hand snaking its way even farther up her skirt.

Bode tasted like beer and his lips were rough and his hand insistent. She pulled away, but he didn't let her go, so she pushed harder. She fought down the first wave of panic. After all, they were in a bar, and surely he would take the hint and just let her go. And if not, she knew what to do: she'd taken a self-defense class at the clinic and she just needed to remember whether she was supposed to go for the throat or the eyes first.

She never got a chance to make a decision. There was a whish of air and a sudden moment, and she felt herself topple back, almost, but not quite, falling off the barstool.

"What the hell?" Lynn said, looking down at the writhing form of Bode. Jackson stood there calmly, almost as if he hadn't moved.

Attracted by the sudden commotion, Tory and Greg materialized behind them.

Bode rose to his feet and for a moment, Lynn thought nothing more was going to happen. But she underestimated Bode's feelings on the matter. Without warning, he charged Jackson, who nimbly sidestepped him. Bode stumbled, almost fell, but Quent, who knew when trouble was brewing in his bar, caught him.

"Hey now, what's happening?" Quent's voice loud and commanding brought the pub to a standstill.

"It didn't seem like he was acting like a gentleman," Jackson said calmly. He looked Bode in the eye. "I believe the lady said no."

"Yeah, is that what you think? Then she shouldn't be such a tease!" Bode shot back. At this, Jackson moved toward him but was stopped by one of Quent's meaty hands.

"There's no fighting in here."

Jackson lowered his arms and took a step back. Lynn fought to catch her breath. It had all happened so fast. She hadn't meant for anyone to take Bode down, but still, the jerk hadn't gotten the picture.

"Come on, let's go," Tory had her arm and was pulling her away.

Lynn walked out of the pub into the cool night air, drawing a deep, deep breath.

"What happened in there?" Tory asked.

"I don't know...Bode, well he was kind of an ass. He put his hand up here, and I mean all the way up here, and when I told him to remove it and said I wasn't that kind of girl, he laughed and said why the hell had I gone out with him if I wasn't interested in sex, because it wasn't like we had anything else in common. And when he didn't take no for an answer, Jackson was there doing some sort of weird ninja trick that had Bode on the ground in no time flat."

"I saw that, and I have to say that was kinda hot," Tory said, nodding. "Imagine that, Jackson Sanders coming to your rescue. And sorry about Bode. Maybe you aren't ready to just jump into bed with someone."

"I didn't need rescuing," Lynn said, ignoring what Tory had said about Bode. Yes, her hormones were itching, but not for what Bode was offering. It had been a little too blunt. And he hadn't taken no for an answer the first time. She'd been just about to tell him that in no uncertain terms, the way she had learned in defense class, but Jackson had just been there, smooth, capable, kind of like James Bond. Ok, so maybe she didn't need the rescuing; but Tory was right—there had been something kind of hot about Jackson stepping in.

"I am sure you didn't, but still, it's not every day a girl gets caught up in a bar fight."

Lynn slowed her pace just a little, shook her head, "I'm not a girl. I'm a grown woman, a doctor; and the last thing I need is be caught up in some sort barroom brawl."

"Whatever. I still think it's kind of hot. And wow, the way Jackson was staring at you, like he couldn't tear himself away."

"Oh please," Lynn snorted.

"Well, it's about time he got over her. You know, he might just be what you need."

"I didn't need any help," Lynn insisted. "He was just being a gentleman, you know because I'm friends with his soon to be sister-in-law."

"Whatever. Anyway, here's my car. I'm going to head home now."

"You ok to drive?" Lynn said.

"I only had one beer the entire night," Tory said. "But let me drive you to your door."

Lynn was about to say no, that the walk would do her good, when a shadow fell upon them, cast by the old-fashioned street lamp.

They turned and saw Jackson walking towards them. He had put on his jacket and to Lynn, he looked tall, dangerous, and very suave. James Bond indeed.

"Ladies, can I walk you home?" he asked, coming to a stop before them.

"This is my car, I was going to head home, but since you and Lynn are heading to the same place, you can make sure she gets home safely," Tory said quickly, shooting a fierce look at Jackson.

"Lynn will be perfectly safe with me," he said to Tory, his voice stiff.

Lynn watched the exchange between Tory and Jackson, puzzled. There was an undercurrent here that she didn't understand, but then it didn't seem to matter because Jackson was looking down at her for confirmation and all she could do was mutter, "Umm, sure," suddenly feeling tongue-tied.

She gave Tory a quick, one-armed hug and watched as her friend jumped into her little Mini Cooper and peeled off.

And she was left standing in the street with Jackson.

"You were heading home, I presume?" Jackson said.

"Yes," Lynn answered, because she didn't really have anywhere else to be. Except for a date with her couch, the Hallmark channel, and some black raspberry ice cream with chocolate sauce.

"Should we go?" He held out an arm in the general direction of the harbor and she fell in step beside him, suddenly aware of the heat emanating from him.

"I guess I should say thank you," Lynn said. "I mean, I was handling it, could have handled it. In fact, I was going to try a move like yours, I mean not like yours, because wow, yours was pretty killer. I didn't even know you were there. Is that because you're a black belt?"

She stopped took a breath, realizing she was babbling. Nervous; why was she so nervous? Jackson had only ever made her irritated, mad, before—not nervous. Ok, so he had made her both. Irritated, nervous, jumpy; you name it, he had caused just about the full spectrum.

"Yes and yes."

"What?"

"Yes, I am sure you could have had handled it, but it annoyed me he wasn't getting the message fast enough. And yes, I was able to do that because I'm a black belt."

"Have you ever done that before?" she asked, not sure if she wanted to know if he made a habit of rescuing other women.

"In a bar?" He glanced down at her and she thought that maybe, for once, his eyes looked less icy, friendly even.

"Yeah."

"No, never in a bar. In competitions, yes. But then I haven't done one of those in many years."

"It doesn't seem like you're out of practice."

"I just finished what you started." His voice was gracious.

"Are you always so much of a gentleman or do you just like dropping guys with an axe kick?"

He stopped then and she was forced to stop with him. "If you're asking if I approve of violence, I do not. But I hate bullies even more. And Bode was bullying you."

"So you would have done the same for anyone?"

She wondered why she was disappointed when Jackson answered with a simple yes and they continued walking. She didn't know why she felt she needed to explain the situation to him, but she did.

"I'm really not the type of girl who goes all the way on the first date." As she said it, she knew it was true. She needed a little bit of romance, even if her hormones were screaming for some therapy. "And that's all he seemed interested in. I mean, he acknowledged that we have nothing in common except a certain level of physical attractiveness...I mean, he practically admitted he was only interested in my body."

"And that upsets you?" Jackson asked dryly.

She looked up at him. His eyes were shrouded in the dark, so she couldn't tell what he was thinking. She swallowed, all of a sudden nervous. She had never imagined walking in the moonlight with Jackson Sanders, and it was putting her on edge. Why did it have to be him that her underused hormones responded to? Why couldn't they do backflips for Nate the accountant, or even Bode the blunt?

They were almost at the harbor and the building that housed their apartments. A few clouds were rolling in, playing hide and seek with the moon. Tomorrow was supposed to be rainy, she remembered, the first real rain of the fall. It would be a good day to huddle in bed, figure out why her professional life seemed to be going so well but her personal life was in shambles. It was because she was book smart and guy stupid, she decided.

They were almost at the stairs that led up to the second-floor balcony. He got there first but stood back, letting her go ahead. She mounted the steps, going up them as quickly as possible, all of a sudden eager to get away from Jackson. Her body was too jumpy, her nervous system tingling—a sure sign her hormones were kicking up into overdrive.

So far, he had shown nothing but irritation or excruciating politeness to her, and she could only assume that his own body and nervous system were not in any way compromised. Like he said, he would have done what he did for anyone. *So don't read too much into it,* she told herself.

The light had been fixed, she noticed, and now there was no mistaking her door from Jackson's, especially now that she had put a new doormat in front of it.

"Here we are," she said, walking to her door, one hand fumbling for her key in her purse.

To her surprise, he didn't stop at his own door and go directly in. Instead, he came until he was standing close to her. As her hands fished the keys from her bag, she felt them tremble slightly. There was something distinctly unnerving having Jackson Sanders standing so close to her, his eyes staring at her face.

Without a word, he leaned in and for one breathless moment, Lynn had a crazy idea that he was going to kiss her, and though she wasn't nearly ready for it, she nonetheless would have wanted it.

Instead, he reached his hand out and took the keys from hers. In a swift, fluid moment, he opened the door to her apartment and the keys were back in her hand.

The distance was back between them now and she let out a breath, confused at what had just happened, or in any case had not happened.

"Have a good night," he said.

"Are you always such a gentleman?" she breathed.

"There's no reason we can't be polite to one another." His voice was steady.

"Yes, of course," she managed to stammer, then added, "thank you."

She waited, but there was nothing but an awkward silence stretching between them. Quickly, before she could embarrass herself further, she let herself into her apartment, shutting the door behind her. She leaned against it and closed her eyes, wondering why she had thought, even for a moment, that he might have wanted to kiss her, and that against all reason, she had wanted him to.

She was just about to move, think about undressing, getting into something comfortable, maybe make a cup of tea, when there was a quiet knock at her door.

Without bothering to look through the peephole, she opened it and there he stood, a sudden burst of moonlight tipping his blond hair silver.

"Yes?"

"I'm not always such a gentleman, Lynn," he said. And he moved in quickly, taking her face in her hands, his lips coming down on hers. It was as if an electric current sprang between them and she felt herself lifted up off her toes and into him, her arms coming around his shoulders as she pulled herself into him.

It seemed to go on forever as they hungrily devoured each other. She heard a sound, a wordless moan, and realized that it must have come from her.

All too soon, he broke free from her, took a step back, his hand firmly at his sides.

"Have a good night," he said. Then turned on his heel and walked to his own door and was gone.

Shocked, Lynn held the door open just a moment longer and then stepped back, shut it, and sunk to the floor, truly wondering what had just happened and how she was ever going to be able to sleep with her body wound up and as tingly as a kid with the chicken pox.

Chapter 24

Jackson paced restlessly in his apartment, wondering just what he'd done, trying to assess just where his feelings were going. He stopped, looking out the window at the harbor. The moon was out now, uncovered by the clouds, and it left a glittering quicksilver trail across the surface, which in the dark, looked still, heavy as if all of Queensbay Harbor was a cauldron of molten silver.

He hadn't meant to kiss her. Or had he? He rubbed his hand through his hair, knowing that he was lying to himself. Ok, so he had meant to kiss her, knowing that if he left and then came back it would definitely unsettle her. And he wanted her unsettled, right? He wanted to know that she was lying awake at night thinking about him. But why? She wasn't his type. He didn't have a type, couldn't have a type. He wanted no strings attached. He liked women who were taller, blonder. Not as enthusiastic. Detached. He remembered how passionately she had spoken about the clinic. He couldn't let himself become involved. He couldn't ever feel again.

He had sworn after Ashley that he wouldn't let his guard down, that he wouldn't let himself care about anyone. It had hurt too much, pushed him too close to the edge. He was willing to offer his bed, companionship, but nothing more. Sure he'd been attracted to women, he wasn't a monk, after all, but he hadn't felt a powerful need for anyone, not like with Lynn. And she had answered with every fiber of her body, to that kiss. No, this was not good at all.

He sat down on the couch, suddenly tired. He looked at his hands. He hadn't landed a punch in a long time against anything more than a training bag. Bode had looked tough, all thick head and muscle, but that only meant he had fallen harder.

There had been a certain satisfaction in knocking the guy down, Jackson thought. He may not have wanted to get tangled up with a woman, but when she said no, you had to respect that. And Lynn had been making it clear that she wasn't interested in a casual, physical acquaintance. Nope, Bode had deserved just what he'd gotten.

And Lynn? She didn't deserve him, not if she really cared. And Jackson had a feeling she could be the type of woman who cared, very, very much.

Chapter 25

It did rain the next day. Lynn awoke early, to the soft patter of rain on the roof. From her window, she could see only gray, as if the whole of Queensbay was covered in a soft blanket. The rain, cloud, and mist hovered over the harbor so that the edges of the docks were ghostly outlines and the hills and bluffs that ringed the town were invisible.

She had the day off. She had been excited for it, but now it stretched in front of her, empty, and she didn't know what to with herself.

She could unpack some more boxes, hang some pictures up on the wall, but she only had one, a print Phoebe had given her. Maybe she should go shopping. There was a gallery or two in town with some affordable photographs. She could browse through their racks, pick up a modest purchase, treat herself to a carbohydrate-heavy lunch at The Golden Pear, maybe hit the library and check out a book she could read.

All of that sounded appealing, except for the weather and her mood, which matched it perfectly. Gray-blue. Lynn was not a melancholy person and she didn't quite know what to do with the feeling that made every action an effort. She rolled back on her pillows and stared up at her white ceiling. What had she been thinking agreeing to a date with Bode? She should have known he'd only be interested in sex. Ok, so maybe that's all she had thought she was interested in. But not in the first hour! He had hadn't even offered to buy her dinner, just a beer and a bowl of free mixed nuts. But at least he had been honest. An asshole but an honest one. She had gone on the date knowing full well that Bode wasn't her type. And that perhaps his only use to her was to make Jackson jealous.

Last night she had been kissed twice, which was twice more than she had been kissed in about two years. And Jackson's kiss had been by far the better one. She hadn't been kissed like that in a long, long time—if ever. It had been amazing: all her senses on overload, every nerve-ending exploding. Not even her first one with Todd Hammerschmitt, her eighth-grade boyfriend for all of two weeks, could compare. He too had needed something. Her science homework. After the big test, he had dumped her for Jessie Unger. Lynn sighed.

No, Jackson's kiss had made her knees go weak, her heart clench and then thump like a bass drum. There had been a roaring in her ears and she had felt every nerve in her body strung tight. It had been amazing. But it was just a kiss. She shouldn't read too much into it. Especially not from someone who was as emotionally damaged as he was supposed to be. He was the definition of fixer upper, and she needed to stay away.

But he had rescued her and walked her home. Had he thought he deserved a kiss for his knight in shining armor routine? She pulled the pillow up over her head and mouthed a silent scream into it. Just because she thought he was cute—there she had admitted it—there was no reason to start building up a fantasy around Jackson. Damaged goods—that's what Tory had all but said.

And now she didn't know what to do next. Her operating playbook had nothing on this. Was she supposed to leave the kiss in the past, pretend it had never happened, treat him coolly and professionally? Like a tenant to the landlord? Had it been a one-time thing? Or did he want to do it again? She curled and uncurled her toes, not able to stop remembering the feeling of being kissed by Jackson.

She knew what she wanted. She could kiss Jackson again and again and never get tired of it. Was it possible that for him it had been just another kiss? That it had all been one sided?

Exasperated, she tossed the pillow aside and swung her feet out onto the floor, deciding that she needed to exercise, burn off some of this energy. Maybe then she would come up with a plan, a strategy for how to handle Jackson without making a fool of herself. Then she remembered. Hitting the gym, where she was likely to run into Bode, was off limits, and with the gray cloak of fog, running outside along the beach was an equally bad idea. Last thing she needed was to sprain or break something.

No. That meant being indoors. Shopping and eating, maybe even a movie, Lynn thought, brightening slightly. She could go see what was playing. It had been a long time since she saw a movie in the theater. Something loud and full of action and explosions. Mindless entertainment. That's what she needed, something where there wouldn't be a trace of romance.

Chapter 26

He was coming out of the hotel when he saw her walking toward her car. She had on tall rubber boots, jeans, and an expensive-looking raincoat with a turtleneck poking through the collar. Her hood was up, protecting her face from the spit-like rain that seemed to envelope them.

"Lynn!" he called after her and he saw her stop, hesitate and then finally turn around to give him a tight smile.

"Hello," he said, coming to stand before her. He didn't trust himself to get close to her. She stood there, hands jammed in the pocket of her coat. He did the same and found himself suddenly at a loss for words. Maybe it had been a bad idea to greet her. Perhaps he should have just slunk away, hoping that they didn't run into each other. Which was a silly hope, since for the moment they were working and living in the same buildings.

"Hi," she said.

"Going out?" he asked.

"Yes," she said, and then the silence hung between them. He could have kicked himself, knowing this wasn't going as planned. Well, he hadn't really planned anything about their meeting. Just knew that there was a part of him that wanted to—no, needed to—see her again.

Since there seemed to be nothing more to say, he saw her turn, as if to go.

"Wait," he said, holding up a hand. "I just wanted to say…" He stumbled for a moment, trying to find the right words. "After last night, I mean with Bode. I wanted to say, that it would be fine if you wanted to use the gym at the hotel. No charge, of course. I checked with Chase. I know it doesn't have all the amenities of the other place, but hey, I figured it would be ok until you found somewhere else to go."

He stopped, taking a breath. Seriously, he had worked and lived in ten countries, could speak four languages passably, and now he was fumbling for words like he was in middle school talking to the first girl he'd met.

A smile, this one genuine, crossed Lynn's face. "Thanks, that would be great. I wasn't sure what to do. I mean, going outside is always an option, unless it's like today, so…" She trailed off and then ended with another, "thanks."

"Anytime." The rain picked up again. There didn't seem to be much point in standing out there, but he couldn't quite bring himself to get away.

"Ok. Well, I'm going to go run some errands," she said, and he watched as she started to back away, then turned and practically ran towards her car.

He stood for a moment more in the rain, watching her go, reminding himself that it was better this way.

Chapter 27

Lynn finished with her patient, a nine-year-old girl who had strep throat. The girl, who had been nervous when she first came in, was now relaxed and happy to know that there wasn't something really wrong with her.

She gave a prescription for antibiotics to the mom and lollipops to the girl and her little sister, who looked at her solemnly with big blue eyes.

She stood, stretched, looked around. It was late in the afternoon and the patients were starting to thin out. The clinic closed early tonight, so soon it would be time for her to go home, Lynn thought. A good thing, since she'd been here since early in the morning. It was a nice fall evening, and the rain, which had lingered all yesterday, had blown out to sea, and in its place was cool, crisp, fall weather. Queensbay seemed shiny and bright under brilliant blue skies dotted by puffy white clouds, everything looking as if it had been freshly scrubbed.

Maybe she'd get out in time for a run, or even a walk; anything, since just getting out would be good. Or she could hang some of the pictures she'd bought and invite Tory and Phoebe over to help out. That might help her keep the thoughts of Jackson out of her mind. The movie the other day had worked, up to a point. The point where the hero—a blond actor with blue eyes and chiseled features—had gone for the obligatory kiss with the female lead. Lynn had almost gotten up and left the theater, but she was in the middle of the row and still had half her popcorn left. So she suffered through it, telling her hormones to calm it down. Going back to work had been a relief, for at least there she could focus.

But now another quiet evening stretched in front of her. Yup, some girlfriend time, take out, a glass of wine would be just what the doctor ordered. Feeling better at the thought of spending time with friends, she headed out towards the small office/break room all the staff shared. She could grab a cup of bad coffee, or better yet some tea, and finish up her paperwork.

She heard his voice, before she saw him. Curious, she walked towards the sound. He was in the director's office, the door slightly open. She slowed and then decided to hurry past, since it was really none of her business what Jackson was doing here. After all, he owned the building, so he had every right to be here.

Sadie, who must have caught a flash of her passing by, called out to her, "Hey, Lynn! Come on in."

Almost reluctantly, she turned on her heel and went to the office. Jackson's presence seemed to overpower the small room. For a moment, all Lynn could sense and feel was him, his scent—the barest hint of good, clean soap and a lightly spicy aftershave. Her insides clenched and she willed herself to focus instead on the ever-pervasive smell of disinfectant, hoping to quell her dancing hormones.

She glanced between the two of them. Sadie was beaming and even Jackson looked as if he was pleased with himself.

"What's going on?" she asked.

"Mr. Sanders," Sadie began.

"Jackson, please," he interrupted smoothly.

Sadie flashed him a smile so wide that Lynn was almost blinded. "Jackson is offering us a new lease. A very reasonable one, that allows us to stay here for as long as we want, and he's promised to start to address the list of repairs and maintenance that Petersen never did."

"What?" Lynn asked, looking at Jackson in disbelief. "Why would you do that?"

"Lynn," Sadie hissed, "I don't think we should question Mr., I mean Jackson's, motives, now should we?"

"No, of course not," Lynn said, hurriedly, shoving her hands into the pockets of her white coat. She glanced over at Jackson who had stood and was gathering up papers, stacking them neatly, and then placing them inside a file folder, which he then placed into his briefcase. He was wearing one of his expensive suits again, one that showed off his broad shoulders. He looked like himself again, professional, aloof, unreadable.

Snapping the briefcase, he picked it up, shook Sadie's hand, and turned to Lynn. One look and her hormones swelled up like a tsunami and had her senses humming. It was his eyes. That had to be it. The way they could look hard and hurt and soulful, as if the mystery that was Jackson was all in there. They called to the healer in her, but he only gave a brief nod and even briefer smile.

"Doctor," he said smoothly as he inclined his head in her direction. "I look forward to working with both of you."

Sadie's profusion of thanks echoed in Lynn's ears as she watched Jackson leave the office. Ok, that was weird. It was like the kiss had never happened, like they hadn't so much as touched. So his offering her the use of the gym at the hotel had been nothing but being...gentlemanly.

How could he ignore her like that? Or worse yet, how could he make her feel like...a horny teenager, without so much as him feeling a tickle of attraction? He couldn't generate this much heat in her without some sort of answering reaction, could he? It had to violate the laws of chemistry, she decided.

"Can you believe it?" Sadie turned and addressed Lynn. "I mean it's like some sort of miracle. The board of directors will be thrilled. The terms are really quite favorable, and I believe that we'll really be able to make a go of it here."

Lynn barely heard her but nodded all the same. She waited a moment, not sure what to do, but then she rushed out, determined to get to the bottom of this. She had to know if the attraction she felt for him was mutual or if he really was so cold that nothing of it was getting to him.

Chapter 28

She caught up to him in the parking lot, where he was just getting into the driver's seat of his BMW.

"Wait," she said as she jogged over to him.

He rolled down the window and looked at her from behind sunglasses. "Can I help you?"

"Why? I don't get it. Did you do it because of me?"

"You?"

It came out like a slap. Lynn realized that she had just made a fool of herself. Hormones, adrenaline, the triumph of the male conqueror, that's what the kiss had been about. Jackson had defeated another man at her expense and her kiss had been the prize. And that meant anything between them had to be one sided.

"Well, I mean…" Lynn stammered, feeling her face turning bright red, before she clutched at the very rationale he had given her. "You said the clinic was paying below market rent and was a losing proposition for you and you wanted to refit the space into a luxury medical spa."

"Upon closer examination of the details, it turns out you have a solid history of paying your rent, which, upon further evaluation, isn't as below market as I thought. So I negotiated a slight increase and in return, I'll begin to address the maintenance issues. Plus, the medical spa is still interested but would prefer an upper floor, with an entrance in the rear, as their clients tend to prefer a bit of anonymity. So as you might say, I was able to work out a win-win."

"A win-win?" Lynn said, thinking over the explanation. "It seems like you made quite an about-face from your previous position."

"You know, Lynn," he said, pulling down his sunglasses and stabbing her with his piercing blue eyes, "I am not as inflexible as you make it seem. Yes, I'm a businessman and I try to make money. But it's not always about squeezing every single cent from people. Plus you always have to balance short-term with the long-term benefits. Sure, I could probably kick you guys out, fix the place up, and find someone who would come in and pay me more in rent. But then how do I know they're a business with staying power? That in six months they won't close up shop and I'll have an empty space until I find a new client? And besides, Queensbay is my home, always has been, and according to some medical professionals I've talked to, the clinic plays an important role in the town."

"Ok," she said, accepting what he said. He moved to turn on the car, and on impulse she reached out to touch his arm, feeling the electric connection that ran sprang up when their skin connected.

She quickly drew her hand back, saw that he had glanced down at where her hand had been and was now looking up at her. Maybe there had been something more to the kiss. On impulse, she said, "I suppose this deserves a thank you."

"I don't need a thank you. I was just being a good citizen," he said but a dark look crossed his face. He had felt it, she was sure, that same spark of connection. But he didn't want to acknowledge it. She took a step back. Whatever was going on, Jackson was fighting it. She looked at him, but he kept his hands tightly fisted around the wheels, eyes straight ahead. She shouldn't push it, shouldn't push him. She'd be asking for humiliation.

"Well then, again thank you." She took another step back, far enough away so that Jackson could safely pull away from the curb without running over her foot. She almost missed it, the look of relief that crossed over his face, the way the tension eased out of his shoulders and relaxed fractionally.

He looked up at her and his face was unreadable. "Goodbye, Lynn," he said. And then he hit the gas and the car took off.

Chapter 29

"Why do you think Jackson changed his mind about the closing the clinic?" Lynn asked Tory. They were in Lynn's apartment, at the breakfast bar, drinking coffee and eating bagels Tory had brought from The Golden Pear. Tory had promised to help her do some shopping for dishes and cookware, something she had been dreading, but Lynn was getting tired of eating off of paper plates and cooking in the microwave.

Tory swallowed her sip of coffee. "Oh, I don't think he grew a conscience if that's what you're thinking."

"What do you mean?"

Tory laughed. "It's because the poor man has been subjected to a steady stream of his friends and family telling him he was a bad person, a terrible citizen, and that if he wanted to stay here and try to forget the past, he needed to let the clinic stay open. First up was Chase—I heard him on the phone giving Jackson an earful, then later Noah Randall stopped by while Jackson was doing something at the hotel. I didn't hear that conversation, but I did hear the one in The Golden Pear where Caitlyn and Darby tag-teamed him about his Scrooge complex."

"Oh." Lynn didn't know why she suddenly felt so deflated. Why should she have thought that Jackson's changing his mind about keeping the clinic open would have anything to do with her? Of course, it made more sense that he would have considered how it would look if he closed the clinic. It had been a calculated move, a strategic decision; nothing to do with his feelings about her.

"What is it?" Tory asked, her voice suddenly sharply curious. "Did you think you had something to do with it?"

Lynn shrugged. She hadn't told Tory about the kiss she couldn't get out of her mind.

"You're not telling me something." Tory looked closely at her and Lynn felt a flush of embarrassment start to crawl up her skin under the intense scrutiny.

"You didn't, did you? Omigod! Did you sleep with Jackson Sanders?"

"I did not." Lynn's hand flew to her throat. "He just kissed me."

"Aha! Gotcha. I knew something happened and since you weren't about to tell me, I had to guess."

"It was just a kiss!" Lynn defended herself.

"He kissed you and you're only just now telling me about it?" Tory looked at her over her coffee and shook her head.

"Sorry that saving lives had to come first." Lynn said, a touch of petulance in her voice.

"There you go. That's always your excuse, you know. That whole 'saving lives' thing. What about me? You know, I fixed someone's hard drive at work the other day—saved a year's worth of data."

"That's impressive too," Lynn answered, doing her best to sound like it was.

"It's how I got the morning off. A little way of Chase saying thank you, plus I worked until four in the morning debugging the customer database last night."

"Wow. Guys must love it when you talk computer speak."

"Only the smart ones." Tory flashed a smile. There was a pause and then she said, "So he is getting over the late, great Ashley."

"Funny, because I don't think he's over her at all." Lynn said, putting down her coffee cup and pushing her bagel away. Suddenly there was heavy feeling in the pit of her stomach as she thought of something. Jackson might not be over Ashley. That would explain why he seemed so determined to ignore whatever was brewing between the two of them.

"Why, what do you mean? He finally came back to town. I mean, he's been away for years. If that doesn't say he's over her then I don't know what does."

"Then he has the most self-restraint of any guy I know." Lynn's mind flashed back to the way it had felt, with her back up against the door, Jackson's hands holding her, the way their lips had met.

"What do you mean?"

"That's it. It's like nothing happened between us. I mean he talks to me, but won't look me in the eye. I can't decide if he hates me or if he's afraid and wants to jump my bones."

Tory smiled. "I'd go with he wants to jump your bones. But supposedly he was pretty messed after the accident. Left town right after the funeral and didn't come back until now."

"What happened?" Lynn had to ask.

Tory shrugged. "I don't know exactly. I was at college so I only got secondhand information. The details were murky, even the newspaper articles were kind of vague. But apparently, it seemed like Jackson and Ashley were out for a ride, going too fast or something and the car crashed. Jackson walked away without a scrape and Ashley didn't."

"You mean people blamed him?"

"Yeah. Well, Mrs. Moran did and she went around town, doing all she could to smear Jackson's name. That's why he left. I mean, things were pretty brutal for him here, from what I gather. I mean, obviously Chase and his friends, his real friends, stood by him, but it wasn't easy. Of course, Ashley came out looking like a saint."

Lynn nodded, thinking that it explained the reaction Jackson had gotten in The Golden Pear. But she caught the underlying bitterness in Tory's words.

"You don't sound like a fan," Lynn said.

"I don't like to speak ill of the dead, but Ashley was one of those girls who had everyone fooled. She was blond and cute and a star soccer player. She raised money for homeless dogs and sick kids. She had a smile for everyone to their face and then a knife for their back. And she had her claws deep into Jackson. I mean, if he so much as said hi to another girl or hung out with the guys instead of being with her, she gave him hell. She was just a real, well, bitch."

"Wow. What did she do to you?" Lynn asked, curious.

Tory looked up with a slightly regretful face. "Let's just say I wasn't always the hot computer chick you see in front of you."

"Oh?"

"In high school I was a scrawny, glasses-wearing computer nerd, and Ashley was the sort of girl who ate my kind for breakfast and spat them out. Not that I wanted her dead, but I am not sure she deserved the storybook ending, or to be memorialized as a saintly do-gooder."

Lynn frowned. Jackson didn't seem the sort of guy who would go for a girl like that; but perhaps cool, blond, and bitchy was exactly his style.

"Well, I for one am glad you're a computer nerd, because seriously I do need your computer skills."

"Doesn't everyone," Tory said.

"I can pay you," Lynn mentioned and she saw Tory's eyes light up. She knew Tory enjoyed working for Chase and his company, but she also remembered Tory had mentioned wanting to start her own computer consulting business. When Caitlyn had told her she should get a website up and running for Healthy Kids Now, Lynn had no idea where to start, but trusted Tory would.

"Do tell." Tory said. And Lynn smiled. Now that the clinic was on steadier feet, Lynn was excited to take her program to the next level. Caitlyn and Phoebe had inspired her to start thinking bigger. She knew she couldn't do it alone, and she was certain Tory was the perfect person to help her.

Chapter 30

"What are you doing here?" Jackson's voice came out of nowhere and she almost dropped her hotdog. He stood eye level with her, but only because she was sitting on the third level of the bleachers. She hoped she didn't have any mustard on her face and fought the urge to send her tongue in an exploratory lick.

"What am *I* doing here? Why are *you* here?" she answered back, looking at him in surprise. Of all the people she had thought she might see at a girls' soccer game, Jackson was the least likely.

He nodded toward the players on the field. "Watching the game."

She looked at the soccer team and then back at him. "Do you often watch girls' soccer teams? Should I be worried?"

"No." He rocked on his heels, and she got the sense that he was embarrassed. She waited, hoping there would be more, so she held his gaze with a questioning one of her own.

"The coach asked me to stop by," he finally said, running a hand through his hair. It was longer than she had seen it, curling slightly over the edge of the collar of his leather jacket. She realized that he wasn't wearing a suit, just jeans and a shirt. Not that she was complaining. Jackson could wear anything, or nothing at all, she was willing to bet, and still be hot. Even his slightly odd behavior was doing nothing to quell her appreciation of that basic fact and the effect it had on her system.

"Are you going to stay and watch?" she asked, patting the empty bleacher next to her.

He gave a smile, but it seemed forced. "Sure."

He took the seat next to her, but perched on its edge as if he was ready to bolt at any moment. Still, his arm grazed hers and he didn't pull back, at least not right away. There was the faintest bit of pressure and she again felt the electric current running between them. He turned and looked at her, an intense, direct blue gaze; she had to look away, shift herself ever so slightly away from him to break their connection.

Lynn put her half-eaten hotdog down. She was still in her scrubs, of course, but she figured she didn't need to add a mustard stain to the patchwork of substances that had already landed on her today.

"You never answered my question. What are you doing here?" he asked, looking straight ahead.

"I'm just stopping by too. I promised that one," Lynn pointed out the girl in pigtails, "number thirty-two, Anna, that I would watch her play once this season."

Jackson watched. "Ok," he said and Lynn knew what he was thinking.

"It's not about how good she is. It's about the fact that she's here at all."

"And why's that?"

"Well, she's one of my first." Lynn said. He looked at her. "One of the first kids I put on my Healthy Kids Now program. Over a year ago, Anna was about twenty-five pounds overweight and drank soda for breakfast and thought a French fry was really a vegetable."

"Ok," he said, watching Anna more intently now.

"Over the past year, she's lost the weight, loves vegetables, exercises for thirty minutes a day, and got straight 'A's last quarter."

"All right, I'm impressed."

"Yeah, she's an amazing kid, now. But she was a tough case, stubborn; didn't want to listen to me, thought she was too smart to hear what I said. So I made her promise to motivate her. I didn't know if it would work, but apparently it did."

"What sort of promise?" he asked.

"If she made the soccer team, I would come watch her play. I think she kind of looked up to me, so I thought the promise would give her some encouragement."

"And did it?" Jackson asked.

"She's out there now. She's their backup player, so she'll only be on the field for another couple of minutes, but…"

"That's not the point," he finished for her.

"And since then, about fifty kids have gone through the program at the clinic alone. I'm working on making it more official, so that other places, like hospitals or schools and even other clinics, can use it."

"Really?" he said.

"You sound surprised?" Lynn countered. She was staring straight ahead, watching Anna, but she felt his gaze on her, so she finally turned and looked at him.

"Actually, I'm not surprised at all. Sounds like a good idea."

She looked at him, suddenly not sure what to say, so she just nodded and looked back at the field, hoping to distract herself.

"Go, Anna!" Lynn called as she watched the girl catch a pass and then dribble it up the field. She made it a respectable halfway before the opposing team managed to swipe the ball from her. But it was a start.

The whistle blew and the coach called for a sub. Anna, her pigtails flying and her face red, came off the field to a round of applause and cheers from her parents. She waved at them and came straight toward Lynn.

Lynn hopped down and gave Anna a big hug. "That was amazing!"

"You watched!"

"A promise is a promise," Lynn said.

A man trailed behind Anna. He had on sweatpants, a visor, and a whistle around his neck.

"This is my coach, Coach Dave," Anna said.

Lynn said hi, but realized that Coach Dave's attention was not on her, but behind her.

"You came," he said. She turned and saw that he was speaking to Jackson, who had risen and was standing uncomfortably behind them.

"Dave," he said moving forward. Lynn watched as Coach Dave pulled Jackson into one of those awkward one-handed hugs that guys always seemed to do.

"Well, Anna did an awesome job today. But let me tell you, without this guy we wouldn't have a field to play on."

Jackson shrugged, but Dave wouldn't be deterred. "Yup, let me tell you up until a few years ago this place was weed lot. But thanks to Jackson and his donation, now the kids have a place to play."

"Least I could do," Jackson said.

Lynn thought that Jackson was embarrassed, since the top of his ears were turning red. She looked around. She hadn't given much thought to the town athletics fields, but she supposed they were pretty nice as far as junior soccer and little league fields went. This field was tidy, neat and small-town picture perfect under a blue autumn sky, the trees ringing it wreathed in their autumnal coats of orange, scarlet, and yellow. There were bleachers, baseball diamonds, and separate fields for soccer. There was the snack shack building that had sold her the forgotten hotdog, plus a playground with little kids swinging and hurtling down slides.

There was even, now that she noticed it, a nice bronze plaque. She had to strain a bit to see the inscription, but then Coach Dave led Jackson over to it, keeping up a running commentary on turf versus grass, number of teams in the league, and other things. Lynn trailed along, watching the rigid set of Jackson's shoulders.

The plaque, when they got to it, affixed to the side of the snack shack, was impressive. It showed the relief of a female soccer player and underneath it read, "Dedicated to the memory of Ashley Moran, beloved athlete. Made possible by the generosity of Jackson Sanders."

"I told you I didn't want any recognition," Jackson said, turning on Dave. Lynn took a step back. She recognized the look in Jackson's eyes. It was similar to the one he'd had after he decked Bode.

Coach Dave slapped Jackson on the back, seemingly oblivious to Jackson's anger, "Oh man, I couldn't let that happen. Without your donation, none of this would have been possible. People deserve to know, man. It can only help you." At this, Coach Dave's hand dropped low.

Jackson drew up himself up so he practically towered above Dave. "I didn't do this to look good. The whole point was that I didn't want anyone to know. Take it down. I'll pay for a new one." Lynn saw that Jackson's mouth was set in a hard, thin line.

Coach Dave seemed about to say something more, but even he had the good sense to realize Jackson was upset.

"Whoa, sure thing, Jax. Whatever you want. Didn't mean to upset you. Just thought…"

Lynn took a step forward and put her hand on Jackson's arm. He turned to look at her, and she saw a flash of anger die down to be replaced by something else. Pain, regret maybe.

"I just don't want to make a big deal about it."

Dave, relieved that Jackson didn't seem like he was going to get any angrier, held up his hands. "Sure, no problem. Like I said, I'll get on it right away."

"Thanks." Jackson turned around and started to walk away. She put an arm out to stop him but he looked down at it, and then up at her and she saw his face was contorted in sadness. She wanted to reach out, to touch him, to smooth his hair and tell him it would be ok, like she did with one of her patients.

He seemed to read her mind because he took a slow step back. "Lynn, I am not one of your patients. What I have can't be healed with some aspirin and rest."

"I know," she started to say but he cut her off.

"No, you don't know. I don't know what you've heard..." He swallowed. "You might think you do know, but you don't, you can't. No one else ever will. I came back home because I couldn't, didn't want to stay away any longer. But not everyone is happy I am here. And I can't drag you down with me, so this," and he held out his hands to encompass her, "can't happen. It's not a good idea," he finished, almost as if he were telling himself.

He took another step back and she stopped, not following him and taking a deep breath. Really how much clearer could he be?

"Ok," she said.

Surprise flashed across his face and she felt a small thrill of satisfaction. Maybe he was disappointed. If so, it would give him something to think about.

There was a call behind her, from Anna, telling Lynn to come watch.

"I have to go. I made a promise," she said.

He looked at her sadly, his hands jammed into the pockets of his coat. "So did I."

Chapter 31

"Looks like things are moving along here," Jake said, leaning in the doorway.

"That they are," Jackson said. He had gotten most of the demolition done on the upstairs space and it was now mostly an open, raw space.

"You've been pretty busy here. You know you could have called me, I would have gotten a crew to come on down, take care of this for you," Jake said.

"I didn't mind doing the demo work myself," Jackson said.

Jake walked in, taking a good look around, testing things like support beams.

"I heard you renewed the lease for some of the tenants," Jake said casually.

"Yeah, Madame Robireux wouldn't be moved. I think she practically threatened to put a hex on me."

Jake shook his head, "That's not who I'm talking about."

Jackson shifted some papers on the sheet of plywood he was still using as a desk.

"Oh, the clinic? I ran the numbers another time and it seemed like it was more beneficial to keep them. I even got them to agree to slight rate increase, and in return I'll start to make sure that all the maintenance items that were neglected under Petersen get addressed." He decided not to mention how he'd been bombarded with all the reasons on why not to close the clinic from Chase, Noah, Caitlyn, and Darby, just to name a few people.

"That's awfully nice of you," Jake said, his voice deceptively innocent.

"What is it?" Jackson finally asked as the silence stretched between them.

"I was just wondering if a certain brunette spitfire about, yay high," he held a hand up to his mid-chest, "had anything to do with it."

"You mean Lynn Masters?"

"Yeah. You know, the lady in the scrubs and the white coat, cures people for a living?"

"I'm not doing it for her. I'm doing it because they're a paying tenant."

"Wouldn't be the first time you did something just because of a pretty face," Jake said, his arms crossed, legs wide apart.

Jackson looked up from his laptop as a sudden thought occurred to him.

"Hey, why are you so interested in Lynn and me? There's nothing there you know, but I didn't think I was crowding in on your territory."

The thought had finally penetrated his brain that maybe the reason Jake was giving him a hard time about her was that he had eyes for Lynn himself. If so, that meant Jackson would have to back down, because that was the guy code, right? Which wouldn't matter since Jackson had no intention of going anyplace with her, did he?

To his relief, Jake gave a little laugh, "No, not my territory. But she's a nice girl. And friends with your brother and Phoebe."

"I know that. And I've barely said two words to her," Jackson said, keeping his voice neutral. Sure he had kissed her; but in truth, they'd never had much of an actual conversation.

"Oh, so you didn't get into a fight at Quent's over her? I just thought I'd heard something about that. You know, you could have let me know; I would have been your backup."

"It wasn't a fight," Jackson said, running his hand through his hair. "The guy didn't stand a chance."

Jake smiled. "That's the Jax I know. I heard you took down that meathead with one swift flying tiger kick."

Jackson shook his head, but he was smiling. "And I keep telling you there's no such thing as a flying tiger kick. The guy was a jerk. Lynn made it clear she didn't want to anything to do with him and he couldn't take no for an answer. That's it."

"Heard you walked her home too," Jake said, throwing himself onto a folding metal chair that Jackson had brought in so he wouldn't have to sit on a box.

Jackson wondered how Jake had found out. Maybe from Tory? "We happen to live next door to each other. It was only natural that I walk her home, make sure that the meathead, Bode didn't get any crazy ideas about following her."

Jake shook his head. "Always the gentleman, Jackson. You know, you'd better be careful."

"What are you trying to say?" Jackson asked, going still.

"I would just hate for things to get messy, bro. I mean you just got back. I don't want you walking out all over again, over another girl. It's not that I don't think you deserve a shot at happiness, but Lynn's a good woman, made a lot of friends—mostly because she's healed them."

"Are you saying she's too good for me?"

"No, I'm saying that you still have a perception problem my friend. Right or wrong, you're still that guy who was driving the car the night his fiancée died."

"And how does that affect my relationship—though there isn't one—with Lynn Masters today?" Jackson was aware his tone was icy.

"People won't want to see her get hurt." Jake shrugged.

"What makes people think I would hurt her?" Jackson asked.

Jake shrugged again. "You've got a reputation, that's all; and she's popular girl. I just don't see it working for you too. So don't let her get under your skin."

"Good thing I'm not looking for anyone to get under my skin."

Jake smiled. "I thought that's what we're all looking for."

Jackson threw a pencil across the table. "Enough. Are you here to grill me on my non-existent love life or do you have another reason for bothering me on an otherwise perfectly good workday?"

"Just so happens I might have a project for us. Turns out one of my clients wants to make her house energy efficient and was thinking about solar panels on her roof, and she started talking to me about these things." Jake a took crumpled piece of paper out of his pocket. "And asked me if I knew anything about them."

Jackson took the piece of paper. It was an article from a magazine about a relatively new type of solar roofing panel. He thought it was a promising way to go and had planned on including them in his product lineup.

"What did you say?"

Jake smiled. "Told her of course I did and that our green building division would be happy to work up a quote."

"Green building division?" Jackson said.

"Well, that's if you think you're ready to be in business."

Jackson felt a wave of relief rush over him. He hadn't known just how much he wanted Jake to be in on this with him.

"Long overdue," Jackson said, holding out his hand, and Jake shook it.

"Better now than never."

Chapter 32

Lynn didn't consider herself a computer whiz, not on par with Tory, but honestly, once she had the last name, it didn't take much searching. The local paper had devoted quite a bit of space to the story. Ashley Moran had been a beloved hometown girl, just as Tory had said. She had been a star high school and college soccer player. She had come back to Queensbay after graduation, where she was coaching the school's junior team. According to the paper, she had liked the beach and boating. Classmates remembered her as pretty, involved in school activities. She'd been a good student…blah, blah, blah…All the usual accolades had been heaped her way. And she'd left behind her parents, a younger sister, Lindsay, and her fiancé, Jackson Sanders.

Lynn sighed and pushed the laptop away. So Jackson had been one half of the town's golden couple. That was the baggage that Tory had been talking about. To have been there when it happened, to be a witness to that. No wonder he'd run away.

She got up, walked over to the breakfast bar, and poured herself another cup of coffee. She had to be at work in half an hour and still needed to take a shower. There was no sense in dwelling on Ashley Moran. It had just been her natural sense of curiosity, she told herself, that had made her look the story up.

But now that she knew, did it change anything with Jackson? He had said they weren't a good idea, but Lynn didn't know if it was because he wanted to protect her from his history in the town or if he had recognized there was something between them and was fighting against it, for whatever reason.

And she had to admit, there was something about the wounded look in Jackson's eyes that spoke to her. Occupational hazard, but she knew she was driven to try and fix people who were hurting. He called to her, and she was pretty certain that the feeling wasn't one sided. But she didn't know what to do about it.

Chapter 33

"I need to see a doctor," Jackson managed to say, through the pain. The woman at the front desk looked up from her computer, coolly assessing him over her half-moon glasses.

"Take a seat; someone will be right with you."

She handed him a clipboard too.

"But I'm bleeding," he said. Maybe he should have driven himself right to the emergency room. It had looked like a lot of blood when the glass had sliced through his hand.

"You're able to walk and talk, so it can't be that bad. Just keep it elevated."

Jackson's mouth dropped open and then he shut it. It hurt like a bitch, but it didn't seem manly to admit that. After all, there was one kid waiting, holding an ice pack over a swollen elbow, who just sat there, legs swinging, not crying or bellyaching.

Stoically, he took a seat. Filling out the paperwork proved to be a problem, since he had to balance the clipboard on his knee and try to fill in all the little spaces with his personal information. He gave up after a moment, and that was all it took.

"Next." Suddenly Lynn appeared in the doorway, hands jabbed into the pockets of her white medical coat.

The woman at the front desk nodded at Jackson and he stood quickly. The move dizzied him and he felt the clipboard drop. He swayed and then she was there, an arm wrapped around his waist.

"Lean into me," she said, guiding him through the door to the back area of the clinic.

"I'm fine," he said impatiently. The dizziness had passed and he felt better, or as good as one could feel with an open wound.

"Keep that hand elevated," was all she said, leading him onto a hospital bed. She dropped him down and then closed the curtain.

He looked at her. Her rich brown hair was pulled back in a ponytail, but a few stray curls escaped, curling around her neck and along her the elegant line of her jaw. She was wearing perfume, nothing heavy, but a light, citrus scent. He closed his eyes and breathed it in. She smelled good, like an angel.

He felt himself being laid down on the exam table while she held his arm up. He opened his eyes, saw her start to unwrap the bloody towel and then he had to close them again.

"How did it happen?" she asked, her voice calm, businesslike, and strangely soothing. If she wasn't upset, it couldn't be that bad. Still there was no hint of warmth in her eyes, and he wondered where was the friendly bedside manner he imagined her having.

"I was working on the upstairs space, trying to get one of those windows unstuck, and it came loose, broke, and the glass got my hand."

She was looking at the cut, face unreadable.

"You were fixing something?" There was a trace of amusement in her voice.

"Sure. Why do you sound surprised?"

Her chocolate brown eyes fixed on him and he was aware that his stomach jumped and not because of the pain. He had kissed her, unplanned, without finesse; and since then she hadn't been far from his mind.

Sure, he could try and lie to himself that it didn't matter, but he was done with that. Part of coming back home had been to start with a clean slate, professionally. He hadn't given a thought to his personal life, only knew that it would be a bad idea to get mixed up with Lynn. She was too passionate for one. And she knew too many of the same people. Ending things would be messy.

Still, he constantly thought about kissing her again, and what it would be like to keep kissing her and let it lead them to where it was meant to be. It must be the blood loss, he thought. He had told her to stay away, that she would be better off keeping her distance. And he meant it. If only it would make it easier for him.

She took a step back as if understanding something of what was in his eyes.

"You just seem like the type to hire someone to do the manual labor, that's all."

"Looks can be deceiving," he managed to answer. "I've worked construction, hands on and around the globe, since I was sixteen. I might be more used to managing people now, but I still know how to use a hammer."

"Are you sure about that?" she answered, but there was a lightness in her voice, an almost teasing quality, and he took hope in it, giving her a smile. She hovered close to him, still looking at his hand, the space between them narrowing until he could feel her breath on him. She looked at him, unblinking and he couldn't look away, knowing at that moment that everything he had told himself about staying away from her was a lie. The attraction between them was thrilling and he thought he would slowly go crazy if he tried to ignore it. But she would have to play by his rules.

Whatever was flowing between them ruptured when a nurse came into the exam area and said, "Suture tray, Doctor."

He saw Lynn take a deep breath and step back. She was back in her doctor mode.

"You need stitches. You're lucky the cut didn't go too deep. I can do it here if you want; or you can go to the emergency room, but you'll likely have to wait."

"Ok."

"Ok, what?"

"You'll do it, right? I mean, sew me up?"

She smiled. "Yes, I can do it. I can even give you something for the pain."

His eyes took in the big glass jar of lollipops. "And a lollipop."

"Only if you're a good patient." The teasing note was definitely in her voice, and despite the pain he found himself relaxing.

#

Her hands were steady. She made sure of that. True, most of her patients were several feet shorter than this one and desperately scared when she had to do something like this. Jackson wore a grim expression, but he was still as she gave him the anesthesia and then stitched up the nasty gash in his hand. He kept a steady gaze on her, his blue eyes reminding her of the sky on the first warm spring day. Something between them had changed, she was sure—some realization on his part of their connection. And this time, instead of freaking him out, he seemed calm about it, accepting.

He was dressed casually, in jeans, work boots, and t-shirt, and smelled faintly of sawdust and soap. The nurse was in and out, and so normally, where Lynn would have kept up a steady stream of chatter with the patient, in an effort to calm him instead she found herself tongue tied, supremely aware of him.

She felt him watching her and finally felt compelled to say something. "You're renovating upstairs?" It was better to stick to small talk.

"Starting to," he said.

"Who's moving in there, the medical spa?"

"The what...?" His brow puckered together. "Maybe. But it's for me."

"You?"

"I need some office space," he said.

"You're doing the work yourself?"

"Some of it. I guess I won't be after this, though."

She hazarded a glance down at him. He hadn't shaved in a day or two and there was light blond stubble on his face. It went well with the dressed-down look.

"No. Probably a bad idea, since you'll have to keep the sutures dry. And the hand will be sore for a while but there shouldn't be any permanent damage."

She finished off the operation and added the bandage. She realized she was still holding his hand and that he made no move to take it from her. From out in the waiting room she could hear the sound of a kid crying, a high-pitched wail, which probably meant a fever. There was the noise of the DVD player that was on a constant loop of kids' cartoons and a steady hum of soothing voices and cranky kids. Other patients were waiting yet she couldn't quite tear herself away from him.

All of that was pushed to the background, and somehow all she could hear was the thud of her own heart and a curious thrum in her own ears. In her hand, she could feel the warmth of Jackson's, feel the beat of his pulse. His eyes held her and she felt as if the ground shifted beneath her, as her stomach jumped and flopped. It was a heady moment, as if a bolt of lightning had hit her, and Lynn took a step back.

He had baggage, she reminded herself. He was older, a sophisticated world traveler. They probably didn't have much in common. Still, her heart was racing and she felt like she could look in his eyes and never get tired. She wanted to know if he could ever look at her in the same way.

"All done?" he asked in surprise.

"Yes," Lynn said. His question broke the spell and she took the moment to turn her back on him, setting down her instruments on the tray, ready to strip off her gloves. She turned to find him standing there, looking down at her.

"I guess it's my turn to thank you."

"You can consider us even," Lynn said. It came out more sharply than she meant it to, but she had a sudden urge to be rid of him. She couldn't stand this push and pull with him. Either he was interested and going to act on it, or he wasn't and they could both be miserable and get on with their lives. But she wasn't going to beg.

"Listen, about the other day," he started to say.

She held up a hand. "You don't need to explain."

"But I think I do. You know, so you can be fully aware of the situation," he said, stepping closer to her. She felt the nearness of his presence, felt as if all the air were being sucked out of her. Years of medical school, years in the ER treating all sorts of life and death situations and now, here was a guy making her feel like a witless first-year med student.

"You don't have to tell me anything," Lynn said. She didn't want to be told that there was no way she could compete with a dead woman.

"Probably because you already know," he said, his voice was laced bitterness.

"What?"

"It's a small town. Not too many secrets. I am sure you probably know I was engaged to be married to someone—Ashley Moran."

Lynn nodded, but Jackson seemed not to see it. "She died in a car crash, and well, some people felt I was to blame for it. But you probably were able to figure that out from what happened at The Golden Pear. After Ash died, it was too hard to stay. I left town and pretty much broke off all contact with anyone from here. My own family, my brother, my best friend."

She had a vision of a younger, grief-stricken Jackson taking flight from town, a backpack slung on his shoulder.

"And now you're back?"

"I'm back."

"Why?" Lynn asked. Jackson was so close she could see the way his jaw clenched.

"Because this is my home, and it's where I belong."

"Oh," Lynn said. There was strength in those words, conviction. But she wasn't sure. It might mean that he was ready to move back to Queensbay, but did it mean he was ready to move onto something new in the relationship department?

He stood still, waiting, but Lynn didn't know what to say.

She was saved by the bell, or rather by another emergency.

"Doctor, things are backing up out here, I think we have a broken arm. Do you want me to re-route some of them to the hospital?"

She tore her gaze away from Jackson. She had a job to do, she reminded herself. Her personal life would have to wait.

"No, we're done here. Please take Mr. Sanders up to the front desk, go over discharge procedures with him."

"Very well. This way, please."

Jackson held back, looking at her for a fraction of a moment, as if searching for an answer. He nodded, gave a rueful smile, and then started to follow the nurse out of the exam area.

He paused, turned and gave her a grin that had her heart skip a beat and her stomach drop and do a flip. "Doctor, there's something you forgot."

Affronted, she said, "What are you talking about?"

"My lollipop. You said if I was a good patient, you'd give me a lollipop."

"A lollipop?"

He nodded and smiled.

She gritted her teeth and walked past him. He took up so much space in her small exam room there was no way that she could go around him. So she had to brush past him, letting their arms touch. The shock went through her body, straight through. She wouldn't have thought he noticed, but he must have because he kept looking at her.

"Lemon? Strawberry? Cherry?"

He gave her a drop-dead gorgeous grin. "I'll take the cherry."

She almost dropped the bottle before she was able to hand him one.

Chapter 34

It had been a bad idea. It had been Tory's of course, because Lynn never would have agreed to this without some serious trash talking from her friend. She hadn't played softball in a while but she remembered enough of it to keep from making a fool of herself. By the fifth innings she even felt she was acquitting herself well. She caught a fly ball and knocked someone from the opposing team out. She'd had more fun than she thought possible playing the game. They'd even managed to squeak out a win.

And that was why she found herself at Quent's doing shots with two guys. It was the shots that were a bad idea, not playing softball. One was named Bob, the other Jeff, she was certain; or maybe their names were Brett and Jerry. The tequila was making them both seem funny, and even Jerry looked mildly attractive. Not Jackson attractive of course, but it had been days since Lynn had seen him and her hormones were in a crazy overdrive cycle, which the tequila was doing nothing to mitigate.

"Wow, I can't believe I got you out!" Tory sidled up to her and threw an arm around her shoulder, carefully turning her away from Brett and Jerry, who were busy reliving the last innings.

"That was fun. Let me know the next time you need a pinch hitter. Or a relief pitcher. Or a whatever."

"So do you think either one of them is cute?" Tory asked, her voice dropping low as she took a sip of the beer she was nursing.

Lynn laughed until saw that Tory was serious. "What do you mean cute? Like *doing it* cute?"

"Yeah, what else? Look, you need to get over Jackson, and the best way is to get right back in there."

"There's no getting over Jackson because there's nothing between us," Lynn pointed out. She had thought that maybe, after she had seen him at the clinic, after that intense moment of connection, that he had rethought the wisdom of staying away, but apparently he was stronger than she thought.

Tory shook her head. "Look, if you're attracted to him and he's attracted to you, and he's not going to give into it and you're not going to push him on it, then you need to move on."

"Hold on there." Lynn spun on her barstool. "Are you saying you think I should give him a push?" Lynn asked.

As she thought about it, she realized that she had always let Jackson pull back, never really shown him what he was giving up. She had let him kiss her once, and then like a dumb damsel in distress hadn't followed up on that, and instead had let herself wait around for a second chance.

Lynn narrowed her eyes, focusing on Tory, who was peeling the label off her beer bottle. "I thought you said he had too much baggage."

Tory shrugged. "I'm not talking about getting into a long term relationship with him, but I'm sure if you gave him a little push you two could find a way to amuse yourselves. After all, you're the one who said it's been a while. You just don't want all of your lady parts freezing up on you, you know, from disuse."

Lynn punched Tory on the arm. "I already told you, that's medically impossible."

"In theory," Tory shot back, rubbing her arm where Lynn had whacked her.

Another round of shots appeared. There was a shout, a happy one, and Brett and Jerry downed their glasses. Two pairs of eyes turned to look at Lynn expectantly. She smiled, reached for the glass and hesitated.

Her stomach lurched at the smell; she didn't want it. Brett and Jerry looked disappointed, but not angry when she made her excuses, gathering up her sweatshirt. She didn't bother to say goodbye to Tory, just knew she needed to get out and get some fresh air.

What had she been thinking? That she was going to meet the right guy in a bar? Seriously. The night air was cool and she walked toward the water and her apartment. Bed sounded good, and so did her old flannel pajamas, along with a cup of ginger tea to ward away any ill effects of the alcohol. And besides, what Tory had said, about giving Jackson a push, was bothering her. Why was she being so patient with him? She'd never be so passive with one of her patients if they were sick, if they needed something; so why was she letting Jackson dictate the terms of their...thing?

"You're muttering to yourself." Jackson appeared almost silently by her side. She jumped, surprised. He had seemed to materialize out of nowhere, but she realized she was closer to their apartment building than she thought, almost in the parking lot. She glanced over. His car was there, the headlights dimming as if he had just pulled in, gotten out, and locked it.

"You've been drinking," he said.

"I had a few drinks. Well, a few shots," she amended. She couldn't help it, she was honest by nature. The thought almost made her start to giggle but she clamped down tight on it. Jackson was standing, looking down at her. From that angle his shoulders looked impossibly broad, his arms thick and muscled. His blue eyes were icy again and perhaps just slightly disapproving.

"Shots? Are you crazy? You must weigh a hundred and ten pounds soaking wet. You can't possibly handle shots."

"A hundred and fifteen," she corrected him. "And I can do shots." She hiccupped, giving lie to her words. Bed was sounding better and better, she thought, and then she looked at Jackson. An entirely different kind of thought crossed her mind. Perhaps the answer had been staring her in the face all along. Maybe Tory was right, maybe she just needed to give him a push.

She swayed a bit, only a little of it fake.

"Here, let's get you home," Jackson said, slipping his arm around her and directing her toward the Annex. He quickly guided her up the stairs and once again opened the door for her. She spun around on the doorstep, fixed him with a look that she hoped screamed 'Come hither,' and invited him in.

She sensed the barest moment of hesitation in him as he thought about it, discarded his concerns, and crossed the threshold.

She had made some improvements to the apartment. She now had dishes, wineglasses, a corkscrew, and even a bottle of wine or two.

"Thanks for helping me. Can I get you a drink?"

She didn't wait for an answer. She had no intention of drinking much more, but Jackson stood there, standing stiff, like a deer caught in the headlights. She may not need one, but he definitely looked like he needed something.

She reached into a drawer and easily found the corkscrew since it was just about the only thing in there. The bottle of wine was in the new wine rack she had bought, a small iron thing with leaves and scrolls on it.

She pulled two glasses down and poured some into each of them.

"You're not going to let me drink alone," she said. All of a sudden, whatever tipsiness she had felt at the bar was rapidly fading in light of the adrenaline and anticipation thrumming through her body.

"I guess not," he said, and he came farther into the apartment and took the glass she handed him.

She swallowed her wine and realized that she wasn't sure what to do next. Small talk? Try to look sexy? All well and good, until she remembered she was wearing a grass stained t-shirt and a pair of athletic pants.

"How's the hand?" she finally managed to say.

He held it up and waved it at her. "Great. I went to my regular doctor like you said. He was impressed, said you had done a great job."

"Thanks," she said and took another small swallow. She looked at the bottle. It had been a gift from someone at the clinic, and even though she was no expert, she was pretty sure she had just offered Jackson Sanders, global world traveler, one hundred percent bona fide rotgut.

She watched him take his own sip and saw when he tried to hide his wince at the taste. He gently set the glass down on the table. She wondered if she should say something about changing into something more comfortable? Did women really do that anymore? What would Savannah Ryan, her favorite movie star of all time, have done?

Lynn suppressed a sigh. Someone as elegant and glamorous as Savannah Ryan wouldn't have been caught dead in a pair of grubby track pants and a stained t-shirt. If possible, it was a step down from her usual attire of grimy scrubs.

Jackson cleared his throat, and made to get up. "Well, if you're ok, I guess I should be going."

Lynn decided it was a what-the-hell-moment. As he started to rise, she moved over to him and put a hand out squarely on his chest. His smooth, muscled, very hard chest, which she could feel through the thin fabric of his shirt.

"No you don't."

"I don't?" he said, confusion in his voice.

"You can't go," she stated, aware that her adrenaline was zooming and her hands were shaking just a little bit. Ok, make that a lot.

He looked down at her, his eyes dark, unreadable. He was tense, she could tell as she didn't move, didn't let anything come between them this time.

"You can't go until you kiss me," she said.

"Lynn, you've been drinking," he said, gently putting his hands over hers. She decided not to take no for an answer. She pushed herself closer to him. She didn't have far to go because he was reaching down for her, his lips rushing to meet hers.

He faltered and then gave in, his mouth covering hers. She wrapped her arms more tightly around him, pulling him in close to her, needing to feel him, feel something. Her fingers found the waistline of his pants, and her fingers sought the button.

Suddenly she found herself pushed away, almost flung back to the other end of the couch. Stung, she curled her feet up, wrapped her arms tight around her.

He was sitting there, his eyes heavy with lust, his breathing labored.

"What's the matter now? Do gentlemen not take advantage of girls who've had a few drinks? I thought that was the basis for just about all sexual intercourse in the western world."

He closed his eyes, took a deep breath and his whole body seemed to still. "Actually, they don't. Lynn you're hurt, you're a little drunk. This isn't a good thing. I don't want to be something you'll regret in the morning."

"How can I regret what I've never gotten?" she said angrily, almost unaware the words had come out. "You think you make all the rules here. But you know what? You can't keep ignoring what's between us."

"Lynn," he said, his voice rough and low with warning.

"No," she said, feeling bold. She wasn't going to let him sneak away with an excuse, she was going to push it.

"Don't try to talk yourself out of it. Just answer me this simple question."

"What?"

"Do you like kissing me?"

"Yes," he breathed. "I like it a lot."

"Then why don't we just go with it."

"Because..."

"I don't care about your past, Jackson. I just care about now. We're two grownups who are attracted to each other. Can't that be enough for now? What if I told you that I am not looking for forever? Just for right now."

"Is that all you really want, Lynn? Something for right now?"

"Yes," she said, knowing part of her was lying. But it was for a good cause, because what she wanted most right now was him. And she didn't care how she got him.

"So you're saying you're willing to have sex with me right now, even if I told you that it would be a bad idea. That I'm not the type of guy who's in it for the long term? That whatever happens between us is a no-strings-attached kind of deal?" He took her hands and looking deeply into her eyes, he kissed one hand, then the other.

"Yes," she whispered. "Will you spend the night?"

He shook his head and give her a slow, wicked smile that more than anything he had done sent her heart pounding and her senses tingling. "Not this night. I would rather you have a clear head for this."

"For what?"

"Just because we can agree to no strings doesn't mean we shouldn't have some expectations. Or anticipation. Or even some romance. When was the last time someone took you out on a real date?"

"What?"

"Not Two for Tacos or Aussie Night at Quent's."

She blinked, struggling to remember. "A while. I mean never. I mean, a guy took me for burgers and milkshakes once," she managed to say.

Jackson laughed. "Then I think it's even more important that we do this right." He paused and his face went serious. "Lynn, I'm not the kind of guy who believes in happily ever after, but I do believe in making the most of right now. And while there might be no strings attached, a gentleman, as you like to call me, still has certain standards to uphold."

"Oh," Lynn said, trying to find the strength to breathe, realizing that she was finding this unbearably sexy. Jackson got up, leaned down and brushed his lips across her forehead, sending an electric thrill through her.

"Does that mean you're going to sleep with me?" Lynn tried not to sound like she was begging.

"Oh, don't worry, I intend to do a lot more than sleep with you," he said, and it was all Lynn could do to keep her mouth from popping open.

"And now, I think you better start sleeping it off. I'll see you tomorrow."

Lynn could barely nod as he gave her a grin that had a bolt of desire shooting down her body until her toes wanted to curl in delight.

Chapter 35

The pounding in Lynn's head woke her up at the same time as the pounding on the door registered. She sat up, aware that she was still in her clothes from the night before, still stretched out on her couch, a blanket twisted around her legs.

Snippets of last night came back as she struggled to her feet, automatically going towards the door.

"I'm coming, I'm coming," she shouted at the unknown knocker, then muttered, "What the hell."

She opened the door to a glorious, sunny, fall day and Tory, her hair shining in the sun like a brownish-gold mane, framed by a backdrop of the glimmering water of the harbor.

"Man, you do look like crap. Maybe trying to meet a guy in a bar isn't the best approach." Tory kept up a running stream of conversation as she dropped a brown paper bag from which a delicious smell wafted up.

Lynn's stomach lurched, which reminded her that she had skipped dinner in favor of tequila shots. She wasn't sure if eating now would be a good thing or not.

Tory hiked herself up at the breakfast bar, uncapping a cup of steaming hot coffee. "Don't worry, I'll share this with you while you brew a cup. The breakfast sandwich is from The Golden Pear by the way. Practically guaranteed to fix whatever ails you."

Lynn, just nodded, went over to the kitchen cabinet, found a glass, and poured some water and drank. It slid down her throat, doing a little to push away the cotton ball feeling in her mouth.

"What happened to you last night?" Tory asked.

With a sigh, Lynn pulled up another stool. Tory pushed over the cup of coffee and the breakfast sandwich.

Over coffee and an egg sandwich, Lynn told Tory about what had happened with Jackson.

"Wow, so Jackson came to your rescue again, and decided you were too drunk to have sex."

Lynn thought back, her memory hazy. "It was perhaps just about my most mortifying moment."

Tory shook her head, was silent for a moment, "No, that's when your prom date doesn't show up because there's a comic convention in town."

Lynn thought for a moment. "Yeah, that's bad too."

They were silent for a moment. "So now what?" Tory asked.

Lynn thought. Just what had been Jackson's words…? *I'm going to do a lot more than sleep with you.* She shivered at the thought and felt herself tighten at the memory. A threat? A promise? Either way it had been hot. Hot enough that she could almost forget he was probably still in love with a dead woman.

"I guess he wants to go on a real date. He said that while he doesn't believe in happily ever after, he does like to show a girl a good time…or words to that effect." Lynn's insides quaked just a little as she thought about what that might mean.

Tory nodded. "At least that's a few points in his favor. He has a job, a car, he's good looking, and he wants to feed you before he sleeps with you. Sounds like a winner to me. Of course, he still has enough baggage to make Paris Hilton look like a light packer, but as long as you know it's a no-strings-attached deal, you should come out of this just fine." Tory seemed to be saying it to reassure herself. She looked at Lynn with concern.

"What do you mean, just fine?"

"I don't want to see you get hurt."

"You're the one who told me I should change my expectations, just go for sex. That's all I've been thinking about for weeks now. I don't think I can turn back now even if I wanted to. What's so wrong with Jackson?"

Tory shrugged. "It could get messy. I mean, he's smooth and polished and you won't feel like he's just in it for the sex. Not until it's too late. And he can definitely afford to buy you dinner. But when it ends, you'll still have to run into each other all the time. Queensbay's a small town. But he'll probably send you flowers."

As if on cue, there was a knock at the door. Lynn got up calling, "Who is it?"

"Delivery," a disembodied voice called back.

Lynn went to the door and came back with a long, white box.

"Oh man, please don't tell me!" Tory said.

Lynn opened the card, looked at it, and felt a smile come over her face.

"OK, so who are they from?"

"Jackson."

"See what I mean? A classy type of guy. You're right. What could be better for you to reopen your foray into the world of sex? An over-muscled man-boy or someone who is going to treat you like a lady and then rock your socks off?"

Lynn nodded. "If Jackson Sanders is so hot and eligible, then why would he be interested in me?"

Lynn held up a hand when she saw that Tory was about to launch into a tirade. "I'm not throwing a pity party, but don't you think he's used to a different kind of woman? I walk around in a uniform that's basically a pair of pajamas. I'm knee deep in snot and vomit half the time. Unless my mother's cooking, I eat ramen noodles and drink cheap wine."

Tory shook her head. "Maybe it's time you thought of yourself differently."

"So what are you saying I need to do?"

"Nothing. I'm saying Jackson must like you just the way you are. So don't sweat it."

Tory looked at the flowers and looked at Lynn. "Ok maybe sweat it a little bit. When you're not working, perhaps it's time we upgraded your wardrobe from scrubs and yoga pants to some tailored pieces and a few more dresses. You know, if he's going to play the grown up game, maybe you should too. Like the gift wrap that will drive him crazy to get to what's underneath, if you know what I mean."

Lynn thought for a moment. "Scrubs really aren't sexy are they?"

Tory shook her head. "Not in the least."

"They are comfortable."

"So are sweatpants, but those aren't real clothes either."

Lynn opened up the box. There were a dozen long-stem yellow roses nestled there. She picked one up, smelled the beautiful, delicate fragrance, and put it down. If this was Jackson's idea of dating, then she was all for it.

Chapter 36

She ran into him just as she was coming out of the hotel gym and almost tried to avoid him. Sweats and scrubs. She couldn't seem to catch a break in the sartorial department when he was around. She remembered what Tory had said. It mattered what she felt like on the inside. Fine, then time to summon her inner sexpot. She closed her eyes, but before anything came to her, she had been spotted.

"Hello," he said.

She stood up a little taller and smiled. He smiled back and she took it as a good sign.

"Hi." There was a pause while she thought about what to say next. He took a step closer to her and she found herself tongue tied. Stay cool, she reminded herself.

"I guess you're feeling fine if you were at the gym," he said as his eyes swept over her tank top and shorts.

"Yes, actually I am. I mean I still have a bit of a headache, but thanks to you—and breakfast—I am feeling better."

He moved closer to her so that they were almost touching. One hand reached up and he took his finger and ran it along her shoulder.

"Lifting weights?" he asked.

She nodded. His light touch sparked the senses all over her body and she told herself it had to be just the leftover adrenaline from her workout.

"Who knew muscles could be so sexy?" he said, his voice pitched so low she almost couldn't hear it.

"Oh," she said and then tried to regroup. "Thank you for the flowers. They're beautiful."

"I figured you could use something to cheer you up," he said. His hand moved up and touched the few strands of hair curling loose from her ponytail. Yup, definitely not the adrenaline, she decided. Her heart was pounding so loud it was a wonder he didn't notice it.

"What are you doing?" she managed to ask.

"I was hoping to get you worked up," he said simply and looked at her, his eyes dark, intense.

Lynn sucked her breath in sharply.

"Is it working?"

She managed to nod.

He leaned down and whispered, with mock seriousness, "So I assume what we discussed last night is still agreeable to you?"

"Very agreeable," she murmured. He took a step back, breaking their connection and she acutely felt the absence of it.

A big smile spread over his face and he said, "Then I would like to take you out on a date."

"Do we have to?" Lynn tipped her head back and managed to make her voice light.

He wagged his finger at her. "No you don't."

"Don't what?"

"Don't sell yourself short. I told you drinks at a pub and Taco Tuesdays does not a date make."

"It does in my book," she said.

"Well then, you've only dated boys."

"And you're not?"

He took a step forward again and she almost jumped in surprise. Careful not to touch her, he bent down and whispered so only she could hear, "I am most assuredly not a boy, and what's more I can take my time to appreciate you."

"Oh," came her breathy response.

"We're going to do this my way. Now, I would like to take you out on a date."

"Yes," she answered simply, because really, what more was there to say?

He leaned back, looked at her. "Wonderful. Shall we say Friday night, then? I'll pick you up at eight?"

"Friday?" Lynn said, "But that's days from now."

"You waited this long, surely you can wait just a little longer? I promise it will be worth it."

"Very well, then." Lynn smiled and decided that two could play at this game. "I'll see you on Friday, then."

"Friday," he said. "And not that you haven't upped my appreciation for scrubs and yoga pants, but I was planning on going to a slightly fancier place," he added.

"I do own other clothes," she lied, giving him another smile. Then she turned on her sneakered heel and went out the door.

He watched her, telling himself that he was jumpy for no reason, that it was just a date, and that he had been on dozens of them before, with women who were a lot more demanding, a lot more sophisticated than Lynn Masters. But not one of those had left him with the tight little curl of anticipation and desire quite the way the thought of spending time with her did.

He wasn't sure just when he decided he couldn't stay away anymore. He was aware that he had been fighting it, fighting her since he had first seen her, and that every time he had been around her, she had grown harder and harder to resist. And that kissing her was like nothing else, so that all the senses seemed to rush from his head, and that it felt right. Ever since he had woken up in that hotel room, aware that he had been dreaming of coming home, he had been living on instinct. And his instincts about Lynn were pushing him toward her.

Chapter 37

It started before she even knew it, in the days leading up to their date. Her cup of coffee at The Golden Pear was on the house, courtesy of Jackson. A tray of cookies showed up at the clinic, to be shared by everyone. There was even a note slipped under her door, with the words 'Can't wait until Friday' scrawled in heavy black ink. The note itself was written on thick, creamy cardstock, with Jackson's name engraved on the top.

Lynn's every nerve thrilled in anticipation as she thought about Jackson and the way his hands had felt against her skin. He hadn't even kissed her again and yet she couldn't stop thinking about him. About the way his shoulders had looked, wide and strong the day at the gym. Or the fluid way he moved, whether he was in a business suit or a pair of jeans. Then there was the way he smelled, of clean soap, with the slightest hint of spicy aftershave. Or the way his blue eyes fixed on her and seemed to read all the secrets written inside of her.

To make it worse, she heard from him, with his presents and his notes, but she didn't see him, or even hear him really. She fought the urge to go to his door and knock, telling herself that she needed to be mature, patient, to allow this game to play out. But she'd barely seen a light on in his place, and try as she might, she hadn't heard a sound, not even the low hum of the television.

So she threw herself into work, focusing on the clinic and refining her plan for her Healthy Kids Now project. Things were progressing nicely and Caitlyn Randall had even promised to help her throw a fundraiser, catered by Darby at The Golden Pear. Work distracted her, but that calm was shattered whenever Tory texted her with questions like what was she going to wear, how was she going to do her hair.

Finally, Lynn gave in and agreed to go shopping with Tory on Thursday night, which was why she was now stuck in the mall, in a too-small dressing room, under unflattering light.

"How dressed up did he say to get?" Tory asked.

"He just said to 'wear something nice,'" Lynn called out, after she stared at herself in the mirror again, deciding that the black dress she was trying on made her legs look too short.

"Hmm, well does that mean you even have to wear a dress?"

"I want to. Don't you think I should? I mean it sort of covers all bases."

"It means easier access," Tory said, a shade too loudly. Lynn poked her head from the dressing room.

"Will you keep it down out there?" she hissed.

"What?" Tory shrugged, her eyes wide and innocent looking. "You know that's what you're thinking about."

"Am not," Lynn said.

"That's just because you've never done it right. If you had, then that's all you would be thinking about."

"I've done it right," Lynn said, wondering just how she had gotten into a conversation like this.

"Really, so you've had incredible, toe curling, over the top orgasm sex?"

Lynn felt her face starting to flame red. She wasn't a prude, but still.

"Ah, I can tell by your silence that you haven't."

"I had a good experience."

Tory shook her head. "If that's all you've had, then you weren't doing it right."

"If sex was that good, nothing else would ever get done. After all, sex is a biological imperative, survival of the species. It's not really about pleasure," Lynn said.

Tory just smiled. "If you think that, then it just proves that you've never done it right. So on Saturday morning, when you're thinking it over, you'll call me and tell me what you really think. Because you will be calling me, pronto, and giving me all the details. And I mean everything."

Lynn said nothing but shimmied into the final dress Tory had selected for her. It was short, but not too short, and a deep, scarlet red. It picked up the dark red highlights in her hair and made her brown eyes dance.

She was silent, admiring herself, the way the dress dipped down into a V in the front and then flared slightly over her hips and out, giving the skirt a kicky bounce.

Tory, made curious by the silence, popped her head into the dressing room and Lynn saw her smile in approval, "Oh, now that's the one."

"Yeah," Lynn said. "I think I found it."

"Great. All we need is to find some underwear," Tory said.

"I have underwear," Lynn pointed out.

"Not the kind I'm thinking of." Tory answered.

"How do you know?"

"A perceptive guess. Come on, let's pay for that and hit Victoria's Secret. I think there's some black lace with your name on it."

Lynn gulped, wondering what she had gotten herself into. Black lace and scrubs didn't exactly go together. But she took a deep breath. A grownup wears grownup underwear, she told herself.

Chapter 38

Lynn tried not to pace. But she was nervous. Her hands felt sweaty and her heart was fluttering. Jackson had slipped one more note under her door, a simple 'see you later,' but all day she had been thinking of him.

She checked the watch. Almost eight. She had declined Tory's offer to come over and help her get dressed, but she had called once in a panic about what to do with her hair. Finally, they had decided on half up and half down, with some tendrils framing her face. The curls, which she had pumped up with the help of her curling iron, fell in luxurious waves down around her face, skimming her shoulders, and touching the bare skin of her back.

Checking herself in the mirror one more time, she sighed in relief. She looked good, she decided, better than good. She had followed a video on the Internet about how to give herself sultry, nighttime eyes using makeup, and the woman staring back at her was nothing like the scrub clad med student she was used to. No, finally she looked like a woman, a sophisticated woman. It was something, she decided, that she could get used to.

There was a knock on the door and she nearly jumped out of her skin, then told herself it was just a date. She had been on them before. Ok, so not many, but she knew how they were supposed to go. They would talk, they would flirt, and they would kiss, and perhaps, hopefully, more. Because this time, she was sure that's what she wanted. Jackson.

Another knock came, and Lynn snapped to attention. "Coming," she said, shaking herself loose of her thoughts.

#

Jackson fingered the collar of his dress shirt, then stilled himself. He wasn't the type of man who made nervous gestures. He had carefully schooled himself to stay calm, to never betray any of the nervousness he felt. In business, appearing calm under pressure was half the battle, and he had earned the respect of more than one grizzled business veteran because he never panicked.

Just why then did his heart leap up when the door opened and Lynn stood there? She leaned against the doorjamb, almost tall in high heels, her petite body looking lean and long in a red dress that hugged her in all the right places. It dipped invitingly low over the swell of her breasts and he wrenched his eyes up, looking at her face.

"You look...amazing," he finished lamely, realizing that she did. There was something slightly different about her, as if she had grown up in the few days he had carefully avoided her. Her dark eyes were smoky with expectancy and her hair curled around her face, begging him to touch it.

She smiled and he was reassured, seeing in it the same girl he had come to know.

"Right on time," she said. "Would you like to come in or should we just go?"

"We can go. I mean, everything is ready," wondering why he suddenly felt tongue-tied.

She nodded and turned and he saw that the dress scooped low in the back, revealing that she probably wasn't wearing a bra, and that her back was toned and muscled. She moved, even in her high heels, with a grace he found compelling. She went over to the breakfast bar, picked up her purse and a jacket.

He came in then and said, "Let me," holding out his hand for her coat. Wordlessly she handed it to him, and he held it so she could step into it.

He let his hand brushed against her cheek, the skin on skin contact sending a delicious tingle of delight through him. Her breath caught, the only indication that she felt it too. She turned and faced him, her head angled up towards him, and he gently brushed his hands along her cheek again.

"Lynn," he said.

"What?" she asked.

He allowed himself to bury his head briefly in the waves of her hair, smelling her shampoo which gave off a flowery scent with a hint of citrus.

"If we don't leave now, we might not ever get out of here," he said.

"Oh," she said as she understood what he was saying. "Maybe that wouldn't be so bad," she said, her voice low and enticing.

"Oh no you don't," he answered, pushing her gently away. "I said I wanted to take you to dinner, so that's what we're going to do."

"What about what I want to do?" She moved closer to him.

"I think that's your hormones talking, and since we're both adults here, we'd be silly to listen to just our hormones."

"As a doctor, I have to tell you that hormones are a powerful force of nature."

He took her hands looking into her eyes. "Don't worry. I have every intention of making sure that our hormones are fully satisfied. You're not getting out of this, Lynn, unless you want to, but we need to make sure we take it slow."

"I thought that's what we have been doing."

"You know there's something to be said about the anticipation," he said, pulling her toward the door. "Or were you the type of kid who went searching for your hidden Christmas presents?"

"Absolutely. And I ripped the paper right off. I bet you were the type of kid who saved all the wrapping paper."

"Folded it too," he said with a wink as he closed the door shut. He still held her hand as he walked her down the catwalk to the steps.

"So where are we going?" she asked.

"My date. I'm not ruining the surprise," he said.

#

They drove out along the coast, away from Queensbay. She was glad that they weren't going to the Osprey Arms, since it meant that they'd be less likely to run into anyone they knew. She felt it was important to have him all to herself.

"This is Sean Callahan's, the chef at the Osprey Arms, other restaurant," he explained as the lights of his car lit up the tower.

"A lighthouse?" she said.

"Yeah. Pretty cool, right? Sean Callahan and Chase were so successful with the Osprey Arms that Sean decided to open this place up. It's out of the way and specializes in locally sourced food. It's only been open a few weeks, but I hear it's getting some great reviews."

"I've heard about it, but haven't been," she said, thinking that this sure beat the heck out of Salsa Salsa.

He pulled up and a valet appeared, opening her door. Remembering to swing her legs out first, before the rest of her, she managed to gracefully exit the car.

"Does the light still shine?" Lynn stopped, looking up at the tall stone tower.

"No. They built an automatic beacon farther out on the coast, years ago. The local historical society bought it from the government but they were having trouble maintaining it, so when Sean and Chase suggested that they rent it and fix it up, everyone was happy."

He put a hand on the small of her back and ushered her into the building.

The tower had a stone house attached to it, what must have once been the lighthouse keeper's cottage. It looked bigger, roomier inside, and she wondered if it had been expanded to accommodate the restaurant. The ceiling stretched up the full two stories and in the corner, you could see the iron stairwell that must lead up to the tower itself.

Whatever windows that had been there had been replaced with large, solid paned ones that looked out over the water. It was dark now, and in the distance lights were winking on, perhaps from the distant shore of Long Island, but more likely from boats still at sea. Without thinking, she felt drawn toward the window and she stepped over to see that they overlooked a cliff that dropped down to a rocky shore.

"Impressive," she said.

"Isn't it?" Jackson said beside her and she heard the pride in his voice.

She had heard that he and his brother were partners on a lot of their projects and she wondered if this was one of them. If so, he had the right to be proud, she thought, taking in the space more carefully. It was light and airy, with beams flying overhead, and a giant hearth, where a fire crackled merrily. It smelled of wood smoke, leather, and richly spiced food. Tables were scattered, simple, rough-hewn, solid wood ones. The whole place seemed inviting and she thought, quietly expensive. This much simplicity cost money.

"How about we take a walk?"

She glanced unconsciously down at her shoes.

He smiled. "I meant a climb. We can go up to the top of the tower."

"Really?" she said, feeling like a kid at Christmas. "The view must be amazing."

"It's nothing to turn your nose up at."

With a hand at the small of her back, he guided her towards the steps and they started up. Luckily, the lighthouse had already been built on a raised bit of land, so the tower itself was short—relatively—for a lighthouse. They made it to the top after climbing the tight, circular staircase. All the way, she was breathlessly aware of Jackson at her back, never too close, never too far away.

Small windows punctuated the sides of the walls as they climbed up, affording glimpses of the dark sky, but the real treat was when they finally ascended to the top platform. It was enclosed in glass and the giant light, while its powerful reflecting lenses, stood dark. There was a small door that led to a parapet outside and Jackson opened it with a key he pulled from his pocket.

"It says 'Do Not Enter,'" Lynn pointed out.

"I know the owner. Besides, the best view is from out here. You're not afraid of heights, I take it?" he asked, his voice light.

"I like to climb rocks," she pointed out as she stepped out onto the iron catwalk. It was covered over with weathered planks, for which she was glad, since it meant that she wouldn't catch her heel.

The moon was on the rise and the sky was dotted with the first stars of the evening, and she could hear the boom of the surf and the surge of the wind in equal measure.

"It's beautiful," she said, taken away.

"Not as beautiful as you," Jackson said. He stood next to her and she leaned into him, thankful for his tall frame and the shelter it provided from the wind. He put an arm around her and she nestled into his warmth, feeling the heat surging between them.

"Truly," he said, his lips somewhere near her ear, "you look amazing tonight." His lips grazed her cheek and she turned towards him, the sudden need for him overwhelming.

"Even doctors can clean up when we have too," she murmured, her neck arching, her lips searching out his. In a moment they met and their lips brushed each other, touched, and then his mouth covered hers and he kissed her.

Their tongues met and she encircled her arms around his neck, standing up into him. His hands came around her waist, pulling her closer while they kissed. She twined her hands in the hair at the back of his neck and allowed herself to lean into his long, lean body.

A moan, which must have been from her, escaped and she welcomed the heat and hunger as she felt his hands, hot on her back.

"We should," he said, finally pulling back, "go back down for dinner."

She nodded, marveling at how his light eyes were darkened with desire. He came in for one final kiss, then took her hand and all but dragged her back into the relative warmth of the interior platform.

He led the way down the stairs this time, the descent leaving her breathless, though not from the exertion. Her stomach was flip-flopping, clenching in anticipation and, she realized, something else, deeper. Two-sided attraction, she decided, was a very powerful turn on.

Dinner proceeded smoothly, with the two of them seated at a cozy table near enough to both the roaring fire and the window. Light music filled the air, and the place started to fill up, the volume going up, but never enough to be distracting.

She was jumpy, too nervous to eat much, but what she did eat was delicious. A crab cake appetizer, a fresh greens salad, and then grilled salmon.

"You know, you don't have to be nervous," Jackson said, somewhere between the salad and the main course, as his hand reached out for hers. She let him cover hers, feeling the warmth and the strength.

"I'm not nervous," she lied.

"Oh really?" he arched one eyebrow.

"Ok, maybe a little. It's just that it's been amazing so far. You, the drive up here, the tower, the food."

"You've never been out to dinner?"

"Of course I have; it's just that you know most med students are, well, a little on the impoverished side, so we usually go for places where the drinks come in plastic cups and the food is usually served in red plastic baskets."

"Truth be told, I've been known to enjoy dinner served in a plastic basket too," he said.

"I find that a bit hard to believe," she said.

"It may have been a while, but there's nothing wrong with it. I just wanted to show you that you're special. That you deserve this."

She looked at him, with his blond hair, the sculpted cheekbones. "You don't have to, you know. I mean this is nice and all, but..."

"Don't," he said.

"What?"

"Don't talk yourself out of what you deserve. Lynn, you're beautiful, accomplished, and hell, I'm betting you've saved a life or two; you're funny, intelligent, and strong; and, well, the list could go on. You deserve the best, so please allow me to treat you that way."

She was speechless, reaching for her wine and taking a sip to cover her emotions. He was right, she thought. She had never demanded much from the guys she had dated, mostly because she had been too absorbed in pursuing her career.

"Thank you…but I'm not impressed," she added.

"Then I guess I'll have to try harder," he said, a playful smile lighting up his cheeks.

"Ok, so you know I'm a doctor and like working with kids, so why don't you tell me what you like to do besides follow me places and play with power tools?"

He shrugged. "Jake Owen and I used to run a lawn mowing service in the summertime, then we got into painting houses, then handyman stuff, all while we were in high school. I went off to college but we kept it up over the summers. Then one year I got an internship with a big construction firm in New York City. As project manager. You know, learning how to build skyscrapers while managing time and budget. I loved it and they offered me a job after college. I was supposed to do it for a year or two and then Jake and I were going to go into business for real, start a full service construction business. Sort of expand on what his dad had started."

Jackson toyed with the stem of his wineglass and Lynn waited.

"Then the company offered me a chance to go to London, to work on a project there. I took it and for the past couple of years I've traveled, managing building sites in Dubai, Hong Kong, even Australia for a while."

"Sounds like you were quite the nomad," Lynn said. She noticed that he didn't mention why he'd left in the first place. Fine, if he didn't want to talk more about Ashley, then she could live with that.

"I was."

"Why did you decide to come back?" she asked, hoping that a question like that wasn't off limits.

He looked down, then up, and his blue eyes were dark but his expression was rueful, "Look, don't think I'm crazy or into this hocus-pocus stuff, but I woke up in my hotel room one morning and all I could see was sand and tall buildings, hot, dirty, dusty. And I thought I had to get out of there. I'd been having a dream, of water, of boats, of Queensbay. I knew it was time. Like I was finally called home."

She looked at him. "For real, you felt a calling?"

"I can't explain it but I just decided to accept it. So far, things have been working out," he said.

"And just like that you quit?"

"Well, almost. I gave them a decent amount of notice, but I also felt like I learned as much as I needed to, plus I sort of got more interested in green construction and remodeling older buildings—you know, bringing things back to life. My employer builds things on a massive scale. I want to do something smaller scale, more environmentally friendly, maybe even self-sustaining energy-wise. Right now, it seems like the next big wave will be solar power, really getting it to catch on, with all sorts of construction, big and small; and I want to see if I can be a part of that."

"So back to Queensbay? What are you going to do now?"

"Well, Jake and I are joining forces. I'm redoing the old Sail Makers' building—in case you haven't noticed," he said with a wink. "And Jake and I will get started on renovating the Osprey Arms soon. It should keep me busy for a while."

"And after that?" Lynn asked curiously, wondering if there really was enough here to keep a man who lived all over the world busily.

"I have my eye on a few projects in the area. Some big, some small. I'm sure I will find things to occupy myself."

Lynn sighed. "Sounds like pretty soon you and Chase will own half the town."

Jackson laughed. "We won't be that bad, but to be honest, Queensbay was on a long, slow, slide for a while. Chase and I, well, we're happy to help bring it back to its former glory."

Her eyes narrowed. "Not you too?"

"What do you mean?"

"Let me guess, you got in early on Noah Randall's IPO?"

He laughed. "Chase and Noah have been friends for a long time. I just rode on their coattails; but yes, it was one of the best investments I ever made."

"And now you and Jake are going to be swinging hammers together?"

Jackson smiled. "Something like that. Truth, I'm more of the sales and marketing guy. And Jake only swings a hammer these days when it's for a friend."

There was a pause but before Lynn could ask another question, he said, "Perhaps you'd like to check out the dessert menu? I've heard the chocolate cake is amazing, as is the upside down walnut apple pie."

Lynn sensed that Jackson wanted to change the subject and decided that it was all right. After all, she wasn't sure he'd want to hear her talk about the correct way to perform a tracheal intubation.

"I'm game for it, if you are."

"Challenge accepted," he said.

She excused herself just after dessert, going to the ladies' room and closing herself in the stall. Dinner was almost over, and this was it, she thought. She hadn't been sure if it would be his place or hers, but she had made sure that she had fresh sheets on her bed. She leaned against the door, savoring the prospect. She was nervous yes, but more than that she was ready, her body humming with excitement.

She let herself out of the stall, stood at the sink. The wind on the tower hadn't done too much damage to her hair, but she rearranged it so the dark waves fell down on her shoulders. She wanted this, she thought, wanted this with him. She took a deep breath, to steady herself, telling herself she was ready.

Jackson was waiting for her, her coat draped over his arm. As he helped her into it, her skin tingled from the brief contact. He took her hand and led them outside. The valet jumped to attention and his car was there in a moment.

He guided into her the passenger seat, and she leaned back in the soft, buttery leather as he got in. The car pulled smoothly away, heading down the coast road back towards Queensbay.

She didn't know what to say, her tongue feeling thick. She almost jumped when she felt his hand reach for hers. He took it gently, brought it to his lips, and kissed it.

Comforted by the gesture, she found her voice. "Thanks for dinner. It was lovely."

"My pleasure," he said, throwing her a glance. They were almost to back to town and he pulled smoothly into a spot. She looked up. The third-story window of her apartment was there, with the small light she had left on, a beacon in the dark.

Before she could open the door, he was there, his hand reaching for her. She let herself be pulled up and into him. She half expected him to kiss her, but he didn't, just letting her linger in his arms while he sent her a lopsided smile that caused her stomach to curl in a tight ball.

She led the way up the steps and when she reached into her purse for the key, he took it from her and in a smooth gesture, unlocked the door and opened it up for her. The door swung wide and she stepped in, turned. He was still standing outside the door, not coming in.

"What are you doing?" she asked.

"Saying good night."

She felt her face fall. "Don't you want to come in?"

"Not tonight," he said.

She took a step back as if she had been slapped. He held up his hands. "I didn't mean it that way."

He stepped closer, but still stayed well outside the door. "More than you know, I want to come in, but then I might not be able to leave."

"Isn't that what you want? It's what I want." Lynn was tired of beating around the bush.

He looked at her, his eyes dark, unreadable. "You know it's what I want. And I'm glad it's what you want to. And believe me, I intend to get there with you."

"Then why don't you come in?"

He took a deep breath and a step back. "Because I'm enjoying the way things are going, Lynn. And truth be told, it's a little fun to watch you beg."

"I'm not begging," she said as she stepped forward, closing the distance between them, "I believe you respect me, if that's what you're worried about." And she did. Whatever happened with Jackson, even if he didn't believe in happily ever after, she knew that he would appreciate her, care for her while it lasted.

"You know I do. But I want you to be sure. That you under-stand the rules. We're attracted to each other, we want to be with each other…"

"And that's it. I got it, no strings attached. But seriously, I'm not sure how much longer I can wait," she told him, as her insides clenched in frustration. Ok, there, she was almost begging.

This time he let her get close to him and she kissed him. He didn't respond at first and then his mouth came down on hers, covering hers with hot heat and possession. His hands twined in her hair and she stood up on her tiptoes. Before she knew it, he had backed her up against the wall in her apartment and was kissing her back, pressed into her. Her brain couldn't think, lost in the heat and passion. She felt the tingle of excitement spread through her as she wrapped her arms around his shoulders.

He pulled away. "Like I said, you should have no doubt that I want you. But, not like this."

She looked around. "We could go inside. I have a couch, a bed…"

He smiled down at her, a suddenly wicked smile that had knees trembling. "Don't worry, I have plans. Do you trust me? I want it to be special. You said, after all, that it's been a while."

"I didn't say that," Lynn said.

"You didn't have to," he said with a sly smile.

"I don't need a trip to Paris or anything like that."

"Now there's an interesting idea," he said as he nuzzled her neck. "But I was thinking that we'd spend the day together tomorrow."

"Ok," she said, surprised and delighted. "I can do that."

"Meet me at the docks, tomorrow, say ten o'clock. How about we go for a boat ride?"

"A boat ride?" she asked. "Isn't it cold out?"

"Dress warmly. I want to show you something."

"Ok, a boat ride. Should I bring anything?"

"No, I've got it covered," he said. "I'll see you tomorrow."

"Fine. If you think you can wait that long." She said it as a challenge, wanting to see if it would make him reconsider.

"Oh, I'm not sure that I'll get much sleep tonight. But like I said, I'm a patient man; I can wait."

She realized she wasn't going to get any more than that from him, so slowly, tantalizing, she closed her door.

She waited, leaning against it, to see if she could hear him. There was a shifting of weight, the slight creak of the floorboards underneath him and then she could sense movement against the door, almost feel where he had placed his hands. She lifted one up, to where she imagined his was.

"Lynn, go to bed. Trust me, I'll be waiting for you tomorrow," his voice came through the door.

And then she heard him go.

With a sigh that did nothing to calm the adrenaline coursing through her, she turned and faced her empty apartment. She had a feeling it was going to be a long night.

Chapter 39

"What do you mean nothing happened?" Tory screeched so loudly that Lynn had to close her eyes. "He took you to the Lighthouse, voted the most romantic restaurant in all of New England, and you barely even kiss good night?"

Lynn sighed. She had finally managed to get to sleep but then she'd an embarrassingly vivid dream and she had woken in the midst of tangled sheets, damp from head to foot, with an aching knot of frustration tied up tight within her. She hadn't been able to sleep after that, and when she got the early morning text from Tory, she had agreed to meet her for a quick cup of coffee before her plans with Jackson.

"He said he's being patient."

"Sounds like he's teasing you," Tory said, and Lynn could almost hear the wheels of her brain turning.

"Though, that's not necessarily a bad thing. I mean, talk about the buildup! You must just be about to explode. I mean, your underused lady parts facing an eruption of cataclysmic proportions."

"Will you shut up!" Lynn said, looking to see if anyone else had heard. Joan Altieri, the proprietor of The Garden Cottage, a local store that sold fancy home goods and knick-knacks, seemed awfully engrossed in her morning paper, which must have been racy enough to have the tops of her ears turning pink.

Even Darby Callahan, all eight and half months pregnant of her, seemed to be hovering near them, wiping a neighboring table down with an unusual thoroughness.

She had thought that meeting with Tory would help calm her, but Lynn was as jumpy as a flea with eczema, and Tory's voice was a little too loud for comfort. It was a small town and if Joan and Darby knew about her and Jackson, it wouldn't be long before all of Queensbay, including her parents, found out. Besides, given what half the town thought of Jackson, maybe keeping their relationship quiet was the way to go.

"What, it's not like everyone isn't after the same thing here. You're due for a good healthy dose of robust exercise."

"Seriously, is that all you think it is?" Lynn hissed.

"It's not the only thing, but it certainly makes this business of living a little more exciting... You know," Tory said, breaking off a piece of her chocolate croissant, dunking it in her coffee, and then holding it half way on route to her lips, "Jackson may have you right where he wants you."

"And what does that mean?"

"Awfully worked up. And focused on one thing. Wow, look who has the one-track mind."

"I do not have a one-track mind," Lynn protested.

"Whatcha thinking about now?" Tory said as the chocolate croissant disappeared between her lips.

Chapter 40

After her breakfast with Tory, she walked slowly home and waited until it was time to go. Her mother had called and left a message, asking her to call her. Lynn was certain that her mother had made it into the café and had heard the gossip.

Lynn decided her mother could wait, but wasn't surprised when her mother sent her a text: *"be safe…and by that I mean use protection"*

Feeling the flames of embarrassment light up her face, she didn't know how to respond to that, so she ignored it. It was the pitfalls of having two parents who were doctors themselves. No beating around the bush when it came to bodily functions. And safety first, always safety first.

Now she was walking along the docks of the marina, enjoying another beautiful fall day. There was a chill in the air but she hardly felt it through her sweater and fleece, which was warm enough to withstand an arctic storm.

Jackson had sent her the slip number so she could find him and as she passed boats big enough to take up residence on, she wondered just how much money Jackson had made investing. He had said boat, not yacht, she was sure of that.

However, the directions led her just past a sleek white motor yacht with tinted windows, around a sloop large enough to have sailed around the world to something much more charming.

"This is yours?" she asked looking it over. Jackson stood in the little cockpit of a gleaming, varnished, antique wood runabout. The hull was a golden brown and the brass trimmings shined bright. Jaunty striped cushions were on the two captain's chairs and the small bench that ran along the back of the cockpit. Everything was orderly and precise in the little boat, which rocked slowly in its slip.

"All mine," he said. He was wearing jeans, boat shoes, and a fleece pullover that hugged his broad shoulders. The sun glinted on his fair hair and there was a definite note of pride in his voice.

"She's beautiful," Lynn acknowledged. Living on the coast might be new to her, and boats somewhat uncharted territory, but even she could see this boat was a classic, something that must have been lovingly restored.

"Thanks. I did most of the work myself, years ago. Well, everything but the engine," he admitted.

"Was it a lot of work?" Lynn said.

"You bet. She was a wreck, literally. Washed up on the shore. I was the first to find her and when the owner decided she was too far gone to fix, I had a hell of a project on my hands. Chase has been looking out for her for me, but I haven't been out since I got back into town."

Lynn could tell that Jackson was just as excited as she was about the prospect of a day on the water.

"Do you need me to cast off?"

"That would be great." Jackson started the engine, and it gave off a low, throaty putt-putt as it idled. Lynn walked to the bow of the boat, untied the line, and then walked to the stern. She loosened it and then did as graceful a flying leap as possible onto the boat, while holding onto the stern line with one hand.

Jackson's arm, the one not manning the steering wheel, caught her and pulled her close. He gave her a quick kiss on the cheek before turning his attention back to the water in front of them.

Lynn thought about the butterflies in her stomach and willed them away. It was a beautiful day, warm for October, and the sky was a clear, deep blue, with large, white clouds scudding across it. In the sun it was lovely, but she was glad she had dressed warmly. There was more than a hint of the changing seasons in the air, of unsettled weather and longer, darker nights.

Jackson guided the boat out through the closely spaced vessels moored close to the marina and then out into the channel. Soon most of the boats would be pulled in for the winter, but there were still a fair number to navigate through.

"You never told me where we were going," she said, raising her voice to be heard above the sound of the engine and the wind. She had pulled her hair back into a ponytail, but some strands whipped across her face and she tucked them behind her ear.

"Here and there," Jackson said.

"Here and there?" Lynn asked. "You don't seem to be a here and there type of guy."

He shrugged. "Not on dry land. But the water's a different story. I thought we'd explore the harbor. Have you been out?"

"Once, with your brother and Phoebe, on Chase's sailboat. My dad's thinking of buying one, so Chase gave him the tour."

"Ahh, Chase and his sailboat. Now tell me," Jackson said as he pushed down on the throttle and the sleek little boat jumped ahead, "Which do you like better..."

Lynn laughed as her hair whipped wildly around her head.

He even let her drive, or steer, the boat. She stood up, so she could have a clear view of the water ahead of them, and he nestled himself behind her, his body blocking the wind, his weight a comforting presence as he showed her the controls, taught her how to pick out a spot on land and use that to guide her.

They moved past the hulking wreck of the Queensbay Show House, its tattered 'Save Me Now' banner flapping in the wind, and then up the shoreline into a sandy cove, and then back out into the main harbor.

She was having so much fun she didn't notice that the white clouds had piled up into a mass of smoky gray ones and that the sun was covered by a milky film that stole its warmth.

"Is it going to rain?" she asked, glancing up as she shivered.

Jackson followed her gaze. "Most likely. But that's ok."

Lynn looked back over her shoulder. It was hard to judge distances over the water, but she felt even if they made all out for the marina, they were still looking at getting a good soaking before they landed.

"I don't think we'll make it back to the marina in time. Don't suppose you have any foul weather gear on board?"

There was a small stowage area in the bow of the boat but it wouldn't really provide much in the way of shelter, Lynn thought.

"I might, but we won't need them," Jackson said, his hand coming down over hers as he slowed the throttle down and nudged the wheel in the direction of the shore.

"We're going to go to the beach?" She knew she wasn't keeping the surprise out of her voice.

"Not quite. We're heading for that dock there. We can tie up there and catch some shelter."

"Won't the owner get mad?" Lynn asked.

Jackson shot her a smile. "He's an old friend. He won't mind."

Lynn was about to argue that they couldn't just go barging in on someone when the first large raindrop splattered on the windshield in front of them. Already the wind had turned colder, more cutting and she thought that it would be nice to get inside.

"Want me to take her in?" Jackson asked, and Lynn handed over the wheel. She set out the bumpers along the gunwales and picked up the bowline, waiting. Jackson guided the boat quickly but gently and cut the engine so they floated up to the dock. Just before they touched, Lynn was out, tying the boat down. The rain was starting to come down a little harder now, the flat surface of the harbor awash with concentric circles as each raindrop landed and disappeared.

Quickly and without much talking, they secured the boat together. He lifted a cushion and she saw there was a compartment under one of the benches. From it he pulled out a bright yellow rain slicker and tossed it to her. She wrapped it around her and in a moment, Jackson was with her on the dock. He grabbed her hand and they all but ran up the long walkway towards the end where the dock landed on the sandy verge.

She looked up. They were along the bluffs of the harbor, where the elevation went almost straight up. She could catch a glimpse of a structure amidst the trees above.

"Hope you don't mind a bit of a climb," he said as he pointed to the set of steps that zigzagged up the steep incline.

"Not a problem." The rain goaded them on and the climb was over before she had even realized it began. The steps opened up to a wide lawn and Lynn got the impression of a low-slung building that hugged the hill it was built into. There were windows, lots of them, and strong, sturdy beams made of warm brown wood and dark metal. Staying close to her, Jackson hurried her up the slope, then to a set of stairs that led to a wide-planked deck that ran along the front of the house.

Still shielding her from the rain, he slid open a door and they plunged into the silence of the house. Lynn stood, letting her racing pulse slow as she took in her surroundings. Windows. She got the impression of lots of windows and open space, metal, and wood trusses. It was sparsely finished because she realized that most of it was new. There was the faint smell of raw wood and new paint, even as there was the smell of something else, like cinnamon and vanilla mixed in as well.

"Is this a new house?"

With a slight shushing sound and a click, the slider door locked into place and Jackson turned to her. "Not quite. It's been completely renovated though. It used to be a traditional ranch, a bit boxy, with nothing special except for this."

He motioned and she was drawn to the window. The sky was completely overcast now, a gunmetal gray that turned the surface of the water to a leaden pewter shade. The rain, which had started in large, single drops had now turned into a single sheet of water pouring down. She shivered, feeling the dampness, glad that they didn't have to go out there again, at least not right away.

"Here," he said, dropping an arm around her shoulder. "Let me start a fire."

He led her down to a sunken living room, where one wall was dominated by a fireplace, surrounded by mellow gray fieldstone. The chimney, in the same stone, went up to the vaulted ceiling above. A sectional couch, in a light cream color, sat across from the fireplace.

Grateful, Lynn sunk into it, while Jackson crouched by the hearth. As she stripped off the raincoat and her damp fleece, she could see that a fire had already been set—paper, kindling, and some nice fat logs. All that needed to be done was to set a match to it. Jackson took a long narrow container, opened it and a match appeared. He struck it on the bottom of the tin and the flame jumped to life. Cupping a hand around it, he maneuvered it closer to the fire and touched it to the paper.

In an instant, the flame caught and there was a crackle as the fire settled in. Almost immediately, she could sense the warmth coming from it, and she moved along the side of the couch to get closer to the blaze.

He turned and looked at her, throwing her a smile. The light in the room was soft and gray, a reflection of the world outside. His blond hair caught the red of the flames as he leaned back on his haunches.

"Sorry about that. The weather wasn't supposed to turn this early in the day. I thought we had until late afternoon."

"Is it supposed to rain for a while?" Lynn asked.

Jackson got up, and reaching past her picked up a soft wool throw in a dark chocolate color. He draped it around her shoulders and she soaked up the warmth.

"Until late tonight."

"I guess we won't be going back out in the boat for a while."

He looked at her. "Not if we don't have to. There's supposed to be a decent amount of wind, with the rain heavy at times. It's not that far back to the marina but there's no sense risking it if we don't need to."

737

"So we're stuck here?" she asked, the realization of the possibilities suddenly dawning on her.

He came up to the couch and leaned a little closer to her. "In a matter of speaking. We're not that far from town, you know. Pretty sure there's a car in the garage, if you want to go home?"

"Your friend, is he coming back anytime soon?"

"Friend?" Jackson said and his face showed a moment of confusion. "Oh, you mean the owner."

Lynn, nodded, wondering why she suddenly felt shy.

"No, I think we're safe from any interruptions," he said, his voice rough.

She felt a flash of desire, of anticipation and tried to hide it by stretching out her legs.

He smiled, as if sensing her unease. "How about something to eat? And some music?"

"Maybe some music," Lynn agreed.

"Good idea. The stereo system is over there. I'll check the kitchen and we'll meet back here?"

Relieved she had something to do, they got up, and Lynn went to the shelf that held the radio. It looked like all she had to do was turn it on. A small screen popped up, allowing her to select a type of music. She scanned through the choices, settling for classic rock.

Satisfied, she turned and wandered back towards the kitchen. This floor seemed to be taken up by one large room that was divided into a kitchen, an eating area, and the sunken living room. Beyond that, there was a set of stairs leading down and a hallway beyond that. She imagined that the rest of the house, things like bathrooms and bedrooms, all had to be down there.

The kitchen was brand new. Dark granite counter tops contrasted with lighter, amber colored wood cabinets. The appliances sparkled and were all top of the line. Lynn knew, since her mother was a spectacular cook and coveted ones like these.

"It still smells like a new house in here," Lynn said snagging one of the stools that ran along the counter.

"Yes, the renovation just finished. Mostly. There's still a few things to do, but it's livable."

"I'm surprised the fridge is stocked," she said, craning her neck for a better look.

"Always be prepared," Jackson said, emerging with a bottle of champagne.

She looked. He had already set out some cheese, crackers, and grapes.

He opened a cabinet without hesitation and pulled out two champagne flutes. She watched as he set them down and expertly opened the bottle. There was a small pop and the white bubbly liquid dribbled into the glasses.

She took the one handed to her. He held out his glass and they clinked. She took a sip, the bubbles hitting her nose.

"You seem awfully familiar with everything in this place," she said.

He gave her a smile and lifted one eyebrow. "I have a good memory."

"Really?"

"I helped build the place."

"With your own hands?"

"Not quite. Let's just say I had a lot of input into the design."

"And the absentee owner?"

"It used to be my grandmother's. She needed to downsize so I bought it from her. At first, I was renting it out, but about a year ago the tenants moved and I decided it was time to remodel a bit.

"I can't quite see a grandmother living here," Lynn said.

"Exactly. Don't get me wrong, I love my grandmother. But the place was stuck in a seventies time warp. I added an addition, finished out the basement, and of course, transformed the space into something a little more modern. I always loved the view, sitting out on the deck."

"Not many people would be able to have the vision to take something like what you're describing and transform it into this."

"Do you like it?" Jackson asked.

"Like it?" Lynn said. "I love it." And she realized she just might have found her style. Everything called to her, from the muted earth tones of the furniture to the darker shades of the wood. Even the exposed steel rafters, painted a dark gray, blended together. The space was not so much sparsely as carefully furnished, with just enough of everything and no extra clutter. It felt restful, simple.

"It's not too modern? My mom took one look and I swear she was ready to give me her glass figurine collection to make it homier."

"Well," Lynn said, looking around, considering. "It definitely looks a bit like a single guy lives here. I mean your TV takes up one whole wall. And while you do have a few books around, they all seem to be on serious subjects."

"I read mostly on my e-reader," Jackson defended himself.

"And there's nothing living here. Not even flowers, which technically aren't living. What about a plant? Shouldn't you have a fern or something?"

He laughed. "I'm a guy. Plants seem awfully girly. And you have to remember to water them."

"Yeah, I'm not much good at keeping things alive—well, except for people," she amended.

"Good thing then," he said giving her a look that had shivers spiraling down her back.

"What about your apartment at the marina?"

He laughed. "I was just there temporarily while they finished some work in here. Chase keeps one for family and friends. I don't really like staying in the actual hotel, so he let me use it."

"That's why it seemed like you haven't been there for a while," Lynn said, thinking that explained the unusual quietness she had noticed.

"Not this week. I've been staying here."

"Did you plan all of this, as a way to get me into your bachelor pad?"

"I can't control the weather, you know. Like I said, I thought the storm was going to come in much later. I figured that we'd have a nice trip around the harbor, maybe anchor, enjoy something to eat, and then I would casually suggest we check out a property I was working on."

"So you did plan for us to wind up here?" Lynn said.

He smiled at her, leaning closer to her. "I told you I had a plan."

His face was just inches from hers. She closed her eyes, breathing in his scent of soap, fresh air, and rain. He smelled good and she could feel heat rolling off of him, surrounding her. She wanted him to kiss her, wanted to wrap herself in him. The weather was cold and dark, and in here it was warm and cozy. Logically she knew Queensbay was only a few miles away, but it felt as if they were in a separate place.

"You shivered," he said, concern in his voice. "Come," he took her hand and pulled her to him. His lips brushed the top of her hair, and he led her back to the couch and the warmth of the fire.

"I'm not fragile, you know."

"I know," he said, his face hovering in front of hers for an instant, so close she could almost feel their lips touch.

"Why are you afraid of hurting me?"

"Who says it's not the other way around," he said, and it took a moment to realize what he was saying.

"Me, hurt you? What are you talking about?"

His blue eyes held hers, dark in the gray light. She could hear that slash of the rain against the windows and saw that the storm had moved further in toward them, sheathing the house in a gray cocoon.

He looked out the window and a rueful smile broke over his face. "Let's just say I think too much about you already."

She felt her stomach jump and flip-flop as she felt the need to be near him. She wasn't sure what she wanted beyond this, the ability to lose herself for a few hours. Anything else could wait.

"Can't we just enjoy the now? Unless of course, you don't find me attractive in that way," she said, easing herself closer to him and looking him in the eye.

Her hand rested on his shoulder and she trailed it with the faintest of touches down the strong length of his arm.

"Lynn," he all but growled.

"What?" she asked, all the innocence she could summon in her voice.

"Don't do that if you don't mean it."

"I mean it," she said, turning so she faced him. She reached first, pulling him closer to her, closing her eyes, bringing her lips to his. There was the barest moment of wavering before his mouth clamped over hers, hot and full of need. His arms came around her, pulling her in close, so she was all but trapped.

The electricity, the crinkle of attraction sparked between them and she found herself melting into him, reaching up to find the soft, silky feel of his hair, pulling him closer to her. He broke the kiss for a moment, his eyes searching hers. She could see the need, the want in them, and she shifted her weight so she was pressed into him, giving him the invitation he needed.

His head came down again, but he scraped his lips over her neck, up her jawline before going to take her mouth again. She moaned and moved her arms down the length of his back, feeling the play of the muscles there.

He leaned over her and she surrendered, leaning herself back onto the couch, allowing her hips to press up to meet him, feeling his own need there.

His hands found the V of skin where her sweater dipped down. She shivered at the dynamic thrill that came over her. His hands worked their way down, finding her nipple through the thin wool of her sweater, the slight pressure working it to attention, sending a flash of desire straight through to her groin.

Slowly, his hands moved further down, to the strip of exposed flesh between the waist of her jeans and the hem of her top. He put his palm there, the full force of the heat of his hand like a brand on her skin. She gasped and he moved it up, under the sweater, along her bare skin until he reached her breast again, this time his fingers slipping under the fabric of her bra, finding her bare nipple, which he rubbed until she could feel it puckered with desire.

Casually, as he kissed her, she could feel his other hand dip into the waist of her jeans, skim along the flat surface of her stomach and then press against her mound. She moaned, feeling lost with lust and desire.

She needed to be in contact with him, she thought, reaching up and pulling his fleece off. He had on a shirt underneath, the stiff, starched cotton molding over him like a second skin. Her fingers fumbled for the buttons, her fingers clumsy in her hurry.

She looked up, saw the laughter and desire in his eyes. Not shy anymore, she lifted herself up, then in a smooth, fluid movement, took off her sweater. He breathed in sharply, his eyes on hers, as he finished off the buttons of his shirt for her. The shirt discarded, they sat there, looking at each other, drinking it in.

Her eyes roved over the broad sweep of his shoulders, to his smooth chest, down to the flat, defined abs of his stomach. She reached out and trailed her fingers down them, ignoring his sharp intake of breath.

"You're sure?" he asked.

She leaned up, pulling him down. "I'm sure," she said as she wrapped herself around him.

Taking that as all the permission he needed, she felt him undo the buttons of her jeans and felt them being slowly pulled off. She shivered as his warm hands replaced them.

She was only in her bra and panties, and his smile was wolfish as he kissed his way up from her ankles, his hands trailing along behind. She felt as if all her neurons were alive, her body filled with a current of desire.

His hand brushed against the silky cloth of her panties. She flexed her hips, but he bent his head down, his teeth scraping against the fabric of her bra. His hands came up and smoothly he flicked open the clasp and she sprang free.

The pad of his thumb circled her nipple, tight with desire, and then she felt his hand slip down, teasing again as he found her panties. He slipped his hand in, slowly, tantalizing, until he found her spot, already wet. He stroked and she felt her need rise up, hot and fast.

She threw her head back and surrendered to the feelings flowing through her. He kissed her neck, his breath warm and hot on her skin. Her hips rose in an involuntary response and her whole body tensed and hummed, drawing tight as her body gathered itself. She grasped him, feeling the hard muscles of his back, her mind emptying of anything but the sensations running through her.

She felt the wave crest over her, felt her body draw tight as a bow as he pushed her towards her climax, her whole body quivering. It came, pushing her over the edge, the waves of satisfaction rolling off her. And then she wanted more. Her hands found the fly of his jeans, and she fumbled, pushing, rolling them down.

As if sensing her impatience, he used a free hand and together, she felt the jeans roll off, until he was left in his boxers, his need for her obvious though the fabric.

"Are you sure?" he asked again.

"Yes," she practically sobbed. She wanted him. There was a moment while he fumbled in the pocket of his discarded jeans and he drew out the square foil wrapped package.

She took it from him and surprised, he leaned back. But she opened it and took her hands to pull down the fabric of his boxers. He was more than ready for her, she thought, as she rolled the condom down the shaft, taking her time.

She glanced up and saw that he had his eyes closed, his jaw clenched.

"Is everything ok?"

He looked down at her. "If you keep that up, I might not make it much longer."

Laughing, she held her hands up. Taking that as her surrender, he grabbed them and pulled them up over her head. Immobile, she looked at him. He released her, his hands trailing down her body until he reached her hips. She angled them up and he entered her, slowly at first and then as the heat and the feeling grew between them, faster, with more assured thrusts.

She felt her blood tingling, her body quaking as her need rose again, her body ready to meet his desire with her own. She grabbed his hips, guiding them in and out and they found a steady rhythm.

She watched his face, saw the climax building in him until she felt it tear through him into her and she allowed herself to follow, both of them reaching the edge and tumbling over it together.

He sank down onto her, a delicious, heavy weight, as she felt her hammering heart start to slow back down.

The silence weighed upon them and she wasn't sure what she should say. Tell the truth, that it had been the most incredible sex of her life, or play it cool and act like toe-curling sex happened to her all the time.

"Wow," he breathed. And then, "I'm sorry. I didn't mean for this to happen on the couch." He rolled off of her, but the seat cushion was wide enough so that he was able to pull her close to him. The throw found its way onto them and she snuggled into him, feeling content, the warmth of his body sealing her happiness.

"I don't think where mattered, just why it took so long," she said, then realized she had forgotten to play it cool. At least she hadn't begged to do it again.

"Good things come to those that wait," he said, and she could hear the smug satisfaction in his voice.

"Then you can just keep those things coming," she said, her fingers tracing lazy circles along the muscled ridge of his arm.

"I am sure that can be arranged," he said, and she felt his lips touch her hair, his hand slide down to leave a streak of heat down her back.

It was still raining out, the storm in full force, the house now fully enveloped by a wall of gray clouds. The music played on the hidden speakers and the fire had burned low. Their glasses of champagne sat forgotten on the coffee table...Lynn felt like she wanted to take this moment and hold it in time. She felt like something had shifted, that everything had changed.

She felt the lassitude slip from her as Jackson's hands became more insistent, felt the curl of desire flare up in her stomach, realized what she wanted as she tilted her head up to meet his, felt and met the heat of his kiss. Yes, she was going to enjoy the moment.

#

Her stomach rumbled, and he found her one of his button-down shirts to put on, and she wore that, her panties, and nothing else as he made something to eat. She hadn't checked the time, didn't know, with the gray clouds, whether it was lunch or dinner; but it didn't matter. She knew neither one of them had any intention of going anyplace.

"You're not a bad cook," she said, tasting the pasta he had cooked with simple efficiency.

"Pasta's not that hard," he said.

"You should meet my mother: the woman can do wonders with pasta." It was out of Lynn's mouth before she could stop herself. She felt a flush of embarrassment, knowing that she had broken the first rule of casual relationships. Never mention the family, especially when they had agreed up front that this wasn't serious.

"I didn't mean it like that. I mean you don't have to meet my mother. In fact, it's probably better that you don't, you know, because who knows what she'd think? Or worse yet, what she'd say to you."

Lynn realized she was babbling, so she took a deep breath and pretended to be very interested in the linguine and vegetables that she had wrapped around her fork.

She felt his gaze on her and looked up, relieved to see that his expression was more amused than angry.

"Meeting your mother..."

"Look, I didn't mean it that way. Or that she would say anything bad. Or who knows, maybe she would. All I meant is she's a good cook. Usually no one can resist that. But it's probably better that we keep this on the down low, if you know what I mean."

She almost missed the sudden tightening of his expression, but then it was replaced with his usual unreadable look.

"The down low?"

"You know, quiet. It's that, well, I mean, some people might think, you..."

"Of course," he said, taking her hand and pulling it to his mouth, and brushing his lips against it. "I understand perfectly. Better not to have too many people intruding into our relationship, right?"

"Exactly," she said, not sure why she felt deflated he had agreed so quickly.

They ate a bit more in silence, then Jackson looked out the window. "It seems that the rain has stopped," he said.

She looked up and saw that the sky had lightened up, flashes of blue showing through ragged tears in the gray clouds. Drawn, she got up and walked to the bank of windows. The whole world looked wet and a breeze had kicked up, frothing the water of the harbor with whitecaps. The sky out to the west showed rays of sun breaking over the horizon. It was late in the afternoon, almost evening.

He came behind and wrapped his arms around her, and she sunk into his warmth, savoring the smell of soap and spice that had come to mean him to her.

"We don't have to go. Tomorrow the weather will be much better and we can take the boat back."

She turned, running her hand up his arm and up to his cheek. "Are you asking me to stay the night?"

"Well, considering I haven't even given you a tour of the whole house, I thought it might be nice."

"Are you just trying to get me into your bedroom?" she asked.

He waggled his eyebrows at her. "That might be part of it."

She turned, linking her arms around him. "I can't think of a better way to spend a weekend."

Chapter 41

She stayed through the weekend. They did little but watch old movies, play ping-pong on the table he had in the basement, and make love. They snatched bits of sleep and he cooked their meals from his well-stocked pantry. She ignored all of her text messages from Tory and her mom, only saying she was ok but busy. The weather for the most part stayed cloudy and gray and she felt safely tucked away in their private little aerie.

Monday morning came all too soon and he drove her down to the village. It wasn't a long drive by any means, but suddenly she was nervous, as if their weekend was ending and with it something more. They would say goodbye of course, but she wondered if it meant goodbye, it was fun, now it's time to move on; or did it mean goodbye until we can do this again? No strings attached had been the agreement but she didn't know how far that extended.

Her stomach felt strangely nervous, jumpy as they rode down from the heights overlooking the Sound and into Queensbay proper.

It was early in the morning. A fine gray mist clung to the trees, even though the sun promised to break through. A hint of colder weather was in the air but she didn't want to think about it. Children were standing in clusters, waiting for their school busses, moms in various states of dress watching over them, most of them clutching coffee cups that sent up clouds of steam into the air.

"Penny for your thoughts," he said.

She gave herself a start. She hadn't realized she'd been looking out the window, drifting away. She looked over at him. He seemed relaxed, comfortable, sitting there in a dark pair of suit pants. He had on a crisp white shirt and jacket but hadn't bothered with a tie.

"Nothing, really. Just watching the kids."

"Remembering what it was like?" he asked.

She nodded. "I always liked school. But we moved a lot when I was young, or it seemed like it, since my dad finished up his training and then served in the army. Fall was exciting but it was sort of like a rollercoaster. Not the excitement of new beginnings, or the change of the seasons, but something more akin to, oh my god, will I fit in, will the kids be nice to me? You know, your standard kid stuff."

He shot her a smile as he slowed down behind a school bus. "Yeah, I know what you mean. Fall was always the time for new clothes, new shoes. It was football season, too, so that was always fun."

"I guess it must have been different, growing up in the same town, going to the same school, year after year," she said.

"There wasn't that sort of rollercoaster anticipation about it, I guess; but you're right, there is something about fall and new beginnings. I always loved the smell of wood smoke, how as the leaves thinned you could start to see everyone's houses. You get your last days out on the water, and then you'd spend your time getting the boat all shipshape."

She laughed. "For a guy who's been all around the world, you seem pretty comfortable with the small town traditions."

"What can I say? I'm a small town guy at heart."

Jackson had said the past was the past, but here in his small town, everything must remind him of her. What had Tory said about Ashley and Jackson? They had been inseparable all throughout high school. Lynn tamped the thought down before she could think any more about it.

They were in the village now, almost at her apartment. She needed to get home, grab her scrubs, and hop into the car to get to the clinic She checked her watch. Just enough time.

Jackson pulled into an empty spot. Lynn swallowed. Best to be brave, to be a grownup, thank him for the good food, the good sex, and all that, and then appear like she could care less if they made plans to see each other tonight, tomorrow, or next month. That had been the deal, right?

She put her hand on the door, ready to bolt out of there with a hurried goodbye, but he was quicker, sliding out of the car and to her side before she could open the door.

He did it for her and held out his hand. Always the gentleman, she remembered as she stood up. The gray skies of the weekend were definitely burning off. It would be sunny today, a wonderful, sunny gorgeous day. A perfect day to be dumped.

"Thanks," she said, not trusting her voice to say much more.

"Do you want me to walk you up? I can drive you to the clinic, but you probably want your own car there."

She nodded, her throat feeling constricted. But it had to be said.

"Thank you for the lovely time this weekend. Perhaps..." she didn't get any further than that because he had both hands on the side of her cheeks and he was looking down at her with a slightly amused expression.

"Did you just call what we had lovely?"

Unsure, she managed to stutter out a yes. He smelled of soap, a hint of spicy aftershave, and his nearness was doing things to her she didn't quite expect.

"Well it was..."

He kissed her, his mouth hot on hers, demanding. It was a full-bodied, full-sensory kiss. His hands twined around her hair and she relaxed into him, wrapping her arms around his broad shoulders, pulling them to her.

"Better than lovely," she said. They came up for air and he looked at her, his eyes hazy with lust.

"Are you sure you have to be at work in half an hour?"

Her head fell back as his lips nuzzled along her throat.

"Absolutely sure," she said.

"When are you off again?"

"Thursday," she said.

"You'll see me then?" he asked, his voice insistent.

"Yes," she managed to whisper, feeling a hot joy spread through her. He wanted to see her, and well, he wanted her.

"Good. Dinner?"

She nodded, "My turn to cook for you."

He raised an eyebrow. "I thought you told me you lived on ramen and coffee?"

"I did. I suddenly found myself interested in developing a more sophisticated palette. Trust me?"

He held up his hand, the one she had stitched up. "With my life...and my stomach."

Suddenly giddy, she laughed, found the strength to break free. "I really do have to get to work," she said.

"I'll watch to make sure you get in," he said. "Wave from the balcony."

Assured, feeling loved and strangely sophisticated, she took a step back, nodded, and tried not to skip as she made her way up to her apartment.

Chapter 42

"Well, well, well." Jackson drew up short as his brother's voice floated behind him.

"Look at who you just drove home. Were you playing doctor?"

Jackson spun around, his hands balled into fists. "That's not funny." He knew Lynn hated jokes like that, and besides there had been nothing funny about what they had just shared.

Chase held up his hands in surrender. "Sorry, brother. I'm just a bit surprised."

"And why's that?" Jackson said, folding his own arms across his chest. They were in the upstairs suite of rooms of the Osprey Arms that Chase had been using for himself before he had moved in with Phoebe. Now it was going to become project central and Jackson had come to discuss plans and budgets with his brother.

"I don't know." Chase ran a hand through his short hair, visibly frustrated. "I just haven't seen you with a girl in a while."

"You haven't seen me in a while, period," Jackson pointed out. "There were plenty of girls along the way. I enjoy being in a relationship, treating a lady right. As long as we both understand the rules."

Chase raised an eyebrow.

"That it will end eventually. I don't intend to settle down and get married."

"Good for you," Chase said, clapping him on the back. "It's bad for your health to keep it all bottled in. I just didn't realize that you were, you know, ready."

Jackson steeled himself. Chase was his brother and probably knew him as well or better than anyone, including Jake. Still there were some things he couldn't even tell Chase, that Chase couldn't know.

"It's been a while. I'm allowed to move on," Jackson said, defending himself.

"I know, and that's great. I mean we all loved Ashley and it was terrible what happened, but..."

"But what?"

"Well, it just seems sudden, you know. You moving back here, which is great, but getting caught up again with a girl, too? Maybe you should take it one step at a time."

Jackson's eyes narrowed. "I already told you, I'm quite comfortable with relationships. Is there a problem with Lynn in particular," he asked, his voice dangerously low.

"Not at all. And that's the point. She's a nice girl."

"She's not a girl," Jackson pointed out, remembering the way her body had moved under him. There had been nothing but a passionate, sexy, strong woman in bed with him the past weekend and he had loved every second of it. Her strong, tight, lithe, athletic body had surprised him in many, many ways. He sucked in a breath and focused on the lecture his big brother was giving him.

"Fine, a woman. But she just got out of med school, just moved out on her own. Hell, I don't think she's ever had a real boyfriend."

"So?" Jackson stilled, watching with hidden amusement as his brother grew more and more uncomfortable. He didn't plan on enlightening Chase that Lynn wasn't as innocent as she seemed.

"So, just don't mess her up," Chase said.

"What?" The word came out of Jackson in a burst of surprise.

"I just mean she's a good friend of my future wife, and I like her and I'm looking out for her."

"You think I would hurt her?" Jackson asked.

"Not on purpose, no, but I don't think Lynn's a casual type of girl, if you know what I mean. And what I saw you two doing out there seemed pretty intense. Are you ready for that, ready to be serious?"

It was Jackson's turn to run his hand through his hair. "Who said anything about being serious? We were just having some fun," he said, echoing the words Lynn said to him.

"That looked like more than fun to me, brother. And look, I know you too. You may say that you can have a casual relationship, but that's not true, not when it really matters. So just be careful for both of your sakes. I don't want to have to pick up the pieces again."

"And what's that supposed to mean?"

"Look, I get it. You were messed up after Ash died and you had to get out of here. But there were whispers and the Morans kept coming around looking for answers. I defended you even though I didn't understand why you left. This was your town too."

"And I'm back now. And Lynn and I are, well, we're taking things as they come." Jackson felt the flash of anger, wishing that people would have enough sense to mind their own business. But that was part of living in a small town. Your business was never fully your own. There were too many interdependent relationships riding on it.

Chase nodded. "Good. You know I hate pulling the big brother act, but you're family, and Lynn's a friend. I just don't want to see it get messy."

"Hey, it's just a mature relationship; no strings attached," Jackson said, knowing even as it came out of his mouth that he was already beyond that, no matter what Lynn said she wanted. Chase was right.

Chase gave a rueful smile. "Somehow it never quite works that way, does it?"

Chapter 43

Lynn checked the index card again. Her mother had written it down in her neat, precise handwriting. The recipe was the Holy Grail, the one her grandmother had passed down through generations of Masters women. A guaranteed man-pleaser, the recipe was supposed to have been the one that had won her grandfather's heart, at least according to Lynn's grandmother.

The ingredient list had looked deceptively simple, she thought, looking at the packages of food crowded over her counter. She and Jackson hadn't seen each other in four days, Lynn thought, not that she was counting, and she had invited him over for a home-cooked dinner. He had asked what he could bring, and she had made what she thought was a sophisticated response. "A bottle of good Bordeaux."

Her mother had said it could go well with the dish. She had wanted to say more, but Lynn had told her that she was being safe and her mother had backed off, knowing that there was only so much honestly you could have with your adult daughter.

Now, as Lynn looked at the recipe she wasn't quite sure where to start.

"At the beginning," she could almost hear her mother say.

All that had seemed well and good as her mother had passed over the card, but now the terms like sauté, blanch, and make the garlic dance had her bewildered. Her mother had offered to show her how to do it, but Lynn confident that this cooking thing couldn't be too hard, had passed on the offer.

So now there was nothing to do but make a start of it. She grabbed one of her new knives, pulled an onion from a bag, and started dissecting it.

The videos helped, she decided. Lynn had caved and used her tablet to search up definitions, techniques, and just about everything having to do with the recipe. She was led down a rabbit hole of videos and articles about fresh versus dried herbs, the proper way to handle a knife, and whether salt was really necessary to make water boil.

It was fascinating to watch, knowing there were people out there who treated cooking as a science. Her mother had always approached it as more of an art, but now Lynn had a better appreciation for how many different steps must have gone into putting a simple weeknight dinner on the table. When she glanced up at the clock she had to stop herself from cursing. Jackson was due here, literally at any moment, and there was an explosion of flour in one corner and what looked like the results of a nasty accident involving decapitated tomatoes in another. The first batch of garlic had burned, and though she'd bought enough to keep a nest of vampires away, there was a lingering, slightly over-roasted smell in the apartment.

And she was still wearing scrubs. She was about to make for the bedroom when the doorbell rang.

"Just a minute," she said and looked around. There wasn't time to do much of anything she thought. Perhaps clean up the flour? There was a short knock, as if to highlight his impatience.

"Ah hell," she muttered and went to open the door. He was standing there, wearing a dark suit, no tie, shirt open at the collar. She thought he might have gotten his hair cut, but she had no time to think because he crossed over the threshold and pulled her toward him, covering her mouth with his, a kiss full of intensity and desire.

All thoughts of a dirty kitchen faded from her mind as her senses took on a life of their own. Perhaps her Nonna was wrong about food being the way to a person's heart. Perhaps all it took was a kiss. His scraped his lips against her chin as she pulled him into her apartment.

She was vaguely aware of the door shutting behind them and of the way his arms encircled her, lifting her up onto her toes, closer to him.

"I missed you," he said as he set her down. She licked her lips and took a step back to gain a measure of steadiness. She told herself that she shouldn't get used to that, that this was, by mutual consent, a fling, meant to be passionate but ultimately destined to flame out. Jackson had all but told her he wasn't ready to love again.

"I can tell," she said.

He smiled down at her and with a fluid gesture, held out a bottle of red. "You said Bordeaux, correct?"

She nodded, taking the bottle and setting it down on the kitchen counter.

"What are we having?" he asked.

"Well," she looked around, and his eyes followed her gaze. "It's supposed to be chicken cacciatore. And I was supposed to have showered and dressed. And not made it look like I was murdering tomatoes."

He looked at her and she was certain that his mouth was twitching, but he said nothing as he went into the kitchen and peeked into the pots and pans.

"It's an old family recipe," she offered.

He took up a spoon, stirred something, and then held it up for a taste.

"Wait," she said, panicky, "Me first. I don't want to poison you."

"Do you really think it's a possibility?"

"There's a first time for everything," she said darkly. She went over, took the spoon from him, and inhaled. Ok, so it didn't smell so bad. Sort of like tomato soup. Sure, not like when her mother was cooking it, but maybe it would taste fine.

Tentatively she took a taste. "Omigod," she said, dropping the spoon and going to fan her mouth.

"What?" he asked.

"Hot," she managed. She needed water, or milk, but she was certain she didn't have any of that, so she went over to the sink, quickly grabbed a cup and switched on the tap.

"How bad can it be?" Jackson asked. She turned in time to see him dip the spoon in, lift it to his mouth, and then take a big swallow.

It took a moment before he too started to cough and sputter and his eyes water. Wordlessly, she filled the glass full of water and handed it to him. He drank it one gulp.

"Were you supposed to use red pepper flakes?"

She nodded. "That's the secret ingredient. The recipe called for a pinch, but I thought I should measure it." She held up the measuring spoon.

He looked at it and burst out laughing. "That's a tablespoon. That's more like a fistful."

She looked at the spoon, looked at the mess, and then because he had started to, she went along with him and soon they were both laughing.

"Maybe you should stick to medicine," he said.

She punched him lightly, but he was too quick for her and caught her hand, using it to pull her towards him. He wrapped his arms around her so his chin nestled on her head.

"We could always go out," she suggested, trying to quell her laughter.

"Or," he said, taking her chin with his hand and lifting it up, "we can just stay in. I'm not that hungry." He dropped his mouth and his lips brushed against her ear. She felt her body respond, a thrill coursing through her. Her Nonna definitely had it wrong. Food had nothing on this.

His mouth moved to hers, insistent, demanding. She reached up into him, hearing herself moan. She wanted this, wanted him. Everything seemed to slip away as his arms came around her. She could taste the sauce on him, the scent of spice and to her it seemed to mean danger. She knew that she shouldn't let herself be so caught up in this, so caught up in him, but when his arms came around her and he pulled her to him, everything else seemed to fall away. For so long she had been focused on her goal that she had let nothing distract her. Now, when Jackson was around, everything but him and her need for him, faded away.

His arms slid down her shoulders, around her back so that he cupped her backside. In one fluid movement, he lifted her up so that her legs were wrapped around him. His teeth raked down her neck.

"Didn't you say you just had a new bed delivered?" he said, his voice a low growl that made her clench tighter around him.

"Something like that," she said.

"Sounds to me like we better go break it in, make sure it's up to standard."

He swung her around and before she knew it, he was carrying her from the living area, down the short hall into her bedroom. She managed a wild glance around, wondering what sort of shape it was in. Thankfully, she had put all of her clothes away and all there was was the bed and its new cover, soft, inviting.

He lowered her down on it, and she felt her head hit the pillows, her hair splaying out around her. She looked up at him. He took off his jacket and tossed it aside. Before he could start on the buttons of his shirt, she rose up, pulled him down and kissing him, began to undo them, one at time. She let her hands roam over his chest as she pulled the shirt away, let her fingers soak up the feel and play of his muscles, feel the strength underneath them.

She tossed the shirt in the corner and her hands hovered over his waist and played with the buckle of his belt. She could feel his want through the soft fabric of his pants as she brushed her hand over him.

He hissed in through his teeth and looked down at her. "Be careful of the game you're playing," he said.

Her fingers fumbled with the belt buckle and she had to use two hands before it slid free. He stopped her before she could go any further.

"Your turn," he said, and the warmth of his fingers burned on her skin as he grabbed the bottom edge of her top and pulled it over her head.

"At least those are easy to get out of," he said with a laugh, as his finger caught the waist of her pants and tugged them down. She was thankful that she had thought to wear matching underwear and bra today.

He smiled, his finger flicking the nub of her nipple under the red lace of her bra. She could feel it harden in response as her back arched up to him.

"Racy, lacy red lingerie. Under scrubs. Will wonders never cease?" he said as he kissed the spot between her breasts and then trailed kisses down the flat surface of her stomach.

"Just like they say, don't judge a book by its cover. Or a girl by her scrubs."

His fingers teased around the edge of her panties and then slowly, almost unbearably slowly, he slid them in to find her wet, moist center.

"Don't worry," he said as his eyes darkened, watching as her body responded to his touch, "I like the whole package."

She almost lost it then, pushed over the edge but she fought the need, letting him stroke her until her desire built up in her, pulling her, pushing her to a crest. She reached for him, her hands finding his fly, and this time he didn't resist as she slid his pants off, tugging them down so he could shrug out of them. He stepped free of them and then tugged down the waist of his boxers so she could see that he was ready for her.

He unhooked her bra and lowered his mouth down to her nipple and took it with his tongue, gently flicking it to rigid attention. His hands slipped her panties off and she couldn't wait any longer, as she moaned his name and raised her hips up to him, almost there. He entered her quickly and together they moved in sync.

She felt her whole body thrum and hum with fulfilled pleasure. She wrapped her legs around him and rose up to meet him. Together their eyes met and he locked his gaze on her. They moved together, finding their rhythm, and together they rode up and over the wave.

\#

They lay tangled next to each other. Lynn felt her heart racing and willed it to calm down. Next to her, Jackson was lying, strong, quiet, the sheet pulled halfway up around him. He lifted up one arm and smiled at her and she felt her heart melt. He was a nice guy, she reminded herself, nothing more. In fact, he couldn't be. She had to remember that before she let herself get too caught up in him. Still, she could imagine lying next to him, like this, on a regular basis.

It was his stomach that gave him away.

She laughed. "I guess I never fed you."

"I appreciate you for your other talents," he answered, a wicked tone in his voice as his hands lightly traced the line of her hip.

"I suppose we could always order in," she said.

"I'm pretty sure Giovanni's pizza delivers," he said.

"And thank goodness for that."

Chapter 44

The fire crackled warm and bright. Lynn looked around the assembled faces and smiled. Logs and chairs were pulled up in a circle around a huge bonfire that had been built on a little slip of beach below Noah and Caitlyn Randall's house. The log next to her was empty, but not for long as Jackson lowered his long form down next to her.

"I brought you a lobster, corn, and some clams," he said handing her a plate. She put her cup down, setting it into the sand so it wouldn't spill.

"Wow, this looks delicious. You cooked this all in a hole in the ground?" she asked.

"Yup, that's the beauty of a proper New England clam bake. It's a bit late in the season, but when you said you'd never been to one, I couldn't resist."

The firelight flickered, casting long shadows across their faces but she could see his smile and catch the twinkle in his eye.

"So, Doctor. How's the food?" Chase asked, settling down easily onto the log next to them and putting an arm around Phoebe, who gave him a kiss on the nose. Across the fire, Caitlyn Randall, lounged in a real chair, while Noah brought her a plate. Caitlyn was smiling but Lynn caught the looks she kept shooting up toward the house, where baby Luke was supposedly sound asleep, under the watchful eye of a trusted babysitter.

Beyond the fire, Sean Callahan, tended to the big hole in the ground from which all their food was emerging. Also in a chair, Darby, looking like a veritable Madonna, sat, her hands across her full belly, smiling every now and then as she felt the baby kick.

Tory was there, with a guy from the rival softball team. Jake Owen was here as well, but flying solo, which didn't seem to bother him at all.

Someone had set up a radio and a steady stream of upbeat music, a mix of classics and contemporary hits, played on.

Lynn held up the lobster by the tail. "What am I supposed to do, just crack it open?" she said, eyeing the hard, spiny shell with curiosity. She figured she was pretty adventurous when it came to food, but somehow she had never eaten a whole lobster before.

"Do you mean," Tory said in mock horror, a hand over her heart, "that you've never eaten a lobster before?"

Lynn looked around the assorted faces of the group, all of whom were looking at her as if she had tentacles and claws herself.

"Well," she said as she began to defend herself, "it's not exactly indigenous west of the Rockies, is it?" she pointed out.

Jackson laughed and pulled her to him, giving her a kiss. "I take pity on you. I will help you slay the big bad lobster."

There was a round of laughter as Jackson picked the lobster up from her plate. He started to explain the proper methodology of eating a lobster to her but she looked up, distracted, feeling someone's gaze on her. It was Chase and his dark eyes were looking at them, staring as if he was seeing something he didn't quite believe. The intensity, the speculation in the gaze made her uncomfortable. All of a sudden, she wondered if it had been such a good idea to make hers and Jackson's relationship public so soon.

It was Jackson who had wanted it; he'd looked so hopeful when he asked if she'd mind, as if he was afraid she'd say no, worried that she would be nervous to be with him. Lynn had told him to stop being silly. As far as she knew, there had been no further incidents like the one at the café, and what's more, she didn't care. All that was in the past, as far as Lynn was concerned.

So with a glee that she hadn't expected, Jackson had organized this party and said it felt good not to be sneaking around. She hadn't tried to dwell too much on what that meant for the definition of their relationship, but she knew she was starting to believe that what was between them was more than a casual thing.

Phoebe caught Chase's attention and it shifted from them. Lynn decided to ignore the shiver of foreboding that ran down her back and turned her thoughts back to Jackson.

It was getting late and the bonfire was starting to wind down. Caitlyn and Darby had left together, climbing the stairs up to Caitlyn's house, Darby moving slowly, saying she needed a real chair and a real bathroom, while Caitlyn had assured everyone they were welcome to stay.

Noah, Jake, Sean, and the rest of the couples were scattered around, on logs or blankets, digesting the enormous meal. It was getting cold, Lynn thought, the warmth of the day slipping quickly away as night settled fully down. The water was a soft whisper of waves lapping gently at the shore. Off along the coast, the lighthouse, the real one, flashed its light in a steady rhythm and the far shore was defined by a flickering line of lights. Conversation was dwindling and when Jackson whispered in Lynn's ear, she nodded, ready to go as well.

He stood up, sand spilling down from him. "I'll start to gather our things," he said.

"I just want to take a quick look at the water," she said and picked her way carefully along the rocky shore, the light from the moon and the fire her only guide, to the water's edge. She hugged her arms tightly around her. She was wearing jeans and a warm coat, but still the air was chilly, and on a whim she bent down and ran her hand through the water. It felt surprisingly warm.

As she rose up, she felt a presence next to her. She looked up, expecting to see Jackson, but it was his brother Chase.

"Don't be fooled. It's way too cold for skinny dipping," he said. His voice was light but even in the shadows she could tell that his face was serious.

"How would you know?" she shot back.

"Experience. You can't live in Queensbay and not be tempted. It feels warm because the water retains the heat of the summer well into the fall. It's always warmer in October than in April, no matter how hot a day you get in the spring."

"Is that something you did a lot?"

"What, skinny dipping?" Chase gave a low chuckle. "Among other things. Small town. We had to find a way to assume ourselves."

Lynn waited. She was friendly with Chase, but there was no way to mistake this for a casual encounter.

The silence seemed to stretch between them so that she had to ask. "Do you have something to say?"

"You seem to be getting along very well with my brother," Chase said.

"I might be," Lynn answered.

"That's good. He needs that."

Lynn waited, sure she knew what was going to be next. A big brotherly warning about not hurting Jackson or he would have to kill her. Or something like that. But what Chase said next surprised her.

"Just be careful, Lynn."

"What do you mean?" Her voice was laced with surprise. Of all the things he could have said, she had not expected that.

He turned to her, his voice pitched low and filled with concern. "You're a nice girl, Lynn, a good friend. I don't want to see Jackson hurt you is all."

"How would he hurt me?" Lynn asked.

"I don't know if Jackson's really ready to love someone again. But you are. You're one of the happiest, most passionate people I know. And you think you can fix people, and most of the time you can. But my brother, I'm not so sure he's fixable or that he'll be able to give you what you deserve. I am only saying this as your friend," Chase said as Lynn took a step back as if she had been slapped.

"Love...Who said anything about love," her voice started out high, but she caught herself and ended in a whisper.

"I see how he looks at you and how you look at him. He's happy; I'll give you that, and I thank you for that. I never thought I would see him that way again after what happened."

"You mean her," Lynn said.

"Yes, Ashley. It destroyed him. And truth be told, I don't know if he's whole yet."

Lynn wanted to scream in frustration. At every turn with Jackson she felt haunted by a dead woman, Jackson's silence about it doing more than anything else to confirm the presence of the saintly, deceased Ashley in his heart than anything. She felt always like it was one step forward and two steps back. Or maybe this was what Jackson had meant all along. He was perfectly capable of being a great boyfriend. But he would never give his heart to her. She ran a hand over her hair, ending in a tug on her ponytail.

She wasn't sure what to say, and thankfully, didn't have to because Jackson came up to them, threw an arm around her shoulder and snuggled her close to him. She leaned into his warm, hard body and let herself be warmed by the dazzling smile he sent her, and thought that maybe she should be happy with what she had. A sexy, attentive man who made love to her but didn't love her as much as she loved him.

"What are you doing out here with my girl, brother?"

"Just advising her against taking a dip," Chase said, laughing easily.

Jackson leaned down, scooped up a rock, and tossed it into the water. In the silver moonlight, Lynn watched as it skipped three hops and the dropped down into the surface, sending its concentric ripples outward.

He looked down at Lynn. "You do have a sense of adventure," he said and his voice was lightly teasing as he shot a look toward Chase.

She took a step back, already sensing what the brothers had in mind.

"It's colder than it looks," she protested. But she was too late.

She screamed for help but it was two against one. Phoebe and Tory came running to her rescue but the girls were outnumbered. Somehow they all managed to end up in the water, fully clothed, wet and shivering but laughing.

#

Later, warm and snug in bed, with Jackson sleeping beside her, Lynn struggled to find her own sense of peace. She and Chase had never finished their conversation but his message had been clear. Jackson was still in love with his dead fiancée. She looked over at his sleeping form, gently tracing the smooth muscles of his back. He shifted but stayed asleep. True, he had made no promises to her, only that he would treat her like a grownup. That she would enjoy herself. That she would feel sexy and sophisticated. And with him, she did. But not once had he mentioned love. And just where did that leave them? Or leave her? Did she truly love him? Or was she just in love with him, in love with the way he made her feel? Was there a difference? And why now, after guarding herself so carefully, making sure there were no distractions, had she fallen for a man who couldn't love her back?

She reached out, wrapping her arms around him, and pulled him close, as if she could divine his intentions through the heat of his body. He stirred, turned toward her so that he was pulling her close to him. Even in his semi-awake stake, she felt his desire for her as his lips found hers.

He pulled back and his eyes were awake, alive. "Can't sleep?" he asked.

She nodded, not trusting herself to speak.

He smiled and scraped his chin against her cheek, the prickly contact causing a shiver of delight to course through her.

"Let's see what we can do about, shall we?" he said, his words breathless against her ears. She shivered again and gave herself over to him, to the sensations of making love. Perhaps Jackson couldn't love her the way she loved him; in which case, her final thought was that she needed to take as much of him as she could get.

Chapter 45

"This will only take a moment," Lynn said as Jackson pulled the car up in front of Darby Callahan's house, a cute little Victorian on one of the main streets of the village. It was later in the day, the café would be closed and Darby said she'd be at home resting.

Lynn needed to drop some paperwork off to Darby, the contract for catering the fundraiser Caitlyn had urged her to set up. The plan was to use the money raised as the seed funds for the Healthy Kids Now foundation. Lynn had wanted to use her own money but when she had mapped out all she wanted to do, she realized that it would take more than she could give. A kickoff event was what was needed, Caitlyn had told her, and so she'd been planning one.

And now it was time to put everything in motion, and she wanted to give Darby all the details before she and Jackson headed out on their errands.

They, she and Jackson, were going furniture shopping. Well, TV shopping. He wanted a new one for his basement and he had asked Lynn to come with him. She had only hesitated a moment, thinking that this was what it was supposed to be like, right? This quiet way they had moved into being a couple. Shopping for electronics during the day and incredible sex at night. Still, they hadn't ever really touched on anything more than that talked-about some kind of future together. She tried not to mind it, not really, trying to remind herself that they had time, that there was no reason for her to rush him on anything, that she should just enjoy being with him.

"I'll come with you. Maybe she'll have some fresh cookies," he said, smiling.

He got out of the car, and his hand found the small of her back as he guided them up the tidy flagstone path towards the front porch steps. There were pots of mums sitting on the steps, in dusky oranges and maroons, reminders that autumn was fully upon them. It was a sunny day, but the weather had turned cold and there was a crispness to the air, overlaid with the smell of a wood fire.

Lynn breathed it in, her feet crunching on a few fallen leaves that hadn't been raked up. Behind her, she could see if she craned her neck the harbor, blue and bright, the light wind kicking up small waves. Jackson had pulled the boat in for the winter, but already she was looking forward to springtime and the chance to get back out on it.

She glanced up at him and he looked down, gave her a quick smile and a kiss before they stepped up the stairs that led to the wide wraparound porch. A wicker chair and couch were still out, their cushions pushed up. Potted plants swung from the porch, twisting and turning in the breeze. The house was freshly painted, a light cream color, with contrasting white woodwork and sharp green shutters. Everything about it looked inviting, and while Lynn was convinced her own style was more contemporary, the house, though compact, was more than charming.

Lynn raised the knocker and let it down once, then again. There was quiet and she knocked again, and finally she heard the sound of feet moving slowly toward them. The bright red door opened and Lynn was taken aback.

"Darby, are you ok?" she asked. Darby, even though she was eight months pregnant, had always looked glowing and strong. But today was a different story. Her face was pale and she was in a pair of sweats and an oversized t-shirt. Her reddish brown hair looked dull and lifeless, pulled back in a ponytail, and her hands were rubbing her giant belly.

"I don't know, I feel..." She took a deep breath and then she doubled over. Lynn saw her face contort in pain and immediately her instincts kicked in. She stepped forward, grabbed a hold of Darby, and guided her into the living room.

"Let's get you someplace where you can lie down."

"I'm having contractions," Darby said, through gritted teeth.

"It's going to be ok," Lynn said, feeling calm and collected. Her specialty wasn't delivering babies, but she had done a rotation in obstetrics and assisted in several births.

"How long have you had them?" Lynn asked, guiding her onto the couch. There was a fire already crackling and Darby must have been resting here, because there was a stack of magazines, a glass of water, and blanket.

"When's your due date?"

"It's supposed to be three weeks from now," Darby said, and Lynn could hear the worry and pain in her voice.

"It's going to be ok. Just tell me how long the contractions have been going on."

"I don't know, I mean, I was tired this morning, so I decided to rest, and I think I might have fallen asleep and then I woke up and there was something that almost felt like cramping. It's been going on for an hour. I've had them before, but they've always passed. But these are worse."

Darby bit her lip as another contraction hit her. Lynn did a mental calculation. The contractions were close together and obviously painful.

Lynn could feel Jackson hovering behind her.

"Where's Sean?" Lynn asked.

Darby shook her head. "At the restaurant. I told him I would be ok." There was worry and fear in her voice.

Lynn took her hand, knelt closer, and looked in Darby's eyes. "You are going to be ok. I'm a doctor, right?"

Darby nodded, then grimaced as another pain hit her.

"I just need to do a quick examination. Jackson," Lynn turned to see him standing there in the doorway, looking scared. "Will you go get my bag from the car—the black one. And call Sean."

"Should I call anyone else?"

Lynn shook her head. "Not just yet; it could be a false alarm." Calling someone or rushing to the hospital might not be a great thing. It all depended on whether or not Darby would rather have her baby at home or by the side of the road.

She could hear Jackson's rapid steps as he went to do as she asked.

"Darby, I am just going to take a look, to see if this is the real thing or another warmup, all right?"

Darby just nodded and Lynn went to work.

#

Jackson had made the phone call to Sean and gotten Lynn's bag from the car and then stood back, wanting to ask if he could help. Then he realized how silly an idea that was. Lynn was in complete control. Calmly, Lynn had told him to call 911 and Darby's doctor, but had also just as calmly told Darby that the baby was coming, sooner rather than later, and that in her best guess, they didn't have time to wait for the ambulance or drive like lunatics to the hospital.

"What do you need? Towels, boiling water?" he asked.

Lynn looked at him from where she was busy helping Darby.

"Towels, lots of them. And yes boil some water. And dump these in," she said, handing him scissors. "And a cup of ice chips," she added as Darby gave a grunt that turned into a scream.

"Go," Lynn said and turned her attention back to Darby.

It was over sooner than he would have thought, but judging by the sounds that Darby had made, it didn't hurt any less because things had been quick.

Sean had come bounding in the door, the ambulance right behind him, but by then Lynn had been coaxing Darby to push, towels spread all about.

Jackson held onto his friend's shoulder, but Sean went right in, going up to Darby, getting behind her and talking to her in a soothing voice.

The EMTs came crashing in and Jackson was jostled out of the way, but not before he heard Lynn's triumphant, "That's it," and one final loud exclamation from Darby, and then there was a moment of silence and then the wail of a baby.

Jackson fell back against the wall, realizing that he was sweaty and that his legs were shaking. He unclenched his palms and looked back in the room. The EMTs were standing around, with all their gear, looking disappointed that they didn't have more to do, and Lynn was handing the baby to Darby, who had tears streaking down her face.

"A beautiful baby girl," Lynn said. "Congratulations." She took a step back as the EMTs jumped in.

Sean was next to his wife, staring in awe at the wrapped bundle in her arms. There was another faint mewl and cry, and then Sean and Darby were laughing.

Lynn looked at Jackson, calmly wiping her hands with a towel. Her hair had escaped her hair clip and she looked flushed from the heat and the adrenaline, but she was smiling.

She came to him and he took her in his arms. "My God, that was amazing. You were amazing," he whispered.

"I didn't do anything. Darby and the baby did all the work."

"You just delivered a baby."

She looked at him, "Well, it's kind of my job."

"And it's amazing, you're amazing," Jackson said. The last of the setting sun came in through the windows, hitting her brown hair, and she stood there, as calm as if she did this every day. Something shifted in Jackson and his stomach dropped. He looked over at Sean and Darby and saw the way they looked at each other and their baby daughter. Then he looked at Lynn, who too, was absorbed the scene.

"I wonder who will have won the baby pool," she said, seemingly oblivious to the fact that she had just participated in a miracle.

Jackson swallowed, not sure how he was going to handle the fact that he was madly, deeply in love with Lynn Masters.

#

They never made it out to find a new TV, but Lynn was happy. The ambulance had taken Darby and the baby, whom they had named Emma, to the hospital, and they had gone too, to fill out some paperwork. A celebratory glass of champagne followed in Darby's hospital room and then they had left the happy family behind as more family and friends crowded in to visit them.

Lynn felt like she was walking on air. It had been pretty cool to deliver a baby, and not just anybody's. A friend's. And not in a hospital room. Not every day you got to do something like that. Yup, these were the days when she was glad of what she did. When all the hard work really and truly paid off.

She leaned back against Jackson, comfortable on the couch. He had been quiet since they had left the hospital, pensive almost.

The adrenaline of the day was slowly wearing off and she felt drowsy.

"Come, I'll carry you to bed," he said, and before she knew it, she had been scooped up and he was carrying her down the hallway towards the bedroom. Part of her wanted to protest that she could walk, but there didn't seem to be much point in it.

Slowly, carefully, he set her down on the bed. There was just one lamp on and she could see the way he looked at her. Suddenly she wasn't tired anymore and felt herself responding to the look, to the hunger, the desire in his eyes.

Their lips met at the same time, coming together, his kiss soft and sweet, which left her wanting more; but when she tried to push the pace, he kept things slow, his hands trailing over her body with a moving tenderness and a careful touch that made her insides coil with intensity.

Delicately, he undressed her, clothes peeling off until she was on the bed, and he looked at her, the hunger replaced by an almost reverent look as his gaze traveled over her. She felt the way his eyes burned into her and realized that something had changed between them. That her fight against her feelings for him was a losing battle. Somewhere along the way she had lost herself in him.

The thought scared her, and then as he kissed her, gentle at first, but then with passion, the heat, the electricity sparked between them. She rose up to meet him, bringing him down to her, giving her whole self to him, letting him give himself to her.

There were no more boundaries, she thought as his hands moved over her, his simple touches leaving her quivering with excitement, her climax building to the breaking point before he finally entered her and together they moved, the motion pushing them both up and over the crest until finally they both hit the edge and tumbled down the other side in an exquisite cascade of feeling.

They held each other in the dim light, not a word said between them, quietly wrapped together. Lynn felt Jackson's breathing deepen as he dropped off to sleep, still holding her tight. She didn't want to move, afraid to wake him, but at the same time her thoughts were racing, tumbling at what it all meant.

Tonight had been different, she could feel that with him. Perhaps it was only because he too had been affected by watching a miracle. Most people, men especially, never got that close to something that amazing. It wasn't her, she told herself, it had to be the situation; she needed to not read too much into it. Doing so would only get her hurt. In the morning, they would be back on familiar ground. And that's where she would try to keep it.

Chapter 46

They had just finished a run and were doing their cool-down walk along the boardwalk. It was cold, but they had dressed in layers. Jackson was trying to convince her that the first snow of the season couldn't be too far behind and she was asking him when they could go skiing. He laughed and mentioned that he knew a guy with a place in Vermont.

"How come you always know a guy?" she grumbled, but she wasn't displeased at the fact that they were making plans for the future, even if it was only for a weekend of skiing. She had visions of snowstorms, roaring fires with blankets and pillows piled high in front of them.

All, in all it was a totally normal day in the life of a perfectly normal couple as they made their way to The Golden Pear to check on the daily soup specials.

"It's just not the same without Darby here," Lynn said, looking over the menu board, inhaling the savory aroma of baked goods and hearty soups.

"Oh well. I guess a new baby means you don't have much time to cook the clams for the chowder."

Darby and Sean were in seventh heaven taking care of Emma, sleep deprived as they were. Darby was taking a much-deserved rest, with her dad and a few key employees picking up the slack at the café.

"She did say not to worry about the Harvest Ball fundraiser. She told me that between her, Sean, and her dad, they would have everything covered."

Jackson smiled. "I hear tickets are a hot commodity for the fundraiser."

Lynn laughed. "Perhaps, but I think people are afraid to say no to Caitlyn. Every day someone orders more tickets and they say Caitlyn told them it was a good cause."

The Harvest Ball was the event she and Caitlyn had planned as the fundraiser for the Healthy Kids Now foundation. It was a kids' costume party, to be held in the high school gym, with games and activities, plus a silent auction with lots of goodies for grownups too. Darby had worked out a healthy, Halloween-themed menu and had seemed to be excited to make hundreds of ghostly cupcakes that were secretly teeming with vitamin-packed pumpkin puree.

Lynn laughed and snuggled into Jackson's arm, which was slung across her shoulder, loving the feeling. They still hadn't talked about anything other than what they planned to do over the weekend. Still, there was the assumption that they would be spending it together. Slowly, Lynn had noticed she'd been spending more than a few weeknights at Jackson's house, where they chatted about their day while he cooked and they watched TV or read together and made love and then woke up to showers, breakfast, and rushing off to their separate workdays.

It was all perfectly perfect; but Lynn wondered how long she could go on with it before she would burst out and demand to know how he really felt, where he saw things going. But something always stopped her, that look in his eyes—the haunted, wounded look that told her he was still hurting and that she wouldn't like the answer if she asked the question. It was cowardice she supposed, because it would hurt too much to know, that after all, she wasn't enough.

#

They picked up their soup, and took it go, sitting on one of the benches overlooking the harbor to eat it.

"You have some pumpkin bisque on your nose," he said, looking down at her. She glanced up and went to reach for it.

"Here let me." He moved in closer with his napkin and paused. She was looking up at him, her dark brown eyes liquid, full of life and laughter.

He ignored the soup and instead angled his head and went down for the kiss. She seemed surprised but pressed herself into it. He took his free hand and snaked it around her back, pulling her closer. She tasted sweet and spicy, like the season, and he couldn't get enough of her.

A small sigh of what he hoped was happiness escaped her. He angled down and brought up his hand to run it along the straight line of her jaw. Her skin was soft and smooth and he felt the small shiver that ran through her.

He broke the kiss and saw the look in her eyes. They were almost finished eating and he knew without asking that they would head back to his house tonight, together, that this had become routine. He liked it, wanted it, and was always disappointed if for some reason she couldn't come to him, if next to him the bed was empty.

He knew that she was starting to wonder, wonder where things were going. Still she never asked, but he could tell in the glances she sent him sometimes, in the brief, clouded looks that crossed her beautiful face when she thought he wasn't looking. He loved her, he knew that; he had admitted it to himself—but what did it mean? He had made a promise to himself never to lose himself again; but with Lynn it was desperately easy to do that.

It was the ghost of Ashley that saved him. Lynn would dance around the subject, but she never pushed it. He let it be that way, letting her think that there was only so much of him to give. He hoped that she would be happy with that but also dreaded the day when she asked for more. Because even though he loved her, he couldn't be in love with her, couldn't give himself to her. And he knew she would never accept less than that, not in the long term. Nor, he admitted, did she deserve it.

#

They walked together, Lynn quiet but unsettled. She knew she had almost said something to him, about what he was thinking back on the bench, but she had chickened out again. So they strolled on, and she almost didn't notice as Jackson slowed and she felt him stiffen beside her.

She looked up, surprised by his sudden stop. He was standing as if frozen, the look on his face as if he had seen a ghost. Lynn followed his gaze. A woman, an attractive middle-aged blond, dressed in black leggings and a brightly patterned top, stood there, almost blocking their way.

"Jackson." Her voice was high, pitched with shock, and Lynn decided that she too looked like she had seen a ghost.

"Mrs. Moran," he said, his voice hoarse. Lynn stood still, looking between the two of them. They were all standing by the water, caught in a chilly breeze. A nor'easter was coming, Tory had predicted earlier that day and Lynn, feeling the sudden heaviness in the air, believed it.

"I didn't expect to see you here," Mrs. Moran said, looking between the two of them.

"I'm back in town. I thought you had moved."

A bitter look came across her face. "So that's why you thought you could come back? What, have you just been waiting all this time for us to leave so you can come in and take over this town? That would be just like you."

"I just...I didn't think I'd meet you," Jackson said, and Lynn could tell he was stumbling to find the right words.

"Well, here we are," Mrs. Moran said, and she turned slightly to include Lynn in the conversation. There was a pause and Lynn realized that the woman was waiting for an introduction. And that Jackson seemed to be tongue tied.

"I'm Lynn Masters. I work at the clinic," she said. She held out her hand.

"Libby Moran." The woman stepped forward, took Lynn's hand, and shook it. Lynn could actually feel the discomfort and tension suspended between Jackson and Libby Moran. Lynn sucked in a deep breath. This was Ashley's mom; it had to be.

"You must be new to town, right?" There was a nasty edge to the woman's voice.

"Relatively," Lynn answered, feeling as if the woman's eyes were searching for answers, and then as if finding one, swiveled and turned to Jackson.

"I can't believe you would dare to come back here, to where she walked and lived, and flaunt your life in my face. You lived, she died," Libby hissed.

Jackson said nothing, his face pale, his eyes sunken. Lynn swallowed, wondering just what to do. She took a step forward, but Jackson's arm held her back.

"I'm sorry, Mrs. Moran. You're right..."

"Libby!" There was a short, bark of a voice and a man, also in his fifties, with thinning light brown hair and watery blue eyes, wearing khakis, boat shoes and a windbreaker, came hurrying up.

Behind him trailed a teenaged girl, gawky all long legs, blond hair and with an endearing bit of awkwardness about her.

"Libby," the man repeated, grabbing the woman by the arm and holding her as she took a step toward Jackson.

He didn't make a move to defend himself, though and the slap took his cheek hard and fast.

"Jackson," the man said, pulling his wife back, "I'm sorry. Libby, you can't do this."

"I can!" she yelled, her voice a wail. "I can and I will. Bill, he lived and she died. How is that fair? It was his fault." Her face dissolved into tears and the man, Mr. Moran, Lynn had to assume, pulled his wife to him and rocked her as her body shook with sobs.

"I'm sorry," he said quietly over his wife's cries. "We had to come back and settle a few things with the house sale. It's hitting her hard."

The girl behind them, whom Lynn thought must be the little sister, Lindsay, stayed still, watching, her eyes darting between her parents and Jackson.

"Come, dear. Come," Bill Moran said soothingly, and Jackson took Lynn's hand and all but pulled them past on the boardwalk, his face set, his shoulders rigid.

Lindsay reached out a hand to touch Jackson's arm and he looked down at it and then her.

"I'm sorry," Jackson said tonelessly.

"Jackson, please, let me..." she said.

He gave a quick shake of head and said, "No, Lindsay. No."

Her father called to her, and she followed, shooting Jackson one last look.

Lynn stood frozen, watching the retreating figures of the Morans. In a moment, they were alone, the only sound the flag flapping and snapping in the wind, the single shriek of a gull as it wheeled above them, catching the currents of the air.

Lynn looked at Jackson, concern flooding her. "Are you ok? You don't look so great."

With a visible shake, he moved, starting to walk and saying, "I'm fine. Sorry, just a friend of my mom's. Haven't seen her in a while. Shall we get home? You said you have to work tomorrow?"

As if nothing had happened, Jackson continued walking. Lynn stopped, wondering if he thought she was stupid. But still she said nothing, thinking that he really did look like he had seen a ghost. It was all the answer she needed—all the answers to her questions about the future. How could she have been so stupid, to think that maybe, just maybe there could have been something permanent with her and Jackson? She saw it now. No, he hadn't built a shrine in his house to his dead fiancée but he had kept one in his heart. With a sudden wrench, Lynn knew that Jackson could never, ever be hers the way she wanted to be his.

They went back to his car, ready to head home. Like a sleepwalker he got into the driver seat and she slid into the passenger seat. Jackson reached to start the car but she put out a hand to stop him. "We need to talk."

Chapter 47

All men dreaded those words. Actually, Lynn thought, just about everyone dreaded those words. They were the words you said to a parent when you were about to tell them that their child was sick—very sick. Only bad news could follow. But she had said them and now she couldn't take them back. She saw the clench of Jackson's jaw.

"Must we?" he countered.

"That was her mother, wasn't it?" Lynn found her voice but barely. "That was Ashley's mother." It was the first time she had said that name to him aloud, and all of a sudden it felt like there was a presence in the car with them. Lynn knew it was just her imagination but she couldn't shake the feeling.

"Yes. I thought she had moved out of town."

"Is that why you thought you could come back? Because you wouldn't have to face her?"

"Something like that." Jackson ducked his head.

"She certainly looked surprised."

"She was like a second mother to me," Jackson said. "And she's angry with me."

"For what? Jackson you're still running. God," Lynn said and her voice gathered force, "how could I be so stupid? Everyone warned me, told me that you weren't ready to move on. But I thought I could fix you. They were right about that too, that I have a God complex. Comes with being a doctor, you see. We're trained to diagnose, treat, prevent things, and if something is wrong, find a way to fix it."

Lynn could feel the tears, the hot burning prick of them starting behind her eyelids. She couldn't, wouldn't cry. It was no more than she deserved, thinking she could replace the love of anyone's life.

"And I thought I could fix you, Jackson. I thought you were fixed. I was just giving you time."

"Lynn," Jackson said. His voice was low but his face was unreadable. He reached for her but she couldn't let him touch her or then she would be undone.

"But you aren't. You can't be fixed."

"You don't understand," he said, and his voice held a tinge of desperation.

"Because you haven't told me. You won't talk about her. You won't talk about it."

"It's complicated," he said.

She laughed. "Yeah, life is complicated. I know when we started we said there would be no strings, a grownup relationship." She saw him swallow, but didn't let him speak. "But I'm past that. I need strings, Jackson; but you don't seem to."

"We've been happy the way we were," he said.

"I know and I am, I was happy. But Jackson, I need more. And if you can't give it, then I need to get out."

"Out," he said, repeating the word, dully.

"I won't compete with a ghost, Jackson. No one can. And until you figure out if you're ready to let her go, then I don't think we have anything left to discuss."

She put a hand on the handle of the door. They were still in downtown Queensbay, near enough so she could walk to her own apartment. The fresh air would do her good, she knew, help fight back the tears that were more than threatening to form. A single one escaped and she knew she had to leave.

Opening the door, she felt Jackson reach for her, but she moved quickly, not wanting to risk his touch pulling her back in.

"Lynn, please don't go." His voice was rough.

She stood outside the car and willed herself to look at him. "Tell me you're over her, that you're ready to move on."

He shifted in his seat, ran his hand through his thick hair. "It's complicated. There's something. I can't...it's not mine to tell."

"You have a secret?" She laughed and knew it sounded as if she were on the edge of hysteria, "Don't worry, Jax," she tossed his hated nickname at him. "It's not a secret that you're just as messed up as everyone said."

She swallowed and didn't care that the tears were streaming down her face. "As a doctor, the hardest thing to learn is that you can't save everyone, no matter how hard you try. And that the only thing, the best thing you can do sometimes, is just to accept that. And this is me, doing that."

She slammed the door and walked a little unsteadily across the parking lot. She thought she heard him shout her name, but she didn't stop to see, just walked faster. Going to her apartment was her first thought but then she realized he would find her there. She needed to be alone, to be away from him. There was only one place to go. To her parents. It was a hike, up to the Heights, but she could do it. She began to move faster, almost running, until she was sure he wasn't behind her. She was soon up the twisting road to the thicket of streets above the harbor. She came to her parents' house. The lights were off, which meant that her parents probably weren't home. All the better, because she didn't think she could handle talking to them right now.

Chapter 48

If her mother was surprised to see her, she said nothing. Perhaps that was because Lynn was muffled under two blankets and a comforter in what had recently been her bedroom. Her mother had checked in, seen her crying but hadn't asked why. Lynn pulled the covers over her head and drifted back into a state, halfway between sleep and awake.

Eventually, Lynn wasn't sure after how long, there was a slight knock at the door and without waiting for an answer, her mother showed herself in, carrying a tray with a steaming cup of tea and toast. She set it down on the nightstand next to Lynn and then leaned in and pulled the covers back. Lynn blinked in the sudden light then tried to pull them back over her, but her mother wouldn't let her.

"Have some tea. Sugar and milk—just what the doctor ordered."

"What kind of doctor," Lynn said, still trying to burrow further into bed. She knew her eyes were swollen and her nose was red. She was in her t-shirt and underwear from the night before, the rest of her clothes dumped on the chair in the corner.

"Dr. Mom, of course," her mother answered tartly. The bed sank under her weight as she sat down on the edge of it. Lynn waited and so did her mother, who apparently wasn't going anywhere.

"I have all day, Lynn."

"So do I," Lynn muttered back. She wanted a good sulk and her mother was interrupting it.

"Good. So you can start it off by telling me what happened?"

"I don't want to," Lynn said.

Her mother reached down and stroked Lynn's hair. "You are in my house. You did come in here, crying. I think if you want me to keep putting Jackson off that you had better tell me what is going on."

At his name, fresh tears threatened and Lynn had to blink them back rapidly. Prepared, her mother handed her a box of tissues.

"What do you mean?"

"He's been calling, wanting to know if you were here. Wanted to know if you were safe. Apparently, you didn't go home to your apartment last night. Or with him," her mother said.

"What did you tell him?"

"That I knew where you were, that's all. He sounded worried."

"He's just being a nice guy, a gentleman," Lynn said.

Her mom looked at her and Lynn saw herself reflected in the chocolate brown eyes, the freckles and even in the dark hair, though Lynn knew her mother's color now came from the bottle. Her eyes were kind, concerned, and Lynn felt like she was a little girl with the flu being told it was all going to be ok.

"Oh, I think that it was more than that. He was very worried, and very relieved to know you were safe."

Lynn drew her knees up, and propped herself back up on the pillows. Her mother handed her the mug of hot tea. Lynn thought about asking for coffee, but knew what her mother would say to that. Tea was her mother's cure-all, from an upset stomach to an upset heart.

She took her first sip after blowing on it to be sure it was cool and it slid down her throat—milky, sweet, and hot—and she instantly felt comforted.

Her mother gave her a smile. "Never argue with Dr. Mom."

"Thank you," Lynn said.

She expected her mother would leave but she didn't. "I don't know exactly what happened. I mean besides some sort of disagreement with Jackson. And I'm guessing it doesn't have to do with the color he wants to paint the clinic walls."

"Oh, Mom. I was so stupid. Everyone warned me, told me that he wasn't ready, that he wasn't over her. And I thought I could fix him, make him whole. I wanted to be the one to show the world he was ready to move on." She knew her mother had heard the story of Jackson and Ashley Moran.

Her mother stroked Lynn's knee through the fabric of the comforter. "Occupational hazard of being a doctor, I guess. The need to mend people?"

"Broken bones, stuffy noses...they're all a lot easier than broken hearts."

Her mother nodded.

"I don't think he is over her, I mean, really over his fiancée. I thought that if I loved him enough, gave him enough love that he would forget about her. He was happy with me, Mom; he would

779

laugh and be playful. We did things together, the little things, like make dinner together, go shopping, and big things like dates, hikes, and boat rides, and we even talked about going skiing together. I felt like he was different than when I first met him, that he had changed, that something in him was better. But I guess it, or I, wasn't enough."

"You don't know that, do you? Did he ever tell you that?"

Lynn shook her head. "I knew from the beginning that it was just casual relationship. He even said he couldn't offer anything more than…"

Lynn's mother held up her hand. "Please, I get the picture. And don't let your father or brother know. One of them will feel honor bound to punch Jackson's lights out."

"But I thought, I don't know, that things were changing between us. And they did up to a point, and then they just stopped. I didn't know why. But last night—God last night—I realized that it would never change. He's still in love with a dead woman. How do you compete with that?"

"I don't know, honey, I don't," her mom said and pulled her close for a hug.

Lynn let herself be surrounded by her mother's comforting arms. Through the hug, Lynn asked, "If dad died, would you get over him?"

Her mother broke the hug and looked at Lynn. "That's a morbid question."

"I know. I'm sorry."

"But I suppose it deserves an answer. I can't imagine a life without him, but I also can't imagine not wanting to live again. And I mean really live, in all ways. And I don't think he would want me to. And I wouldn't want that from him either. No. I expect that I might be able to move on, eventually. It wouldn't ever be the same, of course, but you do move on, even if things are different. That's life. You have to move on, Lynn. Either by yourself or not."

"I can't make that decision for him," she said.

"No, but have you really given him the chance to know what the choice really is?"

Chapter 49

The Harvest Ball was a resounding success. Lynn could see that and knew it was no thanks to her. She still felt as if she were moving through a layer of mud, everything clouded and fuzzy, her thoughts still on Jackson. But it was her friends and family who rallied to her cause. Darby and her staff had come through, providing veggie burgers designed to look like monsters, chicken hotdogs shaped like spiders, and cupcakes cleverly loaded with shredded carrots and pumpkin puree and decorated like ghosts.

The games and stations were being manned by the local high school service clubs, and the little kids were running to and fro, in their costumes, thrilled. Caitlyn was selling raffle tickets and Lynn's mother was quietly bidding up the silent auction items. Phoebe was doing face painting and Tory was showing a softer side at the jump rope station, thrilling the kids with her Double Dutch skills.

Lynn's dad came up and dropped an arm around Lynn's shoulder as he surveyed the controlled chaos. "Pretty impressive turnout."

"I guess it helped it's raining out. Nothing else for kids and parents to do."

"Lynn," her father rebuked, "it's not like you to be so glum. Come on, this is impressive. Everything you've done is impressive. I know I didn't give it much thought when you started the program at the clinic, but I can't believe what you're doing here. And I heard you've been asked to present your results at a conference in December?"

Lynn nodded. Tory's website and the new materials she had printed had gotten the notice of the local paper, which had written an article on the program, and from there she'd been asked to talk to a local moms club about it. And next up was a meeting of the regional medical association. Things were taking off faster than she could have imagined.

"Like I said, looks like you have the whole town here," her dad said. "And I better go stop your mother from outbidding everyone at the silent auction. If I've told her once, I've told her a hundred times that we don't need his and her massages."

Lynn almost laughed. "There's always a first time."

Her father kissed the top of her head and went off to find her mom. Lynn looked around. The turnout was better than she could have hoped, but her dad was wrong. The whole town wasn't here. Jackson was nowhere to be seen, but she hadn't expected him, of course. After all, what would a guy like Jackson do at a school full of kids? She had to remember that she had no right to expect him here.

He had tried calling her, and she had answered once. It had been an awkward, strained conversation, just a few ordinary questions about her day before she made her excuses and hung up. Since then, she had dodged his calls, managed to time things so she didn't run into him at the clinic. She had felt like such a fool, cried all her tears that she didn't think she could handle seeing him. Being told in person what she already knew would make it no better.

Phoebe came over. "Oh my. I've used up all my face painting materials, can you believe it?"

Lynn checked her watch. "We only have another twenty minutes, so I think it's ok. Maybe you can help Tory out at the jump rope station."

Phoebe shook her head, "Promise if I trip and fall you'll give me free medical advice. It's been a long time since I used a jump rope."

Lynn managed a smile, but Phoebe, her eyes filled with concern, pulled Lynn in for a hug.

"Usually you're the one giving out hugs, but this time you look like you need one," she said.

Lynn closed her eyes, fighting back the tears as her friend held her close.

"I'm sorry he's not here. I thought maybe he would but…"

"It's not your problem. I knew what I was getting into." Lynn took a deep breath and felt the tears subside for the moment. She needed to hold it together.

"Still, it doesn't mean we can't curse his name."

Lynn laughed bitterly. "You're going to be related to him."

"Doesn't matter. I'll still take your side." Phoebe broke the hug and looked at Lynn. "Have you talked to him, I mean really talked to him? He's…he's not himself."

"What good would it do, Phoebe? I mean, do I need to hear it out loud, that he's just not over her? I'm not sure I could take it."

"Are you sure that's what he said?" Phoebe asked softly.

Lynn shook her head. "He didn't have to."

Phoebe nodded, but kept her arm around Lynn and drew her toward the ticket booth. "Maybe you two just need a little more time to work things through."

Lynn didn't say anything else.

#

"You made nearly eight thousand dollars," Caitlyn said, looking at her calculator in satisfaction.

The Harvest Ball was over, and the gymnasium was mostly clean and quiet, with only one table and a few chairs left. Caitlyn, who had agreed to act as her temporary treasurer, had just finished counting all the proceeds from the day.

"Wow," Lynn said, gratified but also amazed. "I can't quite believe it. I mean, there were a lot of kids here, but we really made that much with the raffle tickets and the silent auction?"

Caitlyn looked up, glanced at Tory and Phoebe, and then said, "Not quite. There were a few straight up donations that added to the total."

"From who?" Lynn asked. "Besides you and Noah?"

"There was one anonymous donation for six thousand dollars."

"What?" Lynn said, her mouth dropping open in shock. "From whom?"

"Well, as I said, it's anonymous," Caitlyn answered, but her gray eyes slid away from Lynn's face.

"You mean you don't know or you won't tell me?" Lynn stood up. "All of a sudden was there a wad of cash dropped into your lap? Or did this 'anonymous' donor use a more traditional payment source like a check or a credit card."

"Look," Caitlyn glanced at Lynn, "he didn't even want me to tell you, but I think you should know."

"Jackson?" Lynn breathed the name.

"Yes. But really, he didn't want you to know, wanted me to tell you that you made it all from raffle tickets. But I can't be dishonest with you."

Lynn looked at the faces of her friends who were watching intently.

"It doesn't change anything," Lynn said. And knew that it didn't, shouldn't. Jackson couldn't buy her forgiveness. She could be thankful for his support, but it didn't make a difference. She wasn't going to forget that he was in a love with another woman and carry on their relationship.

Tory gave a short laugh. "You are stubborn. I think the man is trying to tell you something."

"I can't be bought, Tory. The money's great, because it's for a good cause. But Jackson can't make himself feel better by giving me money. I don't think he's a bad person. He doesn't have to prove that to me."

It was something else entirely. She knew Jackson could be generous, could be a gentleman. But he couldn't be hers. And she was just going to have to live with that.

Chapter 50

"I am not going to serve you another one." Paulie the bartender was implacable, wiping down a glass as he stood behind the bar of the Osprey Arms.

"You do know who I am, don't you?" Jackson said, trying to focus on Paulie. But there appeared to be more than one of him.

"Yup, you're the guy my boss told me to cut off," Paulie said, putting the dry glass down and picking up another one.

"I'll sleep in an empty room. Please, just give me another drink."

Paulie just shook his head. Jackson started to get up, figuring he would head to Quent's and grab a beer there. He would still find an empty room at the hotel to sleep in. He knew well enough that he was in no condition to drive, but still a man had a right to drown his sorrows.

"Just what do you think you're doing?" Jake appeared next to him and Jackson tried to push against his friend, but Jake still retained enough of his quarterback bulk to stop him.

"Paulie has cut me off," Jackson said, glaring at Paulie.

"Chase told me to," Paulie said in his defense. "Jackson's been here every night for a week eating French fries and drinking beer, and he's had enough."

"What happened? I haven't seen you in days. I thought you and I were supposed to be starting a business together." Jake's voice was annoyed as he plopped Jackson back onto the barstool that he had so recently tried to vacate.

"I've been busy," Jackson said, his own voice sounding thick in his ears.

"Paulie, will you get us coffee and water please?" Jake said, turning his barstool so that it faced Jackson.

"Sure thing," Paulie nodded, and in a moment there were two cups of steaming black coffee and two pints of water in front of them.

"Pick one and get started," Jake said.

"What are you trying to do?"

"Sober you up. Find out what the hell is going on, though judging by your condition I'm going to make a wild-ass guess that it's woman trouble."

"A whole heap," Jackson said, hearing the misery in his own voice.

"I thought you and Lynn were happy," Jake said carefully.

"We were. And then I ruined it." Jackson decided to start with the coffee. He had a sip, decided that it was mistake on a stomach full of beer and Scotch, and tried the water instead.

"What did you do? Ask her to play doctor? I hear real ones hate it when you do." Jake's voice was light, teasing.

Jackson said nothing, too sunk in his own gloom to know what to say. God he was miserable without her. But she wouldn't talk to him, let alone let him explain. She wouldn't return his phone calls. He had wanted to go to her fundraiser tonight, but he just couldn't bring himself to see her, not if he didn't know that she would want to see him. But he knew she wanted the one thing he couldn't give.

"What are you muttering about?"

"She thinks I'm still in love with Ashley. Says she won't compete with a ghost."

"Don't know any good woman who would," Jake said, adding cream to his coffee and taking a sip.

"How can I be in love with a ghost? It doesn't even make sense," Jackson said.

"What have you told her?"

"I haven't told her anything. It's what everyone else says. That it hit me hard, that I have baggage, that she was the love of my life. What is Lynn supposed to believe?"

"What you tell her," Jake said simply.

"But I can't."

"Why not?"

"Because it's even worse than that. I'm not still in love with Ashley. I haven't been, not since…" Jackson faltered. He'd made a promise that he still intended to keep.

"Ok, so if you're not still in love with Ashley, what's wrong with Lynn? If you just don't feel that way about her, let her down easy. It will be messy and it will make Chase and Phoebe's wedding complicated, but you'll get through it. Lynn's passionate but reasonable. She'll move on eventually."

"It's not that."

"Then what is it?"

"After Ashley died, I realized that I'd spent years of my life loving someone who didn't love me back, who used me to feed her ego, telling me how important I was to her, how she couldn't live without me. And I bought it hook, line, and sinker. Hell, she was even cheating on me, and I think I knew it, and I made excuses for her. What a sap I was."

"Ok," Jake said neutrally, "so you're not, or haven't been, in love with Ashley for a long time but…"

"But I told myself I would never make that mistake again. That I wouldn't ever love anyone again, you know, get so wrapped up in them that I lost myself."

Jake nodded sagely. "The self-preservation vow. I think we've all made it when we've gotten burned. But no man is an island, you know. What I don't get is why you left then, if you weren't all torn up about Ashley. I mean, when did you realize this?"

"About three months before she died."

They turned and swiveled at the same time, looking at the speaker. Libby Moran stood there, her blond hair pulled back in a twist, dressed in wool slacks and a blouse, clutching a purse in front of her like it was a shield. Her eyes were sad, but they were no longer accusing.

Mrs. Moran's eyes were wide and so bright that for a moment Jackson thought she was going to cry, but then she blinked rapidly and the moment was over.

"Jackson, I am so sorry."

"No, Mrs. Moran. You don't have to do this," Jackson said desperately.

"Lindsay told me everything, and then Bill spoke to the police captain. God, Jackson why did you do it?"

"I…"

Libby looked at Jake. "Did you know?"

Jake held up his hands in bewilderment and Jackson sagged against the barstool.

"Look, Mrs. Moran, you don't have to apologize."

She closed her eyes, blinked back what he thought were tears and then took a deep breath. "Lindsay told me everything. About the breakup, Ashley wanting to leave, Tucker Wolff, and how you told the police you'd been driving. But why?"

Jackson closed his eyes, memories of that night flooding back. Why had he done it? If he'd known how the Morans would blame him, how everyone would look and point and whisper, would he have the courage to do it again?

"I didn't want you to think of Ashley that way. I wanted you to remember her, well, the way she was."

Libby's head sank down and her eyes closed briefly. "Thank you. I don't know what to think. I mean, I knew something was different, was up with Ashley; but I wouldn't have thought all that. And I blamed you, all these years."

"It's ok," Jackson said. "Mrs. Moran, you don't have to do this."

"No, I do. I never would have let you do it if I knew what it would cost you. Why did you let me blame you?"

Mrs. Moran didn't wait for an answer but rushed on. "I know Ashley broke up with you months before she died. And that she was running off with Tucker Wolff. That's why he was in the car with her, not you, right?"

Jackson couldn't say anything, just nodded.

"Lindsay told me how Ashley broke off the engagement and of her plans to go away with Tucker Wolff. But still, that night, you were there for her like you'd always been, covering for her, saving her from her mistakes, doing the right thing. I know she was drinking that night, driving wild with Tucker. And if people had known that you two weren't together or that Tucker was involved, they would have talked."

Jackson didn't know if he could say anything, could only feel the pounding in his chest, feel the relief rising in him. He had kept the secret for so long, kept silent about him and Ashley because he wanted to protect the Morans, because they were good people and had been like second parents to him. It had been a simple decision and had felt right at the time, to help a grieving family. But then they had turned on him. Hell, it had felt like the whole town had turned on him and they were all serving up the sentimental bullshit about how wonderful Ashley had been. It had been too much. He'd had to get out. He'd been wounded, and then he had gotten angry. Angry at them, angry at Ashley, angry at himself for letting himself love her.

Mrs. Moran reached out and took Jackson's hand in her both of hers. "So again, I want to say thank you. It did make it easier to blame someone else, not her. And you owe us nothing, Jackson. You deserve to come home, to find some happiness. You will find no judgment from us and if I hear even a whisper of it from anyone else, I will give them my two cents, even if it's from afar."

"Not everyone needs to know; it doesn't matter," Jackson said, but already he wanted to find a way to unburden himself.

Mrs. Moran smiled sadly and looked at Jake. "It does. You gave Ashley everything, more I think than she deserved. Ashley was driving the car, she had been drinking. I am trying to get around to accepting that, and I will. But I do know that you deserve to have a full and rich life, without her memory holding you back, here or wherever you go."

Jackson sagged. Loving Ashley had been a rollercoaster of highs and lows, and there had been that edge to it of neediness, as if Ashley had only been happy if she knew you were worrying about her. It had taken him a while to realize that it wasn't love. It had been selfishness.

There was a pause, and before the silence could become awkward, Libby Moran took a step back, clutched her bag, and smiled brightly. "I have to be going. Bill and Lindsay are waiting for me. We're just about wrapped up here in town, so I am not sure when we'll see each other again."

She nodded and slipped out as Jackson sat there stunned, not sure what this meant. For five years of his life he'd been keeping a secret and now he'd just been told that it was no longer important. That it was time to move on. But what did that mean? Did it even matter?

Jake, who had risen from his stool as Mrs. Moran left, sat back down and fixed Jackson with a stare.

"And what, my friend, was that about?"

Jackson looked up. The bar was comfortably crowded but they were tucked back along the far corner of the bar, private enough. Mrs. Moran had said she trusted him to know who could be told.

"Sit back and order another cup of coffee. This is going to take a while."

#

Jake took a sip of his lukewarm coffee, watching Jackson finish his story. It made sense and it explained a whole hell of a lot of things. He'd known something had been wrong with Jackson back then. Just as he had noticed that the ever-present Ashley was no longer so ever present. Still, to think she'd been running around with Tucker Wolff, behind Jackson's back. After the accident, Tucker had quietly slipped out of town too, joined the Navy. Jake had never given much thought to that. Now it all made sense.

"So you let the Morans think you were with Ashley when she crashed? And that everything was hunky-dory between the two of you?"

"I thought it would make it easier for them to grieve. I never thought they would blame me the way they did. And to tell them would have been to destroy the memory of their daughter."

"But Tucker Wolff?"

"I guess Ashley still had a thing for him, and when she came home from college, there he was, here—ready to fill her with promises to go off and see the world and take her with him. Turns out Ashley never quite bought into the whole living our life out here. Tucker Wolff was just her way out."

Jake almost winced but didn't. He thought it was a pretty fair assessment of Ashley's character, but it would do no good to say that now. He did, however, decide to ask the question that had been on his mind for five years. "So do you think if Ash had lived…that you would have gotten back together? That it was a temporary case of cold feet?"

Jackson took a sip of coffee and then said evenly, "No. Ashley and I wanted very different things. She thought living here was confining. She wanted to travel, to have adventures. She liked the thrill of the chase. That isn't me. Yes, I left; but because I felt I had to, not because I wanted to. Ashley wouldn't have been happy living here. And as it turns out, I wasn't happy not living here."

"So what are you going to do about her?"

"About Lynn?" Jackson ran a hand through his hair.

"Yeah, her. How do you feel about her? Do you love her?" It was a simple question and it deserved a simple answer.

"Yes, I love her. I told her that I couldn't be anything more than a…"

"Friends with benefits," Jake finished for him.

"Something like that. And now…"

"And now you two are in love. I don't understand what the problem is. It's not rocket science. You two are crazy about each other, you want to spend time with each other, you love each other."

"The last time I loved someone I lost myself. In more ways than one. You said it yourself, remember. She consumed me."

"Is that what you're afraid of? It's not that you still love someone else, is it? You're afraid you'll love Lynn too much, that she'll use you the way Ashley did?"

Jackson looked at his friend, not surprised that he had guessed the truth.

"So that's it. You're not all caught up in Ashley, you're just too afraid to love again. Well let me ask you, do you feel that way with Lynn?"

"No," Jackson said quietly, and realized that the water and the coffee were beginning to have their effect. "It feels different. Steady, constant. I mean, don't get me wrong, it's exciting too but I don't feel like I'm dancing on the edge of a flame. I don't know if that's love or companionship. I've only experienced moods and passions so fierce they engulf you or well, not that this makes me a standup guy, but you know, just simple physical attraction. This is something different. But it doesn't matter because..." he muttered.

How could he go back and tell Lynn about Ashley? She had said she didn't want to compete with a dead woman. Well she had, but not the way she thought. Would she think that his lying to her was worse than the truth, that he didn't think he could ever love that way again? Would she think it meant he wasn't capable of it?

"I think it does. And it should. Look, like Mrs. Moran said, you did your duty. You stood by them when they needed it most. They moved forward, moved on. If, God forbid, the situation had been reversed, I don't think Ashley would be down here swearing off men."

"I am not swearing off women...It's just with Lynn, it's..."

"Different," Jake said. "Face it. With Lynn you're a better man. Happier, chiller, you know, all around less broody and all that. Why? I don't know. Maybe she smiles and you see rainbows and unicorns. Or maybe she tells really funny jokes. Or really dirty ones. Or she can cook, or maybe she just gets you. I don't know how, but whatever it is it works. And maybe you've lived so long working on not caring that you're afraid of what it feels like. But this time, it might just be the real deal."

"When did this become the Tao of Jake?"

Jake shrugged. "Look, man. It's one thing to want to run around and sample all the fish in the sea when you're seventeen. But add in a few years and you realize that there's more to life than sitting in a dark bar listening to crap music and drinking beer with other guys. If you feel something for Lynn, something real, well then you should go for it. Tell her the truth and let her decide. You owe her that much."

"Yeah," Jackson said.

Jake picked up his glass of water. Listening was thirsty work. "The truth will set you free, man. It will set you free."

Chapter 51

The truth did set him free. He told Chase the next morning, making him take a walk out along the docks so that he could move around. Somehow it seemed easier to talk about if he didn't have to sit in a chair and feel like he had been called into the principal's office.

Chase said nothing at first, and then, "Wow. That is some heavy baggage you've been carrying around."

Jackson looked up as a gull circled the sky. He found himself glancing up toward the Osprey Arms annex and what would be Lynn's apartment. The blinds were closed, he couldn't see anything. But it didn't matter, she was sure to be at work. After all, that is what he had done—lose himself in work when he didn't want to deal.

"It feels good to be free. I mean, I don't intend to shout it to the whole world, but I know when I left that I let you down too, left you with the family business to run. Not that, as it turned out, you needed me."

Chase smiled, an eyebrow quirked up. "I'm just glad to have you back. It's been fun, but it will be more fun with you around. You're staying right?"

Jackson smiled and shook his head. "I never want to leave again."

"Good," Chase said, and leaned over the railing so he could peer into the depths of the water lapping at the dock below. "Now we just have to fix your love life."

"What?" Jackson sputtered. Really, he was glad to be honest with his brother but this was pushing it.

"Don't try to deny it." Chase waggled a finger at Jackson. "You're crazy about her. And miserable without her."

Jackson shoved his hands in the pocket of the coat he had put on against the autumn chill. "It's too late there. I screwed it up. She thinks I'm..."

"An emotionless hard-hearted bastard in love with somebody else."

"Something like that."

"But she's pretty miserable too; I have that on good authority."

"She's just mad," Jackson said, shaking his head. He couldn't let himself get his hopes up.

"I like Lynn, I really do. And not just because she's friends with my bride to be. Did I ever tell you about the time she saved my life?" Chase laughed at the expression on Jackson's face. "Ok, so it was just a paper cut. But seriously, I think when two people are in, how shall we say, in sync with one other, then just about anything can be fixed."

Jackson sighed. He knew he wasn't going to escape the brotherly advice, solicited or not. "What's your idea, big brother?"

Chase smiled. "It's time for the grand gesture, my friend. Think big, think wow, and then prepare tell the truth and grovel. That should do it."

"What should I get, a skywriter to say I'm sorry? What do you mean by a grand gesture?"

Chase shrugged. "How the hell should I know what Lynn wants? She's not my girl. Though it seems like money isn't the way to her heart. Apparently, she was unmoved by your donation."

Jackson sighed. "It was supposed to be anonymous. I didn't want her to think I was trying to buy her forgiveness."

"Classic guy move, thinking you can throw money at a problem. I think this time you need to figure it out. She's your girl after all. For Phoebe it would probably be a new set of drawing pencils or fancy new sheets. Seriously. But you have to figure out what's going to melt Lynn's heart, if you know what I mean, long enough for you to get down on your knees and beg. Got it?"

Jackson nodded. He thought he might just be finally getting it.

Chapter 52

"Next." Lynn barely looked up as the next patient entered the small exam area. If she thought that she had managed to put Jackson out of mind, she realized she had been mistaken.

"You." Lynn couldn't keep the surprise out of her voice.

"Doctor." Lindsay Moran stepped into the exam room and hesitated, as if waiting for Lynn to say something.

The nurse, as if she could feel the tension, looked at Lynn. Lynn swallowed, then waved her away, taking the proffered chart. She was a professional and she was pretty sure that anything Lindsay had couldn't fluster her. She just needed to remain detached, above it all, and she would do just fine.

Lindsay smiled shyly as the nurse left them alone and took a seat on the examining table, as if she had all the time in the world.

"Do your parents know you're here?" Lynn asked.

"I'm eighteen so it doesn't matter, and this isn't because I'm sick. We're leaving today and this seemed like the fastest way to get to you. I tracked down Chase and he told me where to find you."

"Ok," Lynn said, not sure where this was going.

"You should give Jackson another chance, you know," Lindsay said, her legs swinging off the side of the table, her eyes, big, blue, round.

"Excuse me?"

"Look, I saw the way you looked at my mom. And the way you looked at Jax. I don't know what you heard about my sister's death, but whatever it was it wasn't Jackson's fault. I told my mom that, and she believes me I think, but I didn't want you holding what you thought you knew against him."

Lynn gave a bitter laugh. "What, that he's in love with a dead woman?" As soon it was out of her mouth, Lynn regretted it. Her hand flew to her mouth, covering it, and she wished with all her heart she could take her words back. "Sorry."

Libby shrugged with a world weariness that Lynn knew could only have come from having suffered a tragedy.

"See, that's what you think you know."

"So what don't I know?"

"Well, everyone thinks she was St. Ashley. But she wasn't."

"I have a brother and he's no saint either, but he's still a good person," Lynn said carefully.

Lindsay shook her head. "No. Ash had some serious issues. Deep down issues. Poor Jackson got suckered right into it. He adored her, worshipped her, and she treated him like a faithful puppy and he put up with it. But he was never happy. Ashley," and here her voice dropped just a bit, "liked drama. She liked to keep Jackson on his toes. It fed her ego, her self-confidence to know that he was always a bit more in love with her than she was with him."

"Did you think this was going to make me feel better?" Lynn asked. She balled her hand into a fist, aware that it was trembling. She took a deep breath, trying to get control of her emotions.

"No. But perhaps you need to give Jackson a chance to explain," Lindsay said.

Lynn closed her eyes, shook her head, wished she could make all of this go away. "I would like for him to, but he won't. Just said I wouldn't understand."

"Yeah, that sounds like Jackson, Mr. Goody-two-shoes. He has a serious knight in shining armor complex."

Lindsay said nothing more, just hopped off the exam table, the white paper crinkling as she did so. She landed neatly on her feet and looked down at Lynn.

"I think that Jackson needs to explain it himself. I knew of course. Can't keep things from a nosy little sister, but he swore me to secrecy, told me it would be better this way. I believed him; only I didn't realize how bad things would get for him."

Lynn shook her head in bewilderment. She had no idea what Lindsay could possibly be talking about.

Lindsay started toward the opening in the curtain that separated them from the rest of the clinic.

"You know, he's happy with you. I could see it, hear it."

"Hear it?"

"Yeah, he sends me emails, little presents sometimes. Nothing weird, don't worry. But he was kind of like a big brother to me when he was with Ashley, and just because my mom went all crazy on him, he never stopped being there for me."

"He talked about me?" Lynn said.

"Sort of. I mean, he hardly ever gave me any details about his personal life, but well, he did mention you, so I thought that was kind of, you know, significant. And I don't know, there was just something in what he did say. You know, like he was happy."

"Happy?" Lynn repeated.

"Yes. He's happy with you. Trust me." And with that she was gone.

Lynn sank slowly to the small rolling stool, needing a moment to calm and pull herself together as the clinic hummed around her.

Happy? Had she truly made Jackson happy? She remembered his smiles, his laughs, the way he teased her, looked out for her, his thoughtfulness, his loving hands. All so different from the stern, serious man she had accused of having ice in his heart and closing down the clinic. He was the man who had given the clinic a new lease on life, who fixed up the ball fields, who made an outrageous donation to something that was important to her.

But could being happy with someone compare to being crazy in love? Was happy a good enough substitute for passion? Lynn's own heart, its breaking, told her the answer. She was crazy in love with Jackson and miserable over it.

Chapter 53

She drove up the driveway, the pit in her stomach growing larger. It was dark early now, and there was a soft glow of a few lamps on in the house, as it sat low slung to the ground. Beyond, she could see shimmering lights on the far bluffs across the expanse of the harbor. The moon sat large and fat in the sky, a harvest moon.

She pulled up in front and just sat in her car, allowing the warmth of the heater to caress her bones, trying to do anything that would postpone the inevitable. Sure, she had thought about calling the items a loss, but then she had told herself to grow a pair. If Jackson wasn't planning on moving and if neither was she, then she was bound to run into him here and there. Better to be mature, to be grownups about it.

So she had to will herself to get out of the car, pulling her barn coat more tightly around her. She had her scrubs on and the thin fabric caught in the wind and it cut right through her. There might still be leaves on the trees and a warm spot of sun in the afternoon, but fall was giving up the ghost, no doubt about it. Winter would be upon them soon.

Shivering, she started up the crushed gravel walkway to the wide redwood planked steps. Maybe he wouldn't be here, she thought, then shook herself. She was not going to weenie out of this. And besides, what Lindsay Moran had said kept coming back to her.

Ringing the doorbell, she rocked on the ball of her heels, pulling on her ponytail. There was the sound of a click and then Jackson's voice over the intercom. "Lynn?"

"Yes," she said, trying to keep the irritation out of her voice. Was he expecting someone else? Maybe he had moved on to another woman he couldn't commit to. The thought stabbed at her heart and she waited for another moment before he answered.

"Come in." The disembodied voice was eerie over the loudspeaker. Behind, the tree branches moaned and scraped together in the wind.

She glanced back and saw only shadows and dark, so she scooted into the inviting warmth of the house.

The lamps were on dim, the fire was crackling in the fireplace, and there was music, something soft and low playing on the stereo.

She looked around for the box of her stuff, hoping that perhaps he had just left it for her up here on the main floor and she could grab it and go.

"Down here," he called, and seeing that there was no obvious pile of stuff, she took a breath and started down the staircase to the bottom floor.

The lights were on brighter here, and she saw that he had been doing some work. It smelled of fresh paint and new wood, but the main room seemed untouched, with its bar area and pool table.

"I'm back here," he called again. Feeling frustrated, wondering what sort of wild goose chase she was being led on, she followed his voice, past the pool table, to the corridor off to the side of the bar. This area had been unfinished, except for the laundry room. It had been a good-sized space, open, broken by only by steel columns and cold concrete.

She stopped, coming to a halt, her mouth not quite working.

"Surprise," he said, looking at her.

"What is this?"

"A rock-climbing wall. Well, a rock-climbing ceiling."

She looked around. It wasn't a tall wall of course, but the room's walls and ceiling had been lined with plywood, painted gray and studded with toe and handholds. One could climb up the walls and then across the ceiling. The floor, she noticed now, was squishy and well padded.

"A rock-climbing room?"

Unsure, she put her hand up and touched one of the toeholds, feeling the smooth plastic.

"Why," she whispered, feeling her throat close up.

He took a step toward her, his hands out. "I think you know why, Lynn. It's a peace offering, a gift, a way to show you that I messed up."

"But nothing has changed," she whispered. "You're still in love with her, and I won't come after a dead woman. I'm sorry, I don't mean to be harsh. But I need you—all of you."

"But you do have me," he said, his arm reaching out to her, stopping her so she wouldn't go. "There's something I need to tell you…"

He took a deep breath and Lynn waited.

"I haven't been in love with Ashley for a long time. Even before she died."

"What...? But..." Lynn took the step back and he didn't stop her.

"I told a lie. To you, to her parents, to my family, to my friends. And I think—I know—I would do it again. It was the right thing to do at the time."

"Why?" she asked, but suddenly the conversation with Lindsay was starting to make sense.

"I thought it was the right thing to do then to protect her memory. To protect her family. I just never thought the lie would overtake me the way it did. Somehow it became the defining point in my life. I was Jackson Sanders, poor Jax who lost his one true love in a car crash. And then, before I knew it, everyone blamed me for killing her. But I wasn't even with her."

Lynn's head was reeling. "I don't understand."

"Ashley broke up with me months before she died. Told me the wedding was off, that she never wanted to live in a small town, that she was made for better things. She even told me she was seeing someone else. At first, I thought it was just cold feet so I begged her, asked her to reconsider. We told nobody—she agreed to that—but she wouldn't see me. The only one who knew was her little sister.

"I was devastated but I also felt, like for the first time in a while, I could breathe. I could be myself. I could take a damn step without worrying what Ashley would think or do or how she would try to twist it into whether or not I really loved her. I realized that I had loved the idea of being in love with her more than actually loving her."

"I..." Lynn started to say but Jackson kept going on.

"I was getting over her, moving on, making plans with Jake for our business, planning on working another year or two to get the experience. I was happy."

"And then what happened?"

"Her parents knew something was wrong. Ashley was staying out late, partying a bit, blowing off work. They came to me. Ashley hadn't told them, so I lied to them, covering for her. But soon I was pissed. Until she came clean to her parents, I was trapped in a lie. I couldn't say hi to a girl or stay out late without half the town giving me looks like I was stepping out on her. But she didn't tell them because it kept them off of her back. And I couldn't do it. Too much of a gentleman, I guess," he said ruefully.

"And then…"

Jackson swallowed. "I got a call one night, from this guy I knew on the police force. There had been an accident and I might want to get there fast. He was doing me a favor, I think. I went to the scene. Ashley was there, in bad shape, still alive, and I thought she might make it. She'd been driving too fast, drinking probably, and there had been a passenger, Tucker Wolff—some guy we had gone to high school with. Of course, he was fine, not a scratch on him."

"Let me guess—that's who she was seeing."

"Exactly, and things were confusing. By then, EMTs and the other cops got there, people just assumed I was with her. It wasn't a cover-up, just not quite the truth. Wolff was able to walk away, and I even gave him my car keys, had him take my car. Everyone made assumptions and I played vague. Some people kept quiet and before I knew it, we had a story going."

"You let it happen?"

"I rode with Ashley to the hospital, and the doctors tried everything they could, but it was too late. Her mom leaned on me for support and it just seemed easier to play along with it, to not let the rumors and the scandals start."

"So you played the grief-stricken fiancé?"

"I was grief stricken, for a while. I did love her once. And for what it's worth, she was a vital, commanding person. But Ashley was selfish in life and in death. And then Mrs. Moran, well she went off the deep end, not that I can blame her. But she kind of took it out on me. So I went from the poor, grief-stricken fiancé to one step above a murderer. The fact that the cops did nothing to me only made her crazier."

"But you could have told the truth at any time, gotten it all to stop," Lynn said.

"And what? Let everyone know Ashley had been stepping out on me? Ruin her memory? There would have been plenty of people who would have liked to see her fall a bit from her pedestal. No way. Ashley was drunk, she was driving that car. Thank God she only hurt herself. I could take the blame if it meant protecting her parents from that kind of truth."

Lynn nodded. "I see."

"Do you? Do you know what this means?"

Lynn wrapped her arms around herself, hugging her close, suddenly cold, and said, "You lied to me as well. You let me believe that you were still in love with her. That we couldn't have a real relationship because you were broken. What's changed?"

Jackson looked at her, his eyes big, bright, intent on her.

"After Ashley died, I vowed I wasn't ever going to get caught up in a relationship like that again. I lost something of myself—when I was with her and even after she died, when I had to leave town. It took me a while to get myself back, to get back to here. To do that I had to stay detached. And it worked. Until you."

He took a step toward her and she almost moved away from him, but didn't, letting his words spill over her.

"Lynn, you broke through that feeling, made me realize that I'd been telling myself a lie to protect myself. I stayed away from relationships, real relationships, because I didn't ever want to be hurt again. But you showed me that things—love—can be different. It can be passionate, but constant, faithful and exciting, committed and true and real."

"But you never said anything," Lynn whispered, not quite believing it.

He took her by her arms and held her so she wouldn't go, his eyes looking down into her. "I thought I knew what love was. That it was crazy, passionate, ups and downs. And with you it is," he said, twining his fingers around her hand, "But it's also warm and even and sexy and full of surprises and joy and happiness and laughter. That's what you've given me. And I don't want to lose it, I don't want to lose you."

"But…"

"From the moment I saw you launch yourself into Petersen's office, to the way you beat me at the rock wall, to our first kiss, I knew I wanted you. On some level, I knew you made me whole. And then I realized I loved you. Slowly, deeply, always. You're the woman who can steer a boat, stitch up a hand, give out lollipops, make kids healthy, and deliver babies. You're an amazing, sexy, beautiful woman. And I want to be with you."

She could feel the electric pull of their connection, the need for him. She had missed him, been miserable at her core every day without seeing him, without knowing that he was waiting for her.

He touched his forehead down to hers but did no more. "I missed you, so much. Every night you weren't here, I would come home and this house would be empty and cold; there was no laughter, no fun, no you."

"Yes," she agreed, still not able to look at him.

"So you missed me too?" he asked, hope lighting his voice.

"From the moment you first kissed me and walked away," she said, knowing that she could finally admit it. "I love you too, all of you. And probably most of all, the knowledge that you will do what's right...even if it hurts you." She could forgive him for keeping his secret, respect what he had done. He was a good man. And he was hers.

He kissed her then, a deep, tender kiss that had her melting into him.

They broke finally, coming up for air.

"I don't want to ever lose you again," he said.

"I'm here. You built me a rock-climbing room."

He smiled. "Marry me."

"What?"

"Marry me. I want to be with you for the rest of my life, Lynn Masters. You're intelligent, compassionate, and beautiful. You make me happy. You make me remember what it's like to have fun. Marry me and we'll go rock climbing and skiing, and kayaking and skinny-dipping on a hot summer night. Whatever you want. But build a life with me, a family, and marry me."

She waited for a just a heartbeat, feeling, seeing all the possibilities, knowing that with Jackson there was everything she wanted: a home, love, adventure.

"Yes, I'll marry you," she said. And he swept her up into his arms.

THE END

Want More Queensbay?

Thanks for checking out the first four books in my small town contemporary romance series. I hope you'll want to keep reading more about Queensbay, starting with Lynn's friend Tory Somers...Will she be able to find true love or will her past hold her back?

Discover Tory & Colby's story in With You...Available on Amazon.com

Read An Excerpt from *With You*

Tory Somers' day started off just as expected. She had woken up to her alarm and the launching of dawn light, which peeked through the sheer curtains that covered her bedroom window. She rose from bed, saw that the sun was pushing its way above the hills to the east of the harbor, suffusing the sky with a pinkish hue and making the water of Queensbay Harbor sparkle as if the day was just waiting for something magical to happen. Too bad she didn't believe in magic, knew instead the sparkle was simply a combination of water and light, a prism effect in action.

She stretched, taking a look around her bedroom. It hadn't gotten old, the feeling that, finally, she was in her own place, not her childhood bedroom in her parents' charming center hall Colonial, but her very own apartment with her very own living room, one and a half bathrooms, a kitchenette and a balcony with a view of the water. Where she was free to come and go as she pleased. It had made sense to live with her parents for a while, after the break up, to save money while she focused on her career. Just as now it made sense to be on her own. All part of her plan.

She relished every minute of her freedom as she headed out for her daily run, showered, ate breakfast and made a cup of coffee to go. She left her apartment in the Annex, next to Queensbay's one and only hotel, the Osprey Arms, to go to work. The Annex was a brick building with white trim, black shutters and a porch that ran around the entire first floor. Soon it would house retail shops, with conference rooms planned for the second floor. The third floor held apartments, only two occupied at the moment, and one belonged all to her. She gave a little wave to her window as she headed across the parking lot to where her most prized possession, her hunter green Mini Cooper, awaited her.

She placed the cardboard box she'd been carrying, her briefcase and her bag in the passenger seat and hopped in, revving the engine and opening the window. It was spring, technically, since that was what the calendar said, and she caught sight of pale yellow buds on a forsythia bush, as sure a sign as any that winter was well and truly over. Still, spring came slowly to the New England coast, and she was glad she had worn a blazer over her blouse and stylish-enough-for-work jeans.

The streets of Queensbay Village were empty this early, the old-fashioned iron and gaslight streetlamps flicking off as she drove past them. The only signs of life were at the Golden Pear, her favorite deli. There, through the large plate glass windows that looked into the shop, she could see villagers were already lined up for their coffee and muffins. Tory thought about stopping, but she wanted to get into work early.

The rest of the village was sleepy-looking in the morning light, the sun just starting to light up the charming mix of styles, from the Colonial era clapboard-sided houses and shops, to the more modern Victorians with their fanciful trim work and bright colors. Queensbay, like many a town along the New England coast, had seen its fortunes rise and fall, just like the tides in the harbor it sat watch over. Now, once again, its fortune was on the rise, and many of the buildings which had fallen into disrepair had been refurbished and refinished. The whole town glowed in anticipation of what could be.

Tory loved it, loved being here. Ok, so it hadn't quite been her plan to return to her hometown after college, or stay so long, but she had found that plans needed to be flexible. Lately, though, Tory was starting to feel as if her plan needed a little updating. She was over what had happened, had moved on, but still career-wise, she had been working her current job for almost five years, an eternity these days, and while things were good, she had started to feel like her life needed a bit of a jumpstart. She didn't want to think about leaving Queensbay, but she couldn't deny the fact that maybe it was time to look elsewhere.

Within moments, she was at work. She found a spot easily enough in the parking lot of the large, warehouse-like building that had once been a sailmaker's loft, though it had been a long time since a sail was stitched there. For many years, it had been a genteelly rundown eyesore at the edge of town, the only tenants a health clinic and Madame Robrieux, Queensbay's one and only psychic. Tory had never visited the great Madame, preferring to make her fortune rather than having it dictated to her.

Now, though, the building was getting a second chance. The new owner had come in and re-sided, painted and given the clinic's rooms a facelift. The second floor was home to a construction company, while the third floor and addition was to be the new corporate headquarters of North Coast Outfitters, the company where Tory worked.

She took the newly refurbished elevator up to the third floor, and the doors opened up onto a dimly lit space. The whole place smelled like sawdust and fresh paint, and it made her smile. At least someone's plan was going according to schedule. Her boss, Chase Sanders, had taken over his family's ship chandlery and t-shirt shop when he had returned home from racing yachts in Europe. In a few short years, he'd turned it into an upscale apparel company for the yachting set—or those that aspired to be. Even though there was still a store down by the harbor, most of their orders came from their website—for which she was mainly responsible, along with a hodgepodge of other technical responsibilities.

The company had grown so big that Chase had decided to move them out of their space above the store and into here, where they would have plenty of room to grow. She'd volunteered to come in and do the setup work on the new computer system, and she expected to have the place mostly to herself, except for the construction crew, which she could dimly hear farther back, in the newer part of the building. Everyone would be moving in over the next couple of days, but for now, she was pretty certain she'd be alone.

"Finally, you're here!" She jumped at the sound of the voice, the coffee in her to-go cup sloshing as her heartrate pounded and then slowed down when she saw who it was.

Chase Sanders, the owner and CEO of North Coast Outfitters, was running his hands up and down the smooth walls, his blue eyes sparkling like a kid on Christmas morning. She could tell that he was excited about the new space, raw and unfinished as it was.

"I was going to check out the new server room you and Horace promised me. See if I could start to set it up," she said as she began to set her stuff down on a desk in one of cubicles. Horace Wentworth was the current Chief Technology Officer and, technically, her direct boss.

But Chase had other ideas.

"Oh no, you don't," he said and grabbed her arm.

"What do you mean?" she asked, propelled along by Chase's energy.

"You're going here," he said. Now he not only looked like a kid on Christmas morning, but he sounded like one too.

He led her to a door, flung it open and turned on the lights.

"Like it?"

"What do you mean? What is it?"

"Your new office."

"For me?" Tory asked, trying to keep her voice cool. She was a computer geek and wasn't used to an office. She'd barely had a desk in the old building, since space had been so tight.

"Yes, for you. Since you're the Chief Technology Officer of the company, I think it's time you had your own office."

"I thought I was your assistant website designer and all-around tech support. Isn't Horace the Chief Technology Officer?" Tory asked carefully, not quite able to breathe. It had been on her plan, toward the bottom of the list: *Be a CTO by 30*. But it had been a stretch goal, something Tory had put down because she wanted to have something to strive for. But this was more than she had expected.

Chase laughed and led her into the office. It was white and came with a desk, two chairs and a bookshelf. There was a window, too— not enormous, but Tory was pretty sure she could glimpse a flash of the blue surface of Queensbay Harbor in the distance. An office, with a view. And her birthday was still months away.

"This is my way of offering you a promotion," Chase said. He walked over to the desk and pulled out the chair, giving it a little wiggle. He was grinning.

"You couldn't have pulled me into a conference room with HR and asked me there?" Tory said, still trying to find her balance. "What if I don't want a promotion? And again, what about Horace?" She was trying to stay calm, and not be carried away on a wave of giddiness. This had to be a joke.

"This is way more fun, and besides, you're more likely to say yes and not ask a lot of silly questions if I take you by surprise."

"Like what kind of questions?" Tory gave in to the temptation. She sat down in the ergonomically correct chair and savored the small feeling of accomplishment it gave her. She'd been working at North Coast Outfitters since just after college, starting out as a sales clerk. Then she had offered to help out with the truly awful website and had found herself promoted to the chief web geek—Chase's title, not hers. Still Horace, who had to be seventy if he was a day, had remained the Chief Technology Officer. He was an old friend of Chase's father whom Chase hadn't had the heart to get rid of.

"Horace's daughter just had a baby, and he wants to spend more time with the grandkids. He's retiring, effective just about now. He said that the only person who could replace him was you."

"He said that, really?" Tory tried to keep the surprise out of her voice. She and Horace hadn't always seen eye to eye. He was a nice enough guy, but she didn't feel he'd been interested enough in some of the newest technology on the market, the kind of stuff that could help North Coast Outfitters outperform its competitors.

"Well, close enough," Chase said with a wave of his hand, as if the details weren't that important. She decided that they weren't, especially if it meant a promotion for her.

"So, what other questions were you afraid I was going to ask?"

"You know, the usual. Being the Chief Technology Officer means a lot more responsibility. It's more than just the website—though that, of course, is huge. You have to support marketing and all their requests for sales data. And I'm told our inventory system sucks."

"I'm the one who told you that," Tory pointed out.

"I know, and you also were the only one who researched alternatives, complete with a cost-benefit analysis, and presented it to me in a way that made sense."

"So … do I have the job because I convinced you I know what I'm doing or because Horace retired and you have no other choice?"

"Let's just say, after a couple of years of working with you, I'm pretty sure you'll handle anything I throw your way. And this is my way of recognizing it. Horace was a good guy, but we both know he was a little old-fashioned. If it hadn't been for you, we would still be taking orders over the phone and faxing them someplace. I know how much you've pushed when it comes to technology, and you've shown that you can manage the team here. I may not be the most computer-savvy guy, but I know when someone else is."

"You're the only person I know who can break a computer just by looking at it," Tory shook her head.

Chase laughed. "Exactly. Hey, I know my own strengths, and deciding which software to pick isn't one of them."

Then he turned serious. "Look, even I can tell that the website you're responsible for makes up more than seventy percent of our sales, and the new inventory system you want to put in will cut down on our order processing costs, and that you've somehow managed to take all the sales reports for the past five years and accurately project demand for the last two seasons, so I'd say you've earned this. And I have to give myself a pat on the back. Who knew when you needed a summer job that you had a degree in computer science and that you are, like, you know, totally brilliant. Besides, I don't want you to leave."

"Leave?" Tory said carefully.

"Don't tell me recruiters haven't been calling you," Chase said, a sly smile crossing his face.

"Well, maybe," Tory kept her voice neutral. Truth was she had been getting tired of working under Horace, of not being able to do as much as she wanted, of not being able to check out all the new technology, so she had been talking, just a little, with a few recruiters.

After Stevie it felt like her life had been in a holding pattern. Sure, she was happy here in Queensbay, but the salaries and opportunities that had been dangled in front of her had been tempting, even if most of them meant a move to Boston or New York City.

"Opportunity knocks, so don't shut the door on it. Besides being good for the company, Phoebe would kill me if you moved away," he added, referring to his fiancée and Tory's friend.

"With a new office? A new title. And more money, right?" As good as everything sounded, she knew that Horace had been making a great deal more money than she had. If she was going to be taking over his job, it was time for a raise.

"Of course. But just remember there's more responsibility and now the whole IT staff reports to you. Means you get to do all their performance reports," Chase said in a whisper. Everyone knew he hated all the paperwork that went into running a company.

"Ok," Tory said, taking a deep breath and letting it out. She could do this. It was what she had wanted, a chance to run the show, to really help build a business, using all the cool technology that was out there. And now Chase was offering her that opportunity.

"Ok?"

"Ok, I accept. You have yourself a new Chief Technology Officer."

"Great, there's some paperwork from HR on the desk. You should read it over, let me know if you have any questions. By the way, Sandy in sales said there's s something wrong with the order processing system, so I think you'd better check it out."

And with that, Chase was gone and Tory was left alone with her new responsibilities. Tory sat stock-still in her office, not quite believing what had just hit her—a freight train or the chance of a lifetime?

Her phone buzzed, and there was a pinging from her tablet. As if on cue, the desk phone started ringing. And so it began. Tory took a deep breath, grabbed her mobile, told the caller to wait, then grabbed the desk phone, told that caller to hold on, and then reached for her tablet to check her email.

Nice new office: check. Great job: check. First trial by fire: check. It was going to be a long day.

About Drea Stein

Drea Stein is the author of contemporary romance. She writes the Queensbay series, set in the quaint New England town of Queensbay. In real life, she lives in rural New Jersey with her husband and children.

Read the other books
in the Queensbay Series:

Book 1: Dinner for Two - Darby and Sean

Book 2: Rough Harbor - Caitlyn and Noah

Book 3: The Ivy House - Phoebe and Chase

Book 4: Chasing a Chance - Lynn and Jackson

Book 5: With You - Tory and Colby

Want to stay in touch? Want the cookie recipe - you know the one - Darby's Famous Better Than You Know What Cookies? Check out www.dreastein.com and get THE COOKIE RECIPE…

Cheers

Drea

75456352R00499

Made in the USA
San Bernardino, CA
30 April 2018